More praise for John Irving
and
THE CIDER HOUSE RULES

"Clearly Irving's best-made book and a book of importance. It is a tour de force, a heavyweight among books, as John Irving must be accounted among writers....He accomplishes his feat with both humanity and wisdom....A moving, sometimes hilarious, and unfailingly entertaining story."
—*St. Petersburg Times*

"With each new novel John Irving displays widening of compass....It is the breadth and spread, the depth of characterization that lift this novel beyond anything that Irving has done before....This may be a novel of Maine, but it carries a far wider meaning."
—*John Barkham Reviews*

"Irving is in top form in this capacious novel of personal discovery....Deft realism in both scene and characterization...*The Cider House Rules* is a mature, entertaining novel."

—*Library Journal*

Also by John Irving
Published by Ballantine Books:

Books

Screenplays

Books published by The Random House Publishing Group are available at quantity discounts on bulk purchases for premium, educational, fund-raising, and special sales use. For details, please call 1-800-733-3000.

THE
CIDER HOUSE
RULES

John Irving

BALLANTINE BOOKS · NEW YORK

For David Calicchio

The Cider House Rules is a work of fiction. Names, characters, places, and incidents are the products of the author's imagination or are used fictitiously. Any resemblance to actual events, locales, or persons, living or dead, is entirely coincidental.

A Ballantine Book
Published by The Random House Publishing Group
Copyright © 1985 by Garp Enterprises, Ltd.

Published in the United States by Ballantine Books, an imprint of The Random House Publishing Group, a division of Random House, Inc., New York, and simultaneously in Canada by Random House of Canada Limited, Toronto.

Ballantine and colophon are registered trademarks of Random House, Inc.

www.ballantinebooks.com

ISBN 0-345-38765-1

This edition published by arrangement with Bantam Books, Inc.

Manufactured in the United States of America

First Ballantine Books Edition: December 1993

49 48 47 46 45 44 43 42 41

Chapters

Conventionality is not morality. Self-righteousness is not religion. To attack the first is not to assail the last.

—*Charlotte Brontë, 1847*

For practical purposes abortion may be defined as the interruption of gestation before viability of the child.

—*H. J. Boldt, M.D., 1906*

The
Cider
House
Rules

1/ The Boy Who Belonged to St. Cloud's

In the hospital of the orphanage—the boys' division at St. Cloud's, Maine—two nurses were in charge of naming the new babies and checking that their little penises were healing from the obligatory circumcision. In those days (in 192__), all boys born at St. Cloud's were circumcised because the orphanage physician had experienced some difficulty in treating uncircumcised soldiers, for this and for that, in World War I. The doctor, who was also the director of the boys' division, was not a religious man; circumcision was not a rite with him—it was a strictly medical act, performed for hygienic reasons. His name was Wilbur Larch, which, except for the scent of ether that always accompanied him, reminded one of the nurses of the tough, durable wood of the coniferous tree of that name. She hated, however, the ridiculous name of Wilbur, and took offense at the silliness of combining a word like Wilbur with something as substantial as a tree.

The other nurse imagined herself to be in love with Dr. Larch, and when it was her turn to name a baby, she frequently named him John Larch, or John Wilbur (her father's name was John), or Wilbur Walsh (her mother's maiden name had been Walsh). Despite her love for Dr. Larch, she could not imagine Larch as anything but a last name—and when she thought of him, she did not think of trees at all. For its flexibility as a first or as a last name, she loved the name of Wilbur—and when she tired of her use of John, or was criticized by her colleague for overusing it, she could rarely come up with anything more original than a Robert Larch or a Jack Wilbur (she seemed not to know that Jack was often a nickname for John).

If he had been named by this dull, love-struck nurse, he probably would have been a Larch or a Wilbur of one kind or another; and a John, a Jack, or a Robert—to make matters even duller. Because it was the other nurse's turn, he was named Homer Wells.

The other nurse's father was in the business of drilling wells, which was hard, harrowing, honest, precise work—to her thinking her father was composed of these qualities, which lent the word "wells" a certain deep, down-to-earth aura. "Homer" had been the name of one of her family's umpteen cats.

This other nurse—Nurse Angela, to almost everyone—rarely repeated the names of her babies, whereas poor Nurse Edna had named three John Wilbur Juniors, and two John Larch the Thirds. Nurse Angela knew an inexhaustible number of no-nonsense nouns, which she diligently employed as last names—Maple, Fields, Stone, Hill, Knot, Day, Waters (to list a few)—and a slightly less impressive list of first names borrowed from a family history of many dead but cherished pets (Felix, Fuzzy, Smoky, Sam, Snowy, Joe, Curly, Ed and so forth).

For most of the orphans, of course, these nurse-given names were temporary. The boys' division had a better record than the girls' division at placing the orphans in homes when they were babies, too young ever to know the names their good nurses had given them; most of the orphans wouldn't even remember Nurse Angela or Nurse Edna, the first women in the world to fuss over them. Dr. Larch made it a firm policy that the orphans' adoptive families *not* be informed of the names the nurses gave with such zeal. The feeling at St. Cloud's was that a child, upon leaving the orphanage, should know the thrill of a fresh start—but (especially with the boys who were difficult to place and lived at St. Cloud's the longest) it was hard for Nurse Angela and Nurse Edna, and even for Dr. Larch, not to think of their John Wilburs and John Larches (their Felix Hills, Curly Maples, Joe Knots, Smoky Waterses) as possessing their nurse-given names forever.

The reason Homer Wells kept his name was that he came back to St. Cloud's so many times, after so many failed foster homes, that the orphanage was forced to acknowledge Homer's intention to make St. Cloud's his home. It was not easy for anyone to accept, but Nurse Angela and Nurse Edna—and, finally, Dr. Wilbur Larch—were forced to admit that Homer Wells *belonged to* St. Cloud's. The determined boy was not put up for adoption anymore.

Nurse Angela, with her love of cats and orphans, once

remarked of Homer Wells that the boy must *adore* the name she gave him because he fought so hard not to lose it.

/ / /

St. Cloud's, Maine—the town—had been a logging camp for most of the nineteenth century. The camp, and—gradually—the town, set up shop in the river valley, where the land was flat, which made the first roads easier to build and the heavy equipment easier to transport. The first building was a saw mill. The first settlers were French Canadians—woodsmen, lumberjacks, sawyers; then came the overland haulers and the river bargemen, then the prostitutes, then the vagrants and the thugs, and (at last) there was a church. The first logging camp had been called, simply, Clouds—because the valley was low and the clouds broke up reluctantly. A fog hung over the violent river until midmorning, and the falls, which roared for three miles upstream from the site of the first camp, produced a constant mist. When the first woodcutters went to work there, the only impediments to their rape of the forest were the black flies and the mosquitoes; these infernal insects preferred the nearly constant cover of clouds in the stagnant valleys of inland Maine to the sharp air of the mountains, or to the crisp sunlight by the bright Maine sea.

Dr. Wilbur Larch—who was not only the doctor for the orphanage and the director of the boys' division (he had also founded the place)—was the self-appointed historian of the town. According to Dr. Larch, the logging camp called Clouds became St. Clouds only because of "the fervent backwoods Catholic instinct to put a Saint before so many things—as if to grant those things a grace they could never quite acquire naturally." The logging camp remained St. Clouds for nearly half a century before the apostrophe was inserted—probably by someone who was unaware of the camp's origin. But by the time it became St. Cloud's, it was more of a mill town than a logging camp. The forest, for miles around, was cleared; instead of logs jamming the river, and the rough camp full of men lamed and crippled by falling from trees or by trees falling on them, one saw the high, orderly stacks of fresh-cut boards drying out in the hazy sun. Overall lay a silty sawdust occasionally too fine to see, but ever-present in the sneezes and wheezes of the town, in the town's perpetually itching noses and in its rasping lungs. The town's wounded now sported stitches instead of bruises and broken bones; they wore gashes (and found ways to flaunt their missing parts) from the mill's many saws. The keen whine of those blades was as constant in St. Cloud's as the fog, the mist, the humidity that overhangs inland Maine in the damp cold of its long, wet, snowed-in winters and in the fetid, stifling heat of its drizzly summers—blessed, only occasionally, by violent thunderstorms.

There was never any spring in that part of Maine, except that period of time in March and April distinguished by thawing mud. The heavy equipment of the lumbering business was immobilized; the work of the town shut down. The impassable roads kept everyone at home—and the springtime river was so swollen, and ran so fast, that no one dared to travel on it. Spring in St. Cloud's meant trouble: drinking trouble, brawling trouble, whoring and raping trouble. Spring was the suicide season. In spring, the seeds for an orphanage were planted and overplanted.

And what of the fall? In his journal—his whatnot diary, his daily record of the business of the orphanage—Dr. Wilbur Larch wrote of the fall. Each of Dr. Larch's entries began, "Here in St. Cloud's . . ."—except for those entries that began, "In other parts of the world . . ." Of the fall, Dr. Larch wrote: "In other parts of the world, fall is for the harvest; one gathers the fruits of spring and summer's labors. These fruits provide for the long slumber and the season of ungrowing that is called winter. But here in St. Cloud's, the fall is only five minutes long."

What sort of climate would anyone expect for an orphanage? Could anyone imagine *resort* weather? Would an orphanage bloom in an *innocent* town?

In his journal, Dr. Larch was demonstratively conservative with paper. He wrote in a small, cramped hand, on both sides of the pages, which were absolutely filled. Dr. Larch was not a man for leaving margins. "Here in St. Cloud's," he wrote, "guess who is the enemy of the Maine forests, the villainous father of the unwanted babies, the reason the river is choked with deadwood and the valley land stripped, unplanted, eroded by the river floods—guess *who* is the insatiable destroyer (first of a logger with his hands pitchy and his fingers mashed; then of a lumberman, a saw-mill slave whose hands are dry and cracked, with some fingers only a memory), and guess *why* this glutton is not satisfied with logs or with lumber . . . guess *who*."

To Dr. Larch, the enemy was paper—specifically, the Ramses Paper Company. There were enough trees for lumber, Dr. Larch imagined, but there would never be enough trees for all the paper the Ramses Paper Company seemed to want or to need—especially if one failed to plant new trees. When the valley surrounding St. Cloud's was cleared and the second growth (scrub pine and random, unmanaged softwoods) sprang up everywhere, like swamp weed, and when there were no more logs to send downriver, from Three Mile Falls to St. Cloud's—because there were no more trees—that was when the Ramses Paper Company introduced Maine to the twentieth century by closing down the saw mill and the lumberyard along the river at St. Cloud's and moving camp, downstream.

And what was left behind? The weather, the sawdust, the scarred, bruised bank of the river (where the big log drives, jamming, had gouged out a raw, new shore), and the buildings themselves: the mill with its broken windows with no screens; the whore hotel with its dance hall downstairs and the bingo-for-money room overlooking the rough river; the few private homes, log-cabin style, and the church, which was Catholic, for the French Canadians, and which looked too clean and unused to belong to St. Cloud's, where it had never been half as popular as the whores, or the dance hall, or even bingo-for-money. (In Dr. Larch's journal, he wrote: "In other parts of the world they play tennis or poker, but here in St. Cloud's they play bingo-for-money.")

And the people who were left behind? There were no Ramses Paper Company people left behind, but there were people: the older, and the less attractive prostitutes, and the children of these prostitutes. Not one of the neglected officers of the Catholic Church of St. Cloud's stayed; there were more souls to save by following the Ramses Paper Company downstream.

In his *A Brief History of St. Cloud's,* Dr. Larch documented that at least one of these prostitutes knew how to read and write. On the last barge downriver, following the Ramses Paper Company to a new civilization, a relatively literate prostitute sent a letter addressed to: WHICHEVER OFFICIAL OF THE STATE OF MAINE WHO IS CONCERNED WITH ORPHANS!

Somehow, this letter actually reached someone. Forwarded many times ("for its curiosity," Dr. Larch wrote, "as much as for its urgency"), the letter was delivered to the state board of medical examiners. The youngest member of this board—"a puppy, right out of medical school," as Dr. Larch described himself—was shown the prostitute's letter as a kind of bait. The rest of the board thought that young Larch was "the one hopelessly naïve Democrat and liberal" among them. The letter said: THERE SHOULD BE A GODDAMNED DOCTOR, AND A GODDAMNED SCHOOL, AND EVEN A GOD-DAMNED POLICEMAN AND A GODDAMNED LAW-YER IN ST. CLOUD'S, WHICH HAS BEEN DESERTED BY ITS GODDAMN MEN (WHO WERE NEVER MUCH) AND LEFT TO HELPLESS WOMEN AND ORPHANS!

The chairman of the state board of medical examiners was a retired physician who thought that President Teddy Roosevelt was the only other man in the world besides himself who had not been made from a banana.

"Why don't you look into this mush, Larch?" the chairman said, little knowing that out of this invitation a state-supported facility—for orphans!—would soon develop. It would one day gain at least partial federal support, and even that most vague and least dependable support offered by "private benefactors."

Anyway, in 190__, as the twentieth century—so young and full of promise—blossomed (even in inland Maine), Dr. Wilbur Larch undertook the task of righting the wrongs of St. Cloud's. He had his work cut out for him. For almost twenty years, Dr. Larch would leave St. Cloud's only once—for World War I, where it is doubtful he was more needed. What better man could be imagined for the job of undoing what the Ramses Paper Company had done than a man named after one of the world's coniferous trees? In his journal—as he was only beginning—Dr. Larch wrote: "Here in St. Cloud's it is high time something was done for the *good* of someone. What better place for improvement could there be—for self-improvement, *and* for the good of all—than a place where evil has so clearly flourished if not altogether triumphed?"

In 192__, when Homer Wells was born and had his little penis snipped and was named, Nurse Edna (who was in love) and Nurse Angela (who wasn't) had in common a pet name of their own for St. Cloud's founder, physician, town historian, war hero (he was even decorated), and director of the boys' division.

"*Saint* Larch," they called him—and why not?

When Wilbur Larch granted Homer Wells permission to

remain at St. Cloud's for as long as the boy felt he belonged there, the doctor was merely exercising his considerable, and earned, authority. On the issue of belonging to St. Cloud's, Dr. Larch was an authority. St. Larch had found his place—in the twentieth century—to be, as he put it, "of use." And that is precisely how Dr. Larch instructed Homer Wells, when the doctor sternly accepted the boy's need to stay at St. Cloud's.

"Well, then, Homer," said St. Larch, "I expect you to be of use."

/ / /

He was nothing (Homer Wells) if not of use. His sense of usefulness appears to predate Dr. Larch's instructions. His first foster parents returned him to St. Cloud's; they thought there was something wrong with him—he never cried. The foster parents complained that they would wake to the same silence that had prompted them to adopt a child in the first place. They'd wake up alarmed that the baby hadn't woken them, they'd rush into the baby's room, expecting to find him dead, but Homer Wells would be toothlessly biting his lip, perhaps grimacing, but not protesting that he was unfed and unattended. Homer's foster parents always suspected that he'd been awake, quietly suffering, for hours. They thought this wasn't normal.

Dr. Larch explained to them that the babies of St. Cloud's were used to lying in their beds unattended. Nurse Angela and Nurse Edna, dearly devoted though they were, could not be rushing to each and every baby the second it cried; crying was not of much use at St. Cloud's (though in his heart of hearts Dr. Larch knew very well that Homer's capacity for withholding tears was unusual even for an orphan).

It was Dr. Larch's experience that foster parents who could so easily be deterred from wanting a baby were not the best parents for an orphan. Homer's first foster parents were so quick to assume they'd been given a wrong one—retarded, a lemon, brain-damaged—that Dr. Larch didn't extend himself to assure them that Homer was a very fit baby, bound to have a courageous long haul in the life ahead.

His second foster family responded differently to Homer's lack of sound—his stiff-upper-lip and bite-the-bullet-while-just-lying-there placidity. His second foster family beat the baby so regularly that they managed to get some appropriately babylike noise out of him. Homer's crying saved him.

If he'd proven himself to be stalwart at resisting tears, now when he saw that tears and howls and shrieks seemed to be what his foster family most desired of him, he tried to be of use and gave, with his whole heart, the lustiest wails he could deliver. He had been such a creature of contentment, Dr. Larch was surprised to learn that the new baby from St. Cloud's was disturbing the peace in the fortunately small and nearby town of Three Mile Falls. It's fortunate that Three Mile Falls was small, because the stories of Homer's cries were the center of the area's gossip for several weeks; and it's fortunate that Three Mile Falls was nearby, because the stories found their way to St. Cloud's and to Nurse Angela and Nurse Edna, who had cornered the gossip market in all those river, wood and paper towns. When they heard the tales of how their Homer Wells was keeping Three Mile Falls awake until the small hours, and how he would wake up the town before it was light, the nurses' good memories did not forsake them; they went straight to St. Larch.

"That's not *my* Homer!" Nurse Angela cried.

"He's not a *natural* at crying, Wilbur," Nurse Edna said—taking every opportunity she had to pronounce that name so dear to her heart: Wilbur! It always made Nurse Angela cross with her (whenever Nurse Edna indulged her desire to call Dr. Larch a *Wilbur* to his face).

"*Doctor* Larch," Nurse Angela said, with pointed and excessive formality, "if Homer Wells is waking up Three Mile Falls, that family you let have him must be burning that boy with their cigarettes."

They weren't *that* kind of family. That was a favorite fantasy of Nurse Angela's—she hated smoking; just the look of a cigarette dangling from anyone's mouth made her remember a French-speaking Indian who'd come to see her father about digging a well and had stuck his cigarette in one of her cat's faces, burning its nose!—the cat, an especially friendly spayed female, had jumped up in the Indian's lap. That cat had been named Bandit—she'd had the classic masked face of a raccoon. Nurse Angela had restrained herself from naming any of the orphans after Bandit—she thought of Bandit as a girl's name.

But the family from Three Mile Falls were not sadists of a very known kind. An older man and his younger wife lived with his grown-up children of a previous marriage; the young wife wanted a child of her own, but she couldn't get pregnant.

Everyone in the family thought it would be nice for the young wife to have her own baby. What no one mentioned was that one of the grown-up children from the previous marriage had had a baby, illegitimately, and she hadn't cared for it very well, and the baby had cried and cried and cried. Everyone complained about the baby crying, night and day, and one morning the grown-up daughter had simply taken her baby and gone. She left only this note behind:

> I'M SICK OF HEARING FROM ALL OF YOU ABOUT HOW MUCH MY BABY CRIES. I GUESS IF I GO YOU WON'T MISS THE CRYING OR ME EITHER.

But they *did* miss the crying—everyone missed that wonderful, bawling baby and the dear, dim-witted daughter who had taken it away.

"Be sure nice to have a baby crying around here again," someone in the family had remarked, and so they went and got themselves a baby from St. Cloud's.

They were the wrong family to be given a baby who wouldn't cry. Homer's silence was such a disappointment to them that they took it as a kind of affront and challenged each other to discover who among them could make the baby cry first; after first they progressed to loudest, after loudest came longest.

They first made him cry by not feeding him, but they made him cry loudest by hurting him; this usually meant pinching him or punching him, but there was ample evidence that the baby had been bitten, too. They made him cry longest by frightening him; they discovered that startling babies was the best way to frighten them. They must have been very accomplished at achieving the loudest and longest in order to have made Homer Wells's crying a legend in Three Mile Falls. It was especially hard to hear anything in Three Mile Falls—not to mention how hard it was to make a legend out of anything there.

The falls themselves made such a steady roar that Three Mile Falls was the perfect town for murder; no one there could hear a shot or a scream. If you murdered someone in Three Mile Falls and threw the body in the river at the falls, the body couldn't possibly be stopped (or even slowed down, not to mention found) until it went three miles downriver to St.

Cloud's. It was therefore all the more remarkable that the whole town heard the kind of crying Homer Wells made.

It took Nurse Angela and Nurse Edna about a year before Homer Wells stopped waking up with a scream or letting out a wail whenever someone crossed his field of vision, or whenever he heard a human sound, even a chair being dragged across the floor, or even a bed creak, a window shut, a door open. Every sight and sound connected with a human being who might possibly be headed in Homer's direction produced a high, stammering shout and such tearful blubbering that anyone visiting the boys' division would have thought that the orphanage was, in fairy-tale fashion, a torture shop, a prison of child molestation and abuse beyond imagining.

"Homer, Homer," Dr. Larch would say soothingly—while the boy burned scarlet and refilled his lungs. "Homer, you're going to get us investigated for murder! You're going to get us shut down."

Poor Nurse Edna and poor Nurse Angela were probably more permanently scarred by the family from Three Mile Falls than Homer Wells was, and the good and the great St. Larch never fully recovered from the incident. He had met the family; he'd interviewed them all—and been horribly wrong about them; and he'd seen them all again on the day he went to Three Mile Falls to bring Homer Wells back to St. Cloud's.

What Dr. Larch would always remember was the fright in all of their expressions when he'd marched into their house and taken Homer up in his arms. The fear in their faces would haunt Dr. Larch forever, the epitome of everything he could never understand about the great ambiguity in the feelings people had for children. There was the human body, which was so clearly designed to *want* babies—and then there was the human mind, which was so confused about the matter. Sometimes the mind didn't want the babies, but sometimes the mind was so perverse that it made other people have babies they knew they didn't want. For whom was this insisting done? Dr. Larch wondered. For whom did some minds insist that babies, even clearly unwanted ones, *must* be brought, screaming, into the world?

And when other minds thought they wanted babies but then couldn't (or wouldn't) take proper care of them . . . well, what were these minds thinking? When Dr. Larch's mind ran away with him on the subject, it was always the fear in those faces of the family from Three Mile Falls that he saw, and Homer Wells's legendary howl that he heard. The fear in that family was fixed in St. Larch's vision; no one, he believed, who had seen such fear should ever make a woman have a baby she didn't want to have. "NO ONE!" Dr. Larch wrote in his journal. "Not even someone from the Ramses Paper Company!"

If you had an ounce of sanity, you would not speak against abortion to Dr. Wilbur Larch—or you would suffer every detail there was to know about the six weeks Homer Wells spent with the family from Three Mile Falls. This was Larch's only way of discussing the issue (which was not even open to debate with him). He was an obstetrician, but when he was asked—and when it was safe—he was an abortionist, too.

By the time Homer was four he didn't have those dreams anymore—the ones that could awaken every living soul in St. Cloud's, the dreams that caused one night watchman to resign ("My heart," he said, "won't take another night of that boy") and that resided so soundly in the memory of Dr. Wilbur Larch that he was known, for years, to hear babies crying in his sleep and to roll over saying, "Homer, Homer, it's all right now, Homer."

At St. Cloud's, of course, babies were always crying in everyone's sleep, but no baby ever woke up crying in quite the manner that Homer Wells managed it.

"Lord, it's as if he was being *stabbed*," Nurse Edna would say.

"As if he was being burned with a cigarette," Nurse Angela would say.

But only Wilbur Larch knew what it was really like—that way that Homer Wells woke up and (in his violent waking) woke everyone else. "As if he were being circumcised," Dr. Larch wrote in his journal. "As if someone were snipping his little penis—over and over again, just snipping it and snipping it."

/ / /

The third foster family to fail with Homer Wells was a family of such rare and championship qualities that to judge humanity by this family's example would be foolish. They were that good a family. They were that perfect, or Dr. Larch would not have let Homer go to them. After the family from Three Mile Falls, Dr. Larch was being especially careful with Homer.

Professor Draper and his wife of nearly forty years lived in

Waterville, Maine. Waterville was not much of a college town in 193—, when Homer Wells went there; but if you compared Waterville to St. Cloud's, or to Three Mile Falls, you would have to say that Waterville was a community of moral and social giants. Though still inland, it was of considerably higher elevation—there were nearby mountains, and from these there were actual vistas; mountain life (like the life on an ocean, or on the plains, or on open farmland) affords the inhabitant the luxury of a view. Living on land where you can occasionally see a long way provides the soul with a perspective of a beneficially expansive nature—or so believed Professor Draper; he was a born teacher.

"Unfarmed valley land," he would intone, "which I associate with forests too low and too dense to provide a view, tends to cramp the uplifting qualities of human nature and enhance those instincts which are mean-spirited and small."

"Now, Homer," Mrs. Draper would say. "The professor is a born teacher. You have to take him with a grain of salt."

Everyone called her Mom. No one (including his grown children and his grandchildren) called him anything but Professor. Even Dr. Larch didn't know what his first name was. If his tone was professorial, at times even officious, he was a man of very regular habits and temperament, and his manner was jocular.

"Wet shoes," the professor once said to Homer, "are a fact of Maine. They are a given. Your method, Homer, of putting wet shoes on a windowsill where they might be dried by the faint appearance, albeit rare, of the Maine sun, is admirable for its positivism, its determined optimism. However," the professor would go on, "a method *I* would recommend for wet shoes—a method, I must add, that is independent of the weather—involves a more reliable source of heat in Maine: namely, the furnace. When you consider that the days when shoes get wet are days, as a rule, when we don't see the sun, you'll recognize the furnace-room method as having certain advantages."

"With a grain of salt, Homer," Mrs. Draper would tell the boy. Even the professor called her Mom; even Mom called him Professor.

If Homer Wells found the professor's conversation abounding in pithy maxims, he didn't complain. If Professor Draper's students at the college and his colleagues in the history department thought that the professor was a sententious bore—and tended to flee his path like rabbits escaping the slow but nose-to-the-ground hound—they could not influence Homer's opinion of the first father figure in his life to rival Dr. Larch.

Homer's arrival in Waterville was greeted by the kind of attention the boy had never known. Nurse Angela and Nurse Edna were emergency providers, and Dr. Larch an affectionate, if stern and distracted, overseer. But Mrs. Draper was a mom's mom; she was a hoverer. She was up before Homer was awake; the cookies she baked while he ate his breakfast were miraculously still warm in his lunch bag at noon. Mom Draper *hiked* to school with Homer—they went overland, disdaining the road; it was her "constitutional," she said.

In the afternoons, Professor Draper met Homer in the school's playground—school's end seemed magically timed to coincide with the professor's last class of the day at the college—and they would tramp home together. In the winter, which in Waterville came early, this was a literal tramping—on snowshoes, the mastery of which the professor placed on a level of learning to read and write.

"Use the body, use the mind, Homer," the professor said.

It's easy to see why Wilbur Larch was impressed with the man. He vigorously represented usefulness.

In truth, Homer liked the routine of it, the *tramp, tramp* of it, the utter predictability of it. An orphan is simply more of a child than other children in that essential appreciation of the things that happen daily, on schedule. For everything that promises to last, to stay the same, the orphan is a sucker.

Dr. Larch ran the boys' division with as many of the simulated manifestations of daily life as are possible to cultivate at an orphanage. Meals were promptly served at the same time, every day. Dr. Larch would read aloud at the same evening hour for the same length of time, even if it meant leaving a chapter in midadventure, with the boys shouting, "More, more, just read the *next* thing that happens!"

And St. Larch would say, "Tomorrow, same time, same place." There would be groans of disappointment, but Larch knew that he had made a promise; he had established a routine. "Here in St. Cloud's," he wrote in his journal, "security is measured by the number of promises kept. Every child understands a promise—*if* it is kept—and looks forward to the next promise. Among orphans, you build security slowly but regularly."

Slow but regular would describe the life that Homer Wells led with the Drapers in Waterville. Every activity was a lesson; each corner of the comfortable old house held something to be learned and then counted upon.

"This is Rufus. He's very old," the professor would say, introducing Homer to the dog. "This is Rufus's rug, this is his kingdom. When Rufus is sleeping on his kingdom, do not wake him—unless you are prepared for him to snap." Whereupon the professor would rouse the ancient dog, who would *snap* awake—and then appear to puzzle over the air he had bitten, tasting in it the Drapers' grown-up children, now married and with children of their own.

Homer met them all for Thanksgiving. Thanksgiving with the Drapers was an experience in family guaranteed to make other families feel inferior. Mom would outdo herself at momness. The professor had a lecture ready on every conceivable subject: the qualities of white meat, and of dark; the last election; the pretension of salad forks; the superiority of the nineteenth-century novel (not to mention other aspects of that century's superiority); the proper texture of cranberry sauce; the meaning of "repentance"; the wholesomeness of exercise (including a comparison between splitting wood and ice skating); the evil inherent in naps. To each laboriously expressed opinion of the professor's, his grown children (two married women, one married man) would respond with a fairly balanced mixture of:

"Just so!"

"Isn't that always the way?"

"Right again, Professor!"

These robotlike responses were punctuated, with equal precision, by Mom's oft-repeated, "Grain of salt, grain of salt."

Homer Wells listened to these steady rhythms like a visitor from another world trying to decipher a strange tribe's drums. He couldn't quite catch on. The seeming constancy of everyone was overwhelming. He wouldn't know until he was much older just which it was that didn't set well with him—the implicit (and explicit) and self-congratulatory do-gooderism, or the heartiness with which life was tediously oversimplified.

Whichever it was, he stopped liking it; it became an obstacle in the path he was looking for that led to himself—to who he was, or should be. He remembered various Thanksgivings at St. Cloud's. They were not so cheery as the Waterville Thanksgiving with the Draper family, but they seemed a lot more real. He remembered how he had felt of use. There were always babies who couldn't feed themselves. There was the likelihood of a snowstorm that would knock out the electricity; Homer was put in charge of the candles and the kerosene lamps. He was also in charge of helping the kitchen staff clear, of helping Nurse Angela and Nurse Edna comfort the crying—of being Dr. Larch's messenger: the most prized responsibility that was conferred in the boys' division. Before he was ten, and long before he would be given such explicit instruction from Dr. Larch, Homer felt full of *usefulness* at St. Cloud's.

What was it about Thanksgiving at the Drapers' that contrasted so severely with the same event at St. Cloud's? Mom had no match as a cook; it couldn't have been the food—which, at St. Cloud's, suffered from a visible and seemingly terminal grayness. Was it the saying of grace? At St. Cloud's, grace was a rather blunt instrument—Dr. Larch not being a religious man.

"Let us be thankful," he would say, and then pause—as if he were truly wondering, What for? "Let us be thankful for what kindness we have received," Larch would say, cautiously looking at the unwanted and abandoned around him. "Let us be thankful for Nurse Angela and for Nurse Edna," he would add, with more assurance in his voice. "Let us be thankful that we've got options, that we've got second chances," he added once, looking at Homer Wells.

The event of grace—at Thanksgiving, at St. Cloud's—was shrouded with chance, with understandable caution, with typically Larchlike reserve.

Grace at the Drapers' was effusive and strange. It seemed somehow connected with the professor's definition of the meaning of "repentance." Professor Draper said that the start of real repentance was to accept yourself as vile. For grace, the professor cried out, "Say after me: I am vile, I abhor myself, but I am thankful for everyone in my family!" They all said so—even Homer, even Mom (who for once withheld her recommended grain of salt).

St. Cloud's was a sober place, but its manner of giving what little thanks it could seemed frank, sincere. Some contradiction in the Draper family occurred to Homer Wells for the first time at Thanksgiving. Unlike St. Cloud's, life in Waterville seemed good—babies, for example, were wanted. Where did "repentance" come from, then? Was there guilt attached to feeling lucky? And if Larch (as Homer had been told) was named from a tree, God (whom Homer heard a lot about in Waterville) seemed to be named from even tougher stuff: maybe from mountain, maybe from ice. If God was sobering in Waterville, the Draper Thanksgiving was—to Homer's surprise —a drunken occasion.

The professor was, in Mom's words, "in his cups." This, Homer deduced, meant that the professor had consumed more than his normal, daily amount of alcohol—which, in Mom's words, made him only "tipsy." Homer was shocked to see the two married daughters and the married son behave as if they were in their cups, too. And since Thanksgiving was special and he was allowed to stay up late—with all the grandchildren— Homer observed that nightly occurrence he had previously only heard as he was falling asleep: the thudding, dragging, shuffling sound, and the muffled voice of reason, which was the professor slurring his protest of the fact that Mom forcibly assisted him upstairs and with astonishing strength lifted him to and deposited him upon the bed.

"Value of exercise!" shouted the grown and married son, before toppling from the green chaise and collapsing upon the rug—beside old Rufus—as if he'd been poisoned.

"Like father, like son!" said one of the married daughters. The other married daughter, Homer noted, had nothing to say. She slept peacefully in the rocking chair; her whole hand— above the second knuckle joints—was submerged in her nearly full drink, which rested precariously in her lap.

The unmanaged grandchildren violated the house's million rules. The professor's passionate readings of various riot acts were seemingly ignored for Thanksgiving.

Homer Wells, not yet ten, crept quietly to his bed. Invoking an especially sad memory of St. Cloud's was a way he frequently forced sleep upon himself. What he remembered was the time he saw the mothers leaving the orphanage hospital, which was within view of the girls' division and which adjoined the boys' division—they were architecturally linked by a long shed, formerly a storage room for spare blades to the circular saw. It was early morning, but it was still dark out and Homer needed the coach lights in order to see that it was snowing. He slept badly and was often awake for the arrival of the coach, which came from the railroad station and delivered to St. Cloud's the kitchen and cleaning staff and the first hospital shift. The coach was simply an abandoned railroad car; set on sled runners in the winter, it was a converted sleigh, pulled by horses. When there wasn't enough snow on the dirt road, the sled runners struck sparks against the stones in the ground and made a terrible grating noise (they were reluctant to change the runners for wheels until they knew the winter was over). A bright light, like a flare, sputtered by the heavily blanketed driver on the makeshift carriage seat; softer lights winked inside the coach car.

This morning, Homer noted, there were women waiting in the snow to be picked up by the coach. Homer Wells didn't recognize the women, who fidgeted the whole time it took the St. Cloud's staff to unload. There seemed to be a certain tension between these groups—the women waiting to board appeared shy, even ashamed; the men and women coming to work seemed, by comparison, arrogant, even superior, and one of them (it was a woman) made a rough remark to the women waiting to leave. Homer couldn't hear the remark, but its effect drove the waiting women away from the coach like a blast of the winter wind. The women who boarded the coach did not look back, or even at each other. They didn't even speak, and the driver, who struck Homer as a friendly man who had something to say to nearly everyone in any weather, had no words for them. The coach simply turned around and glided across the snow to the station; in the lit windows, Homer Wells could see that several of the women had their faces in their hands, or sat as stonily as the other kind of mourner at a funeral—the one who must assume an attitude of total disinterest or else risk total loss of control.

He had never before seen the mothers who had their unwanted babies at St. Cloud's and then left them there, and he didn't see them very clearly this time. It was unquestionably more meaningful that he first saw them as they were taking their leave rather than arriving, full-bellied and undelivered of their problems. Importantly, Homer knew they did not look delivered of *all* their problems when they left. No one he had seen looked more miserable than those women; he suspected it was no accident that they left in darkness.

When he tried to put himself to sleep, Thanksgiving night

with the Drapers in Waterville, Homer Wells saw the mothers leaving in the snow, but he also saw more than he'd actually seen. On the nights he couldn't sleep, Homer rode in the coach to the station with the women, he boarded the train with them, he went to their homes with them; he singled out *his* mother and followed *her*. It was hard to see what she looked like and where she lived, where she'd come from, if she'd gone back there—and harder still was to imagine who his father was, and if she went back to *him*. Like most orphans, Homer Wells imagined that he saw his missing parents often, but he was always unrecognized by them. As a child he was embarrassed to be caught staring at adults, sometimes affectionately, other times with an instinctual hostility he would not have recognized on his own face.

"You stop it, Homer," Dr. Larch used to say to him at those times. "You just cut it out."

As an adult, Homer Wells would still get caught staring.

But on Thanksgiving night in Waterville, he stared so hard into his *real* parents' lives that he almost found them before he fell asleep, exhausted. He was abruptly awakened by one of the grandchildren, an older boy; Homer had forgotten he was going to share his bed with him because the house was crowded.

"Move over," the boy said. Homer moved over. "Keep your pecker in your pajamas," the boy told Homer, who had no intention of taking it out. "You know what *buggering* is?" the boy asked, then.

"No," Homer said.

"Yes, you do, Pecker Head," the boy said. "That's what you all do at Saint Cloud's. You bugger yourselves. All the time. I'm telling you, you try to bugger me and you'll go back there without your pecker," the boy said. "I'll cut off your pecker and feed it to the dog."

"You mean Rufus?" Homer Wells asked.

"That's right, Pecker Head," the boy said. "You want to tell me again you don't know what buggering is?"

"I don't know," Homer said.

"You want me to show you, don't you?" the boy asked.

"I don't think so," Homer said.

"Yes, you do, Pecker Head," the boy said, and he then tried to bugger Homer Wells. Homer had never seen or heard of anyone being so abused at St. Cloud's. Although the older boy had learned his style of buggery at a private school—a very good one—he had never been educated in the kind of crying that Homer Wells had been taught by the family from Three Mile Falls. It seemed to Homer that it was a good time for crying, loudly—if one wanted to escape the buggery—and his crying immediately awakened the one adult in the Draper household who had merely gone to sleep (as opposed to passing out). In other words, Homer woke Mom. He woke all the grandchildren, too, and since several of them were younger than Homer, and all of them had no knowledge of Homer's capacity for howls, his crying produced sheer terror among them—and even aroused Rufus, who snapped.

"What in Heaven's name?" Mom asked, at Homer's door.

"He tried to bugger me, so I let him have it," said the private school boy. Homer, who was struggling to get his legendary howls under control—to send them back to history—didn't know that grandchildren are believed before orphans.

"Here in St. Cloud's," wrote Dr. Larch, "it is self-defeating and cruel to give much thought to ancestors. In other parts of the world, I'm sorry to say, an orphan's ancestors are always under suspicion."

Mom hit Homer as hard as any representative of the failed family from Three Mile Falls ever hit him. She then banished him to the furnace room for the remainder of the night; it was at least warm and dry there, and there was a fold-out cot, which in the summers was used for camping trips.

There were also lots of wet shoes—a pair of which even belonged to Homer. Some of the wet socks were almost dry, and fit him. And the assortment of wet snowsuits and hardy tramping clothes gave Homer an adequate selection. He dressed himself in warm, outdoor clothes, which were—for the most part—nearly dry. He knew that Mom and the professor thought too highly of family ever to send him back to St. Cloud's over a mere buggery; if he wanted to go back, and he did, he'd have to leave on his own initiative.

In fact, Mom had provided Homer with a vision of how his alleged buggery would be treated and, doubtlessly, cured. She'd made him kneel before the fold-out cot in the furnace room.

"Say after me," she said, and repeated the professor's strange version of grace. " 'I am vile, I abhor myself,' " Mom said, and Homer had said it after her—knowing that every word was untrue. He'd never liked himself so much. He felt he was on the track to finding out who he was, and how he could be of use, but he knew that the path led back to St. Cloud's.

When Mom kissed him good night, she said, "Now, Homer, don't mind what the professor has to say about this. Whatever he says, you just take it with a grain of salt."

Homer Wells didn't wait to hear the text of the professor's lesson regarding buggery. Homer stepped outside; even the snow didn't stop him. In Waterville, in 193__, it was no surprise to see so much snow on the ground for Thanksgiving; and Professor Draper had very carefully instructed Homer on the merits and methods of snowshoeing.

Homer was a good tramper. He found the town road fairly easily, and the bigger road after that. It was daylight when the first truck stopped; it was a logging truck. This seemed, to Homer, appropriate to where he was going. "I belong to Saint Cloud's," he told the driver. "I got lost." In 193__ every logger knew where St. Cloud's was; this driver knew it was in the other direction.

"You're going the wrong way, kid," he advised the boy. "Turn around and look for a truck going the other way. What are you, *from* Saint Cloud's?" the driver asked. Like most people, he assumed that orphans were always running away *from* the orphanage—not running *to* it.

"I just belong there," Homer Wells said, and the driver waved good-bye. In Dr. Larch's opinion, this driver—in order to be so insensitive as to let a boy go off alone in the snow— simply had to be an employee of the Ramses Paper Company.

The next driver was also driving a logging truck; it was empty, it was heading back to the forest for more logs, and St. Cloud's was more or less on the way.

"You an orphan?" the driver asked Homer, when he said he was going to St. Cloud's.

"No," Homer said. "I just belong there—for now."

In 193__, it took a long time to drive anywhere in Maine, especially with snow on the roads. It was growing dark when Homer Wells returned to his home. The quality of the light was the same as the early morning when he'd seen the mothers leaving their babies behind. Homer stood at the hospital entrance for a while and watched the snow fall. Then he went and stood at the entrance to the boys' division. Then he went back and stood outside the hospital entrance, because there was better light there.

He was still thinking of exactly what to say to Dr. Larch when the coach from the railroad station—that unmerry sleigh—stopped at the hospital entrance and let out a single passenger. She was so pregnant that the driver at first appeared concerned she might slip and fall; then the driver appeared to realize why the woman had come here, and it must have struck him as immoral that he should actually help a woman like that through the snow. He drove off and left her making her careful way toward the entrance, and toward Homer Wells. Homer rang the bell at the entrance for the woman, who didn't seem to know what to do. It occurred to him that she was hoping for a little time to think of what she too wanted to say to Dr. Larch.

To anyone seeing them there, this was a mother with her son. There was just that kind of familiarity in the way that they looked at each other, and in the clear recognition between them—they knew perfectly well what the other was up to. Homer was worried what Dr. Larch would say to him, but he realized that the woman was more worried than he was—the woman didn't know Dr. Larch; she had no idea what sort of place St. Cloud's was.

More lights were turned on inside, and Homer recognized the divine shape of Nurse Angela coming to open the door. For some reason, he reached out and took the pregnant woman's hand. Maybe it was the tear frozen to her face that the new light had allowed him to see, but he wanted a hand to hold himself. He was calm—Homer Wells—as Nurse Angela peered into the snowy night in disbelief while she struggled to open the frozen door. To the pregnant woman, and to her unwanted child, Homer said, "Don't worry. Everyone is nice here."

He felt the pregnant woman squeeze his hand so hard that it hurt. The word "Mother!" was strangely on his lips when Nurse Angela finally got the door open and seized Homer Wells in her arms.

"Oh, *oh*!" she cried. "Oh, *Homer*—my Homer, *our* Homer! I knew you'd be back!"

And because the pregnant woman's hand still firmly held Homer's hand—neither one of them felt able to let go—Nurse Angela turned and included the woman in her embrace. It seemed to Nurse Angela that this pregnant woman was just another orphan who belonged (like Homer Wells) exactly where she was.

/ / /

What he told Dr. Larch was that he'd felt of no use in Waterville. Because of what the Drapers had said, when they'd called Larch to say that Homer had run away, Homer had to explain about the buggery—afterward, St. Larch explained all about buggery to Homer. The professor's drinking surprised Dr. Larch (he was good, as a rule, at detecting that), and the prayers baffled Larch. Dr. Larch's note to the Drapers was of a brevity the professor's own language rarely allowed.

"Repent," the note said. Larch might have left it at that, but he couldn't resist adding, "You *are* vile, you *should* abhor yourselves."

Wilbur Larch knew that a fourth foster family for Homer Wells would not be easy to find. The search took Dr. Larch three years, by which time Homer was twelve—almost thirteen. Larch knew what the danger would be: it would take Homer a great many years to feel as comfortable anywhere else as he felt at St. Cloud's.

"Here in St. Cloud's," Larch wrote in his journal, "we have only one problem. That there will always be orphans is not in the category of a problem; that is simply not to be solved—one does the best one can with that, one takes care of them. That our budget will always be too small is also not a problem; that won't be solved, either—an orphanage goes down to the wire; by definition, that is what should happen. And it is *not* a problem that every woman who gets pregnant doesn't necessarily want her baby; perhaps we can look ahead to a more enlightened time, when women will have the right to abort the birth of an unwanted child—but some women will always be uneducated, will always be confused, will always be frightened. Even in enlightened times, unwanted babies will manage to be born.

"And there will always be babies, who *were* very much wanted, who will *end up* orphans—by accident, by both planned and random acts of violence, which are not problems either. Here in St. Cloud's we would waste our limited energy and our limited imagination by regarding the sordid *facts* of life as if they were problems. Here in St. Cloud's we have only one problem. His name is Homer Wells. We have been very successful with Homer. We have managed to make the orphanage his home, and that is the problem. If you try to give an institution of the state, or of any government, anything like the love one is meant to invest in a family—and if the institution is an orphanage and you *succeed* in giving it love—then you will create a monster: an orphanage that is not a way-station to a better life, but an orphanage that is the first and last stop, and the only station the orphan will accept.

"There is no excuse for cruelty, but—at an orphanage—perhaps we are obliged to withhold love; if you fail to withhold love at an orphanage, you will create an orphanage that no orphan will willingly leave. You will create a Homer Wells—a true orphan, because his only home will always be at St. Cloud's. God (or whoever) forgive me. I have made an orphan; his name is Homer Wells and he will belong to St. Cloud's forever."

By the time Homer was twelve, he had the run of the place. He knew its stoves and its wood boxes, its fuse boxes, its linen closets, its laundry room, its kitchen, its corners where the cats slept—when the mail came, who got any, everyone's name, who was on what shift; where the mothers went to be shaved when they arrived, how long the mothers stayed, when—and with what necessary assistance—they left. He knew the bells; in fact, he rang them. He knew who the tutors were; he could recognize their style of walking from the train station, when they were still two hundred yards away. He was even known at the girls' division, although the very few girls older than he was frightened him and he spent as little time there as he could—going only on errands for Dr. Larch: messages and delivering medicines. The director of the girls' division was not a doctor, so when the girls were sick, either they visited Dr. Larch at the hospital or Larch went to the girls' division to visit them. The director of the girls' division was Boston Irish and had worked for a while at The New England Home for Little Wanderers. Her name was Mrs. Grogan, although she never mentioned Mr. Grogan, and no one seeing her would have an easy time imagining that there had ever been a man in her life. She may have preferred the sound of Missus to the sound of Miss. At The New England Home for Little Wanderers she had belonged to a society called God's Little Servants, which had given Dr. Larch pause. But Mrs. Grogan showed no signs of seeking members for such a society in St. Cloud's; perhaps she was too busy—in addition to her duties as director of the girls' division, she was responsible for arranging what little education was available for the orphans.

If there was an orphan who remained at St. Cloud's past the

sixth grade level of school, there was no school to go to—and the only school for grades one through six was in Three Mile Falls; this was only a one-station stop on the train from St. Cloud's, but in 193__ the trains were often delayed, and the Thursday engineer was notorious for forgetting to stop at the St. Cloud's station (as if the sight of so many abandoned buildings convinced him that St. Cloud's was still a ghost town, or perhaps he disapproved of the women who got off the train there).

The majority of the pupils in the one-room schoolhouse in Three Mile Falls thought themselves superior to the occasional orphans in attendance; this feeling prevailed the most strongly among those students who came from families where they were neglected or abused, or both, and thus grades one through six, for Homer Wells, were comprised of experiences more combative than educational. He missed three Thursdays out of four, for years, and at least one other day (every week) because of a late train; in the winters, he missed a day a week because he was sick. And when there was too much snow, the trains didn't run.

The three tutors suffered the same perils pressed upon train service in those years, because they all came to St. Cloud's from Three Mile Falls. There was a woman who taught math; she was a bookkeeper for a textile mill—"a real-life accountant," Nurse Edna claimed—but she refused to have anything to do with algebra or geometry, and she firmly preferred addition and subtraction to multiplication and division (Homer Wells would be a grown man before Dr. Larch would discover that the boy had never learned the multiplication table).

Another woman, a well-to-do plumber's widow, taught grammar and spelling. Her method was rigorous and messy. She presented great clumps of uncapitalized, misspelled, and unpunctuated words, and demanded that the clumps be put into proper sentences, meticulously punctuated and correctly spelled. She then corrected the corrections; the final document—she employed a system of different-colored inks—resembled a much-revised treaty between two semiliterate countries at war. The text itself was always strange to Homer Wells, even when it was finally correct. This was because the woman borrowed heavily from a family hymnal, and Homer Wells had never seen a church or heard a hymn (unless one counted Christmas carols, or the songs Mrs. Grogan sang—and the plumber's widow was not such a fool that she used Christmas carols). Homer Wells used to have nightmares about deciphering the passages that the plumber's widow concocted.

> o lorde mi got wen i en ausum wundor
> konsider al the wurlds thi hends hav mad . . .

Or there was this one:

> o ruck of eges clift fur me let mi hid misulf en theee . . .

And so forth.

The third tutor, a retired schoolteacher from Camden, was an old, unhappy man who lived with his daughter's family because he couldn't take care of himself. He taught history, but he had no books. He taught the world from memory; he said the dates weren't important. He was capable of sustaining a rant about Mesopotamia for a full half hour, but when he paused for breath, or for a sip of water, he would find himself in Rome, or in Troy; he would recite long, uninterrupted passages from Thucydides, but a mere swallow would transport him to Elba, with Napoleon.

"I think," Nurse Edna once remarked to Dr. Larch, "that he manages to give a sense of the scope of history."

Nurse Angela rolled her eyes. "Whenever I try to listen to him," she said, "I can think of a hundred good reasons for war."

She meant, Homer Wells understood, that no one should live so long.

It is easy to understand why Homer was more fond of doing chores than he was fond of education.

Homer's favorite chore was selecting, for Dr. Larch, the evening reading. He was supposed to estimate a passage that would take Dr. Larch exactly twenty minutes to read; this was difficult because when Homer read aloud to himself, he read more slowly than Dr. Larch, but when he simply read to himself, he read more quickly than Dr. Larch could read aloud. At twenty minutes an evening, it took Dr. Larch several months to read *Great Expectations,* and more than a year to read *David Copperfield*—at the end of which time, St. Larch announced to Homer that he would start at the beginning of *Great Expectations* again. Except for Homer, the orphans who'd first heard *Great Expectations* had moved on.

Almost none of them understood *Great Expectations* or *David Copperfield,* anyway. They were not only too young for the Dickensian language, they were also too young to comprehend the usual language of St. Cloud's. What mattered to Dr. Larch was the idea of reading aloud—it was a successful soporific for the children who didn't know what they were listening to, and for those few who understood the words and the story, the evening reading provided them with a way to leave St. Cloud's in their dreams, in their imaginations.

Dickens was a personal favorite of Dr. Larch; it was no accident, of course, that both *Great Expectations* and *David Copperfield* were concerned with orphans. ("What in hell else would you read to an orphan?" Dr. Larch inquired in his journal.)

And so Homer Wells was familiar with the vision of that gibbet in the marshland—"with some chains hanging to it which had once held a pirate"—and Homer's imagination of the orphan, Pip, and the convict, Magwitch . . . the beautiful Estella, the vengeful Miss Havisham . . . provided him with sharper details when, falling asleep, he would follow the ghostly mothers who left St. Cloud's in the cover of darkness, and boarded the horse-drawn coach car, or, later, the bus which replaced the coach, and gave Homer Wells his first sensation of the passage of time, of progress. Soon after the bus replaced the coach, all bus service in St. Cloud's was discontinued. Thereafter, the mothers walked; this gave Homer further understanding of progress.

The mothers he saw in his sleep never changed. But the men who had not bothered to accompany them to St. Cloud's—where were they? Homer liked the part in *Great Expectations* when Pip is just starting out and he says that "the mists had all solemnly risen . . . and the world lay spread before me." A boy from St. Cloud's knew plenty about "mists"—they were what shrouded the river, the town, the orphanage itself; they drifted downriver from Three Mile Falls; they were what concealed one's parents. They were the clouds of St. Cloud's that allowed one's parents to slip away, unseen.

"Homer," Dr. Larch would say, "one day you'll get to see the ocean. You've only been as far as the mountains; they're not nearly as spectacular as the sea. There's fog on the coast—it can be worse than the fog here—and when the fog lifts, Homer . . . well," said St. Larch, "that's a moment you must see."

But Homer Wells had already seen it, he'd already imagined it—"the mists . . . all solemnly risen." He smiled at Dr. Larch and excused himself; it was time to ring a bell. That was what he was doing—bell-ringing—when his fourth foster family arrived at St. Cloud's to fetch him. Dr. Larch had prepared him very well; Homer had no trouble recognizing the couple.

They were, in today's language, sports-oriented; in Maine, in 193—, when Homer Wells was twelve, the couple who wanted to adopt him were simply thought fanatical about everything that could be done outdoors. They were a white-water-canoeing couple, an ocean-sailing couple—a mountain-climbing, deep-sea-diving, wilderness-camping couple. A one-hundred-mile (at forced-march-pace) tramping couple. Athletes—but not of organized sports; they were not a sissy-sport couple.

The day they arrived at St. Cloud's, Homer Wells rang the bell for ten o'clock fourteen times. He was transfixed by them—by their solid, muscular looks, by their loping strides, by his safari hat, by her bushwhacking machete in a long sheath (with Indian beads) at her cartridge belt. They both wore boots that looked lived in. Their vehicle was a homemade pioneer of what would years later be called a camper; it looked equipped to capture and contain a rhino. Homer instantly foresaw that he would be made to hunt bears, wrestle alligators—in short, live off the land. Nurse Edna stopped him before he could ring fifteen o'clock.

Wilbur Larch was being cautious. He didn't fear for Homer's mind. A boy who has read *Great Expectations* and *David Copperfield* by himself, twice each—and had each word of both books read aloud to him, also twice—is more mentally prepared than most. Dr. Larch felt that the boy's physical or athletic development had been less certain. Sports seemed frivolous to Larch when compared to the learning of more necessary, more fundamental skills. Larch knew that the St. Cloud's sports program—which consisted of indoor football in the dining hall when there was bad weather—was inadequate. In good weather, the boys' and girls' divisions played tag, or kick the can, or sometimes Nurse Edna or Nurse Angela pitched for stickball. The ball was composed of several socks wrapped in adhesive tape; it moved poorly. Larch had nothing against an outdoor life; he also knew nothing about one. He guessed that a little of its wasted energy (wasted to Larch) would be good for Homer—possibly such physical activity might enhance the boy's sense of humor.

The couple's name was a source of humor for Nurse Edna and Nurse Angela. Their married name was Winkle—he was called Grant, she was called Billy. They were members of Maine's very small money class. Their business, as they ridiculously called it, didn't make a cent, but they didn't need to make money; they were born rich. Their needless enterprise consisted of taking people to the wilderness and creating for them the sensation that they were lost there; they also took people shooting down rapids in frail rafts or canoes, creating for them the sensation that they would surely be bashed to death before they drowned. The Winkles were in the business of manufacturing sensations for people who were so removed from any sensations of their own making or circumstances that only high (but simulated) adventure could provoke any response from them at all. Dr. Larch was not impressed with the Winkles' "business"; he knew that they were simply rich people who did exactly what they wanted to do and needed to call what they did something more serious-sounding than play. What impressed Larch with the Winkles was that they were deliriously happy. Among adults—and among orphans—Wilbur Larch noted that delirious happiness was rare.

"In other parts of the world," Dr. Larch wrote, "delirious happiness is thought to be a state of mind. Here in St. Cloud's we recognize that delirious happiness is possible only for the totally mindless. I would call it, therefore, that thing most rare: a state of the soul." Larch was often facetious when he discussed the soul. He liked to tease Nurse Edna and Nurse Angela in the operating room, where the subject of the soul could catch the dear nurses off-guard.

Once, with a body open on the table, Larch pointed dramatically to a smooth, maroon shape beneath the rib cage and above the belly's viscera; it looked like a three-pound loaf of bread, or a slug with two great lobes. "Look!" Larch whispered. "You rarely see it, but we've caught it napping. Look quickly before it moves!" The nurses gaped. "The *soul*," Larch whispered reverentially. In fact, it was the body's largest gland, empowered with skills also ascribed to the soul—for example, it could regenerate its own abused cells. It was the *liver*, which Larch thought more of than he thought of the soul.

But whether the delirious happiness of the Winkles was a state of mind or a state of the soul, Wilbur Larch wished that some of it could rub off on Homer Wells. The Winkles had always wanted a child—"to share the world of nature with us," they said, "and just to make a child happy, of course." Looking at them, Dr. Larch had his own ideas as to why they could not successfully breed. Lack of the essential concentration, Larch thought; Larch suspected that the Winkles never stopped moving long enough to mate. Perhaps, he speculated, looking at Billy Winkle, she is not really a woman.

Grant had a plan. He has no face, Dr. Larch noticed, trying to discern the man's blunt features, somewhere between his blond beard and his blonder hair. The hair was cropped in bangs, completely concealing a low forehead. The cheeks, or what Larch could see of them, were a ridge, the eyes hidden behind them. The rest was beard—a blond underbrush that Dr. Larch imagined Billy Winkle needed her machete to hack through. Grant's plan was that they borrow Homer for a little moose-watching. The Winkles were going on a canoe trip and portage through the northern State Forest, the principal fun of which was to see moose. A secondary pleasure would be introducing Homer Wells to a little white water.

St. Larch felt that such a trip, in the massive hands of the Winkles, wouldn't be dangerous for Homer. He felt less sure that Homer would want to stay with these people, to actually be adopted by them. He hardly worried that the Winkles' craziness would bother the boy, and it wouldn't have. What boy is troubled by perpetual adventure? What Wilbur Larch suspected was that the Winkles would bore Homer to tears, if not to death. A camping trip in the State Forest—white water now and then, a moose or two—might give the boy an idea of whether or not he could stand Grant and Billy forever.

"And if you have a good time in the woods," Grant Winkle told Homer cheerfully, "then we'll take you out on the ocean!" They probably ride whales, Homer imagined. They tease sharks, Dr. Larch thought.

But Dr. Larch wanted Homer to try it, and Homer Wells was willing—he would try anything for St. Larch.

"Nothing dangerous," Larch said sternly to the Winkles.

"Oh, no, cross our hearts!" cried Billy; Grant crossed his, too.

Dr. Larch knew there was only one road that ran through

the northern State Forest. It was built by, and remained the property of, the Ramses Paper Company. They were not allowed to cut the trees in the State Forest, but they could drive their equipment through it en route to the trees that were theirs. Only this—that Homer was going anywhere near where the Ramses Paper Company was operating—troubled Dr. Larch.

Homer was surprised at how little room there was in the cab of the homemade safari vehicle that the Winkles drove. The equipment it carried was impressive: the canoe, the tent, the fishing gear, the cooking miscellany, the guns. But there was little room for the driver and the passengers. In the cab, Homer sat on Billy's lap; it was a big lap but strangely uncomfortable because of the hardness of her thighs. Homer had felt a woman's lap only once before, during St. Cloud's annual three-legged race.

Once a year the boys' and girls' divisions amused the town with this race. It was a fund-raiser for the orphanage, so everyone endured it. The last two years Homer had won the race—only because his partner, the oldest girl in the girls' division, was strong enough to pick him up and run with him in her arms across the finish line. The idea was that a boy and a girl of comparable age fastened *his* left leg to *her* right; they then hopped toward the finish line, on each of their free legs, dragging the miserable so-called third leg between them. The big girl from the girls' division hadn't needed to drag Homer— she cheated, she just carried him. But last year she had fallen at the finish line, pulling Homer into her lap. By mistake, trying to get out of her lap, he'd put his hand on her breast and she'd sharply pinched what the private school boy in Waterville had called his pecker.

Her name was Melony, which was, like several of the orphans' names in the girls' division, a typographical error. Melony's name had been, officially, Melody—but the girls' division secretary was a terrible typist. The mistyping was a fortunate mistake, actually, because there was nothing melodious about the girl. She was about sixteen (no one really knew her exact age), and there was in the fullness of her breasts and in the roundness of her bottom very much the suggestion of melons.

In the long ride north, Homer worried that Billy Winkle might pinch his pecker, too. He watched the houses disappear, and the farm animals; other cars and trucks were gone from the roads. Soon it was just a road, a single road—most often, it ran alongside water; the water ran fast. Ahead of them—for hours, it seemed—loomed a mountain that had snow on the top, although it was July. The mountain had an Indian name.

"That's where we're going, Homer!" Grant Winkle told the boy. "Just under all that snow, there's a lake."

"The moose are crazy about the lake," Billy told Homer, "and you'll be crazy about the lake, too."

Homer didn't doubt it. It was an adventure. Dr. Larch had told him he didn't have to stay.

The Winkles stopped for the night before it got dark. Between the single road and the rushing water, they pitched a tent with three rooms in it. They lit a cookstove in one of the rooms, and Billy did one hundred sit-ups in another room (Homer held her feet) while Grant caught some brook trout. It was such a cool evening, there weren't any bugs; they kept the lamps running long after dark, with the tent flaps open. Grant and Billy told adventure stories. (In his journal, Dr. Larch would later write, "What the hell else would they tell?")

Grant told about the sixty-year-old lawyer who had hired them to show him a bear giving birth. Billy showed Homer her bear scars. And then there was the man who had asked the Winkles to cast him adrift at sea in a small boat—with only one oar. This man had been interested in the sensation of survival. He wanted to see if he could find his way back to land, but he wanted the Winkles to observe him and rescue him if he was getting into real trouble. The trick to that was not letting the man know he was being observed. At night—when the fool fell asleep and drifted farther out to sea—the Winkles would cautiously tow him toward shore. But in the morning—once, even within sight of land—the man always found a way to get lost again. They finally had to rescue him when they caught him drinking salt water; he'd been so disappointed, he gave them several bad checks before he finally paid his adventure fee.

"Adventure fee" was Billy's name for it.

Homer thought it might make his would-be adoptive parents self-conscious if he told them any stories about life at St. Cloud's—or worse, about Thanksgiving in Waterville. He felt he had to contribute something to the campfire spirit of this present adventure, but the only good stories he knew were *Great Expectations* and *David Copperfield*. Dr. Larch had let him take the copy of *Great Expectations* with him; it was Homer's favorite of the two. Homer asked the Winkles if he could read them a little of his favorite story. Of course, they said, they'd love it; they'd never been read to, not that they could remember. Homer was a little nervous; as many times as he'd read *Great Expectations,* he'd never read aloud to an audience before.

But he was wonderful! He even mastered what he guessed was Joe Gargery's accent, and by the time he got to the part where Mr. Wopsle cries out, " 'No!' with the feeble malice of a tired man," Homer sensed he had found the proper voice for the whole tale—he felt he might also have discovered his first talent. Unfortunately, talented though he was, his reading put the Winkles fast asleep. Homer kept reading by himself, through the end of Chapter 7. Maybe it's not my reading, Homer thought; maybe it's the Winkles—all her sit-ups, all his trout-catching, all the fierce rigor of the indisputably great outdoors.

Homer attempted to arrange the Winkles' sleeping bag—a huge, single bag—comfortably around them. He blew out the lamps. He went to his own room in the vast tent and crawled into his own sleeping bag. He lay with his head by the open tent flap; he could see the stars; he could hear the nearby crashing water. It did not remind him of Three Mile Falls, because the stream here was so different from that river. It was just as fast, but it ran through a deep, narrow gorge—sparkling clean, round-bouldered, with glossy pools where Grant had caught the trout. It was not unpleasant imagining further adventures with the Winkles, but Homer had more trouble imagining a moose. Exactly how big would a moose be? Bigger than the Winkles?

Homer exhibited no mistrust, and certainly no fear, of the Winkles. He felt for them only a detached wariness—he was sure they weren't dangerous but they were of a slightly altered species. He fell asleep confusing the Winkles, in his child's mind, with moose. In the morning he woke up to the sound of what he was sure *were* moose—only to discover that it was the Winkles in the tent room next to his. The Winkles appeared to greet the morning vigorously. Although Homer had never heard human beings make love, or moose mate, he knew perfectly well that the Winkles were mating. If Dr. Larch had been present, he might have drawn new conclusions concerning the Winkles' inability to produce offspring. He would have concluded that the violent athleticism of their coupling simply destroyed, or scared to death, every available egg and sperm.

Homer politely feigned sleep. The Winkles then roused him playfully. Like large dogs, they burst into his room on all fours, tugging at his sleeping bag with their teeth. They were going to swim! they told him. They were such large people, Homer wondered at the sheer abundance of their active flesh. He also wondered how they intended to swim in the raging stream without being bashed against the boulders and swept away. Homer didn't know how to swim—not even in calm water.

But the Winkles were old hands at outdoor feats of skill, and they were cunning with equipment. They threw a line across the rapids; it was called a survival rope, they told Homer. The rope attached to a rakelike cluster of spikes, which Grant Winkle neatly lodged among the rocks on the far shore of the roaring river; he then strung a second rope to this one, and then a third. These additional ropes were complicated, with metal eyelets and hooks and adjustable safety straps that went around the Winkles themselves and held them tightly at their waists. With the assistance of this truly adventuresome gear, the Winkles were able to bounce, semi-suspended, into the thick of the rapids—where they were tossed about like bathtub toys while remaining safely in the same place, attached to each other and to the so-called survival rope. It was fun for Homer to watch them. The water seemed to swallow them completely at times—streaming sheets of it would engulf them and suck them down. Yet they would emerge in seconds, bouncing, appearing to walk across the churning, rolling foam. They played in midstream like giant, blond otters. Homer was very nearly convinced of their mastery of the elements—at least of water—and felt himself to be on the verge of asking them to let him try the game of showering in the rapids when it occurred to him that they couldn't hear him. If he'd called out to them—even if he'd screamed—the *whoosh* of the turbid water all around the Winkles would have drowned out any noise he could muster.

He had resolved, therefore, to remain sitting on the shore and watch his would-be adoptive parents play, when the ground began to shake under him. He knew this more from certain badly told stories, in badly written children's books, than from the felt recognition of the moving ground itself; in those children's books, when something terrible is about to happen, the ground *always* shakes. He almost chose not to believe it, but the ground was unmistakably trembling; a dull hammering reached his ears.

Homer watched the Winkles more closely, believing them to be in control of everything. The Winkles continued to play in the rapids; they heard nothing, they didn't feel the ground shake because they weren't on the ground.

Oh my God, a *moose* is coming! thought Homer Wells. He stood up. He watched his feet hop—all by themselves—on the jumping ground. It is a *herd* of moose! he thought. To add to the hammering sound, Homer now heard sharper noises: cracks, some as startling as pistol shots. He looked at the Winkles and could tell that they'd heard these harsh slaps, too. Whatever it was that was coming, the Winkles were familiar with it; their entire attitude changed—they were no longer playful. They seemed to be struggling, and on their faces (now disappearing in the rushing white froth) their expressions were both knowledgeable and frightened. When they got a second to look (between plunges into the rapids), they looked upstream.

So did Homer—in time to see the log drive when it was about twenty-five yards away. The trees along the shoreline were occasionally snapped off as cleanly as kindling snapped over a knee—by a random log as big as a telephone pole but stouter, hurtling out of the water, striking a boulder and spinning for twenty feet through the air, leveling a patch of forest wherever it crashed and rolled on. The mass of logs, each as big as telephone poles, moved swiftly downstream with a wall of water in front of it. This water was not like the clear water of the river, but muddy with turmoil, clogged with slabs of bark, messy with whole chunks of ground that had been gouged out of the shore. The Ramses Paper Company called it a modest log drive; they said there'd been no more than four hundred, maybe seven hundred logs in that particular drive downriver.

Homer Wells was still running when he reached the road, where he was safe. He turned in time to see the logs surge by. A line from the tent had been attached to the Winkles' survival rope, and the entire tent and everything in it (Homer's copy of *Great Expectations,* too) were swept downstream in the pounding flow and charge of logs. The Ramses Paper Company wouldn't recover Billy's and Grant's bodies for three days; they found them nearly four miles away.

Homer Wells was fairly calm. He looked upstream, waiting

for more of anything; upstream was clearly the direction whatever might come next would come from. After a while, he
relaxed; he examined the Winkles' safari vehicle, which looked
naked without the tent and the kitchen equipment. He found
some fishing gear, but he didn't dare to fish; it meant standing
too close to the stream. He found some guns, but he had no
idea how they worked (he felt comforted that the guns were
there, however). He chose the biggest, most dangerous-looking
one—a twelve-gauge, double-barrel shotgun—and dragged it
around with him.

He was quite hungry by midafternoon, but before it was dark
he heard a logging truck coming nearer and nearer; he knew it
was a full one because of the straining sound of the gears. It
was also a piece of luck (on the order of his not knowing how
to swim, and therefore not joining the Winkles in their sport)
that the truck was going Homer's way.

"Saint Cloud's," he told the baffled driver, who was impressed with the shotgun.

It was a Ramses Paper Company truck, and Dr. Larch was at
first furious to see it pull up to the hospital entrance. "Unless
this is an absolute emergency," he told the smitten Nurse
Edna, "I will not do a stitch of work on anyone from that
company!" Larch was actually disappointed to see Homer
Wells, and alarmed to see the shotgun. Homer had the bewildered expression on his face of the many patients Larch had
observed emerging from the spell of ether.

"You didn't give the Winkles much of a chance, Homer,"
Dr. Larch said gravely. Then Homer explained why he'd come
back so soon.

"You mean the Winkles are *gone*?" Dr. Larch asked.

"Swept away," said Homer Wells. *"Whoosh!"*

That was when Wilbur Larch gave up on finding Homer
Wells a home. That was when Dr. Larch said that Homer
could stay at St. Cloud's for as long as Homer felt he belonged
there. That was when St. Larch said, "Well, then, Homer, I
expect you to be of use."

For Homer Wells, this was easy. *Of use,* he felt, was all that
an orphan was born to be.

2/ The Lord's Work

A child of Maine, Wilbur Larch was born in Portland in 186__—the son of a sullen, tidy woman who was among the staff of cooks and housekeepers for a man named Neal Dow, the mayor of Portland and the so-called father of the Maine law that introduced Prohibition to that state. Neal Dow once ran for the presidency as the candidate of the Prohibition Party, but he won barely ten thousand votes—proving that the general voter was wiser than Wilbur Larch's mother, who worshiped her employer and saw herself more as his co-worker for temperance reform than as his servant (which she was).

Interestingly, Wilbur Larch's father was a drunk—no small feat in the Portland of Mayor Dow's day. It was permitted to advertise beer in the shop windows—Scotch ale and bitter beer, which Wilbur Larch's father consumed copiously; it was necessary, he claimed, to drink these weak brews by the bucketful in order to get a buzz on. To young Wilbur, his father never looked drunk—he never staggered or fell or lay in a stupor, he never shouted or slurred his speech. Rather, he had about him the appearance of one perpetually surprised, of one given to frequent and sudden revelations that would stop him in his tracks, or in midsentence, as if something had just come to him (or had just escaped him) that had preoccupied him for days.

He shook his head a lot, and all his life dispensed this misinformation: that the nineteen-thousand-ton ship the *Great Eastern*, which was built in Portland, was destined to sail the North Atlantic between Europe and Maine. It was the opinion of Wilbur Larch's father that the two best wharves in Portland Harbor had been built specifically for the *Great Eastern*, that the new and huge hotel in Portland had been built expressly to house the *Great Eastern*'s passengers, and that someone evil or at least corrupt or just plain foolish was responsible for keeping the *Great Eastern* from returning to her home port in Maine.

Wilbur Larch's father had worked as a lathe operator during the building of the *Great Eastern,* and perhaps the complaining noise of that machinery and the constant buzz he felt from all the beer he consumed had deceived him. The *Great Eastern* had not been built for voyages to and from Portland; she was originally intended for the route to Australia, but the many delays in getting her to sea drove her owners to bankruptcy and she was purchased for use on the North Atlantic route for which she proved unsuitable. She was, in fact, a failure.

So Wilbur Larch's father had an addled memory of his days as a lathe operator, and he had considerable loathing for temperance reform, his wife's beliefs and his wife's employer, Mayor Neal Dow himself. In the opinion of Wilbur Larch's father, the *Great Eastern* didn't return to Portland because of Prohibition—that curse which had limited him to a bilious dependency on Scotch ale and bitter beer. Since Wilbur knew his father only in the man's later years, when the *Great Eastern* was gone and his father was a porter in the Portland station of the Grand Trunk Railway, he could only imagine why working a wood-turning machine had been the high point of his father's life.

As a boy, it never occurred to Wilbur Larch that his father's missing fingers were the result of too many Scotch ales and bitter beers while operating the lathe—"just accidents," his father said—or that his mother's zeal for temperance reform might be the result of a lathe operator's demotion to porter. Of course, Wilbur realized later, his parents were servants; their disappointment made Wilbur become what his teachers called a whale of a student.

Although he grew up in the mayor's mansion, Wilbur Larch always used the kitchen entrance and ate his meals with the great prohibitionist's hired help; his father drank his meals, down at the docks. Wilbur Larch was a good student because he preferred the company of books to overhearing his mother's talk of temperance with Mayor Dow's servants.

He went to Bowdoin College, and to Harvard Medical School—where a fascination with bacteria almost deterred him from practicing medicine, almost turned him into a laboratory animal, or at least a bacteriologist. He had a gift for the field, his professor told him, and he enjoyed the careful atmosphere of the laboratory; also, he had a burning desire to learn about bacteria. For nearly a year of medical school young Wilbur carried a bacterium that so offended and pained him that he was driven by more than scientific curiosity to discover its cure. He had gonorrhea: a gift, indirectly, from his father. The old man, in his beer buzz, had been so proud of Wilbur that he sent him to medicine school in 188__ with a present. He bought the boy a Portland whore, setting up his son with a night of supposed pleasure in one of the wharfside boardinghouses. It was a present the boy had been too embarrassed to refuse. His father's selfish nostalgia allowed him so few gestures toward his son; his mother's bitter righteousness was selfish in her own way; young Wilbur was touched that his father had offered to give him anything.

In the boardinghouse—the wood dry with salt and a sea-damp clinging to the curtains and to the bedspread—the whore reminded Wilbur of one of his mother's more attractive servant-colleagues; he shut his eyes and tried to imagine that he was embarking on a forbidden romance in a back room of the mayor's mansion. When he opened his eyes, he saw the candle-light deepening the stretch marks across the whore's abdomen; he didn't know they were stretch marks, then. The whore seemed unconcerned whether Wilbur noticed the stretch marks or not; in fact, as they fell asleep with his head on her stomach, he was vaguely wondering if the woman's wrinkles would transfer to his face—marking him. A sharp, unpleasant smell awakened him and he moved quickly off the woman, without disturbing her. In a chair in the room, the one where she'd put her clothes, someone was smoking a cigar—Wilbur saw the end glow brighter with each inhalation. He assumed that a man—the whore's next customer—was politely waiting for him to leave, but when he asked if there was a fresh candle to light (he needed to locate his clothes), it was a young girl's voice that answered him.

"You could have had me for less," was all she said. He could not see her distinctly but—since there was no fresh candle—she lit his way to his clothes by puffing earnestly on her cigar, casting both a red glow and a haze of smoke over his search. He thanked her for her help, and left.

On the morning train to Boston, he was embarrassed to

meet the whore again. A chatty woman in the daylight, she was carrying a bandbox with the authority of a chronic shopper; he felt obliged to give her his seat on the overcrowded train. A young girl was traveling with the whore—"my daughter," the whore said, indicating the girl with a jab of her thumb. The daughter reminded Wilbur that they'd already met by breathing her astonishingly foul cigar breath into his face. She was a girl not quite Wilbur's age.

The whore's name was Mrs. Eames—"She rhymes with screams!" Wilbur's father had told him. Mrs. Eames told Wilbur she was a widow who lived a proper life in Boston, but that in order to afford such a life she found it necessary to sell herself in some out-of-the-way town. She begged Wilbur to allow her to keep her appearances and her reputation intact—in Boston. Wilbur not only assured her that her reputation was safe with him; he also, unasked, paid her more money of his own, on the spot, than his father had originally paid the woman. The amount of the original payment, he learned later—when his father told Wilbur that Mrs. Eames was a proper *Portlander* of good reputation who occasionally was obliged to sell herself in *Boston* so that she might afford to keep up her appearances in Portland. As an old favor to Wilbur's father, she had allowed—"Just this once!"—the exception of lowering herself in her hometown.

Wilbur's father didn't know that Mrs. Eames had a daughter, who—by her own confession—cost less than her mother and made no pretense of keeping up appearances in either Boston or Portland. The sullen girl never spoke on the train ride into Boston's North Station; her cigar breath and her scornful gaze spoke for her. Wilbur never told his father that there was some contradiction regarding *which* town Mrs. Eames had a good reputation in, and he never told his father that he caught the clap from Mrs. Eames, who might not have known she had it.

At medical school, Wilbur learned that gonorrhea could live in the Fallopian tubes of females for years. Only the appearance of an abscess in the pelvis might allow the woman to know that she carried the disease. The symptomatology, the discharge and so forth, could go unnoticed for a long time. It did not go unnoticed in Wilbur Larch; the bacterial infection, in these prepenicillin days, lived on for months in young Wilbur, giving him his passionate interest in bacteriology before burning itself out. It left his urethra scarred and his prostate rocky. It left him fond of ether, too—because the ether sleeps he occasionally administered to himself relieved him of the burning sensation he experienced, both when he urinated and when he dreamed. This singular and painful encounter with sexual pleasure—in combination with Wilbur's memory of his parents' loveless marriage—convinced the would-be doctor that a life of sexual abstinence was both medically and philosophically sound.

In the same year, 188__, that Wilbur Larch became a doctor, Neal Dow died. In grief, Wilbur Larch's mother shortly followed her temperance hero to the grave. A few days later, Wilbur's father auctioned every item from their servants' rooms in the former mayor's mansion and rode the Grand Trunk Railway to Montreal, a town less temperance-minded than Portland, and where Wilbur Larch's father pushed his liver beyond limits. His body was returned to Portland on the same Grand Trunk Railway that had carried the former lathe operator away. Wilbur Larch met the train; he played the porter to his father's remains. From the near-cadavers of the cirrhotic that he had seen during his first internship, young Dr. Larch knew exactly what must have been his father's condition at the end. Cirrhosis turns the liver to a mass of scars and lumps, the skin reflects the bile of jaundice, the stools lighten, the urine darkens, the blood doesn't clot. Dr. Larch doubted that his father would have even noticed the accompanying impotence.

/ / /

How moving to conclude that young Larch chose to be an obstetrician because the loss of his parents inspired him to bring more children into the world, but the road that led Larch to obstetrics was strewn with bacteria. The demonstrator of bacteriology at Harvard Medical School, a Dr. Harold Ernst, is best remembered as one of the first college baseball pitchers to throw a curve ball; he was also the first college baseball player to become a bacteriologist. In the early morning laboratory, before Dr. Ernst—the former curve-ball pitcher—would arrive to set up his demonstrations, young Wilbur Larch would be all alone. He didn't feel alone in the presence of so many bacteria growing in the little Petri dishes, in the presence of the bacteria inhabiting his urethra and his prostate gland.

He would milk a drop of pus from his penis onto an ordinary stained slide. Magnified more than a thousand times, the villains he spotted every morning under the microscope were still smaller than common red ants.

Years later Larch would write that the gonococci looked stooped, like too-tall visitors in an igloo. ("They bend," he wrote, "as if they have waists and are bowing to each other.")

Young Larch would stare at his pus until Dr. Ernst would arrive and greet his little living experiments all over the lab (as if they were his old baseball teammates).

"Honestly, Larch," the famous bacteriologist said one morning, "the way you look into that microscope, you appear to be plotting revenge!"

But it was not the smirk of vengeance that Dr. Ernst recognized on Wilbur Larch's face. It was simply the intensity with which Larch was emerging from his ether-daze. The young medical student had discovered that the light, tasty vapor was a safe, effective killer of his pain. In his days spent fighting the dancing gonococci, Larch had become quite a knowledgeable imbiber of ether. By the time the fierce bacteria had burned themselves out, Larch was an ether addict. He was an open-drop-method man. With one hand he held a cone over his mouth and nose; he made this mask himself (by wrapping many layers of gauze around a cone of stiff paper); with his other hand, he wet the cone. He used a quarter-pound ether can punctured with a safety pin; the drops that fell from the elbow of the safety pin fell in exactly the correct size and at exactly the correct rate.

It was the way he would give ether to his patients, too, except that he gave himself much less; when the hand that held the ether can felt unsteady, he put the can down; when the hand that held the cone over his mouth and nose dropped to his side, the cone fell off his face—it wouldn't stay in place if no one held it. He felt nothing of the panic that a patient being anesthetized with ether experiences—he never approached the moment when there wasn't enough air to breathe. Before that happened, he always dropped the mask.

When young Dr. Larch first set out from the South Branch of the Boston Lying-In to deliver babies in the poor districts of the city, he had a place in his mind where the peace of ether resided. Although he carried the ether can and the gauze cone with him, he didn't always have time to anesthetize the patient. The woman's labor was often too far advanced for the ether to help her. Of course he used it when he had the time; he would never share the opinion of some of his elder colleagues that ether was a deviation from the given—that children *should* be brought forth in pain.

Larch delivered his first child to a Lithuanian family in a cold-water, top-floor apartment—the surrounding streets littered with squashed fruit and tattered vegetables and horse droppings. There was no ice to put on the abdomen, over the uterus, in case of postpartum hemorrhage. There was a pot of water already boiling on the stove, but Larch wished he could sterilize the entire apartment. He sent the husband out for ice. He measured the woman's pelvis. He mapped out the fetus. He listened to its heartbeat while he watched a cat toying with a dead mouse on the kitchen floor.

There was a would-be grandmother present; she spoke Lithuanian to the woman in labor. To Dr. Larch she spoke a strange language of gestures, which suggested to him that the would-be grandmother was feebleminded. She indicated that a large mole on her face was either a source of hysterical pleasure or hysterical pain—Larch couldn't tell which; perhaps she simply wanted him to remove it, either before or after he delivered the baby. She found several ways to exhibit the mole—once by holding a spoon under it, as if it were about to fall; once capping it with a teacup and revealing it suddenly, as if it were a surprise or a kind of magician's trick. But the zeal she brought to each revelation of the mole suggested to Wilbur Larch that the old woman simply forgot that she had already shown him her mole.

When the husband returned with the ice, he trod on the cat, which voiced its disapproval in tones that made Wilbur Larch think the child was being born. Larch was grateful not to have to use the forceps; it was a short, safe, loud delivery, following which the husband refused to wash the baby. The grandmother offered, but Larch feared that her combination of excitement and feeblemindedness would cause an accident. Indicating (as well as he could, without the benefit of Lithuanian) that the child should be washed in warm water and soap—but *not* boiled in the pot on the stove, and *not* held head down under the cold-water tap—Larch turned his attention to the afterbirth, which refused to come away. The way the patient kept bleeding, Larch knew he would soon be faced with serious hemorrhage.

He begged the husband to hack him some ice—the strong

fellow had brought a whole block, borrowing the ice company's tongs for this purpose and standing in the kitchen with the tongs on his shoulder in a menacing fashion. The block of ice could cool the uteri of several bleeding patients; to apply it whole, to a single patient, would likely crush the uterus, if not the patient. At this moment the grandmother lost her grip on the soapy child and dropped it among the dishes soaking in the cold-water sink; this happened the instant that the husband again trod upon the cat.

Seizing the moment, when he saw that the grandmother and the husband were distracted, Larch grasped the top of his patient's uterus through her abdominal wall and squeezed hard. The woman screamed and grabbed his hands; the grandmother, abandoning the baby among the dishes, tackled Larch at the waist and bit him between the shoulder blades. The husband retrieved the child from the sink with one hand, but he raised the ice tongs over Larch with the other. Whereupon, lucky Wilbur Larch felt the placenta separate. When he calmly pointed to its appearance, the grandmother and the husband seemed more in awe of it than of the child. After washing the baby himself and giving the mother some ergot, he bowed a wordless good-bye. Leaving the apartment, he was surprised to hear a commotion almost the instant he closed the door: the grandmother, the iced patient, the husband—all shouting in Lithuanian—and the baby giving forceful voice to its first family quarrel. It was as if the delivery, and Dr. Larch's entire appearance, had been only a brief interruption to a life of unintelligible turmoil.

Larch navigated the dark stairs and groped his way outside; he stepped on a rotting head of lettuce, which gave under his foot with the disquieting softness of a newborn baby's skull. This time he did not confuse the cat's terrible yowl with the sounds a child can make. He looked up in time to see the object flying through the window of the Lithuanian apartment. He was in time to dodge it. It had clearly been hurled at him, and Larch wondered what particular, perhaps Lithuanian, offense he had caused these poor people. Larch was shocked to see that the object thrown from the window—and now dead on the ground at his feet—was the cat. But he was not *that* shocked; for a passing second, he feared it might have been the child. He had been told by his professor of obstetrics at Harvard that "the tensile strength of the newborn" was "a marvel," but Larch knew that the tensile strength of a cat was also considerable and he noted that the beast had failed to survive its fall.

"Here in St. Cloud's," Dr. Larch would write, "I am constantly grateful for the South End of Boston." He meant he was grateful for its children and for the feeling they gave him: that the act of bringing them into this world was perhaps the safest phase of their journey. Larch also appreciated the blunt reminder given him by the prostitutes in the South End. They recalled for him the painful gift of Mrs. Eames. He could not see the prostitutes without imagining their bacteria under the microscope. And he could not imagine those bacteria without feeling the need for the giddy warmth of ether—just a sniff; just a light dose (and a light doze). He was not a drinking man, Dr. Larch, and he had no taste for tobacco. But now and then he provided his sagging spirits with an ether frolic.

/ / /

One night, when Wilbur was dozing in the South End Branch of the Boston Lying-In, he was informed by one of the doctors that there was an emergency arrival, and that it was his turn. Although she had lost a lot of weight and all of her youthfulness since Larch had last seen her, he had no trouble recognizing Mrs. Eames. She was so frightened, and in such intense pain, that she had difficulty catching her breath, and more trouble telling the nurse-receptionist her name.

"Rhymes with screams," said Dr. Larch helpfully.

If Mrs. Eames recognized him right away, she didn't let on. She was cold to the touch, her pulse was very fast, and her abdomen was as hard and white as the knuckles of a tight fist; Larch could detect no signs of labor, and he couldn't hear the heartbeats of the fetus, which Larch couldn't help imagining as having features similar to Mrs. Eames's sullen teen-age daughter. How old would she be now? he wondered. Still about his own age—that much he had time to remember before attending to his diagnosis of Mrs. Eames: hemorrhage within the abdomen. He operated as soon as the house officer could locate the necessary donors for the transfusion.

"Missus Eames?" he asked her softly, still seeking some recognition from her.

"How's your father, Wilbur?" she asked him, just before he operated.

Her abdomen was full of blood; he sponged away, looking

for the source, and saw that the hemorrhage issued from a six-inch rupture in the back of the uterus. Larch performed a Caesarean section and delivered a stillborn child—the pinched, scornful face of which forcibly reminded him of the cigar-smoking daughter. He wondered why Mrs. Eames had come here alone.

To this point in the operation, young Larch felt in charge. Despite his memories of the woman opened up before him—and his memories of her transmitted disease, which he was only recently rid of—he felt he was handling a fairly manageable emergency. But when he tried to sew up Mrs. Eames's uterus, his stitches simply pulled through the tissue, which he noticed was the texture of a soft cheese—imagine trying to put stitches in Muenster! He had no choice then; he had to remove the uterus. After all the transfusions, Larch was surprised that Mrs. Eames's condition seemed pretty good.

He conferred with a senior surgeon in the morning. At the Boston Lying-In it was standard that an obstetrician's background was surgical—Larch had interned in surgery at Mass General—and the senior surgeon shared young Larch's bafflement with the disintegrating consistency of Mrs. Eames's uterus. Even the rupture was a puzzle. There was no scar of a previous Caesarean section that could have given way; the placenta could not have weakened the wall of the uterus because the afterbirth had been on the other side of the uterus from the tear. There had been no tumor.

For forty-eight hours Mrs. Eames did very well. She consoled young Wilbur on the death of his parents. "I never knew your mother, of course," she confided. She again expressed her concern that Wilbur consider her reputation, which Wilbur assured her he would (and *had*—by refraining from expressing his fears to the senior surgeon that the condition of Mrs. Eames might somehow be the result of gonorrhea). He briefly wondered which story Mrs. Eames was using at the moment, regarding her reputation: whether she was claiming to live a proper life in Portland or in Boston; whether a third city was now involved and necessarily a third fictitious life.

On the third day after the removal of her strange uterus, Mrs. Eames filled up with blood again, and Wilbur Larch reopened her wound; this time he was quite afraid of what he'd find. At first, he was relieved; there was not as much blood in her abdomen as before. But when he sponged the blood away, he perforated the intestine, which he had hardly touched, and when he lifted up the injured loop to close the hole, his fingers passed as easily through the intestine as through gelatin. If all her organs were this same fragile jelly, Larch knew Mrs. Eames wouldn't live very long.

She lived three more days. The night she died, Larch had a nightmare—his penis fell off in his hands; he tried to sew it back on but it kept disintegrating; then his fingers gave way in a similar fashion. How like a surgeon! he thought. Fingers are valued above penises. How like Wilbur Larch!

This helped to strengthen Larch's conviction regarding sexual abstinence. He waited for whatever had destroyed Mrs. Eames to claim him, but the autopsy, which was performed by a distinguished pathologist, seemed off the track.

"Scurvy," the pathologist said.

So much for pathologists, thought Wilbur Larch. Scurvy indeed!

"Missus Eames was a prostitute," Larch told the pathologist respectfully. "She wasn't a sailor."

But the pathologist was sure about it. It had nothing to do with the gonorrhea, nothing to do with the pregnancy. Mrs. Eames had died of the sailor's curse; she had not a trace of Vitamin C, and, the pathologist said, "She had destruction of connective tissue and the tendency to bleed that goes with it." Scurvy.

Though this was a puzzle, it convinced Larch that it wasn't a venereal puzzle and he had one good night's sleep before Mrs. Eames's daughter came to see him.

"It's not my turn, is it?" he sleepily asked the colleague who roused him.

"She says you're her doctor," the colleague told him.

He did not recognize Mrs. Eames's daughter, who had once cost less than Mrs. Eames; now, she would have charged more than her mother could get. If, on the train, she had seemed only a few years younger than Wilbur, now she seemed several years older. Her sullen teen-age quality had matured in a brash and caustic fashion. Her makeup, her jewelry, and her perfume were excessive; her dress was slatternly. Her hair—in a single, thick braid with a sea-gull feather stuck in it—was so severely pulled back from her face that the veins in her temples seemed strained, and her neck muscles were tensed—as if a violent lover had thrown her to her back and held her there by her strong, dark pigtail.

She greeted Wilbur Larch by roughly handing him a bottle of brown liquid—its pungent odor escaping through a leaky cork stopper. The bottle's label was illegibly stained.

"That's what did her in," the girl said with a growl. "I ain't having any. There's other ways."

"Is it Miss Eames?" Wilbur Larch asked, searching for her memorable cigar breath.

"I said there's *other* ways!" Miss Eames said. "I ain't so far along as she was, I ain't *quick*."

Wilbur Larch sniffed the bottle in his hand; he knew what "quick" meant. If a fetus was quick it meant the mother had felt it move, it meant the mother was about half through her gestation period, usually in her fourth or fifth month; to some doctors, with religion, when a fetus was quick it meant it had a soul. Wilbur Larch didn't think anyone had a soul, but until the middle of the nineteenth century, the common law's attitude toward abortion was simple and (to Wilbur Larch) sensible: before "quickening"—before the first, felt movement of the fetus—abortion was legal. More important, to the doctor in Wilbur Larch, it was not dangerous to the mother to perform an abortion before the fetus was quick. After the third month, whether the fetus was quick or not, Wilbur Larch knew it had a grip on the uterus that required more force to break.

For example, the liquid in the bottle Wilbur Larch was holding had not provided sufficient force to break the grip that Mrs. Eames's fetus had on her—although, apparently, it had exerted enough force to kill the fetus and turn Mrs. Eames's insides to mush.

"It's gotta be pure poison," Mrs. Eames's tough daughter remarked to Wilbur Larch, who dabbed a little of his beloved ether on the bottle's stained label, cleaning it up enough to read.

FRENCH LUNAR SOLUTION

Restores Female Monthly Regularity!

Stops Suppression!

(Suppression, young Larch knew, was a euphemism for pregnancy.)

Caution: Dangerous to Married Women!

Almost Certainly Causes Miscarriages!

the label concluded; which, of course, was why Mrs. Eames had taken it and taken it.

Larch had studied the abuse of aborticides in medical school. Some—like the ergot Larch used to make the uterus contract after delivery, and pituitary extract—directly affected the uterus. Others ruined the intestines—they were simply drastic purgatives. Two of the cadavers Larch had worked with in medical school had been victims of a rather common household aborticide of the time: turpentine. People who didn't want babies in the 1880s and 1890s were also killing themselves with strychnine and oil of rue. The French Lunar Solution Mrs. Eames had tried was oil of tansy; she had taken it for such a long time, and in such amounts, that her intestines had lost their ability to absorb Vitamin C. Thus did she turn herself into Muenster. She died, as the pathologist had correctly observed, of scurvy.

Mrs. Eames could have chosen several other ways of attempting to abort the birth of another child. There were stories that a rather notorious abortionist in the South End was also the district's most successful pimp. Because he charged nearly five hundred dollars for an abortion, which very few poor women could afford, in their indebtedness they became his whores. His quarters—and others like his—were called, simply, "Off Harrison"—appropriately vague, but not without meaning. One of the facilities of the South Branch of the Boston Lying-In was established *on* Harrison Street, so that "Off Harrison," in street language, correctly implied something unofficial—not to mention, illegal.

It did not make much sense to have an abortion "Off Harrison," as Mrs. Eames, perhaps, had reason to know. Her daughter also knew the methods of that place, which was why she gave Wilbur Larch a chance to do the job—and gave herself a chance to have the job done well.

"I said I ain't quick," Mrs. Eames's daughter told young Larch. "I'd be easy. I'd get out of here in just a couple of minutes."

It was after midnight at the South Branch. The house officer was asleep; the nurse-practitioner, an anesthetist, was also asleep. The colleague who had woken Larch—he'd gone to sleep, too.

The dilation of the cervix at any stage of pregnancy usually leads to uterine contractions, which expel the contents of the uterus. Larch also knew that any irritant to the uterus would usually have the desired effect: contraction, expulsion. Young Wilbur Larch stared at Mrs. Eames's daughter; his legs felt rocky. Perhaps he was still standing with his hand on the back of Mrs. Eames's seat on that swaying train from Portland, before he knew he had the clap.

"You want an abortion," Wilbur Larch said softly. It was the first time he had spoken the word.

Mrs. Eames's daughter took the sea-gull feather out of her pigtail and jabbed Larch in the chest with the quill end. "Shit or get off the pot," she said. It was with the words "shit" and "pot" that the sour stench of cigar reached him.

Wilbur Larch could hear the nurse-anesthetist sleeping—she had a sinus condition. For an abortion, he wouldn't need as much ether as he liked to use for a delivery; he would need only a little more than he routinely gave himself. He also doubted it was necessary to shave the patient; patients were routinely shaved for a delivery and Larch would have preferred it for an abortion, but to save time, he could skip it; he would *not* skip ether. He would put red merthiolate on the vaginal area. If he'd had a childhood like Mrs. Eames's daughter, he wouldn't have wanted to bring a child into the world, either. He would use the set of dilators with the Douglass points—rounded, snub-nosed points, they had the advantage of an easy introduction into the uterus and eliminated the danger of pinching tissue in withdrawal. With the cervix dilated to the desired size, he doubted that—unless Mrs. Eames's daughter was well along in her third or fourth month—he would need to use forceps, and then only for the removal of placenta and the larger pieces. A medical school textbook had referred, euphemistically, to the products of conception: these could be scraped from the wall of the uterus with a curette—perhaps with two different-sized curettes, the small one to reach into the corners.

But he was too young, Wilbur Larch; he hesitated. He was thinking about the time for recovery from ether that he would need to allow Mrs. Eames's daughter, and what he would say to his colleagues, or to the nurse if she woke up—or even to the house officer if it turned out to be necessary to keep the girl until the morning (if there was any excessive bleeding, for example). He was surprised by the sudden pain in his chest; Mrs. Eames's savage daughter was stabbing him with the sea-gull feather again.

"I ain't quick! I ain't *quick,* I said!" the Eames girl screamed at him, stabbing him again and again, until the feather bent in her hand; she left it stuck in his shirt. In turning away from him, her heavy braid brushed his face—the braid's odor over-whelmingly conveying smoke. When she was gone and Larch plucked the sea-gull feather from his breast, he noticed that the oil of tansy—the French Lunar Solution—had spilled on his hands. Its smell was not unpleasant, but it momentarily over-powered the smell Larch liked and was used to—it over-powered the ether; it put an end to his peace of mind.

/ / /

They did not use ether "Off Harrison." They didn't concern themselves with pain there. For pain "Off Harrison," they used music. An outfit called The German Choir practiced *Lieder* in the front rooms "Off Harrison." They sang passionately. Per-haps Mrs. Eames's daughter appreciated it, but she made no mention of the music when she was brought back to the South Branch a week later. No one was sure how she got there; she appeared to have been flung against the door. She also ap-peared to have been beaten about the face and neck, perhaps for failing to pay the usual abortion fee. She had a very high fever—her swollen face was as hot and dry to the touch as bread fresh from the oven. From the fever and the tenseness of her abdomen, rigid as glass, the house officer and the night nurse suspected peritonitis. The reason they woke Wilbur was that Mrs. Eames's daughter had a piece of paper pinned to the shoulder of her dress.

DOCTOR LARCH—
SHIT OR GET
OFF THE POT!

Pinned to her other shoulder—like a mismatched epaulette, pulling her dress askew—was a pair of ladies' underwear. They were her only pair. It was discovered she wasn't wearing any. Apparently, her panties had been pinned there in a hurry; that way they wouldn't be lost. Wilbur Larch didn't need to exam-ine Mrs. Eames's daughter very thoroughly in order to discover that the abortion attempt had failed. A fetus with no heartbeat was imprisoned in her uterus, which had suffered some hay-wire contraction and was in a state of spasm. The hemorrhage and infection could have come from any of the several methods employed "Off Harrison."

There was the water-cure school, which advocated the use of an intrauterine tube and syringe, but neither the tube nor the water was sterile—and the syringe had many other uses. There was a primitive suction system, simply an airtight cup from which all the air could be sucked by a foot-operated pump; it had the power to abort, but it also had the power to draw blood through the pores of the skin. It could do a lot of damage to soft tissue. And—as the little sign said on the door. "Off Harrison," WE TREAT MENSTRUAL SUPPRESSION ELECTRICALLY!—there was the McIntosh galvanic battery. The long leads were hooked up to the battery; the leads had intravaginal and intrauterine attachments on insulated, rubber-covered handles; that way the abortionist wouldn't feel the shock in his hands.

When Mrs. Eames's daughter died—before Dr. Larch could operate on her and without her having further words with him (beyond the "Shit or get off the pot!" note that was pinned to her shoulder), her temperature was nearly 107. The house officer felt compelled to ask Larch if he knew the woman. The note certainly implied an intimate message.

"She was angry with me for not giving her an abortion," Wilbur Larch replied.

"Good for you!" said the house officer.

But Wilbur Larch failed to see how this was good for anyone. There was a widespread inflammation of the membranes and viscera of the abdominal cavity, the uterus had been perforated twice, and the fetus, which was dead, was true to Mrs. Eames's daughter's prediction: it had not been quick.

In the morning, Dr. Larch visited "Off Harrison." He needed to see for himself what happened there; he wanted to know where women went when doctors turned them down. On his mind was Mrs. Eames's daughter's last puff of cigar breath in his face as he bent over her before she died—reminding him, of course, of the night he needed her puffing cigar to find his clothes. If pride was a sin, thought Dr. Larch, the greatest sin was moral pride. He had slept with someone's mother and dressed himself in the light of her daughter's cigar. He could quite comfortably abstain from having sex for the rest of his life, but how could he ever condemn another person for having sex?

/ / /

The German Choir blasted him at the door with the little sign that promised the return of menstruation electrically. There was a harsh and out-of-tune piano—no oboe, no English horn, no mezzo-soprano—yet Larch thought the music was remindful of Mahler's *Kindertotenlieder*. Years later, when he first heard the scream-concealing sound of the water rushing through Three Mile Falls, he would remember the abortionist's songs that pumped like jism "Off Harrison." He beat on the door—he could have screamed—but no one heard him. When he opened the door and stepped inside, no one bothered to look at him; The German Choir kept singing. The only instrument was a piano, and there were not nearly enough chairs for the women, and there were only a few music stands; the men stood huddled in two groups, far from the women; there weren't enough copies of the sheet music to go around. The choir conductor stood by the piano. A lean, bald man without a shirt, he wore a dirty-white shirt collar (perhaps to catch the sweat) and kept his eyes half closed, as if in prayer, while his arms wildly pummeled the air—as if the air, which was full of cigar smoke and the urinelike stink of cheap draft beer, were hard to move. The choir pursued the man's wild arms.

A fussy or critical God, thought Wilbur Larch, would strike us all dead. Larch walked behind the piano and through the only open door. He entered into a room with nothing in it—not a piece of furniture, not a window. There was only a closed door. Larch opened it and found himself in what was obviously the waiting room—at least people appeared to be waiting there. There were even newspapers and fresh flowers and an open window; four people sat in pairs. No one read the papers or sniffed the flowers or looked out the window; everyone looked down and continued to look down when Wilbur Larch walked in. At a desk, with only a pad of paper and a cashbox on it, sat an alert man eating something that looked like navy beans out of a bowl. The man appeared young and strong and indifferent; he wore a pair of work overalls and a sleeveless undershirt; around his neck, like a gym instructor's whistle, hung a key—obviously to the cashbox. He was as bald as the choir conductor; Larch considered that their heads were shaved.

Without looking at Wilbur Larch, the man, who might have been one of the choir sitting out a song or two, said: "Hey, you don't come here. You just have the lady come by herself, or with a lady friend."

In the front room, Wilbur Larch heard them singing something about someone's "dear mother"—wasn't that what *"mütterlein"* meant?

"I'm a doctor," Dr. Larch said.

The cashbox man kept eating, but he looked up at Larch. The singers took a deep breath, and in the split-second silence Larch heard the man's swift, skillful spoon scrape against the bowl—and, from another room, the sound of someone retching, quickly followed by the splash of vomit in a metal basin. One of the women in the waiting room began to cry, but before Larch could identify which of the women it was, the singers caught their breath and bore down again. Something about Christ's blood, Larch thought.

"What do you want?" the man asked Larch.

"I'm a doctor, I want to see the doctor here," Larch said.

"No doctor here," the man said. "Just you."

"Then I want to give advice," Larch said. "Medical advice. Free medical advice."

The man studied Larch's face; he appeared to think that a response to Larch's offer could be found there. "You're not the first one here," the man said, after a while. "You wait your turn."

That seemed to satisfy both men for the moment, and Larch looked for a seat—taking a chair precisely between the two-somes of women already in the room. He was too shocked by everything to be surprised when he recognized one of the couples: the Lithuanian woman whose child he'd delivered (his first delivery) sat mutely with her mole-faced mother. They wouldn't look up at him; Larch smiled at them and nodded. The woman was very pregnant—too pregnant for an easy abortion, under the safest of circumstances. Larch realized, with panic, that he couldn't convey this to her; she spoke only Lithuanian. She would associate him with delivering only live babies! Also, he knew nothing of what might have become of her first baby—nothing of what her life with that baby had been, or was now. He tapped his foot nervously and looked at the other couple—also, clearly, a mother and her daughter, but both of them were younger than the Lithuanians and it was hard to tell which of them was pregnant. This abortion, at least, looked easier to perform. The daughter looked too young to be pregnant, but then why, Larch wondered, had the mother brought the girl here? Did she need the company so badly, or was this meant as a lesson? Watch out—this could happen to you! In the front room, the singers grew hysterical on the subject of God's love and something that sounded like "blinding destiny"—*verblendenen Geschike*.

Wilbur Larch stared at the shut door, behind which he had heard unmistakable vomiting. A bee, crazily out of place, buzzed in the open window and seemed to find the flowers fakes; it buzzed straight out again. When Larch looked at the Lithuanian couple, he saw that the grandmother had recognized him—and she had discovered a new way to exhibit her mole, which had grown additional and longer hairs and had slightly changed color. Pinching her fingers to either side of the mole, the grandmother inflamed the surrounding skin and made the mole appear to explode from her face—like a boil come to a head, about to burst. The pregnant woman seemed not to notice her mother's charmless demonstration, and when she stared at Larch she appeared not to recognize him; for Larch, there was only Lithuanian written on her face. Perhaps, Larch thought, her husband threw her baby out the window and drove her mad. For a moment Larch thought that the choir might be Lithuanian, but he recognized something about a battle between *Gott und Schicksal*—clearly German, clearly God and Fate.

The scream that cut through the shut door had no difficulty rising above the voices declaring that God had won. The young girl jumped from her seat, sat down, hugged herself, cried out; she put her face in her mother's lap to muffle her cries. Larch realized she'd been the one to cry before. He also realized that she must be the one needing the abortion—not her mother. The girl didn't look older than ten or twelve.

"Excuse me," Larch said to the mother. "I'm a doctor."

He felt like an actor with good potential who'd been crippled with a single stupid line—it was all he had to say. "I'm a doctor." What followed from that?

"So you're a doctor," the mother said, bitterly, but Larch

was happy to hear she didn't speak Lithuanian. "So what help are you?" the mother asked him.

"How many months is she?" Larch asked the mother.

"Maybe three," the mother said suspiciously. "But I already paid them here."

"How old is she?" Larch asked.

The girl looked up from her mother's lap; a strand of her dirty-blond hair caught in her mouth. "I'm fourteen," she said defensively.

"She'll *be* fourteen, next year," the mother said.

Larch stood up and said to the man with the cashbox key, "Pay them back. I'll help the girl."

"I thought you came for advice," the man said.

"To give it," Dr. Larch said.

"Why not take some while you're here?" the man said. "When you pay, there's a deposit. You don't get a deposit back."

"How much is the deposit?" Larch asked. The man shrugged; he drummed his fingers on the cashbox.

"Maybe half," he said.

"Eure ganze Macht!" the choir sang. "Your whole power," translated Wilbur Larch. Many medical students were good in German.

When the evil door opened, an old couple, like someone's bewildered grandparents, peered anxiously into the waiting room—both confusion and curiosity on their faces, which, like the faces of many old couples, had grown to resemble each other. They were small and stooped, and behind them, on a cot—as still as a painting—a woman lay resting under a sheet, her eyes open but unfocused. The vomit basin had been placed on a towel on the floor, within her reach.

"He says he's a doctor," the cashbox man said, without looking at the old couple. "He says he came to give you free medical advice. He says to pay these ladies back. He says he'll take care of the young lady himself."

By the way that the old white-haired woman had become a presence—or, stronger, a *force*—in the doorway between the waiting room and the operating theater, Larch realized that *she* was in charge; the old white-haired man was her assistant. The old woman would have looked at home in a pleasant kitchen, baking cookies, inviting the neighborhood children to come and go as they pleased.

"Doctor Larch," Dr. Larch said, bowing a little too formally.

"Oh, yes, Doctor Larch," the old woman said, neutrally. "Come to shit or to get off the pot?"

The abortionist was known in the neighborhood "Off Harrison" as Mrs. Santa Claus. She was not the original author of that remark—or of that note. Mrs. Eames's daughter had written that herself, before she went to see Mrs. Santa Claus; she knew enough about the dangers "Off Harrison" to know that she might be in no shape to write anything at all after Mrs. Santa Claus finished with her.

Larch was unprepared for Mrs. Santa Claus—specifically, for her attitude. He had imagined that in any meeting with an abortionist *he* (Dr. Larch) would take charge. He still tried to. He walked into the operating theater and picked up something, just to demonstrate his authority. What he picked up was the suction cup with a short hose running to the foot pump. The cup fitted neatly into the palm of his hand; he had no trouble imagining what else it fitted. To his surprise, when he had attached the cup to his palm, Mrs. Santa Claus began stepping on the foot pump. When he felt the blood rushing to his pores, he popped the cup out of his palm before the thing could raise more than a blood blister on the heel of his hand.

"Well?" Mrs. Claus asked, aggressively. "What's your advice, Doctor?" As if in reply, the patient under the sheet drew Larch to her; the woman's forehead was clammy with sweat.

"You don't know what you're doing," Dr. Larch said to Mrs. Santa Claus.

"At least I'm doing something," the old woman said with hostile calm. "If you know how to do it, why don't you do it?" Mrs. Santa Claus asked. "If you know how, why don't you teach me?"

The woman under the sheet looked groggy, but she was trying to pull herself together. She sat up and tried to examine herself; she discovered that, under the sheet, she still wore her own dress. This knowledge appeared to relax her.

"Please listen to me," Dr. Larch said to her. "If you have a fever—if you have more than just a little bleeding—you must come to the hospital. Don't wait."

"I thought the advice was for *me*," Mrs. Santa Claus said. "Where's *my* advice?"

Larch tried to ignore her. He went out to the waiting room

and told the mother with her young daughter that they should leave, but the mother was concerned about the money.

"Pay them back!" Mrs. Santa Claus told the cashbox man.

"They don't get the deposit back," the man said again.

"Pay them back the deposit, too!" the old woman said angrily. She came into the waiting room to oversee the disgruntled transaction. She put her hand on Dr. Larch's arm. "Ask her who the father is," Mrs. Santa Claus said.

"That's none of my business," Larch said.

"You're right," the old woman said. "That much you got right. But ask her, anyway—it's an interesting story."

Larch tried to ignore her; Mrs. Santa Claus grabbed hold of both the mother and her daughter. She spoke to the mother. "Tell him who the father is," she said. The daughter began to snivel and whine; Mrs. Santa Claus ignored her; she looked only at the mother. "Tell him," she repeated.

"My husband," the woman murmured, and then she added —as if it weren't clear—"her father."

"Her father is the father," Mrs. Santa Claus said to Dr. Larch. "Got it?"

"Yes, I've got it, thank you," Dr. Larch said. He needed to put his arm around the thirteen-year-old, who was sagging; she had her eyes shut.

"Maybe a third of the young ones are like her," Mrs. Santa Claus told Larch nastily; she treated him as if *he* were the father. "About a third of them get it from their fathers, or their brothers. Rape," Mrs. Santa Claus said. "Incest. You understand?"

"Yes, thank you," Larch said, pulling the girl with him— tugging the sleeve of the mother's coat to make her follow.

"Shit or get off the pot!" Mrs. Santa Claus yelled after them.

"All you starving doctors!" the cashbox man hollered. "You're all over."

The choir was singing. Larch thought he heard them say *"vom keinen Sturm erschrecket"*—frightened by no storm.

In the empty room that separated the songs from the abortions, Larch and the mother with her daughter collided with the woman who'd been under the sheet. She was still groggy, her eyes were darting, and her dress was plastered with sweat to her back.

"Please remember!" Larch said to her. "If there's a fever, if there's more than a little blood . . ." Then he saw the woman's underwear pinned to the shoulder of her dress. That reminding epaulette was the badge of "Off Harrison," a kind of ribbon for bravery. Obviously, the woman didn't know that her panties were there. Larch imagined that the South End was sprinkled liberally with these staggering women, their panties pinned to their shoulders, marking them as indelibly as that long-ago Puritan New England "A" upon their bosoms.

"Wait!" Larch cried, and grabbed for the underwear. The woman didn't want to wait; as she pulled herself free of his grasp, the pin opened and stuck Larch in the hand. After she'd gone, he put her panties in his suit-jacket pocket.

He led the mother and her daughter through the room that was always so heady with song, but the choir was taking a beer break. The lean, bald conductor had just dipped into his frothy stein when he looked up and saw Dr. Larch leaving with the women; a moustache of foam whitened his lip and a dab of the white froth shone on the end of his nose. The conductor raised his stein toward Dr. Larch, offering a toast. "Praise the Lord!" the conductor called. "You keep on saving those poor souls, Doc!"

"Danke schön!" the choir called after him. Of course they could not have been singing Mahler's *Songs on the Death of Children,* but those were the songs Wilbur Larch had heard.

/ / /

"In other parts of the world," wrote Dr. Wilbur Larch upon his arrival in St. Cloud's, "an ability to act before you think—but to act nonetheless correctly—is essential. Perhaps there will be more time to think, here in St. Cloud's."

In Boston, he meant, he was a hero; and he wouldn't have lasted long—being a hero. He took the young girl and her mother to the South Branch. He instructed the house officer to write up the following:

"This is a thirteen-year-old girl. Her pelvis is only three and a half inches in diameter. Two previous, violent deliveries have lacerated her soft parts and left her with a mass of unyielding scar tissue. This is her third pregnancy as a result of incest—as a result of rape. If allowed to come to term, she can be delivered only by Caesarean section, which—given the child's delicate state of health (she *is* a child), not to mention her state of mind—would be dangerous. Therefore, I've decided to give her an abortion."

"You have?" the house officer asked.

"That's right," Wilbur Larch said—and to the nurse-anesthetist, he said, "We'll do it immediately."

The abortion took only twenty minutes; Larch's light touch with ether was the envy of his colleagues. He used the set of dilators with the Douglass points and both a medium-sized and a small curette. There was, of course, no mass of unyielding scar tissue; there were no lacerated soft parts. This was a first, not a third pregnancy, and although she was a small girl, her pelvis was certainly greater than three and a half inches in diameter. These fictional details, which Wilbur Larch provided for the house officer, were intended to make the house officer's report more convincing. No one at the Boston Lying-In ever questioned Larch's decision to perform this abortion—no one ever mentioned it, but Dr. Larch could tell that something had changed.

He detected the dying of conversations upon his entering a room. He detected a general aloofness; although he was not exactly shunned, he was never invited. He dined alone at a nearby German restaurant; he ate pig knuckles and sauerkraut, and one night he drank a beer. It reminded him of his father; it was Wilbur Larch's first and last beer.

At this time in his life Wilbur Larch seemed destined to a first-and-last existence; one sexual experience, one beer, one abortion. But he'd had more than one experience with ether, and the news, in the South End—that there was an alternative to Mrs. Santa Claus and the methods practiced "Off Harrison" —traveled fast. He was first approached while standing at a fruit-vendor's cart, drinking fresh-squeezed orange juice; a tall, gaunt woman with a shopping bag and a laundry basket materialized beside him.

"I ain't quick," the woman whispered to Wilbur Larch. "What's it cost? I ain't quick, I swear."

After her, they followed him everywhere. Sleepily, at the South Branch, he was always saying to one colleague or another, "It's not my turn, is it?" And always the answer was the same: "She says you're her doctor."

A child of Maine, Wilbur Larch was used to looking into people's faces and finding their eyes; now he looked down, or away; like a city person, he made their eyes hunt for his. In the same mail with his catalogue of surgical instruments from Fred Halsam & Co. he received a copy of Mrs. W. H. Maxwell's *A Female Physician to the Ladies of the United States*. Until late in

187__, Mrs. Maxwell had operated a woman's clinic in New York. "The authoress has not established her hospital simply for the benefit of lying-in women," she wrote. "She believes that in view of the uncharitableness of general society towards the erring, it is fit that the unfortunate should have some sanctuary to which to flee, in whose shade they may have undisturbed opportunity to reflect, and hiding forever their present unhappiness, nerve themselves to be wiser in the future. The true physician's soul cannot be too broad and gentle."

Of course, Wilbur Larch saw that the South End was mercilessly full of evidence of uncharitableness towards the erring and that he had become, in the view of the erring, the sanctuary to which to flee.

Instead, *he* fled. He went home to Maine. He applied to the Maine State board of medical examiners for a useful position in obstetrics. While they sought a position for him in some developing community, they liked his Harvard degree and made him a member of their board. Wilbur Larch awaited his new appointment in his old hometown of Portland, that safe harbor—the old mayor's mansion where he had spent the half life of his childhood, the salty boardinghouse where he had caught his dose of life from Mrs. Eames.

He wondered if he would miss the South End: the palmist who had assured him he would live a long time and have many children ("Too many to count!"), which Larch understood as confirmation that, in seeking to become an obstetrician, he had made the right choice; the fortune teller who had told young Larch that he would never follow in his father's footsteps, which was all right with Wilbur Larch, who had no knowledge of lathes, no fondness for drink, and was sure that his liver wouldn't be the culprit of his final undoing; and the Chinese herb doctor who had told Larch that he could cure the clap by applying crushed green leaves and bread mold to his penis. The quack was almost right. The chlorophyll in the plants would destroy the bacteria that contributed to gangrene but it wouldn't kill the dance couples in the pus cells, those lively gonococci; the penicillin, extracted from some bread molds, would. Years later, Larch would dream that if only Dr. Harold Ernst, Harvard Medical School's bacteriologist and curve-ball pitcher, and the Chinese herb doctor from the South End had put their heads together . . . well, what wouldn't they have cured?

"They would not have cured orphans," wrote Dr. Larch when he woke from that dream.

And the orphans of the South End: Wilbur Larch remembered them from the branch hospitals of the Boston Lying-In. In 189__, less than half the mothers were married. In the institution's charter it was written that no patient would be admitted "unless a married woman or one recently widowed, and known to be of good moral character." The benevolent citizen groups who had first contributed thousands of dollars to provide for a lying-in hospital for the poor . . . *they* had insisted; but in truth almost everyone was admitted. There was an astonishing number of women claiming to be widows, or claiming marriage to sailors off to sea—gone with the *Great Eastern,* Wilbur Larch used to imagine.

In Portland, he wondered, why were there no orphans, no children or women in need? Wilbur Larch did not feel of much use in the tidy town of Portland; it is ironic to think that while he waited to be sent somewhere where he was needed, a prostitute's letter—about abandoned women and orphans—was making its way to him from St. Cloud's.

But before the letter arrived, Wilbur Larch had another invitation. The pleasure of his company was requested by a Mrs. Channing-Peabody of the Boston Channing-Peabodys, who spent every summer on their coastal property just east of Portland. The invitation suggested that perhaps young Larch missed the Boston society to which he'd doubtlessly become accustomed and would enjoy some tennis or croquet, or even some sailing, before a dinner with the Channing-Peabodys and friends. Larch had been accustomed to *no* Boston society. He associated the Channing-Peabodys with Cambridge, or with Beacon Hill—where he was never invited—and although he knew that Channing and Peabody were old Boston family names, he was unfamiliar with this strange coupling of the two. For all Wilbur Larch knew about this level of society, the Channings and the Peabodys might be throwing a party together and for the purpose of the invitation had agreed to hyphenate their names.

As for sailing, Wilbur Larch had never been on the water—or in it. A child of Maine, he knew better than to learn to swim in that water; the Maine water, in Wilbur Larch's opinion, was for summer people and lobsters. And as for tennis or croquet, he didn't own the proper clothing. From a watercolor of some strange lawn games, he had once imagined that striking a wooden ball with a wooden mallet as hard as he could would be rewarding, but he wanted time to practice this art alone and unobserved. He regretted the expense of hiring a driver to take him to the Channing-Peabody summer house, and he felt uncomfortably dressed for the season—his only suit was a dark, heavy one, and he hadn't worn it since the day of his visit "Off Harrison." As he lifted the big brass door knocker of the Channing-Peabody house (choosing to introduce himself formally, rather than wandering among the people in their whites at play at various sports around the grounds), he felt the suit was not only too hot but also needed a pressing, and he discovered in the jacket pocket the panties of the woman who'd aborted the birth of her child "Off Harrison." Wilbur Larch was holding the panties in his hand and staring at them—remembering their valiant, epaulette position, their jaunty bravery on the woman's shoulder—when Mrs. Channing-Peabody opened the door to receive him.

He could not return the panties to his jacket pocket quickly enough so he stuffed them into the pocket in the attitude of a handkerchief he'd just been caught blowing his nose in. By the quick way Mrs. Channing-Peabody looked away from them, Larch knew she'd seen the panties for what they were: women's underdrawers, plain as day.

"Doctor Larch?" Mrs. Channing-Peabody said cautiously, as if the panties had provided her with a clue to Larch's identity.

I should simply leave now, Wilbur Larch thought, but he said, "Yes, Doctor Larch," and bowed to the woman—a great gunship of a woman, with a tanned face and a head helmeted in silver-gray hair, as sleek and as dangerous-looking as a bullet.

"You must come meet my daughter," the woman said. "And all the rest of us!" she added with a booming laugh that chilled the sweat on Wilbur Larch's back.

All the rest of them seemed to be named Channing or Peabody or Channing-Peabody, and some of them had first names that resembled last names. There was a Cabot and a Chadwick and a Loring and an Emerald (who had the dullest brown eyes), but the daughter whom Mrs. Channing-Peabody had designated to meet Dr. Larch was the plainest and youngest and least healthy-looking of the bunch. Her name was Missy.

"Missy?" Wilbur Larch repeated. The girl nodded and shrugged.

They were seated at a long table, next to each other. Across from them, and about their age, was one of the young men in tennis whites, either the Chadwick or the Cabot. He looked cross, or else he'd just had a fight with Miss Channing-Peabody, or else he would rather have been seated next to her himself. Or maybe he's just her brother and wishes he were seated farther away from her, thought Wilbur Larch.

The girl looked unwell. In a family of tans, she was pale; she picked at her food. It was one of those dinners where the arrival of each course caused a complete change of dishes, and as the conversation lapsed and failed, or at least grew fainter, the sound of china and silverware grew louder, and a tension mounted at the dinner table. It was not a tension caused by any subject of conversation—it was a tension caused by no subject of conversation.

The rather senile retired surgeon who was seated on Wilbur's other side—he was either a Channing or a Peabody—seemed disappointed to learn that Larch was an obstetrician. Still, the old codger insisted on knowing Dr. Larch's preferred method of expelling the placenta into the lower genital tract. Wilbur Larch tried, quietly, to describe the expression of placenta to Dr. Peabody or Dr. Channing, or whoever he was, but the old man was hard of hearing and insisted that young Larch *speak up*! Their conversation, which was the dinner table's only conversation, thus progressed to injuries to the perineum—including the method of holding back the baby's head to prevent a perineal tear—and the proper mediolateral incision for the performance of an episiotomy when a tear of the perineum seems imminent.

Wilbur Larch was aware that Missy Channing-Peabody's skin was changing color beside him. She went from milk to mustard to spring-grass green, and almost back to milk before she fainted. Her skin was quite cool and clammy, and when Wilbur Larch looked at her, he saw that her eyes were almost completely rolled up into her head. Her mother and the cross young man in tennis whites, the Cabot or the Chadwick, whisked her away from the table—"She needs *air*," Mrs. Channing-Peabody announced, but air was not in short supply in Maine.

Wilbur Larch already knew what Missy needed. She needed

an abortion. It came to him through the visible anger of young Chadwick or Cabot, it came to him over the babbling senility of the old surgeon inquiring about "modern" obstetrical procedure, it came to him through the absence of other conversation and through the noise of the knives and the forks and the plates. That was why he'd been invited: Missy Channing-Peabody, suffering from morning sickness, needed an abortion. Rich people needed them, too. Even rich people, who, in Wilbur Larch's opinion, were the last to learn about anything, *even rich people* knew about him. He wanted to leave, but now it was his fate that held him. Sometimes, when we are labeled, when we are branded, our brand becomes our calling; Wilbur Larch felt himself called. The letter from the prostitute from St. Cloud's was on its way to him and he would go there, but first he was being called to perform—here.

He rose from the table. The men were being sent to some special room—for cigars. The women had gathered around someone's baby—a nurse or a governess (a *servant,* thought Wilbur Larch) had brought a baby into the dining room, and the women were having a look. Wilbur Larch had a look, too. The women made room for him. The baby was rosy-looking and cheerful, about three months old, but Dr. Larch noticed the forceps mark on its cheek: a definite indentation, it would leave a scar. I can do better work than this, he thought.

"Isn't that a darling baby, Doctor Larch?" one of the women asked him.

"It's too bad about that forceps mark," Larch said, and that shut them all up.

Mrs. Channing-Peabody took him out into the hall. He let her lead him to the room that had been prepared for him. On the way she said, "We have this little problem."

"How many months along is she?" he asked Mrs. Channing-Peabody. "Is she *quick?*"

Quick or not, Missy Channing-Peabody had certainly been prepared. The family had converted a small reading room into an operating theater. There were old pictures of men in uniform, and books (looking long untouched) stood at attention. In the grim room's foreground was a solid table appropriately set with cotton batting and rubber sheeting, and Missy herself was lying in the correct examining position. She was already shaved, already swabbed with the bichloride solution. Someone had done the necessary homework; perhaps they'd pumped the senile family surgeon for details. Dr. Larch saw the alcohol, the green soap, the nail brush (which he proceeded, immediately, to use). There was a set of six metal dilators, and a set of three curettes in a leather-covered, satin-lined case. There was chloroform and a chloroform inhaler, and this one mistake—that they didn't know Wilbur Larch's preference for ether—made Larch almost forgive them.

What Wilbur Larch could not forgive was the obvious loathing they felt for him. There was an old woman in attendance, perhaps some faithful household servant who had played midwife to countless little Channing-Peabodys, maybe even midwife to Missy. The old woman was particularly chisel-faced and sharp-eyed when she looked at Larch, as if she expected him to congratulate her—at which moment she would not acknowledge that he'd spoken to her—for her precision in readying the patient. Mrs. Channing-Peabody herself seemed unable to touch him; she did offer to hold his coat, which he let her take before he asked her to leave.

"Send that young man," Larch told her. "He should be here, I think." He meant the particularly hostile young man in tennis whites, whether he was the outraged brother or the guilty lover or both. These people need me but they hate me, Larch was thinking, as he scrubbed under his nails. While he let his arms soak in the alcohol bath, he wondered how many doctors the Channing-Peabodys must know (how many must be in the family!), but they would never have asked one of their kind for help with this "little problem." They were too pure for it.

"You want my help?" the sullen young man asked Larch.

"Not really," Larch replied. "Don't touch anything and stand to my left. Just look over my shoulder, and be sure you can see everything."

That class-conscious look of scorn had all but left young Chadwick's (or young Cabot's) face when Wilbur Larch went to work with the curette; with the first appearance of the products of conception, the young man's expression opened—that certain, judgmental air was not discernible in any aspect of his face, which seemed softened and resembled his tennis whites in its color.

"I have made this observation about the wall of the uterus," Dr. Larch told the ghostly young man. "It is a good, hard, muscular wall, and when you've scraped it clean, it responds with a gritty sound. That's how you know when you've got all of it—all the products of conception. You just listen for that gritty sound." He scraped some more. "Can you hear it?" he asked.

"No," the young man whispered.

"Well, perhaps 'sound' isn't the right word," Wilbur Larch said. "Perhaps it's more like a gritty feeling, but it's a sound to me. *Gritty,*" he said, as young Cabot or young Chadwick attempted to catch his own vomit in his cupped hands.

"Take her temperature every hour," Larch told the rigid servant who held the sterile towels. "If there's more than a little bleeding, or if she has a fever, I should be called. And treat her like a princess," Wilbur Larch told the old woman and the ashen, empty young man. "No one should be allowed to make her feel ashamed."

He would have departed like a gentleman after he looked under Missy's eyelids at her chloroform gaze; but when he put his coat on, he felt the envelope bulge in the breast pocket. He didn't count the money, but he saw there were several hundred dollars. It was the mayor's mansion all over again, the servants' quarters treatment; it meant the Channing-Peabodys wouldn't ask him back for tennis or croquet or a sail.

He promptly handed about fifty dollars to the old woman who had bathed Missy's genitals with the bichloride solution and had covered her with a sterile vulval pad. He gave about twenty dollars to the young tennis player, who had opened the door to the patio to breathe a little of the garden air. Larch was going to leave. Then, when he shoved his hands in his coat pockets and found the panties again, on an impulse he grabbed the placenta forceps and took the instrument with him. He went off looking for the old surgeon, but there were only servants in the dining room—still clearing the table. He gave each of them about twenty or thirty dollars.

He found the senile doctor asleep in a reading chair in another room. He opened the mouth of the forceps, clamped the pair of panties from "Off Harrison" in it, and then clamped the whole business to the old snorer's lapel.

He found the kitchen, and several servants busy in it, and gave away about two hundred dollars there.

He went out on the grounds and gave the last of the money, another two hundred dollars, to a gardener who was on his knees in a flower bed by the main door. He would have liked to have handed the empty envelope back to Mrs. Channing-Peabody; the grand lady was hiding from him. He tried to fold the envelope and pin it to the main door under the big brass door knocker; the envelope kept blowing free in the wind. Then he got angry and wadded it up in a ball and threw it into a manicured circle of green lawn, which served as a rotary for the main driveway. Two croquet players on a far lawn held up their game and stared first at the crumpled envelope and then at the blue summer sky, as if a lightning bolt, at the very least, were momentarily expected to strike Larch dead.

On his way back to Portland, Wilbur Larch reflected on the last century of medical history—when abortion was legal, when many more complex procedures than a simple abortion were routinely taught medical students: such things as utero decapitation and fetal pulverization (these in lieu of the more dangerous Caesarean section). He mumbled those words to himself: utero decapitation, fetal pulverization. By the time he got back to Portland, he had worked the matter out. He was an obstetrician; he delivered babies into the world. His colleagues called this "the Lord's work." And he was an abortionist; he delivered mothers, too. His colleagues called this "the Devil's work," but it was *all* the Lord's work to Wilbur Larch. As Mrs. Maxwell had observed: "The true physician's soul cannot be too broad and gentle."

Later, when he would have occasion to doubt himself, he would force himself to remember: he had slept with someone's mother and dressed himself in the light of her daughter's cigar. He could quite comfortably abstain from having sex for the rest of his life, but how could he ever condemn another person for having sex? He would remember, too, what he *hadn't* done for Mrs. Eames's daughter, and what that had cost.

He would deliver babies. He would deliver mothers, too.

In Portland, a letter from St. Cloud's awaited him. When the Maine State board of medical examiners sent him to St. Cloud's, they could not have known Wilbur Larch's feeling for orphans—nor could they have known his readiness to leave Portland, that safe harbor from which the *Great Eastern* had sailed with no plans for return. And they would never know that in the first week Wilbur Larch spent in St. Cloud's, he founded an orphanage (because it was needed), delivered three babies (one wanted, two inevitable—one would be another orphan), and performed one abortion (his third). It would take Larch some years to educate the population regarding birth control—the ratio would endure for some time: one abortion for every three births. Over the years, it would go to one in four, then to one in five.

During World War I, when Wilbur Larch went to France, the replacement physician at the orphanage would not perform abortions; the birth rate would climb, the number of orphans would double, but the replacement physician said to Nurse Edna and to Nurse Angela that he was put on this earth to do the Lord's work, not the Devil's. This feeble distinction would later prove useful to Nurse Angela and to Nurse Edna, and to Dr. Wilbur Larch, who wrote his good nurses from France that he had seen the real Devil's work: the Devil worked with shell and grenade fragments, with shrapnel and with the little, dirty bits of clothing carried with a missile into a wound. The Devil's work was gas bacillus infection, that scourge of the First World War—Wilbur Larch would never forget how it crackled to the touch.

"Tell him," Larch wrote Nurse Angela and Nurse Edna, "tell that fool [he meant his replacement] that the work at the orphanage is *all* the Lord's work—everything you do, you do *for* the orphans, you deliver *them!*"

And when the war was over, and Wilbur Larch came home to St. Cloud's, Nurse Edna and Nurse Angela were already familiar with the proper language for the work of St. Cloud's—the Lord's work *and* the Devil's work, they called it, just to keep it straight between themselves which operation was being performed when. Wilbur Larch went along with it—it was useful language—but both nurses were in agreement with Larch: that it was *all* the Lord's work that they were performing.

It was not until 193__ that they encountered their first problem. His name was Homer Wells. He went out into the world and came back to St. Cloud's so many times that it was necessary to put him to work; by the time a boy is a teen-ager, he should be of use. But would he understand? the nurses and Dr. Larch wondered. Homer had seen the mothers come and go, and leave their babies behind, but how long before he started counting heads—and realized that there were more mothers coming and going than there were babies left behind? How long before he observed that not all the mothers who came to St. Cloud's were visibly pregnant—and some of them didn't even stay overnight? Should they tell him? the nurses and Dr. Larch wondered.

"Wilbur," Nurse Edna said, while Nurse Angela rolled her eyes, "the boy has the run of the place—he's going to figure it out for himself."

"He's growing older every minute," Nurse Angela said. "He's learning something new every day."

It was true that they never let the women recovering from the abortions rest in the same room with the new mothers, who were gaining their strength to leave their babies behind; that was something even a child could observe. And Homer Wells was frequently in charge of emptying the wastebaskets—*all* the wastebaskets, even the operating-room wastebaskets, which were leakproof and taken directly to the incinerator.

"What if he looks in a wastebasket, Wilbur?" Nurse Edna asked Dr. Larch.

"If he's old enough to look, he's old enough to learn," St. Larch replied.

Perhaps Larch meant: if he's old enough to recognize what there was to be seen. After the Lord's work, or after the Devil's, much that would be in the wastebasket would be the same. In most cases: blood and mucus, cotton and gauze, placenta and pubic hair. Both nurses told Dr. Larch there was no need to shave a patient for an abortion, but Larch was fussy; and if it was all the Lord's work, he thought, let it all look the same. The wastebaskets that Homer Wells would carry to the incinerator held the history of St. Cloud's: the clipped ends of the silk and gut sutures, fecal matter and soap suds from the enemas, and what Nurse Edna and Nurse Angela feared Homer Wells would see—the so-called products of conception, a human fetus, or a recognizable part thereof.

And that is how Homer Wells (an unlucky thirteen) would discover that both the quick and the not quick were delivered at St. Cloud's. One day, walking back from the incinerator, he saw a fetus on the ground: it had fallen from the wastebasket he'd been carrying, but when he saw it, he assumed it had fallen from the sky. He bent over it, then he looked for the nest it might have dropped from—only there were no trees. Homer Wells knew that birds didn't deliver their eggs in flight—or that an egg, while falling, couldn't lose its shell.

Then he imagined that some animal had miscarried—in an orphanage, around a hospital, one heard that word—but *what* animal? It weighed less than a pound, it was maybe eight inches long, and that shadow on its almost translucent head was the first phase of hair, not feathers; and those were almost eyebrows on its scrunched face; it had eyelashes, too. And were those *nipples*—those little pale pink dots emerging on that chest the size of a large thumb? And those slivers at the fingertips and at the toes—those were *nails*! Holding the whole thing in one hand, Homer ran with it, straight to Dr. Larch. Larch was sitting at the typewriter in Nurse Angela's office; he was writing a letter to The New England Home for Little Wanderers.

"I found something," Homer Wells said. He held out his hand, and Larch took the fetus from him and placed it on a clean white piece of typing paper on Nurse Angela's desk. It was about three months—at the most, four. Not quite quick, Dr. Larch knew, but almost. "What is it?" Homer Wells asked.

"The Lord's work," said Wilbur Larch, that saint of St. Cloud's, because that was when he realized that this was also the Lord's work: teaching Homer Wells, telling him everything, making sure he learned right from wrong. It was a lot of work, the Lord's work, but if one was going to be presumptuous enough to undertake it, one had to do it perfectly.

3/ Princes of Maine, Kings of New England

"Here in St. Cloud's," Dr. Larch wrote, "we treat orphans as if they came from royal families."

In the boys' division, this sentiment informed his nightly blessing—his benediction, shouted over the beds standing in rows in the darkness. Dr. Larch's blessing followed the bedtime reading, which—after the unfortunate accident to the Winkles—became the responsibility of Homer Wells. Dr. Larch wanted to give Homer more confidence. When Homer told Dr. Larch how he had loved reading to the Winkles in their safari tent—and how he thought he had done it well, except that the Winkles had fallen asleep—the doctor decided that the boy's talent should be encouraged.

In 193__, almost immediately after seeing his first fetus, Homer Wells began reading *David Copperfield* to the boys' division, just twenty minutes a crack, no more, no less; he thought it would take him longer to read it than it took Dickens to write it. Faltering at first—and teased by the very few boys who were near his own age (no boy was older)—Homer improved. Every night he would murmur aloud to himself that book's opening passage. It had the effect of a litany—on occasion, it allowed him to sleep peacefully.

> Whether I shall turn out to be the hero
> of my own life, or whether that station will
> be held by anybody else, these pages must show.

"Whether I shall turn out to be the hero of my own life," Homer whispered to himself. He remembered the dryness in his eyes and nose in the furnace room at the Drapers' in Waterville; he remembered the spray from the water that had swept the Winkles away; he remembered the cool, damp, curled-in-on-itself beginning that lay dead in his hand. (That thing he had held in his hand could not have been a hero.)

And after "lights out," and Nurse Edna or Nurse Angela had asked if anyone wanted a last glass of water, or if anyone needed a last trip to the potty—when those dots of light from the just-extinguished lamps still blinked in the darkness, and every orphan's mind was either sleeping, dreaming, or lingering with David Copperfield's adventures—Dr. Larch would open the door from the hall, with its exposed pipes and its hospital colors.

"Good night!" he would call. "Good night—you Princes of Maine, you Kings of New England!" (That thing Homer had held in his hand was no prince—it hadn't lived to be king.)

Then, bang!—the door would close, and the orphans would be left in a new blackness. Whatever image of royalty that they could conjure would be left to them. What princes and kings could they have seen? What futures were possible for them to dream of? What royal foster families would greet them in sleep? What princesses would love them? What queens would they marry? And when would they escape the darkness left with them after Larch closed the door, after they could no longer hear the retreating squeaks of Nurse Edna's and Nurse Angela's shoes? (That thing he had held in his hand could not have heard the shoes—it had the smallest, most wrinkled ears!)

For Homer Wells, it was different. He did not imagine leaving St. Cloud's. The Princes of Maine that Homer saw, the Kings of New England that he imagined—they reigned at the court of St. Cloud's, they traveled nowhere; they didn't get to go to sea; they never even saw the ocean. But somehow, even to Homer Wells, Dr. Larch's benediction was uplifting, full of hope. These Princes of Maine, these Kings of New England, these orphans of St. Cloud's—whoever they were, they *were* the heroes of their own lives. That much Homer could see in the darkness; that much Dr. Larch, like a father, gave him.

Princely, even kingly behavior was possible, even at St. Cloud's. That seemed to be what Dr. Larch was saying.

Homer Wells dreamed he was a prince. He lifted up his eyes to *his* king: he watched St. Larch's every move. It was the astonishing coolness of the thing that Homer couldn't forget.

"Because it was dead, right?" he asked Dr. Larch. "That's why it was cool, right?"

"Yes," said Dr. Larch. "In a way, Homer, it was never alive."

"Never alive," said Homer Wells.

"Sometimes," Dr. Larch said, "a woman simply can't make herself stop a pregnancy, she feels the baby is already a baby—from the first speck—and she has to have it—although she doesn't want it and she can't take care of it—and so she comes to us and has her baby here. She leaves it here, with us. She trusts us to find it a home."

"She makes an orphan," said Homer Wells. "Someone has to adopt it."

"Someone usually adopts it," Dr. Larch said.

"Usually," said Homer Wells. "Maybe."

"Eventually," Dr. Larch said.

"And sometimes," said Homer Wells, "the woman *doesn't* go through with it, right? She doesn't go through with having the baby."

"Sometimes," said Dr. Larch, "the woman knows very early in her pregnancy that this child is unwanted."

"An orphan, from the start," said Homer Wells.

"You might say," said Wilbur Larch.

"So she kills it," said Homer Wells.

"You might say," said Wilbur Larch. "You might also say that she stops it before it becomes a child—she just stops it. In the first three or four months, the fetus—or the embryo (I don't say, then, 'the child')—it does not quite have a life of its own. It lives off the mother. It hasn't developed."

"It's developed only a little," said Homer Wells.

"It hasn't moved, independently," said Dr. Larch.

"It doesn't have a proper nose," said Homer Wells, remembering it. On the thing he had held in his hand, neither the nostrils nor the nose itself had developed to its downward slope; the nostrils pointed straight out from the face, like the nostrils of a pig.

"Sometimes," said Dr. Larch, "when a woman is very strong and knows that no one will care for this baby if she has it, and she doesn't want to bring a child into the world and try to find it a home—she comes to me and I stop it."

"Tell me again, what's *stopping* it called?" asked Homer Wells.

"An abortion," Dr. Larch said.

"Right," said Homer Wells. "An abortion."

"And what you held in your hand, Homer, was an aborted fetus," Dr. Larch said. "An embryo, about three to four months."

"An aborted fetus, an embryo, about three to four months," said Homer Wells, who had an irritating habit of repeating the pigtails of sentences very seriously, as if he were planning to read *them* aloud, like *David Copperfield*.

"And that's why," Dr. Larch said patiently, "some of the women who come here don't *look* pregnant . . . the embryo, the fetus, there's just not enough of it to show."

"But they all *are* pregnant," said Homer Wells. "All the women who come here—they're either going to have an orphan, or they're going to stop it, right?"

"That's right," Dr. Larch said. "I'm just the doctor. I help them have what they want. An orphan or an abortion."

"An orphan or an abortion," said Homer Wells.

/ / /

Nurse Edna teased Dr. Larch about Homer Wells. "You have a new shadow, Wilbur," she said.

"*Doctor* Larch," Nurse Angela said, "you have developed an echo. You've got a parrot following you around."

"God or whatever, forgive me," wrote Dr. Larch. "I have created a disciple, I have a thirteen-year-old *disciple*."

By the time Homer was fifteen, his reading of *David Copperfield* was so successful that some of the older girls in the girls' division asked Dr. Larch if Homer might be persuaded to read to them.

"Just to the older girls?" Homer asked Dr. Larch.

"Certainly not," said Dr. Larch. "You'll read to all of them."

"In the girls' division?" Homer asked.

"Well, yes," Dr. Larch said. "It would be awkward to have all the girls come to the boys' division."

"Right," said Homer Wells. "But do I read to the girls first or to the boys first?"

"The girls," Larch said. "The girls go to bed earlier than the boys."

"They do?" Homer asked.

"They do here," Dr. Larch said.

"And do I read them the same passage?" Homer asked. He was, at the time, in his fourth journey through *David Copperfield*, only his third aloud—at Chapter 16, "I Am a New Boy in More Senses Than One."

But Dr. Larch decided that girl orphans should hear about

girl orphans—in the same spirit that he believed boy orphans should hear about boy orphans—and so he assigned Homer the task of reading aloud to the girls' division from *Jane Eyre.*

It struck Homer immediately that the girls were more attentive than the boys; they were an altogether better audience—except for the giggles upon his arrival and upon his departure. That they should be a better audience surprised Homer, for he found *Jane Eyre* not nearly so interesting as *David Copperfield;* he was convinced that Charlotte Brontë was not nearly as good a writer as Charles Dickens. Compared to little David, Homer thought, little Jane was something of a whiner—a sniveler—but the girls in the girls' division always cried for more, for just one more scene, when, every evening, Homer would stop and hurry away, out of the building and into the night, racing for the boys' division and Dickens.

The night between the boys' and girls' division frequently smelled of sawdust; only the night had kept the memory of the original St. Cloud's intact, dispensing in its secretive darkness, the odors of the old saw mills and even the rank smell of the sawyers' cigars.

"The night sometimes smells like wood and cigars," Homer Wells told Dr. Larch, who had his own memory of cigars; the doctor shuddered.

The girls' division, Homer thought, had a different smell from the boys', although the same exposed pipes, the same hospital colors, the same dormitory discipline prevailed. On the one hand, it smelled sweeter; on the other hand, it smelled sicker—Homer had difficulty deciding.

For going to bed, the boys and girls dressed alike—undervests and underpants—and whenever Homer arrived at the girls' division, the girls were already in their beds, with their legs covered, some of them sitting up, some of them lying down. The very few with visible breasts were usually sitting with their arms folded across their chests to conceal their development. All but one—the biggest one, the oldest one; she was both bigger and older than Homer Wells. She had carried Homer across the finish line of a particularly famous three-legged race—she was the one called Melony, who was meant to be Melody; the one whose breasts Homer had mistakenly touched, the one who'd pinched his pecker.

Melony sat for the reading Indian-style—on top of her bed covers, her underpants not quite big enough for her, her hands on her hips, her elbows pointed out like wings, her considerable bosom thrust forward; a bit of her big, bare belly was exposed. Every night, Mrs. Grogan, who directed the girls' division, would say, "Won't you catch cold outside your covers, Melony?"

"Nope," Melony would say, and Mrs. Grogan would sigh—it was almost a groan. That was her nickname: Mrs. Groan. Her authority rested in her ability to make the girls think that they caused her pain by doing harm to themselves or each other.

"Oh, that hurts me to see that," she would tell them when they fought, pulled hair, gouged eyeballs, bit each other in the face. "That really hurts me." Her method was effective with the girls who liked her. It was not effective with Melony. Mrs. Grogan was especially fond of Melony, but she felt she was a failure at making Melony like her.

"Oh, it hurts me, Melony, to see you catching cold—outside your covers," Mrs. Grogan would say, "only partially clothed. That really hurts me."

But Melony would stay put, her eyes never leaving Homer Wells. She was bigger than Mrs. Grogan, she was too big for the girls' division. She was too big to be adopted. She's too big to be a *girl,* thought Homer Wells. Bigger than Nurse Edna, bigger than Nurse Angela—almost as big as Dr. Larch—she was fat, but her fat looked solid. Although he had not competed in the three-legged race for several years, Homer Wells also knew that Melony was strong. Homer had decided not to compete as long as he would be paired with Melony—and he would be paired with her as long as he was the oldest boy and she was the oldest girl.

In reading aloud from *Jane Eyre,* Homer needed to keep his eyes off Melony; one look at her would remind him of having his leg tied to hers. He sensed that she resented his withdrawal from the annual competition. He was also afraid that she might sense how he *liked* her heaviness—how fat, to an orphan, seemed such good fortune.

The sweeter passages of *Jane Eyre* (too sweet, for Homer Wells) brought tears to the eyes of the girls in the girls' division, and drew the most plaintive sighs and moans from Mrs. Grogan, but these same, sweeter passages extracted from Melony the most tortured breathing—as if sweetness provoked in her an anger barely restrainable.

The end of Chapter Four provided Melony with too much anger to restrain.

" 'That afternoon lapsed in peace and harmony,' " Homer Wells read to them; hearing Melony hiss at the words "peace" and "harmony," he bravely read on. " 'And in the evening Bessie told me some of her most enchanting stories, and sang me some of her sweetest songs,' " Homer continued, glad there was only one more sentence to get through; he saw Melony's broad chest heave. " 'Even for me [chirped little Jane Eyre], life had its gleams of sunshine.' "

" 'Gleams of sunshine'!" Melony shouted in violent disbelief. "Let her come here! Let her show *me* the gleams of sunshine!"

"Oh, how it hurts me, Melony—to hear you say that," Mrs. Grogan said.

"Sunshine?" Melony said with a howl. The younger girls crawled all the way under their bed covers; some of them began to cry.

"The pain this causes me, I don't know if I can bear it, Melony," Mrs. Grogan said.

Homer Wells slipped away. It was the end of the chapter, anyway. He was due at the boys' division. This time the giggles attendant on his departure were mixed with sobs and with Melony's derision.

"Gleams!" Melony called after him.

"How this hurts us *all,*" Mrs. Grogan said more firmly.

Outside, the night seemed full of new scents to Homer Wells. Mingled with the sawdust smell and the rank cigars, was that a waft of the raucous perfume drifting over him from the former whore hotel? And something like sweat from the bingo-for-money room? The river itself gave off a smell.

In the boys' division, they were waiting for him. Some of the smaller ones had fallen asleep. The others were open-eyed—seemingly, open-mouthed, like baby birds; Homer felt he was rushing from nest to nest, his voice feeding them as they always cried for more. His reading, like food, made them sleepy, but it often woke Homer up. He usually lay awake after the nightly benediction—the *ince* in "Princes" and the *ing* in "Kings" still rang in the dark room. Sometimes he wished he could sleep in the baby room; the constant waking and crying there might be more rhythmic.

The older orphans had their irritating habits. One of Nurse

Edna's John Wilburs slept on a rubber sheet; Homer would lie awake, waiting to hear him wet his bed. Some nights Homer would wake the child, march him to the toilet, point his tiny pecker in the right direction and whisper, "*Pee,* John Wilbur. Pee *now.* Pee *here.*" The child, asleep on his feet, would hold it back, waiting for the welcoming rubber sheet, that familiar dent and warm puddle in the bed.

Some nights, when he felt irritable, Homer Wells would simply stand by John Wilbur's bedside and whisper his command in the boy's ear: "Pee!" With almost instantaneous results!

More upsetting was Nurse Angela's name-child, the sickly little Fuzzy Stone. Fuzzy had a cough, a constant dry hack. He had wet, red eyes. He slept inside a humidified tent; a waterwheel cranked by a battery and a fan to distribute the vapor ran all night. Fuzzy Stone's chest sounded like a tiny, failing motor; the damp, cool sheets enclosing him fluttered through the night like the tissue of a giant, semi-transparent lung. The waterwheel, the fan, Fuzzy Stone's dramatic gasps—they merged in Homer's mind. If one of the three were to stop, Homer doubted he'd know which two were still alive.

Dr. Larch told Homer that he suspected Fuzzy Stone was allergic to dust; that the boy was born and slept in a former sawmill was doubtlessly not the best thing for him. A child with chronic bronchitis was not easily adoptable. Who wants to take home a cough?

When Fuzzy Stone's coughing was too much for Homer Wells, when the various engines that struggled to maintain Fuzzy were too much on Homer's mind—lungs, waterwheel and fan—Homer would quietly seek out the baby room. Nurse Angela or Nurse Edna was always there, usually awake and tending to one of the babies. Sometimes, when the babies were quiet, even the nurse on duty was sleeping, and Homer Wells would tiptoe past them all.

One night he saw one of the mothers standing in the baby room. She did not appear to be looking for her baby in particular; she was just standing in her hospital gown in the middle of the baby room, her eyes closed, absorbing the smells and sounds of the baby room through her other senses. Homer was afraid the woman would wake up Nurse Angela, who was dozing on the duty bed; Nurse Angela would have been cross with her. Slowly, as Homer imagined you might assist a sleep-walker, he led the woman back to the mothers' room.

The mothers were often awake when he went to peek in on them. Sometimes he would get someone a glass of water.

The women who came to St. Cloud's for the abortions rarely stayed overnight. They required less time to recover than the women who had delivered, and Dr. Larch discovered that they were most comfortable if they arrived in the morning, shortly before light, and left in the early evening, just after dark. In the daytime, the sound of the babies was not so prevailing because the noise the older orphans made, and the talk among the mothers and the nurses, confused everything. It was the sound of the newborn babies that, Dr. Larch observed, upset the women having the abortions. At night—except for John Wilbur's peeing and Fuzzy Stone's cough—the waking babies and the owls made the only sounds at St. Cloud's.

It was a simple enough observation to make: the women having abortions were not comforted to hear the cries and prattle of the newborn. You could not plan the exact hour for a delivery, but Larch tried to plan the abortions for the early morning, which gave the women the whole day to recover and allowed them to be gone by evening. Some of the women traveled a long way—in these cases, Larch recommended that they come to St. Cloud's the night before their abortions, when he could give them something strong to help them sleep; they'd have the whole of the next day to recover.

If one of those women spent the night, it was never in the room with the expectant or delivered mothers. Homer Wells—in his insomniac tour of St. Cloud's—saw that, in sleep, the expressions of these overnight visitors were no more nor less troubled than the expressions of the women who were having (or who'd already had) babies. Homer Wells would try to imagine his own mother among the faces of the sleeping and the wakeful women. Where was she waiting to get back to—when the pain of her labor was behind her? Or was there no place she wanted to go? And what, when she was lying there, was his father thinking—if he even knew he was a father? If she even knew who he was.

These are the things the women would say to him:

"Are you in training to be a doctor?"

"Are you going to be a doctor when you grow up?"

"Are you one of the orphans?"

"How old are you? Hasn't anyone adopted you yet?"

"Did someone send you back?"

"Do you like it here?"

And he would answer:

"I might become a doctor."

"Of course Doctor Larch is a good teacher."

"That's right: one of the orphans."

"Almost sixteen. I *tried* being adopted, but it just wasn't for me."

"I *wanted* to come back."

"Of course I like it here!"

One of the women—very expectant, her belly huge under a taut sheet—asked him, "Do you mean, if someone wanted to adopt you, you wouldn't go?"

"I wouldn't go," said Homer Wells. "Right."

"You wouldn't even consider it?" the woman asked. He almost couldn't look at her—she seemed so ready to explode.

"Well, I guess I'd think about it," Homer Wells said. "But I'd probably decide to stay, as long as I can help out around here—you know, be of use."

The pregnant woman began to cry. "Be of use," she said, as if *she'd* learned to repeat the pigtails of sentences from listening to Homer Wells. She pulled down the sheet, she pulled up her hospital gown; Nurse Edna had already shaved her. She put her hands on her great belly. "Look at that," she whispered. "You want to be of use?"

"Right," said Homer Wells, who held his breath.

"No one but me ever put a hand on me, to feel that baby. No one wanted to put his ear against it and listen," the woman said. "You shouldn't have a baby if there's no one who wants to feel it kick, or listen to it move."

"I don't know," said Homer Wells.

"Don't you want to touch it or put your ear down to it?" the woman asked him.

"Okay," said Homer Wells, putting his hand on the woman's hot, hard belly.

"Put your ear down against it, too," the woman advised him.

"Right," Homer said. He touched his ear very lightly to her stomach but she strongly pressed his face against her; she was like a drum—all pings! and pongs! She was a warm engine—shut off, but still tapping with heat. If Homer had been to the ocean, he would have recognized that she was like the tide, like surf—surging in and out and back and forth.

"No one should have a baby if there's no one who wants to sleep with his head right there," the woman whispered, patting the place where she roughly held Homer's face. Right *where*? Homer wondered, because there was no comfortable place to put his head, no place between her breasts and her belly that wasn't round. Her breasts, at least, looked comfortable, but he knew that wasn't where she wanted his head. He found it hard to imagine, from all the noise and motion inside her, that the woman was carrying only one baby. Homer Wells thought that the woman was going to give birth to a tribe.

"You want to be of use?" the woman asked him, crying gently now.

"Yes. Be of use," he said.

"Sleep right here," the woman told him. He pretended to sleep with his face against the noisy boulder, where she held him snug. He knew when her water had broken before she knew it—she had fallen that soundly asleep. He went and found Nurse Edna without waking the woman, who before dawn delivered a seven-pound baby girl. Since neither Nurse Edna nor Nurse Angela was in charge of naming the girl orphans, after a few days someone gave her a name— probably Mrs. Grogan, who favored Irish names, or if Mrs. Grogan had momentarily exhausted her supply, the secretary who typed badly and was responsible for "Melony" instead of "Melody"; she also enjoyed naming the little girls.

Homer Wells never knew which one she was, but he kept looking for her, as if his nighttime vigil with his face upon the mother's jumping belly might have given him the senses necessary to recognize her child.

He never would recognize her, of course. All he had to go on was the fluid sound of her, and how she'd moved under his ear, in the dark. But he kept looking; he watched the girls in the girls' division as if he expected her to do something that would give her away.

He even admitted his private game to Melony once, but Melony was, typically, derisive. "Just what do you think the kid's going to do so you'll know which one she is?" Melony asked. "Is she going to gurgle, is she going to fart—or kick you in the ear?"

But Homer Wells knew he was just playing a game by

himself, with himself; orphans are notorious for interior games. For example, one of the oldest games that orphans play is imagining that their parents want them back—that their parents are looking for them. But Homer had spent an evening with the mystery baby's mother; he'd heard all about the mystery baby's father—and his lack of interest in the matter. Homer knew that the mystery baby's parents *weren't* looking for her; that may have been why he decided *he'd* look for her. If that baby girl was growing up, and if she was playing the old orphans' game, wouldn't it be better if there was at least *someone* who was looking for her—even if it was just another orphan?

/ / /

Dr. Larch tried to talk to Homer about Melony's anger.

"Anger is a funny thing," Dr. Larch began, believing that anger was an *un*funny thing.

"I mean, I agree, the passage about the 'gleams of sunshine' —okay, it's sappy," Homer said. "It's one of those things—it makes you wince when you read it, but it's just what Jane would say, it's just like her, so what can you do?" Homer asked. "But Melony was *violent* about it."

Dr. Larch knew that Melony was one of the few orphans still at St. Cloud's who was not born at St. Cloud's. She'd been left at the hospital entrance one early morning when she'd been four or five; she was always so big for her age, it had been hard to tell how old she was. She hadn't talked until she was eight or nine. At first, Larch thought she might be retarded, but that wasn't the problem.

"Melony was always angry," Dr. Larch tried to explain. "We don't know about her origins, or her early years, and she may not know herself what all the sources of her anger are." Larch was deliberating—whether or not he should tell Homer Wells that Melony had been adopted and had been returned more times than Homer. "Melony had several unfortunate experiences in foster homes," Dr. Larch said cautiously. "If you have the opportunity to ask her about her experiences—and if she wants to talk about them—it might provide her with a welcome release for some of her anger."

"Ask her about her experiences," said Homer Wells, shaking his head. "I don't know," he said. "I never tried to *talk* to her."

Dr. Larch already regretted his suggestion. Perhaps Melony

would remember her first foster family and tell Homer about them; they had sent her back because she allegedly bit the family dog in an altercation concerning a ball. It wasn't just the one fracas that upset the family; they claimed that Melony repeatedly bit the dog. For weeks after the incident, she would creep up on the animal and surprise it when it was eating, or when it was asleep. The family accused Melony of driving the dog crazy.

Melony had run away from the second and third families, alleging that the men in the families, either fathers or brothers, had taken a sexual interest in her. The fourth family claimed that Melony had taken a sexual interest in a younger, female child. In the case of number five: the husband and wife eventually separated because of Melony's relationship with the husband—the wife claimed that her husband had seduced Melony, the husband claimed that Melony had seduced (he said "attacked") him. Melony was not ambiguous about the matter. "No one seduces me!" she told Mrs. Grogan proudly. In the case of number six: the husband had died of a heart attack shortly after Melony's arrival, and the wife had sent the girl back to St. Cloud's because she felt unequipped for the task of raising Melony alone. (Melony's only remark to Mrs. Grogan had been: "You bet she's unequipped!")

All this, suddenly, Dr. Larch imagined Homer hearing first-hand from Melony; the vision disturbed him. He feared that he had made Homer Wells his apprentice—an attendant to the gritty operation of St. Cloud's—while at the same time he could not resist screening the boy from some of the harder truths.

It was so like Nurse Angela, of course, to call Homer Wells "angelic," and so like Nurse Edna to speak of the boy's "perfection" and of his "innocence," but Dr. Larch worried about Homer's contact with the damaged women who sought the services of St. Cloud's—those departing mothers in whose characters and histories the boy must be seeking some definition of his own mother. And the troubled women who were scraped clean and went away leaving no one behind (just the products of conception)—what impression did they make on the boy?

Homer Wells had a good, open face; it was not a face that could hide things—every feeling and thought was visible upon it, the way a lake in the open reflects every weather. He had a good hand for holding and eyes you could confess to; Dr. Larch was worried about the specific details of the life stories Homer would be exposed to—not simply the sordidness but also the abundant rationalizations he would hear.

And now Melony, the undisputed heavyweight of the girls' division, had disturbed the boy with her anger—with what Dr. Larch suspected was only the tip of the iceberg of her power; her potential for educating Homer Wells seemed to be both terrible and vast.

Melony began her contribution to Homer's education the very next evening when he read to the girls' division. Homer had arrived early (hoping to leave early), but he found the girls' dormitory quarters in disarray. Many of the girls were out of their beds—some of them shrieking when they saw him; their legs were bare. Homer was embarrassed; he stood under the hanging bulb in the communal bedroom, searching the room without success for Mrs. Grogan, who was always nice to him, and clutching his copy of *Jane Eyre* in both hands—as if the wild girls were likely to tear it away from him.

He did notice that Melony was already in her usual position, in her expected, brief attire. He met her eyes, which were piercing but withholding opinion; then he looked down, or away, or at his hands holding *Jane Eyre*.

"Hey, you," he heard Melony say to him—and he heard a subsequent hush fall among the other girls. "Hey, you," Melony repeated. When he looked up at her, she was kneeling on her bed and shoving toward him the biggest bare ass he'd ever seen. A blue shadow (perhaps a bruise) discolored one of Melony's straining thighs; between the bulging, flexed cheeks of her intimidating buttocks, a single dark eye stared at Homer Wells. "Hey, *Sunshine*," Melony said to Homer, who blushed the color of the sun at sunrise or sunset. "Hey, Sunshine," Melony crooned sweetly to him—thus giving to the orphan Homer Wells her own name for him: *Sunshine*.

/ / /

When Homer told Dr. Larch what Melony had done to him, Dr. Larch reconsidered the wisdom of allowing Homer to read to the girls' division. But to remove this chore from the boy's duties would constitute, Larch felt, a kind of demotion; Homer might suffer a sense of failure. The work at an orphanage is fairly decisive; when Wilbur Larch felt *in*decisive, regarding Homer Wells, he knew he was suffering from the natural feelings of a father. The thought that he had allowed himself to become a father and a sufferer of a father's indecision so depressed Dr. Larch that he sought the good peace of ether—to which he was becoming, steadily, more accustomed.

There were no curtains at St. Cloud's. The hospital dispensary was a corner room; it had a south window and an east window, and it was the east window, in Nurse Edna's opinion, that made Dr. Larch such an early riser. The slim, white-iron hospital bed never looked slept in; Dr. Larch was the last to bed and the first to rise—enhancing the rumor that he never slept at all. If he slept, it was generally agreed that he slept in the dispensary. He did his writing at night, at the typewriter in Nurse Angela's office. The nurses had long ago forgotten why this room was called Nurse Angela's office; it was St. Cloud's only office room, and Dr. Larch had always used it for his writing. Since the dispensary was where he slept, perhaps Dr. Larch felt the need to say that the office belonged to someone else.

The dispensary had two doors (one leading to a toilet and shower), which in such a small room created a problem with furniture. With a window on the south end and on the east wall, and a door on the north and on the west, there was no wall one could put anything *against;* the stark bed fit under the east window. The closed and locked cupboards with their frail glass doors formed an awkward maze around the dispensary counter in the middle of the room; it seemed fitting, for a dispensary, that the medicines and the ether cans and the hardware of small surgery should occupy the most central space, but Larch had other reasons for arranging the room this way. The labyrinth of cabinets in the middle of the room not only left access to the hall and bathroom doors; it also blocked the bed from view of the hall door, which, like all the doors in the orphanage, had no lock.

The cluttered dispensary afforded him some privacy for his ether frolics. How Larch liked the heft of that quarter-pound can. Ether is a matter of experience and technique. Imbibing ether is pungent but light, even though ether is twice as heavy as air; inducing ether anesthesia—bringing one's patients through the panic of that suffocating odor—is different. With his more delicate patients, Larch often preceded his ether administration with five or six drops of oil of orange. For himself, he required no aromatic preparation, no fruity disguise. He was always conscious of the bump the ether can made when he set it on the floor by the bed; he was not always conscious of the moment when his fingers lost their grip on the mask; the cone—by the force of his own exhalations—fell from his face. He was usually conscious of the limp hand that had released the cone; oddly, that hand was the first part of him to wake up, often reaching for the mask that was no longer there. He could usually hear voices outside the dispensary—if they were calling him. He was confident that he would always have time to recover.

"Doctor Larch?" Nurse Angela or Nurse Edna, or Homer Wells, would ask, which was all Larch needed to be brought back from his ether voyage.

"Right here!" Larch would answer. "Just resting."

It was the dispensary, after all; don't the dispensaries of surgeons always smell of ether? And for a man who worked so hard and slept so little (if he slept at all), wasn't it natural that he would need an occasional nap?

It was Melony who first suggested to Homer Wells that Dr. Larch possessed certain remote habits and singular powers.

"Listen, Sunshine," Melony told Homer, "how come your favorite doctor doesn't look at women? He doesn't—believe me. He won't even look at me, and every male everywhere, every time, looks at me—men and boys look at me. Even you, Sunshine. You look at me." But Homer Wells looked away.

"And what's the smell he carries around?" Melony asked.

"Ether," said Homer Wells. "He's a doctor. He smells like ether."

"You're saying this is normal?" Melony asked him.

"Right," said Homer Wells.

"Like a dairy farmer?" Melony asked slyly. "He's *supposed* to smell like milk and cowshit, right?"

"Right," said Homer Wells, cautiously.

"Wrong, Sunshine," Melony said. "Your favorite doctor smells like he's got ether inside him—like he's got ether instead of blood."

Homer let this pass. The top of his dark head measured up to Melony's shoulder. They were walking on the tree-stripped and eroded riverbank in the part of St. Cloud's where the abandoned buildings had remained abandoned; the river there had eroded not only the bank but also the foundations of these buildings, which in several cases did not have proper foundations or even cellar holes—some of these buildings were set on posts, which were visible and rotting in the gnawing water at the river's edge.

The building Homer and Melony preferred had a porch that had not been designed to overhang the river, though it hung over the river now; through the porch's broken floorboards, Homer and Melony could watch the bruise-colored water rush by.

The building had been a kind of dormitory for the rough men who worked in the saw mills and lumberyards of the old St. Cloud's; it was not a building of sufficient style for the bosses or even the foremen—the Ramses Paper Company people had kept rooms in the whore hotel. It was a building for the sawyers, the stackers, the yardmen—the men who broke up the logjams, who drove the logs downstream, who hauled the logs and cut lumber overland; the men who worked the mills.

Usually, Homer and Melony stayed outside the building, on the porch. Inside, there were only an empty communal kitchen and the countless, sordid bunkrooms—the ruptured mattresses infested with mice. Because of the railroad, hoboes had come and gone, staking out their territory in the manner of dogs, by peeing around it, thus isolating the mattresses least overrun by the mice. Even with the window glass gone and the rooms half filling with snow in the winters, there was no ridding the inside of that building from the smell of urine.

One day, when the weak spring sun had lured a black snake, sluggish with cold, to warm itself on the floorboards of the porch, Melony said to Homer Wells, "Watch this, Sunshine." With surprising quickness of hand for such a big girl, she seized the napping snake behind its head. It was a milk snake— almost three feet long, and it twined around Melony's arm, but Melony held it the proper way, tightly, behind the head, not choking it. Once she had caught it, she seemed to pay no attention to it; she watched the sky as if for a sign and went on talking to Homer Wells.

"Your favorite doctor, Sunshine," Melony said. "He knows more about you than you know. And more about me than I know, maybe."

Homer let this pass. He was wary of Melony, especially now that she had a snake. She could grab hold of me just as quickly, he was thinking. She could do something to me with the snake.

"You ever think about your mother?" Melony asked, still

searching the sky. "You ever wish you knew who she was, why she didn't keep you, who your father was—you know, those things?"

"Right," said Homer Wells, who kept his eyes on the snake. It wound itself around Melony's arm; then it uncoiled itself and hung like a rope; then it thickened and thinned, all by itself. Tentatively, it explored around Melony's big hip; appearing to feel more secure, it settled around her thick waist—it could just reach.

"I was told I was left at the door," Melony said. "Maybe so, maybe not."

"I was born here," said Homer Wells.

"So you were told," Melony said.

"Nurse Angela named me," Homer offered in evidence.

"Nurse Angela or Nurse Edna would have named you if you'd been *left*," Melony said. She still watched the sky, she remained indifferent to the snake. She's bigger than I am, she's older than I am, she knows more than I do, thought Homer Wells. And she has a snake, he reminded himself, letting Melony's last remark pass.

"Sunshine," Melony said absently. "Just think about it: if you were born here in Saint Cloud's, there's got to be a record of it. Your favorite doctor knows who your mother is. He's got to have her name on file. You're written down, on paper. It's a law."

"A law," Homer Wells said flatly.

"It's a law that there's got to be a record of you," Melony said. "In writing—a record, a file. You're history, Sunshine."

"History," said Homer Wells. He had an image of Dr. Larch sitting at the typewriter in Nurse Angela's office; if there were records, that was where they would be.

"If you want to know who your mother is," Melony said, "all you got to do is look her up. You just look up your file. You could look me up while you were at it. A smart reader like you, Sunshine—it wouldn't take you much time. And any of it would make more interesting reading than *Jane Eyre.* My file alone is more interesting than that, I'll bet. And who knows what's in yours?"

Homer allowed himself to be distracted from the snake. He looked through a hole in the porch floorboards at some passing debris; a broken branch, perhaps, or a man's boot—maybe a man's leg—was swept by in the river. When he heard a whistling sound, like a whip, he regretted taking his eyes from the snake; he ducked; Melony was still concentrating on the sky. She was swinging the snake around and around her head, yet her attention was entirely on the sky—not on any sign that appeared there, either, but on a red-shouldered hawk. It hung above the river in that lazy-seeming, spiral soaring of hawks when they are hunting. Melony let the snake sail out over the river, the hawk following it; even before the snake struck the water and started swimming for its life, for shore, the hawk began to dive. The snake didn't fight the current, it raced with it, trying to find the angle that would bring it safely under the eroded bank or into the tangled bracken.

"Watch this, Sunshine," Melony said. A long ten yards offshore the hawk seized the swimming snake and carried it, writhing and striking, aloft. "I want to show you something else," Melony said, already turning her attention from the sky, now that the outcome was clear.

"Right," said Homer Wells—all eyes, all ears. At first the weight and movement of the snake appeared to make the hawk's rising a struggle, but the higher the hawk rose, the more easily it flew—as if the higher air had different properties from the air down where the snake had flourished.

"Sunshine!" Melony called impatiently. She led him inside the old building and upstairs to one of the darker bunkrooms. The room smelled as if there might be someone in it—possibly, someone alive—but it was too dark to see either the mice-invaded mattresses or a body. Melony forced open a ragged shutter hanging by one hinge and knelt on a mattress against a wall that the open shutter had brought to light. An old photograph was tacked to the wall, in line with what had once been the head of someone's bed; the tack had rusted and had bled a rusty path across the sepia tones of the photograph.

Homer had looked at other photographs, in other rooms, though he had neglected this one. The ones he remembered were baby pictures, and pictures of mothers and fathers, he presumed—the kind of family photographs that are always of interest to orphans.

"Come look at this, Sunshine," Melony said. She was trying to pick the tack loose with her fingernail, but the tack had been stuck there for years. Homer knelt beside Melony on the rotting mattress. It took awhile for him to grasp the content of the photograph; possibly, he was distracted by his awareness that he had not been as physically close to Melony since he'd last been tied to her in the three-legged race.

Once Homer had understood the photograph (at least, he understood its subject, if not its reason for existing), he found it a difficult photograph to go on looking at, especially with Melony so close to him. On the other hand, he suspected he would be accused of cowardice if he looked away. The photograph reflected the cute revisions of reality engineered in many photographic studios at the turn of the century; the picture was edged with fake clouds, with a funereal or reverential mist; the participants in the photograph appeared to be performing their curious act in a very stylish Heaven or Hell.

Homer Wells guessed it was Hell. The participants in the photograph were a leggy young woman and a short pony. The naked woman lay with her long legs spread-eagled on a rug—a wildly confused Persian or Oriental (Homer Wells didn't know the difference)—and the pony, facing the wrong way, straddled her. His head was bent, as if to drink or to graze, just above the woman's extensive patch of pubic hair; the pony's expression was slightly camera-conscious, or ashamed, or possibly just stupid. The pony's penis looked longer and thicker than Homer Wells's arm, yet the athletic-looking young woman had contorted her neck and had sufficient strength in her arms and hands to bend the pony's penis to her mouth. Her cheeks were puffed out, as if she'd held her breath too long; her eyes bulged; yet the woman's expression remained ambiguous—it was impossible to tell if she was going to burst out laughing or if she was choking to death on the pony's penis. As for the pony, his shaggy face was full of faked indifference—the placid pose of strained animal dignity.

"Lucky pony, huh, Sunshine?" Melony asked him, but Homer Wells felt passing through his limbs a shudder that coincided exactly with his sudden vision of the photographer, the evil manipulator of the woman, the pony, the clouds of Heaven or the smoke of Hell. The mists of nowhere on this earth, at least, Homer imagined. Homer saw, briefly, as fast as a tremble, the darkroom genius who had created this spectacle. What lingered with Homer longer was his vision of the man who had slept on this mattress where he now knelt with Melony in worship of the man's treasure. This was the picture some woodsman had chosen to wake up with, the portrait of pony and woman somehow substituting itself for the man's family.

This was what caused Homer the sharpest pain; to imagine the tired man in the bunkroom at St. Cloud's, drawn to this woman and this pony because he knew of no friendlier image—no baby pictures, no mother, no father, no wife, no lover, no brother, no friend.

But in spite of the pain it caused him, Homer Wells found himself unable to turn away from the photograph. With a surprisingly girlish delicacy, Melony was still picking at the rusty tack—in such a considerate way that she never blocked Homer's view of the picture.

"If I can get the damn thing off the wall," she said, "I'll give it to you."

"I don't want it," said Homer Wells, but he wasn't sure.

"Sure you do," Melony said. "There's nothing in it for *me*. I'm not interested in ponies."

When she finally dug the tack out of the wall, she noticed that she'd broken her nail and torn her cuticle; a fine spatter of her blood newly marred the photograph—quickly drying to a color similar to the streak of rust that ran down the pony's mane, across the woman's thigh. Melony stuck the finger with the broken nail in her mouth and handed the photograph to Homer Wells.

Melony allowed her finger to tug a little at her lower lip, pressing it against her lower teeth. "You *get* it, don't you, Sunshine?" she asked Homer Wells. "You see what the woman's doing to the pony, right?"

"Right," said Homer Wells.

"How'd you like me to do to you what that woman is doing to that pony?" Melony asked him. She stuck her finger all the way into her mouth, then, and closed her lips around it, over the second knuckle joint; in this fashion she waited for his answer, but Homer Wells let the question pass. Melony took her wet finger out of her mouth, then, and touched its tip to Homer's still lips. Homer didn't move; he knew that if he looked at her finger, his eyes would cross. "If you'd like me to do that to you, Sunshine," Melony said, "all you've got to do is get me my file—get me my records." She pressed her finger against his lips a little too hard.

"Of course, while you're looking up the file on me you can look up yourself—if you're interested," Melony added. She took her finger away. "Give me your finger, Sunshine," she said, but Homer Wells, holding the photograph in both hands, decided to let this request pass. "Come on," Melony coaxed. "I won't hurt you." He gave her his left hand, keeping the photograph in his right; he actually extended his closed fist to her so that it was necessary for her to open his hand before she could slip his left index finger into her mouth. "Look at the picture, Sunshine," she told him; he did as he was told. She tapped his finger against her teeth while she managed to say, "Just get me the file and you know what you'll get. Just keep the picture and think about it," Melony said.

What Homer thought was that the anxiety of looking at the photograph with his finger in Melony's mouth, kneeling beside her on the mattress home of countless mice, would be eternal. But there was such a startling *thump!* on the roof of the building—like a falling body, followed by a lighter thump (as if the body had bounced)—that Melony bit down hard on his finger before he could, instinctively, retrieve it from her mouth. Still on their knees, they lurched into each other's arms; they hugged each other and held their breath. Homer Wells could feel his heart pound against Melony's breasts. "What the hell was *that*?" Melony asked.

Homer Wells let the question pass. He was imagining the ghost of the woodsman whose photograph he clutched in his hand, the actual body of the saw-mill laborer landing on the roof, a man with a rusty ripsaw in each hand, a man whose ears would hear, in eternity, only the whine of those lumberyard blades. In that *thump!* of dead weight upon the roof of the abandoned building, Homer himself heard the snarling pitch of those long-ago saws—but what was that sharp, almost human noise he heard singing above the buzz? It was the sound of cries, Homer imagined: the paper-thin wails of the babies on the hill, those first orphans of St. Cloud's.

His hot cheek felt the flutter of the pulse in Melony's throat. The lightest, most delicate footsteps seemed to walk the roof—as if the body of the ghost, after his fall, were changing back to spirit.

"Jesus!" Melony said, shoving Homer Wells away from her so forcefully that he fell against the wall. The noise Homer made caused the spirit on the roof to scurry, and to emit a piercing, two-syllable shriek—the easily identified whistle of the red-shouldered hawk.

"Kee-yer!" the hawk said.

The hawk's cry was apparently not recognizable to Melony,

who screamed, but Homer knew instantly what was on the roof; he rushed down the stairs, across the porch to the wrecked rail. He was in time to see the hawk ascending; this time the snake appeared easier to carry—it hung straight down, as true as a plumb line. It was impossible to know if the hawk had lost control of the snake, or if the bird had dropped the snake intentionally—realizing that this was a sure, if not entirely professional, way to kill it. No matter: the long fall to the roof had clearly finished the snake, and its dead weight was easier to bear away than when it had lived and writhed in the hawk's talons and had repeatedly struck at the hawk's breast. Homer noted that the snake was slightly longer and not quite as thick as the pony's penis.

Melony, out of breath, stood on the porch beside Homer. When the hawk was out of sight, she repeated her promise to him. "Just keep the picture and think about it," she repeated.

Not that Homer Wells needed any instruction to "think about it." What a lot he had to think about!

/ / /

"Adolescence," wrote Wilbur Larch. "Is it the first time in life we discover that we have something terrible to hide from those who love us?"

For the first time in his life, Homer Wells was hiding something from Dr. Larch—and from Nurse Angela and Nurse Edna. And with the photograph of the pony with its penis in the woman's mouth, Homer Wells was also hiding his first misgivings concerning St. Larch. With the photograph, he hid his first lust—not only for the woman who gagged on the pony's amazing instrument but also for the inspired promise Melony had made him. Hidden with the photograph (under his hospital-bed mattress, pinned against the bedsprings) were Homer's anxieties concerning what he might discover in the so-called files—in the imagined record of his birth at St. Cloud's. His own mother's history lay in hiding with that photograph, which Homer found he was more and more drawn to.

He took it out from under the mattress and looked at it three or four times a day; and at night, when he couldn't sleep, he looked at it in candlelight—a drowsy light in which the woman's eyes appeared to bulge less violently, a light in the flicker of which Homer imagined he could see the woman's cheeks actually move. The movement of the candlelight appeared to stir the pony's mane. One night when he was looking at the picture, he heard John Wilbur wet his bed. More often, Homer looked at the picture to the accompaniment of Fuzzy Stone's dramatic gasps—the cacophony of lungs, waterwheel and fan seemed appropriate to the woman-and-pony act that Homer Wells so fully memorized and imagined.

Something changed in Homer's insomnia; Dr. Larch detected the difference, or else it was the deception within him that made Homer Wells conscious of Dr. Larch's observations of him. When Homer would tiptoe down to Nurse Angela's office, late at night, it seemed to him that Dr. Larch was *always* at the typewriter—and that he would always notice Homer's careful movement in the hall.

"Anything I can do for you, Homer?" Dr. Larch would ask.

"Just can't sleep," Homer would reply.

"So what's new?" Dr. Larch would ask.

Did the man write all night? In the daytime, Nurse Angela's office was busy—it was the only room for interviews and phone calls. It was full of Dr. Larch's papers, too—his correspondence with other orphanages, with adoption agencies, with prospective parents; his noteworthy (if occasionally facetious) journal, his whatnot diary, which he called *A Brief History of St. Cloud's.* It was no longer "brief," and it grew daily—every entry faithfully beginning, "Here in St. Cloud's . . ." or, "In other parts of the world . . ."

Dr. Larch's papers also included extensive family histories— but only of the families who adopted the orphans. Contrary to Melony's belief, no records were kept of the orphans' actual mothers and fathers. An orphan's history began with its date of birth—its sex, its length in inches, its weight in pounds, its nurse-given name (if it was a boy) or the name Mrs. Grogan or the girls' division secretary gave it (if it was a girl). This, with a record of the orphans' sicknesses and shots, was all there was. A substantially thicker file was kept on the orphans' adoptive families—knowing what he could about those families was important to Dr. Larch.

"Here in St. Cloud's," he wrote, "I try to consider, with each rule I make or break, that my first priority is an orphan's future. It is for his or her future, for example, that I destroy any record of the identity of his or her natural mother. The unfortunate women who give birth here have made a very difficult decision; they should not, later in their lives, be faced with making this decision again. And in almost every case the orphans should be spared any later search for the biological parents; certainly, the orphans should, in most cases, be spared the discovery of the actual parents.

"I am thinking of them, always of them—only of the orphans! Of course they will, one day, want to know; at the very least, they will be curious. But how does it help anyone to look forward to the past? How are orphans served by having their past to look ahead to? Orphans, especially, must look ahead to their futures.

"And would an orphan be served by having his or her biological parent, in later years, regret the decision to give birth here? If there were records, it would always be possible for the real parents to trace their children. I am not in the business of reuniting orphans with their biological beginnings! That is the storytelling business. I am in the business *for* the orphans."

That is the passage from *A Brief History of St. Cloud's* that Wilbur Larch showed to Homer Wells, when he caught Homer in Nurse Angela's office going through his papers.

"I was just looking for something, and I couldn't find it," Homer stammered to Dr. Larch.

"I know what you were looking for, Homer," Dr. Larch told him, "and it is not to be found."

That is what the note said, the one Homer passed to Melony when he went to the girls' division to read *Jane Eyre*. Each night they had repeated a wordless habit: Melony would stick her finger in her mouth—she appeared to stick it halfway down her throat, her eyes bulging in mockery of the woman with the pony—and Homer Wells would simply shake his head, indicating that he hadn't found what he was looking for. The note that said "Not to Be Found" provoked a look of profound suspicion on Melony's restless countenance.

"Homer," Dr. Larch had said, "I don't remember your mother. I don't even remember *you* when you were born; you didn't *become* you until later."

"I thought there was a law," Homer said. He meant Melony's law—a law of records, or written history—but Wilbur Larch was the only historian and the only law at St. Cloud's. It was an orphanage law: an orphan's life began when Wilbur Larch remembered it; and if an orphan was adopted before it became memorable (which was the hope), then its life began with whoever had adopted it. That was Larch's law. After all, he had taken the necessary responsibility to follow the common law regarding when a fetus was quick or not yet quick; the rules governing whether he delivered a baby or whether he delivered a mother were *his* rules, too.

"I've been thinking about you, Homer," Dr. Larch told the boy. "I think about you more and more, but I don't waste my time—or yours—thinking about who you were before I knew you."

Larch showed Homer a letter he was writing—it was still in the typewriter. It was a letter to someone at The New England Home for Little Wanderers, which had been an orphanage even longer than St. Cloud's.

The letter was friendly and familiar; Larch's correspondent appeared to be an old colleague if not an old friend. There was in the tone of Larch's argument, too, the sparkle of frequent debate—as if the correspondent were someone Larch had often used as a kind of philosophical opponent.

"The reasons orphans should be adopted before adolescence is that they should be loved, and have someone to love, before they embark on that necessary phase of adolescence: namely deceitfulness," Larch argued in the letter. "A teen-ager discovers that deceit is almost as seductive as sex, and much more easily accomplished. It may be especially easy to deceive loved ones—the people who love you are the least willing to acknowledge your deceit. But if you love no one, and feel that no one loves you, there's no one with the power to sting you by pointing out to you that you're lying. If an orphan is not adopted by the time he reaches this alarming period of adolescence, he may continue to deceive himself, and others forever.

"For a terrible time of life a teen-ager deceives himself; he believes he can trick the world. He believes he is invulnerable. An adolescent who is an orphan at this phase is in danger of never growing up."

Of course, Dr. Larch knew, Homer Wells was different; he *was* loved—by Nurse Angela and Nurse Edna, and by Dr. Larch, in spite of himself—and Homer Wells not only knew that he was loved, he also probably knew that he loved these people. *His* age of deceit might be blessedly brief.

Melony was the perfect example of the adolescent orphan Larch described in his letter to The New England Home for Little Wanderers. This also occurred to Homer Wells, who had asked Melony—*before* he gave her the note that her history was "Not to Be Found"—what she wanted to find her mother for.

"To kill her," Melony had said without hesitation. "Maybe I'll poison her, but if she's not as big as I am, if I'm much stronger than she is, and I probably am, then I'd like to strangle her."

"To strangle her," repeated Homer Wells uncontrollably.

"Why?" Melony asked him. "What would *you* do if you found *your* mother?"

"I don't know," he said. "Ask her some questions, maybe."

"Ask her some questions!" Melony said. Homer had not heard such scorn in Melony's voice since her response to Jane Eyre's "gleams of sunshine."

Homer knew that his simple note—"Not to Be Found" —would never satisfy her, although Homer had found Dr. Larch, as usual, to be convincing. Homer was also holding back; he was still deceiving Dr. Larch, and himself, a little. The photograph of the woman with the pony was still pinned between his mattress and his bedsprings; it had grown almost soft with handling. Frankly, Homer was full of regret. He knew he could not produce Melony's history and that without it he would be denied the pony's seemingly singular experience.

/ / /

"What does he mean, 'Not to Be Found'?" Melony screamed at Homer; they were on the sagging porch of the building where the woman and the pony had spent so many years. "What he means is, he's playing God—he gives you your history, or he takes it away! If that's not playing God, what is?"

Homer Wells let this pass. Dr. Larch, Homer knew, played God in other ways; it was still Homer's cautious opinion that Dr. Larch played God pretty well.

"Here in St. Cloud's," Dr. Larch wrote, "I have been given the choice of playing God or leaving practically everything up to chance. It is my experience that practically everything is left up to chance much of the time; men who believe in good and evil, and who believe that good should win, should watch for those moments when it is possible to play God—we should seize those moments. There won't be many.

"Here in St. Cloud's there may be more moments to seize than one could find in the rest of the world, but that is only because so much that comes this way has been left to chance already."

"Goddamn him!" Melony screamed; but the river was ever-loud, the empty building had heard much worse than this in its day, and Homer Wells let this remark pass, too.

"Too bad for you, Sunshine," Melony snapped at him. "Isn't it?" she insisted. He kept his distance.

"So!" she yelled—of which the Maine woods, across the river, managed only a short echo of the "o!" She lifted her heavy leg and kicked a whole section of the wrecked porch rail into the river. "So, this is *it!*" Melony cried, but the forest was too dense to manage even a clipped echo of the "it!" The Maine woods, like Homer Wells, let Melony's remark pass. "Jesus!" Melony cried, but the forest repeated nothing; the old building might have creaked—possibly, it sighed. It was difficult to destroy that building; time and other vandals had already destroyed it; Melony was looking for possible parts of the building she could still destroy. Homer followed her at a safe distance.

"Sunshine," Melony said, finding a small pane of glass that hadn't been smashed—and smashing it. "Sunshine, we've got *nobody*. If you tell me we've got each other, I'll kill you."

It had not occurred to Homer to offer this or any other suggestion to Melony; he kept silent.

"If you tell me we've got your favorite Doctor Larch, or this whole place," she said—stamping her foot through a floorboard, trying to pry the floorboard loose with both hands—"if you tell me that, I'll torture you before I kill you."

"Right," said Homer Wells.

With the floorboard in both hands, Melony attacked the banister of the main staircase; the banister was knocked apart easily, but the banister post, which anchored the whole railing in the downstairs hall, remained upright. Melony dropped the floorboard and seized the banister post in a bear hug.

"Goddamn you!" she screamed—at Dr. Larch, at her mother, at St. Cloud's, at the world. She wrestled the post to the floor; it was still attached to a main support beam, under the floorboards, but Melony swung a piece of the banister railing like a club until she was able to knock the post free. When she tried to lift the post, and couldn't, she turned to Homer Wells.

"Can't you see I need help?" she said to him.

Together, they lifted the post; using it as a battering ram, they knocked down the kitchen wall.

"Why aren't you angry?" she asked Homer. "What's wrong with you? You're never going to find out who did this to you! Don't you care?"

"I don't know," said Homer Wells. Together, they ran the post head-on into what appeared to be a fairly major beam; maybe it supports the second floor, thought Homer Wells. They hit the beam three blows, bouncing off in a different direction each time; with the fourth try, they cracked it. Something in the building above them appeared to shift. Melony dropped her share of the banister post and bear-hugged the cracked beam; she tried to run with the beam, her momentum carrying her over the doorsill, out onto the porch. One of the upstairs' bunkrooms fell downstairs, into the kitchen; when that happened, the porch roof partially collapsed, and what remained of the porch railing was launched into the river. Even Melony seemed impressed with this much destruction; she took Homer Wells by the hand and almost gently led him upstairs—more than half the upstairs was still upstairs, including the bunkroom where the pony and the woman had entertained a former woodsman of St. Cloud's.

"Help me," Melony said softly to Homer Wells. They went to the window and together managed to wrest the shutter free of the one hinge that held it; they watched it fall straight through the porch roof and pass even more easily through the porch floorboards before it splashed in the river. "Neat, huh?" Melony asked dully.

She sat on the mattress where they'd been kneeling when the snake hit the roof. "Help me," Melony said again; she indicated to Homer that he should sit beside her.

"Help me, or I'm going to run away," she told him, "help me, or I'm going to kill someone." These notions seemed vaguely parallel if not equal to her. Homer realized that it was not easy for him, in the case of Melony, "to be of use," but he tried.

"Don't kill anyone," he said. "Don't run away."

"Why stay?" she countered. "*You're* not staying—I don't mean you'll run away, I mean someone will adopt you."

"No, they won't," Homer said. "Besides, I wouldn't go."

"You'll go," Melony said.

"I won't," Homer said. "Please, don't run away—please don't kill anyone."

"If I stay, you'll stay—is that what you're saying?" Melony asked him. Is that what I mean? thought Homer Wells. But Melony, as usual, gave him no time to think. "Promise me you'll stay as long as I stay, Sunshine," Melony said. She moved closer to him; she took his hand and opened his fingers and put his index finger in her mouth. "Lucky pony," Melony whispered, but Homer Wells wasn't sure if the pony had been so lucky. The old building gave a groan. Melony slid his index finger in and out of her mouth. "Promise me you'll stay as long as I stay, Sunshine," she said.

"Right," said Homer Wells. She bit him. "I *promise,*" Homer said. More of the upstairs fell into the kitchen; there was a sympathetic shriek from the twisted beams that still supported what was left of the porch roof.

What was it that distracted him—when Melony, finally, found his tiny penis and put it into her mouth? He was not afraid that the old building would collapse and kill them both; this would have been a reasonable fear. He was not thinking about the history of the mattress they were lying on; its history was violent—even by Melony's standards. He was not thinking of his own lost history, and he wasn't thinking that his being with Melony was or wasn't a betrayal of Dr. Larch. In part, the noise distracted Homer; there was the noise that Melony made with her mouth—and her breathing—and then there was his own breathing. The racket of this passion reminded him of little Fuzzy Stone and the energy of those mechanisms that struggled to keep Fuzzy alive. That such wet, breathy effort was made in Fuzzy's behalf seemed to emphasize how fragile his life was.

Homer grew only a little bigger in Melony's mouth; when he started to grow smaller, Melony increased her efforts. Homer's major distraction was the photograph itself, which he saw very clearly. He could even see the dust-free rectangle on the wall where the photograph had been. If the photograph had, at first, inspired him to imagine this act with Melony, now the photograph directly blocked his ability to perform at all. If the woman in the photograph had, at first, encouraged him to think of Melony, now the woman, and Melony, seemed only abused. The pony's brute insensitivity remained the same: the dumb beast's inappropriate passivity. Homer felt himself grow tinier than he felt he'd ever been.

Melony was humiliated; she shoved him away. "Goddamn you!" she screamed at him. "What's wrong with you, anyway? And don't you tell me there's anything wrong with me!"

"Right," Homer said, "there isn't."

"You *bet* there isn't!" Melony cried, but her lips looked

sore—even bruised—and he saw tears in the anger in her eyes. She yanked the mattress out from under him; then she folded it in half and threw it out the window. The mattress fell on the roof and stuck half through the hole the shutter had made. This seemed to enrage Melony: that the mattress hadn't passed cleanly through to the river. She began to dismantle the bunk bed nearest her, crying while she worked. Homer Wells, as he had retreated from her outrage at the "gleams of sunshine," retreated from her now. He sneaked down the weakened stairs; when he stepped on the porch, it gave a sharp creak and slumped in the direction of the river, momentarily throwing him off-balance. He heard what sounded like several bunk beds, or a part of a wall, landing on the roof above him; he fled for open ground. Melony must have seen him through the upstairs window.

"You promised me, Sunshine!" she screamed at him. "You promised you wouldn't leave me! As long as I stay, you stay!"

"I promise!" he called to her, but he turned away and started down the river, along the bank, heading back to the occupied buildings of St. Cloud's and to the orphanage on the hill above the river. He was still on the riverbank, near the water's edge, when Melony managed to dislodge the overhanging porch (the porch roof went with it); he stood and watched what looked like half the building float downstream. Homer imagined that Melony—given time enough—could possibly rid the landscape of the entire town. But he didn't stay to watch her ongoing efforts at destruction. He went directly to his bed in the sleeping room of the boys' division. He lifted his mattress; he intended to throw the photograph away, but it was gone.

"It wasn't me," said Fuzzy Stone. Although it was midday, Fuzzy was still in the sleeping room, imprisoned in his humidified tent. That meant, Homer knew, that Fuzzy was having a kind of relapse. The tent, at night, was Fuzzy's home, but when Fuzzy spent the day in the tent, the tent was referred to as his "treatment." He had to have what Dr. Larch called "tests" all the time, too, and every day, everyone knew, he had to have a shot. Homer stood next to the flapping, breathing, gasping contraption and asked Fuzzy Stone where the photograph was. Homer was informed that John Wilbur had wet his bed so thoroughly that Nurse Angela had told him to lie down on Homer's bed while she replaced the ruined mattress. John

Wilbur had found the photograph; he showed it to Fuzzy and to a few of the other boys who were around—among them, Wilbur Walsh and Snowy Meadows; Snowy had thrown up.

"Then what happened?" Homer asked Fuzzy, who was already out of breath. Fuzzy was nine; next to Homer Wells, he was the oldest orphan in the boys' division. Fuzzy said that Nurse Angela had come back with a fresh mattress for John Wilbur and *she* had seen the photograph; naturally, she'd taken it away. Of course, John Wilbur had told her where he'd found it. By now, Homer knew, Nurse Edna would have seen it, and Dr. Larch would have seen it, too. It crossed Homer's mind to go find John Wilbur and hit him, but the boy was too small—he would only pee; there would be this new evidence against Homer.

"But what *was* it?" Fuzzy Stone gasped to Homer.

"I thought you saw it," Homer said.

"I saw it, but what *was* it?" Fuzzy repeated. He looked genuinely frightened.

Snowy Meadows had thought that the woman was eating the pony's intestines, Fuzzy explained; Wilbur Walsh had run away. John Wilbur had probably peed some more, thought Homer Wells. "What were they *doing*?" Fuzzy Stone pleaded. "The woman," Fuzzy said with a gasp, "how *could* she? How could she *breathe*?" Fuzzy asked breathlessly. He was wheezing badly when Homer left him. In the daylight Fuzzy seemed almost transparent, as if—if you held him up to a bright enough source of light—you could see right through him, see all his frail organs working to save him.

Dr. Larch was not in Nurse Angela's office, where Homer had expected to find him; Homer was thankful that Nurse Edna and Nurse Angela were not around; he felt especially ashamed to face them. Outside the hospital entrance he could see Nurse Angela talking to the man who hauled away the nonburnable trash. The issue of their conversation was John Wilbur's old mattress. Homer went to the dispensary to see if Dr. Larch was there.

It had been quite a day for Wilbur Larch, who had reclined on his hospital bed in the dispensary with a gauze cone that was more heavily saturated with ether than was his usual habit. The reported vandalism to the so-called sawyer's lodge had upset Larch less than it had disturbed certain townspeople who had witnessed the damage done by Homer and Melony—mostly by Melony, Dr. Larch was sure. What are abandoned buildings for? Dr. Larch wondered—if not for kids to vandalize, a little? The report that half the building had floated downriver was surely exaggerated.

He inhaled and thought about what had really upset him: that photograph. That woman with the pony.

Larch was not bothered that Homer Wells had the picture; teen-agers were interested in that kind of thing. Larch knew that Homer never would have shown it to the younger boys; that Homer had kept such a photograph meant to Wilbur Larch that it was time Homer was given more serious, adult responsibilities. It was time to step up the apprenticeship.

And the photograph itself—to Larch—was not that upsetting. After all, he had worked in the South End. Such photographs were everywhere; in Wilbur Larch's days at the Boston Lying-In, such pictures cost a dime.

What troubled Larch was the particular woman in the photograph; he had no trouble recognizing Mrs. Eames's brave daughter. Larch had seen her cheeks puffed out before—she was a veteran cigar smoker, no stranger to putting terrible things in her mouth. And when she'd been brought to his door with acute peritonitis, the result of whatever unspeakable injuries she had suffered "Off Harrison," her eyes had bulged then. To look at the photograph reminded Larch of the life she must have had; it reminded him, too, that he could have eased the pain of her life—just a little—by giving her an abortion. The photograph reminded Larch of a life he could have—even if only momentarily—saved. Mrs. Eames's tragic daughter should have been his first abortion patient.

Wilbur Larch looked at the photograph and wondered if Mrs. Eames's daughter had been paid enough for posing with the pony to be able to afford the abortion fee "Off Harrison." Probably not, he concluded—it wasn't even a very good photograph. Whoever had posed the participants had been careless with the young woman's stunning, dark pigtail; it could have been draped over her shoulder, or even been made to lie near her breast, where its darkness would have accented the whiteness of her skin. It could have been flung straight back, behind her head, which at least would have emphasized the pigtail's unusual thickness and length. Obviously, no one had been thinking about the pigtail. It lay off to the side of Mrs. Eames's daughter's face, curled in a shadow that was cast by one of the pony's stout, short, shaggy legs. In the photograph, the pigtail was lost; you had to know Mrs. Eames's daughter to know what that dark shape off to the side of the woman's straining face was.

"I'm sorry," Larch said, inhaling. Mrs. Eames's daughter did not respond, so he said again, "I'm sorry." He exhaled. He thought he heard her calling him.

"Doctor Larch!"

"Rhymes with screams," Wilbur Larch murmured. He took the deepest possible breath. His hand lost touch with the cone, which rolled off his face and under the bed.

"Doctor Larch?" Homer Wells said again. The smell of ether in the dispensary seemed unusually strong to Homer, who passed through the labyrinth of medicine chests to see if Dr. Larch was on his bed.

"Shit or get off the pot!" he heard Dr. Larch say. (Inhale, exhale.) "I'm sorry," Dr. Larch said when he saw Homer beside his bed. He sat up too fast; he felt very light-headed; the room was swimming. "I'm sorry," he repeated.

"That's okay," said Homer Wells. "I'm sorry I woke you up."

"Rhymes with screams," said Wilbur Larch.

"Pardon me?" said Homer Wells.

In the closed dispensary, a fragrant mothball sent its vapory messages everywhere.

"Sit down, Homer," said Dr. Larch, who realized that Homer was already sitting beside him on the bed. Larch wished his head was clearer; he knew this was an important confrontation for the boy. Homer expected to be reprimanded, and not in uncertain terms, but Larch feared he might not be in the best shape for sounding certain.

"Vandalism!" Larch launched in. "Pornography!" Now there's a start, he thought, but the boy sitting beside him just waited patiently. Larch took a gulp of what he hoped was clearer air; the fragrance of ether was still heavily present in the dispensary; the air in the immediate vicinity was alternately drowsy and sparkling with little stars.

"Vandalism is one thing, Homer," Larch said. "And pornography—quite another."

"Right," said Homer Wells—growing older, learning something new every day.

"More central to our relationship, Homer, is the issue of you deceiving me. Right?"

"Right," Homer said.

"Fine," Larch said.

The stars sparkled so brightly on the ceiling of the dispensary that for a moment Dr. Larch thought that their dialogue was taking place under the nighttime firmament. He tipped his head back, to escape the fumes, but he lost his balance and fell back on the bed.

"Are you okay?" Homer asked him.

"Fine!" Larch boomed heartily. Then he started to laugh.

It was the first time Homer Wells had heard Dr. Larch laugh.

"Listen, Homer," Dr. Larch said, but he giggled. "If you're old enough to vandalize whole buildings and masturbate to pictures of women giving blow jobs to ponies, then you're old enough to be my assistant!" This struck Larch as so funny that he doubled up on the bed. Homer thought it was a funny thing to say, too, and he began to smile. "You don't get it, do you?" Larch asked, still giggling. "You don't get what I mean." He lay on his back and waved his feet in the air while the firmament of stars circled above them. "I'm going to teach you surgery!" Larch shouted at Homer, which dissolved both of them into tears of laughter. "Obstetrical procedure, Homer," Larch said; Homer, now, fell back on the bed, too. "The Lord's work *and* the Devil's, Homer!" Larch said, hooting. "The *works*!" he screamed. Homer started to cough, he was laughing so hard. He was surprised when Larch—like a magician—produced the photograph of the woman and the pony and waved it in front of him. "If you're old enough even to contemplate this," Larch said, "you're old enough to have a grown-up's job!" This cracked up Larch so completely that he had to hand the photograph to Homer Wells—or else he would have dropped it.

"Listen, Homer," Larch said. "You're going to finish medical school before you start high school!" This was especially funny to Homer, but Dr. Larch suddenly grew serious. He snatched the photograph back from Homer. "Look at this," he commanded. They sat on the edge of the bed and Larch held the photograph steady on his knee. "I'll show you what you don't know. Look at that!" he said, pointing to the pigtail, obscured in the shadow of the pony's leg. "What is it?" he asked Homer Wells. "Teen-agers: you think you know everything," Larch said threateningly. Homer caught the new tone of voice; he paid close attention to this part of the picture he'd never looked at before—a stain on the rug, maybe, or was it a pool of blood from the woman's ear?

"Well?" Larch asked. "It's not in *David Copperfield.* It's not in *Jane Eyre,* either—what you need to know," he added almost nastily.

The medical slant of the conversation convinced Homer Wells that it *was* a pool of blood in the photograph—that only a doctor could recognize it so positively. "Blood," Homer said. "The woman's bleeding." Larch ran with the photograph to the lamp at the dispensary counter.

"Blood?" Larch said. "Blood!" He looked the photograph all over. "That's not blood, you idiot! That's a pigtail!" He showed the photograph once more to Homer Wells; it would be Homer's last look at the photograph, though Dr. Larch would look at it often. He would keep it attached to the pages of *A Brief History of St. Cloud's;* he did not keep it for pornographic interest but because it reminded him of a woman he had abused twice. He had slept with her mother in front of her, and he had not provided her with a service that she had every right to request. He had not been a proper doctor to her, and he wanted to remember her. That he was forced to remember her with a pony's penis in her mouth made Dr. Larch's mistakes all the more forcefully mistakes to him; Larch liked it that way.

He was a hard man—on himself, too.

He took a harder line toward Homer Wells than the hilarity of his promises to the boy at first suggested—to teach him "the works," as Larch called it, was not so funny. Surgery, obstetrical procedure—even a normal birth, even the standard D and C—required considerable background and preparation.

"You think it's tough to look at a woman with a pony's penis in her mouth, Homer?" Larch asked him the next day— when he was not under the influence of ether. "You ought to look at something that's harder to understand than that. Here," Larch said, handing Homer the well-worn copy of *Gray's Anatomy,* "look at this. Look at it three or four times a day, and every night. Forget pony penises, and learn this."

"Here in St. Cloud's," wrote Dr. Wilbur Larch, "I have had little use for my *Gray's Anatomy;* but in France, in World War I, I used it every day. It was the only road map I had over there."

Larch also gave Homer his personal handbook of obstetrical procedure, his notebooks from medical school and from his internships; he began with the chemistry lectures and the standard textbook. He set aside a corner of the dispensary for a few easy experiments in bacteriology, although the sight of Petri dishes caused Larch flashes of no uncertain pain; he was not fond of the world there was to be seen under the microscope. Larch was also not fond of Melony—specifically, he was not fond of her apparent hold on Homer Wells. Larch assumed that they slept together; he assumed that Melony had initiated him, which was true, and now forced him to continue, which was not the case. In time, they would sleep together, albeit routinely, and that hold that Dr. Larch imagined Melony had on Homer was balanced by a hold Homer had on Melony (Homer's promise to her, which Larch couldn't see). He saw Melony as Mrs. Grogan's responsibility, and he was unaware how his responsibility for Homer Wells might cloud his other responsibilities.

He sent Homer to the river to catch a frog; then he made Homer dissect it, although not everything in the frog could be properly accounted for in *Gray's Anatomy*. It was Homer's first visit to the river since he had fled from Melony's destruction of the so-called sawyers' lodge, and Homer was impressed to see that truly half the building was gone.

Homer was also impressed with the first live birth he was asked to observe—not so much with any special skill that seemed to be required of Dr. Larch, and not with the formal, efficient procedures carried out by Nurse Angela and Nurse Edna. What impressed Homer was the process that was already so much under way before Dr. Larch's procedure began; what impressed Homer was how much had happened to the woman and her child that was, internally, just their natural progress— the actual rhythm of the labor (you could set a watch to it), the power of the woman's pushing muscles, the urgency of the child to be born. The most unnatural thing about it, to Homer Wells, was how clearly hostile the child found the environment in which it first exercised its lungs—how clearly unfriendly, though not unexciting, the child's new world was to the child, whose first choice (had it been given a choice) might have been to remain where it was. Not a bad reaction, Melony might have observed, had she been there. However much Homer enjoyed having sex with Melony, he was troubled that the act was more arbitrary than birth.

When Homer went to read *Jane Eyre* to the girls' division, Melony seemed subdued to him, not defeated or even resigned; something in her had been tired out, something about her look was worn down. She had been wrong, after all, about the existence of her history in Dr. Larch's hands—and being wrong about important things is exhausting. She had been humiliated, too—first by the incredible shrinking penis of little Homer Wells, and second by how quickly Homer appeared to take sex with her for granted. And, Homer thought, she must be *physically* tired—after all, she had single-handedly obliterated a sizable chunk of the man-made history of St. Cloud's. She had pushed half a building into the flow of time. She has a right to look worn out, thought Homer Wells.

Something in the way he read *Jane Eyre* struck Homer as different too—as if this or any story were newly informed by the recent experiences in his life: a woman with a pony's penis in her mouth, his first sexual failure, his first routine sex, *Gray's Anatomy,* and a live birth. He read with more appreciation of Jane's anxiety, which had struck him earlier as tedious. Jane has a right to be anxious, he thought.

It was unfortunate timing—after what he and Melony had been through together—that he encountered that passage in the middle of Chapter Ten, where Jane imagines how it might be to leave her orphanage, where she realizes that the real world is "wide," and that her own existence is "not enough." Did Homer only imagine there was a new reverence in the girls' division when he read this section—that Melony, especially, seemed poised above the sentences, as if she were hearing them for the first time? And then he hit this line:

I tired of the routine of eight years in one afternoon.

His mouth went dry when he read it; he needed to swallow, which gave the line more emphasis than he wanted to give it. When he tried to begin again, Melony stopped him.

"What was that? Read that again, Sunshine."

" 'I tired of the routine of eight years in one afternoon,' " Homer Wells read aloud.

"I know just how she feels," Melony said bitterly, but quietly.

"It hurts me to hear you say that, Melony," Mrs. Grogan began softly.

"I know just how she feels!" Melony repeated. "And so do

you, Sunshine!" she added. "Little Jane should try fifteen or sixteen or seventeen years," Melony announced loudly. "She should try it and see if she doesn't 'tire' of *that* routine!"

"You'll only hurt yourself, dear, if you keep on like that," Mrs. Grogan said. And indeed, this seemed true; Melony was crying. She was such a big girl—to put her head in Mrs. Grogan's lap and allow her to stroke her hair—but she just went on crying, quietly. Mrs. Grogan could not remember when she'd last held Melony's head in her lap. Homer caught the look from Mrs. Grogan: that he should leave. It was not the end of the chapter, not even the end of the scene, or even of a paragraph. There was more to read; the next line began:

I desired liberty . . .

But it would have been cruel to continue. Jane Eyre had already made her point. Homer and Melony had already had several such afternoons—those days that tire you out about your whole life!

This night the air between the girls' and boys' division seemed odorless and void of history. It was simply dark outside.

When he went back to the boys' division, Nurse Angela told him that John Wilbur was gone—*adopted!*

"A nice family," Nurse Angela told Homer happily. "The father of the family used to be a bed-wetter. They're going to be very sympathetic."

As was Dr. Larch's habit, when someone was adopted, his routine benediction to the boys in the darkness was altered slightly. Before he addressed them as "Princes of Maine," as "Kings of New England," he made an oddly formal announcement.

"Let us be happy for John Wilbur," Wilbur Larch said. "He has found a family. Good night, John," Dr. Larch said, and the boys murmured after him:

"Good night, John!"

"Good night, John Wilbur."

And Dr. Larch would pause respectfully before saying the usual: "Good night, you Princes of Maine—you Kings of New England!"

Homer Wells looked at a little of *Gray's Anatomy* in the candlelight allowed him before he tried to go to sleep. It was not just John Wilbur's peeing that was missing from the night;

something else was gone. It took Homer a while to detect what was absent; it was the silence that finally informed him. Fuzzy Stone and his noisy apparatus had been taken to the hospital. Apparently, the breathing contraption—and Fuzzy—required more careful monitoring, and Dr. Larch had moved the whole business into the private room, next to surgery, where Nurse Edna or Nurse Angela could keep a closer eye on Fuzzy.

It was not until Homer Wells had some experience with dilatation and curettage that he would know what Fuzzy Stone resembled: he looked like an embryo—Fuzzy Stone looked like a walking, talking fetus. That was what was peculiar about the way you could almost see through Fuzzy's skin, and his slightly caved-in shape; that was what made him appear so especially vulnerable. He looked as if he were not yet alive but still in some stage of development that should properly be carried on inside the womb. Dr. Larch told Homer that Fuzzy had been born prematurely—that Fuzzy's lungs had never adequately developed. Homer would not have a picture of what this meant until he confronted the few recognizable parts in his first look at the standard procedure for removing the products of conception.

"Are you listening, Homer?" Wilbur Larch asked, when the procedure was over.

"Yes," Homer Wells said.

"I'm not saying it's *right,* you understand? I'm saying it's her choice—it's a woman's choice. She's got a right to have a choice, you understand?" Larch asked.

"Right," said Homer Wells.

When he couldn't sleep, he thought about Fuzzy Stone. When Homer went down to the private room, next to surgery, he couldn't hear the breathing apparatus. He stood very still and listened; he could always track Fuzzy down by his sound—lungs, waterwheel and fan—but the silence Homer Wells listened to made a more startling noise to him than the sound of that snake hitting the roof while his finger was in Melony's mouth.

Poor Melony, he thought. She now listened to *Jane Eyre* as if it were her life story being told to her, and the only thing she ever said to Homer Wells was to remind him of his promise. ("You won't leave here before I do, remember? You promised.")

"Where is he?" Homer asked Dr. Larch. "Where's Fuzzy?"

Dr. Larch was at the typewriter in Nurse Angela's office, where he was—very late—almost every night.

"I was thinking of a way to tell you," Larch said.

"You said I was your apprentice, right?" Homer asked him. "If that's what I am, I should be told. If you're teaching me, you can't leave anything out. Right?"

"That's right, Homer," Dr. Larch agreed. How the boy had changed! How does one mark the passage of time in an orphanage? Why hadn't Larch noticed that Homer Wells needed a shave? Why hadn't Larch taught him to do that? I am responsible for everything—if I am going to be responsible at all, Larch reminded himself.

"Fuzzy's lungs weren't strong enough, Homer," Dr. Larch said. "They never developed properly. He was susceptible to every respiratory infection that I ever saw."

Homer Wells let it pass. He regretted that Fuzzy had seen the photograph. Homer was growing up; he was starting the process of holding himself responsible for things. That photograph had upset Fuzzy Stone; there was nothing Homer, or even Dr. Larch, could have done for Fuzzy's lungs, but the photograph hadn't been necessary.

"What are you going to tell the little ones?" Homer asked Dr. Larch.

Wilbur Larch looked at Homer; God, how he loved what he saw! Proud as a father, he had trouble speaking. His affection for Homer Wells had virtually etherized him. "What do you think I should say, Homer?" Dr. Larch asked.

It was Homer's first decision as an adult. He thought about it very carefully. In 193__, he was almost sixteen. He was beginning the process of learning how to be a doctor at a time when most boys his age were learning how to drive a car. Homer had not yet learned how to drive a car; Wilbur Larch had never learned how to drive a car.

"I think," said Homer Wells, "that you should tell the little ones what you usually tell them. You should tell them that Fuzzy has been adopted."

Wilbur Larch watched Homer carefully. In *A Brief History of St. Cloud's,* he would write, "How I resent fatherhood! The feelings it gives one: they completely ruin one's objectivity, they wreck one's sense of fair play. I worry that I have caused Homer Wells to skip his childhood—I worry that he has absolutely skipped being a child! But many orphans find it easier to skip childhood altogether than to indulge themselves as children when they are orphans. If I helped Homer Wells to skip his childhood, did I help him skip a bad thing? Damn the confusion of feeling like a father! Loving someone as a parent can produce a cloud that conceals from one's vision what correct behavior is." When he wrote that line, Wilbur Larch saw the cloud created in the photographer's studio, the cloud that so falsely edged the photograph of Mrs. Eames's daughter with the pony; he launched off into a paragraph on "clouds." (The terrible weather in inland Maine; "the *clouds* of St. Cloud's," and so forth.)

When Homer Wells suggested to Dr. Larch that he tell the little ones that Fuzzy Stone had been adopted, Larch knew that Homer was right; there were no clouds around that decision. The next night, Wilbur Larch followed the advice of his young apprentice. Perhaps because he was lying, he forgot the proper routine. Instead of beginning with the announcement about Fuzzy Stone, he gave the usual benediction; he got the whole business out of order.

"Good night, you Princes of Maine—you Kings of New England!" Dr. Larch addressed them in the darkness. Then he remembered what he was supposed to say. "Oh!" he said aloud, in a startled voice that caused one of the little orphans to leap in his bed in fright.

"What's wrong?" cried Snowy Meadows, who was always throwing up; he did not throw up only when confronted with the image of a woman with what he thought was a pony's intestines in her mouth.

"Nothing's wrong!" Dr. Larch said heartily, but the whole room of boys was charged with anxiety. Into this jumpy atmosphere, Larch tried to say the usual about the unusual. "Let us be happy for Fuzzy Stone," Dr. Larch said. Homer Wells knew what was meant when it was said that you could hear a pin drop. "Fuzzy Stone has found a family," Dr. Larch said. "Good night, Fuzzy."

"Good night, Fuzzy!" someone said. But Homer Wells heard a pause in the air; it had all been done out of order, and not everyone was completely convinced.

"Good night, Fuzzy!" Homer Wells said with authority, and a few of the little voices followed him.

"Good night, Fuzzy!"

"Good night, Fuzzy Stone!"

Homer Wells also knew what was meant when it was said that silence could be deafening. After Dr. Larch had left them, little Snowy Meadows was the first to speak.

"Homer?" Snowy said.

"Right here," said Homer Wells in the darkness.

"How could anyone adopt Fuzzy Stone, Homer?" Snowy Meadows asked.

"Who could do it?" said little Wilbur Walsh.

"Someone with a better machine," said Homer Wells. "Someone who had a better breathing machine than the one Doctor Larch built for Fuzzy. It's a family that knows all about breathing machines. It's the family business," he added. "Breathing machines."

"Lucky Fuzzy!" someone said in a wondering voice.

Homer knew he had convinced them when Snowy Meadows said, "Good night, Fuzzy."

Homer Wells, not yet sixteen—an apprentice surgeon, a veteran insomniac—walked down to the river that had carried away so many pieces of the history of St. Cloud's. The loudness of the river was a comfort to Homer, more comforting than the silence in the sleeping room that night. He stood on the riverbank where the porch to the sawyers' lodge had been, where he'd seen the hawk come from the sky more quickly than the snake could swim to shore—and the snake had been very fast.

If Wilbur Larch had seen Homer there, he would have worried that the boy was saying good-bye to his own childhood—too soon. But Dr. Larch had ether to help him sleep, and Homer Wells had no cure for his insomnia.

"Good night, Fuzzy," Homer said over the river. The Maine woods, typically, let the remark pass, but Homer insisted that he be heard. "Good night, Fuzzy!" he cried as loud as he could. And then louder, "Good night, Fuzzy!" He yelled it and yelled it—the grown-up boy whose crying had once been a legend upriver in Three Mile Falls.

"Good night, Fuzzy Stone!"

4/ Young Dr. Wells

"In other parts of the world," wrote Wilbur Larch, "there is what the world calls 'society.' Here in St. Cloud's we have no society—there are not the choices, the better-than or worse-than comparisons that are nearly constant in any society. It is less complicated here, because the choices and comparisons are either obvious or nonexistent. But having so few options is what makes an orphan so desperate to encounter society—*any* society, the more complex with intrigue, the more gossip-ridden, the better. Given the chance, an orphan throws himself into society—the way an otter takes to the water."

What Wilbur Larch was thinking of, regarding "options," was that Homer Wells had no choice concerning either his apprenticeship or Melony. He and Melony were doomed to become a kind of couple because there was no one else for them to couple with. In society, it would have mattered if they were suited for each other; that they were *not* suited for each other didn't matter in St. Cloud's. And since Homer had exhausted the resources of the dismal tutors employed at St. Cloud's, what else was there for him to learn if he didn't learn surgery? Specifically, obstetrical procedure. And what was far simpler for Dr. Larch to teach him: dilatation and curettage.

Homer Wells kept his notes in one of Dr. Larch's old medical school notebooks; Larch had been a cramped, sparse notetaker—there was plenty of room. In Larch's opinion, there was no need for Homer to have a notebook of his own. Wilbur Larch had only to look around him to see what paper cost. The trees were gone; they had been replaced by orphans—all for paper.

Under the heading "D&C," Homer wrote: "The woman is most secure in stirrups." In Dr. Larch's procedure, she was also shaved.

"The VAGINAL area is prepared with an ANTISEPTIC SOLUTION," wrote Homer Wells; he did a lot of CAPITAL-IZING—it was related to his habit of repeating the ends of sentences, or key words. "The UTERUS is examined to esti-mate its size. One hand is placed on the ABDOMINAL WALL; two or three fingers of the other hand are in the VAGINA. A VAGINAL SPECULUM, which looks like a duck's bill, is inserted in the VAGINA—through which the CERVIX is visi-ble. (The CERVIX," he wrote parenthetically, as if to remind himself, "is the necklike part of the lower, constricted end of the UTERUS.) The hole in the middle of the CERVIX is the entrance of the UTERUS. It is like a cherry Life Saver. In PREGNANCY the CERVIX is swollen and shiny.

"With a series of METAL DILATORS, the CERVIX is dilated to admit entrance of the OVUM FORCEPS. These are tongs with which the doctor grabs at what's inside the UTERUS. He pulls what he can out."

What this was (what Homer meant) was blood and slime. "The products of conception," he called it.

"With a CURETTE," noted Homer, "the WALL OF THE UTERUS is scraped clean. One knows when it's clean when one hears a gritty sound."

And that's all that was entered in the notebook concerning dilatation and the process of curetting. As a footnote to this procedure, Homer added only this: "The WOMB one reads about in literature is that portion of the GENITAL TRACT in which the FERTILIZED OVUM implants itself." A page num-ber was jotted in the margin of this notebook entry—the page in *Gray's Anatomy* that begins the section "The Female Organs of Generation," where the most useful illustrations and de-scriptions can be found.

By 194__, Homer Wells (not yet twenty) had been a midwife to countless births and the surgical apprentice to about a quarter as many abortions; he had delivered many children himself, with Dr. Larch always present, but Larch had not allowed Homer to perform an abortion. It was understood by both Larch and Homer that Homer was completely able to perform one, but Larch believed that Homer should complete medical school—a *real* medical school—and serve an internship in another hospital before he undertook the operation. It was not that the operation was complicated; it was Larch's opinion that Homer's *choice* should be involved. What Larch meant

was that Homer should know something of society before he
made the decision, by himself, whether to perform abortions or
not.

What Dr. Larch was looking for was someone to sponsor
Homer Wells. Larch wanted someone to send the boy to
college, not only in order for Homer to qualify for admission
to medical school but also in order to expose Homer to the
world outside St. Cloud's.

How to advertise for such a sponsor was a puzzle to Wilbur
Larch. Should he ask his colleague and correspondent at The
New England Home for Little Wanderers if he could make use
of their large mailing list?

> ACCOMPLISHED MIDWIFE &
> QUALIFIED ABORTIONIST
> SEEKS SPONSOR FOR COLLEGE YEARS
> —PLUS MEDICAL SCHOOL EXPENSES!

Where was the society where Homer Wells could fit in?
wondered Wilbur Larch.

Mainly, Larch knew, he had to get his apprentice away from
Melony. The two of them together: how they depressed Larch!
They struck the doctor as a tired and loveless married couple.
What sexual tensions Melony had managed to conduct between them in the earlier years of their angry courtship seemed
absent now. If they still practiced a sexual exchange, they
practiced infrequently and without enthusiasm. Over lunch
they sat together without speaking, in plain view of the girls' or
of the boys' divisions; together they examined the well-worn
copy of *Gray's Anatomy* as if it were the intricate map they had
to follow if they were ever to find their way out of St. Cloud's.

Melony didn't even run away anymore. It appeared to Dr.
Larch that some wordless, joyless pact bound Homer and
Melony together. Their sullenness toward each other reminded
Dr. Larch of Mrs. Eames's daughter, who would spend eternity
with a pony's penis in her mouth. Melony and Homer never
fought; they never argued; Melony seemed to have given up
raising her voice. If there was still anything sexual between
them, Larch knew that it happened randomly, and only out of
the keenest boredom.

Larch even got Melony a job as live-in help for a well-to-do
old woman in Three Mile Falls. It may have been that the

woman was a cranky invalid who would have complained about anyone; she certainly complained about Melony—she said Melony was "insensitive," that she was never "forthcoming" with conversation, and that, in regard to such physical attentions as helping her in and out of her bath, the girl was "unbelievably rough." Dr. Larch could believe it, and Melony herself complained; she said she preferred to live at St. Cloud's; if she had to have a job, she wanted one she could go to and then leave.

"I want to come home at night," she told Mrs. Grogan and Dr. Larch. Home? Larch thought.

There was another job, in town, but it required that Melony know how to drive. Although Dr. Larch even found a local boy to teach Melony, her driving thoroughly frightened the young man and she needed to take the driver's examination for her license three times in order to pass it once. She then lost the job—delivering parts and tools for a building contractor. She was unable to account for more than two hundred miles that had accumulated in one week on the delivery van's odometer.

"I just drove to places because I was bored," she told Dr. Larch, shrugging. "And there was a guy I was seeing, for a couple of days."

Larch fretted that Melony, who was almost twenty, was now unemployable and unadoptable; she had grown dependent on her proximity to Homer Wells, although whole days passed when there didn't appear to be a word between them—in fact, no intercourse beyond mere presence was observable for weeks in succession (if Melony's presence could ever be called "mere"). Because of how much Melony depressed Dr. Larch, Dr. Larch assumed that her presence was depressing to Homer Wells.

Wilbur Larch loved Homer Wells—he had never loved anyone as he loved that boy, and he could not imagine enduring a life at St. Cloud's without him—but the doctor knew that Homer Wells had to have an authentic encounter with society if the boy was going to have a chosen life at all. What Larch dreamed of was that Homer would venture out in the world and then choose to come back to St. Cloud's. But who would choose such a thing? Larch wondered.

Maine had many towns; there wasn't one as charmless as St. Cloud's.

Larch lay down in the dispensary and sniffed a little ether. He recalled Portland's safe harbor; his mind ticked off the towns, either east or inland from Portland, and his lips tried the towns with the good, Maine names.

(Inhale, exhale.) Wilbur Larch could almost taste those towns, their vapory names. There was Kennebunk and Kennebunkport, there was Vassalborough and Nobleboro and Waldoboro, there was Wiscasset and West Bath, Damariscotta and Friendship, Penobscot Bay and Sagadahoc Bay, Yarmouth and Camden, Rockport and Arundel, Rumford and Biddeford and Livermore Falls.

/ / /

East of Cape Kenneth, the tourist trap, lies Heart's Haven; inland from the small, pretty harbor town that's called a haven squats the town of Heart's Rock. The rock in Heart's Rock is named for the uninhabited rock island that appears to float like a dead whale in the otherwise perfect harbor of Heart's Haven. It is an eyesore island, unloved by the people of Heart's Haven; perhaps they were moved to name the eyesore town of Heart's Rock after their bird-beshitted and fish-belly-white rock. Nearly covered at high tide, and lying fairly flat in the water, it lists slightly—hence its name: Dead Whale Rock. There is no actual "rock" in Heart's Rock, which is not a town deserving to be looked down upon; it is only five miles inland, and from some of its hills the ocean is visible; in most of the town, the sea breeze is refreshingly felt.

But compared to Heart's Haven, every other town is a mongrel. When condemning Heart's Rock, the people of Heart's Haven do not mention the simple quaintness of the town's only stores—Sanborn's General Store and Titus Hardware and Plumbing. The people of Heart's Haven are more likely to mention Drinkwater Lake, and the summer cottages on its murky shores. A not-very-fresh freshwater lake, more of a pond—because by mid-July the bottom is cloudy and rank with algae—Drinkwater Lake is Heart's Rock's only offering to summer people. People who summer on Drinkwater Lake have not traveled far; they may live elsewhere in Heart's Rock—or, even more rustically, in Kenneth Corners. The summer camps and cottages that dot the lakeshore are also used during the hunting-season weekends in the fall. The cottages and camps have names of a striving wishfulness. Echo's End, and Buck's Last Stand (this one is decked with antlers); there is one called Endless Weekend, with a floating dock; one called Wee Three, suggesting inhabitants of an almost unbearable cuteness; and a frank sort of place called Sherman's Hole in the Ground, which is an accurate description.

In 194__ Drinkwater Lake was already cluttered, and by 195__ it would become intolerably busy with powerboats and water skis—propellers fouled and oars festooned with the slime-green algae stirred up from the bottom. The lake is too woodsy to let the wind through; sailboats always die on the dead-calm surface, which is perfect for hatching mosquitoes, and over the years the accumulated children's urine and gasoline would give the lake an unwell, glossy sheen. There are wonderfully remote lakes in Maine, but Drinkwater Lake was never one of them. The occasional, bewildered canoeist looking for the wilderness would not find it there. The wild-hearted, departed Winkles would not have favored the place. You would not willingly drink the water of Drinkwater Lake, and there are many tiresome jokes on that subject, all conceived in Heart's Haven, where the habit of judging Heart's Rock by its single, sorry body of water is long-standing.

When Homer Wells would first see Drinkwater Lake, he would imagine that if there were ever a summer camp for the luckless orphans of St. Cloud's, it would be situated in the bog that separates Echo's End from Sherman's Hole in the Ground.

/ / /

Not all of Heart's Rock was so ugly. It was a town of stay-put people on fairly open, neatly farmed land; it was dairy-cow country, and fruit-tree country. In 194__, the Ocean View Orchard on Drinkwater Road, which connected Heart's Rock to Heart's Haven, was pretty and plentiful—even by the standards of the spoiled and hard-to-please of Heart's Haven. Although the Ocean View Orchards were in Heart's Rock, there was a Heart's Haven look to the place; the farmhouse had flagstone patios, the grounds were landscaped with rose bushes—like the Heart's Haven homes on the more elegant coast—and the lawns spreading from the main house to the swimming pool, all the way to the nearest apple orchard, were kept up and fussed over by the same yard gangs who made the Heart's Haven lawns look so much like putting greens.

The owner of Ocean View Orchards, Wallace Worthington, even had a Heart's Haven kind of name—meaning, it was not a local-sounding name. Indeed not, because Wallace Worthington was from New York; he'd fled investments for apple farming just before everyone's investments crashed, and if he didn't know all there was to know about apples—being a gentleman farmer, in soul and in bones (and in clothes)—he knew almost everything about money and had hired the right foremen to run Ocean View (men who *did* know apples).

Worthington was a perpetual board member at the Haven Club; he was the only member whose position on the board was never voted—and the only Heart's Rock resident who was a Haven Club member. Since his orchard employed half the locals of Heart's Rock, Wallace Worthington had the rare distinction of being appreciated in both towns.

Wallace Worthington would have reminded Wilbur Larch of someone he might have met at the Channing-Peabodys', where Dr. Larch went to perform his second abortion—the rich people's abortion, as Larch thought of it. Wallace Worthington would strike Homer Wells as what a *real* King of New England should look like.

You'd have to live in Heart's Rock or in Heart's Haven—and be familiar with the social histories of the towns—to know that Wallace Worthington's wife was not every inch a queen; she certainly looked like a queen and conducted herself, every inch, as such. But the townspeople knew that Olive Worthington—although a Heart's Haven native—had come from the wrong part of town. Society is so complex that even Heart's Haven had a wrong part to it.

Olive Worthington was born Alice Bean; to the knowledgeable, she was Bruce Bean's (the clam-digger's) daughter; she was Bucky Bean's (the well-digger's) clever sister—which falsely implied that Bucky wasn't clever; he was at least cleverer than his father, Bruce. Well-digging (the business of Nurse Angela's father, the business that yielded Homer Wells a name) was good-paying work: well-digging beats clam-digging by dollars and by miles, as they say in Maine.

Olive Worthington grew up selling clams out of the back of a pickup truck that leaked ice. Her mother, Maud, never talked; she kept a cracked makeup mirror on a chopping block at the crowded corner of a kitchen counter—her cosmetics, which fascinated her, mingled with stray clams. A large clam shell was her only ashtray. Sometimes the black and gritty skin discarded from the neck of a cleaned clam clung to a bottle of her Blush-Up. She died of lung cancer when Olive was still in high school.

Alice Bean became a Worthington by marrying Wallace

Worthington; she became an Olive by altering her own name at the town clerk's office in Heart's Haven. It was a willful, legal change-of-name form that she filled out—easy to do, in part because it required the changing of only two letters to make an Alice into an Olive. There was no end to the way the locals liked to play with the name *Olive,* as if they were moving around in their mouths the disagreeable pits of that odd food; and behind her back, there were many who still called her Alice Bean, though only her brother Bucky would call Olive Alice to her face. Everyone else respected her enough to say Olive if that's what she wanted to hear, and it was agreed that although she married a Worthington, and therefore had married into apples and money, she had got no bargain in Wallace.

Cheerful, fun-loving, a good-timer, Wallace Worthington was generous and kind. He adored Olive and everything about her—her gray eyes and her ash-blond hair turning softly to pearl, and her college-learned New British accent (which was often imitated at the Haven Club). Her brother Bucky's success as a well-digger had paid for Olive's college accent, without which she might not have enticed Wallace Worthington to notice her. It may have been gratitude that caused Olive to tolerate Bucky calling her Alice to her face. She even tolerated his predictable appearances at Ocean View Orchards—his boots always muddy with that clay-colored muck from the middle of the earth, the stuff only well-diggers find. Olive tried not to cringe while he tromped about the house in those boots, calling her "Alice Baby," and on hot summer days he would dive into the swimming pool in all his clothes, leaving only those middle-earth boots out of the bright water (which he left sloshing in Atlantic turmoil and clay-colored at the edges). Bucky Bean could leave a ring on a swimming pool the way a dirty child could ring a bathtub.

For all that Olive Worthington had been spared, by escaping the Alice Bean in herself, there was something wrong with Wallace Worthington. Despite his being a real gentleman, and excellent at teasing the Republicans at the Haven Club, and fair to his orchardmen (he provided them with health insurance policies at his expense at a time when most farm workers were living below the standard of minimum *everything*)—despite Wallace Worthington's lovable flamboyance (all the farm and personal vehicles at Ocean View Orchards bore his monogram on a big, red apple!), despite *everything* that was grand about

Wallace, he appeared to be drunk all the time, and he exhibited such a childish quality of hyperactivity and restlessness that everyone in Heart's Haven and in Heart's Rock agreed that he must certainly be no prize to live with.

He was drunk at the Haven Club when he lowered the net at center court (which he could not seem to adjust properly) by cutting through it with the saw blade of his jackknife. He was drunk again at the Haven Club when Dr. Darryrimple had his stroke; Wallace tossed the old gentleman into the shallow end of the pool—"to revive him," he said later. The old fellow nearly drowned in addition to suffering his stroke, and the offended Darryrimples were so outraged that they canceled membership. And Wallace was drunk in his own orchards when he drove his Cadillac headlong into the five-hundred-gallon Hardie sprayer, dousing himself and his oyster-white convertible with chemicals that gave him a rash in his lap and permanently bleached the Cadillac's scarlet upholstery. He was drunk again when he insisted on driving the tractor that towed the flatbed with half of Ira Titcomb's beehives on it, promptly dumping the load—the honey, the hives, and millions of angry bees—at the intersection of Drinkwater Road and Day Lane (getting himself badly stung). Also stung were Everett Taft and his wife, Dot; and Dot's kid sister, Debra Pettigrew, who were working in the Day Lane orchard at the time of the accident.

Yet no one doubted that Wallace Worthington was faithful to Olive—the cynics saying that he was too drunk to get it up with anyone else, and possibly too drunk to get it up with Olive. It was clear he had gotten it up with her at least once; he had produced a son, just turning twenty in 194_, as big and handsome and charming as his father, with his mother's smoky eyes and with not quite her former blondness (his was tawny, not ash); he even had a bit of her New British accent. Wallace Worthington, Junior, was too good-looking ever to be called Junior (he was called Wally). From the day of Wally's birth, Wallace Worthington was called Senior, even by Olive and eventually by Wally.

And this is only a beginning to an understanding of the societies of Heart's Haven and Heart's Rock. If he had known only this much, Dr. Larch might have tried to keep Homer Wells away from the place; he might have guessed that Homer's life would get complicated there. What did an orphan know about gossip, or care about class? But to Wilbur Larch

Heart's Haven and Heart's Rock were very pretty names, improved by ether.

If Dr. Larch had spent some time around Senior Worthington, Larch might have figured out that the man was unfairly judged; of course he drank too much—many people who drink at all drink too much. But Senior was not a drunk. He bore the classic, clinical features of Alzheimer's disease, and Wilbur Larch would have spotted it for what it was—a progressive organic brain syndrome. Alzheimer's presenile dementia is marked by deterioration of intellect, failure of memory and a striking appearance of rapid aging in a patient in middle life, symptoms that become progressively more severe over a period of just a few years and terminate in death. Restlessness, hyperactivity, defective judgment are other hallmarks of the disease. But as keen as the wit in Heart's Haven was, the townspeople didn't know the difference between drunkenness and Alzheimer's disease; they were dead-sure they had the Worthingtons figured out.

They misjudged Olive Worthington, too. She had earned her name. She might have been desperate to leave the clam level of life, but she knew what work was; she had seen how quickly the ice in the pickup melted, how short a time the clams could be kept cool. She knew hustle, she knew know-how. She saw, instantly, that Wallace Worthington was good about money and weak on apples, and so she took up apples as her cause. She found out who the knowledgeable foremen were and she gave them raises; she fired the others, and hired a younger, more reliable crew. She baked apple pies for the families of the orchardmen who pleased her, and she taught their wives the recipe, too. She installed a pizza oven in the apple mart and soon could turn out forty-eight pies in one baking, adding greatly to the business over the counter at harvest time—formerly reserved for apple cider and apple jelly. She overpaid for the damages to Ira Titcomb's beehives and soon was selling apple blossom honey over the counter, too. She went to the university and learned everything about cross-pollination and how to plant a new-tree orchard; she learned more about mousing, and suckering, and thinning, and the new chemicals than the foremen knew, and then she taught them.

Olive had a vision of her silent mother, Maud, mesmerized by her own fading image in the makeup mirror—clams everywhere around her. The little cotton balls dabbed with cosmetics (the color of the clay on her brother Bucky's terrible boots) were flecked with the ashes from the cigarettes overstuffing the clam-shell ashtray. These images strengthened Olive. She knew the life she had escaped, and at Ocean View Orchards she more than earned her keep; she took the farm out of Senior's careless hands, and she ran it very intelligently for him.

At night, coming back from the Haven Club (she always drove), Olive would leave Senior passed out in the passenger seat and put a note on her son Wally's pillow, asking him, when he got home, to remember to carry his father up to bed. Wally always did so; he was a golden boy, not just a picture of one. The one night that young Wally had drunk too much to carry his father to bed, Olive Worthington was quick to point out to her son the error of his ways.

"You may resemble your father, with my permission, in every aspect but in his drunkenness," she told Wally. "*If* you resemble him in that aspect, you will lose this farm—and every penny made by every apple. Do you think your father could prevent me from doing that to you?"

Wally looked at his father, whom he had allowed to sleep all night in the passenger seat of the Cadillac, now mottled by spraying chemicals. It was obvious to the boy that Senior Worthington could prevent nothing.

"No, Mom," Wally said to his mother respectfully—not just because he was educated and polite (he could have taught tennis *and* manners at the Haven Club, and taught them well), but also because he knew his mother, Olive Worthington, hadn't "married into" anything more than a little working cash. The *work* had been supplied by her; Wilbur Larch would have respected that.

The sadness was that Olive, too, misjudged poor Senior, who was only a tangential victim of alcoholism and a nearly complete victim of Alzheimer's disease.

There are things that the societies of towns know about you, and things that they miss. Senior Worthington was baffled by his own deterioration, which he also believed to be the result of the evils of drink. When he drank less—and still couldn't remember in the morning what he'd said or done the evening before; still saw no relenting of his remarkably speeded-up process of aging; still hopped from one activity to the next, leaving a jacket in one place, a hat in another, his car keys in the lost jacket—when he drank less and *still* behaved like a fool, this bewildered him to such an extreme that he began to drink more. In the end, he would be a victim of both Alzheimer's disease *and* alcoholism; a happy drunk, with unexplained plunges of mood. In a better, and better-informed, world, he would have been cared for like the nearly faultless patient that he was.

In this one respect Heart's Haven and Heart's Rock resembled St. Cloud's: there was no saving Senior Worthington from what was wrong with him, as surely as there had been no saving Fuzzy Stone.

/ / /

In 193__, Homer Wells began *Gray's Anatomy*—at the beginning. He began with osteology, the skeleton. He began with bones. In 194__, he was making his third journey through *Gray's Anatomy*, some of which he shared with Melony. Melony showed a wayward concentration, though she confessed interest in the complexity of the nervous system, specifically the description of the twelfth or hypoglossal nerve, which is the motor nerve of the tongue.

"What's a motor nerve?" Melony asked, sticking out her tongue. Homer tried to explain, but he felt tired. He was making his sixth journey through *David Copperfield*, his seventh through *Great Expectations*, his fourth through *Jane Eyre*. Only last night he had come to a part that always made Melony cringe—which made Homer anxious.

It's near the beginning of Chapter Twelve, when Jane shrewdly observes, "It is vain to say human beings ought to be satisfied with tranquillity: they must have action; and they will make it if they cannot find it."

"Just remember, Sunshine," Melony interrupted him. "As long as I stay, you stay. A promise is a promise."

But Homer Wells was tired of Melony making him anxious. He repeated the line, this time reading it as if he were personally delivering a threat.

" 'It is vain to say human beings ought to be satisfied with tranquillity: they must have action; and they will make it if they cannot find it.' " Mrs. Grogan looked taken aback at the ominousness in his voice.

He copied the line in a handwriting nearly as orderly and cramped as Dr. Larch's; Homer typed it on Nurse Angela's typewriter, making only a few mistakes. And when Wilbur Larch was "just resting" in the dispensary, Homer crept up on the tired saint and placed the piece of paper with the quotation from *Jane Eyre* on Dr. Larch's rising and falling chest. Dr. Larch felt less threatened by the actual text of the quotation than he felt a general unease: that Homer knew Dr. Larch's ether habit so exactly that the boy could approach his bed undetected. Or am I using a little more of this stuff than I used to? Larch wondered.

Was it meant as a message that Homer had used the ether cone to hold the *Jane Eyre* quotation to Larch's chest?

"History," wrote Dr. Larch, "is composed of the smallest, often undetected mistakes."

He may have been referring to something as small as the apostrophe that someone added to the original St. Clouds. His point is also illuminated by the case of the heart in both Heart's Haven and in Heart's Rock, a case similar in error to how Melody became forever a Melony. The explorer credited with the discovery of the fine, pretty harbor at Heart's Haven—a seafaring man named Reginald Hart—was also the first settler of Heart's Rock to clear land and try to be a farmer. The general illiteracy of the times, and of the times following Reginald Hart's death, prevailed; no one knew of any written difference between one heart and another. The first settlers of Heart's Haven and Heart's Rock, probably never knowing that Reginald *Hart* had been given the name of a *deer,* quite comfortably named their towns after an organ.

"A hollow muscular organ of conical form," as Homer Wells could recite, by rote, from *Gray's Anatomy,* " . . . enclosed in the cavity of the PERICARDIUM." By 194__, Homer had looked at each of the hearts in the three cadavers Dr. Larch had acquired for him (each cadaver outliving its usefulness for exploratory purposes in about two years' time).

The cadavers were female; it hardly served Dr. Larch's purpose—in the process of educating Homer Wells in obstetrical procedure and procedures of a related kind—to have his student examining male cadavers. There was always a problem getting a body (once one was delivered in water that was supposed to be ice; another had to be disposed of because the embalming fluid had clearly been old or too weak). Homer remembered the three cadavers distinctly. It was not until the third body that he developed enough of a sense of humor to give the body a name; he called her Clara after David Copperfield's wimpish mother—that poor, weak woman who'd allowed herself and young David to be so bullied by the terrible Mr. Murdstone.

"You should call her Jane," Melony advised Homer; Melony was alternately sick of Jane Eyre and completely identified with her.

"I could have called her Melony," Homer responded, but humor was not reliably to be found in Melony, who preferred to play her own jokes.

Body number two provided Homer with the essential practice that prepared him for his first Caesarean section; for that one, he had felt Dr. Larch's eyes so riveted to his hands that his hands seemed not his own—they moved with such smooth purpose that Homer was sure that Dr. Larch had discovered a way to make that perfect, no-bigger-than-necessary incision in the uterus with his mind (no need for using hands, at all).

The harangue that developed at the railroad station over the arrival of the body Homer would call Clara gave Homer his first experience with eclamptic convulsions—or puerperal convulsions, as they were called in Wilbur Larch's days at the Boston Lying-In. At the exact moment that Dr. Larch was at the railroad station arguing with the stationmaster about the release form for the unfortunate Clara, Homer Wells was at St. Cloud's trying to locate, exactly, the inferior thyroid vein on body number two. Although he didn't know it, he had a good excuse for having, momentarily, lost his way; body number two was wholly shopworn, and many things were hard to locate within it. He would have consulted his *Gray's* in another minute or two, but just then Nurse Edna burst upon him—shrieking (as she always did when she saw Homer with body number two; it was as if she'd caught him up to something with Melony).

"Oh, *Homer!*" she cried, but she couldn't speak; she flapped her arms in an agitated, chickenlike fashion before she managed to point Homer in the direction of the dispensary. He ran there as quickly as he could, finding a woman lying on the dispensary floor—her eyes staring so wildly and so steadily unseeing that at first he mistook her for the body he knew Dr. Larch was trying to liberate from the stationmaster. Then the woman began to move, and Homer Wells knew she was quite close to becoming a cadaver; the convulsions began with a twitching in her face, but they spread rapidly through all the muscles of her frame. Her face, which had been flushed, turned a shiny blue-black; her heels struck the floor with such force that both her shoes flew off—Homer saw instantly that her ankles were hugely swollen. Her jaws were set; her mouth and chin were wet with a frothy spittle, laced with blood because she'd bitten her tongue—which was at least preferable to her swallowing it. Her respiration was hardworking; she expelled air with a hiss, and the spray splashed Homer's face with a violence he'd not felt since he stood back from the bank and watched the Winkles being swept away.

"Eclampsia," Homer Wells said to Nurse Edna. It derives from the Greek; Dr. Larch had told him that the word refers to the flashes of light a patient sees at the onset of the puerperal convulsions. With any sensible prenatal care, Homer knew, eclampsia was usually avoidable. There was an easily detected rise in blood pressure, the presence of albumin in the urine, swelling of the feet and hands, headaches, vomiting, and of course those spots and flashes in the eyes. Bed rest, diet, reduction of fluid intake, and free catharsis usually worked; but if they didn't, the bringing on of premature labor almost always prevented the convulsions and often produced a living baby.

But the patients Dr. Larch saw were not women who sought or even understood prenatal care. This patient was very last-minute—even by the standards of Dr. Larch's practice.

"Doctor Larch is at the railroad station," Homer told Nurse Edna calmly. "Someone has to get him. You and Nurse Angela should stay to help me."

In lifting the woman and carrying her to the delivery room, Homer felt the woman's moist, cold skin and was reminded of body number one and body number two (the latter, he recalled, had been left on the examining table in the room now used for his anatomical studies, near the boys' division kitchen). In the last century, Homer Wells knew, a doctor would have given this patient an ether anesthesia and would have dilated the mouth of the womb to effect a forcible delivery—a method that usually caused the patient's death.

At the Boston Lying-In Wilbur Larch had learned to fortify the heart muscle with doses of digitalis, which helped prevent the development of fluid in the lungs. Homer listened to the woman's watery breathing and realized he might be too late, even if he correctly remembered the procedure. He knew that one had to be conservative with eclampsia; if he was forced to deliver the woman prematurely, he must allow the labor to develop as naturally as possible. The woman just then moaned; her head and heels whacked the operating table in unison, her pregnant belly seemed to levitate—and one of her arms, without will, without purposeful direction, flew up and hit Homer in the face.

He knew that sometimes a woman had only one puerperal convulsion; it was recorded that a few patients had survived as many as a hundred. What Homer didn't know, of course, was whether he was observing this woman's second convulsion or her ninetieth.

When Nurse Edna returned to the delivery room with Nurse Angela, Homer instructed the nurses to administer morphine to the patient; Homer himself injected some magnesium sulphate into a vein, to lower her blood pressure at least temporarily. In the interval between her last and what Homer knew would be her next convulsion, he asked Nurse Edna to take a urine sample from the woman and he asked Nurse Angela to examine the specimen for traces of albumin. He asked the woman to tell him how many convulsions she had already suffered; but although the woman was coherent and could even answer questions intelligently, she couldn't pinpoint the number of convulsions. Typically, she remembered nothing of the convulsions themselves—only their onset and their draining aftereffects. She estimated she was at least a month away from expecting her baby.

At the onset of her next convulsion, Homer gave the woman a light ether sedation, hoping he might reduce the violence of the fit. This fit was different in character from the last, though Homer doubted it was any less violent; the woman's motion was slower, but—if anything—more powerful. Homer lay across her chest, but her body abruptly jackknifed—lifting him off the operating table. In the next interval, while the woman was still relaxed under the ether sedation, Homer's investigations showed him that the neck of the patient's womb was not shortened, its mouth was not dilated; labor hadn't begun. He contemplated beginning it, prayed that he wouldn't have to make this decision, wondered why it was taking so long to find Dr. Larch.

An orphan with a bad cold had been assigned to locate Larch at the railroad station; he returned with a thick rivulet of snot in each nostril and strung across one cheek, like a welt from a whiplash. His name (Nurse Angela's, of course) was Curly Day, and he wetly announced that Dr. Larch had boarded the train to Three Mile Falls—in order to chase down and capture the body that the stationmaster (in a pique of perversity prompted by religious outrage) had forwarded to the next stop. The stationmaster had simply refused to accept the cadaver. Larch, in a rage now surpassing the stationmaster's, had taken the next train after it.

"Oh-oh," Nurse Edna said.

Homer gave his patient her first dose of digitalis; he would repeat this periodically until he could see its effects on the woman's heartbeat. While he waited with the woman for her next seizure, he asked her if she had decided to put her baby up for adoption, or if she had come to St. Cloud's only because it was the nearest hospital—in short, was this a baby she very much wanted, or one she didn't want?

"You mean it's going to die?" the woman asked.

He gave her Dr. Larch's best "Of course not!" kind of smile; but what he thought was that it was likely the baby would die if he didn't deliver it soon, and likely the woman would die if he rushed the delivery.

The woman said she had hitchhiked to St. Cloud's because there was no one in her life to bring her, and that she didn't want to keep the baby—but that she wanted it, very much, to live.

"Right," Homer said, as if this decision would have been his own.

"You seem kinda young," the woman said. "I'm not going to die, am I?" she asked.

"That's right, you're not," said Homer Wells, using Dr. Larch's smile again; it at least made him look older.

But in twelve hours, when Dr. Larch had not returned and when the woman was arching her body on the operating table, suffering what was her seventh seizure, Homer Wells could not remember the exact expression that produced the reassuring smile.

He looked at Nurse Angela, who was trying to help him hold the woman, and he said, "I'm going to start her labor. I'm going to rupture the bag of waters."

"I'm sure you know what's best, Homer," Nurse Angela said, but her own imitation of Dr. Larch's confidence-inspiring smile was very poor.

In twelve more hours the patient's uterine contractions commenced; Homer Wells would never remember the exact number of convulsions the woman experienced in that time. He was beginning to worry more about Dr. Larch than about the woman, and he had to fight down his fear of something happening to Dr. Larch in order to concentrate on his job.

Another ten hours after the onset of the woman's contractions, she delivered herself of a boy—four pounds, eleven ounces, in good condition. The mother's improvement was rapid—as Homer had expected. There were no more convulsions, her blood pressure returned to normal, the traces of albumin in her urine were minimal.

In the evening of the day after the morning when he had gone to the station to retrieve the body that the stationmaster would neither keep nor relinquish, Wilbur Larch—together with the rescued cadaver soon to be called Clara—returned tired and triumphant to St. Cloud's. He had followed the body to Three Mile Falls, but the stationmaster there had registered such horror that the body was never unloaded from the train; it had traveled on, and Larch had traveled after it, arriving at the next, and at the next station, always a train behind. No one wanted Clara, except to put her in the ground, and it was thought that this should not be the responsibility of a stationmaster—who would surely not accept, at his station, a body that no one came forward for. Clara was a body clearly not intended for the ground. The unearthly sloshing sound of the embalming fluid, the leathery skin, the outer-space colors of the occasionally exposed arteries and veins—"Whatever that is, I don't want it here," said the stationmaster in Three Mile Falls.

And so Clara went from Three Mile Falls to Misery Gore, to Moxie Gore, to East Moxie—on and on. Larch got in a terrible row with the stationmaster in Harmony, Maine, where Clara had stopped for a few minutes—giving the railroad personnel the fright of their lives—before she'd been sent on.

"That was *my* body!" Larch screamed. "It had *my* name on it, it is intended for the instruction of a student of medicine who is training with *me* in *my* hospital in Saint Cloud's. It's *mine*!" Larch yelled. "Why are you sending it in the wrong direction? Why are you sending it *away* from me?"

"It came here, didn't it?" the stationmaster said. "It didn't get taken at Saint Cloud's, it appears to me."

"The stationmaster in Saint Cloud's is crazy!" Larch hollered; he gave a little hop—a little jump, which made him appear a little crazy, too.

"Maybe he is, maybe he isn't," said the stationmaster in Harmony. "All I know is, the body come here and I sent it on."

"For Christ's sake, it's not haunted!" Larch said with a wail.

"Didn't say it was," said the stationmaster. "Maybe it is, maybe it isn't—wasn't here long enough to tell."

"Idiots!" Larch shouted, and took the train. In Cornville (where the train didn't stop), Wilbur Larch screamed out the window at a couple of potato farmers who were waving at the train. "Maine is full of *morons*!" he yelled, riding on.

In Skowhegan, he asked the stationmaster just where in Hell he thought the damn body was going. "Bath, I suppose," the Skowhegan stationmaster said. "That's where it came from, and if nobody wants it at the other end, that's where it's going back to."

"Somebody *does* want it at the other end!" screamed Wilbur Larch. "*I* want it."

The body had been sent to the hospital in St. Cloud's from the hospital in Bath; a woman who was a willing body-donor had died, and the pathologist at Bath Memorial Hospital knew that Wilbur Larch was looking for a fresh female.

Dr. Larch caught up with Clara in Augusta; Augusta was very sophisticated, for Maine, and the stationmaster simply saw that the body was going the wrong way. "Of *course* it's going the wrong way!" Wilbur Larch cried.

"Damnedest thing," the stationmaster said. "Don't they speak English up in your parts?"

"They don't *hear* English!" Larch yelled. "I'd like to send a cadaver to every damn one of those towns—one a day!"

"That sure would rile up a bunch of folks," the stationmaster said dryly, wondering how "riled up" Dr. Larch was going to get.

On the long ride back to St. Cloud's with Clara, Dr. Larch didn't calm down. In each of the towns that offended him—in Harmony, especially, but in East Moxie and in Moxie Gore, and in all the rest of them, too—he offered his opinions to the respective stationmasters while the train paused at the stations.

"Moronville," he told the stationmaster in Harmony. "Tell me *one* thing that's *harmonious* here—*one* thing!"

"It was pretty harmonious before you and your damn body got here," the stationmaster said.

"Moronville!" Larch shouted out the window as the train pulled away. "Idiotsburg!"

To his great disappointment, when the train arrived in St. Cloud's, the stationmaster was not there. "Lunch," someone told Dr. Larch, but it was early evening.

"Perhaps you mean supper?" Dr. Larch asked. "Perhaps the stationmaster doesn't know the difference," he said nastily; he hired the help of two louts to lug Clara up the hill to the boys' division.

He was surprised by the disarray in which Homer Wells had left body number two. In the excitement of the emergency, Homer had forgotten to put body number two away, and Larch ordered the two oafs to carry Clara in there—not preparing the simpletons for the shopworn cadaver exposed on the table. One of the clods ran into a wall. Terrible crying out and jumping around! Larch went shouting through the orphanage, looking for Homer.

"Here I am, running after a new body for you—across half the damn state of Maine—and you leave a mess like that just lying out in the open where any fool can fall upon it! *Homer!*" Dr. Larch yelled. "Goddamn it," he muttered to himself, "there is no way a teen-ager is going to be an adult ahead of his own, good time—no way you can expect a teen-ager to accept adult responsibilities, to do an adult's Goddamn *job!*" He went muttering all over the boys' division, looking for Homer Wells, but Homer had collapsed on Larch's white-iron bed in the dispensary and had fallen into the deepest sleep. The aura of ether surrounding that spare bed under that eastern window might have enhanced Homer's drowsiness, but he scarcely needed ether to sleep; he had been up for nearly forty hours with the eclampsia patient—delivering her and her child.

Nurse Angela interrupted Dr. Larch before he could find Homer Wells and wake him up.

"What's happening around here?" Larch demanded to know. "Is no one the least bit interested in where in Hell I've been? And why has that boy left his body looking like a war casualty? I go away overnight and just look at this place."

But Nurse Angela straightened him out. She told him it had been the worst case of puerperal convulsions she'd ever seen, and she had seen some—in her time. Wilbur Larch had seen some, too. In his days at the Boston Lying-In, he'd lost a lot of women to eclampsia, and even in 194__, about a quarter of the deaths in childbirth were credited to these convulsions.

"Homer did this?" Larch asked Nurse Angela and Nurse Edna; he was reading the report; he had examined the mother, who was fine, and the premature baby boy, who was normal and healthy.

"He was almost as calm as you, Wilbur," Nurse Edna said admiringly. "You can be real proud of him."

"He is an angel, in my opinion," Nurse Angela said.

"He looked a little grim when he had to break the water," Nurse Edna remembered, "but he did everything just right."

"He was as sure as snow," Nurse Angela said.

He did almost everything right, Wilbur Larch was thinking; it really was amazing. Larch thought it was a slight error that Homer had failed to record the exact number of convulsions in the second twelve-hour period (especially after correctly counting them in the first twelve hours), and Homer had not mentioned the number or the severity of the convulsions (or if there *were* any) in the ten-hour period after the patient's labor contractions began and before she delivered. Minor criticism. Wilbur Larch was a good teacher; he knew that this criticism was better withheld. Homer Wells had performed all the hard parts correctly; his procedure had been perfect.

"He's not even twenty—is he?" Larch asked. But Nurse Edna had gone to bed, she was exhausted; in her dreams she would mingle Homer's heroism with her already considerable love for Larch; she would sleep very well. Nurse Angela was still up, in her office, and when Dr. Larch asked her why the premature baby had not been named, she told Larch that it was Nurse Edna's turn and Nurse Edna had been too tired.

"Well, it's just a matter of form," said Wilbur Larch. "*You* name it, then—I want it named. It won't kill you to go out of turn, will it?"

But Nurse Angela had a better idea. It was Homer's baby—he had saved it, and the mother. Homer Wells should name this one, Nurse Angela said.

"Yes, you're right, he should," Dr. Larch replied, filling with pride in his wonderful creation.

Homer Wells would wake to a day of naming. In the same day he would be faced with naming body number three *and* his first orphan. He would name the new body Clara, and what else could he have named a baby boy except David Copperfield? He was reading *Great Expectations* at the time and he preferred *Great Expectations* to *David Copperfield* as a book. But he would not name anyone Pip, and he didn't care for the character of Pip as much as he cared for little David. It was an easy decision, and he woke that morning very refreshed and capable of more demanding decisions than that one.

He had slept almost through the night. He woke only once on the dispensary bed, aware that Dr. Larch was back; Larch was in the room, probably looking at him, but Homer kept his eyes closed. He somehow knew Larch was there because of the sweet scent of ether, which Larch wore like cologne, and because of the steadiness of Larch's breathing. Then he felt Larch's hand—a doctor's hand, feeling for fever—pass very lightly over his forehead. Homer Wells, not yet twenty—quite accomplished in obstetrical procedure and as knowledgeable as almost any doctor on the care of "the female organs of generation"—lay very still, pretending to sleep.

Dr. Larch bent over him and kissed him, very lightly, on his lips. Homer heard Larch whisper, "Good work, Homer." He felt a second, even lighter kiss. "Good work, my boy," the doctor said, and then left him.

Homer Wells felt his tears come silently; there were more tears than he remembered crying the last time he had cried—when Fuzzy Stone had died and Homer had lied about Fuzzy to Snowy Meadows and the others. He cried and cried, but he never made a sound; he would have to change Dr. Larch's pillowcase in the morning, he cried so much. He cried because he had received his first fatherly kisses.

Of course Melony had kissed him; she didn't do it much anymore, but she had. And Nurse Edna and Nurse Angela had kissed him silly, but they kissed everyone. Dr. Larch had never kissed him before, and now he had kissed him twice.

Homer Wells cried because he'd never known how nice a father's kisses could be, and he cried because he doubted that Wilbur Larch would ever do it again—or would have done it, if he'd thought Homer was awake.

Dr. Larch went to marvel at the good health of the eclampsia patient and at her thriving, tiny child—who, in the morning, would become the orphan David Copperfield ("David Copperfield, *Junior*," Dr. Larch would enjoy saying). Then Larch went to the familiar typewriter in Nurse Angela's office, but he couldn't write anything. He couldn't even think, he was so agitated from kissing Homer Wells. If Homer Wells had received his first fatherly kisses, Dr. Larch had given the first kisses he had *ever* given—fatherly, or otherwise—since the day in the Portland boardinghouse when he caught the clap from Mrs. Eames. And the kisses he gave to Mrs. Eames were more in the nature of explorations than they were gifts of love. Oh God, thought Wilbur Larch, what will happen to me when Homer has to go?

/ / /

Where he would go was hardly a place of comparable excitement, of comparable challenge, of comparable sadness, of comparable gloom; but where he would go was nice, and what would Homer Wells, with his background, make of *nice?* Wouldn't it simply seduce him? Wouldn't anyone rather have *nice?*

What did Heart's Haven or Heart's Rock know of trouble, and what did anyone do there to be of use?

Yes, Olive Worthington suffered her brother Bucky's intrusions—his well-digging slime in her swimming pool and his trekking across her rugs. Big deal. Yes, Olive worried if young Wally would have gumption, if he would really learn and contribute to the apple-growing business—or would the pretty boy become, like Senior, a good-timer turning pathetic? But what were these worries compared to the business of St. Cloud's? Compared to the Lord's work and the Devil's work, weren't these concerns trivial? Wasn't life in *nice* places shallow?

But trouble can come to nice places, too; trouble travels, trouble visits. Trouble even takes holidays from the places where it thrives, from places like St. Cloud's. The trouble that visited Heart's Haven and Heart's Rock was a fairly trivial and common form of trouble; it began, as trouble often does, with falling in love.

"Here in St. Cloud's," wrote Wilbur Larch, "I don't imagine that anyone falls in love; it would be too evident a luxury, to fall in love here." Larch didn't know that Nurse Edna had been in love with him from day one, but he was correct in supposing that it hadn't been exactly love that passed between Melony and Homer Wells. And what clung to each of them after the first passion had passed was surely not love. And that picture of Mrs. Eames's daughter with the pony's penis in her mouth: that photograph was the oldest resident of St. Cloud's—and surely it had no love in it. That picture was as far from love as Heart's Haven and Heart's Rock were from St. Cloud's.

"In other parts of the world," wrote Wilbur Larch, "I imagine that people fall in love all the time."

If not all the time, a lot. Young Wally Worthington, for example, thought he'd been in love twice before he was twenty, and once when he was twenty-one; now, in 194__ (he was just three years older than Homer Wells), Wally fell full-force in love for the fourth time. He didn't know that this time would be for keeps.

The girl young Wally's heart would select for life was a lobsterman's daughter; he was no ordinary lobsterman, and it was no surprise to anyone that he had an extraordinary daughter. Raymond Kendall was so good at lobstering that other lobstermen, through binoculars, watched him pull and bait a pot. When he changed his mooring lines, they changed theirs. When he didn't go to sea but stayed at home, or at his dock mending pots, they stayed home, too, and mended theirs. But they couldn't match him; he had so many pots in the water that his personalized black and orange buoys gave the Heart's Haven harbor the razzle-dazzle of collegiate competition. Once a contingent of Yale men from the Haven Club beseeched Raymond Kendall to change his colors to blue and white, but Kendall only muttered that he didn't have time for games. Other contingents from the Haven Club would beseech him; the subject was rarely the color of his lobster buoys.

The Haven Club faced the far jetty of Heart's Haven Harbor, where Raymond Kendall's lobster pound and dock were long established. Kendall lived above the pound, which might have enticed a more superficial man to comply with the Haven Club's requests that he beautify his immediate environs. His establishment was considered, by summer people's standards, an eyesore on a harborfront of otherwise natural and/or expensively groomed beauty. Even his bedroom window was hung with buoys in various stages of repainting. The lobster pots undergoing repairs were piled so high on his dock that it was impossible, from shore, to see if boats were moored on the far side of the dock. The parking lot for the lobster pound was nearly full—and not of customers' cars (there was never enough room for the customers); it was full of the various trucks and cars that Raymond Kendall was "working on," and full of the vast and oily inboard engines for his lobster boats.

Everything surrounding the harborfront property of Raymond Kendall was teeming with a messy mechanic's condition of total overhaul; everything was in progress, incomplete, dismantled, still wet, waiting for parts—and, for noise, there were the constant grinding sounds of the generator that ran the water tanks for the lobsters in the pound and the greasy belching of an inboard engine idling at the dock. And then there was the smell: of tarred rope, of that slightly-different-from-fishy fishiness that a lobster has, of the fuel and motor oil that slicked the ocean at his dock (which was matted with seaweed, studded with periwinkles, festooned with yellow oil-skin suits hung out to dry). Raymond Kendall *lived* his work; he liked his work in evidence around him; the jetty end of Heart's Haven Harbor was his artist's studio.

He was not just an artist with lobster, he also was an expert at fixing things—at keeping everything anyone else would throw away running. If asked, Raymond Kendall wouldn't tell you he was a lobsterman; it was not that he was ashamed of it, but he was prouder of his qualities as a mechanic. "I'm just a tinkerer," he liked to say.

And if the Haven Club complained about the constant evidence of his tinkering, which they strongly felt tarnished their splendid view, they didn't complain too much; Raymond Kendall fixed what belonged to them, too. For example, he repaired the filter system for their swimming pool—in the days when no one had pools, when no one else would have touched it and Ray Kendall himself had never seen a filter system before. "I suppose it just does what you'd think it should," he said, taking ten minutes with the job.

It was rumored that the only thing Ray Kendall threw away was uneaten food, which he threw overboard or off the end of his dock. "Just feeding the lobsters, which feed me," he would say to anyone who complained. "Just feeding the sea gulls, who are hungrier than you and me."

It was rumored he had more money than Senior Worthington; there was almost no evidence of his spending any—except on his daughter. Like the children of the Haven Club members, she went to a private boarding school; and Raymond Kendall paid the considerable annual dues for a Haven Club membership—not for himself (he went to the club only on request: to fix things) but for his daughter, who'd learned to swim in the heated pool there, and who'd taken her tennis lessons on the same courts graced by young Wally Worthington. Kendall's daughter had her own car, too—it looked out of place in the Haven Club parking lot. It was a lobster-pound-parking-lot sort of car, a mishmash of the parts that were still serviceable from other cars; one of its fenders was unpainted and was attached with wires; it had a Ford insignia on its hood and a Chrysler emblem on the trunk, and the passenger-side door was sealed completely shut. However, *its* battery never went dead in the Haven Club lot; it was never *this relic* that wouldn't start; when one of the Haven Club members had a car that wouldn't start, he went looking for Raymond Kendall's daughter, who kept jumper cables in her sturdy wreck and had been taught by her father how to use them.

Some of the fabulous money Raymond Kendall was rumored to have, and to hoard, was paid him as salary by Olive Worthington; in addition to his lobstering, Ray Kendall kept the vehicles and machinery of the Ocean View Orchards running. Olive Worthington paid him a full foreman's salary because he knew almost as much about apples as he knew about lobsters (and he was indispensable as the farm's mechanic), but Ray refused to work more than two hours a day. He picked his own two hours, too—sometimes coming first thing, saying it was a bad time to go to sea, and sometimes showing up at the end of the workday, just in time to hear the orchardmen's complaints about what was wrong with the nozzle of the Hardie or with the pump of the Bean sprayer, or what was plugged in the carburetor of the Deere tractor, or out of tune with the International Harvester. He saw instantly what was crooked in the mower blades, fucked up in the forklift, jammed in the conveyor, dead in the pickup, or out of alignment in the cider mill. Raymond Kendall did in two hours what another mechanic would have spent a day doing a half-assed job of, and he almost never came to Olive and told her that she had to get a new this or a new that.

It was always Olive who made the first suggestion: that something should be replaced.

"Isn't the clutch on the Deere always in need of adjustment, Ray?" she would politely ask him. "Would you recommend its replacement?"

But Raymond Kendall was a surgeon among tinkerers—he had a doctor's hearty denial of death—and he found replacing something an admission of weakness, of failure. He would almost always say, "Well, now, Olive—if I fixed it before, I can fix it again. I can always just go on fixing it."

Olive respected Raymond Kendall's contempt for people who didn't know their own work and had "no capacity for work of any kind, anyhow." She agreed with him completely, and she also appreciated that he never included in his contempt either Senior or her father, Bruce Bean. Besides, Senior Worthington knew enough about managing money with his left hand that he'd been very successful without working more than an hour a day—usually on the telephone.

"The crop," Olive would say, of her beloved apples, "can survive bad weather even at blossom time." By which she meant wind; a stiff offshore breeze would keep Ira Titcomb's bees in their hives, and the wild bees would be blown back into the woods, where they pollinated everything but apple trees. "The crop can even survive a bad harvest," Olive said. She might have meant rain, when the fruit is slippery, gets dropped, gets bruised, is then good only for cider; or even a hurricane, which is a real danger for a coastal orchard. "The crop could even survive something happening to *me*," Olive claimed—at which modesty both Senior Worthington and young Wally would voice protest. "But what the crop could never survive," Olive would say, "is losing Ray Kendall." She meant that without Raymond nothing would work, or that they'd have to buy new *everything*, which soon wouldn't work any better than the old stuff that only Ray could keep running.

"I doubt very much, Mother," said young Wally, "if either Heart's Haven or Heart's Rock could survive without Raymond Kendall."

"I'll drink to that," Senior Worthington said, and promptly did so, causing Olive to look tragic and inspiring young Wally to change the subject.

Despite the fact that Ray Kendall worked two hours every day at Ocean View, he was never seen to eat an apple; only rarely did he eat lobster (he preferred chicken or pork chops, or even hamburger). During a Haven Club regatta, several sailors claimed that they could smell Ray Kendall frying hamburger aboard his lobster boat while he was pulling in his pots.

But whatever legend of the work ethic Ray represented, and

whatever griping was done on account of the evidence of his work with which Raymond Kendall preferred to surround himself, no fault could be found with his beautiful daughter—except the fault of her name, which was not her fault (who would ever have named herself a Candice, and therefore been a Candy to all?) and which everyone knew had been the name of her dead mother, and therefore was not the mother's fault, either. Candice "Candy" Kendall was named after her mother, who had died in childbirth. Raymond had named his daughter in memory of his departed wife, whom everyone had liked and who, in her day, had kept the environs of the lobster pound and the dock slightly better picked up. Who could find fault with any name that was given out of love?

You had only to know her to know that she was not a Candy; she was lovely, but never falsely sweet; she was a great and natural beauty, but no crowd-pleaser. She had daily reliability written all over her, she was at once friendly and practical—she was courteous, energetic, and substantial in an argument without ever being shrill. She complained only about her name, and she was always good-humored about it (she would never hurt her father's feelings—or anyone else's feelings, willingly). She appeared to combine her father's enraptured embrace of the work ethic with the education and the refinements he had allowed her—she took to both labor and sophistication with ease. If other girls at the Haven Club (or in the rest of Heart's Haven and Heart's Rock) were jealous of the attention young Wally Worthington gave to her, there was still no one who disliked her. If she'd been born an orphan, even at St. Cloud's, half the population *there* would have fallen in love with her.

Even Olive Worthington liked her, and Olive was suspicious of the girls who dated Wally; she questioned what they wanted from him. She could never forget how much she had wanted to get out of her life and into a Worthington's green and apple-bright existence at Ocean View, and this memory of her younger self gave Olive an eye for girls who might be more interested in the Ocean View life than they were interested in Wally. Olive knew this wasn't the case with Candy, who seemed to think that her own life above Ray Kendall's crawling, live-lobster pound was perfect; she was as fond of her father's orneriness as she was deservedly proud of his industry. She was well cared for by the latter. She wasn't looking for money, and she preferred taking Wally for an ocean swim—off her father's treacherous and crowded dock—to swimming in the Haven Club pool or in the Worthingtons' private swimming pool, where she knew she was welcome. In truth, Olive Worthington thought that Candy Kendall might be too good for her son, whom she knew to be rather unsettled, or at least *not* industrious—she would grant you he was charming and genuinely good-natured.

And then there was the uncertain pain that Candy caused in Olive's memory of her mother, Maud (frozen among her cosmetics and clams): Olive envied Candy her perfect love of *her* mother (whom she'd never seen); the girl's absolute goodness made Olive feel guilty for how much she despised her own origins (her mother's silence, her father's failure, her brother's vulgarity).

Candy worshiped at the little shrines to her mother that Raymond Kendall constructed—there were actual altarpieces assembled—all over the upstairs rooms of the lobster pound, where they lived above the gurgle of the lobster tank. And everywhere were gathered the photographs of Candy's young mother, many taken with Candy's young father (who was so unrecognizably youthful, whose smile was so unrecognizably constant in the pictures that Candy looked at Ray, at times, as if he were as much a stranger to her as her mother).

Candy's mother was said to have smoothed out Ray's rough edges. She'd had a sunny spirit, she'd kept on top of everything, she'd had the boundless energy that Raymond Kendall possessed for his work and Candy had in abundance for everything. On the coffee table, in the kitchen, alongside a disassembled magneto case and ignition system (for the Evinrude), was a triptych of pictures of Ray and Candice at their wedding, which had been the only time Ray Kendall had attended an event at the Haven Club when he was not dressed to repair something.

In Ray's bedroom, on the night table, next to the broken toggleswitch to the Johnson (the inboard Johnson; there was an outboard, too), was a picture of Candice and Ray—both in their oilskin slickers, both pulling pots, on a rough sea (and it was clear to anyone, especially to Candy, that Candice was pregnant *and* hard at work).

In her own bedroom, Candy kept the picture of her mother when her mother had been Candy's age (which was Homer

Wells's age, exactly): young Candice Talbot, of the Heart's Haven Talbots—the long-standing Haven Club Talbots. She was in a long white dress (for tennis, of all things!), and she looked just like Candy. The picture was taken the summer she met Ray (an older boy, strong and dark and determined to fix everything, to make everything *work*); if he had seemed a hick, or a little too serious, he was at least not grim about his ambitions, and alongside him the boys at the Haven Club had appeared as court dandies, as spoiled, upper-class fops.

Candy had her mother's blondness; it was darker than Wally's blondness—and much darker than her mother's and than Olive Worthington's former blondness. She had her father's dark skin and dark brown eyes, and her father's height. Ray Kendall was a tall man (a disadvantage for a lobsterman, and for a mechanic, he used to say good-naturedly, because of the strain on the lower back when pulling lobster pots—there is nearly constant lifting in that work—and because of a mechanic's need to crawl under and bend over things). Candy was extremely tall for a woman, which intimidated Olive Worthington—just a bit—but was felt by Olive as only a mild flaw in Olive's near-perfect satisfaction with Candy Kendall as the correct match for Wally.

Olive Worthington was fairly tall herself (taller than Senior, especially when Senior was staggering), and she looked in a somewhat unfriendly fashion upon everyone who was taller than she. Her son, Wally, was taller than she, too, which Olive still found difficult at times—especially when she desired to reprimand him.

"Is Candy taller than you, Wally?" she asked him once, a sudden alarm in her voice.

"No, Mom, we're exactly the same height," Wally told his mother. That was another thing that slightly bothered her about the two of them being together: they seemed so alike physically. Was their attraction to each other a form of narcissism? Olive worried. And since each of them was an only child, were they seeing in each other the brother or sister they always wanted? Wilbur Larch would have got along with Olive Worthington; she was a born worrier. Together they could have outworried the rest of the world.

They shared the concept that there *was* a "rest of the world," by which they meant the *whole* rest of the world—the world outside their making. They were both smart enough to know why they feared this other world so much: they fully understood that, despite their considerable efforts, they were only marginally in control of the worlds of their own delicate making.

When Candy Kendall and Wally Worthington fell in love with each other, in the summer of 194__, everyone in Heart's Haven and in Heart's Rock always knew they would—it was a wonder only that it had taken them this long to discover it themselves. For years, both towns had thought them perfect for each other. Even crusty Raymond Kendall approved. Ray thought Wally was unfocused, but that was not the same as lazy, and anyone could see the boy was good-hearted. Ray also approved of Wally's mother; he had a thorough liking for the way Olive Worthington respected work.

Everyone felt sorry for how out of it poor Senior seemed, how his drinking (they thought) had aged him overnight. "It won't be long, Alice, before the guy's pissing his pants in public," the charmless Bucky Bean said to Olive.

And Candy thought that Olive Worthington would be a perfect mother-in-law. When Candy dreamed of her own mother—grown older than she'd been allowed to grow in this life; grown naturally older in a better world—she always thought her mother would have aged to resemble Olive Worthington. Candy hoped, at least, that her mother would have managed Olive's refinement, if not perhaps her college-learned New British. Candy would be going to college in a year, she assumed, and she had no intentions of learning an accent there. But except for the accent, Candy thought Olive Worthington was wonderful; it was sad about Senior, but the man was certainly sweet.

So everyone was happy with this love affair that was as certain to become a marriage made in heaven as any love affair Heart's Haven and Heart's Rock had seen. It was understood that Wally would finish college first, and that Candy would be allowed to finish college—if she wanted to—before they got married. But with Olive Worthington's instincts for worry, one might have assumed that Olive would have foreseen the possible causes for a change of plans. After all, it was 194__; there was a war in Europe; there were many people who thought that more than Europe would be involved before long. But Olive had a mother's wish to keep war out of her mind.

Wilbur Larch had the war in Europe very much in his mind; he had been in the last war, and he foresaw that if there was another war, it might coincide with Homer Wells's being the right age to go. Since that would be the wrong age to be, the good doctor had already taken some pains to see that Homer Wells wouldn't have to go to a war, if there was one.

Larch was, after all, the historian of St. Cloud's; he wrote the only records that were kept there; he usually wrote the not-so-simple history of the place but he had tried his hand at fiction, too. In the case of Fuzzy Stone, for example—and in the other, very few cases of orphans who had died in his care—Wilbur Larch hadn't liked the actual endings, hadn't wanted to record the actual outcomes to those small, foreshortened lives. Wasn't it fair if Larch took liberties—if he occasionally indulged himself with happy endings?

In the case of the few who had died, Wilbur Larch made up a longer life for them. For example, the history of F. Stone read like a case study of what Wilbur Larch *wished* for Homer Wells. Following Fuzzy's most successful adoption (every member of the adoptive family was scrupulously described) and the most successful treatment and cure imaginable of Fuzzy's respiratory difficulties, the young man would pursue an education at none other than Bowdoin College (Wilbur Larch's own alma mater) and study medicine at Harvard Medical School—he would even follow Larch's footsteps to internships at Mass General and at the Boston Lying-In. Larch intended to make a devoted and skilled obstetrician out of Fuzzy Stone; the orphan's fictional history was as carefully done as everything Wilbur Larch did—allowing a possible exception for his use of ether, and Larch was especially pleased to note that some of his fictional history was more convincing than what had actually happened to some of the others.

Snowy Meadows, for example, would be adopted by a family in Bangor by the name of Marsh. Who would believe that a Meadows became a Marsh? Wilbur Larch was pleased with himself for making up better stories than that. The Marshes were in the furniture business, and Snowy (who had been unimaginatively named Robert) would attend the University of Maine only briefly before marrying some local flower and going into the Marsh family furniture business as a salesman.

"It's for keeps," Snowy would write Dr. Larch, about the girl who caused him to drop out of school. "And I really love the furniture business!"

Whenever he wrote to Dr. Larch, Snowy Meadows, alias

Robert Marsh, would always ask, "Say, what's happened to Homer Wells?" The next thing you know, Larch thought, Snowy Meadows will suggest a reunion! Larch grumbled to himself for days, trying to think of what to say to Snowy Meadows about Homer; he would have liked to brag about Homer's perfect procedure with the eclampsia patient, but Larch was aware that his training of Homer Wells—and the business of the Lord's work and the Devil's work in St. Cloud's—would not meet with everyone's approval.

"Homer is still with us," Larch would write to Snowy, ambiguously. Snowy is a sneaky one, Larch concluded—Snowy Meadows also never failed to ask, in each of his letters, about Fuzzy Stone.

"What's happening with Fuzzy, these days?" Snowy always asked, and Wilbur Larch would carefully check the history he had written for Fuzzy—just to keep Snowy up to date.

Larch ignored Snowy's requests for Fuzzy Stone's address. Dr. Larch was convinced that the young furniture salesman, Robert Marsh, was a dogged sort of fool, who—if he had any of the other orphans' addresses—would bother everyone about starting an Orphan Club or an Orphan Society. Larch even complained to Nurse Edna and to Nurse Angela about Snowy Meadows, saying, "I wish someone out of Maine had adopted *that* one, someone far away. That Snowy Meadows is so stupid, he writes to me as if I ran a boarding school! The next thing you know, he'll expect me to publish an alumni magazine!"

This was a somewhat unfeeling remark to make to Nurse Edna and to Nurse Angela, Larch realized later. These two dear but sentimental ladies would have jumped at the idea of an alumni magazine; they missed every orphan they ever gave away. If things were up to them, there would be reunions planned every year. Every *month*! Larch thought, and groaned.

He lay down in the dispensary. He thought about a slight modification he had been shrewd enough to make in the history of Homer Wells; he would tell Homer about it one day, if the situation demanded it. He was very pleased with himself for this slight fiction that he had so skillfully blended with the actual history of Homer Wells. Of course, he'd included nothing of the medical training; he had incriminated himself by what he'd written about the abortions, many times, but Larch knew well enough that Homer Wells should be left out of *that* written history. What Wilbur Larch had written about Homer

Wells was that the boy had a heart defect, a heart that was damaged and weakened from birth. Larch had even taken the trouble to make this the first entry about Homer, which necessitated his locating some older-looking paper and painstakingly revising, and retyping, all the earlier—and actual—history. But he managed to work in the heart defect in the correctly casual places. The reference was always vague and uncharacteristically lacking in medical precision; the words "defect" and "damaged" and "weakened" would not have convinced a good detective, or even a good doctor, whom Wilbur Larch imagined he might one day need to convince. In fact, he worried a little if he could convince Homer of it—given what the boy had learned. But Larch would face that if and when the situation arose.

The situation Larch was thinking of was war, the so-called war in Europe; Larch, and many others, feared that the war wouldn't stay there. ("I'm sorry, Homer," Larch imagined having to tell the boy. "I don't want you to worry, but you have a bad heart; it just wouldn't stand up to a war.") What Larch meant was that his own heart would never stand up to Homer Wells's going to war.

The love of Wilbur Larch for Homer Wells extended even to his tampering with history, a field wherein he was an admitted amateur, but it was nonetheless a field that he respected and also loved. (In an earlier entry in the file on Homer Wells—an entry that Dr. Larch removed, for it lent an incorrect tone of voice, or at least a tone of voice unusual for history—Dr. Larch had written: "I love nothing or no one as much as I love Homer Wells. Period.")

Thus Wilbur Larch was more prepared for how a war could change important plans than Olive Worthington was prepared for it. The other and more probable cause for a change in the wedding plans of her son and Candy Kendall—another way in which the young lovers' plans could be changed—*had* been foreseen by Olive. It was an unwanted pregnancy. A pity that it was not foreseen by either Candy or Wally.

Thus, when Candy got pregnant (she'd been a virgin, naturally), she and Wally were much distressed, but they were also surprised. Olive would have been distressed (had she known), but she wouldn't have been surprised. Getting pregnant would never have surprised Wilbur Larch, who knew that it happened, and happened by accident, all the time. But Candy

Kendall and Wally Worthington, so full of beauty and of the moment and of their own rightness for each other, simply couldn't believe it. They were not the sort of people who would have been ashamed or unable to tell their parents; they were simply stunned at the prospect of having to derail their perfect plans—of *having* to get married ahead of schedule.

Did Wally Worthington *need* a college degree to inherit his parents' apple orchard? Of course not. Did Candy Kendall *need* to go to college at all? She didn't. Wouldn't she refine herself, and educate herself, if left to her own means? Of course she would! And Wally wasn't much of a student, anyway, was he? Of course he wasn't. He was a botany major, but only at the insistence of his mother—Olive thought that the study of plants might stimulate her son to become more excited and more knowledgeable about apple-growing.

"It's just that we're not *ready,*" Candy said to Wally. "I mean, we aren't, are we? Do *you* feel ready?"

"I love you," Wally said. He was a brave boy, and true, and Candy—who had not cried a single tear at the surprising discovery that she was with child—loved him, too.

"But it's just not the right time for us, is it, Wally?" Candy asked him.

"I want to marry you, anytime," he said truthfully, but he added something that she hadn't thought of. *He* had thought of the war in Europe, even if his mother had missed it. He said, "What if there's a war—I mean, what if we get involved in it?"

"What if *what*?" said Candy, truly shocked.

"I mean, if we were at war, I'd go—I'd have to, I'd *want* to," Wally said. "Only, if there was a child, it wouldn't feel right—going to a war."

"When would it feel right to go to a war, Wally?" Candy asked him.

"Well, I mean, I'd just have to, that's all—if we had one," he said. "I mean, it's our country, and besides, for the experience—I couldn't miss it."

She slapped his face, she started to cry—in a rage. "For the *experience*! You'd want to go to war for the *experience*!"

"Well, not if we had a child—that's when it wouldn't feel right," Wally said. "Would it?" He was about as innocent as rain, and about as thoughtless.

"What about *me*?" Candy asked, still shocked—and shocked,

further, that she had slapped him. She put her hand very softly where his cheek was so red. "With or without a child, what would it be like for me if you went to a war?"

"Well, it's all 'What if,' isn't it?" Wally asked. "It's just something to think about," he added. "About the business of the child, especially—I think. If you see what I mean," he said.

"I think we should try *not* to have the baby," Candy told him.

"I won't have you going to one of those places where there's no real doctor," Wally said.

"Of course not," she agreed. "But aren't there any real doctors who do it?"

"It's not what I've heard," Wally admitted. He was too much of a gentleman to tell her what he'd heard: that there was a butcher in Cape Kenneth who did you for five hundred dollars. You went to a parking lot and put a blindfold around yourself and waited; you went alone. Someone picked you up and took you to the butcher; you were brought back when the butcher was through—you were blindfolded throughout. And what was worse, you had to appear absolutely hysterical in front of some fairly dignified and local doctor before the doctor would even tell you where the parking lot was and how you got in contact with the butcher. If you didn't act upset enough, if you weren't completely crazy, the doctor wouldn't put you in touch with the butcher.

That was the story Wally had heard, and he wanted no part of any of it for Candy. He doubted if Candy could act upset enough, anyway. Wally would have the baby instead of any of that; he'd marry Candy and be happy about it, too; it was what he wanted, one day, anyway.

The story Wally had heard was partially true. You did have to go to the fairly dignified and local doctor, and you did have to work yourself up into a frenzy, and if the doctor thought you were ready to drown yourself, only then would he tell you the location of the parking lot and how to approach the butcher. What Wally didn't know was the more human part of the story. If you were calm and collected and well-spoken and obviously sane, the doctor would skip the whole story about the parking lot and the butcher; if you looked like a reasonable woman—someone who wouldn't turn him in, later—the doctor would simply give you an abortion, right there in his office, for five hundred dollars. And if you acted like a nut, he also gave you an abortion—right there in his office—for five hundred dollars. The only difference was that you had to stand around blindfolded in a parking lot and *think* that you were being operated on by a butcher; that's what acting crazy got you. What was decidedly unjust, in either case, was that the doctor charged five hundred dollars.

But Wally Worthington was not seeking the correct information about that doctor, or that so-called butcher. He hoped to get advice about another abortionist, somewhere, and he had a vague plan concerning the people he'd ask. There was little point in seeking the advice of the members of the Haven Club; he'd been told that one member had actually taken a cruise to Sweden for an abortion, but that was out of the question for Candy.

Wally knew the orchardmen at Ocean View were the sort of men who might have need of a less extravagant remedy; he also knew that they liked him and that, with few exceptions, they could be trusted to keep what Wally thought was a reliable, manly confidence about the matter. He went first to the only bachelor on the orchard crew, supposing that bachelors (and this one was also a notorious ladies' man) might have more use for abortionists than married men. Wally approached a member of the apple crew named Herb Fowler, a man only a few years older than Wally—he was good-looking in a too-thin, too-cruel kind of way, with a too-thin moustache on his dark lip.

Herb Fowler's present girlfriend worked in the packinghouse during harvest; during the times of the year when the apple mart was open, she worked with the other mart women. She was younger than Herb, just a local girl, about Candy's age—her name was Louise Tobey, and the men called her Squeeze Louise, which was apparently okay with Herb. He was rumored to have other girlfriends, and he had the appalling habit of carrying lots of prophylactics on him—at all times of the day and night—and when anyone said anything at all about sex, Herb Fowler would reach into his pocket for a rubber and flip it at the speaker (all rolled up in its wrapper, of course). He'd just flip a prophylactic and say, "See these? They keep a fella free."

Wally had already had several rubbers flipped at him, and he was tired of the joke, and he was not in the best humor to have the joke played on him again in his present situation—but he imagined that Herb Fowler was the right sort of man to ask, that, despite the rubbers, Herb Fowler was always getting girls in trouble. One way or another, Herb looked·like trouble for every girl alive.

"Hey, Herb," Wally said to him. It was a rainy, late-spring day; college was out, and Wally was working alongside Herb in the storage cellar, which was empty in the spring. They were varnishing ladders, and when they finished the ladders, they would start painting the tracks for the conveyors that ran nonstop when the packinghouse was in full operation. Every year, everything was repainted.

"Yup, that's my name," Herb said. He kept a cigarette so fixedly drooped from his lips that his eyes were always squinted half shut, and he kept his long face tipped up and back so that he could inhale the trail of smoke through his nose.

"Herb, I was wondering," Wally said. "If you got a girl pregnant, what would you do about it. Knowing your view," Wally smartly added, "about keeping yourself free." That stole Herb's punch line and probably made Herb cross; he had a rubber half out of his pocket, ready to flip at Wally while delivering his usual remark on the subject, but Wally's saying it for him forced him to arrest the motion of his flipping hand. He never brought the rubber out.

"Who'd you knock up?" Herb asked, instead.

Wally corrected him. "I didn't say I'd knocked up anybody. I asked you what *you'd* do—*if.*"

Herb Fowler disappointed Wally. All he knew about was the same mysterious parking lot in Cape Kenneth—something about a blindfold, a butcher and five hundred dollars.

"Maybe Meany Hyde would know about it," Herb added. "Why don'tcha ask Meany what *he'd* do if *he* knocked anybody up?" Herb Fowler smiled at Wally—he was not a nice character—but Wally wouldn't satisfy him; Wally just smiled back.

Meany Hyde *was* a nice man. He'd grown up with a bunch of older brothers who beat him up and otherwise abused him steadily. His brothers had nicknamed him Meany—probably just to confuse him. Meany was ever-friendly; he had a friendly wife, Florence, who was one of the packinghouse and apple mart women; there had been so many children that Wally couldn't remember all their names, or tell one from the other, and therefore he found it hard to imagine that Meany Hyde even knew what an abortion was.

"Meany listens to everything," Herb Fowler told Wally. "Don'tcha ever watch Meany? What's he *do,* except listen."

So Wally went to find Meany Hyde. Meany was waxing the press boards for the cider press; he was generally in charge of the cider mill, and because of his nice disposition, he was often in charge of overseeing all the cider house activities—including the dealings with the migrant workers who lived in the cider house during the harvest. Olive made a point of keeping Herb Fowler at a considerable distance from those poor migrant workers; Herb's disposition was not so agreeable.

Wally watched Meany Hyde waxing for a while. The sharp but clean odor of the fermented cider and the old cider apples was strongest on a wet day, but Meany seemed to like it; Wally didn't mind it, either.

"Say, Meany," Wally said, after a while.

"I thought you forgot my name," Meany said cheerfully.

"Meany, what do you know about abortion?" Wally asked.

"I know it's a sin," Meany Hyde said, "and I know Grace Lynch has had one—and in her case, I sympathize with her—if you know what I mean."

Grace Lynch was Vernon Lynch's wife; Wally—and everyone else—knew that Vernon beat her. They had no children; it was rumored that this was the result of Vernon's beating Grace so much that Grace's organs of generation (as Homer Wells knew them) were damaged. Grace was one of the pie women during the harvest and when the apple mart was humming; Wally wondered if she'd be working today. There was lots to do in the orchards on a good day in late spring; but when it was raining, there was just painting and washing, or fixing up the cider house to get it ready for the harvest.

It was just like Meany Hyde to be waxing the press boards too early. Someone would probably tell him to wax them again, just before it was time for the first press. But Meany didn't like painting or washing up, and when it rained, he could kill whole days fussing over his beloved cider press.

"Who do you know needs an abortion, Wally?" Meany Hyde asked.

"A friend of a friend," Wally said, which would have prompted a rubber from Herb Fowler's pocket, but Meany was nice—he took no pleasure in anyone else's bad luck.

"That's a shame, Wally," Meany said. "I think you should speak to Grace about it—just don't speak to her when Vernon's around."

Wally didn't have to be told that. He had often seen the bruises on the backs of Grace Lynch's arms where Vernon had grabbed her and shook her. Once he had seized her by the arms and yanked her toward him, lowering his head in order to butt her in the face. This had happened, Wally knew, because Senior had paid for Grace's dental work (she'd told Senior and Olive that she'd fallen downstairs). Vernon had also beaten up a black man, one of the migrants, in the orchard called Old Trees, several harvests ago. The men had been telling jokes, and the black man had offered a joke of his own. Vernon hadn't liked a black man telling jokes that had anything to do with sex—he'd told Wally, in fact, that black people should be prevented from having sex.

"Or pretty soon," Vernon had said, "there'll be too many of them."

In the Old Trees orchard, Vernon had snapped the man off his ladder, and when the man picked himself off the ground, Vernon held both his arms and butted him in the face over and over again, until Everett Taft, who was one of the foremen, and Ira Titcomb, the beekeeper, had to pull Vernon off. The black man had taken over twenty stitches in his mouth, in his lips, and in his tongue; everyone knew Grace Lynch hadn't lost her teeth falling down any stairs.

It was Vernon who should have had Meany's name, or something worse.

"Wally?" Meany asked him, as he was leaving the cider house. "Don't tell Grace *I* told you to ask her."

So Wally went looking for Grace Lynch. He drove the pickup through the muddy lane that divided the orchard called Frying Pan, because it was in a valley, and was the hottest to work in, from the orchard called Doris, after someone's wife. He drove to the building called Number Two (it was simply the second building for keeping the larger vehicles; the sprayers were sheltered in Number Two because the building was more isolated, and the sprayers—and the chemicals that went inside them—stank). Vernon Lynch was painting in there; he had a spray gun with a long, needlelike nozzle and he was hosing down the Hardie five-hundred-gallon sprayer with a fresh coat of apple red. Vernon wore a respirator to protect himself from the paint fumes (it was the same mask the men wore when they sprayed the trees), and he wore his foul-weather gear—the complete oilskin suit. Wally somehow knew it was Vernon, although not a single feature of Vernon was visible. Vernon had a way of attacking his work that made his actions unmistakably his, and Wally noticed that Vernon was painting the Hardie as if he were wielding a flamethrower. Wally drove on; he didn't want to ask Vernon where his wife was today. Wally shuddered as he imagined several of Vernon's leering responses.

In the empty, off-season apple mart, three of the mart women were smoking cigarettes and talking. They didn't have much to do; and when they saw the boss's son coming, they didn't throw down their coffee cups, stamp out their cigarettes and disperse·in different directions. They just stepped a little away from one another and smiled at Wally sheepishly.

Florence Hyde, Meany's wife, didn't even pretend to be busy at anything; she dragged on her cigarette, and called out to Wally. "Hi, honey!"

"Hi, Florence," Wally said, smiling.

Big Dot Taft, who'd miraculously run a mile, getting stung all the while, the night Senior had dumped Ira Titcomb's bees, put out her cigarette and picked up an empty crate; then she put the crate down and wondered where she'd left her broom. "Hi, cutey," Dot said to Wally cheerfully.

"What's new?" Wally asked the women.

"Nothing new here," said Irene Titcomb, Ira's wife. She laughed and turned her face away. She was always laughing— and turning away the side of her face with the burn scar, as if she were meeting you for the first time and could keep the scar a secret. The accident had happened years ago, and there couldn't have been anyone in Heart's Haven or Heart's Rock who hadn't seen Irene Titcomb's scar and didn't know the exact details of how she got it.

One night Ira Titcomb had sat out in his yard all night with an oil torch and a shotgun; something had been getting into his hives—probably a bear or a raccoon. Irene had known this was Ira's plan, yet she was surprised when she woke up, hearing him calling her. He was on the lawn and waving the lit torch under her window; all she saw was the torchlight. He asked her to make him some bacon and eggs, if she wouldn't mind, because he was so bored waiting for whatever it was he intended to shoot that he'd gotten hungry.

Irene was humming to herself, watching the bacon fry, when Ira came to the kitchen window and tapped on the pane to find out if the food was ready. Irene was unprepared for the vision of Ira in his beekeeper suit, moving out of the darkness and into the faint light from the kitchen window with fire in his hands. She had seen her husband in his beekeeper suit many times, but she hadn't imagined that he'd be wearing it while he waited to shoot a bear or a coon. She'd never seen the way the suit glowed in firelight, or at night, either.

Ira had worn the suit because he'd imagined that his shotgun blast might rip into one of the hives and loose a few bees. He had no intention of scaring his wife, but poor Irene looked out the window and saw what she thought was a flaming white apparition! No doubt *this* was what had been molesting the hives! The ghost of a beekeeper of bygone days! It had probably killed poor Ira and was now coming for her! The frying pan flew up in her hands, splashing the hot bacon grease on her face. Irene was lucky she didn't blind herself. Oh, those at-home accidents! How they surprise you.

"Whatcha want, big boy?" Big Dot Taft asked Wally. The apple mart women teased and flirted with Wally endlessly; they thought he was gorgeous and a lot of fun, and these three had known him since he was a little boy.

"He wants to take us for a ride!" cried Irene Titcomb, still laughing—her face still turned away.

"Why don't you take us to a movie, Wally?" Florence Hyde asked him.

"Oh, God, what I wouldn't do for you, Wally," Dot Taft said, "if you took me to a movie!"

"Don't you want to make us happy, Wally?" Florence asked him, whining a little.

"Maybe Wally's going to *fire* us!" Irene Titcomb shrieked, and that broke up the three of them. Dot Taft roared so loud that Florence Hyde inhaled her cigarette the wrong way and began to cough, which made Dot roar some more.

"Is Grace here today?" Wally asked casually, when the women calmed down.

"Oh, God, he wants Grace!" Dot Taft said. "What's she got that we haven't got?"

Bruises, Wally thought. Broken bones, false teeth—certainly genuine aches and pains.

"I just want to ask her something," Wally said, smiling shyly—his shyness was deliberate; he handled himself very smoothly around the mart women.

"I'll bet she'll say 'No!' " Irene Titcomb said, giggling.

"No, everyone says 'Yes!' to Wally," Florence Hyde teased. Wally allowed the laughter to subside.

Then Dot Taft said, "Grace is cleaning the pie oven."

"Thank you, ladies," Wally said, bowing, blowing them kisses, backing away.

"You're bad, Wally," Florence Hyde told him. "You just came here to make us jealous."

"That Grace must have a hot oven," Dot Taft said, and this started more laughter and coughing.

"Don't get burned, Wally," Irene Titcomb called after him, and he left the mart women chattering and smoking at a higher pitch than when he'd found them.

He was not surprised that Grace Lynch had drawn the worst job for a rainy day. The other women sympathized with her, but she was not one of them. She stood apart, as if she were afraid everyone might suddenly turn on her and beat her as badly as Vernon did, as if the beatings she'd already survived had cost her the necessary humor for trading stories equally with Florence and Irene and Dot.

Grace Lynch was much thinner and a little younger than these women; her thinness was unusual among the regular women. Even Herb Fowler's girlfriend (Squeeze Louise) was heftier than Grace, and Dot Taft's kid sister, Debra Pettigrew—who was fairly regular in pie season, and when the assembly line to the packinghouse was running—even Debra had more flesh on her than Grace had.

And since she had needed new teeth, Grace was even tighter-lipped than usual; there was a grim concentration to the narrow line of her mouth. Wally couldn't remember ever seeing Grace Lynch laugh—and some form of yucking it up was essential to relieve the boredom of the life of the apple mart women. Grace was simply the cowed dog among them. She didn't look as if she took any pleasure from eating pie—or from eating anything at all. She didn't smoke, and in 194__ everyone smoked—even Wally. She was noise-shy and flinched around the machinery.

Wally hoped she was wearing long sleeves so that he wouldn't have to look at the bruises on her arms, but she was half in one of the deep shelves of the pie oven when Wally found her; she was wearing a long-sleeved shirt, but both sleeves were rolled up above her elbows to spare the shirt some of the oven-black. Wally startled her with her head in the oven, and half her body, too, and Grace made a little cry and banged one of her elbows against the door hinge as she withdrew in too much of a hurry.

"Sorry I scared you, Grace," Wally said quickly—it was hard to walk up on Grace without making her bump into something. She said nothing; she rubbed one elbow; she folded and unfolded her thin arms, hiding her very slight breasts or, by keeping her arms in constant motion, concealing her bruises. She wouldn't look Wally in the eye; as poised as Wally was, he always felt a terrific tension when he tried to talk with her; he felt she might suddenly run away from him or throw herself at him—either with her claws out, or kissing him with her tongue stabbing.

He wondered if she mistook his inescapable search for the new bruises on her body for a sexual interest; maybe that was part of the problem between them.

"That poor woman is just crazy," Ray Kendall had told Wally once; maybe that was all.

"Grace?" Wally asked, and Grace trembled. She was squeezing a wad of steel wool so tightly that the dirty suds streaked down one arm and wet the waist of her shirt and the bony hip of her denim work jeans. A single tooth, probably false, appeared out of her mouth and clenched a tiny piece of her lower lip. "Uh, Grace," Wally said. "I've got a problem."

She stared at him as if this news frightened her more than anything anyone had ever told her. She looked quickly away and said, "I'm cleaning the oven." Wally thought he might have to grab her to keep her from crawling back *in* the oven. He suddenly realized that all his secrets—that *anyone's* secrets—were entirely safe with Grace Lynch. There was absolutely nothing she dared to say, and no one in her life to tell it to—if she ever got up the courage.

"Candy is pregnant," Wally said to Grace, who wobbled as if a wind had come up—or the strong ammonia fumes of the oven cleaner had overpowered her. She looked at Wally again with her eyes as round as a rabbit's.

"I need advice," Wally said to her. It occurred to him that if Vernon Lynch saw him talking to Grace, Vernon would probably find that just cause for giving Grace another beating. "Please just tell me what you know, Grace," Wally said.

Grace Lynch spat it out from between her very tight lips. "Saint Cloud's," she hissed; it was a loud whisper. Wally thought it was someone's name—the name of a saint? Or else a kind of nickname for an exceptionally evil abortionist—St. Cloud's! Grace Lynch, it was clear, had no luck. If she'd been to an abortionist, wouldn't it have to be the worst abortionist one could imagine?

"I don't know the doctor's name," Grace confided, still whispering and not looking up at Wally anymore—she would never again look up at him. "The place is called Saint Cloud's, and the doctor's good—he's kinda gentle, he makes it okay." For her, this was virtually a sermon—at least a speech. "But don't make her go alone—okay, Wally?" Grace said, actually reaching out and touching him—but recoiling the instant she made contact, as if Wally's skin were hotter than the pie oven when it was fired up.

"No, I won't make her go alone, of course," Wally promised her.

"You ask for the orphanage when you get off the train," Grace said. She climbed back in the oven before he could thank her.

Grace Lynch had gone to St. Cloud's alone. Vernon hadn't even known she was going, or he would probably have beaten her for it. Since she'd been gone overnight, he'd beaten her for that, but perhaps it was a lesser beating by his standards.

Grace had arrived in the early evening, just after dark; as was customary, she'd not been housed with the expectant mothers; she'd been so jittery that Dr. Larch's sedation had not affected her very much and she'd been awake through the night, listening to everything. It had been before Homer's days as an apprentice, so if Homer had seen her, he would never remember her, and when—one day—Grace Lynch would see Homer Wells, she wouldn't recognize him.

She'd had the standard D and C at a proper and safe time in her pregnancy, and there'd been no complications—except in her dreams. There had never been any serious complications following any abortion Dr. Larch had ever performed, and no permanent damage from any of the operations—unless it was something so interior, so very much in the mind, that Dr. Larch couldn't have been responsible for it.

Still—though Nurse Edna and Nurse Angela had made her feel welcome, and Larch had been, as Grace had told Wally, gentle—Grace Lynch hated to think of St. Cloud's. It was not so much for her own experience, or because of her own trouble, but because of the atmosphere of the place in the long night she'd stayed awake. The dense air hung like a great weight, the disturbed river smelled like death, the cries of the babies were weirder than the cries of loons—and there were owls, and someone peeing, and someone walking around. There was a far-off machine (the typewriter), and a shout from another building—just one long wail (possibly, that had been Melony).

After Wally had visited with her, Grace balked at finishing the pie oven job. She felt sick to her stomach—it was like the cramps she'd had that time—and she went out to the apple mart and asked the women there if they'd finish the oven for her; she just didn't feel well, she said. Nobody teased Grace. Big Dot Taft asked her if she'd like a ride home, and Irene Titcomb and Florence Hyde (who had nothing to do, anyway) said they'd tackle the oven "in two shakes," as they say in Maine. Grace Lynch went to find Olive Worthington; she told Olive she wasn't feeling well and was going home early.

Olive was her usual kind self regarding the matter; when she saw Vernon Lynch later, she gave Vernon a glare—hard enough for Vernon to feel discomforted by it. He was cleaning the nozzle for the spray gun down at Number Two when Olive cruised past him in the faded pickup. Olive's look was such that Vernon wondered for a moment if he'd been fired, if that look was all the notice he was going to get. But the thought quickly passed, the way thoughts tended to pass through Vernon Lynch. He looked at the muddy tracks left by Olive's pickup and said something typical.

"Suck my dick, you rich bitch," Vernon Lynch said. Then he continued to clean out the spray-gun nozzle.

That night Wally sat on Ray Kendall's dock with Candy and told her what little he knew about St. Cloud's. He didn't know, for example, that there was an apostrophe. He'd not bothered to apply to Harvard; his grades weren't good enough to get him into Bowdoin; the University of Maine, where he was halfheartedly majoring in botany, hadn't taught him a thing about grammar.

"I knew it was an orphanage," Candy said. "That's all I knew."

It was clear to them both that no good excuse could be invented for their being gone overnight, so Wally arranged to borrow Senior's Cadillac; they would have to leave very early in the morning and return in the evening of the same day. Wally told Senior it was the best time of year to explore the coast, and maybe drive a little inland; the coast would have more tourists as the summer progressed, and inland it would get too hot for a comfortable drive.

"I know it's a workday," Wally told Olive. "What's one day matter, Mom? It's just to have a little adventure with Candy—just a day off."

Olive wondered if Wally would ever amount to anything.

Ray Kendall had his own work to worry about. He knew Candy would be happy to take a drive with Wally. Wally was a good driver—if a trifle fast—and the Cadillac, Ray knew better than anyone, was a safe car. Ray did all the work on it.

The night before their trip, Candy and Wally went to bed early, but each of them was awake through the night. Like most truly loving young couples, they found themselves worrying about what effect this experience would have on the other. Wally worried that an abortion would make Candy unhappy, or even uncomfortable with sex. Candy wondered if Wally would feel the same way about her after all this was over.

That same night Wilbur Larch and Homer Wells weren't sleeping either. Larch sat at the typewriter in Nurse Angela's office; through the window, he saw Homer Wells walking around outside, with an oil lamp in the darkness. What is the matter now? Larch wondered, and went to see what Homer was doing.

"I couldn't sleep," Homer told Larch.

"What is it this time?" Dr. Larch asked Homer.

"Maybe it's just an owl," said Homer Wells. The oil lamp didn't project very far into the darkness, and the wind was strong, which was unusual for St. Cloud's. When the wind blew out the lamp, the doctor and his assistant saw that they were backlit by the light shining from the window of Nurse Angela's office. It was the only light for miles around, and it made their shadows gigantic. Larch's shadow reached across the stripped, unplanted plot of ground, up the barren hillside, all the way into the black woods. Homer Wells's shadow touched the dark sky. It was only then that both men noticed: Homer had grown taller than Dr. Larch.

"I'll be damned," Larch muttered, spreading his arms, so that his shadow looked like a magician about to reveal something. Larch flapped his arms like a big bat. "Look!" he said to Homer. "I'm a sorcerer!"

Homer Wells, the sorcerer's apprentice, flapped his arms, too.

The wind was very strong and fresh. The usual density in the air above St. Cloud's had lifted; the stars shone bright and cold; the memory of cigar smoke and sawdust was missing from this new air.

"Feel that wind," said Homer Wells; maybe the wind was keeping him up.

"It's a wind coming from the coast," Wilbur Larch said; he sniffed, deeply, for traces of salt. It was a rare sea breeze, Larch was sure.

Wherever it's from, it's nice, Homer Wells decided.

Both men stood sniffing the wind. Each man thought: What is going to happen to me?

5/ Homer Breaks a Promise

The stationmaster at St. Cloud's was a lonely, unattractive man—a victim of mail-order catalogues and of an especially crackpot mail-order religion. The latter, whose publication took an almost comic book form, was delivered monthly; the last month's issue, for example, had a cover illustration of a skeleton in soldier's clothes flying on a winged zebra over a battlefield that vaguely resembled the trenches of World War I. The other mail-order catalogues were of a more standard variety, but the stationmaster was such a victim of his superstitions that his dreams frequently confused the images of his mail-order religious material with the household gadgets, nursing bras, folding chairs, and giant zucchinis he saw advertised in the catalogues.

Thus it was not unusual for him to be awakened in a night terror by a vision of coffins levitating from a picture-perfect garden—the prize-winning vegetables taking flight with the corpses. There was one catalogue devoted entirely to fishing equipment; the stationmaster's cadavers were often seen in waders or carrying rods and nets; and then there were the undergarment catalogues, advertising bras and girdles. The flying dead in bras and girdles especially frightened the stationmaster.

The most particularly crackpot aspect of the mail-order religion was its insistence on the presence of the growing numbers of the restless, homeless, unsaved dead; in areas of the world more populated than St. Cloud's, the stationmaster imagined that these luckless souls were crowding the sky. The arrival of Dr. Larch's "Clara" fitted ominously into the stationmaster's pattern of night terrors and contributed to his especially stricken appearance upon the arrival of every new train—although Larch had assured the moron that there would be no new bodies arriving for at least a year or two.

To the stationmaster, the notion of Judgment Day was as tangible as the weather. He hated the first train of the morning the most. It was the milk train; and in any weather, the heavy cans were covered with a cold sweat. The empty cans, which were put on the train, produced a kind of death knell, a hollow bonging noise, as they tapped the wooden station platform or were handed up the iron stairs. The first train of the morning was the mail train, too; although the stationmaster was eager for new catalogues, he never lost his fear of the mail—of what might be coming his way: if not another cadaver, sloshing in embalming fluid, then the monthly warning from the mail-order religion that Judgment Day was at hand (always sooner than it was last expected, and always with more terrifying verve). The stationmaster lived to be shocked.

A hole in a tomato could cause him to escalate his predawn bouts of feverish prayer; dead animals (of whatever cause) made him tremble—he believed the creatures' souls clogged the air he needed to breathe or were capable of invading his body. (They were certainly capable of contributing to his sleeplessness, for the stationmaster was as veteran an insomniac as Wilbur Larch and Homer Wells and was without the benefit of ether, youth or education.)

This time it was the wind that awakened him, he was sure; something like a bat was blown off-course and struck his house. He was convinced that a flying animal had died violently against his wall and that its rabid soul was circling around outside, seeking entry. Then the wind made a moaning sound as it funneled through the spokes of the stationmaster's bicycle. A sudden gust knocked the bicycle off its kickstand; it clattered on the brick path, its little thumb bell dinging feebly—as if one of the world's restless souls had failed in an attempt to steal it. The stationmaster sat up in bed and screamed.

He had been advised in the monthly mail-order religious publication that screaming was of some, if not certain, protection against homeless souls. Indeed, the stationmaster's scream was not without effect; its shrillness dislodged a pigeon from the eaves of the house, and (since no pigeon desires to fly at night) the bird hopped and scrabbled its way noisily across the stationmaster's roof looking for a quieter corner. The stationmaster lay on his back, staring straight up at his roof; he expected the wandering soul to descend at any moment upon him. The pigeon's coo was the cry of another tortured sinner, the stationmaster was sure. He got up and stared out of his bedroom window, his nightlight weakly illuminating the small plot he had recently tilled for his vegetable garden. The freshly turned earth shocked him; he mistook it for a ready grave. It gave him such a turn that he quickly dressed himself and tramped outside.

Another thing he had learned from his mail-order religion was that the souls of the dead cannot invade an active body. You mustn't be caught sleeping, or even standing still; that was the main thing. And so the stationmaster boldly set out for a brisk walk through St. Cloud's. He muttered threateningly at the would-be ghosts he saw everywhere. "Go away," he growled—at this building, at that sound, at every unclear shadow. A dog barked in one house. The stationmaster surprised a raccoon busy with someone's garbage, but live animals didn't bother him; he hissed at the coon and appeared satisfied when the coon hissed back. He chose to stay away from the abandoned buildings where, he remembered, that fat nightmare of a girl from the orphanage had caused so much damage. He knew that in *those* buildings the lost souls were both numerous and fierce.

He felt safer around the orphanage. Though he was frightened of Dr. Larch, the stationmaster became fairly aggressive in the presence of children and their imagined souls. Like most easily frightened people, the stationmaster was something of a bully when he perceived that he had the upper hand. "Damn kids," he muttered, passing the girls' division. He had trouble thinking of the girls' division without imagining doing terrible things with that great big ruffian-girl—the destroyer, he called her. He'd had more than one night terror regarding her; she was often the model of the many bras and girdles in his dreams. He paused only briefly by the girls' division, sniffing deeply—he thought he might catch some scent of Melony, the building wrecker—but the wind was too strong; the wind was everywhere. It is a Judgment Day wind! he thought, and walked quickly on. He was not going to stand still long enough for some terrible soul to enter him.

He was on the wrong side of the boys' division to see the lighted window in Nurse Angela's office, but he could look over the building, up the hillside, and see the light from the window illuminating the eroded, unplanted hill. He couldn't see where the light was coming from, and this disquieted him; it seemed eerie how a light from nowhere was making the stripped hill glow all the way into the black edge of the woods.

The stationmaster could have wept at his own timidity, but he cursed himself instead; so much of his sleep was lost to fear, and the first train of the morning was such an early train. For most of the year, the train arrived when it was still dark. And those women who were on it, sometimes . . . the stationmaster shuddered. Those women in the loose clothes, always asking where the orphanage was—some of them back the same evening, their faces like ash, the color of so many of the faces in the stationmaster's night terrors. Very nearly, he thought, the color of Clara's face, though the stationmaster didn't know her name. His one look at Clara had been so brief that it was unfair he should be doomed to see her so many times *since;* and each time, he saw more of her—in his dreams.

When the stationmaster heard what he thought were voices, he looked over the boys' division at the lit hillside above St. Cloud's, and that was when he saw the towering shadows of Wilbur Larch and Homer Wells—stretching, in the case of one, to the woods' dark edge and, in the case of the other, stretching into the sky. The two giant figures flapped their huge, hill-spanning arms; whipped by the wind, the stationmaster caught the word "sorcerer!" It was then he knew that he could walk, or even run, all night—but he would *not* escape, not this time. The last thought that the stationmaster had was that the time for him, and for all the world, had come.

/ / /

The next morning, the sea breeze still stirred St. Cloud's. Even Melony noticed it; her usual grouchiness was suspended— she had trouble waking up, although she'd passed a wakeful night. She'd had the impression that all night an animal was prowling the grounds of the girls' division, probably getting into the trash. And she'd been able to observe the two women walking up the hill from the train station in the predawn glow. The women were not speaking to each other—they probably didn't know each other; they had certainly guessed each other's circumstances. The women walked head down. They were both overdressed for the spring; Melony watched the wind press their baggy winter coats against the women's bodies. They don't *look* pregnant, Melony observed; she reminded herself to be on hand, at her favorite window, to watch the women heading down the hill for the evening train. With what they were giving up, Melony thought, one might expect their returning steps to be lighter; and, after all, they were heading downhill. But every time, the women walked more heavily down the hill than they had walked up it—it appeared they'd been given something to carry away with them. Their gait was quite the contrary from what one might expect in the gait of women who'd been, truly, scraped clean.

Scraped *not* so clean, maybe, Melony thought. Although Homer Wells had told her nothing, what trouble could exist that Melony couldn't see? Whatever there was that glimmered of wrong, that shone of mistake—of loss, of hope abandoned, of the grim choices that were possible—Melony had an eye expertly trained to see this, and more.

She'd not yet set foot outdoors but she could tell something different was in the wind. She could not see the body of the stationmaster; he had fallen in the weeds by the delivery entrance to the boys' division—which was little used; there was a separate delivery entrance for the hospital.

From his window-on-the-world, from Nurse Angela's office, Dr. Larch could not have seen the weeds where the stationmaster lay stiffening, either. And it was not the stationmaster's departed soul that troubled Larch that morning. He'd had other sleepless nights; sea breezes were rare, but he had felt them. There'd been a fight in the girls' division that had required some stitching in one girl's lip and in another girl's eyebrow, but Wilbur Larch wasn't worried about those girls. Homer Wells had done a very neat job with the lip; Larch had handled the eyebrow, which presented more of a problem with permanent scarring.

And the two women who were waiting for their abortions were very early in their respective pregnancies, and—in Nurse Edna's judgment—both seemed robust and sane. And there was an almost cheerful woman from Damariscotta—she'd just begun her contractions, which appeared perfectly normal; she'd had one previous delivery, very routine, and so Larch anticipated no difficulty with her. He was thinking he'd have Homer deliver the Damariscotta woman because it looked straightforward and because the woman, Nurse Angela had said, had taken a particular liking to Homer; she had talked up a storm to him every second he'd been around her.

So what's wrong? thought Wilbur Larch. Or if not wrong, different?

So what if the mail was late and the dining hall said there'd been no milk delivery? Larch didn't know—and wouldn't have cared—that the train station had been more than usually disorganized in the stationmaster's absence; he didn't know that the stationmaster was missing. Wilbur Larch had noticed no disturbance among the souls crowding the sky above St. Cloud's. With the work he felt was his calling, Dr. Larch could not afford too rigorous a contemplation of the soul.

Previous to this morning, Homer Wells had not been presented with an occasion to contemplate the soul. A study of the soul had not been a part of his training. And since there were no windows in the room where Homer conducted his studies of Clara, it was not the stationmaster—or his soul—that suddenly presented itself to Homer Wells.

Dr. Larch had asked Homer to prepare a fetus for an autopsy.

A woman from Three Mile Falls had been stabbed, or she had stabbed herself; this was not unusual in Three Mile Falls but the pregnancy of the woman was nearly full-term—and the possibility of delivering a live baby from the dead woman had been unusual, even for Dr. Larch. He had attempted to rescue the child but the child—or, rather, the embryo, nearly nine months—had not escaped one of the stab wounds. Like its mother, the child (or the fetus, as Dr. Larch preferred) had bled to death. It would have been a boy—that much was clear to Homer Wells, or even to the untrained eye; whatever one called it, it was very nearly a fully developed baby. Dr. Larch had asked Homer to help him determine (more exactly than "bled to death") the source of the fetus's bleeding.

Homer Wells borrowed Dr. Larch's sternum shears before he realized that a pair of heavy scissors was all he needed to open the fetus's sternum. He cut straight up the middle, noticing immediately the slashed pulmonary artery; to his surprise, the wound was less than half an inch away from a wide-open ductus—in the fetus, the ductus arteriosus is half the size of the aorta, but Homer had never looked inside a fetus before; in the *born,* within ten days, the ductus becomes nothing but a fibrous thread. This change is initiated not by any mystery but by the first breath, which closes the ductus and opens the lungs. In the fetus, the ductus is a shunt—the blood bypasses the lungs on its way to the aorta.

It should not have been a shock for Homer Wells to see the evidence that a fetus has little need for blood in its lungs; a fetus doesn't breathe. Yet Homer was shocked; the stab wound, at the base of the ductus, appeared as a second eye alongside the little opening of the ductus itself. The facts were straightforward enough: the ductus was wide open because this fetus had never taken its first breath.

What was the life of the embryo but a history of development? Homer attached a tiny, needle-nosed clamp to the severed pulmonary artery. He turned to the section in *Gray's* devoted to the embryo. It was another shock for him to remember that *Gray's* did not begin with the embryo; it ended with it. The embryo was the last thing considered.

Homer Wells had seen the products of conception in many stages of development: in rather whole form, on occasion, and in such partial form as to be barely recognizable, too. Why the old black-and-white drawings should have affected him so strongly, he could not say. In *Gray's* there was the profile view of the head of a human embryo, estimated at twenty-seven days old. Not quick, as Dr. Larch would be quick to point out, and not recognizably human, either: what would be the spine was cocked, like a wrist, and where the knuckles of the fist (above the wrist) would be, there was the ill-formed face of a fish (the kind that lives below light, is never caught, could give you nightmares). The undersurface of the head of the embryo gaped like an eel—the eyes were at the sides of the head, as if they could protect the creature from an attack from any direction. In eight weeks, though still not quick, the fetus has a nose and a mouth; it has an expression, thought Homer Wells. And with this discovery—that a fetus, as early as eight weeks, has an *expression*—Homer Wells felt in the presence of what others call a soul.

He displayed the pulmonary artery of the baby from Three Mile Falls in a shallow, white enamel examining tray; he used two clamps to hold the chest incision open, and one more clamp to lift and expose the lacerated artery. The baby's cheeks appeared deflated; someone's invisible hands appeared to press its small face at its sides; it lay on its back, resting on its elbows—its forearms held stiffly perpendicular to its chest. The tiny fingers of its hands were slightly open—as if the baby were preparing to catch a ball.

Homer Wells did not care for the tattered appearance of the stump of the umbilical cord, which was also too long; he clipped it again, and tied it off neatly. There was a little caked blood on the tiny penis, and Homer cleaned this away. A spot of old blood on the bright white edge of the enamel tray came off easily with just a cotton swab dabbed with alcohol. The color of the dead baby, especially against the whiteness of the tray, was of something sallow-going-gray. Homer turned to the sink and vomited rather deftly in it. When he ran the faucet to clean the sink, the old pipes pounded and howled; he thought it was the pipes, or his dizziness, that made the room—the whole building—tremble. He wasn't thinking about the wind from the coast—how strong it was!

He wasn't blaming Dr. Larch, either. Homer felt there was nothing as simple as anyone's fault involved; it was not Larch's fault—Larch did what he believed in. If Wilbur Larch was a saint to Nurse Angela and to Nurse Edna, he was both a saint and a father to Homer Wells. Larch knew what he was doing—and for whom. But that quick and not-quick stuff: it didn't work for Homer Wells. You can *call* it a fetus, or an embryo, or the products of conception, thought Homer Wells, but whatever you call it, it's alive. And whatever you do to it, Homer thought—and whatever you call what you do—you're killing it. He looked at the severed pulmonary artery, which was so perfectly displayed in the open chest of the baby from Three Mile Falls. Let Larch call it whatever he wants, thought Homer Wells. It's his choice—if it's a fetus, to him, that's fine. It's a baby to me, thought Homer Wells. If Larch has a choice, I have a choice, too.

He picked up the spotless tray and carried it into the hall, like a proud waiter carrying a special dish to a favorite guest. Curly Day, forever snot-nosed, was cruising in the corridor between the dispensary and Nurse Angela's office. He was not allowed to be playing there, but Curly Day had a bored-every-minute look about him; he had the attention span of a rabbit. At the moment, Curly was dragging a cardboard carton through the corridor. It was the carton the new enema bags had come in; Homer recognized the carton because he had unpacked it.

"Whatcha got?" Curly Day asked Homer, who held the tray and the dead baby from Three Mile Falls at shoulder level;

Curly Day came up to Homer's waist. When Homer got close to the carton, he saw that it was not empty; David Copperfield, Junior, was in the bottom of the carton—Curly Day was giving him a ride.

"Get out of here, Curly," Homer said.

"Gomer!" cried David Copperfield.

"It's *Homer,* you idiot," Curly Day said.

"Gomer!" David Copperfield cried.

"Get out of here, please," Homer told them.

"Whatcha got?" Curly asked Homer. He reached upward, for the edge of the tray, but Homer picked off his dirty little hand; he grabbed Curly at the wrist and twisted Curly's arm behind his back. Homer balanced the tray and its contents expertly; Curly Day tried to struggle.

"Ow!" Curly cried. David Copperfield tried to stand up in the bottom of the carton, but he lost his balance and sat down.

Homer lifted Curly Day's arm behind his back—just slightly higher than the right-angle mark—which caused Curly to bend over and rest his forehead on the edge of the enema-bag carton. "Cut it out," Curly said.

"You're leaving, Curly—right?" Homer asked.

"Yeah, yeah," Curly said, and Homer let him go. "Tough guy," Curly said.

"Right," said Homer Wells.

"Gomer!" David Copperfield managed to say.

Curly Day wiped his nose on his disheveled sleeve. He jerked the carton so suddenly that David Copperfield rolled on his side. "Ack!" little Copperfield cried.

"Shut up," Curly said to his cargo. He shuffled away from Homer Wells, to whom he gave a look of peevish sorrow, of aimless complaint—nothing more. His body bobbed from side to side as he made his way with the carton containing David Copperfield. Homer noted that Curly's shoes were on the wrong feet, and one of them was untied, but he decided it would be unworthy criticism to mention this to Curly, who was as buoyant as he was messy—and wasn't his buoyancy more important than his carelessness, especially since he was an orphan?

"Good-bye, Curly," Homer said to the boy's slouched back; Curly's untucked shirt hung to his knees.

"See ya, Homer," Curly said, keeping his face turned away. When he passed the dispensary door, Nurse Edna appeared and scolded him.

"You're not supposed to be playing here, Curly," she said.

"Yeah, yeah," Curly said. "I'm going, I'm going."

"Medna!" David Copperfield cried in a muffled voice from the bottom of the enema-bag carton.

"It's *Edna,* you little scum," Curly said.

Then Homer was at the door of Nurse Angela's office, which was open. He could see Dr. Larch at the typewriter; the doctor wasn't writing; there wasn't even any paper in the machine. Dr. Larch was just looking out the window. In the doctor's trancelike expression Homer recognized the peaceful distance that ether provided in those moments when Homer had found the doctor "just resting" in the dispensary. Perhaps the state of mind that ether occasionally allowed Dr. Larch to enjoy was, increasingly, a state of mind that Larch could summon by just looking out a window. Homer assumed that Dr. Larch used a little ether because he was in some kind of pain; he suspected that almost everyone in St. Cloud's was in some kind of pain, and that Larch, as a doctor, was especially qualified in remedying it. The smell of ether was so cloying and nauseating to Homer Wells that it was no remedy he would have chosen. It hadn't yet occurred to him: what an addiction was. The state of a dream was so present on Wilbur Larch's face that Homer Wells paused in the doorway before continuing his gruesome presentation; he almost turned around and took the baby from Three Mile Falls away with him.

But no one encounters the presence of a soul so casually that one can permit the accompanying sense of mission to pass without remarking upon it; and a sense of mission usually requires a gesture more demonstrative than a passing remark. In the doorway of Nurse Angela's office, Homer hesitated; then he stepped forward and clunked the metal tray down on top of the typewriter. The dead baby from Three Mile Falls was level with Dr. Larch's throat—it was close enough to bite, as they say in Maine.

"Doctor Larch?" Homer Wells said. Larch looked away from his dream; he stared over the baby at Homer. "The source of the bleeding was the pulmonary artery, which was completely severed—as you see," Homer said, as Larch looked down at the display upon the typewriter. He stared at the baby as if it were something he'd written—come to life (and then to death) at his bidding.

Outside the hospital, someone was screaming, but the wind

whipped the words to a muddle; the screamer's message sounded confused.

"Goddamn!" said Wilbur Larch, staring at the severed artery.

"I have to tell you that I *won't* perform an abortion, not ever," Homer Wells said. This followed, logically, from the severed artery; in Homer's mind, it followed, but Dr. Larch looked confused.

"You won't?" Larch said. "You *what?*"

Outside, the screaming was louder but no more distinct. Homer Wells and Dr. Larch just stared at each other—the baby from Three Mile Falls occupying the space between them.

"I'm coming, I'm coming," they heard Nurse Angela say.

"It's that Curly Day," Nurse Edna was explaining to Nurse Angela. "I just had to kick him and the Copperfield kid out of here."

"Not ever," Homer Wells said.

"You disapprove?" Dr. Larch asked Homer.

"I don't disapprove of you," Homer Wells said. "I disapprove of *it*—it's not for me."

"Well, I've never forced you," Dr. Larch said. "And I never will. It's all your choice."

"Right," said Homer Wells.

A door opened, but what Curly Day was caterwauling about was no clearer. Dr. Larch and Homer Wells heard the test tubes in the rack by the dispensary door tinkle; over these chimes, and for the first time holding its own with the wind, the word "Dead!" came through to them.

"Dead! Dead! Dead!" Curly Day was screaming, his announcement punctuated by the unintelligible, monosyllabic utterances of young Copperfield.

"Who's dead, dear?" Nurse Angela asked Curly sweetly.

Curly Day had discovered that the stationmaster was dead; Curly didn't know it was the stationmaster—Curly hadn't taken a long enough look.

"A guy is dead!" Curly said to Nurse Angela and Nurse Edna.

Wilbur Larch, who heard this distinctly, got up from the desk and walked past Homer Wells, into the hall.

"And if it's all the same to you," Homer Wells said to him, "I'd like permission to *not* be there, when you do what you have to do. I want to be of use in any other way, and I'm not disapproving of you," Homer said. "If it's okay, I just don't want to watch it."

"I'll have to think about that, Homer," Dr. Larch said. "Let's see who's dead, shall we?" As Homer followed Larch down the hall, he noted that the door to the delivery room was closed, and that the door light was on—which meant that Nurse Edna or Nurse Angela had prepared the two women who were waiting for their abortions. The woman from Damariscotta, whose contractions were still slow and regular, probably wouldn't be needing the delivery room until long after Larch was through the two abortions. Homer agreed with Dr. Larch that it was cruel to make the women waiting for the abortions wait any longer than was necessary, especially after they'd been prepared, and so Homer opened the delivery room door and poked his head inside without really looking at either woman. He announced, "The doctor will be right with you— please don't worry."

Homer Wells regretted his timing; before he could close the delivery room door, Curly Day began his "Dead!" chant all over again.

Curly Day possessed the kind of restlessness that would always lead him to unwanted discoveries. He had tired of dragging David Copperfield around in the enema-bag carton, and therefore he had conceived of launching young Copperfield (in the carton) off the loading platform at the boys' division delivery entrance. It had been a struggle to get the carton and Copperfield up the ramp; but once elevated above the little-used driveway and the tall weeds, Curly imagined that Copperfield might be taught how to almost fly. Surely it wasn't such a high drop; in the carton, especially, it wouldn't be much of a fall. And the weedy hill that sloped away from the loading platform would probably allow the enema-bag carton to slide. Curly did foresee the possible damage to the carton—the destruction of which would leave him in the company of David Copperfield, all alone, and the prospect of Copperfield without a carton or another plaything was powerfully boring. But Curly was already tired of the possible uses of Copperfield *with* (or *in*) the carton; he had exhausted the safe things there were to do, and Copperfield was not complaining. Copperfield didn't know he was on the brink of the loading platform; he couldn't see over the sides of the carton. When Curly pushed the carton and Copperfield over the edge, he was careful to keep the carton in an upright position, thus preventing Copperfield from landing on his head. The carton landed on one corner, which collapsed; and young Copperfield was propelled down the bank of tall weeds. Like an unsteady chick staggering out of its shell, he came briefly to his feet before he fell and rolled, again and again. From the platform, Curly Day watched the weeds waving at him; if the weeds indicated Copperfield's whereabouts, they were too tall for Curly to actually see Copperfield.

Copperfield was not injured, but he was disoriented. He couldn't see Curly, and he couldn't see the carton—which he'd grown rather fond of. When he stopped rolling, he tried to stand, but dizziness, in combination with the uneven ground, unbalanced him, and he sat down. What he sat on was something hard and round, like a stone, but when he looked at what it was, he saw it was the stationmaster's head—face up, eyes open, a strangely accepting terror in the frozen expression.

An older child, or even an adult, might have been upset at sitting on the dead stationmaster's face, but young David Copperfield viewed it much as he viewed the rest of the world: with more curiosity than surprise. However, when he touched the face and felt its coldness, the correctness of the child's sensibilities was apparent: the coldness was surely wrong. Young Copperfield leaped away, rolled, came to his feet, ran, fell, rolled again. Finally on his feet, he began to yelp like a dog. Curly Day began to track him through the tall weeds.

"Hang on, hang on, don't get excited!" Curly called to the boy, but Copperfield ran and fell in circles, barking strangely. "Stay in one place so I can find you!" Curly yelled. He stepped on something that rolled under his shoe; it felt like a freshly fallen branch that had not yet settled into the ground; it was the stationmaster's arm. In an attempt to catch his balance, Curly put his hand on the stationmaster's chest. The wide-eyed, unflinching face, which the tall weeds sheltered from the wind, stared past Curly, undisturbed. And then, in the plot of weeds, there were two barking dogs, who moved as if trapped in a maze. It was a testimony to something basically brave and responsible in Curly Day that the boy did not bolt from the weeds until he found David Copperfield.

Melony, at her window, watched the inexplicable thrashing through the weeds; at any time, she could have yelled out to Curly Day and told him the whereabouts of David Copperfield— she could see by the movement of the weeds which yelping animal was where. But she let them fend for themselves. Only when Curly Day was dragging young Copperfield up the drive-way, around the boys' division toward the hospital entrance, did Melony feel inclined to comment.

"Hey, Curly, your shoes are on the wrong feet!" Melony called. "You jerk!" But the wind was too strong. Curly couldn't hear her; she couldn't hear what Curly was yelling. She spoke just one more word out the window, to no one in particular; she felt that the wind allowed her to say exactly what she felt, from the heart, as loudly as she chose, although she did not even bother to speak loudly. "Boring," she said.

But things became more interesting to Melony when Wilbur Larch and Homer Wells—and Nurse Edna and Nurse Angela—appeared in the driveway by the boys' division delivery en-trance. They were clearly searching the plot of tall weeds.

"What are you looking for?" Melony yelled out the window, but either the noise of the wind or the intentness with which the searchers plunged through the weeds caused her question to be ignored. She decided to go see for herself.

Melony felt uneasy about the way this day was developing, but at the same time she felt grateful that something seemed to be happening—that anything at all was happening was vaguely all right with Melony.

This was not a feeling shared by either Candy Kendall or Wally Worthington, who for the last three hours had main-tained an awkward silence—their sense of anticipation was too keen to conceal with conversation. It had still been dark when they'd left the coast at Heart's Haven and ventured inland—away from the wind, although the wind was still surprisingly strong. Wally had studied the map so excessively the night before that the white Cadillac moved as purposefully away from the sea as an oyster or its pearl washing resolutely ashore. It was really too windy, even inland, for the top to be down, but Wally preferred the Cadillac when it was a proper convert-ible, and also—with the top down, with the rush of the wind so noisily in the car—the absence of conversation between him and Candy was less obtrusive. Candy preferred it, too; her honey-blond hair was all around her face—such wild swirls of hair surrounded her face at times that she knew Wally couldn't see her expression. Wally knew what her expression was, any-way; he knew her very well.

Wally glanced at the unread book in Candy's lap; she picked it up to read every so often, but when she returned the book to her lap, the same page was dog-eared. The book was *Little Dorrit* by Charles Dickens. It was required summer reading for all the girls in Candy's would-be graduating class; Candy had begun it four or five times, but she had no idea what the book was about, or whether she even liked it.

Wally, who was no reader, didn't bother to notice the name of the book; he just watched the same dog-eared page and thought about Candy. He was also thinking about St. Cloud's. He was already (in his mind) through the abortion; Candy was recovering nicely; the doctor was telling jokes; all the nurses were laughing. There were enough nurses to win a war, in Wally's imagination. All of them were young and pretty. And the orphans were amusing little tykes, with the appropriate gaps in their toothy smiles.

In the trunk of Senior Worthington's gliding Cadillac, Wally had three apple crates crammed full of goodies for the orphans. If it had been the proper season, he would have brought them apples and cider; in the spring there weren't any fresh apples, and there wasn't any cider, but Wally had provided the next best thing—in his opinion. He had loaded the Cadillac with jars and jars of the Worthingtons' best apple-cider jelly and crab-apple jelly, and with half-gallon jugs of Ira Titcomb's best apple-blossom honey. He imagined arriving for this abortion like Santa Claus (an unfortunate image, if one considered Wilbur Larch's memory of the abortion place "Off Harrison").

Wally imagined that Candy was sitting up after her abortion, with that relief on her face of someone who had just had a nasty splinter removed; oddly, Wally populated the abortion room itself with the aura of celebration one associates with the birth of a *welcome* child. The air of Wally's wishful thinking was rich with congratulation—and through the lighthearted scene traipsed the cute waifs of St. Cloud's, each with his or her own jar of jelly. Little honey-carriers, as happy as bear cubs!

Candy closed her book and returned it to her lap again, and Wally felt he had to say something.

"How's the book?" he said.

"I don't know," Candy said, and laughed.

He pinched her thigh; something caught in his throat when he tried to laugh with her. She pinched his thigh in return—a pinch of the exact same passion and pressure as the one he'd given her. Oh, how relieved he was that they were so alike!

Through the ever-poorer, gawking towns, as the sun rose and rose, they drove like lost royalty—the oyster-white Cadillac with its dazzling passengers was a head-turner. That scarlet upholstery, so curiously mottled by Senior's accident with the chemicals, was unique. Everyone who saw them pass would not forget them.

"Not much farther," Wally said. This time he knew better than to pinch her thigh; he simply let his hand rest in her lap, near *Little Dorrit*. Candy put her hand on top of his, while Melony—stalking through the girls' division lobby with more than usual purpose—caught Mrs. Grogan's generous and watchful eye.

"What's going on, dear?" Mrs. Grogan asked Melony.

"I don't know," Melony said, shrugging. "You can bet it ain't a new boy in town, or nothing," which was a mild remark for Melony; Mrs. Grogan thought, How the girl has mellowed. She *had* mellowed—a little. A *very* little.

Something about the big young woman's determination made Mrs. Grogan follow her outside. "My, what a wind!" Mrs. Grogan exclaimed. Where have *you* been? Melony thought, but she didn't utter a word; the degree that she had mellowed could be confused with not caring much anymore.

"It's the stationmaster," said Homer Wells, who was the first to find the body.

"That moron!" Wilbur Larch muttered.

"Well, he's dead, anyway," Homer informed Dr. Larch, who was still struggling through the weeds, en route to the body. Dr. Larch refrained from saying that by dying in this manner the stationmaster was intending a further inconvenience to the orphanage. If Wilbur Larch was mellowing, he was also mellowing very little.

St. Cloud's was not a place that mellowed you.

Homer Wells looked over the weeds that concealed the dead stationmaster and saw Melony striding toward him.

Oh, please! he felt his heart say to him. Oh, please, let me *leave*! The powerful wind swept his hair away from his face; he leaned his chest into the wind, as if he stood on the deck of a ship heading into the wind, slicing through the waves of an ocean he'd not yet seen.

/ / /

Wilbur Larch was thinking about the weak heart he had invented for Homer Wells. Larch was wondering how he should tell Homer about having a weak heart without frightening the young man or reminding him of the vision frozen upon the face of the stationmaster. What in Hell had that fool imagined he'd seen? Dr. Larch wondered, as he helped the others lug the stationmaster's stiffened body to the hospital entrance.

Curly Day, who enjoyed being kept busy, had already been sent to the railroad station; young Copperfield had gone with him, which slowed Curly down considerably—yet Curly was grateful for the company. Curly was slightly confused about the message he was sent to deliver, and Copperfield at least presented Curly with a model listener. Curly practiced the message he thought he was supposed to deliver by saying it aloud to David Copperfield; the message had no visible effect on Copperfield, but Curly found the repetition of the message soothing and the practice helped him to understand it, or so he thought.

"The stationmaster is dead!" Curly announced, dragging Copperfield down the hill—Copperfield's head either nodding agreement or just bouncing loosely between the boy's jerking shoulders. The downhill pace was hard for Copperfield, whose balance wasn't the best, and his left hand (grasped in Curly Day's hand) was pulled high above his left ear.

"Doctor Larch says he had a heart attack for several hours!" Curly Day added, which didn't sound quite right to him, but after he repeated it a few times it sounded more reasonable. What Larch had said was that the stationmaster appeared to have had a heart attack several hours ago, but Curly's version felt more or less correct to Curly—the more he said it.

"Tell the relatives and friends that there's soon gonna be an automobile!" said Curly Day, and David Copperfield bobbed in agreement. This didn't sound right to Curly, either, no matter how many times he repeated it, but he was sure he'd been told to say something like that. The word was "autopsy," not "automobile"; Curly had part of the word right. Perhaps, he thought, there was some special car coming to carry the dead. It made a little sense, and a little sense was sense enough for Curly Day—and more sense than Curly saw in most things.

"Dead!" David Copperfield cried happily as they approached the train station. Two of the usual oafs were lounging on the bench that faced away from the tracks; they were the sort of louts who hung around the station all day, as if the station were a house of beautiful women and the women were known to grant favors to all the town's untidy and unemployed. They paid no attention to Curly Day and David Copperfield. ("Dead!" David Copperfield called out to them, with no effect.)

The assistant to the stationmaster was a young man who had modeled his particularly unlikable officiousness upon the officiousness of the stationmaster, so that he had a completely inappropriate old-fart, complaining, curmudgeonly aspect to his youthfulness—this in combination with the mean-spiritedness of a dogcatcher who enjoys his work. He was a stupid young man, who shared with the stationmaster an aspect of the bully: he would holler at children to keep their feet off the benches, but he would simper before anyone better dressed than himself and he tolerated any rudeness from anyone who had any advantage over him. He was without exception cold and superior to the women who got off the train and asked for directions to the orphanage, and he had not once taken the arm of even one of those women and offered his assistance when they mounted the stairs to the return train; and that first step was a high one—many of the women who'd been scraped clean had obvious trouble with that first step.

This morning the stationmaster's assistant was feeling especially virtuous and disagreeable. He had given fifteen cents to one of the louts to go to the stationmaster's house and find him, but the clod had returned with no more information than that the stationmaster's bicycle had fallen over and been left where it had fallen. Ominous, thought the assistant, but frustrating. He was half irritated at having to do the stationmaster's chores, which he'd done poorly, and half thrilled at the prospect of being in charge. When he saw those two dirty urchins from the orphanage crossing the main road in front of the station and coming his way, the stationmaster's assistant felt his authority swell. Curly Day, wiping his nose on one arm, dragging David Copperfield with the other, seemed on the verge of speaking, but the stationmaster's assistant spoke first.

"Beat it," he said. "You don't belong here."

Curly halted; young Copperfield collided with him and staggered from the suddenness of the collision. Curly fully believed he "belonged" nowhere, but he gathered his confidence and delivered, quite loudly, his rehearsed message: "The stationmaster is dead! Doctor Larch says he had a heart attack for several hours! Tell the relatives and friends that there's soon gonna be an automobile!"

Even the oafs took notice. The assistant was stricken by a flood of sudden and conflicting feelings: that the stationmaster was dead might mean that he, the assistant, would be the next stationmaster; that it was possible for someone to suffer a heart attack lasting several hours was unimaginably painful; and what was this promise—or threat—about an automobile?

What relatives, what friends? the two louts wondered.

"What's that about an automobile?" the assistant asked Curly Day. Curly suspected that he'd made a mistake but decided to bluff it out. It was not advisable to display weakness or indecision before a bully, and Curly's crafty instincts for survival led him to choose confidence over the truth.

"It means there's a car coming for him," said Curly Day. The two clods looked mildly impressed; they had not thought the stationmaster was important enough to warrant a car to carry him away.

"You mean a hearse?" asked the assistant. There was a hearse in Three Mile Falls—he had seen it once: a long, black car that moved slowly enough to have been pulled by mules.

"I mean a car," said Curly Day, for whom the word "hearse" meant nothing at all. "I mean an *automobile*."

No one moved, no one spoke; perhaps the symptoms of the special heart attack, reputed to last for several hours, were slowly beginning in all of them. They were all just waiting for the next event of the day, when Senior Worthington's oyster-white Cadillac crept into view.

In the many poor and isolated towns they had driven through, Wally and Candy had drawn more than their share of stares, but they were still unprepared for the stunned gaping of the stationmaster's assistant and the extremes of gawking they provoked from the two louts who sat on the bench in front of the station house as if they'd been nailed there.

"Here we are: Saint Cloud's," Wally said to Candy with a clearly false enthusiasm. Candy could not help herself; she reached for his leg and gripped him at midthigh—*Little Dorrit* plunged from her lap, grazing her locked-together ankles on its way to the Cadillac's floor. The faces of Curly Day and David Copperfield were what struck Candy with the most force. In spite of his grime and dishevelment, Curly Day's face was shining—his smile was a lucky beam of sunlight; it pierced the garbage and revealed the hidden glitter. It was the hugeness of the expectation in Curly's dirty face that took Candy's breath away; her eyes swam, her vision blurred—but not before the wide-openness of David Copperfield's mouth astonished her. From the teardrop shape of his fat lower lip there hung a clear, healthy string of drool, suspended nearly to his tight little fists, which he clenched against his stomach as if the blinding white Cadillac had knocked the wind out of him, as solidly as a punch.

Wally wasn't sure, but he thought that the stationmaster's assistant appeared to be in charge of this strange assemblage of people. "Excuse me," Wally said to the assistant, whose mouth didn't move, whose eyes didn't blink. "Could you tell me the way to the orphanage?"

"You sure got here in a hurry," said the assistant lifelessly. A *white* hearse! he was thinking. Not to mention the beauty of the body snatchers; the assistant found he was unable to look at the girl; his mind's eye would never forget its actual brief glimpse of her.

"Pardon me?" Wally said. The man is deranged, Wally was thinking; I should be talking to someone else. A passing look at the oafs upon the bench was enough to tell Wally that he should not ask them anything. And the littlest child, with the crystal string of slobber now winking like an icicle in the sunlight and reaching nearly to the grass-stained dimples on the child's knees, appeared to be too young for speech. "Hello," Wally ventured pleasantly.

"Dead!" said David Copperfield, the drool dancing like tinsel on a Christmas tree.

Not him, Wally thought, and sought the eyes of Curly Day; Curly's eyes were easy to find—they were riveted on Candy. "Hello," Candy said to him, and Curly Day swallowed visibly—and with apparent pain. The wet end of his nose looked raw, but he rubbed it vigorously anyway.

"Could *you* tell us the way to the orphanage?" Wally asked Curly Day, who, unlike the louts and the assistant, knew that this Cadillac and these angelic specimens of the living had not been sent to retrieve the unwanted body of the dead stationmaster. They want the *orphanage,* thought Curly Day. They've come here to *adopt* someone! his pounding heart told him. Oh, God, thought Curly Day—let it be me!

David Copperfield, in his typical trance, reached his hand out to touch the perfect monogram on the Cadillac's door: Senior Worthington's gold monogram on the face of a gleaming Red Delicious apple—with a leaf of spring-green brightness, the artless shape of a tear. Curly batted young Copperfield's hand away.

I got to take charge of things, Curly was thinking, if I want them to pick me.

"*I'll* show you the orphanage," said Curly Day. "Give us a ride."

Candy smiled and opened the rear door for them. She was a little surprised when Curly picked up young Copperfield and shoved him in the car—not on the seat but on the floor. Copperfield seemed content on the floor; in fact, when he touched the strangely mottled scarlet upholstery of the seat, he pulled back his hand with alarm—he'd never touched leather before—and he jumped as if he feared the seat might be alive. It had been a startling day for young Copperfield: most of the morning confined in an enema-bag carton; his first attempt at flight; his long fall through the weeds; and then sitting on that dead man's face. What next? young Copperfield wondered. When the Cadillac began to move, he screamed. He'd never been inside a car before.

"He don't know about cars," Curly Day explained to Candy. Curly himself had never felt leather before either, but he tried to sit on the luxurious seat as if he were born to ride forever in this fashion. He didn't realize that the bleached-out stains that striped the scarlet were the result of an accident with chemicals—it would often be Curly Day's misfortune to mistake an accident for something artistically intended.

"Slow down, Wally," Candy said. "The little one is frightened." She leaned over the front seat and extended her arms to young Copperfield, whose howling abruptly ceased. He recognized the way her hair fell forward to either side of her face—this together with her outstretched arms and a certain comfort in her smile were familiar to Copperfield from Nurse Angela and Nurse Edna. Men, Copperfield thought, picked you up in one arm and carried you over a hip; by "men" he meant Homer Wells and Dr. Larch. Curly Day sometimes lugged Copperfield around in this fashion, but Curly wasn't quite strong enough and often dropped him.

"Come here, come here, don't be afraid," Candy said to Copperfield, swinging him over the seat and putting him in her lap. Copperfield smiled and touched Candy's hair; he had never felt blond hair before, he wasn't quite sure if it was real.

He had never smelled anyone who smelled this good either; he drove his face into the side of her neck and took a great big sniff of her. She actually hugged him, even kissed him on the blue dent of his temple. She looked at Wally and almost cried.

Curly Day, sick with envy, gripped the leather seat and wondered what he could say that would make them want *him*. Why would anyone want me? he began to wonder, but he fought off the thought. He sought Wally's eyes in the Cadillac's rearview mirror; it was too painful for him to see the way Candy held David Copperfield.

"You're one of the orphans?" Wally asked—he hoped, tactfully.

"You bet!" Curly Day said, too loudly; he sounded too enthusiastic about it, he thought. "I'm not just one of the orphans," he blurted out suddenly, "I'm the *best* one!" This made Candy laugh; she turned around in the front seat and smiled at him, and Curly felt he was losing his grip on the leather upholstery. He knew he should say something else, but his nose was running so violently he was sure that whatever he said would be grotesque; before he could drag his sleeve across his face, there was her hand with her handkerchief extended to him. And she wasn't just handing the handkerchief to him, he realized; she was actually pressing the handkerchief to his nose and holding it correctly in place.

"Blow," Candy said. Only once had anyone done this for Curly Day—Nurse Edna, he thought. He shut his eyes and blew his nose—at first, cautiously.

"Come on," Candy said. "Really blow it!" He really blew it—he blew his nose so emphatically that his head was instantly clear. The delicious scent of her perfume made him giddy; he shut his eyes and wet his pants. Then he lost control and flung himself back in the huge scarlet seat. He saw that he'd blown his nose all over her hand—and she didn't even look angry; she looked concerned, and that made him pee even harder. He couldn't stop himself. She looked completely surprised.

"Left or right?" Wally asked heartily, pausing at the driveway to the boys' division delivery entrance.

"Left!" Curly shouted; then he opened the rear door on Candy's side, and said to her, "I'm sorry! I don't even wet my bed. I never have! I ain't a bed-wetter. I just got a cold! And I got excited! I'm just having a bad day. I'm really *good*!" he cried. "I'm the *best* one!"

"It's all right, it's all right, get back in," she said to him, but Curly was already sprinting through the weeds and around the far corner of the building.

"The poor kid just wet his pants," Candy said to Wally, who saw the way Candy held David Copperfield in her lap and felt himself breaking.

"Please," he whispered to her, "you don't have to do this. You can have the baby. I *want* the baby—I want *your* baby. It would be fine. We can just turn around," he pleaded with her.

But she said, "No, Wally. I'm all right. It's not the time for us to have a baby." She put her face down on David Copperfield's damp neck; the boy smelled both sweet and mildewed.

The car stood still. "Are you sure?" Wally whispered to her. "You don't have to." She loved him for saying just the right thing at the right time, but Candy Kendall was more practical than Wally Worthington, and she had her father's stubbornness when her mind was made up; she was no waffler.

"The boy said you go left," Candy said to Wally. "Go left."

Mrs. Grogan, across the road in the girls' division entrance, observed the Cadillac's hesitation. She had not seen Curly Day flee from the car and she did not recognize the small child in the pretty girl's lap. Mrs. Grogan assumed that the child belonged to the pretty girl—she wondered if she'd ever seen a girl that pretty. And her young man was certainly handsome—almost too handsome for a husband, as they say in Maine.

In Mrs. Grogan's opinion, they looked too young to be adopting anyone—too bad, she mused, because they certainly seemed well off. A Cadillac meant nothing to Mrs. Grogan; it was the people themselves who appeared expensive to her. She was puzzled by how charmed she felt to be looking at these lovely people. Her few glimpses of the very rich had not charmed Mrs. Grogan in the past; those glimpses had only made her feel bitter—on behalf of the unadopted girls. She was all for her girls, Mrs. Grogan was; there was nothing personal in her bitterness—and very little that was personal in her whole life, really.

The car stood still, giving Mrs. Grogan a long view. Oh, the poor dears, she thought. They are *not* married, they have had this child together, either he or she is being disinherited—they have both, clearly, been disgraced—and now they have come to give up their child. But they are hesitating! She wanted to rush out and tell them: keep the child! Drive away! She felt paralyzed by the drama she was imagining. Don't do it! she whispered, mustering the strength for an enormous telepathic signal.

It was the signal Wally felt when he told Candy that she didn't have to. But then the car started up again—it was not turning around, it was heading straight for the hospital entrance of the boys' division—and Mrs. Grogan's heart sank. Boy or girl? she wondered, numbly.

What the fuck is going on? wondered Melony, at her bitter window.

Because of the harsh overhead light in the dormitory, Melony could see her own face reflected in the window; she watched the white Cadillac halt on her upper lip. Curly Day escaped across her cheek, and the pretty blond girl's arms enclosed David Copperfield at Melony's throat.

It was as close as Melony came to looking in a mirror. It was not that she was troubled by the heaviness of her face, or how close together her eyes were, or how her hair rebelled; it was her own expression that upset her—the vacantness, the absence of energy (formerly, she imagined, she had at least had energy). She couldn't remember when she'd last looked at herself in a mirror.

What troubled her, now, was that she'd just seen this familiar vacantness on the face of Homer Wells when he'd lifted the stationmaster's body—it wasn't the absence of strain, it was that look of zero surprise. Melony was afraid of Homer. How things had changed! she thought. She'd wanted to remind him of his promise. You won't leave, will you? she'd almost asked. You'll take me, if you run away, she'd wanted to say, but her familiarity wth his new expression (because it was her nearly constant expression, she was sure) had paralyzed her.

Now who are these pretty people? she wondered. Some car, she thought. She'd not seen their faces, but even the backs of their heads had discomforted her. The man's blond hair had contrasted so perfectly with the smooth, tanned back of his neck that it had given her a shiver. And how could the back of the girl's head be so perfect—the bounce and swing of her hair so accurate? Was there some trick to aligning the length of the hair so exactly with the girl's straight but small shoulders? And it was positively graceful how she'd picked up young Copperfield and held him in her lap—that little runt, thought Melony. She must have said the word "runt" half aloud, because her breath fogged the window at that instant; she lost sight of her own mouth and nose. When the window cleared, she saw the car move on, toward the hospital entrance. People like that are too perfect to need an abortion, Melony imagined. They're too perfect to fuck, she thought bitterly. They're too clean to do it. The pretty girl wonders why she can't get pregnant. She doesn't know you have to fuck first. They're considering adopting someone, but they won't find anyone here. There's no one who's good enough for them, thought Melony—hating them. She spat straight into her own dull reflection and watched her spit run down the pane. She hadn't the energy to move. There was a time, she thought, when I would have at least gone outdoors and poked around the Cadillac. Maybe they would leave something in the car—something good enough to steal. But now, not even the thought of something to steal could move Melony from her window.

/ / /

Dr. Larch had performed the first abortion with Nurse Edna's assistance; Larch had asked Homer to check on the contractions of the expectant mother from Damariscotta. Nurse Angela was assisting Larch with the second abortion, but Dr. Larch had insisted on Homer's presence, too. He had supervised Homer's ether application; Dr. Larch had such a light touch with ether that the first abortion patient had been speaking to Nurse Edna throughout the operation and yet the woman hadn't felt a thing. She talked and talked: a kind of airy list of non sequiturs to which Nurse Edna responded with enthusiasm.

Homer had put the second woman out, and he was clearly cross with himself for sedating the woman more heavily than he'd meant to. "Better safe than sorry," Nurse Angela said encouragingly—her hands on the woman's pale temples, which she instinctively smoothed with her soft hands. Larch had asked Homer to insert the vaginal speculum, and Homer now stared darkly at the woman's shiny cervix, at the puckered opening of the uterus. Bathed in a clear mucus, it had an aura of morning mist, of dew, of the pink clouds of a sunrise gathered around it. If Wally Worthington had peered through the speculum, he would have imagined that he was viewing an apple in some pale, ethereal phase of its development. But what is that little opening? he might have wondered.

"How's it look?" Larch asked.

"It looks fine," said Homer Wells. To his surprise, Larch handed him the cervical stabilizer—a simple instrument. It was for grabbing the upper lip of the cervix and stabilizing the cervix, which was then sounded for depth and dilated.

"Didn't you get what I told you?" Homer asked Dr. Larch.

"Do you disapprove of touching the cervix, Homer?" Larch asked.

Homer reached for the lip of the woman's cervix and seized it, correctly. I won't touch a single dilator, he thought. He won't make me.

But Larch didn't even ask. He said, "Thank you, that's a help." He sounded and dilated the cervix himself. When he asked for the curette, Homer handed it to him.

"You remember that I asked you if it was necessary for me to even be here?" Homer asked quietly. "I said that, if it was all the same to you, I'd just as soon not watch. You remember?"

"It's necessary for you to watch," said Wilbur Larch, who listened to the scrape of his curette; his breathing was shallow but regular.

"I believe," said Dr. Larch, "that you should participate to the degree of watching, of lending some amateur assistance, of understanding the process, of learning how to perform it— whether you ever choose to perform it or not.

"Do *I* interfere?" Larch asked. "When absolutely helpless women tell me that they simply *can't* have an abortion, that they simply *must* go through with having another—and yet another—orphan: do I interfere? Do I?

"I do not," he said, scraping. "I deliver it, Goddamn it. And do you think there are largely happy histories for the babies born here? Do you think the futures of these orphans are rosy? Do you?

"You don't," Larch said. "But do I resist? I do not. I do not even recommend. I give them what they want: an orphan or an abortion," Larch said.

"Well, I'm an orphan," said Homer Wells.

"Do I insist that we have the same ideas? I do not," Dr. Larch said.

"You wish it," said Homer Wells.

"The women who come to me are not helped by *wishes*," said Wilbur Larch. He put down the medium-sized curette and held out his hand for a smaller one, which Homer Wells had ready for him and handed to him automatically.

"I *want* to be of use," Homer began, but Dr. Larch wouldn't listen.

"Then you are not permitted to hide," Larch said. "You are not permitted to look away. It was you who told me, correctly, that if you were going to be of use, if you were going to participate at all, you had to know everything. Nothing could be kept from you. *I* learned that from *you*! Well, you're right," Larch said. "You *were* right," he added.

"It's alive," said Homer Wells. "That's the only thing."

"You are involved in a process," said Dr. Larch. "Birth, on occasion, and interrupting it—on other occasions. Your disapproval is noted. It is legitimate. You are welcome to disapprove. But you are not welcome to be ignorant, to look the other way, to be *un*able to perform—should you change your mind."

"I won't change my mind," said Homer Wells.

"All right, then," said Dr. Larch, "should you, against your will, but for the life of the mother, for example . . . should you *have* to perform."

"I'm not a doctor," said Homer Wells.

"You are not a complete physician," said Dr. Larch. "And you could study with me for another ten years, and you still wouldn't be complete. But regarding all the known complications arising in the area of the female organs of generation, regarding those organs—you can be a complete surgeon. Period. You are already more competent than the most competent midwife, damn it," said Wilbur Larch.

Homer had anticipated the extraction of the small curette; he handed Larch the first of several sterile vulval pads.

"I will never make you do what you disapprove of, Homer," said Dr. Larch, "but you will watch, you will know how to do what I do. Otherwise, what good am I?" he asked. "Aren't we put on this earth to work? At least to learn, at least to watch? What do you think it means, to be of use?" he asked. "Do you think you should be left alone? Do you think I should let you be a *Melony*?"

"Why don't you teach *her* how to do it?" Homer Wells asked Dr. Larch.

Now *there's* a question, Nurse Angela thought, but the woman's head moved slightly in Nurse Angela's hands; the woman moaned, and Nurse Angela touched her lips to the woman's ear. "You're just fine, dear," she whispered. "It's all over now. You just rest."

"Do you see what I mean, Homer?" Dr. Larch asked.

"Right," Homer said.

"But you don't agree, do you?" Larch asked.

"Right again," said Homer Wells.

You damn sullen self-centered self-pitying arrogant untested know-nothing *teen-ager*! thought Wilbur Larch, but instead of any of that, he said to Homer Wells, "Perhaps you're having second thoughts about becoming a doctor."

"I never really had a first thought about that," Homer said. "I never said I wanted to be a doctor."

Larch looked at the blood on the gauze—the right amount of blood, he thought—and when he held out his hand for a fresh pad, Homer had one ready. "You don't want to be a doctor, Homer?" Dr. Larch asked.

"Right," said Homer Wells. "I don't think so."

"You've not had much opportunity to look at other things," Larch said philosophically; his heart was aching. "It's my fault, I know, if I've made medicine so unattractive."

Nurse Angela, who was much tougher than Nurse Edna, felt that she might cry.

"Nothing's your fault," Homer said quickly.

Wilbur Larch checked the bleeding again. "There's not much to do here," he said abruptly. "If you wouldn't mind just staying with her until she's out of the ether—you did give her rather a wallop," he added, looking under the woman's eyelids. "I can deliver the Damariscotta woman, when she's ready. I didn't realize you didn't like the whole business," Larch said.

"That's not true," Homer said. "*I* can deliver the Damariscotta woman. I'd be happy to deliver her." But Wilbur Larch had turned away from the patient and left the operating room.

Nurse Angela glanced quickly at Homer; it was a fairly neutral look, certainly not withering, or even faintly condemning, but it wasn't sympathetic either (or even friendly, thought Homer Wells). She went after Dr. Larch, leaving Homer with the patient making her way out of the ether.

Homer looked at the spotting on the pad; he felt the woman's hand graze his wrist as she said groggily, "I'll wait here while you get the car, honey."

In the boys' shower room, where there were several toilet stalls, Wilbur Larch put cold water on his face and looked for

evidence of his tears in the mirror; he was no more a veteran of
mirrors than Melony was, and Dr. Larch was surprised by his
appearance. How long have I been so *old*? he wondered.
Behind him, in the mirror, he recognized the pile of sodden
clothes upon the floor as belonging to Curly Day. "Curly?" he
asked; he'd thought he was alone, but Curly Day was crying
too—in one of the toilet stalls.

"I'm having a very bad day," Curly announced.

"Let's talk about it," Dr. Larch suggested, which coaxed
Curly out of the stall. He was dressed in more or less fresh
clothes, but Larch recognized that the clothes weren't Curly's.
They were some of Homer's old clothes, too small for Homer
now, but still trying much too large for Curly Day.

"I'm trying to look nice for the nice couple," Curly explained. "I want them to take me."

"*Take* you, Curly?" Dr. Larch asked. "*What* nice couple?"

"You know," said Curly, who believed that Dr. Larch knew
everything. "The beautiful woman? The white car?"

The poor child is having visions, thought Wilbur Larch, who
picked Curly up in his arms and sat him down on the edge of
the sink where he could observe the boy more closely.

"Or are they here to adopt someone else?" Curly asked
miserably. "I think the woman likes Copperfield—but he can't
even talk!"

"No one's adopting anyone today, Curly," Dr. Larch said. "I
don't have any appointments today."

"Maybe they've just come to look," Curly suggested. "They're
just gonna take the best of us."

"It doesn't work like that, Curly," Dr. Larch said, alarmed.
Does the child think I run a *pet* shop? Larch wondered. Does
he think I let people come here and *browse*?

"I don't know how anything works," Curly said, and he
started to cry again.

Wilbur Larch, with his fresh memory of how old he looked
to himself in the mirror, thought for a moment that his job was
too much for him; he felt himself slipping, he felt himself
wishing that someone would adopt *him*—would just take him
away. He held Curly Day's wet face against his chest; he shut
his eyes and saw those spots he saw most regularly when he
inhaled the ether, only those spots quite harshly reminded him
of the spotting he was familiar with from his many viewings of
the sterile vulval pads.

He looked at Curly Day and wondered if Curly ever would be adopted, or if Curly was in danger of becoming another Homer Wells.

Nurse Angela paused by the door to the boys' shower room; she listened to Dr. Larch comforting Curly Day. She was more worried about Dr. Larch than she was worried about Curly; a kind of stubborn goading had developed between Dr. Larch and Homer Wells that Nurse Angela had never expected to see existing between two people who so clearly loved and needed each other. It distressed her that she was powerless to intervene. She heard Nurse Edna calling her and was grateful for the interruption; she decided it would be easier to talk to Homer than to Dr. Larch; she'd not decided what should be said to either of them.

Homer watched the second abortion patient emerge from the ether; he moved her from the operating table to a portable bed; he put up the safety rails on the bed in case the woman was groggy. He looked in another room and saw that the first abortion patient was already sitting up, but he decided both women would rather be alone for a moment, and so he left the second patient in the operating room. It wasn't time to deliver the Damariscotta woman, anyway, he was sure. The tiny hospital felt especially cramped and overcrowded to him, and he longed for a room of his own. But first, he knew, he had to apologize for hurting Dr. Larch's feelings—it had all just slipped out of him, and it made him almost cry to think that he had caused Dr. Larch any suffering. He went straight across the hall to the dispensary, where he could see what he thought were Dr. Larch's feet extending off the foot of the dispensary bed; the dispensary medicine cabinets blocked the rest of the bed from view. He spoke to Dr. Larch's feet, which to Homer's surprise were larger than he remembered them; he was also surprised that Dr. Larch—a neat man—had left his shoes on and that his shoes were muddy.

"Doctor Larch?" Homer said. "I'm sorry." When there was no response, Homer thought crossly to himself that Dr. Larch was under an unusually ill-timed ether sedation.

"I'm sorry, and I love you," Homer added, a little louder. He held his breath, listening for Larch's breathing, which he couldn't hear; alarmed, he stepped around the cabinets and saw the lifeless stationmaster stretched out on Larch's bed. It did not occur to Homer that this had been the first time someone had said "I love you" to the stationmaster.

There'd been no better place to put him. Nurse Edna and Nurse Angela had moved him out of the operating room. It would have been cruel to expect one of the abortion patients to tolerate his presence, or to put him alongside the expectant mother, and certainly it would have been upsetting to the orphans if the stationmaster had been stretched out on one of the dormitory beds.

"Goddamn it," Homer said.

"What's that?" Larch asked. He was carrying Curly Day and calling to Homer from the dispensary door.

"Nothing," Homer Wells said. "Never mind."

"Curly's been having a very bad day," Dr. Larch explained.

"That's too bad, Curly," Homer said.

"Someone's come here to adopt someone," Curly said. "They're sort of *shopping*."

"I don't think so, Curly," Dr. Larch said.

"Tell them I'm the best one, okay, Homer?" Curly asked.

"Right," said Homer Wells. "You're the best."

"Wilbur!" Nurse Edna was calling. She and Nurse Angela were chattering at the hospital entrance door.

They traipsed out to see what was going on: the doctor, his unwilling apprentice, and the next-to-oldest orphan in the boys' division.

There was a small but busy crowd around the Cadillac. The trunk was open and the handsome young man was dispensing presents to the orphans.

"Sorry it's not the season for apples, kids," Wally was saying. "Or cider. You could all use a little cider!" he said cheerfully, handing out the jars of honey, the crab-apple and apple-cider jelly. The eager, dirty hands were grabbing. Mary Agnes Cork, the next-to-oldest orphan in the girls' division, was getting more than her share. (Melony had taught her how to dominate the front of a line.) Mary Agnes was a popular name with Mrs. Grogan, and Cork was the county in Ireland where Mrs. Grogan had been born. There'd been a number of little Corks in the girls' division.

"There's plenty to go around!" Wally said optimistically, as Mary Agnes put two honeys and one crab-apple down her blouse—then reached for more. A boy named Smoky Fields had opened his jar of apple-cider jelly and was eating it out of the jar with his hand. "It's really good on toast, in the morning," Wally said cautiously, but Smoky Fields stared at Wally as if toast was not a regular item on his diet or reliably available in the morning. Smoky Fields intended to finish the jar of jelly on the spot. Mary Agnes spied a horn-rim barrette on the convertible's backseat—it was one that Candy had put aside. Mary Agnes turned to face Candy, then dropped a second jar of crab-apple jelly at Candy's feet.

"Oops," Candy said, bending to pick up the jelly for her while Mary Agnes stole the barrette—little John Walsh observing her deft moves, admiringly. A trace of blood, or maybe rust, on Mary Agnes's bare shin caught Candy's eye and made her feel queasy; she needed to restrain herself from wetting her finger and trying to rub the streak away. When she stood up and handed the girl her jar of jelly, Candy felt a little dizzy. Some grown-ups were coming out of the hospital entrance, and their presence helped Candy compose herself: I've not come here to play with the children, she thought.

"I'm Doctor Larch," the old man was saying to Wally, who seemed transfixed by the determination with which Smoky Fields was devouring the jarful of apple-cider jelly.

"Wally Worthington," Wally said, pumping Dr. Larch's hand, handing him a jar of Ira Titcomb's honey. "Fresh from Ocean View Orchards. That's in Heart's Rock, but we're very near the coast—we're in Heart's Haven, almost."

"Heart's Haven?" said Wilbur Larch, examining the honey. A sea breeze seemed to spring off the boy—as distinctive, Larch thought, as fresh, crisp hundred-dollar bills. Whose face was on a hundred-dollar bill? Larch tried to imagine.

"Tell her," Curly Day said to Homer Wells, pointing to Candy, but there was no need to point. Homer Wells had seen her, and only her, from the moment he emerged from the hospital entrance. Young Copperfield clung to her leg, but this didn't seem to impede her gracefulness—and nothing could interfere with her radiance. "Tell her I'm the best one," Curly said to Homer.

"Hello," Candy said to Homer because he was the tallest person present; he was as tall as Wally. "I'm Candy Kendall," she said to him. "I hope we're not interrupting anything." You are interrupting two abortions, one birth, one death, two autopsies and an argument, thought Homer Wells, but all he said was, "He's the best one." Too mechanically! thought Curly Day. He lacks conviction!

"Me," Curly said, stepping between them. "He means me. I'm the best."

Candy bent over Curly and ruffled his sticky hair. "Of course you are!" she said brightly. And straightening up, she said to Homer, "And do you work here? Or are you one of . . ." Was it polite to say *them*? she wondered.

"Not exactly," Homer mumbled, thinking: I work here, *in*exactly, and I am *in*exactly one of them.

"His name's Homer Wells," Curly told Candy, since Homer had failed to introduce himself. "He's too old to adopt."

"I can see that!" Candy said, feeling shy. I should be talking to the doctor, she thought awkwardly; she was irritated with Wally for creating such a crowd.

"I'm in the apple business," Wally was saying to Dr. Larch. "It's my father's business. Actually," he added, "my mother's business."

What does this fool want? thought Wilbur Larch.

"Oh, I love apples!" Nurse Edna said.

"I would have brought lots of apples," Wally said, "but it's the wrong time of year. You should have your own apples." He indicated the barren hillside stretching behind them. "Look at that hill," he said. "It's washing away. You ought to plant it. I could even get you the trees. In six or seven years, you'd have your own apples; you'd have apples for more than a hundred years."

What do I want with a hundred years of apples? thought Wilbur Larch.

"Wouldn't that be pretty, Wilbur?" Nurse Edna asked.

"And you could get your own cider press," Wally suggested. "Give the kids fresh apples and fresh cider—they'd have lots to do."

They don't need things to *do*, thought Dr. Larch. They need places to *go*!

They're from some charity, thought Nurse Angela cautiously. She put her lips close to Dr. Larch's ear and whispered, "A sizable donation," just so Dr. Larch wouldn't be rude to them.

They're too young to give their money away, thought Wilbur Larch.

"Bees!" Wally was saying. "You should keep bees, too. Fascinating for the kids, and a lot safer than most people think. Have your own honey, and give the kids an education—bees are a model society, a lesson in teamwork!"

Oh shut up, Wally, Candy was thinking, although she understood why he couldn't stop babbling. He was unused to an environment he couldn't instantly brighten; he was unused to a place so despairing that it insisted on silence. He was unused to absorbing a shock, to simply taking it in. Wally's talk-a-mile-a-minute style was a good-hearted effort; he believed in improving the world—he had to fix everything, to make everything better.

Dr. Larch looked around at the children stuffing themselves with honey and jelly. Have they come here to play with the orphans for a day and to make everyone sick? he wondered. He should have looked at Candy; then he would have known why they were there. He was not good at looking in women's eyes, Wilbur Larch; he had seen too much of them under the harsh lights. Nurse Angela at times wondered if Dr. Larch even knew how he tended to overlook women; she wondered if this was an occupational hazard among obstetricians, or if men with a tendency to overlook women were drawn to the obstetrical field.

Homer Wells did not overlook women; he looked right into their eyes, which might have been why, Nurse Angela thought, he seemed to find their position in the stirrups so troubling. Funny, she thought, how he has seen everything that Dr. Larch does, yet he will not watch me or Nurse Edna shave anyone. He was so adamant in arguing with Dr. Larch about shaving the women for abortions. It wasn't necessary, Homer always said, and the women surely didn't *like* to be shaved.

"*Like* it?" Dr. Larch would say. "Am I in the *entertainment* business?"

Candy felt helpless; no one seemed to understand why she was standing there. Children were colliding with her at hip level, and this awkward, darkly handsome young man, who was surely her own age but seemed somehow older . . . was she supposed to tell *him* why she'd come to St. Cloud's? Couldn't anyone tell just by looking at her? Then Homer Wells looked at her in that way; their eyes met. Candy thought that he had seen her many times before, that he'd watched her grow up, had seen her naked, had even observed the act responsible for the particular trouble she was now presenting for cure. It was shattering to Homer to recognize in the expression of the beautiful stranger he had fallen in love with something as familiar and pitiable as another unwanted pregnancy.

"I think you'd be more comfortable inside," he murmured to her.

"Yes, thank you," Candy said, not able to look in his eyes now.

Larch, seeing the girl walk toward the hospital entrance—recognizing that deliberate way of walking that predictably happens to someone who's watching her own feet—thought suddenly, Oh, it's just another abortion, that's all this is about. He turned to follow the girl and Homer, just as Smoky Fields finished the jar of jelly and began to eat a jar of honey. Smoky ate with no apparent satisfaction; but he ate so methodically that even when he was jostled by a nearby orphan, he never took his eyes from his little paw as it scooped its way into the jar. When he was severely jostled, a kind of growl—or gurgle—caught in his throat, and he hunched his shoulders forward as if to protect the jar from other predators.

Homer led the way to Nurse Angela's office; at the threshold he saw the dead baby's hands reaching above the edge of the white enamel examining tray, which still rested on Nurse Angela's typewriter. The baby's hands were still waiting for the ball, but Homer's reflexes were quick enough; he turned full circle in the doorway, pushing Candy back into the hall. "This is Doctor Larch," Homer said to Candy, introducing them while he herded them down the hall to the dispensary. Wilbur Larch did not remember that there was a dead baby on top of the typewriter in Nurse Angela's office.

He said crossly to Homer, "Shouldn't we let Miss Kendall sit down?" He didn't remember that the dead stationmaster was in the dispensary, either, and when he saw the moron's muddy shoes, he pulled Homer aside and whispered harshly to him. "Have you no feeling for this poor girl?" Homer whispered back that he thought the partial view of a dead man was preferable to the whole view of a dead baby.

"Oh," Wilbur Larch said.

"I'll deliver the woman from Damariscotta," Homer added to Dr. Larch, still whispering.

"Well, don't be in too big a hurry," Larch whispered.

"I mean I won't have anything to do with *this* one," Homer whispered back, looking at Candy. "I won't even look at her, do you understand?"

Dr. Larch regarded the young woman. He thought he understood, a little. She was a very pretty young woman, even Dr.

Larch could see that, and he'd not seen Homer so agitated in anyone's presence before. Homer fancies he's in love! thought Dr. Larch. Or he fancies that he'd like to be. Have I been utterly insensitive? Larch wondered. Is the boy still enough of a boy to need to romanticize women? Or is he enough of a man to desire to *romance* women, too?

Wally was introducing himself to Homer Wells. Wilbur Larch thought, Here's the one with apples for brains; why is *he* whispering? It didn't occur to Dr. Larch that Wally thought, by his partial view of the stationmaster, that the stationmaster was asleep.

"If I could have just a moment's peace with Miss Kendall," said Wilbur Larch, "we can all meet each other another time. Edna will assist me with Miss Kendall, please, and Angela— would you help Homer with the Damariscotta woman? *Homer,*" Dr. Larch explained to Wally and to Candy, "is a very accomplished *midwife.*"

"You *are?*" Wally said to Homer enthusiastically. "Wow."

Homer Wells maintained silence. Nurse Angela, bristling at the word "midwife"—at the condescension she quite correctly heard in Dr. Larch's tone—touched Homer's arm very gently and said to him, "I'll give you a count of the contractions." Nurse Edna, whose uncritical love for Dr. Larch beamed forth ever brightly, cheerfully pointed out that various people had to be moved both from and to various beds if a room was to be made ready for Candy.

"Please do it, then," Dr. Larch said. "If I could just have a moment alone with Miss Kendall," he repeated, but he saw that Homer seemed riveted; Homer was unaware that he was staring at Candy. The boy has gone gaga on me, thought Wilbur Larch, and he saw no indication that Apple Brains intended to leave the dispensary. "If I could just explain a little of the process to Miss Kendall," Wilbur Larch said to Wally (it appeared hopeless to address Homer). "I'd like her to know about the bleeding, later—for example," Larch added, intending that the word "bleeding" would have some effect on Wally's apple-bright complexion. It did—perhaps in combination with the overpowering atmosphere of ether in the dispensary.

"Is someone going to *cut* her?" he asked Homer pathetically; Homer caught Wally's arm and pulled him abruptly away. He pulled him so quickly along the hall and got him outdoors so fast that Wally almost escaped being sick at all. As it was, completely owing to Homer's good reflexes, Wally didn't throw up until the two of them were behind the boys' division—on the particular hillside Wally had suggested planting with apple trees, the very hillside where Homer Wells's shadow had only recently outdistanced Dr. Larch's.

The two young men walked up and down and across the hill, in straight lines—respecting the rows of trees Wally was planting in his imagination.

Homer, politely, explained the procedure that Candy would undergo, but Wally wanted to talk about apple trees.

"This hill is perfect for your standard forty-by-forty plot," Wally said, walking forty feet in one direction, then making a perfect right-angle turn.

"If she's in the first three months," Homer noted, "there really shouldn't be any work with the forceps, just the standard dilatation—that means dilating the opening to the uterus—and then curetting—that's scraping."

"I'd recommend four rows of McIntosh, then one row of Red Delicious," Wally said. "Half of the trees should be Macs. I'd mix up the rest—maybe ten percent Red Delicious, another ten or fifteen percent Cortlands and Baldwins. You'll want a few Northern Spies, and I'll throw in some Gravensteins— they're a great apple for pies, and you get to pick them early."

"There's no actual cutting," Homer told Wally, "although there will be some bleeding—we call it spotting, actually, because it's usually not very heavy bleeding. Doctor Larch has a great touch with ether, so don't worry—she won't feel a thing. Of course, she'll feel something afterward," admitted Homer. "It's a special sort of cramp. Doctor Larch says that the other discomfort is psychological."

"You could come back to the coast with us," Wally told Homer. "We could load a truck full of baby trees, and in a day or two we could come back here and plant the orchard together. It wouldn't take too long."

"It's a deal," said Homer Wells. The *coast,* he thought. I get to see the coast. And the girl. I get to ride in that car with that girl.

"*A midwife,* gosh," Wally said. "I guess you're probably going to be a doctor?"

"I don't think so," said Homer Wells. "I don't know yet."

"Well, apples are in my family," Wally said. "I'm going to college, but I really don't know why I bother."

College, thought Homer Wells.

"Candy's father is a lobsterman," Wally explained, "but she's going to go to college, too."

Lobster! thought Homer Wells. The bottom of the sea!

From the bottom of the hill, Nurse Angela was waving to them.

"Damariscotta is ready!" she called to Homer Wells.

"I have to go deliver someone's baby," Homer told Wally.

"Gosh," Wally said. He seemed reluctant to leave the hill. "I think I'll stay up here. I don't think I want to hear anything," he added; he gave Homer a likable and confessional smile.

"Oh, there's not much noise," Homer said; he wasn't thinking of the Damariscotta woman; he was thinking of Candy. He thought of the gritty sound the curette made, but he'd spare his new friend that detail.

He left Wally on the hill and jogged toward Nurse Angela; he looked back at Wally once and waved. A boy his own age! A boy his own size! They were the same height, although Wally was more muscular—from sports, Dr. Larch had guessed. He has the body of a hero, Dr. Larch thought, remembering the heroes he had tried to help in France, in World War I. Lean but well muscled: that was a hero's body—and shot full of holes, thought Wilbur Larch. He didn't know why Wally's body reminded him of this.

And Wally's face? Wilbur Larch was thinking. It was handsome in a finer way than Homer's face, which was also handsome. Although Wally's body was stronger, his bones were somewhat sharper—and more delicate. There wasn't a trace of anger in Wally's eyes; they were the eyes of good intentions. The body of a hero, and the face . . . the face of a benefactor! concluded Wilbur Larch, brushing aside a blond curl of pubic hair that had not gone directly into the refuse bag but had clung to Candy's inner thigh, near her raised, bent knee. He exchanged the medium-sized curette for the smaller one, noting that the girl's eyelids were fluttering, noting Nurse Edna's gentle thumbs—massaging the girl's temples—and the girl's slightly parted lips; she had been remarkably relaxed for such a young girl, and under ether she was even more composed. The beauty in her face, Larch thought, was that she was still free of guilt. It surprised Larch: how Candy looked as if she would always be free of it.

He was aware of Nurse Edna observing the scrutiny he was

giving to the girl, and so he bent once more to the view the speculum afforded him and finished his task with the small curette.

A benefactor, thought Wilbur Larch. Homer has met his benefactor!

Homer Wells was thinking on parallel lines. I have met a Prince of Maine, he was thinking; I have seen a King of New England—and I am invited to his castle. In all his journeys through *David Copperfield,* at last he understood young David's first vision of Steerforth. "He was a person of great power in my eyes," young Copperfield observed. "No veiled future glanced upon him in the moonbeams. There was no shadowy picture of his footsteps, in the garden that I dreamed of walking in all night."

"No veiled future," thought Homer Wells. I am going to the *coast!*

"Push," he said to the woman from Damariscotta. "Is Damariscotta on the coast?" he asked the woman, whose neck was taut with straining—who held Nurse Angela's hand in a white-knuckled grip.

"Near it!" the woman cried, and shoved her child forth into St. Cloud's—its slick head captured perfectly in the palm of Homer's confident right hand. He slipped the heel of his hand under the baby's fragile neck; his left hand lifted the baby's bottom as he guided the baby "outdoors"—as Dr. Larch would say.

It was a boy. *Steerforth,* Homer Wells would name this one—his second solo delivery. Homer cut the cord and smiled to hear young Steerforth's healthy bawling.

Candy, coming out of ether, heard the baby's cries and shuddered; if Dr. Larch had seen her face at that moment, he might have detected some guilt upon it. "Boy or girl?" she asked, her speech slurred. Only Nurse Edna heard her. "Why is it crying?" Candy asked.

"It was nothing, dear," Nurse Edna said. "It's all over."

"I would like to have a baby, one day," Candy said. "I really would."

"Why, of course, dear," Nurse Edna told her. "You can have as many as you want. I'm sure you'd have very beautiful children."

"You'd have Princes of Maine!" Dr. Larch told Candy suddenly. "You'd have Kings of New England!"

Why, the old goat, Nurse Edna thought—he's flirting! Her love for Larch felt momentarily ruffled.

What a strange idea, Candy thought—I can't see what they would look like. Her mind drifted for a while. Why is the baby crying? she wondered. Wilbur Larch, cleaning up, noticed another curly clump of her pubic hair; it was the same tawny tone of Candy's skin, which was doubtlessly why Nurse Edna had missed it. He listened to the cries of the Damariscotta woman's baby and thought that he mustn't be selfish; he must encourage Homer to make friends with this young couple. He stole a look at the dozing girl; opportunity shone from her like light.

And people will always eat apples, he thought—it must be a nice life.

The apple enameled on the Cadillac's door—and mono-grammed in gold—was of special interest to Melony, who managed to prod herself into action; she tried to steal the apple on the door before she realized it wouldn't come off. Mary Agnes's arrival at the girls' division—with her scrawny arms hoarding jars of jelly and honey—had prompted Melony to go see for herself what was going on. She thought, sourly, how it was typical how nothing had been left for her—not even a glimpse of the beautiful people; she wouldn't have minded another look at them. There was nothing worth stealing, she could see at a glance—just an old book; it was fate, she would think later, that the title of the book and the name of its author were visible to her. The book appeared discarded on the car's floor. *Little Dorrit* meant nothing to Melony, but Charles Dickens was a name she recognized—he was a kind of hero to Homer Wells. Without thinking that this was her life's first unselfish act, she stole the book—for Homer. At the time, she wasn't even thinking how it might impress him, how it might gain for her some favorable light in his eyes. She thought only generously: Oh look, a present for Sunshine!

It meant more to her than she could ever admit to herself: that Homer had promised never to leave St. Cloud's without her.

Then she saw Wally; he was walking toward the Cadillac, in the direction of the hospital entrance, but he kept turning around to look at the hill. In his mind, he saw the orchard at harvest time—the long ladders were in the trees, the pickers were the orphans themselves. The bushel crates were stacked in the rows between the trees; in one row a tractor towed a flatbed trailer already heavy with apples. It looked like a good crop.

Where will they get a tractor? Wally wondered. He tripped, caught his balance, looked where he was walking—toward the abandoned Cadillac. Melony was gone. She'd lost her nerve. The thought of confronting that handsome young man, alone—she wasn't sure if she could have tolerated his indifference. If he'd been clearly appalled by her appearance, that wouldn't have bothered Melony; she rather enjoyed her ability to shock people. But she could not bear the thought that he might not even notice her. And if he'd handed her a jar of honey, she'd have cracked his skull with it. Nobody honeys me, she thought—*Little Dorrit* slipped inside her shirt, against her thudding heart.

She crossed the road between the boys' and girls' divisions just as the stationmaster's assistant was climbing the same road, toward the hospital. At first she didn't recognize him—he was so dressed up. To Melony he was just a simpleton in overalls, a busybody who tried to fashion for himself an air of self-importance out of what Melony imagined was the world's stupidest job: watching for trains to arrive, and then watching them leave. The loneliness of the railroad station depressed Melony; she avoided the place. You went there for one thing: to leave. But to stand there all day, imagining leaving—could there be anything sadder, or more stupid, than that? And now here was this oaf, still wearing his year-long effort to grow a moustache, but dressed to kill—well, no, Melony realized: he's dressed for a funeral.

That was it: the plain but ambitious boy had been impressed by the white Cadillac; he'd conceived that the stationmaster's job was his for the taking if he exhibited a proper and adult solemnity regarding the stationmaster's passing. He was terrified of Dr. Larch, and the idea of pregnant women made him feel furtive; but he had imagined that paying his respects at the orphanage, where the stationmaster's body reposed, was a grueling but necessary rite of passage. The spit-up smell he associated with babies made him nauseous, too; an unusual bravery had guided him to the orphanage, giving his silly, young face an almost adult countenance—except for the silky smudge that marred his upper lip and made all his efforts at manhood ridiculous. He had also burdened himself for the uphill climb by carrying all the catalogues; the stationmaster wouldn't be needing them now, and his assistant imagined that he could ingratiate himself to Dr. Larch by bringing the catalogues as a present—a kind of peace offering. He had not bothered to consider what use Wilbur Larch would have for seeds and lingerie, or how the old doctor would respond to declarations regarding the peril of souls—his own and many restless others.

The two orphans the stationmaster's assistant most despised were Homer and Melony. Homer, because his serenity gave him a confident, adult appearance that the assistant felt powerless to achieve; and Melony, because she mocked him. Now, to make a bad day worse, here was Melony—blocking his way.

"What's that on your lip? A fungus?" Melony asked him. "Maybe you should wash it." She was bigger than the stationmaster's assistant, especially now that she stood uphill from him. He tried to ignore her.

"I've come to view the body," he said with dignity—had he any sense, he should have known these words were ill chosen for presentation to Melony.

"Wanna view *my* body?" she asked him. "I'm not kidding," she added, when she saw how lost he was, and frightened. Melony had an instinct for pressing any advantage, but she relented when her adversary was too easy. She saw that the stationmaster's assistant would go on standing in the road until he dropped from fatigue, and so she stepped aside for him, and said, "I *was* kidding."

He stumbled ahead, blushing, and had almost turned the corner by the boys' division when she called after him, "You'd have to *shave* before I'd *let* you!" He staggered slightly, causing Melony to marvel at her power; then he turned the corner and felt himself uplifted by the gleaming Cadillac—by what he mistook for the white hearse. If, at that moment, a choir had erupted into heavenly voice, the assistant would have fallen to his knees, the catalogues spilling around him. The same light that blessed the Cadillac seemed to shine forth from the blond hair of the powerful-looking young man: the driver of the hearse. Now *there* was a responsibility that awed the stationmaster's assistant!

He approached Wally carefully. Wally was leaning on the Cadillac, smoking a cigarette and intently visualizing an apple orchard in St. Cloud's. The stationmaster's assistant, who looked like a mortician's ghoulish lackey, surprised Wally.

"I've come to view the body," the assistant said.

"The body?" Wally said. "*What* body?"

A fear of embarrassing himself almost paralyzed the station-master's assistant. The world, he imagined, was brimming with etiquette beyond his grasp; obviously, it had been tactless to mention the body of the deceased to the very man who was responsible for safely driving the dead away.

"A thousand pardons!" the assistant blurted; it had been something he'd read.

"A thousand *what*?" Wally said, growing alarmed.

"How thoughtless of me," said the stationmaster's assistant, bowing unctuously and sliding toward the hospital entrance.

"Has someone *died*?" Wally asked anxiously, but the assis-tant managed to slip inside the hospital entrance, where he quickly hid himself in a corner of the wall and wondered what to do next. Clearly, he'd upset the high-strung and fine-tuned feelings of the hearse driver. This is a delicate business, the assistant thought, trying to calm himself. What mistake will I make next? He cowered in the corner of the hall, where he could smell ether wafting from the nearby dispensary; he had no idea that the body he wished to "view" was less than fifteen feet from him. He thought he could smell babies, too—he heard one bawling. He thought that babies were born while women had their legs straight up, the soles of their feet facing the ceiling; this vision pinned him to the corner of the hall. I smell blood! he imagined, struggling to control his panic. He clung to the wall like so much plaster—so much so that Wally failed to notice him when he came in the hospital entrance, worried about who had died. Wally entered the dispensary, as if drawn to the ether—although he quickly felt his nausea returning. He apologized to the feet of the stationmaster.

"Oh, excuse me," Wally whispered, reeling back into the hall.

He heard Nurse Angela talking to Candy, who was already able to sit up. Wally barged in on them, but the look of relief on his face—to see that Candy was not the person rumored to be dead—was so touching to Nurse Angela that she wasn't even cross with him for intruding.

"Please come in," she said to Wally, in her best hospital voice, which was first-person plural. "We're feeling much bet-ter now," Nurse Angela said. "We're not quite ready to jump around, but we're sitting up nicely—aren't we?" she asked

Candy, who smiled. Candy was so clearly glad to see Wally that Nurse Angela felt she should leave them alone. St. Cloud's did not have a great and tender history regarding the presence of couples in that operating room, and Nurse Angela was both surprised and happy to see a man and a woman who loved each other. I can clean up later, she thought—or I'll ask Homer to do it.

Homer and Dr. Larch were talking. Nurse Edna had taken the Damariscotta woman back to her bed in the maternity ward, and Dr. Larch was examining the baby Homer Wells had delivered—young Steerforth (a name Larch had already criticized; there was some villainy in the character of Steerforth—or had Homer forgotten that part?—and there was also a death by drowning; it was more of a brand than a name, in Dr. Larch's opinion). But they weren't talking anymore about Steerforth.

"Wally said it would take just a couple of days," Homer Wells was saying. "We'll have to load a truck, I guess. There's going to be forty trees. And I'd like to see the coast."

"Of course, you should go, Homer—it's a great opportunity," Dr. Larch said. He poked Steerforth in the belly with a finger; then he tempted Steerforth into gripping one of his other fingers; then he shone a little light in Steerforth's eyes.

"I'd be gone just two days," Homer Wells said.

Wilbur Larch shook his head; at first Homer thought there was something wrong with Steerforth. "*Maybe* just two days, Homer," Dr. Larch said. "You should be prepared to take advantage of the situation, you should not let an opportunity pass you by—in just two days."

Homer stared at Dr. Larch, but Larch was peering into Steerforth's ears. "If this young couple likes you, Homer, and if you like them ... well," Larch said, "I think you'll be meeting their parents, too, and if their parents like you ... well," said Dr. Larch, "I think you should try to *make* their parents like you."

He would not look at Homer, who was staring at him; Dr. Larch examined the tied end of the umbilical while Steerforth cried and cried.

"I think we both know it would do you good to get away for more than two days, Homer," Dr. Larch said. "You understand, I'm not talking about an adoption, I'm talking about the possibility of a summer job—for a start. Someone might offer you the means to stay away for more than two days—that's all I'm saying—if that's an attractive prospect." Dr. Larch looked at Homer; they stared at each other.

"Right," Homer finally said.

"Of course, you might *want* to come back in two days!" Larch said heartily—but they looked away from each other, as they chose to look away from the likelihood of that. "In which case," Larch said, washing his hands, "you know you're always welcome here." He left the room, and Homer with the baby—too quickly, again, for Homer to say how much he loved him. The cowering stationmaster's assistant watched Wilbur Larch take Nurse Angela and Nurse Edna into the dispensary.

Perhaps, despite the stationmaster's presence, the etherized atmosphere of the dispensary was comforting to Wilbur Larch, and helped him say to his loyal nurses what he needed to say.

"I want to pool our resources," said Wilbur Larch. "I want the boy to have as much money as we can scrounge together, and whatever there is in the way of clothing that looks halfway decent."

"Just for two days, Wilbur?" Nurse Edna asked.

"How much money does the boy need for two days?" Nurse Angela asked.

"It's an opportunity for him, don't you see?" Dr. Larch asked. "I don't think he'll be back here in two days. I hope he *doesn't* come back—at least, not that soon," said Wilbur Larch, whose breaking heart reminded him of what he'd forgotten: the story of Homer's "weak" heart. How could he tell him? Where and when?

He crossed the hall to see how Candy was coming along. He knew that she and Wally wanted to leave as soon as possible; they had a long drive ahead of them. And if Homer Wells is leaving me, thought Wilbur Larch, he'd better leave me in a hurry—although twenty years, Dr. Larch knew, wasn't what most would have called a hurried departure. Homer had to leave in a hurry, now, because Dr. Larch needed to see if he would ever get over it.

I don't think so, he thought. He checked the spotting on the sterile vulval pad—while Wally looked at the ceiling, at his hands, at the floor. "You're doing just fine," Dr. Larch told Candy. He was about to tell her that Homer could advise her about any cramps she suffered, and that Homer could also check her for spotting, but he wanted to leave Homer free of that responsibility. Also, Dr. Larch couldn't at the moment have said Homer's name.

"They're taking *you*?" Curly Day asked Homer, when Curly saw Homer packing.

"I'm *not* being adopted, Curly," said Homer Wells. "I'll be back in just two days."

"They're taking *you*!" said Curly Day; his face looked so stricken, Homer had to turn away.

Dr. Larch was an amateur historian, but he nonetheless understood the power of information that is received indirectly. For that reason, he told Candy and Wally about Homer's weak heart. It was not only easier for Dr. Larch than lying to Homer; in the long run, Larch suspected, the story would be more convincing.

"I've never let him go before—not even for just two days—without saying just a little about his *condition*," Dr. Larch told Candy and Wally. A wonderful word: *condition*. The effect of the word in a doctor's mouth is truly astonishing. Candy seemed to forget she'd just had an abortion; the color came back to Wally's face. "It's his heart," said Wilbur Larch. "I've not told him about it because I haven't wanted to worry him. It's the sort of condition that could be made worse by his worrying about it," Dr. Larch confided to these two good-hearted innocents, who gave him their rapt attention.

"Just so he's not exposed to anything too strenuous, or to anything too violent in the way of exercise—or to anything too shocking," said Wilbur Larch, who had created a perfect history for someone who simply needed to be careful—who needed to stay out of danger. Larch had given his favorite orphan a history that he hoped would keep him safe. He was aware that it was a history a father would construct for his son—if a father could make his son believe it.

Homer Wells, at the moment, couldn't construct a history or anything else that would be soothing to Curly Day, who buried himself under several pillows and a blanket and sobbed.

"What do *you* need to be adopted for?" Curly cried. "You're practically a *doctor*!"

"It's just for two days," Homer Wells repeated; with each repetition his promise sounded less and less likely.

"They're taking *you*! I can't believe it!" cried Curly Day.

Nurse Angela came and sat beside Homer on Curly's bed. Together they regarded the sobbing mound under the blanket.

"It's just for two days, Curly," Nurse Angela said lamely.

"Doctor Larch said Homer was here to *protect* us!" Curly cried. "Some protection!"

Nurse Angela whispered to Homer: that if he'd go clean up the operating table, she'd sit with Curly until he felt better; she'd not wanted to clean up the table while the nice young couple needed to be alone. "Your friends seemed to be having a nice moment together," Nurse Angela whispered to Homer Wells. My *friends*! he thought. Is it possible I'm going to be having *friends*?

"You're *not* the best one, Homer!" Curly cried, under the blanket.

"Right," Homer said; he tried to pat Curly, but Curly stiffened and held his breath. "I'll see you, Curly," Homer said.

"Traitor!" cried Curly Day. Curly seemed to recognize Nurse Angela's touch; his rigid body relaxed, and he gave himself over to a steady sobbing.

Nurse Edna had finally stopped young Steerforth from crying, or she had simply outlasted the baby, who was now washed and dressed and almost asleep in Nurse Edna's arms. He had taken enough of the formula to satisfy Nurse Edna, and so she put him in his bed and finished cleaning the room where he'd been delivered. As soon as she'd put a fresh sheet on the table—she was just wiping the gleaming stirrups—Dr. Larch lurched into the room with the stationmaster's stiff body a somewhat pliable plank over his shoulder.

"Wilbur!" Nurse Edna said critically. "You should let Homer help you with that."

"It's time to get used to not having Homer around," Dr. Larch said curtly, dropping the stationmaster's body on the table. Oh, dear, Nurse Edna thought, we're in for a ferocious time of it.

"I don't suppose you've seen the sternum shears," Dr. Larch asked her.

"The snips?" she asked.

"They're called *shears,*" he said. "If you'd just undress him— I'll ask Homer."

Homer knocked before he entered the operating room, where Candy had dressed herself, with Wally's fumbling help, and now stood leaning against him in what struck Homer as an oddly formal pose—as if the couple had just finished a dance competition and were awaiting the judges' applause.

"You can relax now," said Homer Wells, not quite able to look at Candy's face. "Maybe you'd like some fresh air. I won't be long; I have to clean the table." As an awkward second thought, he added to Candy, "You're feeling all right, aren't you?"

"Oh, yes," she said, her eyes passing over Homer very quickly; she smiled reassuringly at Wally.

That was when Dr. Larch came in and asked Homer if he knew where the sternum shears were.

"They're with Clara," Homer admitted. "I'm sorry," he added quickly. "I had them there because I thought I might need them for the autopsy. On the fetus," he added.

"You don't use sternum shears on a fetus," Dr. Larch said.

"I know—I used the scissors," said Homer Wells, who was aware that the words "fetus" and "autopsy" fell like drops of blood on Wally and Candy. "I'll go get the shears for you," Homer said to Dr. Larch.

"No, finish what you're doing here," Larch said. "You two should get some fresh air," he said to Wally and Candy, who took his suggestion for a command—which it was. They left the operating room; on their way down the hall to the hospital entrance, they would have spotted the stationmaster's assistant, lurking in his corner, had the assistant not been so unnerved by the sight of Dr. Larch carrying the stationmaster's body out of the dispensary that he had cautiously attempted to follow this troubling vision. In his fear, he made a wrong turn and found himself in the dispensary. He was staring at the mud on the sheet at the foot of the bed when Wally led Candy outdoors.

"If you're so sure it was his heart," Homer Wells was asking Dr. Larch, "why are you in such a hurry to do the autopsy?"

"I like to keep busy," Larch said, surprised by the barely restrained anger in his own voice. He might have told Homer, then, that he loved him very much and that he needed something very active to occupy himself at this moment of Homer's departure. He might have confessed to Homer Wells that he wanted very much to lie down on his own bed in the dispensary and administer a little ether to himself, but that he couldn't very well have done that while the stationmaster had occupied his bed. He wanted to take Homer Wells in his arms, and hug him, and kiss him, but he could only hope that Homer understood how much Dr. Larch's self-esteem was dependent on his self-control. And so he said nothing; he left Homer alone in the operating room while he went to find the sternum shears.

Homer scrubbed the table with disinfectant. He had sealed the refuse bag when he noticed the almost transparent blondness of the clump of pubic hair that clung to his pantleg—a tight, clean curl of Candy's especially fine hair was caught on his knee. He held it up to the light, then put it in his pocket.

Nurse Edna was crying as she undressed the stationmaster. Dr. Larch had told her and Nurse Angela that there would be no hoopla of heartfelt well-wishing upon the departure of Homer Wells—nothing that would lead Candy and Wally to suspect that Homer Wells was even considering he might be gone more than two days. "Nothing," Dr. Larch had said. No hugs, no kisses, thought Nurse Edna, weeping. Her tears had no influence on the expression of the stationmaster, whose face remained seized by fear; Nurse Edna completely ignored the stationmaster. She devoted herself to her misery at being forbidden to gush over saying good-bye to Homer Wells.

"We will all appear casual about his leaving," Dr. Larch had said. "Period."

Casual! Nurse Edna thought. The stationmaster was down to his socks when Dr. Larch walked in with the sternum shears.

"There will be no crying," he said sternly to her. "Do you want to give everything away?" She yanked off the stationmaster's socks and threw them at Dr. Larch; then she left him alone with the body.

Homer Wells gave the operating table a thorough inspection, a final examination—a last look. He transferred the cluster of Candy's pubic hair from his pocket to his wallet; he once more counted the money Dr. Larch had given him. There was almost fifty dollars.

He went back to the boys' sleeping room; Nurse Angela still sat on the edge of the bed where Curly Day was still sobbing. She kissed Homer without altering the motion of her hand, which was rubbing Curly Day's back through the blanket; Homer kissed her, and left her without a word.

"I can't believe they took *him,*" murmured Curly Day through his tears.

"He'll be back," whispered Nurse Angela soothingly. *Our* Homer! she thought—I know he'll be back! Doesn't he know where he belongs?

Nurse Edna, attempting to compose herself, stepped into the dispensary, where she encountered the trembling stationmaster's assistant.

"May I help you?" Nurse Edna asked, pulling herself together.

"I've come to view the body," mumbled the assistant.

From across the hall, Nurse Edna heard the familiar crack of the sternum shears, splitting the stationmaster's chest. She doubted that the assistant would care to view the body in its present state. What she said to the assistant was, "Doctor Larch isn't finished with the autopsy."

"I brought some catalogues for Doctor Larch," the assistant said, handing the mess to Nurse Edna.

"Why, thank you," she said, but the young goon in his funeral finery showed no signs of leaving. Perhaps the ether in the dispensary air was unraveling him. "Would you like to wait?" Nurse Edna asked him. He stared at her. "To view the body," she reminded him. "You could wait in Nurse Angela's office." He nodded gratefully as Nurse Edna pointed the way down the hall. "The last door on your right," she told him. "Just make yourself comfortable."

Unburdened of the stationmaster's catalogues, the assistant had a lighter, more relaxed step as he aimed himself toward Nurse Angela's office. He was pleased to see there was a choice of chairs to sit in. Naturally, he would not choose the desk chair, behind the typewriter, but there were two lower, more comfortable-looking chairs positioned in front of the desk and the typewriter. They were the chairs that the prospective foster parents sat in when they were being interviewed. They were unmatched paisley easy chairs, and the stationmaster's assistant chose the lower, more overstuffed one. He regretted his decision as soon as he felt how very low the chair was; everything in the cluttered office seemed to loom over him. If Dr. Larch had been sitting at the desk, at the typewriter, he would have towered over the assistant in his low-sunk chair.

The assistant saw a white enamel sort of pan, or tray, upon the typewriter, but he was seated so very low that he couldn't view the pan's contents. Two tiny hands reached above the edge of the examining tray, but only the fingertips of the dead baby from Three Mile Falls were visible to the stationmaster's assistant. He had never seen a fetus before, or even a newborn baby; he was unprepared for how small the fingers can be. He kept looking around the room, from his sunken and growingly uncomfortable position, but his eyes kept coming back to the fingertips sticking above the rim of the examining tray. He couldn't believe he was really looking at *fingers*.

Whatever that is, it looks like *fingers,* he thought. Gradually, he stopped looking at other things in the room. He stared at the fingertips; a part of his mind said, Get up and see what that is! Another part of his mind made his body feel sunken into the easy chair and held down there by a great weight.

It can't be *fingers!* he thought; he kept staring, he kept sitting.

Nurse Edna wanted to tell Dr. Larch that he should, for once, let his feelings speak for him—that he should tell Homer Wells what he felt—but she stood quietly listening at the operating room door. The stationmaster's chest cracked a few more times. This didn't discomfort her—Nurse Edna was a professional—and she could tell by the precision of the snaps she heard that Dr. Larch had chosen to occupy his emotions with a task. It's *his* decision, she told herself. She went outside to see how that nice young couple were doing.

The young man was doing whatever young men do while peering under the hoods of cars, and the girl was resting, semi-reclined in the Cadillac's spacious backseat. The convertible top was still down. Nurse Edna bent over Candy and whispered to her, "You're as pretty as a picture!" Candy smiled warmly. Nurse Edna could see how exhausted the girl was. "Listen, dear," Nurse Edna said to her. "Don't be shy—if you're worried about your spotting," Nurse Edna said to her confidentially, "or if you have any peculiar cramps, speak to Homer about it. Promise me you won't be shy about it, dear. And most certainly, if you run a fever—promise me," Nurse Edna said.

"I promise," Candy said, blushing.

Melony was struggling to inscribe the copy of *Little Dorrit* she had stolen for Homer when she heard Mary Agnes Cork throwing up in the bathroom.

"Shut up!" Melony called, but Mary Agnes went on retching. She'd eaten two jars of apple-cider jelly, one jar of honey and another of crab-apple jelly. She thought it was the honey that did it.

Smoky Fields had already thrown up. He'd eaten all his jars, of everything, and a jar belonging to one of the little Walshes. He lay miserably in his bed, listening to Curly Day crying and Nurse Angela talking on and on.

TO HOMER "SUNSHINE" WELLS
FOR THE PROMISE
YOU MADE ME

Melony wrote. She glanced out her window, but there was nothing going on. It wasn't dark; it wasn't time for the two women she'd watched arrive in the morning to be heading downhill for their return train—to wherever.

LOVE, MELONY

Melony added, as Mary Agnes groaned and heaved again.

"You dumb little bitch pig!" Melony called.

Homer Wells walked into the operating room when Wilbur Larch had successfully exposed the stationmaster's heart. Larch was not surprised to see no evidence of heart disease, no dead-muscle tissue ("No infarction," he said to Homer, without looking up at him)—in short, no damage to the heart of any kind.

"The stationmaster had a healthy heart," Dr. Larch announced to Homer Wells. No "massive" heart attack had dropped the stationmaster, as Larch had suspected. It appeared there had been a very sudden change in the heart's rhythm. "*Arrhythmia,* I think," Dr. Larch said to Homer Wells.

"His heart just stopped, right?" Homer asked.

"I think that he suffered some shock, or fright," said Wilbur Larch.

Homer Wells could believe that—just by looking at the stationmaster's face. "Right," he said.

"Of course there could be a clot in the brain," said Wilbur Larch. "Where should I look?" he asked Homer familiarly.

"The brain stem," said Homer Wells.

"Right," Wilbur Larch said. "Good boy."

When Homer Wells saw the stationmaster's brain stem exposed, he felt that Dr. Larch was busy enough—with both hands—for it to be safe to say what Homer wanted to say.

"I love you," said Homer Wells. He knew he had to leave the room, then—while he could still see the door—and so he started to leave.

"I love you, too, Homer," said Wilbur Larch, who for another minute or more could not have seen a blood clot in the brain stem if there had been one to see. He heard Homer say "Right" before he heard the door close.

In a while, he could make out the brain stem clearly; there was no clot.

"Arrhythmia," Wilbur Larch repeated to himself. Then he

added, "Right," as if he were now speaking for Homer Wells. Dr. Larch put his instruments aside; he gripped the operating table for a long time.

Outside, Homer Wells stuck his bag in the Cadillac's trunk, smiled at Candy in the backseat, helped Wally raise the convertible's top; it would be dark soon, and especially cold for Candy in the backseat if they left the top down.

"See you in two days!" Nurse Edna said to Homer, too loudly.

"Two days," Homer repeated, too quietly. She pecked his cheek; he patted her arm. Nurse Edna then turned and trotted to the hospital entrance; both Candy and Wally appeared impressed that the woman could move so quickly. When she was inside the hospital, Nurse Edna went directly to the dispensary and threw herself on the bed; if she had a soft heart, she had a strong stomach—it hardly mattered to her that the stationmaster's body had spent much of the day on that bed, or that the mud from his boots had soiled the top sheet.

Dr. Larch was still gripping the operating table when he heard the stationmaster's assistant scream. There was just one scream, followed by a prolonged series of whimpers. Homer and Candy and Wally never heard the scream; Wally had already started the car.

The assistant had waited the longest time before forcing himself out of the deep, low chair. He had not wanted to look more closely at the contents of the white enameled examining tray, but the little fingers had beckoned to him and he had felt himself drawn to the tray, where a full and close-up view of the opened-up fetus had caused him (like Curly Day) to wet his pants. He screamed when he discovered that his legs wouldn't move; the only way he could manage to leave Nurse Angela's office was on all fours; he went whimpering down the hall like a beaten dog. Dr. Larch blocked his way at the operating room door.

"What is the matter with you?" Larch asked the assistant scathingly.

"I brought you all his catalogues!" the stationmaster's assistant managed to say while still on all fours.

"Catalogues?" said Larch, with evident distaste. "Stand up, man! What's wrong with you?" He seized the quaking assistant under his armpits and drew him, trembling, to his feet.

"I just wanted to view the body," the assistant protested weakly.

Wilbur Larch shrugged. What is this fascination the world has with death? he wondered, but he stepped aside, ushering the assistant into the operating room where the stationmaster, with his heart and his brain stem very well exposed, was instantly in view.

"A sudden change in the heart's rhythm," Wilbur Larch explained. "Something frightened him to death." It was not hard for the assistant to imagine being frightened to death, although he thought that the stationmaster appeared to have been run over by a train—or else had fallen victim to the same evil responsible for the hideous baby upon the typewriter.

"Thank you," the assistant whispered to Dr. Larch, then ran so fast down the hall and outdoors that the sound of his footsteps roused Nurse Edna from her weeping; her own crying had prevented her from hearing the assistant's screams or his whimpers.

It seemed to Nurse Angela that nothing would console Curly Day, and so she attempted to make herself comfortable on his narrow bed, believing she was in for a long night.

Dr. Larch sat in his usual place, at the typewriter; the fetus displayed by Homer Wells disturbed him not in the slightest. Perhaps he appreciated that Homer had left something behind that would need attention—busy work, busy work, give me busy work, thought Wilbur Larch. Just before night fell, he leaned forward in his chair enough to turn on the desk lamp. Then he settled back in the chair in which he had spent so many evenings. He appeared to be waiting for someone. It was not yet dark but he could hear an owl outside—very distinctly. He knew the wild wind from the coast must have dropped.

When it was still light, Melony looked out her window and saw the Cadillac pass. The passenger side of the car faced the girls' division, and Melony had no trouble recognizing Homer Wells in the passenger seat—his profile turned to her. He sat rigidly, as if he were holding his breath; he was. If he had seen her—or worse, if he had needed to speak to her in order to finalize his escape—he knew he couldn't have succeeded in saying to her that he would be back in just two days. Melony knew what a lie was and what a promise was, and she knew the instant that a promise was broken. She saw a flash of the beautiful girl with the long legs in the backseat of the car, and she supposed that the handsome young man was driving; she had a longer, better look at the profile of Homer Wells. When she slammed the stolen copy of *Little Dorrit* shut, the ink was still wet and her inscription was smudged. She threw the book against the wall, which only Mrs. Grogan heard—Mary Agnes was still violently ill and too much surrounded by her own noise.

Melony put herself straight to bed without her dinner. Mrs. Grogan, worried about her, went to Melony's bed and felt her forehead, which was feverish, but Mrs. Grogan could not coax Melony to drink anything. All Melony said was, "He broke his promise." Later, she said, "Homer Wells has left Saint Cloud's."

"You have a little temperature, dear," said Mrs. Grogan, but when Homer Wells didn't come to read *Jane Eyre* aloud that evening, Mrs. Grogan started paying closer attention. She allowed Melony to read to the girls that evening; Melony's voice was oddly flat and passionless. Melony's reading from *Jane Eyre* depressed Mrs. Grogan—especially when she read this part:

> . . . it is madness in all women to let a secret love kindle within them, which, if unreturned and unknown, must devour the life that feeds it . . .

Why, the girl didn't bat an eye! Mrs. Grogan observed.

Nurse Angela had hardly any more success, reading aloud to the boys' division from Dickens. Dickensian description was too strenuous for her—she got lost in the longer passages—and when she had to keep going back to the beginning, she saw that the boys were losing interest.

Nurse Edna tried her best with the nightly benediction; Dr. Larch refused to leave Nurse Angela's office; he said he was listening to an owl, and he wanted to keep listening. Nurse Edna felt extremely self-conscious with the benediction, which she'd never fully understood in the first place—she took it to be a kind of private joke between Dr. Larch and the universe. Her voice was too shrill, and startled sick little Smoky Fields out of sleep, and produced a long, loud wail from Curly Day—before Curly returned to his more steady sobbing.

"Good night, you Princes of Maine! You Kings of New England!" Nurse Edna peeped. Where is Homer? several voices whispered, while Nurse Angela continued to rub Curly Day between his shoulder blades in the darkness.

Nurse Edna, extremely agitated by Dr. Larch's behavior, got up the nerve to march right down to Nurse Angela's office. She was going to walk right in and tell Dr. Larch that he should go give himself a good snort of ether and then get a good night's sleep! But Nurse Edna grew more timid as she approached the solitary light shining from the office. Nurse Edna hadn't known about the fetal autopsy, either, and when she rather cautiously peered into Nurse Angela's office, she was given quite a turn by the gruesome fetus. Dr. Larch just sat at the typewriter, unmoving. He was composing in his mind the first of many letters he would write to Homer Wells. He was attempting to gentle his anxieties and calm his thoughts. Please be healthy, please be happy, please be careful, Wilbur Larch was thinking—the darkness edging in around him, the supplicant hands of the murdered baby from Three Mile Falls reaching out to him.

6/ Ocean View

For the first two weeks that Homer Wells was gone from St. Cloud's, Wilbur Larch let the mail pile up unanswered, Nurse Angela struggled with the longer and denser sentences of Charles Dickens (which had a curious effect on the boys' attention; they hung on her every word, holding their breath for the errors they anticipated), and Mrs. Grogan suffered Melony's deadpan rendition of Charlotte Brontë. Near the end of Chapter Twenty-seven, Mrs. Grogan could detect a bare minimum of Jane Eyre's "indomitable" spirit in Melony's voice.

" 'I care for myself,' " Melony read. " 'The more solitary, the more friendless, the more unsustained I am, the more I will respect myself.' "

Good girl, thought Mrs. Grogan, please be a good girl. She told Dr. Larch that, although Melony's reading voice depressed her, Melony should be encouraged; she should be given more responsibility.

Nurse Angela said she'd be glad to give up on Dickens. Dr. Larch surprised them all. When Homer Wells had been gone for three weeks, Dr. Larch announced that he didn't give a damn who read what to whom. He had ceased to care about the benediction altogether, and so Nurse Edna—although it would never feel quite natural to her—persisted with the nightly salutation to the imagined Princes of Maine, "the dear little Kings of New England."

Mrs. Grogan became so firmly transfixed by Melony's reading voice that she now accompanied Melony to the boys' division and listened, with the nervous boys, to Melony read Dickens. Melony's voice was too even-pitched for Dickens; she plodded her way—she made no mistakes but she never adjusted her cadence; she presented bustle and sunshine with the same heavy speech she used for gloom and fog. By her stern countenance, Mrs. Grogan saw that Melony was analyzing as she read—but the subject of her analysis was not Charles Dickens; Melony was searching through Dickens for specific characteristics she associated with Homer Wells. Sometimes, by the intense concentration on Melony's face, Melony seemed close to discovering Homer's whereabouts in the England of another century. (Dr. Larch had told Melony that Homer's actual whereabouts were not her business.)

Never mind that Melony murdered every moment of Dickensian wit with her ferocity, or that the rich and colorful details of character and place were turned uniformly drab by her voice. "The girl has no lilt," Nurse Edna complained. Never mind: the boys were terrified of Melony, and their fears made them pay more attention to her than they had ever paid to Homer Wells. Sometimes the interest in the literature isn't in the literature—the boys' division was an audience like any other: self-interest, personal memories, their secret anxieties crept into their perceptions of what they heard (regardless of what Charles Dickens had done and what Melony did to him).

Not feeling completely comfortable with leaving the girls' division unattended while she trotted to the boys' to hear Melony read, Mrs. Grogan developed the habit of following the excerpt from *Jane Eyre* with a short prayer that clung, both lovely and ominous, to the pale and stained bedspreads on which the moonlight glowed long after Melony and Mrs. Grogan had left the girls to themselves. Even Mary Agnes Cork was struck silent—if not exactly rendered well behaved—by Mrs. Grogan's prayer.

If Mrs. Grogan had known that the prayer was English in origin, she might not have used it; she had heard it on the radio and memorized it, and she always spoke it to herself before she allowed herself to sleep. The prayer was written by Cardinal Newman. When Melony started reading to the boys, Mrs. Grogan made her personal prayer public.

"Oh Lord," she said in the hall light, in the open doorway, while Melony stood restlessly beside her. " 'Oh Lord, support us all the day long, until the shadows lengthen and the evening comes, and the busy world is hushed, and the fever of life is over, and our work is done. Then in thy mercy grant us a safe lodging, and a holy rest, and peace at the last.' "

"Amen," Melony would say—not quite facetiously, but cer-

tainly not reverentially. She said it the way she read from
Charlotte Brontë and from Charles Dickens—it gave Mrs.
Grogan a chill, although the summer nights were warm and
humid and she needed to take two steps for every one of
Melony's, just to keep pace with Melony on her determined
journey to the boys' division. The way Melony said "Amen"
was the way she said everything. Hers was a voice without a
soul, Mrs. Grogan thought—her teeth chattering as she sat in a
chair in the boys' division, slightly out of the light, behind
Melony, watching her broad back. Something in Mrs. Grogan's
transfixed appearance may have been responsible for the rumor
begun in the boys' division, possibly by Curly Day: that Mrs.
Grogan had never gone to school, was actually illiterate, was
incapable of reading even a newspaper to herself—and was,
therefore, in Melony's control.

The little boys, lying frightened in their beds, felt that they
were in Melony's control, too.

Nurse Edna was so disquieted by Melony's reading that she
couldn't wait to launch into her Princes of Maine and Kings of
New England refrain (even if she didn't know what it meant).
Nurse Edna suggested that Melony was to blame for an increase in nightmares in the boys' division and that she should
be removed from her responsibilities as reader. Nurse Angela
disagreed; if Melony persisted in casting an evil presence, it
was because she'd not been given enough responsibility. Also,
Nurse Angela said, maybe there weren't more nightmares: with
Homer Wells gone (it had now been a month), perhaps it was
simply that Nurse Edna and Nurse Angela heard those suffering from night terrors—in the past, Homer heard them first
and tended to them.

Mrs. Grogan was in favor of increasing Melony's responsibilities; she felt the girl was at the threshold of a change—she
might either rise above her own bitterness or descend more
deeply into it. It was Nurse Angela who suggested to Dr. Larch
that Melony might be of use.

"Of *more* use, you mean?" Dr. Larch asked.

"Right," Nurse Angela said, but Dr. Larch didn't appreciate
anyone imitating the speech habits of Homer Wells; he gave
Nurse Angela such a look that she never said "Right" again.
He also didn't appreciate the suggestion that Melony could be
taught to replace Homer—not even in usefulness.

Nurse Edna took up Melony's cause. "If she were a *boy,*

Wilbur," Nurse Edna said, "you would already have given her more to do."

"The hospital is connected to the boys' division," Larch said. "It's impossible to keep what's happening here a secret from the boys. But the *girls* are another matter," he concluded weakly.

"Melony knows what's happening here," Nurse Angela said.

Wilbur Larch knew he was cornered. He was also angry at Homer Wells—he had given the boy permission to extend his time away from St. Cloud's as long as possible, but he hadn't expected he wouldn't *hear* from Homer (not a word!) in nearly six weeks.

"I don't know that I have the patience to work with a teen-ager, anymore," Larch said peevishly.

"I think Melony is twenty-four or twenty-five," Mrs. Grogan said.

How could someone that old still be in an orphanage? Larch wondered. The same way that *I* can still be here, he answered himself. Who else would take the job? Who else would take Melony? "All right. Let's ask her if she's interested," Larch said.

He dreaded the meeting with Melony; he couldn't help himself, but he blamed her for whatever sullenness had crept into Homer's personality—and the rebellion Homer had manifested toward him recently. Larch knew he was being unfair, and this made him feel guilty; he began to answer the mail.

There was a long (albeit businesslike) letter from Olive Worthington, and a check—a rather sizable donation to the orphanage. Mrs. Worthington said she was happy her son had been so "taken" by the good work at St. Cloud's that he'd seen fit to bring one of Dr. Larch's "boys" home with him. It was fine with the Worthingtons that Homer stay through the summer. They frequently hired "schoolboy help," and she was frankly grateful that her son Wally had "the opportunity to mingle with someone his own age—but of less fortunate circumstances." Olive Worthington wanted Larch to know that she and her husband thought Homer was a fine boy, polite and a good worker, and that he seemed "altogether a sobering influence on Wally." She concluded that she hoped "Wally might even learn the value of a day's work from his proximity to Homer," and that Homer had "clearly profited from a rigorous education"—she based this judgment on Homer's ability to learn the apple business "as if he were used to more demanding studies."

Olive wanted Dr. Larch to know that Homer had requested to be paid in the form of a monthly donation to St. Cloud's, minus only what she fairly judged were his expenses; since he shared a room with Wally and could fit into Wally's clothes, and since he ate his meals with the Worthington family, Olive said the boy's expenses were minimal. She was delighted that her son had "such manly and honorable company" for the summer, and she was pleased to have the opportunity to contribute what little she could to the well-being of the orphans of St. Cloud's. "The kids," Olive said (it was how she referred to Wally and Candy), " . . . tell me you are doing great things there. They're so happy they stumbled upon you."

Wilbur Larch could tell that Olive Worthington didn't know she had an accomplished obstetrician tending to her apple trees, and he grumbled to himself about the "rigorous education" he felt had been quite wasted on Homer Wells—given his present occupation—but Dr. Larch calmed himself sufficiently to compose a cordial, albeit formal, letter in response to Mrs. Worthington.

Her donation was very gratefully received, and he was glad that Homer Wells was representing his upbringing at St. Cloud's in so positive a manner—he would expect no less of the boy, which Mrs. Worthington might be so kind as to tell him. Also, that it would be nice if Homer would write. Dr. Larch was happy that there was such healthy summer employment for Homer; the boy would be missed at St. Cloud's, where he had always been of use, but Larch emphasized his pleasure at Homer's good fortune. He congratulated Olive Worthington on the good manners and the generosity of her son; he said he would welcome those "kids" back at St. Cloud's—anytime. What luck—for everyone!—that they had "stumbled upon" the orphanage.

Wilbur Larch gritted his teeth and tried to imagine a harder place to stumble upon than St. Cloud's; he managed a supreme effort at concentration and proceeded with the part of the letter he had waited more than a month to write.

"There is one thing I must tell you about Homer Wells," Wilbur Larch wrote. "There is a problem with his heart," the doctor wrote; he elaborated. He was more careful than he'd been when he discussed Homer's heart defect with Wally and

Candy; he tried to be as precise but as elusive as he knew he'd eventually have to be when he described the ailment to Homer Wells. His letter to Olive Worthington about Homer's heart was a kind of warm-up exercise. He was sowing seeds (an infuriating phrase, but he found himself thinking it—ever since his inheritance of the stationmaster's catalogues); he wanted Homer treated with kid gloves, as they say in Maine.

Olive Worthington had mentioned that Homer was taking driving lessons from Wally and swimming lessons from Candy—the latter in the Haven Club's heated pool. The latter—swimming lessons from that girl!—made Wilbur Larch growl, and he concluded his cautionary advice about Homer's heart with the suggestion that Homer "take it easy with the swimming."

Dr. Larch did not share Olive Worthington's opinion that "every boy should know how to drive and swim"; Dr. Larch could do neither.

"Here in St. Cloud's," he wrote, to himself, "it is imperative to have good obstetrical procedure, and to be able to perform a dilatation and curettage. In other parts of the world, they learn how to drive and swim!"

He showed Olive Worthington's letter to Nurse Angela and Nurse Edna, who both wept over it. They were of the opinion that Mrs. Worthington sounded "charming" and "warm" and "intelligent," but Larch grumbled how it was strange that *Mr.* Worthington was so little in view; what was the matter with him? "What's his wife running the farm for?" Larch asked his nurses, who both scolded him for his readiness to assume there was something wrong whenever a woman was in charge of anything. They reminded him that he had an appointment with Melony.

Melony had been working herself into a proper state of mind for her meeting with Dr. Larch. She prepared herself by lying in her bed and reading over and over again the inscription she had written in the stolen copy of *Little Dorrit:*

> TO HOMER "SUNSHINE" WELLS
> FOR THE PROMISE
> YOU MADE ME
> LOVE, MELONY

Then she tried, again and again, to begin the book through her angry tears.

The image of the staring, blazing sun in Marseilles—the oppressive glare—was both dazzling and mystifying to Melony. What experience did she have to help her comprehend a sun of that brightness? And the coincidence of so much *sunshine* (considering her nickname for Homer Wells) was too much for her. She read, got lost, began again, got lost again; she grew angrier and angrier.

Then she looked in her canvas bag of toilet articles and saw that the horn-rim barrette, which Mary Agnes had stolen from Candy—and which Melony had snatched out of Mary Agnes's hair and taken for herself—had been stolen again. She marched to Mary Agnes Cork's bed and retrieved the elegant barrette from under Mary Agnes's pillow. Melony's hair was cropped too short for her to be able to use the barrette, which she was not exactly sure how to use, anyway. She jammed it into her jeans' pocket; this was uncomfortable—her jeans were so tight. She went into the girls' shower room, where Mary Agnes Cork was washing her hair, and she turned the hot water up so hot that Mary Agnes was nearly scalded. Mary Agnes flung herself out of the shower; she lay red and writhing on the floor, where Melony twisted her arm behind her back and then stepped with all her weight on Mary Agnes's shoulder. Melony didn't mean to break anything; she was repelled by the sound of Mary Agnes's collarbone giving way, and she stepped quickly away from the younger girl—whose naked body turned from very red to very white. She lay on the shower room floor, shivering and moaning, not daring to move.

"Get dressed and I'll take you to the hospital," Melony said. "You broke something."

Mary Agnes trembled. "I can't move," she whispered.

"I didn't mean to," Melony said, "but I told you to keep outta my stuff."

"Your hair's too short," Mary Agnes said. "You can't wear it, anyway."

"You want me to break something else?" Melony asked the girl.

Mary Agnes tried to shake her head, but she stopped. "I can't move," she repeated. When Melony bent over to help her up, Mary Agnes screamed, "Don't touch me!"

"Suit yourself," Melony said, leaving her there. "Just keep outta my stuff."

In the lobby of the girls' division, on her way to her meeting with Dr. Larch, Melony told Mrs. Grogan that Mary Agnes had "broken something." Mrs. Grogan naturally assumed that Melony meant that Mary Agnes had broken a lamp, or a window, or even a bed.

"How are you liking the book, dear?" Mrs. Grogan asked Melony, who always carried *Little Dorrit* with her; she'd not been able to get past the first page.

"It starts kinda slow," said Melony.

When she got to Nurse Angela's office, where Dr. Larch was waiting for her, she was slightly out of breath and sweating.

"What's the book?" Dr. Larch asked her.

"*Little Dorrit* by Charles Dickens," Melony said; she felt the barrette bite into her leg when she sat down.

"Where'd you get it?" Dr. Larch asked her.

"It was a gift," Melony said—which was not exactly a lie.

"That's nice," said Wilbur Larch.

Melony shrugged. "It starts kinda slow," she said.

They eyed each other for a moment, cautiously. Larch smiled a little. Melony tried to smile but she was unsure how this looked on her face—so she stopped. She shifted in the chair; the barrette in her pocket hurt her a little less.

"He's not coming back, is he?" Melony asked Dr. Larch, who regarded her with the respect and wariness you feel for someone who has read your mind.

"He has a summer job," Larch said. "Of course, some other opportunity might develop."

Melony shrugged. "He might go to school, I suppose," she said.

"Oh, I *hope* so!" Larch said.

"I suppose you want him to be a doctor," Melony said.

Larch shrugged. It was his turn to feign indifference. "If he wants to be," he said.

"I broke someone's arm, once," Melony said. "Or maybe it was something in the chest."

"The chest?" Larch asked. "When did you do this?"

"Not too long ago," Melony said. "Pretty recently. I didn't mean to."

"How did it happen?" Dr. Larch asked her.

"I twisted her arm behind her back—she was on the floor— and then I stepped on her shoulder, the same shoulder of the arm I twisted."

"Ouch," said Dr. Larch.

"I heard it," Melony said. "Her arm or her chest."

"Perhaps her collarbone," Larch suggested. Given the position, he guessed it would be the collarbone.

"Well, whatever it was, I heard it," Melony said.

"How did that make you feel?" Wilbur Larch asked Melony, who shrugged.

"I don't know," Melony said. "Sick, I guess, but strong," she added. "Sick and strong," she said.

"Perhaps you'd like to have more to do?" Larch asked her.

"Here?" Melony asked.

"Well, here, yes," Larch said. "I could find more things for you to do here—more important things. Of course, I could also inquire for you about jobs—outside, I mean. Away from here."

"You want me to go, or do more chores, is that it?"

"*I* don't want you to do anything you don't want to do. You told me you didn't want to leave, once—and I'll never force you. It's just that I thought you might be looking for a change."

"You don't like how I read, huh?" Melony asked. "Is that it?"

"No!" Dr. Larch said. "I want you to keep reading, but that's only one of the things you might do here."

"You want me to do what Homer Wells did?"

"Homer did a lot of *studying*," Dr. Larch said. "Perhaps you could assist Nurse Angela and Nurse Edna, and me. Perhaps you'd be interested in just *observing*—to see if you liked it."

"I think it's sick," Melony said.

"You disapprove?" Larch asked, but Melony looked genuinely puzzled.

"What?" she asked.

"You don't believe we should perform the abortions, is that it?" Larch asked. "You don't believe in terminating a birth, in aborting the fetus?"

Melony shrugged. "I just think it would make me sick," she repeated. "Delivering babies—yuck," she said. "And cutting babies out of people—yuck, again."

Larch was confused. "But it's not that you think it's wrong?" he asked.

"What's wrong about it?" she asked him. "I think it's sick. Blood, people leaking stuff out of their bodies—ick," Melony said. "It smells bad around here," she added, meaning the hospital air—the aura of ether, the scent of old blood.

Wilbur Larch stared at Melony and thought, Why, she's just a big child! She's a baby thug!

"I don't want to work around the hospital," Melony said flatly. "I'll rake leaves, or something—stuff like that is okay, if you want me to work more, for my food or something."

"I want you to be happier than you are, Melony," Dr. Larch said cautiously. He felt miserable for how neglected the creature before him was.

"Happier!" said Melony; she gave a little jump in her chair and the stolen barrette dug into her. "You must be stupid, or crazy." Dr. Larch wasn't shocked; he nodded, considering the possibilities.

He heard Mrs. Grogan calling him from the hall outside the dispensary.

"Doctor Larch! Doctor Larch!" she called. "Wilbur?" she added, which gave Nurse Edna a tremor, because she felt a certain possessiveness regarding the use of that name. "Mary Agnes has broken her arm!" Larch stared at Melony, who for the first time managed a smile.

"You said this happened 'not too long ago'?" Larch asked her.

"I said 'pretty recently,' " Melony admitted.

Larch went into the dispensary, where he examined Mary Agnes's collarbone, which was broken; then he instructed Nurse Angela to prepare the child for X ray.

"I slipped on the shower room floor," Mary Agnes moaned. "It was real wet."

"Melony!" Dr. Larch called. Melony was hanging around in the hall. "Melony, would you like to observe how we set a broken bone?" Melony walked into the dispensary, which was a small, crowded area—especially with Nurse Edna and Mrs. Grogan standing there, and with Nurse Angela leading Mary Agnes away for her X ray. Seeing everyone together, Larch realized how old and frail he and his colleagues looked alongside Melony. "Would you like to participate in the setting of a broken bone, Melony?" Larch asked the sturdy and imposing young woman.

"Nope," Melony said. "I got things to do." She waved the copy of *Little Dorrit* a trifle threateningly. "And I gotta look at what I'm gonna read tonight," she added.

She went back to the girls' division, to her window there,

while Dr. Larch set Mary Agnes's collarbone. Melony tried again to comprehend the power of the sun in Marseilles.

"The very dust was scorched brown," she read to herself, "and something quivered in the atmosphere as if the air itself were panting." Oh, Sunshine, she thought, why didn't you take me anywhere? It wouldn't have to have been to France, although that would have been nice.

She daydreamed as she read and therefore she missed the transition between the "universal stare" of the sun in Marseilles and the atmosphere of the prison in the same town. Suddenly, she discovered she was in the prison. "A prison taint was on everything . . ." she read. "Like a well, like a vault, like a tomb, the prison had no knowledge of the brightness outside . . ." She stopped reading. She left *Little Dorrit* on her pillow. She stripped a pillowcase off a bed neater than her own, and into the pillowcase she stuffed her canvas bag of toilet articles and some clothes. She also put *Jane Eyre* in the bag.

In Mrs. Grogan's rather Spartan room, Melony had no difficulty locating Mrs. Grogan's purse—she robbed Mrs. Grogan of her money (there wasn't much), and also took Mrs. Grogan's heavy winter coat (in the summer, the coat would be useful if she had to sleep on the ground). Mrs. Grogan was still at the hospital, worrying about Mary Agnes Cork's collarbone; Melony would have liked to say good-bye to Mrs. Grogan (even after robbing her), but she knew the train schedule by heart—actually, she knew it by ear; the sound of every arrival and departure reached her window.

At the train station she bought a ticket only as far as Livermore Falls. She knew that even the new and stupid young stationmaster would be able to remember that, and he would tell Dr. Larch and Mrs. Grogan that Melony had gone to Livermore Falls. She also knew that once she was on the train she could purchase a ticket to some place much farther away than Livermore Falls. Can I afford Portland? she wondered. It was the coast that she would need to explore, eventually—because, below the Cadillac's gold monogram on that Red Delicious apple, inscribed (also in gold) against the vivid green background of the apple leaf, she had been able to read OCEAN VIEW ORCHARDS. That had to be within sight of the coast, and the Cadillac had a Maine license plate. It mattered not to Melony that there were thousands of miles of coastline in the state of Maine. As her train pulled away from St. Cloud's,

Melony said to herself—so vehemently that her breath fogged the window and obscured the abandoned buildings in that forsaken town from her view—"I'm gonna find you, Sunshine."

/ / /

Dr. Larch tried to comfort Mrs. Grogan, who said she wished only that she'd had more money for Melony to steal. "And my coat's not waterproof," Mrs. Grogan complained. "She should have a real raincoat in this state."

Dr. Larch tried to reassure Mrs. Grogan; he asserted that Melony was not a little girl. "She's twenty-four or twenty-five," Larch reminded Mrs. Grogan.

"I think her heart is broken," said Mrs. Grogan miserably.

Dr. Larch pointed out that Melony had taken *Jane Eyre* with her; he accepted this as a hopeful sign—wherever Melony went, she would not be without guidance, she would not be without love, without faith; she had a good book with her. If only she'll keep reading it, and reading it, Larch thought.

The book that Melony had left behind was a puzzle to both Mrs. Grogan and Dr. Larch. They read the dedication to Homer "Sunshine" Wells, which touched Mrs. Grogan deeply.

Neither of them had any luck reading *Little Dorrit,* either. Mrs. Grogan never would get to the "villainous" prison; the staring sun in Marseilles outstared her, it was too powerfully blinding. Dr. Larch, who—in the absence of Homer Wells *and* Melony—resumed his responsibilities as the nightly reader to both the boys' and the girls' divisions, attempted to read *Little Dorrit* to the girls; wasn't the main character a girl? But the contrast between the scorched air in the Marseilles sun and the tainted air in the Marseilles prison created such a powerful sleeplessness among the girls that Larch was relieved to give up on the book in Chapter Three, which had an unfortunate title, for orphans: "Home." He began the description of London on a Sunday evening—hounded by church bells.

" 'Melancholy streets, in a penitential garb of soot,' " read Dr. Larch, and then he stopped; we need no more melancholy here, he thought.

"Wouldn't we rather wait, and read *Jane Eyre* again?" Dr. Larch asked; the girls nodded eagerly.

Knowing that the beautiful boy with the face of a benefactor must have a mother with the heart for *benefiting* those who existed in (as she had written herself) "less fortunate circumstances," Dr. Larch wrote Olive Worthington.

> My Dear Mrs. Worthington,
> Here in St. Cloud's, we depend on our few luxuries and imagine (and pray) they will last forever. If you would be so kind, please tell Homer that his friend Melony has left us—her whereabouts are unknown—and that she took with her our only copy of *Jane Eyre.* The orphans in the girls' division were accustomed to hearing this book read aloud—in fact, Homer used to read to them. If Homer could discover a replacement copy, the little girls and I would remain in his debt. In other parts of the world, there are bookshops . . .

Thus, Larch knew, he had accomplished two things. Olive Worthington herself would send him a replacement *Jane Eyre* (he doubted very much that it would be a secondhand copy), and Homer would receive the important message: Melony was out. She was loose in the world. Larch thought that Homer should know this, that he might want to keep an eye open for her.

As for *Little Dorrit,* Nurse Edna read Melony's inscription and wept. She was not a big reader, Edna; she penetrated no farther than the inscription. Nurse Angela had already been defeated by Dickens; she blinked once, briefly, at the sun in Marseilles and failed to turn the page.

For years Candy's unread copy would rest in Nurse Angela's office; those nervously awaiting interviews with Dr. Larch would pick up *Little Dorrit* as they would pick up a magazine—restlessly, inattentively. Larch rarely kept anyone waiting past the first glare of the sun. And most preferred to scan the odd assortment of catalogues. The seeds, the fishing equipment, the stupendous undergarments—the latter modeled in an otherworldly way: on those headless, legless, armless stumps that were the period's version of the standard dressmaker's dummy.

"In other parts of the world," Dr. Larch began once, "they have nursing bras." But this thought led him nowhere; it fell as a fragment into the many, many pages of *A Brief History of St. Cloud's.*

Little Dorrit seemed condemned to an unread life. Even Candy, who replaced her stolen copy (and always wondered what happened to it), would never finish the book, although it was required reading for her class. She, too, could not navigate past the sun's initial assault on her senses; she suspected her difficulty with the book arose from its power to remind her of her discomfort on the long journey to and from St. Cloud's—and of what had happened to her there.

She would especially remember the ride back to the coast—how she'd stretched out in the backseat, with only the dash lights of the Cadillac and the glowing ash end of Wally's cigarette shining bright but small in the surrounding darkness. The tires of the big car hummed soothingly; she was grateful for Homer's presence because she didn't have to talk to—or listen to—Wally. She couldn't even hear what Wally and Homer were saying to each other. "Life stories," Wally would say to her later. "That kid's had quite a life, but I should let him tell you."

The drone of their conversation was as rhythmic as the tire song, but—as weary as she was—she couldn't sleep. She thought about how much she was bleeding—maybe more than she should be, she worried. Between St. Cloud's and the coast, she asked Wally three times to stop the car. She kept checking her bleeding and changing the pad; Dr. Larch had given her quite a few pads—but would there be enough, and how much bleeding was too much? She looked at the back of Homer's head. If it's worse tomorrow, or as bad the next day, she thought, I'll have to ask him.

When Wally went to the men's room and left them alone in the car, Homer spoke to her, but he didn't turn around. "You're probably having cramps, about as bad as you get with your period," he said. "You're probably bleeding, but not like you bleed during your period—nothing near what it is, at your heaviest time. If the stains on the pad are only two or three inches in diameter, that's okay. It's expected."

"Thank you," Candy whispered.

"The bleeding should taper off tomorrow, and get much lighter the next day. If you're worried, you should ask me," he said.

"Okay," Candy said. She felt so strange: that a boy her own age should know this much about her.

"I've never seen a lobster," said Homer Wells, to change the subject—to allow her to be the authority.

"Then you've never eaten one, either," Candy said cheerfully.

"I don't know if I want to eat something I've never seen," Homer said, and Candy laughed. She was laughing when Wally got back in the car.

"We're talking about lobsters," Homer explained.

"Oh, they're hilarious," Wally said, and all three of them laughed.

"Wait till you see one!" Candy said to Homer. "He's never seen one!" she told Wally.

"They're even funnier when you see them," Wally said. Candy's laughter hurt her; she stopped very suddenly, but Homer laughed more. "And wait till they try to talk to you," Wally added. "Lobsters really break me up, every time they try to talk."

When he and Wally stopped laughing, Homer said, "I've never seen the ocean, you know."

"Candy, did you hear that?" Wally asked, but Candy had released herself with her brief laughter; she was sound asleep. "You've *never* seen the ocean?" Wally asked Homer.

"That's right," said Homer Wells.

"That's not funny," said Wally seriously.

"Right," Homer said.

A little later, Wally said, "You want to drive for a while?"

"I don't know how to drive," Homer said.

"Really?" Wally asked. And later still—it was almost midnight—Wally asked, "Uh, have you ever been with a girl—made love to one, you know?" But Homer Wells had also felt released: he had laughed out loud with his new friends. The young but veteran insomniac had fallen asleep. Would Wally have been surprised to know that Homer hadn't laughed out loud with friends before, either? And possibly Homer would have had difficulty characterizing his relationship with Melony as a relationship based on making love.

What a new sense of security Homer had felt in that moment of laughter with friends in the enclosed dark of the moving car, and what a sense of freedom the car itself gave to him—its seemingly effortless journeying was a wonder to Homer Wells, for whom the idea of motion (not to mention the sense of change) was accomplished only rarely and only with enormous strife.

"Candy?" Wally whispered. And a little later, he whispered, "Homer?" He rather liked the idea of steering these two through the blackened world, of being their guide through the night, and their protector from whatever lay just beyond the headlights' reach.

"Well, buddy," Wally said to the sleeping Homer Wells, "it's high time you had some *fun*."

Wilbur Larch, almost a month later—still waiting to hear from Homer Wells and too proud to write the first letter—wondered about the "fun" Homer was having. Swimming lessons! he thought. What does one wear for swimming in a heated pool? How do they heat the pool, and how much do they heat it?

In 194__, the pool at the Haven Club was the first heated swimming pool in Maine. Although Raymond Kendall thought it was ridiculous to heat water for purposes other than cooking and bathing, he had invented the heating system for the Haven Club pool. It was just an exercise in mechanics for Ray.

"If you learn to swim in the ocean," Ray told Homer, "you'll learn the proper response for a body to make to all that water."

"But *you* don't know how to swim, Daddy," Candy said.

"That's what I mean," Ray said, winking at Homer Wells. "You set foot in the ocean, or fall in, you'll have enough sense never to set foot in it again—it's too cold!"

Homer liked Candy's father, perhaps because surgery is the mechanics of medicine and Homer's early training had been surgical. He made instant identification with the machinery with which Ray Kendall worked, both the apple farm equipment and the mechanisms for hauling the lobsters and keeping them alive.

Contrary to Wally's promise to him regarding the humor of lobsters, Homer was unamused by his first look at the creatures. They crammed the tank in Ray Kendall's lobster pound, crawling over each other, their claws pegged shut so that they wielded them underwater like ineffective clubs. Homer knew he had seen a good reason for learning how to swim. If one ever fell in the sea, one wouldn't want to fall to the bottom where these creatures lived. It was some while before Homer learned that the lobsters did not cover the ocean's floor in such density as they occupied the tank. The first question that leaped to his mind did not concern how a lobster ate or how it multiplied—but why it lived at all.

"There's got to be something that picks up what's lying around," Ray Kendall advised Homer.

"It's the garbage monster of the ocean's floor," Wally said, laughing—he always laughed when he discussed lobster.

"The sea gull cleans up the shore," Ray Kendall said. "The lobster cleans up the bottom."

"Lobsters and sea gulls," Candy said, "they take what's left over."

Wilbur Larch might have observed that they were given the orphan's share. This occurred to Homer Wells, who discovered he could spend time watching lobsters, with dread, and sea gulls, with pleasure—while watching both with awe and respect.

Years later, when she became the proud owner of the first TV set in Heart's Rock, Olive Worthington would say that Homer Wells was the only person who ever pulled up a chair and sat down in front of the tank in Ray Kendall's lobster pound "as if he were watching the news on television."

Homer pulled lobster pots with Candy's father on Sundays—not for money but to be out on the water and to be around Ray. Six days a week Homer worked with Wally in the orchards. The ocean was visible from only one of Ocean View's several orchards but the presence of the sea was felt throughout the farm, especially in the early-morning fog, and when a sea breeze freshened the summer heat—and because of the sea gulls who circled inland and occasionally perched in the trees. They were more partial to blueberries than to apples but their presence was an irritation to Olive, who from her early years among the clams had no love for the raucous birds, and who fought with the gulls over the small plot of blueberries she was cultivating—the blueberries were protected with low-hung nets, but the gulls and the crows were smart enough to walk under the nets.

Among orphans, thought Homer Wells, sea gulls are superior to crows—not in intelligence or in personality, he observed, but in the freedom they possess and cherish. It was in looking at sea gulls that it first occurred to Homer Wells that he was free.

Wilbur Larch knew that freedom was an orphan's most dangerous illusion, and when he finally heard from Homer, he scanned the oddly formal letter, which was disappointing in its lack of detail. Regarding illusions, and all the rest, there was simply no evidence.

"I am learning to swim," wrote Homer Wells. (I know! I know! Tell me about it! thought Wilbur Larch.) "I do better at driving," Homer added.

"Mrs. Worthington is very nice." (I could have guessed that! thought Wilbur Larch.) "She knows everything about apples.

"Candy's father is very nice, too," Homer Wells wrote to Dr. Larch. "He takes me out on his lobster boat, and he is teaching me how an engine works." (Do you wear a life jacket on the lobster boat? Wilbur Larch wanted to know. You think an *engine* is so special? I could teach you how the *heart* works, thought Wilbur Larch—his own heart teaching him about itself, and much more than its function as a muscle.)

"Candy and Wally are wonderful!" Homer wrote. "I go everywhere with them. I sleep in Wally's room. I wear his clothes. It's great that we're the same size, although he is stronger. Candy and Wally are getting married, one day, and they want to have lots of children." (Tell me about the swimming lessons, thought Wilbur Larch. Watch out for the swimming lessons.)

"Poor Mr. Worthington—everyone calls him Senior," Homer wrote. (Ah-*ha*! thought Wilbur Larch. So something isn't perfect, is it? What's "poor" about Mr. Worthington?)

He asked Nurse Angela and Nurse Edna what they thought of the name "Senior." They agreed it was different.

"It sounds stupid to me," said Wilbur Larch.

Nurse Angela and Nurse Edna told him he wasn't being fair. The boy had departed with his blessings—more, with his encouragement. They agreed Homer could have written something and sent it sooner than six weeks, but they argued that this indicated only how happy he was—how busy and how glad to be busy, too. And what experience did Homer Wells have with writing letters, or with writing of any kind? they wanted to know.

"You want him to be a doctor, Wilbur," Nurse Edna said, "but it's his life."

"Do you expect him to be a writer, too?" Nurse Angela chimed in.

"And never get married?" Nurse Edna asked dangerously.

I expect him to be of *use*, thought Wilbur Larch tiredly. And I want him with me; this last wish he knew was unfair. In the dispensary, he rested from the summer heat. All that glass and steel were somehow cooling, and the ether fumes evaporated more slowly in the humidity. He seemed to be traveling both farther away and for longer in his ether dreams now. When he came out of the ether, he seemed to come out of it more slowly. I'm getting older, he repeated to himself.

A beautiful and untouched copy of *Jane Eyre* arrived from Mrs. Worthington, and Wilbur Larch read more spiritedly to the girls—the newness of the story refreshed him. It even enlivened his weary approach to the sad conclusion to *Great Expectations*. (He never believed the part about Pip and Estella being happy ever after; he never believed that about anyone.)

A pattern of correspondence slowly developed between Wilbur Larch and Homer Wells. Homer would sketch the barest facts of his life in Heart's Rock and Heart's Haven; he would give Dr. Larch a glimpse, like the far-off visibility of the ocean from the one orchard at Ocean View where sighting the sea was possible. He would send Dr. Larch a page, maybe two pages once a week or every other week. To this speck on the horizon Dr. Larch would respond with the full orchestration of the written word: questions (which would never be answered) regarding the specificity that was lacking in Homer's last letter ("What precisely is the matter with Mr. Worthington?") and a flood of details concerning the daily grimness of St. Cloud's. As much as Dr. Larch disdained the gossipy instinct of Snowy Meadows for "keeping up" with the orphanage, Dr. Larch provided Homer Wells with a virtual alumni newsletter and with a calendar of hospital and social events. His letters to Homer Wells were longer than his longest entries in *A Brief History of St. Cloud's,* and they were written and mailed the day following Dr. Larch's receipt of the most minimal scrawl from Homer.

"You can't expect the boy to keep up with you, Wilbur," Nurse Edna advised Dr. Larch.

"You can't expect him to *compete* with you," Nurse Angela said.

"What the hell is wrong with this Senior Worthington character?" Dr. Larch asked.

"Homer said it was a drinking problem, Wilbur," Nurse Edna reminded him.

"What do you want to know—the brand of hooch?" Nurse Angela asked.

But what Wilbur Larch expected from his young apprentice was only what he thought he had taught him: clinical analysis, the exact definition of characteristics associated with light, medium, or heavy drinking. Are we talking about a guy who makes a fool out of himself at parties? Wilbur Larch wondered. Or is this something severe and chronic?

Because Homer Wells had never seen a drunk before, he was—at first—even more easily deceived by Senior Worthington's appearance than Senior's immediate family and friends were; and Homer was as ready as they were to accept Senior's deterioration in cognition as the natural result of alcoholism. A man long admired in Heart's Rock and Heart's Haven, especially for the sweetness of his disposition, Senior had become short-tempered, irritable and even aggressive on occasion. Following the incident with the grasshopper pie, Olive wouldn't allow him to go to the Haven Club without her: Senior had plastered an entire grasshopper pie against the chest of a nice, young lifeguard and needed to be restrained, then, from further smearing the pale-green ingredients on the rump of a nice, young waitress. "He was showing off," Senior said of the lifeguard. "He was just *standing there*," he explained.

"And the waitress?" Olive asked. Senior appeared confused and began to cry.

"I thought she was someone else," he said faintly. Olive had taken him home; Wally had made up to the waitress; it was Candy who had charmed and reassured the lifeguard.

Senior became lost driving to other than routine places; Olive never allowed him to have the car unless Wally or Homer went with him. Eventually, he became lost trying to get to familiar places; Homer had to lead him back to Ocean View from Ray Kendall's lobster pound—even Homer, who was unfamiliar with the network of small roads to and from the coast, could tell that Senior had made a wrong turn.

Senior made terrible mistakes in any complex motor task. While cleaning the carburetor for the Cadillac—a simple job, which Ray Kendall had demonstrated for him many times—Senior inhaled the gas and little carbon particles in the tubes (he sucked *in* instead of blowing *out*).

Senior's recent memory was so severely impaired that he wandered for an hour through his own bedroom unable to dress himself; he constantly confused his sock drawer with the drawer for Olive's underwear. One morning he became so enraged at his mistake that he appeared at the breakfast table with each foot tightly tied up in a bra. Normally friendly to Homer and tender to Wally and Olive, he shouted an accusation at Wally—that his own son was wearing his father's socks, which he had taken without his father's permission!—and he ranted at Olive for turning his domicile into a foundling home without asking his permission regarding *that*.

"You'd be better off at Saint Cloud's than in this house of thieves," he told Homer.

Upon saying this, Senior Worthington burst into tears and begged Homer's forgiveness; he put his head on Homer's shoulder and wept. "My brain is sending poison to my heart," he told Homer, who thought it strange that Senior didn't seem to drink before the late afternoon—yet he appeared to be drunk nearly all the time.

Sometimes it went like this. Senior would not drink for three days—a part of him able to observe that his silliness flourished no less ardently. Yet he would forget to make this point to Olive, or to anyone else, until he'd broken down and had a drink; by the time he remembered to say he had *not* been drinking, he was drunk. Why do I forget everything? he wondered, and then forgot it.

Yet his long-range memory was quite intact. He sang college songs to Olive (the lines of which she herself was unable to remember), and he sweetly recalled for her the romantic evenings of their courtship; he told Wally stories of Wally as a baby; he entertained Homer by cheerfully recounting the planting of some of the older-tree orchards, including the lone orchard from which the sea was visible.

"It was where I wanted to build the house, Homer," Senior said. It was lunchtime. Wally and Homer had been suckering in the orchard: stripping the inner limbs off the tree or any new, sprouting branches (or "suckers") that are turned inward—the ones not reaching out to the sun. Wally had heard the story; he was distracted; he poured some Coca-Cola on an anthill. Suckering exposes as many of the limbs as possible to the light; it lets the light come through the tree.

"You don't allow an apple tree to grow every which way," Wally had explained to Homer.

"Like a boy!" Senior had shouted, laughing.

"Olive thought it was too windy for a house here," Senior told Homer. "Women are disturbed by the wind more than men are disturbed by it," Senior confided. "That's a fact. Anyway . . ." He paused. He gestured to the sea, as if it were a far-off audience and he meant to include it by the sweep of his hand. He turned to the apple trees around them. . . . They were a slightly more intimate audience, paying closer attention. "The wind . . ." he started to say, and paused again, perhaps waiting for the wind to contribute something. "The house . . ." he started to say.

"You can see this orchard from the second floor of our house. Did you know that?" he asked Homer.

"Right," Homer said. Wally's room was on the second floor. From Wally's window, he could see the orchard from which the sea was visible, but the sea wasn't visible from Wally's window—or from any other window in the house.

"I called the whole place Ocean View," Senior explained, "because I thought the house was going to be here. Right here," he repeated. He looked down at the foaming Coca-Cola that Wally was slowly pouring onto the anthill.

"You use poison oats and poison corn to kill the mice," Senior said. "It stinks." Wally looked up at him; Homer nodded. "You scatter the stuff for the field mice, but you have to find the holes and put it in the tunnels if you want to kill the pine mice," he said.

"We know, Pop," Wally said softly.

"Field mice are the same as meadow mice," Senior explained to Homer, who had already been told this.

"Right," Homer said.

"Meadow mice girdle a tree, and pine mice eat the roots," Senior recited, from his distant memory.

Wally stopped pouring the Coke on the anthill. He and Homer didn't know why Senior had joined them for their lunch break; they'd been suckering in the ocean orchard all morning, and Senior had just shown up. He was driving the old jeep that didn't have any license plates; it was strictly for driving around the orchards.

"Pop?" Wally asked him. "What are you doing out here?"

Senior stared blankly at his son. He looked at Homer; he hoped Homer might tell him the answer. He regarded his audience—the apple trees, the far-off ocean.

"I wanted to build the house here, *right here*," he said to Wally. "But your bossy bitch of a have-it-all-her-own-way mother wouldn't let me—she wouldn't let me, the *cunt*!" he cried. "Clam-digger cunt, well-digger *pussy*!" he shouted. He stood up, he looked disoriented; Wally stood up with him.

"Come on, Pop," he said. "I'll drive you home."

They took Wally's pickup. Homer followed them in the old

jeep; it was the vehicle he had learned to drive in after Wally had assured him that he couldn't hurt it.

Alcohol, thought Homer Wells; it sure can destroy you.

Senior had all the other symptoms, too. He was fifty-five; he looked seventy. He had periods of paranoia, of grandiosity, of confabulation. His few obnoxious traits—which he'd always had—were exaggerated; in his case, nose-picking, for example. He could explore a nostril for an hour; he put boogers on his pants or on the furniture. Olive's vulgar brother, Bucky Bean, claimed that Senior could have been a well-digger. "The way he roots into his snoot," Bucky said, "I could use him to dig a well."

The Haven Club's lifeguard, whose chest had received the full force of the grasshopper pie, turned out to be not completely mollified. He objected to Candy giving Homer swimming lessons in the shallow end of the pool in the late afternoon. The pool was crowded then, he complained; swimming lessons were regularly scheduled in the early morning—and he—the lifeguard—regularly administered them—for a fee. He was not convinced that he should be flexible about the matter. Homer worked at Ocean View all day, Candy argued. In the late afternoon, when Wally played tennis after work, was the ideal time for Candy to give Homer instructions.

"Ideal for *you*," the lifeguard argued with Candy; he had a crush on her, it was plain. It was one thing to be jealous of Wally Worthington—everyone was—but quite another to have to suffer the attentions Candy Kendall gave to the hard-luck case from St. Cloud's. At the Haven Club—never in Candy's presence, or in the presence of any of the Worthingtons— Homer was referred to not as the foundling or as the orphan, but as "the hard-luck case from St. Cloud's"—sometimes "the Worthingtons' hard-luck case" was the way it was put.

Homer said he wouldn't mind practicing in the Worthingtons' private pool at Ocean View, but it was nice that he and Candy could be at the Haven Club when Wally finished playing tennis; they could then go off together, to the beach, to Ray Kendall's dock, to wherever. Also, at the Worthingtons' pool there would be Senior to deal with; more and more Olive tried to keep Senior home, away from the Haven Club. She found she could pacify him best by feeding him gin and tonics and keeping him *in* the pool—floating on a rubber raft. But the real reason it was a bad idea (everyone felt) for Homer to learn to swim in the Worthingtons' unheated pool was that the cold water might be a shock to his heart.

Olive decided that she would take over Homer's lessons from Candy; she knew that the lifeguard at the Haven Club wouldn't dare to complain to her; she and Candy and Wally agreed that the unheated experience might be too severe for Homer.

"I don't want to be any trouble for you," Homer said, puzzled and, doubtlessly, disappointed that the hands under his stomach as he paddled back and forth were Olive's and not Candy's. "It's not too cold for me in your pool, Wally," Homer said.

"It's harder to learn when it's cold," Candy said.

"Yes, that's right," Olive said.

"Well, I want to swim in the ocean, as soon as I learn how," Homer told them. "It's a lot colder in the ocean than it is in your pool."

Oh my, Olive worried. She wrote Dr. Larch about "the heart problem," which made Larch feel guilty and slightly trapped. Actually, he wrote to her, cold water doesn't provide the kind of shock he was anxious about; the kind of shock associated with an accident—"for example, a near-drowning" —was more the kind of shock he felt that Homer must try to avoid.

What lies! Larch thought, but he mailed the letter to Mrs. Worthington anyway, and Olive found that Homer learned to swim very rapidly. "He must have been right on the verge of picking it up when I took over from you," she told Candy; but in truth, Homer learned more quickly from Olive because the lessons themselves were not as pleasurable.

With Candy, he might have never learned to swim; at least he could have prolonged it and made the lessons last the rest of the summer.

Homer Wells would have made that summer last the rest of his life if he could have. There was so much about his life at Ocean View that made him happy.

He was not ashamed that he loved the Worthingtons' wall-to-wall carpeting; he'd come from bare wood walls and many layers of linoleum, between which one could feel the sawdust shift underfoot. One couldn't claim that the Worthingtons' walls were hung with art, but Homer had not seen pictures on walls before (except the portrait of the pony woman); even the crowning cuteness of the oil painting of the cat in the flower bed (in Wally's bathroom) appealed to Homer—and the flower-bed wallpaper behind the painting appealed to him, too. What did he know about wallpaper or art? He thought all wallpaper was wonderful.

He felt he would never stop loving Wally's room. What did he know about varsity letters and footballs dipped in liquid gold and inscribed with the score of an important game? And tennis trophies, and old yearbooks and the ticket stubs tucked into the molding of the mirror (from the first movie Wally took Candy to)? What did he know about movies? Wally and Candy took him to one of Maine's first drive-in movies. How could he ever have imagined that? And what did he know about people who came together every day, and worked together, by apparent choice? His fellow workers at Ocean View were a marvel to Homer Wells; at first, he loved them all. He loved Meany Hyde the most, because Meany was so friendly and had such a fondness for explaining how everything was done—even things that Homer—or anyone else—could have seen how to do without being told. Homer especially loved listening to Meany explain the obvious.

He loved Meany Hyde's wife, Florence—and the other women who spent the summer making the apple mart and the cider house ready for the harvest. He loved Big Dot Taft, although the jiggle in the backs of her arms reminded him of Melony (whom he never thought about, not even when he heard that she had left St. Cloud's). He liked Big Dot Taft's kid sister, Debra Pettigrew, who was his own age, and pretty, although there was something determined about her chubbiness that suggested she had the capacity for one day becoming as big as Big Dot.

Big Dot's husband, Everett Taft, showed Homer all about mowing. You mowed the rows between the trees twice a summer; then you raked and hayed the rows; then you baled the hay and sold it to the dairy farm in Kenneth Corners. You used the loose hay for mulch around the younger trees. At Ocean View, everything was used.

Homer liked Ira Titcomb, the beekeeper and the husband of Irene of the wondrous burn scar: it was Ira who explained to Homer about the bees. "They like at least sixty-five degrees, no wind, no hail, no frost," Ira said. "A bee lives about thirty days and does more work than some men do all their lives—I ain't sayin' who. All honey is," said Ira Titcomb, "is fuel for bees."

Homer learned that bees prefer dandelions to apple blossoms, which was why you mowed the dandelions down just before you brought the bees into the orchard. He learned why there had to be more than one kind of tree in an orchard, for cross-pollinating—the bees had to carry the pollen from one kind of tree to another. He learned it should be nighttime when you put the hives out in the orchard; at night the bees were asleep and you could close the little screen door at the slat at the bottom of the box that contained the hive; when you carried the hives, the bees woke up but they couldn't get out. The hives were light when they were carried off the flatbed trailer and distributed through the orchards, but they were heavy with honey when they had to be picked up and loaded back on the trailer a week later. Sometimes a hive could be too heavy to lift alone. If the hives were jostled, the bees inside began to hum; you could feel them stirring through the wood. If honey had leaked through the slats, a lone bee might get gobbed up in the leaking honey, and that was the only way you could get stung.

Once when Homer hugged a hive to his chest, and carefully walked it to the flatbed's edge, he felt a vibration against the taut boards containing the hive; even in the cool night air, the boards were warm; the activity of the hive generated heat—like an infection, Homer thought suddenly. He recalled the taut belly of the woman he had saved from convulsions. He thought of the activity in the uterus as producing both a heat and a hardness to the abdomen. How many abdomens had Homer Wells put his hand on before he was twenty? I prefer apple farming, he thought.

At St. Cloud's, growth was unwanted even when it was delivered—and the process of birth was often interrupted. Now he was engaged in the business of growing things. What he loved about the life at Ocean View was how everything was of use and that everything was wanted.

He even thought he loved Vernon Lynch, although he'd been told how Vernon beat his wife and Grace Lynch had a way of looking at Homer that did alarm him. He could not tell from her look if it was need or suspicion or simply curiosity that he saw—Grace gave out the kind of look you go on feeling after you've stopped looking back.

Vernon Lynch showed Homer how to spray. It was appropriate that Vernon Lynch was in charge of the pesticides, of extermination.

"As soon as there's leaves, there's trouble," Vernon told him. "That's in April. You start sprayin' in April and you don't stop till the end of August, when you're ready to start pickin'. You spray every week or ten days. You spray for scab and you spray for insects. We got two sprayers here, one's a Hardie and one's a Bean, and both of them hold five hundred gallons. You wear the respirator because you don't want to breathe the shit, and the respirator don't do you no good if it don't fit tight." Saying this, Vernon Lynch tightened the respirator around Homer's head; Homer could feel his temples pound. "If you don't keep washin' out the cloth in the mask, you could choke," Vernon said. He cupped his hand over Homer's mouth and nose; Homer experienced airlessness. "And keep your hair covered if you don't want to go bald." Vernon's hand remained clamped over Homer's mouth and nose. "And keep the goggles on if you don't want to go blind," he added. Homer considered struggling, decided to conserve his strength, contemplated fainting, wondered if it was true or just an expression that lungs exploded. "If you got what they call an open wound, like a cut, and the shit gets in there, you could get sterile," said Vernon Lynch. "That means no more nasty hard-ons." Homer tapped his shoulder and waved to Vernon, as if he were signaling something too complicated to be communicated by normal means. I can't breathe! Hello! I can't breathe! Hello out there!

When Homer's knees started to wobble, Vernon ripped the mask off his face—the head strap raking his ears upward and tangling his hair.

"Got the picture?" Vernon asked.

"Right!" Homer called out, his lungs screaming.

He even liked Herb Fowler. He'd been with Herb less than two minutes when the prophylactic sailed his way and struck him in the forehead. All Meany Hyde had said was, "Hi, Herb, this here is Homer Wells—he's Wally's pal from Saint Cloud's." And Herb had flipped the rubber at Homer.

"Wouldn't be so many orphans if more people put these on their joints," Herb said.

Homer Wells had never seen a prophylactic in a commercial wrapper. The ones that Dr. Larch kept at the hospital, and distributed to many of the women, in handfuls, were sealed in something plain and see-through, like wax paper; no brand names adorned them. Dr. Larch was always complaining that he didn't know where all the rubbers were going, but Homer knew that Melony had helped herself on many occasions. It had been Melony, of course, who had introduced Homer to prophylactics.

Herb Fowler's girlfriend, Louise Tobey, was doubtlessly professional in handling Herb's prophylactics. When Homer touched himself, he thought about Squeeze Louise—he imagined her dexterity with a prophylactic, her fast and nimble fingers, the way she held a paint brush and clenched her teeth, slapping the paint on thick on the apple-mart shelves, blowing a lock of her hair off her forehead with a puff of breath that was bitter with cigarettes.

Homer didn't allow himself to masturbate when Candy was on his mind. He lay not touching himself in Wally's room, with Wally breathing deeply and sleeping peacefully beside him. Whenever Homer did imagine that Candy was sleeping beside him, they were never touching each other intimately—they were just holding tightly to each other in a grip of chaste affection. ("Nothing genital," as Melony used to say.)

Candy smoked, but she was so mannered and exaggerated that she often dropped her cigarette in her lap, jumping up and furiously brushing away the sparks, always laughing.

"Oh, what a clod!" she'd cry. If so, thought Homer Wells, only when you're smoking.

Louise Tobey wolfed in a cigarette; she sucked in a cloud of smoke and blew so little back, Homer wondered where it went. The older apple-mart women were constant smokers (all except Grace Lynch, who had resolved not to part her lips—not for any reason), but Florence and Irene and Big Dot Taft had been smoking so long, they appeared offhanded about it. Only Debra Pettigrew, Dot's kid sister, smoked with Candy's infrequency and awkwardness. Squeeze Louise smoked with a quick, sure violence that Homer imagined must have been inspired by Herb Fowler's rough-and-ready use of rubbers.

In all of Heart's Rock and Heart's Haven—from the briny gurgle of lobstering life to the chlorine security of the Haven Club pool; from the bustle of the making ready in the apple mart to the work in the fields—there was nothing that caused Homer a single, sharp reminder of St. Cloud's, nothing until the first rainy day, when they sent him, with a small crew of scrubbers and painters, to the cider house.

Nothing about the building, from the outside, prepared him. On or in various farm vehicles, he had lumbered past it often—a long, thin, one-story, shed-roofed building in the shape of an arm held at a right angle; in the elbow of the building, where there was a double-door entrance, were the cider mill and the press (the grinder, the pump, the pump engine and the grinder engine, and the thousand-gallon tank).

One wing of the building was studded with refrigeration units; it was a cold-storage room for the cider. In the other wing was a small kitchen, beyond which were extended two long rows of iron hospital-style beds, each with its own blanket and pillow. Mattresses were rolled neatly on each of the more than twenty beds. Sometimes a blanket on wire runners enclosed a bed, or a section of beds, in the semi-privacy that Homer Wells associated with a hospital ward. Unpainted plywood shelves between the beds formed primitive but stable wardrobe closets, which contained those twisted, goose-necked reading lamps wherever there was the occasional electrical outlet. The furniture was shabby but neat, as if rescued or rejected from hospitals and offices where it had been exposed to relentless but considerate use.

This wing of the cider house had the functional economy of a military barracks, but it had too many personal touches to be institutional. There were curtains, for example, and Homer could tell that they would have been adequate, if faded, at the Worthingtons' dining-room windows—which was where they'd come from. Homer also recognized a particularly exaggerated peacefulness in a few of the flowery landscape paintings and animal portraits that were hung on the plasterboard walls—in such unlikely places (at times, too high; at times, too low) that Homer was sure they'd been hung to hide holes. Maybe boot holes, maybe fist holes, perhaps whole-head holes; there seemed to Homer Wells to radiate from the room a kind of dormitory anger and apprehension he recognized from his nearly twenty years in the boys' division at St. Cloud's.

"What is this place?" he asked Meany Hyde, the rain pelting on the tin roof above them.

"The cider house," said Meany.

"But who *sleeps* here—who stays here? Do people *live* here?" Homer asked. It was remarkably clean, yet the atmosphere of use was so prevalent, Homer was reminded of the old bunkrooms in St. Cloud's where the woodsmen and sawyers had dreamed out their exhausted lives.

"It's crew quarters, for the pickers," Meany Hyde said. "Durin' the harvest, the pickers stay here—the migrants."

"It's for the colored folks," said Big Dot Taft, plopping down the mops and pails. "Every year, we make it nice for them. We wash everythin' and we give everythin' a fresh coat of paint."

"I gotta wax the press boards," Meany Hyde said, sliding away from what he thought was the women's work—although Homer and Wally would perform it regularly most rainy days of the summer.

"Negroes?" Homer Wells asked. "The pickers are Negroes?"

"Black as night, some of them," said Florence Hyde. "They're okay."

"They're nice!" called Meany Hyde.

"Some of them are nicer than others," said Big Dot Taft.

"Like other people I know," Irene Titcomb said, giggling, hiding her scar.

"They're nice because Mrs. Worthington is nice to them!" Meany Hyde yelled from the spattered vicinity of the cider press.

The building smelled like vinegar—old cider that had turned. It was a strong smell, but there was nothing stifling or unclean about it.

Debra Pettigrew smiled at Homer over the bucket they were sharing; he cautiously returned her smile while wondering where Wally was working today, in the rain, and imagining Ray Kendall at work. Ray would either be out on the choppy sea in his glistening sou'wester or else working on the wiring of the International Harvester in the building called Number Two.

Grace Lynch was scrubbing the linoleum counters in the kitchen of the cider house; Homer marveled that he had not noticed her there before, that he hadn't even known she was part of their crew. Louise Tobey, sucking a cigarette down to its nub and flicking the butt out the picking crew-quarters' door, remarked that her mop wringer was "out of joint."

"It's jammed, or somethin'," Squeeze Louise said crossly.

"Louise's mop wringer is out of joint," Big Dot Taft said mockingly.

"Poor Louise—jammed your mop wringer, huh?" said Florence Hyde, who laughed, which caused Big Dot Taft to roar.

"Oh, cut it out!" Louise said. She kicked her mop wringer.

"What's going on out there?" called Meany Hyde.

"Louise has got an overworked *wringer*!" said Big Dot Taft. Homer looked at Louise, who was cross; then he looked at Debra Pettigrew, who blushed.

"Are you overusin' your poor wringer, Louise?" Irene Titcomb asked.

"Louise, you must be stickin' too many mops in your wringer, darlin'," said Florence Hyde.

"Be nice, all of you!" cried Meany Hyde.

"Too much of *one* mop, that's for sure," said Big Dot Taft. Even Louise found that funny. When she looked at Homer Wells, he looked away; Debra Pettigrew was watching him, so he looked away from her, too.

When Herb Fowler came by, at the lunch break, he walked into the cider house and said, "Whew! You can smell niggers in here a whole year later."

"I think it's just vinegar," Meany Hyde said.

"You tellin' me you can't smell niggers?" Herb Fowler asked. "You smell 'em?" Herb asked Louise. She shrugged. "How about you?" Herb asked Homer. "Can't you smell 'em?"

"I can smell vinegar, old apples, old cider," Homer said.

He saw the rubber sailing toward him in time to catch it.

"You know what niggers do with those?" Herb asked him. He flipped another rubber to Louise Tobey, who caught it without the slightest effort—she expected prophylactics to be flying in her direction hourly. "Show him what a nigger does with it, Louise," Herb said. The other women were bored; they'd seen this demonstration all their lives; Debra Pettigrew looked nervously at Homer Wells and deliberately away from Louise; Louise herself seemed nervous and bored at the same time. She ripped the rubber out of its wrapper and stuck her index finger in it—her fingernail poked out the rubber, her nail's fine edge next to the nipplelike end.

"One year I told the niggers that they should just stick their joints into these rubbers if they didn't want to be catchin' diseases or havin' any new babies," Herb said. He grabbed Louise's finger in the rubber sheath and held it out for everyone to see. "And the next year, all the niggers told me that the rubbers didn't work. They said they stuck their fingers in there, like I showed 'em, and they *still* got diseases and new babies every time they turned around!"

No one laughed; no one believed it; it was an old joke to all of them, except to Homer Wells; and the idea of people having babies every time they turned around was not especially funny to Homer.

When Herb Fowler offered to drive them all to the diner on Drinkwater Road for a hot lunch, Homer said he didn't want to go; Mrs. Worthington made his lunch, and Wally's, every morning, and Homer felt obliged to eat his—he always enjoyed it. He also knew the crew was not supposed to leave the orchards for a lunch break, especially not in any of the Ocean View vehicles, and Herb Fowler was driving the green van that Olive used most often. It wasn't a *hard* rule, but Homer knew that if Wally had been working in the cider house Herb wouldn't have suggested it.

Homer ate his lunch, appropriately, in the cider house kitchen; when he glanced into the long room with the two rows of narrow beds, he thought how much the rolled mattresses and blankets resembled people sleeping there—except the shapes upon the iron beds were too still to be sleepers. They are like bodies waiting to be identified, thought Homer Wells.

Even though it was raining, he went outside to look at the collection of dead cars and junked tractor-and-trailer parts that festooned the dirt driveway in front of the cider house. In the back was a churned-up area of discolored weeds where the mash, or the pomace, was flung after the press. A pig farmer from Waldoboro drove all the way just to have it, Meany Hyde had told Homer; the mash was great for pigs.

Some of the dead cars had South Carolina plates. Homer Wells had never looked at a map of the United States; he had seen a globe, but it was a crude one—the states weren't marked. He knew South Carolina was a long way south; the Negroes came from there in trucks, Meany Hyde had said, or they drove their own cars, but some of their cars were so old and beaten up that they died here; Meany wasn't sure how all the Negroes got back to South Carolina.

"They pick grapefruits down in Florida, I think," Meany said, "and peaches when it's peach time somewhere else, and apples here. They travel around, just pickin' things."

Homer watched a sea gull that was watching him from the roof of the cider house; the gull was so drawn in upon itself that Homer was reminded it was raining and went back inside.

He rolled down one of the mattresses and stretched out on

it, placing both the pillow and the blanket under his head. Something invited him to smell the blanket and the pillow, but he could detect nothing more than the aura of vinegar and a scent he categorized as simply old. The blanket and pillow felt more human than they smelled, but the deeper he pushed his face into them, the more human their smell became. He thought about the strain on Louise Tobey's face, and how her finger had stretched itself out in the rubber, and the way her nail had looked ready to slice through. He recalled the mattress in the sawyers' lodge in St. Cloud's, where Melony had introduced him to the way he felt now. He took himself out of his work jeans and masturbated quickly, the springs of the old iron bed creaking sharply. Something in his vision seemed clearer after he had finished. When he sat up on the bed, he spotted the other body that had taken the liberty of resting in the cider house. Even with her body curled so tightly in upon itself—like the gull in the rain or like a fetus or like a woman with cramps—Homer had no trouble recognizing Grace Lynch.

Even if she hadn't been watching him, even if she'd never been turned in his direction, she surely could not have mistaken the rhythm of the old bed springs—or even, Homer thought, the detectable sharpness of the odor of the semen he cupped in his hand. He stepped quietly outdoors and held his hand out in the rain. The sea gull, still huddled on the cider house roof, took a sudden interest in him—there was a history of successful scavenging associated with this place. When Homer went back in the cider house, he saw that Grace Lynch had fixed her mattress the way it had been and was standing by the window with her face pressed into the curtain. You had to look twice to see Grace Lynch; he wouldn't have seen her standing there if he hadn't already known she was in the room.

"I been there," Grace Lynch said softly, without looking at Homer. "Where you come from," she explained. "I been there—I don't know how you managed a night's sleep."

Her thinness was especially sharp, even knifelike in what dead, gray light the rainy day provided at that window; she drew the faded curtain around her narrow shoulders like a shawl. She wouldn't look at Homer Wells, and nothing in her brittle, shivering stance could have been interpreted as beckoning, yet Homer felt himself drawn to her—in the way we are urged, especially in gloomy weather, to seek the familiar. In St. Cloud's, one grew accustomed to victims, and the attitude of a victim shone stronger than reflected sunlight from Grace Lynch. Homer felt such a contradictory glow shining forth from her that he was impelled to go to her and hold her limp, damp hands.

"Funny," she whispered, still not looking at him. "It was so awful there, but I felt real safe." She put her head on his chest and stuck her sharp knee between his legs, twisting her bony hip into him. "Not like here," she whispered. "It's dangerous here." Her thin bony hand slipped into his pants, as skittish as a lizard.

The noisy arrival of the green van containing the escapees—to a hot lunch—saved him. Like a startled cat, Grace sprang crazily away from him. When they all came through the door, she was digging the grit from a seam in the linoleum on the kitchen counter—using a wire brush that Homer hadn't noticed she'd had in her hip pocket. Like so much of Grace Lynch, it had been concealed. But the tension in the look she gave him at quitting time—when he rode back to the apple mart on Big Dot Taft's jolly lap—was enough to tell Homer Wells that whatever was "dangerous" had not deserted Grace Lynch and that he could travel far but never so far that the victims of St. Cloud's would ever desert him.

/ / /

The night after Grace Lynch attacked him, Homer had his first date with Debra Pettigrew; it was also the first time he went to the drive-in movie with Candy and Wally. They all went in Senior's Cadillac. Homer and Debra Pettigrew sat in the splotched backseat where only a couple of months ago poor Curly Day had lost control of himself; Homer was unaware that the purpose of drive-in movies was, ultimately, for losing control of oneself in the backseats of cars.

"Homer's never been to a drive-in before," Wally announced to Debra Pettigrew when they picked her up. The Pettigrews were a large family who kept dogs—many dogs, mostly chained; some were chained to the bumpers of the several undriven, believed-to-be-dead cars that so permanently occupied the front lawn that the grass grew through the drive shafts and the axle bearings. As Homer stepped gingerly around the snapping dogs en route to Debra's front door, the dogs lunged against the unbudging cars.

The Pettigrews were a large family in both numbers and in flesh; Debra's fetching chubbiness was but a slight reminder of the family's potential for girth. At the door, Debra's mother greeted Homer massively—she of the monstrous genes responsible for the likes of Debra's sister, Big Dot Taft.

"De-BRA!" shrieked Debra's mother. "It's your BEAU! Hi, sweetie-pie," she said to Homer. "I've heard all about how nice you are, and what good manners you've got—please excuse the mess." Debra, blushing beside her, tried to hurry Homer outside as forcefully as her mother wished to usher him in. He glimpsed several huge people—some with remarkably swollen faces, as if they'd lived half their lives underwater or had survived incredible beatings; all with wide, friendly smiles, which contradicted the untold viciousness of the dogs barking in such a frenzy at Homer's back.

"We have to go, Mom," Debra whined, shoving Homer out the door. "We can't be late."

"Late for *what*?" someone cackled from the house, which shook with heavy laughter; coughs followed, which were followed by labored sighing before the dogs erupted in such force that Homer thought the noise of them would be sufficient to keep him and Debra from ever reaching the Cadillac.

"Shut UP!" Debra yelled at the dogs. They all stopped, but only for a second.

When Wally said, "Homer's never been to a drive-in before," he had to shout to be heard over the dogs.

"I've never been to a movie before," Homer admitted.

"Gosh," said Debra Pettigrew. She smelled nice; she was much neater and cleaner than she looked in her apple-mart clothes; Debra dressed with a certain pert orderliness for working, too. Her chubbiness was restrained, and as they drove to Cape Kenneth, her usual good nature emerged so warmly that even her shyness disappeared—she was a *fun* girl, as they say in Maine. She was nice-looking, relaxed, good-humored, hardworking and not very smart. Her prospects, at best, included marriage to someone pleasant and not a great deal older or smarter than herself.

In the summers, the Pettigrews occupied one of the new houses on the overcrowded, mucky shore of Drinkwater Lake; they'd managed to make the new place look lived-in—on its rapid way to ramshackle—almost instantly. The lawn had appeared to grow its dead cars overnight, and the dogs had survived the move from the Pettigrews' winter house in Kenneth Corners without losing a bit of their territorial savagery.

Like all the cottages around Drinkwater Lake, the Pettigrews' had been named—as if the houses themselves were orphans, delivered incomplete and in need of further creation. The Pettigrews' house was named "All of Us!"

"The exclamation point is what kills me," Wally had said to Homer when they pulled up at the car-and-dog lot. "As if they're proud of their overpopulation." But Wally was very respectful once Debra joined them in the car.

This mannerism of what he'd seen of society struck Homer Wells quite forcefully; people, even nice people—because, surely, Wally was nice—would say a host of critical things about someone to whom they would then be perfectly pleasant. At St. Cloud's, criticism was plainer—and harder, if not impossible, to conceal.

The drive-in movie in Cape Kenneth was nearly as new to Maine as the Haven Club's heated pool and was a lot less practical. Drive-in movies would never be a great idea for Maine; the night fog along the coast lent to many a joyful film the inappropriately ghoulish atmosphere of a horror movie. In later years, people groping for rest rooms and the snack bar would fail to find their cars when they attempted to return to them.

The other problem was mosquitoes. In 194__, when Homer Wells went to his first drive-in movie, the hum of the mosquitoes in the night air of Cape Kenneth was far more audible than the sound track. Wally was relatively successful in preventing the mosquitoes from taking over the car because he always brought with him an aerosol pump sprayer with which he frequently doused the car—and the air surrounding the cars. The pump can was loaded with the insecticide they sprayed the apples with. Thus the air in and surrounding the Cadillac was rendered poisonous and foul but fairly free of mosquitoes. The hiss and stench of the spray aroused frequent complaints from Wally's fellow moviegoers in the cars nearest the Cadillac— until they were being bitten so badly by mosquitoes that they stopped protesting; some of them politely asked if they could borrow the device for the purpose of poisoning their own cars.

There was no snack bar at the Cape Kenneth drive-in in 194__, and there were no rest rooms. The men and boys took turns urinating against a dank cement wall at the rear of the drive-in pit; atop the wall were perched several small and uncouth boys (Cape Kenneth locals, too young or too poor for cars), who used the wall to watch the movie even though they were well beyond the possibility of hearing it. Occasionally, when the movie was dissatisfying, they peed from the top of the wall onto the luckless people who were peeing against it.

Girls and women were not expected to pee at the drive-in, and consequently were better behaved than the men and boys—the women drank less, for example, although their behavior inside the cars could not be monitored.

It was wondrous—this whole experience—for Homer Wells. He was especially acute at noticing what human beings did for pleasure—what (there could be no mistake about it) they *chose* to do—because he had come from a place where choice was not so evident, and examples of people performing for pleasure were not plentiful. It amazed him that people suffered drive-in movies by choice, and for pleasure; but he believed that, if he failed to see the fun in it, it was entirely his failure.

What he was most unprepared for was the movie itself. After people honked their horns and blinked their headlights and exhibited other less endearing forms of impatience—Homer heard what was, unmistakably, the sound of someone vomiting against a fender—a gigantic image filled the sky. It is something's mouth! thought Homer Wells. The camera backed, or rather, lurched away. Something's head—a kind of horse! thought Homer Wells. It was a camel, actually, but Homer Wells had never seen a camel, or a picture of one; he thought it was a horribly deformed horse—a mutant horse! Perhaps some ghastly fetus-phase of a horse! The camera staggered back farther. Mounted by the camel's grotesque hump was a black-skinned man almost entirely concealed in white wrapping—bandages! thought Homer Wells. The ferocious black Arab nomad brandished a frightening curved sword; whacking the lumbering camel with the flat of the blade, he drove the beast into a faulty, staggering gallop across such endless sand dunes that the animal and its rider were soon only a speck on the vast horizon. Suddenly, *music!* Homer jumped. *Words!* The titles, the names of the actors were written in the sand by an invisible hand.

"What was that?" Homer asked Wally. He meant: the animal, its rider, the desert, the credits—everything!

"Some dumb Bedouin, I think," Wally said.

A Bedouin? thought Homer Wells.

"It's a kind of horse?" he asked.

"*What* horse?" asked Debra Pettigrew.

"The animal," Homer said, sensing his mistake.

Candy turned around in the front seat and looked at Homer with heartbreaking affection. "That's a camel, Homer," she said.

"You've never seen a camel!" Wally shouted.

"Well, where *would* he see a camel?" Candy snapped at him.

"I was just surprised," Wally said defensively.

"I've never seen a Negro, either," Homer said. "That was one, wasn't it?—on the camel."

"A Negro Bedouin, I guess," Wally said.

"Gosh," said Debra Pettigrew, who looked at Homer a little fearfully, as if she suspected him of simultaneously existing on another planet, in another life-form.

Then the credits were over. The black man on the camel was gone and would never be seen again. The desert was also gone; apparently, it had served its uncertain function—it would never be seen again, either. It was a pirate movie. Great ships were blasting each other with cannons; swarthy men with uncut hair and baggy pants were doing terrible things to nicer-looking men, who were better-dressed. None of the men was black. Perhaps the camel's rider had been a kind of omen, thought Homer Wells. His exposure to storytelling, through Charles Dickens and Charlotte Brontë, had ill prepared him for characters who came from and traveled nowhere—or for stories that made no sense.

The pirates stole a chest of coins and a blond woman from the ship of pleasanter aspect before they sank the ship and sailed away in their own foul vessel, on which they coarsely attempted to make merry with drunkenness and song. They appeared to enjoy leering at the woman, and taunting her, but some mysterious and totally unseen force kept them from actually harming her—for a whole hour, during which they harmed nearly everyone else and many of themselves. The woman, however, was reserved for more teasing, yet she protested her fate bitterly, and Homer had the feeling that he was supposed to lament for her.

A man who apparently adored the complaining woman pursued her across the ocean, through burning harbor towns and charmless inns of suggested but never visualized lewdness. As the fog rolled in, there was much of the movie that was never visualized, although Homer remained riveted to the image in the sky. He was only partially aware that Wally and Candy were uninterested in the movie; they had slumped from sight in the front seat and only occasionally did Candy's hand appear, gripping—or lolling on—the back of the seat. Twice Homer heard her say, "No, Wally," once with a firmness he had never heard in her voice before. Wally's frequent laughter continued at intervals, and he whispered and murmured and gurgled in his throat.

Homer was occasionally aware of Debra Pettigrew being less interested in the pirate movie than he was; when he looked at her, he was surprised to find her looking at him. Not critically but not very affectionately either. She appeared to be more and more amazed to see him, as the picture went on and on. Once she touched his hand; he thought she wanted something, and regarded her politely. She just stared at him; he looked back at the movie.

The blond woman was forever barring her door against her captors, and they were always breaking into her room despite her efforts; they seemed to break into her room for the single purpose of demonstrating to her that she couldn't bar them out. Once in the room, they taunted her in the usual fashion and then retreated—whereupon she attempted to bar their way again.

"I think I've missed something," Homer Wells announced after more than an hour had passed. Candy sat up in the front seat and looked at him, her genuine concern quite apparent despite the wild tangle her hair was in.

"What have you missed?" Wally asked—sleepily, Homer thought.

Debra Pettigrew, prettily, leaned close to Homer and whispered in his ear. "I think you've missed *me,*" she said. "I think you've forgotten I'm here."

Homer had meant he'd missed something in the story; he stared at Debra in a particularly uncomprehending way. Debra kissed him, very neatly—very dryly—on his mouth. She sat back in the seat and smiled at him.

"Your turn," she said.

Wally, at this moment, opened the front door and sprayed lethal fumes all around the Cadillac—much of the stuff drifting back through the open door. Candy and Wally, and Debra, too, coughed in a very dramatic fashion, but Homer stared at

Debra Pettigrew—the idea of the drive-in movie slowly coming to him.

He cautiously kissed Debra on her dry little mouth. She kissed him back. He settled himself more comfortably beside her, and she put her head on his shoulder, one hand on his chest. *He* put one hand on *her* chest, but she pushed it away. He knew he was still missing something, but he proceeded, tentatively, to discover the rules. He kissed her neck; this was acceptable—she snuggled against his neck and something new and daring (and wet) licked him at the throat (her tongue!); Homer permitted his tongue to venture into the poisoned air. He took a moment, contemplating the uses of his tongue; he decided to kiss her on her mouth and to suggest, gently, the application of his tongue there, but this was somewhat tensely rejected—her own tongue pushed his away; her teeth blocked further entry.

He was beginning to see it was a yes-no set of rules he had encountered; he was permitted to rub her tummy, but not to touch her breasts. The hand on her hips was allowed to remain there; the hand on her thigh, in her lap, was moved on. She put her arms around him and hugged him; her kisses were friendly and sweet; he began to feel like a well-treated pet— certainly better treated than most of the Pettigrew dogs.

"No!" Candy said, so loudly that both Homer and Debra Pettigrew flinched; then Debra giggled and cuddled against him. By straining his neck and rolling his eyes toward the back of his head, Homer Wells could manage to see the movie.

At last, the tireless lover had tracked the blond woman to yet another place of bondage; the stupid woman had barred herself in again, but this time she was attempting to keep herself untouched by her rescuer. It was quite frustrating to watch him hack and flail at her door.

From one of the cars in the hazardous fog around them, someone yelled, "*Leave* her!" Another person cried, "*Kill* her!" All Homer felt sure of was that no one would ever *fuck* her—she seemed protected from both sex and death by something as shifty as the Cape Kenneth fog—nor would any of them in the Cadillac pursue much adventure beyond the pleasure afforded to cherished household pets.

This feeling caused Homer to remember the affection Dr. Larch had for him—and Nurse Edna and Nurse Angela had for him, too. When the movie was over, he realized he was crying; he realized that although he loved where he was, he loved Dr. Larch more than anyone else—at this point in his life, he still loved Larch more than he loved Candy—and he realized that he missed Larch, too—while at the same time he hoped he would never again set foot in St. Cloud's.

It was an overwhelming confusion that inspired his weeping, but Debra Pettigrew mistook the cause; she thought the movie had moved him to tears.

"There, there," she said in a mothering tone, hugging him. Candy and Wally leaned over the front seat. Candy touched his head.

"It's okay. You can cry. I cry at lots of movies," she said.

Even Wally was deeply respectful. "Hey, buddy," he said. "We know this must all be a shock to you." His poor *heart,* sweet Wally was thinking. You dear boy, Candy thought, please watch out for your *heart.* She put her cheek against Homer's cheek and kissed him near his ear. It was a very sudden surprise to her, how much she enjoyed that kiss of friendship; it surprised Homer Wells, too. Despite the little dry kisses that Debra Pettigrew gave him in abundance, he felt a remarkable difference surge through him at the instant of Candy's kissing him. It was a feeling that rushed him from nowhere—and he knew, looking at Wally's fond and handsome face, that it was a feeling with nowhere to go. Was that what love was, and how it came to you—leaving you no options for its use? Like the black-skinned nomad on the camel: where did he belong in a movie about pirates?

I am that black-skinned rider on that camel, thought the orphan, Homer Wells. What was he called?

Later, after he'd taken Debra Pettigrew home and had nearly been eaten by her dogs, he asked Wally. Homer sat up front in the Cadillac—Candy in the middle of the seat between them.

"A Bedouin," Wally said.

I'm a *Bedouin*! thought Homer Wells.

When Candy fell asleep, she slumped against Wally's shoulder, but this bothered his driving; he pushed her very gently in Homer's direction. The rest of the way to Heart's Haven, she slept with her head on Homer's shoulder, her hair lightly touching his face. When they got to Ray Kendall's lobster pound, Wally shut off the car and whispered, "Hey, Sleepy." He kissed Candy on the lips, which woke her up. She sat bolt upright, for a second disoriented, and she looked accusingly at both Wally and Homer, as if she weren't sure which one of them had kissed her. "Easy," Wally said to her, laughing. "You're home."

Home, thought Homer Wells. He knew that for the Bedouin—come from nowhere, going nowhere—there was no home.

/ / /

In August of that same summer another Bedouin left what had been home for him; Curly Day departed St. Cloud's for Boothbay, where a young druggist and his wife had recently moved and had plunged into a life of community service. Dr. Larch had his doubts about the young couple, but he had more doubts regarding Curly Day's resilience to another winter in St. Cloud's. The end of the summer was the last good time for visits from adoptive families; the good weather in the early fall was brief. And Curly's general positivism had been in decline since the departure of Homer Wells; Curly could never be convinced that Homer had not somehow stolen the beautiful couple whom a kinder fate had intended for him.

The druggist and his wife were not a beautiful couple. They were well off and good-hearted; but they had not been born to a life of ease, and it seemed unlikely that they would ever adjust to anything resembling gracious living. They had *striven* to their station in life, and their idea of helping their fellow man seemed rooted in the notion that their fellow man should be taught how to *strive.* They had requested an older orphan; they wanted someone capable of doing a few hours' work in the drugstore after school.

They saw their childlessness as entirely God's decision and agreed that God had meant for them to find a foundling and educate him in the methods of self-support and self-improvement, for which the foundling would be broadly rewarded by inheriting the young couple's pharmacy, and with it the means to care for them in their apparently eagerly anticipated old age.

They were practical and Christian people—albeit grim when they reviewed for Larch their earlier efforts to have a child of their own. Before he met the couple—at a time when he had only corresponded with them by mail—Larch had hoped he might persuade them to allow Curly to keep his first name. When an orphan gets to be as old as Curly, Larch argued, the name has more than casual significance. But Larch's hopes sank when he saw the couple; the young man was prematurely bald—so perfectly bald that Larch wondered if the fellow had not suffered from the application of an untested pharmaceutical product—and the young wife's hair was fine and lank. The couple seemed shocked at the wealth of Curly Day's curly hair, and Larch imagined that their first family trip would probably include a visit to the barber.

Curly himself seemed as unenthusiastic about the couple as the couple were unenthusiastic about his name, yet he wanted to leave St. Cloud's—badly. Larch saw that the boy still hoped for an adoption as dazzling as the one he'd imagined, for a couple as glittering with the promise of another life as Candy and Wally were. Of the very plain young couple from Boothbay, Curly Day said to Dr. Larch: "They're okay. They're nice, I guess. And Boothbay *is* on the coast. I think I'd like the ocean."

Larch did not say to the boy that the couple adopting him did not appear to be a boating couple, or a beach couple, or even a fishing-off-a-dock couple; he suspected them of thinking that a life of *playing* with, on, or in the sea was frivolous, something for tourists. (Larch thought that way himself.) Larch expected that the drugstore remained open every daylight hour of the summer, and that the hardworking young couple remained in the store every minute—selling tanning oil to summer people while they themselves stayed as pale as the winter, and were proud of it.

"You can't be too choosy, Wilbur," Nurse Edna said. "If the boy gets sick, there'll be lots of pills and cough medicines around."

"He'll still be Curly to me," Nurse Angela said defiantly.

Worse, Larch imagined: he'll always be Curly to Curly. But Larch let him go; it was high time for him to be gone—that was the main reason.

The couple's name was Rinfret; they called Curly "Roy." And so Roy "Curly" Rinfret took up residence in Boothbay. Rinfret's Pharmacy was a harborfront store; the family lived several miles inland, where the sea was out of sight. "But not out of *scent*," Mrs. Rinfret had maintained; she declared that, when the wind was right, the ocean could be smelled from the house.

Not with Curly's nose, Dr. Larch imagined: Curly's nose was such a constant streamer, Dr. Larch suspected that Curly had no sense of smell at all.

"Let us be happy for Curly Day," Dr. Larch announced to

he boys' division one evening in August in 194__—over David Copperfield's steady sobs. "Curly Day has found a family," Dr. Larch said. "Good night, Curly!"

"G'night, *Burly*!" young Copperfield cried.

When Homer Wells received the letter telling him the news of Curly's adoption, he read it again and again—in the moonlight streaming through Wally's window, while Wally slept.

A druggist! thought Homer Wells. He'd been upset enough by the news to talk about it with Wally and Candy. They'd sat in the moonlight, earlier that evening, throwing snails off Ray Kendall's dock. *Ploink! Ploink!* went the periwinkles; Homer Wells talked and talked. He told them about the litany—"Let us be happy for Curly Day," and so forth; he tried to explain how it had felt to be addressed as a Prince of Maine, as a King of New England.

"I guess I imagined someone who looked like you," Homer said to Wally.

Candy remembered that Dr. Larch had said this to her, too; that he'd told her that her babies would be these princes, these kings. "But I didn't know what he meant," she said. "I mean, he was nice—but it was unimaginable."

"It still is unimaginable to me," Wally said. "I mean, what you saw," he said to Homer. "What all of you imagined—it must have been different, for each of you." Wally was unwilling to accept the notion that someone who looked like himself would ever be adequate to the expression.

"It sounds a little mocking," Candy said. "I just can't see what he meant."

"Yeah," Wally agreed. "It sounds a little cynical."

"Maybe it was," said Homer Wells. "Maybe he said it for himself and not for us."

He told them about Melony, but not everything about her. He took a deep breath and told them about Fuzzy Stone; he imitated the breathing contraption admirably—he had them both so roaring with laughter at the racket he was making that they drowned out the insignificant *ploink* of the snails dropping into the sea. Wally and Candy didn't know they were at the end of the story until Homer simply arrived at it. "Fuzzy Stone has found a new family," he repeated to them. "Good night, Fuzzy," he concluded hollowly.

There wasn't a sound, then, not even a snail; the sea lapped at the dock posts; the boats moored around them rocked on the water. When a line was pulled taut and yanked out of the water, you could hear the water drip off the line; when the thicker ropes were stretched, they made a noise like grinding teeth.

"Curly Day was the first boy I circumcised," Homer Wells announced—just to change the subject from Fuzzy Stone. "Doctor Larch was there when I did it," Homer said, "and a circumcision is no big deal—it's really easy." Wally felt his own penis inch toward itself like a snail. Candy felt a cramp knot in her calf and she stopped swinging her legs off the edge of the dock; she drew her heels up to her buttocks and hugged her knees. "Curly was the first one," Homer said. "I made it a little lopsided," he confessed.

"We could drive up to Boothbay and see how he's doing," Wally suggested.

What would we see? Candy wondered. She imagined Curly peeing all over the Cadillac again, and telling them again that he was the best one.

"I don't think that would be a good idea," Homer said.

He went with Wally back to Ocean View and wrote Dr. Larch a long letter—his longest so far. He tried to tell Larch about the drive-in movie, but the letter degenerated into a critique of the movie itself, and so he tried to change the subject.

Should he tell him about Herb Fowler carrying all the prophylactics? (Although Dr. Larch approved of everyone using prophylactics, he would hardly have approved of Herb Fowler.) Should he tell Larch that he had learned the real purpose of the drive-in? Wasn't it to tease oneself and one's date into a state of sexual frenzy—which neither of you were allowed to act upon? (Dr. Larch would certainly not think highly of that.) Should he tell Dr. Larch what Grace Lynch had said and done, or how he dreamed about her—or how he imagined he was falling in love, or already had fallen in love, with Candy (which he knew was forbidden)? And how do I say, "I miss you"? he wondered—when I don't mean, "I want to come back!"?

And so he ended the letter in his fashion; he ended it inexactly. "I remember when you kissed me," he wrote to Dr. Larch. "I wasn't really asleep."

Yes, thought Dr. Larch, I remember that, too. He rested in the dispensary. Why didn't I kiss him more—why not all the time? In other parts of the world, he dreamed, they have drive-in movies!

/ / /

He always used more ether than he should have before the annual meeting of St. Cloud's board of trustees. He'd never quite understood what a board of trustees was for, and his impatience with the routine inquiries was growing. In the old days, there'd been the Maine State board of medical examiners; they'd never asked him any questions—they never wanted to hear from him. Now it appeared to Wilbur Larch that there was a board of trustees for everything. This year there were two new board members who'd never before seen the orphanage, and so the meeting had been scheduled to take place in St. Cloud's—the board usually met in Portland. The new members wanted to see the place; the old members agreed they should refresh themselves with the atmosphere.

It was a perfect August morning, with more indications of September in the air's crispness than there were indications of the stifling carry-over of July's humidity and hazy heat; but Larch was irritable.

"I don't know, 'exactly,' what a drive-in movie is," he said crossly to Nurse Angela. "Homer doesn't say, 'exactly.'"

Nurse Angela looked frustrated. "No, he doesn't," she agreed, going over the letter again and again.

"What do you do with your cars when you're watching the movie?" Nurse Edna asked.

"I don't know," Dr. Larch said. "I assume that if you drive *into* something to see the movie, you must stay in your cars."

"But *what* do you drive into, Wilbur?" Nurse Edna asked.

"That's what I don't know!" Larch shouted.

"Well, aren't we in a lovely mood?" Nurse Angela said.

"Why would you want to bring your car to a movie in the first place?" Nurse Edna asked.

"I don't know the answer to that, either," Dr. Larch said tiredly.

Unfortunately, he looked tired during the trustees meeting, too. Nurse Angela tried to present some of the orphanage's priorities for him; she didn't want him to get bad-tempered with anyone on the board. The two new members seemed in an awful hurry to demonstrate that they already understood everything—and Nurse Angela detected Dr. Larch looking at these younger members with something of the look he had formerly reserved for Clara, in the days when Larch would discover that Homer's cadaver hadn't been put away properly.

The new woman on the board had been appointed for her abilities at fund-raising; she was especially aggressive. She'd been married to a Congregationalist missionary who'd committed suicide in Japan, and she had returned to her home state of Maine with a zeal for putting her considerable energies to work for something "doable." Japan had not been at all "doable," she kept saying. Maine's problems, by comparison, were entirely surmountable. She believed that all Maine needed—or lacked—was organization, and she believed every solution began with "new blood"—a phrase, Nurse Angela observed, that caused Dr. Larch to pale as if his own blood were trickling away from him.

"That's an unfortunate expression for those of us familiar with hospital work," Dr. Larch snapped once, but the woman—Mrs. Goodhall—did not look sufficiently bitten.

Mrs. Goodhall expressed, albeit coldly, her admiration for the severity and the duration of Dr. Larch's "undertaking" and her respect for how much experience Larch and his assistants had with administering St. Cloud's; perhaps they all could be invigorated by a *younger* assistant. "A young intern—a willing toiler, and with some new ideas in the obstetrical field," Mrs. Goodhall suggested.

"I keep up with the field," Dr. Larch said. "And I keep up with the number of babies born here."

"Well, then, how about a new administrative assistant?" Mrs. Goodhall suggested. "Leave the medical practice to you—I'm talking about someone with a grasp of some of the newer adoption procedures, or just someone who could handle the correspondence and the interviewing for you."

"I could use a new typewriter," Dr. Larch said. "Just get me a new typewriter, and you can keep the assistant—or give the assistant to someone who's *really* doddering around."

The new man on the board was a psychiatrist; he was rather new at psychiatry, which was rather new in Maine in 194__. His name was Gingrich; even with people he had just met, he had a way of assuming he understood what pressure they were under—he was quite sure that everyone was under some pressure. Even if he was correct (about the particular pressure you were under), and even if you agreed with him (that there indeed *was* a certain pressure, and indeed you were under it),

ne had a way of assuming he knew *other* pressures that preyed
upon you (which were always unseen by you). For example,
nad he seen the movie that began with the Bedouin on the
camel, Dr. Gingrich might have assumed that the captive woman
was under great pressure to marry someone—although it was
clearly her opinion that all she wanted was to get free. His eyes
and introductory smile communicated a cloying sympathy that
you perhaps did not deserve—as if he were imparting by the
imposed gentleness of his voice and the slowness with which he
spoke, the assurance that everything is much more subtle than
we can suppose.

The older members of the board—all men, all as elderly as
Larch—were intimidated by this new man who spoke in whis-
pers and by this new woman who was so loud. In tandem, they
seemed so sure of themselves; they viewed their new roles on
the board not as learning experiences, or even as an introduction to orphanage life, but as opportunities for taking charge.

Oh dear, Nurse Edna thought.

There's going to be trouble, as if we need any, Nurse Angela
thought. It wouldn't have hurt to have a young intern around,
or an administrative assistant, either; but she knew that Wilbur
Larch was protecting his ability to perform the abortions. How
could he accept new appointees without knowing the person's
beliefs?

"Now, Doctor Larch," Dr. Gingrich said softly, "surely you
know we don't think of you as doddering."

"Sometimes I think of myself as doddering," Larch said
defensively. "I suppose you might think so, too."

"The *pressure* you must be under," Dr. Gingrich said. "Someone with all your responsibilities should have all the help he
can get."

"Someone with my responsibility should stay responsible,"
Larch said.

"With the *pressure* you must be under," said Dr. Gingrich,
"it's no wonder you find it hard to delegate even a little of that
responsibility."

"I have more use for a typewriter than for a delegate,"
Wilbur Larch said, but when he blinked his eyes he saw those
bright stars that populated both a clear Maine night and the
firmament of ether, and he wasn't sure which stars they were.
He rubbed his face with his hand, and caught Mrs. Goodhall
scribbling something on the impressively thick pad before her.

"Let's see," she said—sharply, by comparison to Dr. Gingrich's wispy voice. "You're in your seventies, now—is that correct? Aren't you seventy-something?" she asked Dr. Larch.

"Right," said Wilbur Larch. "Seventy-something."

"And how old is Missus Grogan?" Mrs. Goodhall asked suddenly, as if Mrs. Grogan weren't present—or as if she were so old that she was incapable of answering for herself.

"I'm sixty-two," Mrs. Grogan said pertly, "and I'm as lively as a spring chicken!"

"Oh, no one doubts you're not *lively*!" said Dr. Gingrich.

"And Nurse Angela?" Mrs. Goodhall asked, not looking up at anyone; the scrutiny of her own writing on the pad before her required every ounce of her exhaustive attention.

"I'm fifty-eight," Nurse Angela said.

"Angela is as strong as an ox!" Mrs. Grogan said.

"We don't doubt it!" said Dr. Gingrich cheerfully.

"I'm fifty-five or fifty-six," Nurse Edna offered, before the question was raised.

"You don't *know* how old you are?" Dr. Gingrich asked meaningfully.

"Actually," said Wilbur Larch, "we're all so senile, we can't remember—we're just guessing. But look at you!" he said suddenly to Mrs. Goodhall, which did get Mrs. Goodhall to raise her eyes from her pad. "I guess you have such trouble remembering things," Larch said, "that you have to write everything down."

"I'm just trying to get the picture of what's going on here," Mrs. Goodhall said evenly.

"Well," Larch said. "I suggest you listen to me. I've been here long enough to have the picture pretty clearly in mind."

"It's very clear what a wonderful job you're doing!" Dr. Gingrich told Dr. Larch. "It's also clear how *hard* a job it is." Such a warm washcloth kind of sympathy was leaking from Dr. Gingrich that Larch felt wet—and grateful that he wasn't sitting near enough to Dr. Gingrich for Dr. Gingrich to touch him; Gingrich was clearly a toucher.

"If it's not asking too much, in the way of your support," Dr. Larch said, "I'd not only like a new typewriter; I'd like permission to keep the old one."

"I think we can arrange that," Mrs. Goodhall said.

Nurse Edna, who was not accustomed to sudden insights—or, despite her years, hot flashes—and was completely inexperinced with the world of omens and signs or even forewarnings, elt a totally foreign and breathtaking violence rise from her tomach. She found herself staring at Mrs. Goodhall with a atred Nurse Edna couldn't conceive of feeling for another uman being. Oh dear, the *enemy*! she thought; she had to xcuse herself—she was sure she was going to be ill. (She was, ut discreetly, out of sight, in the boys' shower room.) Only David Copperfield, still mourning the departure of Curly Day, nd still struggling with the language, spotted her.

"Medna?" young Copperfield asked.

"I'm fine, David," she told him, but she was not fine. I have een the *end,* she thought with an unfamiliar bitterness.

Larch had seen it, too. Someone will replace me, he real-:ed. And it won't be long. He looked at his calendar; he had wo abortions to perform the next day, and three "probables" ear the end of the week. There were always those who just howed up, too.

And what if they get someone who won't perform one? he hought.

When the new typewriter arrived, it fit—just in time—into is plans for Fuzzy Stone.

"Thank you for the new typewriter," Larch wrote to the oard of trustees. It had arrived "just in time," he added, ecause the old typewriter (which, if they remembered, he vanted to keep) had completely broken down. This was not :rue. He had the keys replaced on the old typewriter, and it ow typed a story with a different face.

What it typed were letters from young Fuzzy Stone. Fuzzy egan by wanting Dr. Larch to know how much he was ooking forward to being a doctor when he grew up, and how nuch Dr. Larch had inspired him to make this decision.

"I doubt that I will *ever* come to feel as you do, regarding bortion," young Fuzzy wrote to Dr. Larch. "Certainly, it is bstetrics that interests me, and certainly your example is esponsible for my interest, but I expect we shall never agree bout abortion. Although I know you perform abortions out of ie most genuine beliefs and out of the best intentions, you nust permit me to honor my beliefs accordingly."

And on and on. Larch covered the years; he wrote into the uture, leaving a few convenient blanks. Larch completed Dr. '. Stone's training (he put him through medical school, he ave him fine obstetrical procedure—even a few variances from

Dr. Larch's procedure, which Dr. Larch had Dr. Stone describe). And always Fuzzy Stone remained faithful to his beliefs.

"I'm sorry, but I believe there is a soul, and that it exists from the moment of conception," Fuzzy Stone wrote. He was slightly pompous-sounding, as he grew up, close to unctuous in his graciousness toward Larch, even capable of condescension at times—the kind of patronizing a young man will indulge in when he thinks he has "developed" beyond his teacher. Larch gave Fuzzy Stone an unmistakable self-righteousness, which he imagined all supporters of the existing law against abortion would feel at home with.

He even had young Dr. Stone propose that *he* replace Dr. Larch—"but not until you're ready to retire, of course!"—and that by this replacement it might be demonstrated to Dr. Larch that the law should be observed, that abortions should *not* be performed, and that a safe and informative view of family planning (birth control, and so forth) could in time achieve the desired effect (". . . without breaking the laws of God or man," wrote a convincingly creepy Fuzzy Stone).

"The desired effect"—both Dr. Larch and Dr. Stone agreed—would be a minimum of unwanted children brought forth into the world. "I, for one, am happy to be here!" crowed young Dr. Stone. He sounds like a missionary! thought Wilbur Larch. The idea of making a missionary out of Fuzzy appealed to Dr. Larch for several reasons—among them: Fuzzy wouldn't need a license to practice medicine if he took his magic to some remote and primitive place.

It exhausted Larch, but he got it all down—one typewriter for Fuzzy that was used for nothing else, and the new one for himself. (He made carbons of his own letters and referred to his "dialogue" with young Dr. Stone in various fragments which he contributed to *A Brief History of St. Cloud's*.)

He imagined that their correspondence ended, quite abruptly, when Larch refused to accept the idea that anyone should replace him who was unwilling to perform abortions. "I will go until I drop," he wrote to Fuzzy. "Here in St. Cloud's, I will never allow myself to be replaced by some reactionary religious moron who cares more for the misgivings suffered in his own frail soul than for the actual suffering of countless unwanted and mistreated children. I am *sorry* you're a doctor!" Larch ranted to poor Fuzzy. "I am sorry such training was wasted on someone who refuses to help the living because of a presump-

uous point of view taken toward the unborn. You are *not* the
proper doctor for this orphanage, and over my dead body will
you ever get my job!"

What he heard from Dr. Stone, after that, was a rather curt
note in which Fuzzy said he needed to search his soul regarding his personal debt to Dr. Larch and his "perhaps larger debt
to society, and to all the murdered unborn of the future"; it
was hard, Fuzzy implied, to listen to his conscience and not
"turn in" Dr. Larch ". . . to the authorities," he added ominously.

What a good story! thought Wilbur Larch. It had taken him
the rest of August of 194—. He wanted to leave the matter all
set up—all arranged—when Homer Wells returned to St. Cloud's
from his summer job.

Wilbur Larch had created a replacement for himself, one
who would be acceptable to the authorities—whoever they
were. He had created someone with qualified obstetrical procedure, and—what better?—an orphan familiar with the place
from birth. He had also created a perfect lie, because the Dr.
F. Stone whom Wilbur Larch had in mind *would* perform
abortions, of course, while at the same time—what better?—he
would be on record for claiming he was *against* performing
them. When Larch retired (or, he knew, if he was ever caught),
he would already have available his most perfect replacement.
Of course, Larch was not through with Fuzzy; such an important replacement might require some revision.

Wilbur Larch lay in the dispensary with both the stars of
Maine and the stars of ether circling around him. He had given
Fuzzy Stone a role in life that was much more strenuous than
Fuzzy ever could have been capable of. How could poor Fuzzy
even have imagined it, as he succumbed to the failure of his
breathing contraption?

Only one problem, thought Wilbur Larch, dreaming with
the stars. How do I get Homer to play the part?

Homer Wells, gazing at the actual stars of Maine and at the
orchards visible in the waning moonlight out Wally's window,
saw something glint—something beyond the orchard from which
he knew the ocean could be viewed. Homer moved his head up
and down in Wally's window, and the glint flashed to him; the
feeble signal reminded him of the night when the deep Maine
woods had not returned his voice to him—when he had yelled
his echoless good night to Fuzzy Stone.

Then he realized where the glint was coming from. There

must be one, small, polished spot on the tin roof of the cider house; he was seeing the waning moon bounce off the roof o the cider house—off a spot no bigger than a knife blade. Thi little glint in the night was one of those things that—even after you identify it—you can't leave alone.

It was no help to him, to listen to Wally's peaceful breath ing. The problem is, Homer Wells knew, I am in love with Candy. It was Candy who suggested he not go back to St Cloud's.

"My father likes you so much," she'd told Homer. "I know he'll give you a job on the boat, or in the pound."

"My mother likes you so much," Wally had added. "I know she'll keep you on in the orchards, especially through harvest And she gets lonely whenever I go back to college. I'll bet she'd be delighted to have you stay right where you are—in my room!"

Out in the orchards, the roof of the cider house flashed to him; the flash was as small and as quick as the one glimpse of an eyetooth Grace Lynch had revealed—her mouth had parted only that much when she'd last looked at him.

How could I *not* be in love with Candy? he wondered. And if I stay here, he asked himself, what can I do?

The roof of the cider house flashed; then it stood dark and still. He had seen the wink of the curette before it went to work; he had seen it at rest in the examining tray, dull with blood, in need of cleaning.

And if I go back to St. Cloud's, he asked himself, what can I do?

In Nurse Angela's office, on the new typewriter, Dr. Larch began a letter to Homer Wells. "I remember nothing so vividly as kissing you," Dr. Larch began, but he stopped; he knew he couldn't say that. He pulled the page from the typewriter, then he hid it deep within *A Brief History of St. Cloud's,* as if it were another particle of history without an audience.

David Copperfield had a fever when he'd gone to bed, and Larch went to check on the boy. Dr. Larch was relieved to feel that young Copperfield's fever had broken; the boy's forehead was cool, and a slight sweat chilled the boy's neck, which Larch carefully rubbed dry with a towel. There was not much moonlight; therefore, Larch felt unobserved. He bent over Copperfield and kissed him, much in the manner that he remembered kissing Homer Wells. Larch moved to the next

ed and kissed Smoky Fields, who tasted vaguely like hot dogs;
et the experience was soothing to Larch. How he wished he
ad kissed Homer more, when he'd had the chance! He went
rom bed to bed, kissing the boys; it occurred to him, he didn't
now all their names, but he kissed them anyway. He kissed all
f them.

When he left the room, Smoky Fields asked the darkness,
"What was *that* all about?" But no one else was awake, or else
o one wanted to answer him.

I wish he would kiss *me,* thought Nurse Edna, who had a
ery alert ear for unusual goings-on.

"I think it's nice," Mrs. Grogan said to Nurse Angela, when
Nurse Angela told her about it.

"I think it's senile," Nurse Angela said.

But Homer Wells, at Wally's window, did not know that Dr.
Larch's kisses were out in the world, in search of him.

He didn't know, either—he could never have imagined it!
—that Candy was also awake, and also worried. If he *does* stay,
f he *doesn't* go back to St. Cloud's, she was thinking, what will
do? The sea tugged all around her. Both the darkness and the
oon were failing.

There came that time when Homer Wells could make out
he boundaries of the cider house, but the roof did not wink to
im, no matter how he moved his head. With no signal flashing
o him, Homer may have thought he was speaking to the dead
when he whispered, "Good night, Fuzzy."

He did not know that Fuzzy Stone, like Melony, was looking
or him.

7/ Before the War

One day that August a hazy sun hung over the coastal road between York Harbor and Ogunquit; it was not the staring sun of Marseilles, and not the cool, crisp sun that blinks on much of the coast of Maine at that time of year. It was a St. Cloud's sunlight, steamy and flat, and Melony was irritated by it and sweating when she accepted a ride in a milk truck that was heading inland.

She knew she was south of Portland, and that there was relatively little of the Maine coast that lay south of Portland yet it had taken her these months to search the apple orchards in this limited vicinity. She was not discouraged, she knew she'd had some bad luck, and that her luck was due to improve. She'd managed to pick the pockets of several citizens of Portland; this tided her over for a while. She'd gotten in trouble with some Navy men whose pockets she'd tried to pick in Kittery. She'd managed not to have sex with the men, but they had broken her nose, which had healed crookedly, and they had chipped her two front teeth—the big uppers. Not that she tended to smile a lot anyway, but she had since adopted a rather closemouthed and tight-lipped expression.

The first two orchards she'd visited were within view of the ocean, but they were not called Ocean View, and no one in either orchard had heard of the Ocean View Orchards. She then found an inland orchard, where someone told her he had heard of an Ocean View, but that he was sure it was just a name: that the place wasn't anywhere near the coast. She took a job washing bottles in a dairy in Biddeford, but she quit it as soon as she'd made some traveling money.

The orchard between York Harbor and Ogunquit turned out to be called York Farm, which looked as plain as its name but Melony told the milk truck driver to let her out there, anyway; it was, at least, an apple orchard; someone might have heard of Ocean View.

The foreman at York Farm took one look at Melony and assumed she was a would-be picker, trying to get work ahead of the migrants.

"You're about three weeks early," he told her. "We're only pickin' the Gravensteins this month, and I don't need help pickin' them—there ain't that many."

"You heard of an orchard called Ocean View?" Melony asked the foreman.

"You used to pick there?" the foreman asked.

"No. I'm just looking for it," Melony said.

"It sounds like a rest home," the foreman said, but when Melony didn't even smile, he stopped being friendly. "You any idea how many places there must be in Maine called Ocean View?" he asked.

Melony shrugged. If they were hiring at York Farm in three weeks, she thought she wouldn't mind staying; some of the other pickers might have heard of the place where Homer Wells had gone.

"You got anything for me to do?" Melony asked the foreman.

"In three weeks—if you know how to pick," he added.

"There can't be much to picking apples," Melony said.

"You think it's easy?" the foreman asked. "Come here," he said, and walked her through the dingy apple mart; two older women were hand-lettering a wooden price list. In the first orchard behind the apple mart, the foreman proceeded to lecture Melony on the art of apple picking.

"You take an apple with its stem," the foreman said. "But just above the stem is the bud for next year's apple. That's the spur," he said. "You pull the spur, you pull two years in one." He demonstrated to Melony how to twist the apple. "Twist, don't pull," he told her.

Melony reached into the tree and twisted an apple free. She did it correctly; she looked at the foreman and shrugged. She took a bite of the apple, which wasn't ripe; she spit out the bite and threw the apple away.

"That's a Northern Spy," the foreman explained. "We pick them last—they're not ready before October."

Melony was bored. She started back toward the apple mart.

"I'll give you ten cents a bushel!" the foreman called after her. "Only a nickel a bushel for drops, or if you bruise the fruit! You look pretty strong!" he said, following after her. "If you get the hang of it, you might pick ninety bushels a day. I've had guys here doin' a hundred bushels. That's ten bucks a day," he said. "Come back in three weeks," he added, stopping next to the women working on the sign in the apple mart; Melony was already back on the road.

"I'll be somewhere else in three weeks," she said to the foreman.

"Too bad," the foreman said. He watched her walk down the road, headed back toward the coast. "She looks strong," he said to one of the women in the mart. "I'll bet she weighs about one-sixty."

"She's just a tramp," the woman said.

About a mile away from the apple mart, Melony walked by an orchard where two workers were picking Gravensteins. One of the men waved to her; Melony started to wave back but thought better of it. She was not more than a hundred yards past the men when she heard their pickup truck coming after her. The truck pulled up next to her, off to the side of the road, and the driver said to her, "You look like you lost your sweetheart. Good thing you found me." The man in the passenger side of the truck opened the door before the truck stopped rolling.

"You better leave me alone, buster," Melony said to the driver, but the other man was already around the truck and coming closer. Melony hopped over the road ditch and ran into the orchard. The man pursued her, whooping. The driver killed the truck motor and joined the chase—he left his door open, he was in such a hurry.

There was nowhere to hide, but the orchards seemed endless. Melony ran down one row between the trees, then up another. The first man to chase her was gaining on her, but she noticed that the driver lagged farther and farther behind; he was a big, slow man, and he was huffing and puffing after he'd passed five or six trees. Melony was huffing and puffing herself, but she ran with a certain, even strength, and although the first, smaller man was gaining on her, she could hear him breathing harder and harder.

She crossed a dirt road into another orchard. Way behind her, maybe two or three hundred yards, she saw that the heavy driver had slowed to a determined walk. "Get her, Charley!" he called to the faster man.

To Charley's surprise, Melony stopped and turned to face him. She caught her breath fairly quickly, then she ran *at* Charley—she moved low to the ground, a kind of animal whine in her throat, and the man called Charley did not have time to stop and catch his breath before she flung herself upon him. They fell together—when she felt her knee against his throat, she jounced on him. He made a choking sound and rolled on his side. Melony jumped up to her feet; she stamped twice on his face, and when Charley managed to turn over, on all fours, she jumped up as high as she could and landed with both feet in the small of his back. He was already unconscious when she pinned his arms behind him and bit his ear; she felt her teeth meet. She let him go and knelt beside him; she caught her breath again; then she spit on him. When she stood up, she saw that the heavy man had managed only to cross the dirt road into the second orchard.

"Charley! Get up!" he said, wheezing, but Charley didn't move. Melony rolled Charley over on his back and undid his belt. She tugged it roughly through the loops until she had the belt off him. The big man, the driver, was now only three or four apple trees away from her. She wound one end of the belt twice around her wrist and fist; when she let her arm hang at her side, the buckle end of the belt touched the top of her foot. The big man stopped, only two trees away from her. "What'd you do to Charley?" he asked her, but Melony started swinging the belt; she swung it around and around her head, faster and faster. The square brass belt buckle began to whistle. Melony advanced on the heavy driver, a man in his late forties or early fifties; his hair was gray and thin, and he had quite a paunch thrust ahead of himself. He stood his ground for a moment and watched Melony come nearer to him. The belt was a broad strap of sweat-and-oil-stained leather; the brass buckle was the size of a man's palm; with its square edges, it hummed through the air like the north wind—it made a sound like a scythe.

"Hey!" the fat man said.

"Hey *what,* buster?" Melony said. She suddenly lowered the belt and cracked the buckle across one of the man's shins, where it lifted up a flap of blue jeans and skin that looked like a torn dollar bill. When the man bent over to grab his legs, she swiped the belt buckle across the side of his face; he sat down suddenly and put his hand to his cheek, where he discovered a gouge the approximate length and thickness of a cigarette. He hadn't the time to contemplate this wound before the belt buckle smacked him squarely across the bridge of his nose—the force of the blow, and his pain, temporarily blinded him. He tried to cover his head with one arm while he groped for Melony with the other, but she found it easy to hit him everywhere, and he quickly drew up his knees to his chest and covered his face and head with both arms. The buckle raked and nicked his spine for a while; then she stopped using the buckle end on him—she just strapped him with the flat end of the belt across the backs of his legs and his ass. It seemed she would never stop.

"Are the keys in that truck, buster?" she asked him between blows.

"Yes!" he cried, but she hit him some more before she left him. She took the belt with her, walking back through the first orchard, occasionally taking a swipe at an apple with the tip of the belt, with which she had developed some skill.

The man called Charley regained consciousness, but he didn't move or open his eyes. "Is she gone, Charley?" the fat man asked after a while, because he hadn't moved or opened his eyes either.

"I *hope* so," Charley said, but neither of the men moved until they heard Melony start the truck.

It crossed her mind that she was in debt to Dr. Larch for once getting her a job where she had learned to drive, but it was a passing thought. She turned the truck around and drove back to the apple mart, where the foreman was surprised to see her.

She told the foreman, in front of the women who were working on the sign, that two of his men had tried to rape her. One of the men, the fat one, was married to the woman who was hand-lettering the sign. Melony said to the foreman that he could fire those two men and give her their jobs. "I can do whatever the two of them do, and better than they do it," Melony said.

Or else, she said to the foreman, he could call the police and she'd tell the police how she'd been attacked. The woman whose husband had assaulted Melony was pale and silent, but the other woman said to the foreman what she'd said earlier: "She's just a tramp. What do you want to listen to her for?"

"I can do everything you do, too," Melony said to the woman. "Especially everything you do on your back. You look like you're shit on your back," Melony said, and she flicked the flat end of the belt toward the woman, who jumped away as if the belt were a snake.

"Hey, that's Charley's belt," the foreman said.

"Right," said Melony; this echo of Homer Wells nearly brought tears to her eyes. "Charley lost it," she added. She went to the truck and took out her bundle—her few things, which were all wrapped in Mrs. Grogan's coat. She used the belt to cinch the coat and its contents more securely together.

"I can't fire those guys," the foreman told her. "They've worked here all their lives."

"So call the police, then," Melony said.

"She's threatening you," the fat man's wife said to the foreman.

"No shit," Melony said.

The foreman got Melony settled comfortably in the cider house.

"You can stay here, at least until the pickin' crew comes," he said. "I don't know if you want to stay here when they're here. Sometimes there's women with them, and sometimes there's kids, but if it's just men, I don't think you want to stay here. They're Negroes."

"It'll do for now, anyway," Melony said, looking around.

There were fewer beds than there were in the Worthingtons' cider house, and it was a lot less neat and clean. York Farm was a much smaller, poorer orchard than Ocean View, and there was no one there who cared very much about the style and shape of the quarters for the migrants; York Farm was without an Olive Worthington. The vinegar smell was stronger in the York Farm cider house, and behind the press were dried clots of pomace that clung to the wall like apple scab. There was no stove in the kitchen section—just a hot plate, which tended to blow the old fuses. There was one fuse box for the pump and grinder and the low-watt, overhead bulbs; the light in the refrigerator was out, but this at least made the mold less visible.

It was fine for Melony, who had contributed, lastingly, to the history of the many wrecked rooms in both the abandoned and the lived-in buildings of St. Cloud's.

"This Ocean View—the one you're lookin' for?" the foreman asked. "How come you're lookin' for it?"

"I'm looking for my boyfriend," Melony told him.

She has a *boyfriend*? the foreman wondered.

He went to see how the men were doing. The fat man, whose wife had accompanied him to the hospital (although she had not spoken to him, and wouldn't for more than three months), sat rather placidly through his stitches, but he grew quite excited when the foreman told him that he'd fixed Melony up in the cider house and had given her a job—at least through the harvest.

"You gave her a job!" the fat man cried. "She's a killer!"

"Then you better keep the fuck out of her way," the foreman told him. "If you get in her way I'll have to fire you—she damn near made me, already."

The fat man had a broken nose and needed a total of forty-one stitches, thirty-seven in his face and four in his tongue where he had bitten himself.

The man called Charley was better off in the stitches department. He required only four—to close the wound in his ear. But Melony had cracked two of his ribs by jumping on him; he had received a concussion from having his head stamped on; and his lower back would suffer such repeated muscle spasms that he would be kept off a ladder through the harvest.

"Holy cow," Charley said to the foreman. "I'd hate to meet the son of a bitch who's her *boyfriend*."

"Just keep out of her way," the foreman advised him.

"Has she still got my belt?" Charley asked the foreman.

"If you ask her for your belt back, I'll have to fire you. Get yourself a new belt," the foreman said.

"You won't see me askin' her for nothin'," Charley said. "She didn't say her boyfriend was coming here, did she?" he asked the foreman, but the foreman said that if Melony was looking for her boyfriend, the boyfriend must not have given her any directions; he must have left her. "And God help him if he left her," the foreman said—over and over again.

"Well," said the woman in the apple mart who had called Melony a tramp. "If you had a woman like that, wouldn't you try to leave her?"

"In the first place," the foreman said, "I wouldn't ever have a woman like that. And in the second place, if I *did* have her, I'd never leave her—I wouldn't dare."

In the cider house at York Farm—somewhere inland from York Harbor, somewhere west of Ogunquit, with several hundred miles of coastline between her and Homer Wells—Melony lay listening to the mice. Sometimes they scurried, sometimes they gnawed. The first mouse bold enough to race across the foot of her mattress was swatted so hard with the buckle end of Charley's belt that it flew across four beds, all in a row, and struck the wall with a soft thud. Melony promptly retrieved it—it was quite dead, its back broken. With the aid of a pencil without a point, Melony was able to prop the dead mouse into a sitting position on her night table, an inverted apple crate, which she then moved to the foot of her bed. It was her belief that the dead mouse might function as a kind of totem, to warn other mice away, and—indeed—no mouse bothered Melony for several hours. She lay in the weak light reading *Jane Eyre*—the empty, dark orchard ripening all around her.

She reread, twice, that passage near the end of Chapter Twenty-seven that concludes: "Preconceived opinions, foregone determinations, are all I have at this hour to stand by: there I plant my foot."

With that she closed the book and turned out the light. Melony lay bravely on her back, her broad nostrils full of the sharp cider-vinegar air—the same air Homer Wells is smelling, she thought. Just before she fell asleep, she whispered—although there were only the mice to hear her—"Good night, Sunshine."

/ / /

The next day it rained. It rained from Kennebunkport to Christmas Cove. There was such a strong northeast wind that the flags on the boats moored at the Haven Club, even though they were saturated with rain, pointed to shore, and made a brisk snapping sound as constant as the chafe of Ray Kendall's lobster boat against the old worn-rubber tires that padded his dock.

Ray would spend the day under the John Deere in Building Number Two; he was, alternately, replacing the tractor's manifold and sleeping. It was the place he slept best: under a large, familiar machine. He was never detected; his legs at times extended from under the vehicle in a posture of such extreme sprawl that he looked dead—run over or crushed. One of the apple workers, startled to see him, would speak out, "Ray? Is that you?" Whereupon, like Dr. Larch brought back from ether, Ray Kendall would wake up and say, "Right here. I'm right here."

"Some job, huh?" the worried party would inquire.

"Yup," Ray would say. "Some job, all right."

The rain came pelting down, the wind so strongly onshore that the gulls moved inland. At York Farm they huddled against the cider house and woke up Melony with their fretting; at Ocean View they squatted together on the tin roof of the cider house, where a crew of scrubbers and painters were at work again.

Grace Lynch, as usual, had the worst job, scouring the thousand-gallon cider tank; she was kneeling inside the vat, and the sound of her movements in there impressed the others with a kind of furtive energy as if an animal were scrounging for a nest or for its dinner. Meany Hyde had left the cider house on what his wife, Florence, called "another bullshit errand." Meany had determined that the fan belt on the conveyor was loose, and so he removed it and said he was taking it to Ray Kendall to see what Ray could do about it.

"So what's Ray gonna do with a loose fan belt?" Florence asked Meany. "Order a new one, or take a piece out of that one—right?"

"I suppose," Meany said warily.

"And what do you need the conveyor for today?" Florence asked.

"I'm just takin' it to Ray!" Meany said peevishly.

"You don't wanna work too much, do you?" Florence said, and Meany shuffled out into the rain; he smiled and winked at Homer Wells as he was climbing into the pickup.

"I got a lazy husband," Florence said happily.

"That's better than some other kinds," said Irene Titcomb—and everyone automatically looked in the direction of the thousand-gallon vat where Grace Lynch was feverishly scrubbing.

Irene and Florence, who had patient, steady hands, were painting the sashes and the window trim in the bedroom wing of the cider house. Homer Wells and Big Dot Taft and Big Dot's kid sister, Debra Pettigrew, were painting the kitchen with broader, more carefree strokes.

"I hope you don't feel I'm crampin' you," Big Dot said to Debra and Homer. "I ain't your chaperone or nothin'. If you want to make out, just go right ahead."

Debra Pettigrew looked embarrassed and cross, and Homer smiled shyly. It was funny, he thought, how you have two or three dates with someone—and just kiss them and touch them in a few odd places—and everyone starts talking to you as if you've got *doing it* on your mind every minute. Homer's mind was much more on Grace Lynch in the vat than it was on Debra Pettigrew, who stood right beside him painting the same wall. When Homer encountered the light switch by the kitchen door, he asked Big Dot Taft if he should just paint all around it or let Florence and Irene, with their smaller brushes, trim it more neatly.

"Just paint right over it," said Big Dot Taft. "We do this every year. We just make it look new and fresh. We're not tryin' to win no neatness contest."

By the light switch, there was a tack that pinned a piece of typing paper to the wall—the type itself was very faint, from long exposure to the sunlight that came through the kitchen's curtainless windows. It was some kind of list; the bottom quarter of the page had been torn away; whatever it was, it was incomplete. Homer pulled the tack out of the wall and would have crumpled the paper and tossed it toward the trash barrel if the top line of type hadn't caught his attention.

CIDER HOUSE RULES

the top line said.

What rules? he wondered, reading down the page. The rules were numbered.

1. Please don't operate the grinder or the press if you've been drinking.

2. Please don't smoke in bed or use candles.

3. Please don't go up on the roof if you've been drinking—especially at night.

4. Please wash out the press cloths the same day or night they are used.

5. Please remove the rotary screen immediately after you've finished pressing and hose it clean WHEN THE POMACE IS STILL WET ON IT!

6. Please don't take bottles with you when you go up on the roof.

7. Please—even if you are very hot (or if you've been

drinking)—don't go into the cold-storage room to sleep.

8. Please give your shopping list to the crew boss by seven o'clock in the morning.

9. There should be no more than half a dozen people on the roof at any one time.

If there were a few more rules, Homer couldn't read them because the page had been ripped off. Homer handed the torn paper to Big Dot Taft.

"What's all this about the roof?" he asked Debra Pettigrew.

"You can see the ocean from the roof," Debra said.

"That ain't it," said Big Dot Taft. "At night you can see the Ferris wheel and the carnival lights in Cape Kenneth."

"Big deal," said Homer Wells.

"It's no big deal to me, either," Big Dot Taft said, "but those darkies really like it."

"They sit up on the roof all night, some nights," Debra Pettigrew said.

"They get drunk up there and fall off, some nights," Florence Hyde announced from the bedroom wing.

"They break bottles up there and cut themselves all up," said Irene Titcomb.

"Well, not every night, they don't," said Big Dot Taft.

"And one night one of them got so drunk and sweaty, running the press, that he passed out in the cold storage and woke up with pneumonia," Debra Pettigrew said.

"You don't exactly 'wake up with' pneumonia," said Homer Wells. "It's more complicated than that."

"Excuse *me*," Debra said sulkily.

"Anyway, nobody pays no attention to them rules," Big Dot Taft said. "Every year Olive writes them up, and every year nobody pays no attention."

"All the pickin' crews we've ever had are just children," said Florence Hyde. "If Olive didn't go shoppin' for them every day, they'd starve."

"They never get themselves organized," Irene Titcomb said.

"One of them got his whole arm caught in the grinder," Big Dot Taft recalled. "Not just his fool hand—his whole arm."

"Yuck," said Debra Pettigrew.

"Yuck is what his arm was, all right," said Florence Hyde.

"How many stitches?" asked Homer Wells.

"You're really curious, you know that?" Debra Pettigrew asked him.

"Well, they don't do no harm, except to themselves," said Irene Titcomb philosophically. "What's it matter if they want to drink too much and roll off the roof? Wasn't nobody ever killed here, was there?"

"Not yet," said Grace Lynch's tight, thin voice, her words strangely amplified because she was speaking from the bottom of the thousand-gallon vat. The combination of the strangeness of her voice and the rareness of her making a contribution of any kind to their conversation made them all silent.

Everyone was just working away when Wally drove up in the green van with Louise Tobey; he dropped Louise off with her own bucket and brush and asked the rest of them if they needed anything—more brushes? more paint?

"Just give me a kiss, honey," said Florence Hyde.

"Just take us to the movies," said Big Dot Taft.

"Just propose to me, just *propose*!" cried Irene Titcomb. Everyone was laughing when Wally left. It was almost lunchtime, and everyone knew that Squeeze Louise had come to work particularly late. She usually arrived with Herb Fowler, more or less on time. Louise looked especially pouty this morning, and no one spoke to her for a while.

"Well, you can be havin' your period, or somethin', and still say good mornin'," said Big Dot Taft after a while.

"Good mornin'," said Louise Tobey.

"La-de-da!" said Irene Titcomb. Debra Pettigrew bumped Homer in the side; when he looked at her, she winked. Nothing else happened until Herb Fowler drove by and offered to take everyone to the Drinkwater Road diner for lunch.

Homer looked at the vat, but Grace Lynch made no appearance over its rim; she just continued her scratching and hissing noises in the vat's bottom. She wouldn't have accepted the invitation, anyway. Homer was thinking he probably should accept it, to get away from Grace Lynch, but he had promised himself to investigate the roof of the cider house—he wanted to find the spot that had glinted to him so mysteriously in the moonlight; and now that he'd heard about the cider house rules and that you could see the ocean—and the Cape Kenneth

Ferris wheel!—from the roof, he wanted to climb up there. Even in the rain.

He went outside with all the others, thinking that Grace Lynch might assume he'd gone with them, and then he told Herb Fowler out in the driveway that he was going to stay. He felt a finger hook him in his blue jeans pocket, one of the front ones, and when Herb and the others had gone, he looked in his pocket and discovered the rubber. The prophylactic's presence in his pocket urged him up on the cider house roof in a hurry.

His appearance there surprised the gulls, whose sudden and raucous flight surprised *him;* he had not noticed them huddled on the slope of the roof that faced away from him—and away from the wind. The roof was slippery in the rain; he had to grip the corrugated grooves with both hands and place his feet very close to each other as he climbed. The pitch of the roof was not too steep, or he wouldn't have been able to climb it at all. To his surprise, he found a number of planks—old two-by-fours—nailed to the seaward side of the roof's apex. Benches! he thought. Even at an angle, they were at least more comfortable to sit on than the tin. He sat there in the rain and tried to imagine the pleasure of the view, but the weather was much too stormy for him to be able to see the farthest orchards; the ocean was completely obscured, and he had to imagine where, on a clear night, the Ferris wheel and the carnival lights in Cape Kenneth would be.

He was getting soaked and was about to climb down when he saw the knife. It was a big switchblade, the blade end stuck into the two-by-four at the top of the roof alongside him; the handle, which was fake horn, was cracked in two places, and when Homer Wells tried to extract the blade from the wood, the handle broke in two in his hands. That was why it had been left there, apparently. With the handle broken, the knife wouldn't close properly; it wasn't safe to carry that way—and, besides, the blade was rusted. The whole roof was rusted, Homer noticed; there was no single spot shiny enough to have reflected the moonlight back to Wally's window. Then he noticed the broken glass; some larger pieces were caught in the corrugated grooves in the tin. It must have been one of those pieces of glass that caught the moon, Homer thought.

Beer bottle glass and rum bottle glass, whiskey bottle glass and gin bottle glass, he supposed. He tried to imagine the black men drinking at night on the roof; but the rain had soaked him through, and the wind now thoroughly chilled him. Inching his way back down the roof—to the edge where the ground was the safest jump—he cut his hand, just a small cut, on a piece of glass he didn't see. By the time he went back inside the cider house, the cut was bleeding freely—quite a lot of blood for such a small cut, he thought, and he wondered if perhaps there was a tiny piece of glass still inside the cut. Grace Lynch must have heard him rinsing the wound in the kitchen sink (if she hadn't heard him on the roof). To Homer's surprise, Grace was still in the thousand-gallon vat.

"Help me," she called to him. "I can't get out."

It was a lie; she was just trying to draw him to the edge of the tank. But orphans have a gullible nature; orphanage life is plain; by comparison, every lie is sophisticated. Homer Wells, although he approached the rim of the cider vat with trepidation, approached steadily. The quickness of her thin hands, and the wiry strength with which they gripped his wrists, surprised him; he nearly lost his balance—he was almost pulled into the tank, on top of her. Grace Lynch had taken all her clothes off, but the extreme definition of her bones struck Homer more powerfully than anything forbidden in her nakedness. She looked like a starved animal contained in a more or less humane trap; humane, except that it was evident, from her bruises, that her captor beat her regularly and hard. The bruises on her hips and thighs were the largest; the thumbprint bruises on the backs of her arms were the deepest purple hue and there was a yellow-to-green bruise on one of her small breasts that looked especially angry.

"Let me go," said Homer Wells.

"I know what they do where you come from!" Grace Lynch cried, tugging on his wrists.

"Right," said Homer Wells. Systematically, he began to peel back her fingers, but she scrambled nimbly up the side of the vat and bit him sharply on the back of his hand. He had to push her, then, and he might have hurt her if they both hadn't heard the splashy arrival of Wally in the green van. Grace Lynch let Homer go and scurried to put on her clothes. Wally sat in the van in the drenching rain and pumped the horn; Homer ran outside to see what he wanted.

"Get in!" Wally shouted. "We've got to go rescue my stupid father—he's in some kind of trouble at Sanborn's."

For Homer Wells, who'd grown up in a world without fathers, it was a shock to hear that anyone who had a father would call his father stupid, even if it was true. There was a peck bag of Gravensteins in the passenger seat of the van; Homer held the apples in his lap as Wally drove down Drink-water Road to Sanborn's General Store. The proprietors, Mildred and Bert Sanborn, were among Senior's oldest friends; he'd been a schoolboy with both of them and had once dated Milly (before he'd met Olive—and before Milly had married Bert).

Titus Hardware and Plumbing was next door to Sanborn's; Warren Titus, the plumber, was standing on the porch of the general store, not letting anyone inside, when Wally and Homer drove into Heart's Rock.

"It's a good thing you're here, Wally," Warren said, when the boys ran up to the porch. "Your Dad's got some wild hair across his ass."

In the store, Homer and Wally saw that Mildred and Bert Sanborn had—for the moment—cornered Senior in a niche of shelves reserved for baking goods; Senior appeared to have littered the floor and much of himself with all the flour and sugar within his reach. His trapped appearance reminded Homer of Grace Lynch.

"What's the trouble, Pop?" Wally asked his father. Mildred Sanborn gave a sigh of relief to see Wally, but Bert wouldn't take his eyes off Senior.

"Trouble Pop," Senior said.

"He got in a rage when he couldn't find the dog food," Bert said to Wally, without looking away from Senior; Bert thoroughly expected Senior to bolt, at any moment, to another part of the store and destroy it.

"What did you want with dog food, Pop?" Wally asked his father.

"Dog food Pop," Senior repeated.

"It's like he don't remember, Wally," Bert Sanborn said.

"We told him he didn't have a dog," Mildred said.

"I remember doing it to you, Milly!" Senior shouted.

"There he goes again," Bert said. "Senior, Senior," he said gently. "We're all your friends here."

"I have to feed Blinky," Senior said.

"Blinky was his dog when he was a boy," Milly Sanborn told Wally.

"If Blinky was still alive, Senior," Bert Sanborn said, "he'd be older than we are."

"Older than we are," Senior said.

"Let's go home, Pop," Wally said.

"Home Pop," Senior said, but he let Homer and Wally lead him to the van.

"I tell you, Wally, it's not booze," said Warren Titus, who opened the side door of the van for them. "It's not on his breath, not this time."

"It's something else, Wally," Bert Sanborn said.

"Who are you?" Senior asked Homer.

"I'm Homer Wells, Mister Worthington," Homer said.

"Mister Worthington," Senior said.

When they'd driven for almost five minutes, in silence, Senior shouted, "Everyone just shut up!"

When they got to Ocean View, Olive met the van in the driveway; she ignored Senior and spoke to Wally. "I don't know what he's had this morning, unless it's vodka; it wasn't on his breath when he left. I wouldn't have let him take the van if I thought he'd been drinking."

"I think it's something else, Mom," Wally said. With Homer's help, he led Senior to the bedroom, got his shoes off and coaxed him to lie down on the bed.

"You know, I drilled Milly once," Senior told his son.

"Sure you did, Pop," said Wally.

"I drilled Milly! I drilled Milly!" Senior said.

Wally tried to humor Senior with a limerick; Senior had taught Wally a lot of limericks, but Senior had difficulty remembering a limerick now, even if Wally talked him through it, line by line.

"Remember the Duchess of Kent, Pop?" Wally asked his father.

"Sure," Senior said, but he didn't say anything more.

"Oh, pity the Duchess of Kent!" Wally began, but Senior just listened. "Her cunt is so dreadfully bent," Wally said.

"Bent?" Senior said.

Wally tried again, two lines at a time.

> Oh, pity the Duchess of Kent!
> Her cunt is so dreadfully bent . . .

"Dreadfully bent!" Senior sang out.

Oh, pity the Duchess of Kent!
Her cunt is so dreadfully bent,
The poor wench doth stammer,
"I need a sledgehammer
To pound a man into my vent."

My God! thought Homer Wells. But Senior appeared to be baffled; he said nothing. Wally and Homer left him when they thought he'd fallen asleep.

Downstairs, Homer Wells told Olive and Wally that he thought it was something neurological.

"Neurological?" Olive said.

"What's that mean?" Wally said.

They heard Senior cry out from upstairs. "Vent!" he shouted.

Homer Wells, who had a habit of repeating the pigtails of sentences, knew that Senior's repetitions were insane. That habit was the first symptom he described in his letter about Senior Worthington to Dr. Larch. "He repeats everything," he wrote to Dr. Larch. Homer also noted that Senior appeared to forget the names of the most common things; he recalled how the man had become stuck asking Wally for a cigarette—he had just kept pointing at Wally's breast pocket. "I think the word for cigarette had escaped him," wrote Homer Wells. Homer had also observed that Senior could not operate the latch on the glove compartment the last time that Homer had driven him to Sanborn's for some simple shopping. And the man had the oddest habit of picking at his clothes all the time. "It's as if he thinks he's got dirt, or hair, or lint on his clothes," wrote Homer Wells. "But there's nothing there."

Olive Worthington assured Homer that the family doctor, a geezer even older than Dr. Larch, was quite certain that Senior's problems were entirely "alcohol-related."

"Doc Perkins is too old to be a doctor anymore, Mom," Wally said.

"Doc Perkins delivered you—I guess he knows what he's doing," Olive said.

"I bet I was easy to deliver," Wally said cheerfully.

I'll bet you were, imagined Homer Wells, who thought that Wally took everything in the world for granted—not in a selfish or spoiled way, but like a Prince of Maine, like a King of New England; Wally was just born to be in charge.

Dr. Larch's letter to Homer Wells was so impressive that Homer immediately showed it to Mrs. Worthington.

"What you have described to me, Homer, sounds like some kind of evolving organic brain syndrome," Dr. Larch wrote. "In a man of this age, there aren't a lot of diagnoses to choose from. I'd say your best bet is Alzheimer's presenile dementia; it's pretty rare; I looked it up in one of my bound volumes of the *New England Journal of Medicine*.

"Picking imaginary lint off one's clothes is what neurologists call *carphologia*. In the progress of deterioration common to Alzheimer's disease, a patient will frequently echo back what is said to him. This is called *echolalia*. The inability to name even familiar objects such as a cigarette is due to a failure to recognize the objects. This is called *anomia*. And the loss of the ability to do any type of skilled or learned movement such as opening the glove compartment is also typical. It is called *apraxia*.

"You should prevail upon Mrs. Worthington to have her husband examined by a neurologist. I know there is at least one in Maine. It's only my guess that it's Alzheimer's disease."

"*Alzheimer's* disease?" asked Olive Worthington.

"You mean it's a *disease*—what's wrong with him?" Wally asked Homer.

Wally cried in the car on the way to the neurologist. "I'm sorry, Pop," he said. But Senior seemed delighted.

When the neurologist confirmed Dr. Larch's diagnosis, Senior Worthington was exuberant.

"I have a disease!" he yelled proudly—even happily. It was almost as if someone had announced that he was cured; what he had was quite incurable. "I have a *disease*!" He was euphoric about it.

What a relief it must have been to him—for a moment, anyway—to learn that he wasn't simply a drunk. It was such an enormous relief to Olive that she wept on Wally's shoulder; she hugged and kissed Homer with an energy Homer had not known since he left the arms of Nurse Angela and Nurse Edna. Mrs. Worthington thanked Homer over and over again. It meant a great deal to Olive (although she had long ago fallen out of love with Senior, if she had ever truly loved him) to know that this new information permitted her to renew her respect for Senior. She was overwhelmingly grateful to Homer and to Dr. Larch for restoring Senior's self-esteem—and for restoring some of her esteem for Senior, too.

All this contributed to the special atmosphere that surrounded Senior's death at the end of the summer, shortly before the harvest; a sense of relief was far more prevalent than was a sense of grief. That Senior Worthington was on his way to death had been certain for some time; that, in the nick of time, he had managed to die with some honor—" . . . of a bona fide disease!" Bert Sanborn said—was a welcome surprise.

Of course, the residents of Heart's Rock and Heart's Haven had some difficulty with the term—Alzheimer was not a name familiar to the coast of Maine in 194__. The workers at Ocean View had particular trouble with it; Ray Kendall, one day, made it easier for everyone to understand. "Senior got *Al's Hammer* disease," he announced. Al's Hammer! Now *there* was a disease anyone could understand.

"I just hope it ain't catchin'," said Big Dot Taft.

"Maybe you got to be rich to get it?" wondered Meany Hyde.

"No, it's neurological," Homer Wells insisted, but that didn't mean anything to anyone except Homer.

And so the men and women at Ocean View developed a new saying as they got ready for the harvest that year. "You better watch out," Herb Fowler would say, "or you'll get Al's Hammer."

And when Louise Tobey would show up late, Florence Hyde (or Irene Titcomb, or Big Dot Taft) would ask her, "What's the matter, you got your period or Al's Hammer?" And when Grace Lynch would show up with a limp, or with a noticeable bruise, everyone would think but never say out loud, "She caught old Al's Hammer last night, for sure."

"It seems to me," Wally said to Homer Wells, "that you ought to be a doctor—you obviously have an instinct for it."

"Doctor Larch is the doctor," said Homer Wells. "I'm the Bedouin."

/ / /

Just before the harvest—when Olive Worthington had put fresh flowers in the bedroom wing of the cider house and had typed a clean page of rules (almost exactly the same rules from the previous years) and had tacked them next to the light switch by the kitchen door—she offered the Bedouin a home.

"I always hate it when Wally goes back to college," Olive told Homer. "And this year, with Senior gone, I'm going to hate it more. I would like it very much if you thought you could be happy here, Homer—you could stay in Wally's room.

I like having someone in the house at night, and someone to talk to in the morning." Olive was keeping her back to Homer while she looked out the bay window in the Worthingtons' kitchen. The rubber raft that Senior used to ride was bobbing in the water within her view, but Homer couldn't be sure if Olive was looking at the raft.

"I'm not sure how Doctor Larch would feel about it," Homer said.

"Doctor Larch would like you to go to college one day," Olive said. "And so would I. I would be happy to inquire, at the high school in Cape Kenneth, if they'd work with you—if they'd try to evaluate what you know and what you need to learn. You've had a very ... *odd* education. I know that Doctor Larch is interested in having you take all the sciences." (Homer understood that her mind must have been recalling this from a letter from Dr. Larch.) "And Latin," said Olive Worthington.

"Latin," said Homer Wells. This was *surely* Dr. Larch's work. *Cutaneus maximus*, thought Homer Wells, *dura mater*, not to mention good old *umbilicus*. "Doctor Larch wants me to be a doctor," Homer said to Mrs. Worthington. "But I don't want to be."

"I think he wants you to have the *option* of becoming a doctor, should you change your mind," Olive said. "I think he said Latin or Greek."

They must have had quite some correspondence, thought Homer Wells, but all he said was, "I really like working on the farm."

"Well, I certainly want you to keep working here," Olive told him. "I need your help—through the harvest, especially. I don't imagine you'd be a full-time student; I have to talk to the high school, but I'm sure they'd view you as something of an experiment."

"An experiment," said Homer Wells. Wasn't everything an experiment for a Bedouin?

He thought about the broken knife he'd found on the cider house roof. Was it there because he was *supposed* to find it? And the broken glass, a piece of which had signaled to him in his insomnia at Wally's window: was the glass on the roof *in order* to provide him with some message?

He wrote to Dr. Larch, requesting Larch's permission to stay at Ocean View. "I'll take biology," Homer Wells wrote, "and anything scientific. But do I have to take Latin? Nobody even speaks it anymore."

Where did he get to be such a know-it-all? wondered Wilbur Larch, who nevertheless saw certain advantages to Homer Wells *not* knowing Latin or Greek, both the root of so many medical terms. Like coarctation of the aorta, Dr. Larch was thinking. It can be a relatively mild form of a congenital heart disorder that could decrease as the patient grew older; by the time the patient was Homer's age, the patient might have no murmur at all and only a trained eye could detect, in an X ray, the slight enlargement of the aorta. In a mild case, the only symptoms might be a hypertension in the upper extremities. So don't learn Latin if you don't want to, thought Wilbur Larch.

As for the *best* congenital heart defect for Homer Wells, Dr. Larch was leaning toward pulmonary valve stenosis. "From infancy, and throughout his early childhood, Homer Wells had a loud heart murmur," Dr. Larch wrote—for the record, just to hear how it sounded. "At twenty-one," he noted elsewhere, "Homer's old heart murmur is difficult to detect; however, I find that the stenosis of the pulmonary valve is still apparent in an X ray." It might be *barely* detectable, he knew; Homer's heart defect was not for everyone to see—that was the point. What was necessary was that it just be there.

"Don't take Latin or Greek if you don't want to," Dr. Larch wrote to Homer Wells. "It's a free country, isn't it?"

Homer Wells was beginning to wonder. In the same envelope with Dr. Larch's letter was a letter Dr. Larch had forwarded to him from good old Snowy Meadows. In Wilbur Larch's opinion, Snowy was a fool, "but a persistent one."

"Hi, Homer, it's me—Snowy," Snowy Meadows began. He explained that his name was now Robert Marsh—"of the Bangor Marshes, we're the big furniture family," Snowy wrote.

The furniture family? thought Homer Wells.

Snowy went on and on about how he'd met and married the girl of his dreams, and how he'd chosen the furniture business over going to college, and how happy he was that he'd gotten out of St. Cloud's; Snowy added that he hoped Homer had "gotten out," too.

"And what do you hear from Fuzzy Stone?" Snowy Meadows wanted to know. "Old Larch says Fuzzy is doing well. I'd like to write Fuzzy, if you know his address."

Fuzzy Stone's *address*! thought Homer Wells. And what did

"old Larch" mean (that "Fuzzy is doing well")? Doing well at *what*? wondered Homer Wells, but he wrote to Snowy Meadows that Fuzzy was, indeed, doing well; that he had misplaced Fuzzy's address for the moment; and that he found apple farming to be healthy and satisfying work. Homer added that he had no immediate plans to visit Bangor; he would surely look up "the furniture Marshes" if he was ever in town. And, no, he concluded, he didn't agree with Snowy that "a kind of reunion in St. Cloud's" was such a hot idea; he said he was sure that Dr. Larch would never approve of such a plan; he confessed that he did miss Nurse Angela and Nurse Edna, and of course Dr. Larch himself, but wasn't the place better left behind? "Isn't that what it's for?" Homer Wells asked Snowy Meadows. "Isn't an orphanage supposed to be left behind?"

Then Homer wrote to Dr. Larch.

"What's this about Fuzzy Stone 'doing well'—doing well at WHAT? I know that Snowy Meadows is an idiot, but if you're going to tell him some stuff about Fuzzy Stone, don't you think you better tell me, too?"

In time, in time, thought Wilbur Larch wearily; he was feeling harassed. Dr. Gingrich and Mrs. Goodhall had prevailed upon the board of trustees; the board had requested that Larch comply with Dr. Gingrich's recommendation of a "follow-up report" on the status of each orphan's success (or failure) in each foster home. If this added paperwork was too tedious for Dr. Larch, the board recommended that Larch take Mrs. Goodhall's suggestion and accept an administrative assistant. Don't I have enough history to attend to, as is? Larch wondered. He rested in the dispensary; he sniffed a little ether and composed himself. Gingrich and Goodhall, he said to himself. Ginghall and Goodrich, he muttered. Richhall and Ginggood! Goodging and Hallrich! He woke himself, giggling.

"What are you so merry about?" Nurse Angela said sharply to him from the hall outside the dispensary.

"Goodballs and Ding Dong!" Wilbur Larch said to her.

He went to Nurse Angela's office, with a vengeance. He had plans for Fuzzy Stone. He called Bowdoin College (where Fuzzy Stone would successfully complete his undergraduate studies) and Harvard Medical School (where Larch intended Fuzzy to do very, very well). He told the registrar's office at Bowdoin that a sum of money had been donated to the orphanage at St. Cloud's for the express purpose of paying the medical school expenses of an exceptional young man or woman who would be willing—more than willing, even dedicated—to serve St. Cloud's. Could Dr. Larch have access to the transcripts of Bowdoin's recent graduates who had gone on to medical school? He told a slightly different story to Harvard Medical School; he wanted access to transcripts, of course, but in this case the sum of money had been donated to establish a training fellowship in obstetrics.

It was the first traveling Wilbur Larch had done since he'd chased after Clara, the first time he'd slept in a place other than the dispensary since World War I; but he needed to familiarize himself with the transcript forms at Bowdoin and at Harvard Medical School. Only in this way could he create a transcript for F. Stone; he begged the use of a typewriter and some paper—"one of your blank transcript forms will make it easier for me"—and pretended to type out the names and credentials of a few interesting candidates. "I see so many who'd be perfect," he told them at Bowdoin and Harvard, "but it's impossible to know if any of them could tolerate Saint Cloud's. We're very isolated," he confessed, thanking them for their help, handing them back their transcripts (Fuzzy's in the proper place, among the S's).

When he had returned to St. Cloud's, Dr. Larch wrote to Bowdoin and Harvard, requesting copies of the transcripts of a few outstanding graduates; he had narrowed the choices down to these few, he told them. A copy of Fuzzy's transcript came in the mail with the others.

When Larch had visited Harvard Medical School, he'd taken a Cambridge post office box in Fuzzy's name. Now he wrote to the postmaster there, requesting the mail for F. Stone be forwarded to St. Cloud's. The P.O. box address would be useful, too, if young Dr. Stone were to pursue his zealous instincts to a mission abroad. Then he sent an empty envelope to the Cambridge address and waited for its return.

When the letter came back to him—when he was sure the system worked—he composed the rest of the history regarding F. Stone and his adoptive family (named Eames) and sent it along to the board of trustees, together with Fuzzy's address. He did not have to invent anything regarding Curly Day; he cringed to write the name Roy Rinfret; and he told the truth regarding Snowy Meadows and most of the others, although he had difficulty typing "the furniture Marshes" without laughing out loud, and when he came to the case of Homer Wells, he thought very carefully about how to word the matter of Homer's heart.

Among the members of the board, there wasn't a heart specialist or a radiologist, or even a surgeon; there was a very old GP who, Dr. Larch felt sure, never read anything at all. Larch didn't count Dr. Gingrich as a doctor; he counted psychiatrists as nothing at all, and he felt confident that he could bully Mrs. Goodhall with the slightest terminology.

He confessed to the board (isn't everyone flattered by a confidence?) that he had refrained from mentioning the matter of Homer's heart to Homer; he admitted to stalling but argued that worrying the boy might contribute to his problem, and he wanted the boy to gain confidence in the outside world before burdening him with this dangerous knowledge—yet he intended to burden Homer with it, shortly. Larch said he *had* informed the Worthingtons of the heart defect; they might therefore be more than usually protective of Homer; he had not bothered to explain the presence of the actual murmur to them, or to detail the exact characteristics of pulmonary valve stenosis. He would be happy to provide the board with such details, should they request them. He had fun imagining Mrs. Goodhall scrutinizing an X ray.

He concluded that he thought the board's request for the follow-up reports had been a good idea and that he had enjoyed himself immensely in preparing them; contrary to needing an administrative assistant to perform such a service, Dr. Larch said he had felt "positively energized" by the "welcome task"—since, he added, following up on his orphans' adoptive lives was always on his mind. And sometimes right off the top of my head, he thought.

He was exhausted, and forgot to circumcise a newborn baby boy whom Nurse Angela had prepared for the operation. He mistook a woman awaiting an abortion for a woman he'd delivered the previous day, and therefore told her that her baby was very healthy and doing fine. He spilled a small amount of ether on his face and needed to irrigate his eye.

He became cross because he had overordered prophylactics —he had far too many rubbers around. Since Melony had left, no one was stealing the rubbers anymore. When he thought of Melony, he became worried, which also made him cross.

He returned to Nurse Angela's office and wrote a report,

which was real, concerning David Copperfield's lisp; he neglected to mention that David Copperfield had been delivered and named by Homer Wells. He wrote a slightly fictitious report on the orphan called Steerforth, remarking that his delivery was so straightforward that Nurse Edna and Nurse Angela had been able to handle it entirely without a doctor's assistance. He wrote the truth about Smoky Fields: the boy hoarded food, a trait that was more common in the girls' division than in the boys', and Smoky was beginning to exhibit a pattern of insomnia that Larch had not witnessed at St. Cloud's "since the days of Homer Wells."

The memory of those days brought instant tears to his eyes, but he recovered himself sufficiently to write that both he and Mrs. Grogan were worried about Mary Agnes Cork: she had exhibited frequent depressions since Melony's departure. He also told the truth about Melony, although he chose not to include any acts of vandalism. Larch wrote of Mary Agnes: "Perhaps she sees herself as inheriting Melony's former position, but she hasn't the dominating character that usually attends any powerful or leadership role." That idiot Dr. Gingrich is going to like that, Larch imagined. "Role," Larch said aloud, scornfully. As if orphans have the luxury of imagining that they have *roles*.

Impulsively, he went to the dispensary and inflated two prophylactics. Got to use these things up in some way, he thought. He used a laundry-marking pen to write the name GINGRICH on one prophylactic and the name GOODHALL on the other. Then he took these jolly balloons and went in search of Nurse Angela and Nurse Edna.

They were in the girls' division, having tea with Mrs. Grogan, when Dr. Larch found them.

"A-ha!" Larch said, surprising the ladies, who were unused to see him making an appearance in the girls' division except for the evening dose of *Jane Eyre*—and even more unused to see him waving marked prophylactics in their faces.

"Doctor Gingrich and Missus Goodhall, I presume!" Larch said, bowing to everyone. Whereupon he took a scalpel and popped the prophylactics. On the floor above them, Mary Agnes Cork heard the noise and sat up in her bed where she had been lying in a sullen depression. Mrs. Grogan was too stunned to speak.

When Dr. Larch left the ladies with their tea and returned to the hospital, Nurse Edna was the first to say something. "Wilbur works so hard," she said cautiously. "Isn't it a wonder that he can find the time to be playful?"

Mrs. Grogan was still struck speechless, but Nurse Angela said, "I think the old man is losing his marbles."

Nurse Edna appeared to be personally wounded by this remark; she returned her teacup to her saucer very steadily before she spoke. "I think it's the ether," she said quietly.

"Yes and no," said Nurse Angela.

"Do you think it's Homer Wells, too?" Mrs. Grogan asked.

"Yes," Nurse Angela said. "It's ether *and* it's Homer Wells, and it's old age, *and* it's those new members on the board. It's just everything. It's Saint Cloud's."

"It's what happened to Melony, too," Mrs. Grogan said, but she burst into tears when she said Melony's name. Upstairs, Mary Agnes Cork heard Melony's name and cried.

"Homer Wells will be back, I just know it," Nurse Angela said, but this so dissolved her in tears that Nurse Edna was obliged to comfort both her and Mrs. Grogan. "There, there," Nurse Edna said to them, but she wondered: where is the young man or the young woman who's going to take care of us all?

"Oh Lord," began Mrs. Grogan. Upstairs, Mary Agnes Cork bowed her head and clasped her hands; by pressing the heels of her hands together at a certain angle, she could revive a little of the pain from her old collarbone injury. "Oh Lord," Mrs. Grogan prayed, "support us all day long, until the shadows lengthen and the evening comes, and the busy world is hushed, and the fever of life is over, and our work is done."

That night, in the darkness, in keeping with the moan of an owl, Nurse Edna whispered "Amen" to herself while she listened to Dr. Larch making his rounds, kissing each of the boys—even Smoky Fields, who hoarded his food and hid it in his bed, which smelled, and who only pretended to be asleep.

/ / /

On the Ferris wheel, high above the carnival grounds and the beach at Cape Kenneth, Homer Wells was trying to spot the roof of the cider house, but it was dark and there were no lights on in the cider house—and even if the cider house had been lit, or there had been the clearest daylight imaginable, the house was too far away. Only the brightest carnival lights, especially the distinctive lights of the Ferris wheel, were visible from the cider house roof; the visibility didn't exist the other way around.

"I want to be a pilot," Wally said. "I want to fly, I really do. If I had my pilot's license, and my own plane, I could do all the spraying at the orchards—I'd get a crop duster, but I'd paint it like a fighter. It's so clumsy, driving those dumb sprayers around behind those dumb tractors, up and down those dumb hills."

It was what Candy's father, Ray, was doing at the moment; Meany Hyde was sick, and Everett Taft, the foreman, had asked Ray if he'd mind driving a night spray—Ray knew the equipment so well. It was the last spray before harvest, and somewhere in the blackened inland greenery that lay below the Ferris wheel, Raymond Kendall and Vernon Lynch were spraying their way through Ocean View.

Sometimes Wally sprayed; Homer was learning how. And sometimes Herb Fowler sprayed, but Herb protested against night spraying. ("I have better things to do at night," he'd say.) It was better to spray at night because the wind dropped in the evenings, especially along the coast.

Wally wasn't spraying tonight because it was his last night home; he was going back to college in the morning.

"You'll look after Candy for me, won't you, Homer?" Wally asked, as they loomed above the rocky coast and Cape Kenneth's crowded beach; the scarce bonfires from the summer's-end beach parties winked; the wheel descended.

Candy would finish her senior year at the girls' academy in Camden; she'd get home most weekends, but Wally would stay in Orono except for Thanksgiving and Christmas and the longer vacations.

"Right," said Homer Wells.

"If I were flying—in the war," Wally said. "*If* I joined, and *if* I flew, I mean, *if* I were in a bomber, I'd rather be in the B-24 than the B-25. I'd rather be *strategic* than *tactical,* bomb things not people. And I wouldn't want to fly a fighter in the war. That's shooting people, too."

Homer Wells didn't know what Wally was talking about; Homer didn't follow the war—he didn't know the news. A B-24 was a four-engine, heavy bomber that was used for strategic bombing—bridges, oil refineries, fuel depots, railroad tracks. It hit industry, it didn't drop its bombs on armies. That was the work of the B-25—a medium, tactical bomber. Wally had studied the war—with more interest than he pursued his botany (or his other courses) at the University of Maine. But the war, which was called—in Maine, in those days—"the war in Europe," was very far from Homer's mind. People with families are the people who worry about wars.

Do Bedouins have wars? wondered Homer Wells. And if they do, do they much care?

He was eager for the harvest to start; he was curious about meeting the migrants, about seeing the Negroes. He didn't know why. Were they like orphans? Did they not quite belong? Were they not quite of sufficient *use*?

Because he loved Wally, he resolved to keep his mind off Candy. It was the kind of bold resolve that his sense of elevation, on the Ferris wheel, enhanced. And this evening there was a plan; Homer Wells—an orphan attached to routine—liked for every evening to have a plan, even if he was not that excited about this one.

He drove Wally, in Senior's Cadillac, to Kendall's Lobster Pound, where Candy was waiting. He left Candy and Wally there. Ray would be out spraying for several hours, and Candy and Wally wanted a private good-bye together before Ray came home. Homer would go pick up Debra Pettigrew and take her to the drive-in in Cape Kenneth; it would be their first drive-in without Candy and Wally, and Homer wondered if the touch-this-but-not-that rules would vary when he and Debra were alone. As he navigated an exact path through the Pettigrews' violent dogs, he was disappointed in himself that he wasn't dying to find out whether Debra would or wouldn't. A particularly athletic dog snapped very loudly, near his face, but the chain around the dog's neck appeared to strangle the beast in midair; it landed solidly on its rib cage, with a sharp groan, and was slow getting to its feet. Why do people want to keep dogs? Homer wondered.

It was a Western movie, from which Homer could only conclude that crossing the country in a wagon train was an exercise in lunacy and sorrow; at the very least, he thought, one should make some arrangements with the Indians before starting out. The film was void of arrangements, and Homer was unable to arrange for the use of Herb Fowler's rubbers, which he kept in his pocket—"in case." Debra Pettigrew was substantially freer than she had ever been before, but her ultimate restraint was no less firm.

"No!" she yelled once.

"There's no need to shout," said Homer Wells, removing his hand from the forbidden place.

"Well, that's the second time you did that particular thing," Debra pointed out—a mathematical certainty (and other certainties) apparent in her voice. In Maine, in 194__, Homer Wells was forced to accept that what they called "necking" was permitted; what they called "making out" was within the rules; but that what he had done with Melony—what Grace Lynch appeared to be offering him, and what Candy and Wally did (or had done, at least once)—to all of that, the answer was "No!"

But how did Candy ever get pregnant? Homer Wells wondered, with Debra Pettigrew's damp little face pressed to his chest. Her hair tickled his nose, but he could just manage to see over her—he could witness the Indian massacre. With Herb Fowler dispensing prophylactics even faster than Dr. Larch passed them out to the women at St. Cloud's, how could Wally have let her get pregnant? Wally was so *provided for;* Homer Wells couldn't understand why Wally was even interested in war. But would an orphan ever worry that he was spoiled, or untested? Is an orphan ever bored, or restless—or are those luxurious states of mind? He remembered that Curly Day had been bored.

"Are you asleep, Homer?" Debra Pettigrew asked him.

"No," he said, "I was just thinking."

"Thinking what?" Debra asked.

"How come Wally and Candy do it, and we don't?" Homer asked her.

Debra Pettigrew appeared to be wary of the question, or at least she was surprised by its bluntness; she was cautious in composing an answer.

"Well," she began philosophically. "They're in love—Wally and Candy. Aren't they?"

"Right," said Homer Wells.

"Well, you never said you were in love—with me," Debra added. "And I never said I was—with you."

"That's right," Homer said. "So it's against the rules to do it if you aren't in love?"

"Look at it this way," said Debra Pettigrew; she bit her lower lip. It was absolutely as hard as she had ever thought. "If you're in love and there's an accident—if somebody gets pregnant, is what I mean; then *if* you're in love, you get married. Wally and Candy are in love, and if they have an accident, they'll get married."

Maybe, thought Homer Wells, maybe the *next* time. But what he said was, "I see." What he thought was, So *those* are the rules! It's about accidents, it's about getting pregnant and not wanting to have a baby. My God, is everything about that?

He considered taking the rubber out of his pocket and presenting it to Debra Pettigrew. If the argument was that an accidental pregnancy was really the only reason for not doing it, what did she think of the alternative that Herb Fowler so repeatedly presented? But by arguing in this fashion, wouldn't he be suggesting that all intimacy could be crudely accounted for—or was crude itself? Or was intimacy crude only for him?

In the movie, several human scalps were dangling from a spear; for reasons unfathomable to Homer Wells, the Indians carried on and on about the spear as if such a spear were a treasure. Suddenly a cavalry officer had his hand pinned to a tree by an arrow; the man went to great lengths (using his teeth and his other hand) to free the arrow from the tree, but the arrow still stuck very prominently through his hand. An Indian with a tomahawk approached the cavalry officer; it looked like the end of him, especially since he insisted on trying to cock his pistol with the thumb of the hand that had the arrow stuck through it.

Why doesn't he use his good hand? Homer Wells wondered. But the thumb worked; the pistol—finally—was cocked. Homer Wells concluded from this demonstration that the arrow had managed to pass through the hand without damaging the branch of the median nerve that goes to the muscles of the thumb. Lucky man, thought Homer Wells, as the cavalry officer shot the approaching Indian in the heart—it must be the heart, thought Homer Wells, because the Indian died instantly. It was funny how he could see the pictures of the hand in *Gray's Anatomy* more clearly than he could see the movie.

He took Debra home, begging her forgiveness for not offering to walk her to her door; one of the dogs was loose, it had broken its chain, and it pawed furiously at the driver's-side window (which Homer had rolled up, just in time). It breathed and slobbered and clicked its teeth against the glass, which became so fogged and smeared that Homer had difficulty seeing when he turned the Cadillac around.

"Cut it out, Eddy!" Debra Pettigrew was screaming at the dog as Homer drove away. "Would you just cut it out, Eddy, *please*!" But the dog chased the Cadillac for nearly a mile.

Eddy? thought Homer Wells. Didn't Nurse Angela name someone Eddy, once? He thought so; but it must have been someone who was adopted quickly—the way it was supposed to be done.

By the time he got to Kendall's Lobster Pound, Ray was home. He was making tea and warming his deeply lined, cracked hands on the pot—under his ragged nails was the mechanic's permanent, oil-black grime.

"Well, look who survived the drive-in!" Ray said. "You better sit a while and have some tea with me." Homer could see that Candy and Wally were out on the dock, huddled together. "Lovebirds don't feel the cold, I guess," Ray said to Homer. "It don't look like they're finished saying good-bye."

Homer was happy to have the tea and to sit with Ray; he liked Ray and he knew Ray liked him.

"What'd you learn today?" Ray asked him. Homer was going to say something about the drive-in rules but he guessed that wasn't what Ray meant.

"Nothing," said Homer Wells.

"No, I'll bet you learned somethin'," Ray said. "You're a learner. I know, because I was one. Once you see how somethin' is done, you know how to do it yourself; that's all I mean." Ray had taught Homer oil changes and lubrications, plugs and points and engine timing, fuel-line maintenance and front-end alignment; he'd shown the boy how to tighten a clutch, and—to Ray's astonishment—Homer had remembered. He'd also shown him a valve job and how to replace the universal. In one summer Homer Wells had learned more about mechanics than Wally knew. But it wasn't just Homer's manual dexterity that Ray was fond of; Ray respected loneliness, and an orphan, he imagined, had a fair share of that.

"Shoot," said Ray, "I'll bet there's nothin' you couldn't learn—nothin' your hands wouldn't remember, if your hands ever got to hold it, whatever it was."

"Right," said Homer Wells, smiling. He remembered the perfect balance in the set of dilators with the Douglass points; how you could hold one steadily between your thumb and index finger just by resting the shaft against the pad of your middle finger. It would move only and exactly when and where you moved it. And how wonderfully precise it was, Homer thought: that the vaginal speculum comes in more than one size; that there was always a size that was just right. And how sensitive an adjustment could be accomplished by just a half turn of the little thumbscrew, how the duck-billed speculum could hold the lips of the vagina open *exactly* wide enough.

Homer Wells, twenty-one, breathing in the steam from the hot tea, sat waiting for his life to begin.

/ / /

In the Cadillac with Wally, driving back to Ocean View—the rock-and-water prettiness of Heart's Haven giving way to the scruffier, more tangled land of Heart's Rock—Homer said, "I was wondering—but don't tell me if you'd rather not talk about it—I was just wondering how it happened that Candy got pregnant. I mean, weren't you using anything?"

"Sure I was," Wally said. "I was using one of Herb Fowler's rubbers, but it had a hole in it."

"It had a hole in it?" said Homer Wells.

"Not a big one," Wally said, "but I could tell it had a hole—you know, it leaked."

"Any hole is big enough," Homer said.

"Sure is," Wally said. "The way he carries the things around with him, it probably got poked by something in his pocket."

"I guess you don't use the rubbers Herb throws at you anymore," said Homer Wells.

"That's right," Wally said.

When Wally was asleep—as peacefully as a prince, as out-to-the-world as a king—Homer Wells slipped out of bed, found his pants, found the rubbers in the pocket and took one to the bathroom where he filled it up with water from the cold water tap. The hole was tiny but precise—a fine but uninterrupted needle of water streamed out of the end of the rubber. The hole was bigger than a pinprick but not nearly so large as a nail would make; maybe Herb Fowler used a thumbtack, or the point of a compass, thought Homer Wells.

It was a deliberate sort of hole, perfectly placed, dead center. The thought of Herb Fowler making the holes made Homer Wells shiver. He remembered the first fetus he'd seen, on his way back from the incinerator—how it appeared to have fallen from the sky. He recalled the extended arms of the murdered fetus from Three Mile Falls. And the bruise that was green-going-to-yellow on Grace Lynch's breast. Had Grace's journey to St. Cloud's originated with one of Herb Fowler's prophylactics?

In St. Cloud's he had seen anguish and the plainer forms of unhappiness—and depression, and destructiveness. He was familiar with mean-spiritedness and with injustice, too. But this is evil, isn't it? wondered Homer Wells. Have I seen evil before? He thought of the woman with the pony's penis in her mouth. What do you do when you recognize evil? he wondered.

He looked out Wally's window—but in the darkness, in his mind's eye, he saw the eroded, still unplanted hillside behind the hospital and the boys' division at St. Cloud's; he saw the thick but damaged, sound-absorbing forest beyond the river that carried away his grief for Fuzzy Stone. If he had known Mrs. Grogan's prayer, he would have tried it, but the prayer that Homer used to calm himself was the end of Chapter 43 of *David Copperfield*. There being twenty more chapters to go, these words were perhaps too uncertain for a prayer, and Homer spoke them to himself uncertainly—not as if he believed the words were true, but as if he were trying to force them to be true; by repeating and repeating the words he might make the words true for *him*, for Homer Wells:

> I have stood aside to see the phantoms of those days go by me. They are gone, and I resume the journey of my story.

But all that night he lay awake because the phantoms of those days were *not* gone. Like the tiny, terrible holes in the prophylactics, the phantoms of those days were not easy to detect—and their meaning was unknown—but they were there.

In the morning Wally left, halfheartedly, for the university in Orono. The next day, Candy left for Camden Academy. The day before the picking crew arrived at Ocean View, Homer Wells—the tallest and oldest boy at Cape Kenneth High School—attended the first class meeting of Senior Biology. His friend Debra Pettigrew had to lead him to the laboratory; Homer got lost en route and wandered into a class called Wood Shop.

The textbook for Senior Biology was B. A. Bensley's *Practical Anatomy of the Rabbit;* the text and illustrations were intimidating to the other students, but the book filled Homer Wells with longing. It was a shock for him to realize how much he missed Dr. Larch's well-worn copy of *Gray's*. Homer, at first glance, was critical of Bensley; whereas *Gray's* began with the skeleton, Bensley began with the tissues. But the teacher of the class was no fool; a cadaverous man was Mr. Hood, but he pleased Homer Wells by announcing that he did not intend to follow the text exactly—the class, like *Gray's,* would begin with the bones. Comforted by what, for him, was routine, Homer relished his first look at the ancient yellowed skeleton of a rabbit. The class was hushed; some students were repulsed. Wait till they get to the urogenital system, thought Homer Wells, his eyes skimming over the perfect bones; but this thought shocked him, too. He realized he was looking forward to getting to the poor rabbit's urogenital system.

He had a lateral view of the rabbit's skull; he tested himself with the naming of parts—it was so easy for him: cranial, orbital, nasal, frontal, mandible, maxilla, premaxilla. How well he remembered Clara and the others who had taught him so much!

/ / /

As for Clara, she was finally put to rest in a place she might not have chosen for herself—the cemetery in St. Cloud's was in the abandoned part of town. Perhaps this was appropriate, thought Dr. Larch, who supervised Clara's burial, because Clara herself had been abandoned—and surely she had been more explored and examined than she had ever been loved.

Nurse Edna was shocked to see the departing coffin, but Nurse Angela assured her that none of the orphans had passed away in the night. Mrs. Grogan accompanied Dr. Larch to the cemetery; Larch had asked her to come with him because he knew that Mrs. Grogan enjoyed every opportunity to say her prayer. (There was no minister or priest or rabbi in St. Cloud's; if holy words were in order, someone from Three Mile Falls came and said them. It was a testimony to Wilbur Larch's increasing isolationism that he refused to send to Three Mile Falls for anything, and that he preferred Mrs. Grogan—if he was forced to listen to holy words at all.)

It was the first burial that Wilbur Larch had wept over; Mrs. Grogan knew that his tears were not for Clara. Larch wouldn't have buried Clara if he'd thought that Homer Wells would ever be coming back.

"Well, he's *wrong*," Nurse Angela said. "Even a saint can make a mistake. Homer Wells *will* be back. He *belongs* here, like it or not."

Is it the ether? Dr. Larch wondered. He meant, was it the ether that gave him the sense, increasingly, that he knew everything that was going to happen? For example, he had anticipated the letter that arrived for F. Stone—forwarded from Fuzzy's P.O. box address. "Is this some sick joke?" Nurse Angela asked, turning the envelope around and around.

"I'll take that, please," Dr. Larch said. It was from the board of trustees, as he had expected. That was why they'd wanted those follow-up reports from him and why they'd requested the addresses of the orphans. They were checking up on him, Larch knew.

The letter to Fuzzy began with cordial good wishes; it said that the board knew a great deal about Fuzzy from Dr. Larch, but they wished to know anything further about Fuzzy's "St. Cloud's experience"—anything, naturally, that he wanted to "share" with them.

The "St. Cloud's experience" sounded to Wilbur Larch like a mystical happening. The attached questionnaire made him furious, although he did amuse himself by trying to imagine which of the questions had been conceived by the tedious Dr. Gingrich and which of them had flowed from the chilling mind of Mrs. Goodhall. Dr. Larch also had fun imagining how Homer Wells and Snowy Meadows and Curly Day—and all the others—would answer the silly questionnaire, but he took the immediate business very seriously. He wanted Fuzzy Stone's answers to the questionnaire to be perfect. He wanted to be sure that the board of trustees would never forget Fuzzy Stone.

There were five questions. Every single one of them was based upon the incorrect assumption that every child must have been at least five or six years old before he—or she—was adopted. This and other stupidities convinced Wilbur Larch that Dr. Gingrich and Mrs. Goodhall were going to be easy adversaries.

1. Was your life at St. Cloud's properly supervised? (Please include in your answer if you ever felt that your treatment was especially affectionate, or especially instructive; we would certainly want to hear if you felt your treatment was ever abusive.)

2. Did you receive adequate medical attention at St. Cloud's?

3. Were you adequately prepared for your new life in a

foster home, and do you feel your foster home was carefully and correctly chosen?

4. Would you suggest any possible improvements in the methods and management of St. Cloud's? (Specifically, would you feel things might have gone more smoothly for you if there had been a more youthful, energetic staff in residence—or perhaps, simply a larger staff?)

5. Was any attempt made to integrate the daily life of the orphanage with the life of the surrounding community?

"*What* community?" screamed Wilbur Larch. He stood at the window in Nurse Angela's office and stared at the bleak hillside where Wally had wanted to plant apple trees. Why hadn't they come back and planted the stupid trees, even if all that business was just to please me? Larch wondered.

"What *community*?" he howled.

Oh yes, he thought, I could have asked the stationmaster to offer them religious instruction—to speak to them about the terrifying chaos of homeless souls hovering in every niche of the sky. I could have asked that worthy gentleman to display his underwear catalogues, too.

I could have asked the family of child beaters from Three Mile Falls to come once a week and give lessons. I could have detained a few of the women having abortions and asked them to reveal, to all of us, why they didn't want to have children at that particular moment in their lives; or I could have invited a few of the mothers back—they could have explained to the children why they were left here! *That* would have been instructive! Oh God, thought Wilbur Larch, what a *community* we could have been—if only I'd been more youthful, more *energetic*!

Oh yes, I have made some mistakes, he thought; and for a black hour or two, he remembered some of them. If only I knew how to build a breathing machine, he thought—if only I could have come up with a different set of lungs for Fuzzy.

And maybe Homer Wells will tell them that he was not "adequately prepared" for his first view of the fetus on the hill. And had there been a way to prepare Homer for Three Mile Falls, for the Drapers of Waterville, or for the Winkles being swept away? What was my choice? wondered Wilbur Larch. I suppose that I could have *not* apprenticed him.

"We are put on this earth to be of use," Wilbur Larch (as Fuzzy Stone) wrote to the board of trustees. "It is better to *do* than to criticize," wrote that young idealist, Fuzzy Stone. "It is better to do anything than to stand idly by." You tell 'em, Fuzzy! thought Dr. Larch.

And so Fuzzy Stone told the board of trustees that the hospital at St. Cloud's was a model of the form. "It was Larch who made me want to be a doctor," Fuzzy wrote. "That old guy, Larch—he's an inspiration. You talk about energy: the guy is as full of pep as a teen-ager.

"You better be careful about sending any young people to St. Cloud's—old Larch will work them so hard, they'll get sick. They'll get so tired out, they'll retire in a month!

"And you think those old nurses don't do a day's work? Let me tell you, when Nurse Angela is pitching for stickball, you'd think you were competing in an Olympic event. You talk about *affectionate*—that's them, all right. They're always hugging and kissing you, but they know how to shake some sense into you, too.

"You talk about *supervised*," Fuzzy Stone wrote. "Did you ever find out that you were being watched by owls? That's Nurse Edna and Nurse Angela—they're *owls,* they don't miss a thing. And some of the girls used to say that Mrs. Grogan knew what they did before they did it—before they even knew they were *going* to do it!

"And you talk about *community*," wrote Fuzzy Stone. "St. Cloud's was something special. Why, I remember people would get off the train and walk up the hill just to look the place over—it must have been because we were such a model community, for that area. I just remember these people, coming and going, coming and going—they were just there to look us over, as if we were one of the marvels of Maine."

One of the marvels of Maine? thought Wilbur Larch, struggling to get control of himself. A stray puff of wind blew in the open window in Nurse Angela's office, carrying some of the black smoke from the incinerator with it; the smoke brought Larch nearer to his senses. I'd better stop, he thought. I don't want to get carried away.

He rested in the dispensary after his historical effort. Nurse Edna looked in on him once; Wilbur Larch was one of the marvels of Maine to her, and she was worried about him.

Larch was a little worried himself, when he woke. Where had the time gone? The problem is that I have to *last,* he thought. He could rewrite history but he couldn't touch time; dates were fixed; time marched at its own pace. Even if he could convince Homer Wells to go to a real medical school, it would take time. It would take a few years for Fuzzy Stone to complete his training. I have to last until Fuzzy is qualified to replace me, thought Wilbur Larch.

He felt like hearing Mrs. Grogan's prayer again, and so he went to the girls' division a little early for his usual delivery of *Jane Eyre.* He eavesdropped in the hall on Mrs. Grogan's prayer; I must ask her if she'd mind saying it to the boys, he thought, then wondered if it would confuse the boys, coming so quickly on the heels of, or just before, the Princes of Maine, Kings of New England benediction. I get confused myself sometimes, Dr. Larch knew.

"Grant us a safe lodging, and a holy rest," Mrs. Grogan was saying, "and peace at the last."

Amen, thought Wilbur Larch, the saint of St. Cloud's, who was seventy-something, and an ether addict, and who felt that he'd come a long way and still had a long way to go.

/ / /

When Homer Wells read the questionnaire sent him by the St. Cloud's board of trustees, he did not know exactly what made him anxious. Of course Dr. Larch and the others were getting older, but they were always "older" to him. It did occur to him to wonder what might happen to St. Cloud's when Dr. Larch was too old, but this thought was so troubling that he tucked the questionnaire and the return envelope to the board into his copy of *Practical Anatomy of the Rabbit.* Besides, it was the day the migrants arrived; it was harvest time at Ocean View, and Homer Wells was busy.

He and Mrs. Worthington met the picking crew at the apple mart, and led them to their quarters in the cider house—more than half the crew had picked at Ocean View before and knew the way, and the crew boss was what Mrs. Worthington called "an old hand." He looked very young to Homer. It was the first year that Mrs. Worthington dealt directly with the picking crew and their boss; the hiring relationship, by mail, had been one of Senior Worthington's responsibilities, and Senior had always maintained that if you kept a good crew boss, year after year, all the hiring—and the necessary taking-charge of the crew during the harvest—would be conducted by the boss.

His name was Arthur Rose, and he looked about Wally'
age—just barely older than Homer—although he must hav
been older; he'd been the crew boss for five or six years. On
year Senior Worthington had written to the old man who'
been his crew boss for as long as Olive could remember an
Arthur Rose had written back to Senior saying he was going t
be the crew boss now—"the old boss," Arthur Rose ha
written, "he's dead tired of traveling." As it turned out, the ol
boss was just dead, but Arthur Rose had done a good job. H
brought the right number of pickers, and very few of them eve
quit, or ran off, or lost more than a day or two of good wor
because of too much drinking. There seemed to be a firr
control over the degree of fighting among them—even whe
they were accompanied by a woman or two. And when ther
was an occasional child among them, the child behaved. Ther
were always pickers who fell off ladders, but there'd been n
serious injuries. There were always small accidents around th
cider press—but that was fast, often late-night work, when th
men were tired or drinking a little. And there was the predict
able clumsiness or drinking that led to the infrequent accident
involved in the almost ritualistic use of the cider house roof.

Running a farm had given Olive Worthington a warm feelin
for the daylight hours and a grave suspicion of the night; th
most trouble that people got into, in Olive's opinion, wa
trouble that they encountered because they stayed up too late.

Olive had written Arthur Rose of Senior's death, and tol
him that the picking-crew responsibility of Ocean View ha
now fallen to her. She wrote him at the usual address—a P.C
box in a town called Green, South Carolina—and Arthur Ros
responded promptly, both with his condolences and with hi
assurance that the crew would arrive as always, on time and i
correct numbers.

He was true to his word. Except when writing his first nam
on an envelope, or when she annually noted it in his Christma
card ("Happy Holidays, Arthur!"), Olive Worthington neve
called him Arthur; no one else called him Arthur, either. Fo
reasons that were never explained to Homer Wells but perhap
for a presence of authority that was necessary for a good crev
boss to maintain, he was *Mister* Rose to everybody.

When Olive introduced him to Homer Wells, that measur
of respect was made clear. "Homer," Olive said, "this is Miste
Rose. And this is Homer Wells," Olive added.

"Glad to know you, Homer," said Mr. Rose.

"Homer has become my good right hand," Olive said affectionately.

"Glad to hear that, Homer!" said Mr. Rose. He shook Homer's hand strongly, although he let go of the hand with unusual quickness. He was no better dressed than the rest of the picking crew, and he was slender, like most of them; yet he managed a certain style with shabbiness. If his jacket was dirty and torn, it was a pinstriped suit jacket, a doubled-breasted model that had, in its history, given someone a degree of sharpness, and Mr. Rose wore a real silk necktie for a belt. His shoes were also good, and good shoes were vital for farm work; they were old, but well oiled, resoled, comfortable-looking and in good condition. His socks matched. His suit jacket had a watch pocket, and in it was a gold watch that worked; he regarded the watch naturally and often, as if time were very important to him. He was so clean-shaven he looked as if he might never have needed a shave; his face was a smooth brick of the darkest, unsweetened, bitter chocolate, and in his mouth he expertly moved around a small, bright-white mint, which always surrounded him with a fresh and alert fragrance.

He spoke and moved slowly—modestly, yet deliberately; in both speech and gesture he gave the impression of being humble and contained. Yet, when one observed him standing still and not speaking, he looked extraordinarily fast and sure of himself.

It was a hot, Indian-summer day, and the apple mart was inland enough to miss what little sea breeze there was. Mr. Rose and Mrs. Worthington stood talking among the parked and moving farm vehicles in the apple-mart lot; the rest of the picking crew waited in their cars—the windows rolled down, an orchestra of black fingers strumming the sides of the cars. There were seventeen pickers and a cook—no women or children this year, to Olive's relief.

"Very nice," Mr. Rose said, about the flowers in the cider house.

Mrs. Worthington touched the rules she'd tacked to the wall by the kitchen light switch as she was leaving. "And you'll point out these to everyone, won't you, please?" Olive asked.

"Oh yes, I'm good at rules," said Mr. Rose, smiling. "You all come back and watch the first press, Homer," Mr. Rose said, as Homer held open the van door for Olive. "I'm sure you got better things to watch—movies and stuff—but if you ever got some time on your hands, you come watch us make a little cider. About a thousand gallons," he added shyly; he scuffed his feet, as if he were ashamed that he might be bragging. "All we need is eight hours, and about three hundred bushels of apples," said Mr. Rose. "A thousand gallons," he repeated proudly.

On the way back to the apple mart, Olive Worthington said to Homer, "Mister Rose is a real worker. If the rest of them were like him, they could improve themselves." Homer didn't understand her tone. Certainly he had heard in her voice admiration, sympathy—and even affection—but there was also in her voice the ice that encases a long-ago and immovable point of view.

/ / /

Fortunately, for Melony, the picking crew at York Farm included two women and a child; Melony felt safe to stay in the cider house. One of the women was a wife and the other woman was the first woman's mother and the cook; the wife picked with the crew, while the old lady looked after the food and the child—who was silent to the point of nonexistence. There was only one shower, and it was outdoors—installed behind the cider house, on a cinder-block platform, under a former grape arbor whose trellises were rotted by the weather. The women showered first, every evening, and they permitted no peeking. The York Farm crew boss was a mild man—it was his wife who came along—and he raised no objections to Melony's sharing the cider house with his crew.

His name was Rather; it was a nickname, stemming from the man's laconic habit of remarking during each activity that he'd rather be doing something else. His authority seemed less certain, or at least less electrical, than the authority commanded by Mr. Rose; no one called him *Mister* Rather. He was a steady but not an exceptionally fast picker, yet he always accounted for over a hundred bushels a day; it took Melony just one day to observe that his fellow workers paid Rather a commission. They gave him one bushel for every twenty bushels they picked.

"After all," Rather explained to Melony, "I get them the job." He was fond of saying that his commission, under the circumstances, was "rather small," but Rather never suggested that Melony owed him anything. "After all, I didn't get you your job!" he told her cheerfully.

By her third day in the field, she was managing eighty bushels; she also assisted as a bottler with the first cider press. Yet Melony was disappointed; she'd found the time to ask if anyone had heard of Ocean View, and no one had.

Perhaps because he viewed everything with slightly less cynicism than Melony brought to each of her experiences, Homer Wells needed a few days to notice the commission Mr. Rose exacted from his crew. He was the fastest picker among them, without ever appearing to rush—and he never dropped fruit; he never bruised the apples by bumping his canvas picking bucket against the ladder rungs. Mr. Rose could have managed a hundred and ten bushels a day on his own, but—even with his speed—Homer realized that his regular hundred and fifty or hundred and sixty bushels a day were very high. He took as his commission only one bushel out of every forty, but he had a crew of fifteen and no one picked fewer than eighty bushels a day. Mr. Rose would pick a very fast half dozen bushels, then he'd just rest for a while, or else he'd supervise the picking technique of his crew.

"A little slower, George," he'd say. "You bruise that fruit, what's it gonna be good for?"

"Just cider," George would say.

"That's right," Mr. Rose would say. "Cider apples is only a nickel a bushel."

"Okay," George would say.

"Sure," Mr. Rose would say, "everythin's gonna be okay."

The third day it rained and no one picked; both apples and pickers slip in the rain, and the fruit is more sensitive to bruising.

Homer went to watch Meany Hyde and Mr. Rose conduct the first cider press, which they directed out of range of the splatter. They put two men on the press, and two bottling, and they shifted fresh men into the rotation almost every hour. Meany watched only one thing: whether the racks were stacked crookedly or whether they were right. When the press boards are stacked crookedly, you can lose the press—three bushels of apples in one mess, eight or ten gallons of cider and the pomace flying everywhere. The men at the press wore rubber aprons; the bottlers wore rubber boots. The whine of the grinder reminded Homer Wells of the sounds he had only imagined at St. Cloud's—the saw-mill blades that were ear-splitting in his dreams, and in his insomnia. The pump sucked, the spout disgorged a pulp of seeds and skin and mashed apples, and even worms (if there were worms). It looked like what Nurse Angela calmly called upchuck. From the big tub under the press, the cider whirred through a rotary screen, which strained it into the thousand-gallon vat where, only recently, Grace Lynch had exposed herself to Homer.

In eight hours of no nonsense, they had a thousand gallons. The conveyor tracks rattled the jugs along, straight into cold storage. A man named Branches was assigned to hose out the vat and rinse off the rotary screen; his name stemmed from his dexterity in the big trees—and his scorn for using a ladder. A man named Hero washed the press cloths; Meany Hyde told Homer that the man had been a kind of hero, once. "That's all I heard. He's been comin' here for years, but he was a hero. Just once," Meany added, as if there might be more shame attached to the rarity of the man's heroism than there was glory to be sung for his moment in the sun.

"I'll bet you was bored," Mr. Rose said to Homer, who lied—who said it had been interesting; eight hours of hanging around a cider mill are several hours in excess of interesting. "You got to come at night to get the real feel of it," Mr. Rose confided. "This was just a rainy-day press. When you pick all day and press all night, then you get the *feel* of it." He winked at Homer, assuming he'd managed to make some secret life instantly clear; then he handed Homer a cup of cider. Homer had been sipping cider all day, but the cup was offered solemnly—some pledge about pressing cider at night was being made on the spot—and so Homer took the cup and drank. His eyes watered instantly; the cider was so strongly laced with rum that Homer felt his face flush and his stomach glow. Without further acknowledgment, Mr. Rose took back the cup and offered the remaining swallows to the man called Branches, who bolted it down without needing to make the slightest adjustment on the spray nozzle of his hose.

When Homer Wells was loading some cider jugs into the van, he saw the cup make its way between Meany Hyde and the man called Hero—all of it under the calm supervision of Mr. Rose, who had not revealed the source of the rum to anyone. The phrase "a gift for concealment" occurred to Homer Wells in regard to Mr. Rose; Homer had no idea where such a phrase had come from, unless it was Charles Dickens or Charlotte Brontë—he doubted he had encountered it in *Gray's Anatomy* or in Bensley's *Practical Anatomy of the Rabbit*.

There were no movements wasted in what movement there was to be seen by Mr. Rose—a quality that Homer Wells had formerly associated only with Dr. Larch; surely Dr. Larch had other, quite different qualities, as did Mr. Rose.

Back at the apple mart, the harvest appeared at a momentary standstill, held up by the rain, which Big Dot Taft and the mart women watched sourly from their assembly-line positions along the conveyor tracks in the packing line.

No one seemed very excited by the cider Homer brought. It was very bland, as the first cider usually is, and too watery—composed, typically, of early Macs and Gravensteins. You don't get a good cider until October, Meany Hyde had told Homer, and Mr. Rose had confirmed this with a solemn nod. A good cider needs some of those last-picked apples—Golden Delicious and Winter Banana, and the Baldwins or Russets, too.

"Cider's got no smoke before October," said Big Dot Taft, inhaling her cigarette listlessly.

Homer Wells, listening to Big Dot Taft, felt like her voice—dulled. Wally was away, Candy was away, and the anatomy of a rabbit was, after Clara, no challenge; the migrants, whom he'd so eagerly anticipated, were just plain hard workers; life was just a job. He had grown up without noticing *when*? Was there nothing remarkable in the transition?

They had four days of good picking weather at Ocean View before Meany Hyde said there would be a night press and Mr. Rose again invited Homer to come to the cider house and "get the feel of it." Homer had a quiet dinner with Mrs. Worthington and only after he'd helped her wash the dishes did he say he thought he'd go to the cider house and see if he could help with the pressing; he knew they would have been hard at work for two or three hours.

"What a good worker you are, Homer!" Olive told him appreciatively.

Homer Wells shrugged. It was a cold, clear night, the very best weather for McIntosh apples—warm, sunny days, and cold nights. It was not so cold that Homer couldn't smell the apples as he walked to the cider house, and it was not so dark that he needed to keep on the dirt road; he could go overland. Because he was not on the road, he was able to approach the cider house unobserved.

For a while he stood outside the range of the lights blazing in the mill room and listened to the sounds of the men working

the press, and talking, and laughing—and the murmur of th
men who were talking and laughing on the cider house roo.
Homer Wells listened for a long time, but he realized tha
when the men were not making an effort to be understood by
white person, he couldn't understand them at all—not eve
Mr. Rose, whose clear voice appeared to punctuate the othe
voices with calm but emphatic interjections.

They were also pressing cider at York Farm that night, bu
Melony wasn't interested; she wasn't trying to understand ei
ther the process or the lingo. The crew boss, Rather, had mad
it clear to her that the men resented her working the press, o
even bottling; it cut into their extra pay. Melony was tired fron
the picking, anyway. She lay on her bed in the bunkroom o
the cider house, reading *Jane Eyre;* there was a man asleep a
the far end of the bunkroom, but Melony's reading light didn'
disturb him—he had drunk too much beer, which was all tha
Rather allowed the men to drink. The beer was kept in th
cold-storage room, right next to the mill, and the men wer
drinking and talking together while they ran the press.

The friendly woman named Sandra, who was Rather's wife
was sitting on a bed not far from Melony, trying to mend
zipper on a pair of one of the men's trousers. The man's nam
was Sammy and he had only one pair of trousers; every s
often he'd wander in from the mill room to see how Sandra'
work was progressing—an overlarge, ballooning pair of under
shorts hanging almost to his knobby knees, his legs below th
knees like tough little vines.

Sandra's mother, whom everyone called Ma and who cooke
plain but large meals for the crew, lay in a big lump on the be
next to Sandra, more than her share of blankets piled on top o
her—she was always cold, but it was the only thing she com
plained about.

Sammy came into the bunkroom, sipping a beer and bring
ing with him the apple-mash odor of the mill room; the splat
ter from the press dotted his bare legs.

"Legs like that, no wonder you want your pants back,'
Sandra said.

"What are my chances?" Sammy asked.

"One, your zipper is jammed. Two, you tore it off you
pants," Sandra said.

"What you in such a hurry with your zipper for?" Ma asked
without moving from her lumped position.

"Shit," Sammy said. He went back to the press. Every once in a while the grinder caught on something—a thick stem or a congestion of seeds—and it made a noise like a circular saw gagging on a knot. When that happened, Ma would say, "There goes somebody's hand." Or, "There goes somebody's whole head. Drunk too much beer and fell in."

Over it all, Melony managed to read. She wasn't being antisocial, in her view. The two women were nice to her once they realized she was not after any of the men. The men were respectful of her work—and of the mark upon her that was made by the missing boyfriend. Although they teased her, they meant her no harm.

She had lied, successfully, to one of the men, and the lie, as she knew it would, had gotten around. The man was named Wednesday, for no reason that was ever explained to Melony—and she wasn't interested enough to ask. Wednesday had asked her too many questions about the particular Ocean View she was looking for and the boyfriend she was trying to find.

She had snagged her ladder in a loaded tree and was trying to ease it free without shaking any apples to the ground; Wednesday was helping her, when Melony said, "Pretty tight pants I'm wearing, wouldn't you say?"

Wednesday looked at her and said, "Yeah, I would."

"You can see everything in the pockets, right?" Melony asked.

Wednesday looked again and saw only the odd sickle shape of the partially opened horn-rim barrette; tight and hard against the worn denim, it dug into Melony's thigh. It was the barrette that Mary Agnes Cork had stolen from Candy, and Melony had stolen for herself. One day, she imagined, her hair might be long enough for the barrette to be of use. Until such a time, she carried it like a pocket knife in her right-thigh pocket.

"What's that?" Wednesday asked.

"That's a penis knife," Melony said.

"A *what* knife?" Wednesday said.

"You heard me," Melony said. "It's real small and it's real sharp—it's good for just one thing."

"What's that?" Wednesday asked.

"It cuts off the end of a penis," Melony said. "Real fast, real easy—just the end."

If the picking crew at York Farm had been a knife-carrying crew, someone might have asked Melony to display the penis knife—just as an object of general appreciation among knife-carrying friends. But no one asked; the story appeared to hold. It allied itself with the other stories attached to Melony and solidified the underlying, uneasy feeling among the workers at York Farm: that Melony was no one to mess with. Around Melony, even the beer drinkers behaved.

The only ill effect of the York Farm picking crew drinking beer while they pressed cider was the frequency of their urinating, which Melony objected to only when they peed too near the cider house.

"Hey, I don't want to hear that!" she'd holler out the window when she could hear anyone pissing. "I don't want to smell it later, either! Get away from the building. What's the matter—you afraid of the dark?"

Sandra and Ma liked Melony for that, and they enjoyed the refrain; whenever they heard someone peeing, they would not fail to holler, in unison, "What's the matter? You afraid of the dark?"

But if everyone tolerated Melony's hardness, or even appreciated her for it, no one liked her reading at night. She was the only one who read anything, and it took a while for her to realize how unfriendly they thought reading was, how insulted they felt when she did it.

When they finished pressing that night and everyone settled into bed, Melony asked, as usual, if her reading light was going to bother anyone.

"The *light* don't bother nobody," Wednesday said.

There were murmurs of consent, and Rather said, "You all remember Cameron?" There was laughter and Rather explained to Melony that Cameron, who had worked at York Farm for years, had been such a baby that he needed a light on, all night, just to sleep.

"He thought animals was gonna eat him if he shut out the light!" Sammy said.

"What animals?" Melony asked.

"Cameron didn't know," somebody said.

Melony kept reading *Jane Eyre,* and after a while, Sandra said, "It's not the *light* that bothers us, Melony."

"Yeah," someone said. Melony didn't get it for a while, but gradually she became aware that they had all rolled toward her in their beds and were watching her sullenly.

"Okay," she said. "So what bothers you?"

"What you readin' about, anyway?" Wednesday asked.

"Yeah," Sammy said. "What's so special 'bout that book?"

"It's just a book," Melony said.

"Pretty big deal that you can read it, huh?" Wednesday asked.

"What?" said Melony.

"Maybe, if you like it so much," Rather said, "*we* might like it, too."

"You want me to read to you?" Melony asked.

"Somebody read to me, once," Sandra said.

"It wasn't me!" Ma said. "It wasn't your father, either!"

"I never said it was!" Sandra said.

"I never heard nobody read to nobody," Sammy said.

"Yeah," somebody said.

Melony saw that some of the men were propped on their elbows in their beds, waiting. Even Ma turned her great lump around and faced Melony's bed.

"Quiet, everybody," Rather said.

For the first time in her life, Melony was afraid. After all her efforts and her hard traveling, she felt she had been returned to the girls' division without being aware of it; but it wasn't only that. It was the first time anyone had expected something of her; she knew what *Jane Eyre* meant to her, but what could it mean to them? She'd read it to children too young to understand half the words, too young to pay attention until the end of a sentence, but they were orphans—prisoners of the routine of being read to aloud; it was the routine that mattered.

Melony was more than halfway in her third or fourth journey through *Jane Eyre*. She said, "I'm on page two hundred and eight. There's a lot that's happened before."

"Just read it," Sammy said

"Maybe I should start at the beginning," Melony suggested.

"Just read what you readin' to yourself," Rather said gently.

Her voice had never trembled before, but Melony began.

" 'The wind roared high in the great tree which embowered the gates,' " she read.

"What's 'embowered'?" Wednesday asked her.

"Like a bower," Melony said. "Like a thing hanging over you, like for grapes or roses."

"It's a kind of bower where the shower is," Sandra said.

"Oh," someone said.

" 'But the road as far as I could see,' " Melony continued, " 'to the right hand and left, was all still and solitary . . .' "

"What's that?" Sammy asked.

"Solitary is *alone*," Melony said.

"Like solitaire, you know solitaire," Rather said, and there was an approving murmur.

"Shut up your interruptin'," Sandra said.

"Well, we got to understand," Wednesday said.

"Just shut up," Ma said.

"Read," Rather said to Melony, and she tried to go on.

" '. . . the road . . . all still and solitary: save for the shadows of clouds crossing it at intervals, as the moon looked out, it was but a long pale line, unvaried by one moving speck,' " Melony read.

"Un-what?" someone asked.

"Unvaried means unchanged, not changed," Melony said.

"I know that," Wednesday said. "I got that one."

"Shut up," Sandra said.

" 'A puerile tear,' " Melony began, but she stopped. "I don't know what 'puerile' means," she said. "It's not important that you know what every word means."

"Okay," someone said.

" 'A puerile tear dimmed my eye while I looked—a tear of disappointment and impatience: ashamed of it, I wiped it away . . .' "

"There, we know what it is, anyway," Wednesday said.

" ' . . . I lingered,' " Melony read.

"You *what*?" Sammy asked.

"Hung around; to linger means to hang around!" Melony said sharply. She began again: " ' . . . the moon shut herself wholly within her chamber, and drew close her curtain of dense cloud; the night grew dark . . .' "

"It's gettin' scary now," Wednesday observed.

" ' . . . rain came driving fast on the wind.' " Melony had changed "gale" to "wind" without their knowing it. " 'I wish he would come! I wish he would come! I exclaimed, seized with hypochondriac foreboding.' " Melony stopped with that; tears filled her eyes, and she couldn't see the words. There was a long silence before anyone spoke.

"*What* was she seized with?" Sammy asked, frightened.

"I don't know!" Melony said, sobbing. "Some kind of fear, I think."

They were respectful of Melony's sobs for a while, and then Sammy said, "I guess it's some kind of horror story."

"What you want to read that before you try to sleep?" Rather asked Melony with friendly concern, but Melony lay down on her bed and turned off her reading light.

When all the lights were out, Melony felt Sandra sit on her bed beside her; if it had been Ma, she knew, her bed would have sagged more heavily. "You ask me, you better forget that boyfriend," Sandra said. "If he didn't tell you how to find him, he ain't no good, anyway." Melony had not felt anyone stroke her temples since Mrs. Grogan in the girls' division at St. Cloud's; she realized she missed Mrs. Grogan very much, and for a while this took her mind off Homer Wells.

When everyone else was asleep, Melony turned her reading light back on; whatever failure *Jane Eyre* might be for someone else, it had always worked for Melony—it had helped her—and she felt in need of its help, now. She read another twenty pages, or so, but Homer Wells would not leave her mind. "I must part with you for my whole life," she read, with horror. "I must begin a new existence amongst strange faces and strange scenes." The truth of that closed the book for her, forever. She slid the book under her bed in the bunkroom in the cider house at York Farm, where she would leave it. Had she just read the passage from *David Copperfield* that Homer Wells so loved and repeated to himself as if it were a hopeful prayer, she would have discarded *David Copperfield,* too. "I have stood aside to see the phantoms of those days go by me." Fat chance! Melony would have thought. She knew that all the phantoms of those days were attached to her and Homer more securely than their shadows. And so Melony cried herself to sleep—she was not hopeful, yet she was determined, her mind's eye searching the darkness for Homer Wells.

She could not have seen him that night—he was so well hidden beyond the range of the lights shining from the mill room at Ocean View. Even if he'd sneezed or fallen down, the sound of the grinder and the pump would have concealed his presence. He watched the red-eyed glow of the cigarettes that darted and paused above the roof of the cider house. When he got cold, he went to watch them pressing and to have a little cider and rum.

Mr. Rose seemed glad to see him; he gave Homer a drink with very little cider in it, and together they watched the orchestra of the pump and grinder. A man named Jack, who had a terrible scar across his throat—a hard-to-survive kind of scar—aimed the spout. A man named Orange slapped the racks in place and received the splatter with a wild kind of pride; his name was Orange because he had tried to dye his hair once, and orange was how it turned out—there was no evidence of that color on him now. The rum had made Jack and Orange both savage about their business and defiantly unwary of the flying mess, yet Homer felt that Mr. Rose, who seemed sober, was still in control—the conductor of both the men and the machinery and operating them both at full throttle.

"Let's try to get out of here by midnight," Mr. Rose said calmly. Jack choked the flow of pomace to the top rack; Orange levered the press into place.

In the other corner of the mill room, two men whom Homer Wells didn't know were bottling at high speed. One of the men began to laugh, and his partner started to laugh with him so loudly that Mr. Rose called out to them, "What's so funny?"

One of the men explained that his cigarette had fallen out of his mouth, into the vat; at this announcement, even Jack and Orange began to laugh, and Homer Wells smiled, but Mr. Rose said quietly, "Then you better fish it out. Nobody wants that muckin' up the cider."

The men were quiet, now; just the machinery went on with its sluicing and screaming. "Go on," Mr. Rose repeated. "Go fish."

The man with the lost cigarette stared into the thousand-gallon vat; it was only half full, but it was still a swimming pool. He took off his rubber boots, but Mr. Rose said, "Not just the boots. Take off *all* your clothes, and then go take a shower—and be quick about it. We got work to do."

"What?" the man said. "I ain't gonna strip and go wash just to go swimmin' in there!"

"You're filthy all over," said Mr. Rose. "Be quick about it."

"Hey, *you* can be quick about it," the man said to Mr. Rose. "You want that butt out of there, you can fish it out yourself."

It was Orange who spoke to the man.

"What business you in?" Orange asked him.

"Hey, *what*?" the man asked.

"What business you in, man?" Orange asked.

"Say, you in the apple business, man," Jack advised the man.

"Say, *what*?" the man asked.

"Just say you in the apple business, man," Orange said.

It was at that moment that Mr. Rose took Homer's arm and said to him, "You got to see the view from the roof, my friend." The tug at his elbow was firm but gentle. Mr. Rose very gracefully led Homer out of the mill room, then outside by the kitchen door.

"You know what business Mistuh Rose is in, man?" Homer heard Orange asking.

"He in the knife business, man," he heard Jack say.

"You don't wanna go in the knife business with Mistuh Rose," Homer heard Orange say.

"You just stay in the apple business, you do fine, man," Jack said.

Homer was following Mr. Rose up the ladder to the roof when he heard the shower turn on; it was an inside shower—more private than the shower at York Farm. Except for their cigarettes, the men on the roof were hard to see, but Homer held Mr. Rose's hand and followed him along the plank on the rooftop until they found two good seats.

"You all know Homer," Mr. Rose said to the men on the roof. There was a blur of greetings. The man called Hero was up there, and the man called Branches; there was someone named Willy, and two or three people Homer didn't know, and the old cook whose name was Black Pan. The cook was the shape of a stew pot; it had required some effort for him to gain his perch on the roof.

Someone handed Homer a bottle of beer, but the bottle was warm and full of rum.

"It's stopped again," Branches said, and everyone stared toward the sea.

The night-life lights of Cape Kenneth were so low along the horizon that some of the lights themselves were not visible—only the reflections from them, especially when the lights were cast out over the ocean—but the high Ferris wheel blazed brightly. It was holding still, loading new riders, letting off the old.

"Maybe it stop to breathe," Branches said, and everyone laughed at that.

Someone suggested that it stopped to fart, and everyone laughed louder.

Then Willy said, "When it gets too close to the ground, it *has* to stop, I think," and everyone appeared to consider this seriously.

Then the Ferris wheel started again, and the men on the roof of the cider house released a reverential moan.

"There it go again!" Hero said.

"It like a star," Black Pan, the old cook, said. "It look real cool, but you get too close, it burn you—it hotter than a flame!"

"It's a Ferris wheel," said Homer Wells.

"It a *what*?" Willy said.

"A *what* wheel?" Branches asked.

"A Ferris wheel," said Homer Wells. "That's the Cape Kenneth Carnival, and that's the Ferris wheel." Mr. Rose nudged him in the ribs, but Homer didn't understand. No one spoke for a long time, and when Homer looked at Mr. Rose, Mr. Rose softly shook his head.

"I heard of somethin' like that," Black Pan said. "I think they had one in Charleston."

"It's stopped again," Hero observed.

"It's letting off passengers—*riders*," said Homer Wells. "It's taking on new riders."

"People *ride* that fuckin' thing?" Branches asked.

"Don't shit me, Homer," Hero said.

Again, Homer felt the nudge in his ribs, and Mr. Rose said, mildly, "You all so uneducated—Homer's havin' a little fun with you."

When the bottle of rum passed from man to man, Mr. Rose just passed it along.

"Don't the name Homer mean nothin' to you?" Mr. Rose asked the men.

"I think I heard of it," the cook Black Pan said.

"Homer was the world's first storyteller!" Mr. Rose announced. The nudge at Homer's ribs was back, and Mr. Rose said, "*Our* Homer knows a good story, too."

"Shit," someone said after a while.

"What kind of wheel you call it, Homer?" Branches asked.

"A Ferris wheel," said Homer Wells.

"Yeah!" someone said. Everyone laughed.

"A fuckin' *Ferris* wheel!" Hero said. "That's pretty good."

One of the men Homer didn't know rolled off the roof. Everyone waited until he was on the ground before they called down to him.

"You all right, asshole?" Black Pan asked.

"Yeah," the man said, and everyone laughed.

When Mr. Rose heard the shower start up again, he knew that his bottle man had found the cigarette and was washing the cider off himself.

"Willy and Hero, you're bottlin' now," said Mr. Rose.

"I bottled last time," Hero said.

"Then you gettin' real good at it," said Mr. Rose.

"I'll press for a while," someone said.

"Jack and Orange are goin' good," Mr. Rose said. "We'll just let them go for a while."

Homer sensed that he should leave the roof with Mr. Rose. They helped each other with the ladder; on the ground Mr. Rose spoke very seriously to Homer.

"You got to understand," Mr. Rose whispered. "They don't want to know what that thing is. What good it do them to know?"

"Okay," said Homer Wells, who stood a long while out of the range of the lights blazing in the mill room. Now that he was more familiar with their dialect, he could occasionally understand the voices from the roof.

"It's stopped again," he heard Branches say.

"Yeah, it takin' on *riders!*" someone said, and everyone laughed.

"You know, maybe it's an army place," Black Pan said.

"What army?" someone asked.

"We almost at war," Black Pan said. "I heard that."

"Shit," someone said.

"It's somethin' for the airplanes to see," Black Pan said.

"Whose airplanes?" Hero asked.

"There it go again," Branches said.

Homer Wells walked back through the orchards to the Worthington house; he was touched that Mrs. Worthington had left the light over the stairs on for him, and when he saw the light under her bedroom door, he said, quietly, "Good night, Missus Worthington. I'm back."

"Good night, Homer," she said.

He looked out Wally's window for a while. There was no way, at that distance, that he could witness the reaction on the cider house roof when the Ferris wheel in Cape Kenneth was shut off for the night—when all the lights went out with a blink, what did the men on the roof have to say about *that*? he wondered.

Maybe they thought that the Ferris wheel came from another

planet and, when all the lights went out, that it had returned there.

And wouldn't Fuzzy Stone have loved to see it? thought Homer Wells. And Curly Day, and young Copperfield! And it would have been fun to ride it with Melony—just once, to see what she would have said about it. Dr. Larch wouldn't be impressed. Was anything a mystery to Dr. Larch?

In the morning, Mr. Rose chose to rest his magic hands between trees; he came up to Homer, who was working as a checker in the orchard called Frying Pan, counting the one-bushel crates before they were loaded on the flatbed trailer and giving every picker credit for each bushel picked.

"I want you to show me that wheel," Mr. Rose said, smiling.

"The Ferris wheel?" said Homer Wells.

"If you don't mind showin' me," said Mr. Rose. "There just can't be no talk about it."

"Right," Homer said. "We better go soon, before it gets any colder and they close it for the season. I'll bet it's pretty cold, riding it now."

"I don't know if I want to ride it until I see it," said Mr. Rose.

"Sure," said Homer.

Mrs. Worthington let him take the van, but when he picked up Mr. Rose at the cider house, everyone was curious.

"We've got to check somethin' in the far orchard," Mr. Rose told the men.

"What far orchard he talkin' about?" Black Pan asked Hero when Homer and Mr. Rose got in the van.

Homer Wells remembered his ride on the Ferris wheel with Wally. It was much colder now, and Mr. Rose was subdued all the way to Cape Kenneth and uncharacteristically drawn into himself as they walked through the carnival together. The summer crowd was gone; some of the carnival events were already closed up tight.

"Don't be nervous," Homer said to Mr. Rose. "The Ferris wheel is perfectly safe."

"I'm not nervous about no wheel," said Mr. Rose. "You see a lot of people my color around here?"

Homer had detected nothing hostile in the looks from the people; as an orphan, he always suspected that people singled him out to stare at—and so he had not felt especially singled out in the company of Mr. Rose. But now he noticed more of the looks and realized that the looks an orphan might detect were only imagined, by comparison.

When they got to the Ferris wheel, there was no line, but they had to wait for the ride in progress to be over. When the wheel stopped, Homer and Mr. Rose got on and sat together in one chair.

"We could each sit in our own chairs, if you prefer," said Homer Wells.

"Keep it like it is," said Mr. Rose. When the wheel began its ascent, he sat very still and straight and held his breath until they were nearly at the top of the rise.

"Over there's the orchard," pointed Homer Wells, but Mr. Rose stared straight ahead, as if the stability of the entire Ferris wheel relied on each rider's maintaining perfect balance.

"What's so special about doin' this?" asked Mr. Rose rigidly.

"It's just for the ride, and the view, I guess," said Homer Wells.

"I like the view from the roof," Mr. Rose said. When they started the descent of the wheel turn, Mr. Rose said, "It's a good thing I didn't eat much today."

By the time they passed ground level and began their ascent again, a substantial crowd had formed—but they didn't appear to be standing in line for the next ride. There were only two couples and one boy by himself sharing the wheel with Homer and Mr. Rose, and when they were at the top of the wheel turn again, Homer realized that the crowd below them had formed to stare at Mr. Rose.

"They come to see if niggers fly," Mr. Rose said, "but I ain't goin' nowhere—not for no one's entertainment. They come to see if the machine is gonna break down, tryin' to carry a nigger—or maybe they wanna see me throw up."

"Just don't do anything," Homer Wells said.

"That's the advice I been hearin' all my life, boy," Mr. Rose said. As they started their descent, Mr. Rose leaned out of the chair—quite dangerously farther than was necessary—and vomited in a splendid arc over the crowd below them. The crowd moved as one, but not everyone moved in time.

When their chair was at the bottom of the descent again, the Ferris wheel was stopped so that the sick man could get off. The crowd had retreated, except for a young man who was especially splattered. As Homer Wells and Mr. Rose were leaving the Ferris wheel grounds, the young man came forward and said to Mr. Rose, "You looked like you *meant* to do that."

"Who means to get sick?" said Mr. Rose; he kept walking, and Homer kept up with him. The young man was about Homer's age; he should have homework, thought Homer Wells—if he's still in school, it's a school night.

"I think you meant to," the young man said to Mr. Rose, who stopped walking away then.

"What business you in?" Mr. Rose asked the boy.

"What?" the young man asked, but Homer Wells stepped between them.

"My friend is sick," Homer Wells said. "Please just leave him alone."

"Your *friend*!" the boy said.

"Ask me what business I'm in," Mr. Rose said to the boy.

"What fuckin' business are you in, *Mister*?" the young man shouted at Mr. Rose. Homer felt himself neatly shoved out of the way; he saw that Mr. Rose was standing, very suddenly, chest to chest with the boy. There was no sour smell of vomit on Mr. Rose's breath, however. Somehow, Mr. Rose had slipped one of those mints in his mouth; the alertness that had been missing when Mr. Rose felt ill was back in his eyes. The boy seemed surprised that he was standing so close to Mr. Rose, and so suddenly; he was a little taller, and quite a bit heavier, than Mr. Rose, yet he looked unsure of himself. "I said, 'What fuckin' business are you in, Mister?' " the boy repeated, and Mr. Rose smiled.

"I'm in the throwin'-up business!" Mr. Rose said in a humble manner. Someone in the crowd laughed; Homer Wells felt a surge of vast relief; Mr. Rose smiled in such a way that allowed the boy to smile, too. "Sorry if any of it got on you," Mr. Rose said nicely.

"No problem," said the young man, turning to leave. After taking a few steps, the boy turned inquisitively in Mr. Rose's direction, but Mr. Rose had grasped Homer Wells by the arm and was already walking on. Homer saw shock on the boy's face. The young man's flannel jacket, which was still zipped shut, was flapping wide open—a single, crisp slash had slit it from the collar to the waist—and every button on the boy's shirt was gone. The boy gaped at himself, and then at Mr. Rose, who did not look back, and then the boy allowed himself to be pulled into the comfort of the crowd.

"How'd you do that?" Homer asked Mr. Rose, when they reached the van.

"Your hands got to be fast," Mr. Rose said. "Your knife got to be sharp. But you *do* it with your eyes. Your eyes keep their eyes off your hands."

The wide-open jacket of the boy made Homer remember Clara and how a scalpel made no mistakes. Only a hand makes mistakes. His chest was cold, and he was driving too fast.

When Homer turned off Drinkwater Road and drove through the orchards to the cider house, Mr. Rose said, "You see? I was right, wasn't I? What good is it—to apple pickers—to know about that wheel?"

It does no good to know about it, thought Homer Wells. And what good would it do Melony to know about it, or Curly Day, or Fuzzy—or any Bedouin?

"Am I right?" Mr. Rose demanded.

"Right," said Homer Wells.

8/ Opportunity Knocks

After the harvest at York Farm, the foreman asked Melony to stay on to help with the mousing. "We have to get the mice before the ground freezes, or else they'll have the run of the orchards all winter," the foreman explained. The men used poison oats and poison corn, scattering the poison around the trees and putting it in the pine mice tunnels.

Poor mice, thought Melony, but she tried mousing for a few days. When she saw a pine mouse tunnel, she tried to conceal it; she never put any poison in it. And she only pretended to scatter the oats and corn around the trees; she didn't like the way the poison smelled. She would dump it into the dirt road and fill her bag with sand and gravel and scatter that instead.

"Have a nice winter, mice," she whispered to them.

It began to get very cold in the cider house; they gave her a wood-burning stove, which Melony vented through a window in the bunkroom; the stove kept the toilet from freezing. The morning the outdoor shower was frozen was the morning Melony decided to move on. She only briefly regretted not being able to stay and save more mice.

"If you're lookin' for another orchard," the foreman warned her, "you won't find any that's hirin' in the winter."

"I'd like a city job for the winter," Melony told him.

"What city?" the foreman asked. Melony shrugged. She had securely strapped up her small bundle of things in Charley's belt; the sleeves of Mrs. Grogan's coat reached only halfway down her forearms, and the coat was an especially tight fit across the shoulders and the hips—even so, Melony managed to look comfortable in it. "There's no real cities in Maine," the foreman told her.

"It won't take much of a city to be a city for me," Melony

said. He watched her walk to the same part of the road where he'd called good-bye to her before. It was that time of year when the trees are bare and the sky looks like lead, and underfoot the ground feels more unyielding every day—yet it's too early for snow, or else there's a freak storm and the snow doesn't last.

For some reason the foreman felt a strong desire to leave with Melony; he surprised himself by muttering out loud, "I hope it snows soon."

"What?" one of the apple-mart women said.

"So long!" the foreman called to Melony, but she didn't answer him.

"Good riddance," said one of the women in the mart.

"The slut," another one said.

"What makes her a slut?" the foreman asked sharply. "Who you seen her sleepin' with?"

"She's just a tramp," one of them said.

"At least she's *interesting*," the foreman snapped. The women regarded him for a moment before one of them spoke up.

"Got a crush on her, do you?" she asked.

"I'll bet you wish you was that boyfriend she's lookin' for," another woman said, which drew a teasing sort of laughter from all the mart women.

"It's not that!" the foreman snapped. "I hope she never finds that boyfriend—for his sake!" the foreman said. "And for hers," he added.

The woman whose fat husband had tried to rape Melony turned away from this conversation. She opened the large, communal thermos on the table next to the cash register; but when she tried to pour herself some coffee, none came out. What came out instead was poison oats and poison corn. If Melony had actually meant to poison any of them, she would have been more restrained in the proportions. It was clearly just a message; and the apple-mart women regarded it as silently as if they were trying to read bones.

"You see what I mean?" the foreman asked them. He picked up an apple from a display basket on the counter and took a healthy chomp; the apple had been left out in the cold so long that it was partially frozen, and so mealy in the foreman's mouth that he instantly spat it out.

It was very cold on the road to the coast, but the walking warmed Melony up; also, since there was no traffic, she had no choice about walking. When she reached the coastal highway, she didn't have to wait long for a ride. A pale but jolly boy driving a panel truck stopped for her.

"Yarmouth Paint and Shellac, at your service," the boy said to Melony; he was a little younger than Homer Wells, and—in Melony's opinion—not nearly so worldly-looking. The truck reeked of wood-stain smells and of varnish and creosote. "I'm a wood-treatment expert," the boy said to her proudly.

At best, a salesman, Melony thought; more likely, a delivery boy. She smiled tightly, not showing her chipped teeth. The boy fidgeted, awaiting some form of greeting from her. I can make anyone nervous in less than a minute, Melony thought.

"Uh, where you goin'?" the boy asked her—the panel truck sloshing along.

"The city," Melony said.

"What city?" the boy asked.

Now Melony allowed her lips to part with her smile—the worried boy now staring at the troubled history of her mouth.

"You tell me," Melony said.

"I gotta go to Bath," the boy said nervously. Melony stared at him as if he'd said he had to *have* a bath.

"Bath," she repeated.

"It's a city, sort of," the wood-treatment expert told her.

It was Clara's city! Dr. Larch or Homer Wells could have told Melony—old Clara had come to St. Cloud's from Bath! But Melony didn't know that, and wouldn't have cared; her relationship to Clara had been unpleasantly envious. Homer Wells knew Clara more intimately than he knew Melony. It might have interested Melony that Bath would put her much closer to Ocean View than she'd been at York Farm—that there might even be residents of Bath who would have heard of an Ocean View Orchards; there were certainly many Bath residents who could have directed her to Heart's Haven or to Heart's Rock.

"You wanna go to Bath?" the boy asked her cautiously.

Again Melony showed him her damaged teeth; she was displaying less of a smile than of the manner in which a dog might show its hackles. "Right," she said.

/ / /

Wally came home for Thanksgiving; Candy had been home for several weekends in the early fall, but Homer had not known how to initiate seeing her without Wally. Wally was surprised that Homer and Candy hadn't seen each other; and, from Candy's embarrassment with Wally's surprise, Homer detected that she had been equally troubled about initiating a meeting with him. But the turkey had to be basted every fifteen minutes, the table had to be set, and Olive was too obviously enjoying having a full house again—there was no time to feel awkward.

Raymond Kendall had shared a Thanksgiving dinner with the Worthingtons before, but never without Senior's semi-presence; Ray went through a few minutes of struggling to be overly polite before he relaxed and talked shop with Olive.

"Dad acts like he's having a date," Candy said to Olive in the kitchen.

"I'm flattered," Olive said, squeezing Candy's arm and laughing. But that was the end of any further nonsense.

Homer volunteered to carve the turkey. He did such a good job that Olive said, "You should be a surgeon, Homer!"

Wally laughed; Candy looked at her plate, or at her hands in her lap, and Ray Kendall said, "The boy's just good with his hands. If you've got good hands, once you do a thing your hands won't forget how."

"That's like you, Ray," Olive said, which moved the attention away from Homer's work with the knife; he carved every bit of meat off the bones as quickly as possible.

Wally talked about the war. He said he'd thought about dropping out of college to go to flying school. "So if there *is* a war—if we get into it, I mean—then I'll already know how to fly."

"You'll do no such thing," Olive said to him.

"Why would you *want* to do such a thing?" Candy asked him. "I think you're being selfish."

"What do you mean, *selfish*?" Wally asked. "A war is for your country, it's serving your country!"

"To you, it's an adventure," Candy said. "That's what's selfish about it."

"You'll do no such thing, anyway," Olive repeated.

"I was too young to go to the last war," Ray said, "and if there's another one, I'll be too old."

"Lucky you!" Olive said.

"That's right," Candy said.

Ray shrugged. "I don't know," he said. "I wanted to go to

the last one. I tried to lie about my age, but someone told on me."

"Now you know better," Olive said.

"I'm not so sure of that," Ray said. "If there's a new one there'll be lots of new weapons—they're buildin' stuff you can't even imagine."

"I try to imagine it," Wally said. "I imagine the war all the time."

"Except the dying, Wally," Olive Worthington said, carrying the turkey carcass out to the kitchen. "I don't think you've imagined the dying."

"Right," said Homer Wells, who imagined the dying all the time. Candy looked at him and smiled.

"You should have called me on the weekends, Homer," she said.

"Yeah, why didn't you?" Wally asked him. "Too busy with Debra Pettigrew, that's why." Homer just shook his head.

"Too busy with the practical anatomy of the rabbit!" Olive called from the kitchen.

"The *what*?" Wally said.

But Olive was wrong. It had taken Homer only about three weeks of Senior Biology to realize that he knew more about the particular animal under scrutiny and its relation to human anatomy than did his cadaverous teacher, Mr. Hood.

It was, as Wilbur Larch could have guessed, the urogenital system that revealed Mr. Hood's deficiencies in comparison to the experience of young Dr. Wells. In discussing the three stages of specialization of the uterus, Mr. Hood became confused. The intrauterine life of the rabbit embryo is only thirty days; between five to eight young are born. In keeping with the primitive nature of the little animal, the rabbit has two complete uteri—the structure of the organ at this stage is called *uterus duplex.* The structure of the organ in the human female, which Homer Wells knew very well—wherein two uterine tubes open into a single uterine cavity—is called *uterus simplex.* The third stage of uterine structure falls between the two—partially fused condition existing in some mammals (sheep, for example); it is called *uterus bicornis.*

Poor Mr. Hood, attempting to reveal the secrets of the uterus upon the chalky blackboard, confused his *duplex* with his *bicornis;* he called a sheep a rabbit (and vice versa). It was a smaller error than if he'd imagined the human female had two complete uteri and had spread this misinformation to the class, but it was an error; Homer Wells caught it. It was the first time he had been put in a position of correcting an authority. "An orphan is especially uncomfortable and insecure in such a position," wrote Dr. Wilbur Larch.

"Excuse me, sir?" said Homer Wells.

"Yes, Homer?" said Mr. Hood. His gauntness, in a certain light, made him appear as exposed as the many rabbit cadavers lying open on the students' laboratory tables. He looked skinned, almost ready for labeling. A kind but weary patience was in his eyes; they were the man's only alert features.

"It's the other way around, sir," said Homer Wells.

"Pardon me?" said Mr. Hood.

"The rabbit has two complete uteri, the rabbit is *uterus duplex*—not the sheep, sir," Homer said. "The sheep's uterus is partially fused together, it's almost one—the sheep is *uterus bicornis*."

The class waited. Mr. Hood blinked; for a moment, he looked like a lizard regarding a fly, but he suddenly retreated. "Isn't that what I said?" he asked, smiling.

"No," the class murmured, "you said it the other way around."

"Well, it's my mistake, then," Mr. Hood said almost cheerfully. "I meant it just the way you said it, Homer," he said.

"Maybe I misunderstood you, sir," Homer said, but the class murmured, "No, you got it right."

The short boy named Bucky, with whom Homer had to share his rabbit cadaver, nudged Homer in the ribs. "How come you know all about cunts?" he asked Homer.

"Search me," said Homer Wells. He had learned that phrase from Debra Pettigrew. It was the one game they played. He would ask her something she couldn't answer. She would say "Search me." And Homer Wells, saying "Okay," would begin to search her. "Not *there*!" Debra would cry, pushing his hand away, but laughing. Always laughing, but always pushing his hand away. There was no way Homer Wells would gain admittance to the *uterus simplex* of Debra Pettigrew.

"Not unless I ask her to marry me," he told Wally, when they were back together in Wally's bedroom, Thanksgiving night.

"I wouldn't go that far, old boy," Wally said.

Homer didn't tell Wally about embarrassing Mr. Hood, or how the man seemed changed by the incident. If Mr. Hood had always been cadaverous, now there was an insomnia about his presence, too—as if he were not only dead but also working too hard; staying up late; boning up on his rabbit anatomy; trying to keep *all* the uteri straight. His tiredness made him slightly less cadaverous, but only because exhaustion is a life-sign; it is at least a form of being human. Mr. Hood began to look as if he were waiting for his retirement, hoping that he could get there.

Where have I seen that look before? wondered Homer Wells.

Nurse Angela or Nurse Edna, or even Mrs. Grogan, could have reminded him; they were all familiar with that look—that strained combination of exhaustion and expectation, that fierce contradiction between grim anxiety and childlike faith. For years that look had penetrated even the most innocent expressions of Wilbur Larch; lately, Nurse Angela and Nurse Edna, and even Mrs. Grogan, had recognized the look in their own expressions.

"What are we waiting for?" Nurse Edna asked Nurse Angela one morning. There was an aura of something pending, some form of inevitable change. These good women were as insulted by the now-famous Goodhall-Gingrich questionnaire as they felt sure Dr. Larch had been; Larch did seem unusually cheered by the remarks of the former Snowy Meadows; the board had thought Snowy's response was so praiseworthy that they'd sent it along for Dr. Larch to see.

To the question of being "properly supervised," Snowy said that Dr. Larch and the nurses never let him out of their sight. To the question regarding whether or not the medical attention was "adequate," Snowy Meadows advised the board to "just ask Fuzzy Stone." In Snowy's opinion, Dr. Larch had *breathed* for Fuzzy. "You never heard a worse set of lungs," said Snowy Meadows, "but old Larch just hooked the kid up to a real life-saver." And to the question of whether or not the foster home was "carefully and correctly chosen," Snowy Meadows claimed that Dr. Larch was a genius at this delicate guesswork. "How could the guy have known that I was going to fit right in with a furniture family? Well, I'm telling you, he did know," Snowy Meadows (now Robert Marsh) wrote to the board. "You know, private property, the world of personal possessions—that doesn't mean the world to everybody. But let me tell you," Snowy Meadows said, "furniture means the world to an orphan."

"One of you must have dropped that boy on his head," Wilbur Larch said to Nurse Edna and to Nurse Angela, although they could tell he was very pleased by Snowy's remarks.

But just to be fair, the board sent Larch Curly Day's slightly less enthusiastic response to the questionnaire. Roy Rinfret of Boothbay was seething with resentment. "I was no more prepared to be adopted by druggists than I was prepared to have my belly-cord cut," wrote Roy "Curly" Rinfret. "The most beautiful couple in the world walked off with someone who didn't even need or want to be adopted, and I got nabbed by druggists!" Curly complained. "You call it being supervised when little children are stumbling over dead bodies?" Curly Day asked the board. "Imagine this: on the day I find a dead man in the grass, the couple of my dreams adopts someone else, Dr. Larch tells me that an orphanage is not a pet store, and shortly thereafter, two druggists hire me to work in their drugstore for free—and you call that being adopted!"

"Why, that ungrateful little snot!" said Nurse Angela.

"Why, Curly Day, aren't you ashamed?" Nurse Edna asked the indifferent air.

"If that boy were here," Nurse Angela said, "I'd take him over my knee, I would!"

And why hasn't our Homer Wells filled out the questionnaire? the women wondered.

Speaking of "ungrateful," thought Wilbur Larch, although he held his tongue.

Nurse Angela did not hold hers. She wrote directly to Homer Wells, which would have irritated Dr. Larch if he'd known. Nurse Angela came right to the point. "That questionnaire is the least you can do," she wrote Homer. "We all could use a little support. Just because you're having the time of your life (I suppose), don't you dare forget how to be of use—don't you forget where you belong. And if you happen to run into any young doctors or nurses who would be sympathetic to our situation, I think you know that you'd better recommend us to them—and them to us. We're not getting any younger, you know."

My dear Homer [wrote Dr. Larch, in the next day's mail],

It's come to my attention that the board of trustees is attempting to communicate with several former residents of St. Cloud's in the form of a ridiculous questionnaire. Answer it as you see fit, but please do answer it. And you must be prepared for some other, more troubling correspondence from them. It was necessary for me to be frank with them regarding the health of the orphans. Although I saw no reason to tell them I had "lost" Fuzzy Stone to a respiratory ailment—what good would that admission do Fuzzy?—I did tell the board about your heart. I felt that if anything ever happened to me, there should be someone who knew. I do apologize for not telling you about your condition. I am telling you now because, reconsidering the matter, I would never want you to hear about your heart from someone else first. Now, DON'T BE ALARMED! I would not even describe your heart as a condition, the condition is so slight: you had a fairly substantial heart murmur as a small child, but this had almost entirely disappeared when I last checked you—in your sleep; you wouldn't remember—and I have delayed even mentioning your heart to you for fear of worrying you needlessly. (Such worrying might aggravate the condition.) You have (or had) a pulmonary valve stenosis, but PLEASE DON'T WORRY! It is nothing, or next to nothing. If you're interested in more details, I can provide them. For now, I just didn't want you being upset by some fool thing you might hear from that fool board of trustees. Aside from avoiding any situation of extreme stress or extreme exertion, I want you to know that you can almost certainly lead a normal life.

A normal life? thought Homer Wells. I am a Bedouin with a heart condition and Dr. Larch is telling me I can lead a normal life? I am in love with my best—and only—friend's girlfriend, but is that what Larch would call "extreme stress"? And what was Melony to me if *not* "extreme exertion"?

Whenever Homer Wells thought of Melony (which was not often), he missed her; then he was angry at himself. Why should I miss her? he wondered. He tried not to think about St. Cloud's; the longer he stayed away, the more extreme life there appeared to him—yet when he thought of it, he missed it, too. And Nurse Angela and Nurse Edna and Mrs. Grogan and Dr. Larch, he missed them all. He was angry at himself for that, too; there were absolutely no signals from his heart to tell him that the life at St. Cloud's was the life he wanted.

He liked the life at Ocean View. He wanted Candy, and some life with her. When she went back to Camden, he tried not to think about her; and since he could not think of Wally without thinking of Candy, he was relieved when Wally went back to Orono—although he had missed Wally all that fall.

"When an orphan is depressed," wrote Wilbur Larch, "he is attracted to telling lies. A lie is at least a vigorous enterprise, it keeps you on your toes by making you suddenly responsible for what happens because of it. You must be alert to lie, and stay alert to keep your lie a secret. Orphans are not the masters of their fates; they are the last to believe you if you tell them that other people are also not in charge of theirs.

"When you lie, it makes you feel in charge of your life. Telling lies is very seductive to orphans. I know," Dr. Larch wrote. "I know because I tell them, too. I love to lie. When you lie, you feel as if you have cheated fate—your own, and everybody else's."

And so Homer Wells answered the questionnaire; he sang a hymn of praise to St. Cloud's. He mentioned the "restoration" of the abandoned buildings of St. Cloud's as one of the many attempts made "to integrate the daily life of the orphanage with the life of the surrounding community." He also lied to Nurse Angela, but it was just a little lie—one of those that are intended to make other people feel better. He wrote to her that he had lost the original questionnaire—which was the only reason he had been so tardy in returning it. Perhaps the board would be kind enough to send him another? (When he received the second questionnaire from the board, he would know it was time to send the one he had so arduously filled out—that way he would appear to have filled it out spontaneously, off the top of his head.)

He wrote with feigned calmness to Dr. Larch. He would appreciate further details regarding his pulmonary valve stenosis. Did Dr. Larch think it necessary, for example, for Homer to have monthly checkups? (Dr. Larch would think it unnecessary, of course.) And were there signs of trouble that Homer himself might detect; were there ways that he could listen for his perhaps-returning murmur? (Calm yourself, Dr. Larch would advise; that was the best thing—staying calm.)

In an effort to calm himself, Homer tacked the extra questionnaire—which he did not fill out—to the wall of Wally's room, right by the light switch, so that the questions regarding life at St. Cloud's occupied a position of ignored authority quite similar to the page of rules that were yearly tacked up in the cider house. As Homer came and went, he regarded those questions he had answered with such able lies—for example, it was quite a kick for him to contemplate "any possible improvements in the methods and management of St. Cloud's" each time he entered and left Wally's room.

At night, now, Homer's insomnia kept time to a new music; the winter branches of the picked apple trees rattling against each other in the early December wind made a brittle *click-clack* sound. Lying in his bed—a moonlight the color of bone starkly outlining his hands folded on his chest—Homer Wells thought the trees might be trying to shake the snow off their branches, in advance of the snow itself.

Perhaps the trees knew that a war was coming, too, but Olive Worthington didn't think about it. She had heard the orchard's winter rattle for many years; she had seen the winter branches bare, then lacy with snow, and then bare again. The coastal winds gave the brittle orchard such a shaking that the clashing trees resembled frozen soldiers in all the postures of saber-rattling, but Olive had heard so many years of this season that she never knew a war was coming. If the trees seemed especially naked to her that December, she thought it was because she faced her first winter without Senior.

"Grown-ups don't look for signs in the familiar," noted Dr. Wilbur Larch in *A Brief History of St. Cloud's,* "but an orphan is always looking for signs."

Homer Wells, at Wally's window, searched the skeletal orchard for the future—his own, mainly, but Candy's too, and Wally's. Dr. Larch's future was certainly out there, in those winter branches—even Melony's future. And what future would there be for the Lord's work? wondered Homer Wells.

/ / /

The war that was about to be did not announce itself in signs at St. Cloud's; both the familiar and the unfamiliar were muted there by ritual and by custom. A pregnancy *terminated* in a birth or in an abortion; an orphan was adopted or was waiting to be adopted. When there was a dry and snowless cold, the loose sawdust irritated the eyes and the noses and the throats of St. Cloud's; only briefly, when the snow lay newly fallen, was the sawdust gone from the air. When there was a thaw, the snow melted down and the matted sawdust smelled like wet fur; when there was a freeze, the sawdust reappeared—dry again, somehow on top of the old snow—and again the eyes itched, the noses ran, and the throats could never quite clear themselves of it.

"Let us be happy for Smoky Fields," Dr. Larch announced in the boys' division. "Smoky Fields has found a family. Good night, Smoky."

"Good night, Thmoky!" said David Copperfield.

"G'night!" young Steerforth cried.

Good night, you little food hoarder, Nurse Angela thought. Whoever took him, she knew, would soon learn to lock the refrigerator.

In the December morning, at the window where Melony once allowed the world to pass both with and without comment, Mary Agnes Cork watched the women walking uphill from the train station. They don't look pregnant, Mary Agnes thought.

On the bleak hill where Wally Worthington once imagined apple trees, young Copperfield attempted to steer a cardboard carton through the first, wet snow. The carton had once contained four hundred sterile vulval pads; Copperfield knew this because he had unpacked the carton—and he had placed young Steerforth *in* the carton, at the bottom of the hill. Near the top, he was beginning to realize his mistake. Not only had dragging Steerforth uphill been difficult, but also the boy's weight—in addition to the wetness of the snow—had turned the bottom of the carton soggy. Copperfield wondered if his make-do sled would even slide—if he ever managed to get the mess to the top.

"Good night, Smoky!" Steerforth was singing.

"Thut up, thupid," David Copperfield said.

Dr. Larch was very tired. He was resting in the dispensary. The gray, winter light turned the white walls gray and for a moment Larch wondered what time of day it was—and what time of year. From now on, he was thinking, let everything I do be for a reason. Let me make no wasted moves.

In his mind's eye he saw the correct angle at which the

vaginal speculum allowed him a perfect view of the cervix. Whose cervix? he wondered. Even in his ether sleep the thumb and index finger of his right hand tightened the screw that held the jaws of the speculum in place, and he saw the astonishing blondness of the little clump of pubic hair caught in the hairs of his own wrist. It was so blond he had nearly missed seeing it against his own pale skin. When he shook his wrist, the little clump was so light that it floated in the air. In his ether swoon his left hand reached for it, just missing it. Oh yes—*her* cervix, thought Wilbur Larch. What was her name?

"She has a toy name," Larch said aloud. "Candy!" he remembered. Then he laughed. Nurse Edna, passing the dispensary, held her breath and listened to the laughter. But even when she didn't breathe, the fumes made her old eyes water. That and the sawdust. That and the orphans—some of them made her eyes water, too.

She opened the door at the hospital entrance to let some fresh air into the hall. On the hill she watched a cardboard carton make an unsteady descent; she knew that sterile vulval pads had been in the carton, but she wasn't sure what was in the carton now. Something heavy, because the carton's descent was clumsy and irregular. At times it picked up speed, sliding almost smoothly, but always some rock or bare patch in the slushy snow would jar it off-course and slow it down. The first small body to roll out of the carton and make its way downhill was Steerforth's; she recognized his overlarge mittens and the ski hat that always covered his eyes. For a while he tumbled almost as fast as the carton, but a large patch of bare, frozen ground finally stopped him. Nurse Edna watched him climb back uphill for one of his mittens.

The second, larger body to be propelled from the carton was obviously David Copperfield's; he rolled free with a large, soggy piece of the carton in both his hands. The carton appeared to disintegrate in flight.

"Thit!" Copperfield cried. At least, Nurse Edna thought, young Copperfield's profanities were improved by his lisp.

"Close that door," said Dr. Larch, in the hall behind Nurse Edna.

"I was just trying to get some fresh air," Nurse Edna said pointedly.

"You could have fooled me," said Wilbur Larch. "I thought you were trying to freeze the unborn."

Maybe that will be the way of the future, Nurse Edna thought—wondering what future ways there would be.

/ / /

In the December swimming pool the raft that Senior Worthington used to ride still floated, windblown from one end of the pool to the other, breaking up the lacy fringes of ice that formed and re-formed around the edges. Olive and Homer had drained out a third of the pool's water, to leave room for rainfall and snow melt.

Senior's cold raft, only partially deflated by the falling temperature, still charged around the swimming pool like a rider-less horse; it galloped wherever the wind urged it. Every day Olive watched the raft out the kitchen window, and Homer wondered when she would suggest getting rid of it.

One weekend Candy came home from Camden, and Homer's confusion regarding what he should do about her mounted. Friday was a bad, indecisive day. He went early to Senior Biology, hoping to persuade Mr. Hood either to let him have his own rabbit for dissection or to assign him a lab partner other than that boy Bucky. Bucky managed to mangle the rabbit's innards whenever he handled them, and Homer found the oaf's constant fixation with everything's reproductive system both silly and maddening. Bucky had lately seized on the fact that marsupials have paired vaginas.

"Twin twats! Can you believe it?" Bucky asked Homer.

"Right," said Homer Wells.

"Is that all you can say?" Bucky asked. "Don't you get it? If you was a hamster, you could fuck another hamster *with your buddy*!"

"Why would I want to do that?" Homer asked.

"Two cunts!" Bucky said enthusiastically. "You got no imagination."

"I doubt that even the hamsters are interested in what you suggest," said Homer Wells.

"That's what I mean, stupid," Bucky said. "What a waste—to give two twats to a hamster! You ever seen 'em run on them little wheels? They're crazy! Wouldn't you be crazy if you knew the girl of your dreams had two twats and she still wasn't interested?"

"The girl of my dreams," said Homer Wells.

It was crazy enough, in Homer's opinion, that the girl of his dreams had two people who loved her.

And so he went early to Senior Biology to request either a

fresh rabbit or a replacement for the obsessed boy named Bucky.

There was a geography class in progress when he got there; and when the class was released, Homer saw that the large maps of the world were still pulled down, covering the blackboard. "May I just look at the maps for a moment, before my next class?" Homer asked the geography teacher. "I'll roll them back up for you."

And so he was left alone with his first accurate view of the world—the whole world, albeit unrealistically flat against a blackboard. After a while he found Maine; he regarded how small it was. After a while he found South Carolina; he stared into South Carolina for a long time, as if the exact whereabouts of Mr. Rose and the other migrants would materialize. He had heard all the talk about Germany, which was easier to find than Maine. He was surprised at the size of England; Charles Dickens had given him the impression of something much bigger.

And the ocean that seemed so vast when you looked at it off Ray Kendall's dock—why the oceans of the world were even more vast than he'd imagined. Yet St. Cloud's, which loomed so large in Homer's life, could not be located on the map of Maine. He was using the geography teacher's magnifying glass when he suddenly realized that the entire class of Senior Biology had filled the seats behind him. Mr. Hood was regarding him strangely.

"Looking for your rabbit, Homer?" Mr. Hood asked. The class enjoyed this joke enormously, and Homer realized he had—at least for that day—lost the opportunity to rid himself of Bucky.

"Look at it this way," Bucky whispered to him, near the end of class. "If Debra Pettigrew had two twats, she might let you in one of them. You see the advantages?"

Unfortunately, the idea of paired vaginas troubled Homer throughout his Friday evening date with Debra Pettigrew. There was a Fred Astaire movie in Bath, but that was almost an hour-long drive, each way, and what did Homer Wells know or care about dancing? He had declined several invitations to attend Debra's dancing class with her; if she wanted to see the Fred Astaire movie, Homer thought she could go with someone who was in her dancing class. And it was getting too cold simply to drive down to the beach and park there. Olive was generous about letting Homer use the van. Soon there would be gas rationing, and a welcome end, in Homer's opinion, to all this restless driving.

He drove Debra Pettigrew out to the carnival site at Cape Kenneth. In the moonlight, the abandoned, unlighted Ferris wheel stood out like scaffolding for the world's first rocket launch, or like the bones of some species from dinosaur times. Homer tried to tell Debra about the knife work of Mr. Rose, but she had her heart set on Fred Astaire; he knew better than to waste a good story on her when she was sulking. They drove to the Cape Kenneth drive-in, which was "closed for the season"; they appeared to be reviewing the scenes of a romance that had happened to other people—and not just last summer, but to another generation.

"I don't know what you've got against dancing," Debra said.

"I don't know, either," said Homer Wells.

It was still early when he drove Debra to her winter home in Kenneth Corners; the same ferocious dogs of the summer were there, with their coats grown thicker, with their hot breath icing on their muzzles. There had been talk between Debra and Homer, earlier, about using the summer house on Drinkwater Lake for some kind of party; the house would be unheated, and they would have to keep the lights off, or someone might report a breaking and entering; but despite these discomforts, surely there was a thrill in being unchaperoned. Why? wondered Homer Wells. He knew he still wouldn't get to Debra Pettigrew—even if she had *two* vaginas. With the dull Friday evening they had spent together, and with the dogs' breath crystallizing on the driver's-side window of the van, there was no talk about such a tempting party this night.

"So what are we doing tomorrow night?" Debra asked, sighing.

Homer watched a dog gnaw at his side-view mirror.

"Well, I was going to see Candy—she's home from Camden," Homer said. "I haven't seen her on a weekend all fall, and Wally did ask me to look after her."

"You're going to see her without Wally?" Debra asked.

"Right," Homer said. The van was so snub-nosed that the dogs could hurl themselves directly against the windshield without having to clamber over the hood. A big dog's paws raked one of the windshield wipers away from the windshield, releasing it with a crack; it looked bent; it wouldn't quite touch the surface of the glass anymore.

"You're going to see her alone," Debra said.

"Or with her dad," Homer said.

"Sure," said Debra Pettigrew, getting out of the van. She left the door open a little too long. A dog with the spade-shaped head of a Doberman charged the open door; it was half in the van, its heavy chest heaving against the passenger-side seat, its frosty muzzle drooling on the gearshift box, when Debra grabbed it by the ear and yanked it back, yelping, out of the van.

"So long," said Homer Wells softly—after the door had slammed, after he had wiped the dog's frothy slobber off the gearshift knob.

He drove by Kendall's Lobster Pound twice, but there was nothing to tell him whether Candy was home. On the weekends when she came home, she took the train; then Ray drove her back, on Sunday. I'll call her tomorrow—Saturday—Homer thought.

When Candy said that she wanted to see the Fred Astaire movie, Homer had no objections. "I always wanted to see him," he said. Bath, after all, was less than an hour away.

On the bridge across the Kennebec River, they could see several big ships in the water and several more in dry dock; the Bath shipyards were sprawled along the shore—a rhythmic hammering and other metal sounds audible even on a Saturday. They were much too early for the movie. They were looking for an Italian restaurant that Ray had told them about—if it was still there; Raymond Kendall hadn't been in Bath in years.

In 194__, especially to an outsider, the city seemed dominated by the shipyards, and by the ships that stood taller than the shipyard buildings, and by the bridge that spanned the Kennebec River. Bath was a workingman's town, as Melony soon discovered.

She found a job in the shipyards and began her winter employment on an assembly line, working with other women— and with an occasional, handicapped man—on the second floor of a factory specializing in movable parts. The movable part to which Melony would devote her energies for the first month of her employment was a hexagonal-shaped sprocket that looked like half a ham, split open lengthwise; Melony did not know the whereabouts of the assembly line that dealt with the other half of the ham. The sprocket arrived on the conveyor belt in front of her, pausing there for exactly forty-five seconds before it was moved on and replaced by a new sprocket. The joint of the sprocket was packed with grease; you could stick your finger in the grease, past the second knuckle. The job was to insert six ball bearings into the grease-packed joint; you pushed each ball bearing into the grease until you felt it hit the bottom; all six fit perfectly. The trick was to get only one hand greasy; a clean hand had an easier time handling the clean ball bearings, which were the size of marbles. The other part of the job was making sure that the six ball bearings were perfect—perfectly round, perfectly smooth; no dents, no jagged metal scraps stuck to them. The odds were that one out of every two hundred ball bearings had something wrong with it; at the end of the day, you turned in the bad ball bearings. If you had a day with no bad ball bearings, the foreman told you that you weren't looking each ball bearing over carefully enough.

You could sit or stand, and Melony tried both positions, alternating them through the day. The belt was too high to make sitting comfortable and too low to make standing any better. Your back hurt in one place when you stood and in another place when you sat. Not only did Melony not know who did what, where, to the other half of the sprocket; she also didn't know what the sprocket was for. What's more, she didn't care.

After two weeks, she had the routine down pat: between twenty-six and twenty-eight seconds to insert the ball bearings and never more than ten seconds to pick six perfect ball bearings. She learned to keep a nest of ball bearings in her lap (when she sat) and in an ashtray (she didn't smoke) when she stood; that way she always had a ball bearing handy in case she dropped one. She had a twelve-to-fourteen-second rest between sprockets, during which time she could look at the person on her left and at the person on her right, and shut her eyes and count to three or sometimes five. She observed that there were two styles of labor on the line. Some of the workers picked their six perfect ball bearings immediately upon finishing a sprocket; the others waited for the new sprocket to arrive first. Melony found faults with both styles.

The woman next to Melony put it this way: "Some of us are pickers, some are stickers," she said.

"I'm not either, or I'm both," Melony said.

"Well, I think you'll have an easier time of it, dearie, if you make up your mind," the woman said. Her name was Doris. She had three children; one side of her face was still pretty, but the other was marred by a mole with whiskers in it. In the twelve or fourteen seconds that Doris had between sprockets, she smoked.

On the other side of Melony was an elderly man in a wheelchair. His problem was that he could not pick up the ball bearings that he dropped, and some of them got caught in his lap blanket or in the wheelchair apparatus, which caused him to rattle when he wheeled himself off for his coffee break or for lunch. His name was Walter.

Three or four times a day, Walter would shout, "Fucking ball bearings!"

Some days, when someone was sick, the assembly line was reassembled and Melony was not pinned between Walter and Doris. Sometimes she got to be next to Troy, who was blind. He *felt* the ball bearings for perfection and daintily poked them into the thick and unseen grease. He was a little older than Melony, but he had always worked in the shipyards; he'd been blinded in a welding accident, and the shipyards owed him a job for life.

"At least I've got security," he would say, three or four times a day.

Some days Melony was put next to a girl about her age, a feisty little chick called Lorna.

"There's worse jobs," Lorna said one day.

"Name one," said Melony.

"Blowing bulldogs," Lorna said.

"I don't know about that," Melony said. "I'll bet every bulldog is different."

"Then how come every man is the same?" Lorna asked. Melony decided that she liked Lorna.

Lorna had been married when she was seventeen—"to an older man," she'd said—but it hadn't worked out. He was a garage mechanic, "about twenty-one," Lorna said. "He just married me 'cause I was the first person he slept with," Lorna told Melony.

Melony told Lorna that she'd been separated from her boyfriend by "a rich girl who came between us"; Lorna agreed that this was "the worst."

"But I figure one of two things has happened," Melony said.

"Either he still hasn't fucked her, because she hasn't let him, and so he's figured out what he's missing. Or else she's let him fuck her—in which case, he's figured out what he's missing."

"Ha! That's right," Lorna said. She appeared to like Melony.

"I got some friends," she told Melony. "We eat pizza, go to movies, you know." Melony nodded; she had done none of those things. Lorna was as thin as Melony was thick, she showed as much bone as Melony showed flesh; Lorna was pale and blond, whereas Melony was dark and darker; Lorna looked frail and she coughed a lot, whereas Melony looked almost as strong as she was and her lungs were a set of engines. Yet the women felt they belonged together.

When they requested that they be put next to each other on the assembly line, their request was denied. Friendships, especially talkative ones, were considered counterproductive on the line. Thus Melony was allowed to work alongside Lorna only when the line was reassembled on a sick day. Melony was made to endure the crackpot homilies of Doris and the lost ball bearings of Wheelchair Walter, as everyone called him. But the enforced separation from Lorna on the work line only made Melony feel stronger in her attachment; the attachment was mutual. That Saturday they put in for overtime together, and they worked side by side through the afternoon.

At about the time that Candy and Homer Wells were crossing the bridge over the Kennebec and driving into downtown Bath, Lorna dropped a ball bearing down the cleavage of Melony's work shirt. It was their way of getting each other's attention.

"There's a Fred Astaire movie in town," Lorna said, snapping her chewing gum. "You wanna see it?"

/ / /

Although her voice lacked the studied heartiness of Dr. Larch's, Mrs. Grogan did her best to inspire a welcome response to her announcement to the girls' division. "Let us be happy for Mary Agnes Cork," she said; there was general sniveling, but Mrs. Grogan pressed on. "Mary Agnes Cork has found a family. Good night, Mary Agnes!"

There were stifled moans, the sound of someone gagging in her pillow and a few of the usual, wracking sobs.

"Let us be *happy* for Mary Agnes Cork!" Mrs. Grogan pleaded.

"Fuck you," someone said in the darkness.

"It hurts me to hear you say that," Mrs. Grogan said. "How that hurts us all. Good night, Mary Agnes!" Mrs. Grogan called.

"Good night, Mary Agnes," one of the smaller ones said.

"Be careful, Mary Agnes!" someone blubbered.

Goodness, yes! thought Mrs. Grogan, the tears running down her cheeks. Yes, be careful.

Larch had assured Mrs. Grogan that the adoptive family was especially good for an older girl like Mary Agnes. They were a young couple who bought and sold and restored antiques; they were too active in their business to look after a small child, but they had lots of energy to share with an older child on the weekends and in the evenings. The young wife had been very close to a kid sister; she was "devoted to girl talk," she told Dr. Larch. (Apparently, the kid sister had married a foreigner and was now living abroad.)

And Wilbur Larch had a good feeling for Bath; he'd always maintained a friendly correspondence with the pathologist at Bath Hospital; good old Clara had come from there. And so it seemed perfectly fine to him that Mary Agnes Cork had gone to Bath.

Mary Agnes was attached to her own name, and so they allowed her to keep it, not just the Mary Agnes but the Cork, too. After all, they were Callahans; a Cork went with a Callahan, didn't it? It sounded a little modern for Mrs. Grogan's tastes, although she allowed herself to be pleased at the thought that she'd named someone for keeps.

Ted and Patty Callahan wanted Mary Agnes Cork to view them as friends. The first friendly thing the young couple did was to take Mary Agnes to her first movie. They were a robust couple, and in their opinion they lived near enough to the movie theater in Bath to walk; it was a long walk, during which Ted and Patty demonstrated some of the basic differences between a fox-trot and a waltz. The December sidewalk was sloppy, but Ted and Patty wanted to prepare Mary Agnes for some of the dazzle of Fred Astaire.

Off the Kennebec a damp, chilling wind was blowing and Mary Agnes felt her collarbone ache; when she tried to join the Callahans at dancing, the old injury felt loose; then it throbbed; then it grew numb. The sidewalk was so slippery, she nearly fell—catching her balance on the fender of a dirty green van. Patty brushed her coat off for her. People were outside the movie house, buying tickets in the failing light. On the sliding panel door of the van, Mary Agnes Cork recognized the apple monogram—the W.W., and the OCEAN VIEW. She had first seen this emblem on a Cadillac—there had been a kind of hunger line; she remembered that beautiful girl standing aloof and that beautiful boy passing out the food. They're *here*! Mary Agnes thought, the beautiful people who took Homer Wells away! Maybe Homer was still with them. Mary Agnes began to look around.

Homer and Candy had not had much luck finding the Italian restaurant that Ray had recommended; they'd found two or three Italian restaurants, each one serving pizza and submarine sandwiches and beer, and each one so overrun with workers from the shipyards that there was no place to sit. They'd eaten some pizza in the van and had arrived at the movie early.

When Homer Wells opened his wallet in front of the ticket booth, he realized that he'd never opened his wallet outdoors—in a winter wind—before. He put his back to the wind, but still the loose bills flapped; Candy cupped her hands on either side of his wallet, as if she were protecting a flame in danger of going out, and that was how she was in a position to catch her own, treasured clump of pubic hair when it blew free from Homer's wallet and caught on the cuff of her coat. They both grabbed for it (Homer letting the wallet fall), but Candy was quicker. Some of the fine, blond hairs may have escaped in the wind, but Candy seized the clump tightly—Homer's hand closing immediately on hers.

They stepped away from the ticket booth; a small line moved into the theater past them. Candy continued to hold her pubic hair tightly, and Homer would not let her hand go—he would not let her open her hand to examine what she held; there was no need for that. Candy knew what she held in her hand; she knew it as much from Homer's expression as from the clump of pubic hair itself.

"I'd like to take a walk," she whispered.

"Right," said Homer Wells, not letting go of her hand. They turned away from the theater and walked downhill to the Kennebec. Candy faced the river and leaned against Homer Wells.

"Perhaps you're a collector," she said, as quietly as she could speak and still be heard over the river. "Perhaps you're a pubic hair collector," she said. "You certainly were in a position to be."

"No," he said.

"This *is* pubic hair," she said, wriggling her tightly clenched fist in his hand. "And it's *mine,* right?"

"Right," said Homer Wells.

"Only mine?" Candy asked. "You kept only mine?"

"Right," Homer said.

"Why?" Candy asked. "Don't lie."

He had never said the words: I am in love with you. He was unprepared for the struggle involved in saying them. No doubt he misunderstood the unfamiliar weight he felt upon his heart—he must have associated the constriction of that big muscle in his chest with Dr. Larch's recent news; what he felt was only love, but what he thought he felt was his pulmonary valve stenosis. He let go of Candy's hand and put both his hands to his chest. He had seen the sternum shears at work—he knew the autopsy procedure—but never had it been so hard and painful to breathe.

When Candy turned to him and saw his face, she couldn't help it—both her hands opened and grasped his hands, the blond wisp of pubic hair flying free; a current of rough air carried it out over the river and into the darkness.

"Is it your heart?" Candy asked him. "Oh God, you don't have to say anything—please don't even think about it!"

"My heart," he said. "You know about my heart?"

"*You* know?" she asked. "Don't worry!" she added fiercely.

"I love you," Homer Wells croaked, as if he were saying his last words.

"Yes, I know—don't think about it," Candy said. "Don't worry about anything. I love you, too."

"You *do?*" he asked.

"Yes, yes, and Wally too," she said. "I love you *and* I love Wally—but don't worry about it, don't even think about it."

"How do you know about my heart?" asked Homer Wells.

"We all know about it," Candy said. "Olive knows, and Wally knows."

Hearing this was more convincing to Homer Wells than even the offhand remarks in Dr. Larch's letter; he felt his heart race out of control again.

"Don't think about your heart, Homer!" Candy said, hugging him tightly. "Don't worry about me, or Wally—or any of it."

"What am I supposed to think about?" asked Homer Wells.

"Only good things," Candy told him. When she looked into his eyes, she said suddenly, "I can't believe that you kept my hair!" But when she saw the intensity of his frown, she said, "I mean, it's okay—I understand, I guess. Don't worry about it, either. It may be peculiar, but it's certainly romantic."

"Romantic," said Homer Wells, holding the girl of his dreams—but only holding her. To touch her more would surely be forbidden—by all the rules—and so he tried to accept the ache in his heart as what Dr. Larch would call the common symptoms of a normal life. This is a normal life, he tried to think, holding Candy as both the night fog off the river and the darkness reached over them.

It was not a night that put them in the mood for a musical.

"We can see Fred Astaire dance another time," Candy said philosophically.

The safety of the familiar drew them toward Raymond Kendall's dock—when they got cold, sitting out there, they could always have some tea with Ray. They drove the van back to Heart's Haven; nobody who knew them saw them come or go.

In the Fred Astaire movie, Mary Agnes Cork ate too much popcorn; her foster family thought that the poor girl was simply overstimulated by her first movie; she could not sit still. She watched the audience more than she watched the dancing; she searched every face in the flickering darkness. It was that pretty girl and that pretty boy she was looking for—and maybe Homer Wells. And so she was unprepared to spot the face in the crowd of the one person she missed most in her narrow world; the sight of that dark, heavy countenance shot such a stab of pain through her old collarbone injury that the popcorn container flew from her hands.

Melony loomed over the sassy blond girl named Lorna—hulking in her seat with the authority of a chronic and cynical moviegoer, looking like a sour critic born to be displeased, although this was her first movie. Even in the projector's gray light, Mary Agnes Cork could not fail to recognize her old brutalizer, the ex-queen and former hit-woman of the girls' division.

"I think you've had enough of that popcorn, sweetheart," Patty Callahan told Mary Agnes, who appeared to have a kernel of the stuff caught in her throat. And for the rest of the evening's frivolous entertainment, Mary Agnes could not keep her eyes off that most dominant member of the audience; in

Mary Agnes Cork's opinion, Melony could have wiped up a dance floor with Fred Astaire, she could have broken every bone in Fred's slender body—she could have paralyzed him after just one waltz.

"Do you see someone you know, dear?" Ted Callahan asked Mary Agnes. He thought the poor girl was so stuffed with popcorn that she couldn't talk.

In the lobby, in the sickly neon light, Mary Agnes walked up to Melony as if a dream led her feet—as if she were captured in the old, violent trance of Melony's authority.

"Hi," she said.

"You talking to me, kid?" Lorna asked, but Mary Agnes was smiling just at Melony.

"Hi, it's *me*!" Mary Agnes said.

"So you got out?" Melony said.

"I've been adopted!" said Mary Agnes Cork. Ted and Patty stood a little nervously near her, not wanting to intrude but not wanting to let her very far from their sight, either. "This is Ted and Patty," Mary Agnes said. "This is my friend, Melony."

Melony appeared not to know what to make of the hands extended to her. The tough little broad named Lorna batted her eyes—some of her mascara sticking one of her eyelids in a frozen-open position.

"This is my friend, Lorna," Melony said awkwardly.

Everyone said Hi! and then stood around. What does the little creep want? Melony was thinking.

And that was when Mary Agnes said, "Where's Homer?"

"What?" Melony said.

"Homer Wells," said Mary Agnes. "Isn't he with you?"

"Why?" Melony asked.

"Those pretty people with the car . . ." Mary Agnes began.

"*What* car?" Melony asked.

"Well, it wasn't the same car, it wasn't the pretty car, but there was the apple on the door—I'll never forget that apple," Mary Agnes said.

Melony put her big hands heavily on Mary Agnes's shoulders; Mary Agnes felt the weight pressing her into the floor. "What are you talking about?" Melony asked.

"I saw an old car, but it had that apple on it," Mary Agnes said. "I thought they was at the movie, those pretty people— and Homer, too. And when I saw you, I thought he would be here for sure."

"Where was the car?" Melony asked, her strong thumbs bearing down on both of Mary Agnes's collarbones. "Show me the car!"

"Is something wrong?" Ted Callahan asked.

"Mind your own business," Melony said.

But the van was gone. In the damp cold, on the slushy sidewalk, staring at the empty curbstone, Melony said, "Are you sure it was *that* apple? It had a double W, and it said Ocean View."

"That's it," Mary Agnes said. "It just wasn't the same car, it was an old van, but I'd know that apple anywhere. You don't forget a thing like that."

"Oh, shut up," Melony said tiredly. She stood on the curb, her hands on her hips, her nostrils flared; she was trying to pick up a scent, the way a dog guesses in the air for the history of intrusions upon its territory.

"What is it?" Lorna asked Melony. "Was your fella here with his rich cunt?"

Ted and Patty Callahan were anxious to take Mary Agnes home, but Melony stopped them as they were leaving. She reached into her tight pocket and produced the horn-rimmed barrette that Mary Agnes had stolen from Candy, which Melony had taken for herself. Melony gave the barrette to Mary Agnes.

"Keep it," Melony said. "You took it, it's yours."

Mary Agnes clutched the barrette as if it were a medal for bravery, for valorous conduct in the only arena that Melony respected.

"I hope I see ya!" Mary Agnes called after Melony, who was stalking away—the escaping Homer Wells might be around the next corner.

"What color was the van?" Melony called.

"Green!" said Mary Agnes. "I hope I see ya!" she repeated.

"You ever hear of an Ocean View?" Melony yelled back at the Callahans; they hadn't. What are apples to antiques dealers?

"Can I see ya sometime?" Mary Agnes asked Melony.

"I'm at the shipyards," Melony told the girl. "If you ever hear of an Ocean View, you can see me."

"You don't know it was him," Lorna said to Melony later. They were drinking beer. Melony wasn't talking. "And you don't know if the rich cunt is still with him."

They stood on the bank of the foggy Kennebec, near the boardinghouse where Lorna lived; when they'd finish a beer, they'd throw the bottle into the river. Melony was good at throwing things into rivers. She kept her face turned up; she was still smelling the wind—as if even that wisp of Candy's pubic hair could not escape her powers of detection.

Homer Wells was also making a deposit in the water. *Ploink!* said the snails he threw off Ray Kendall's dock; the sea made just the smallest sound in swallowing snails. *Ploink! Ploink!*

Candy and Homer sat with their backs against opposite corner posts at the end of the dock. If they'd both stretched out their legs to each other, the soles of their feet could have touched, but Candy sat with her knees slightly bent—in a position familiar to Homer Wells from his many views of women in stirrups.

"Is it okay?" Candy asked quietly.

"Is what okay?" he asked.

"Your heart," she whispered.

How could he tell? "I guess so," he said.

"It'll be okay," she said.

"What will be okay?" asked Homer Wells.

"Everything," Candy said hurriedly.

"Everything," repeated Homer Wells. "Me loving you—that's okay. And you loving me, *and* Wally—that's okay, too? Right," he said.

"You have to wait and see," Candy said. "For everything—you have to wait and see."

"Right."

"I don't know what to do, either," said Candy helplessly.

"We have to do the right thing," Homer Wells said. Wally would want to do the right thing, and Dr. Larch was doing what he thought was the right thing, too. If you could be patient enough to wait and see, the right thing must present itself—mustn't it? What else does an orphan do, anyway, but wait and see?

"I can be patient," said Homer Wells.

Melony could be patient, too. And Ray Kendall, at his window above his dock—he could be patient, too. A mechanic is also patient; a mechanic has to wait for something to break before he can fix it. Ray stared at the distance between his daughter's feet and the feet of Homer Wells; it was not much of a distance, and he had observed his daughter on his dock many times in Wally's arms, and, before that, when Candy and Wally had also sat on that dock with their feet not touching.

They were three good kids, Ray was thinking. But he was a mechanic; he knew better than to interfere. When it breaks, then he would fix it; he felt sorry for them all.

"I can drive you back to school tomorrow," Homer said.

"My dad can drive me back," Candy said. "I think he likes to."

Olive Worthington looked at the clock on her night table and turned out her reading lamp; Homer never stayed out this late with Debra Pettigrew, she was thinking. Olive had no trouble imagining Candy's attraction to Homer Wells; Olive had the greatest respect for Homer's diligence. She had seen him be a better student—and of the rabbit, of all things!—than Wally had ever been, and she knew he was a reliable and friendly companion, too. Olive fumed to herself. She felt that typical contradiction a parent so often feels: completely on her son's side—she even wanted to warn him, to help his cause—but at the same time Wally could stand to be taught a lesson. Just maybe not *this* lesson, Olive thought.

"Well, thank goodness, they are three nice people!" she said aloud, her own voice in the empty house surprising her and thoroughly waking her up. Some hot chocolate would be soothing, she thought; and when Homer comes home, he can have some with me.

But in the kitchen Olive was struck by how the fog, shot through with a cloudy moonlight, made the raft in the swimming pool look quite ghostly. The raft was poised at the side of the pool, half in the water and half out, like a very gray and shadowy photograph of itself. The image disturbed her, and Olive decided she'd had enough of that raft. She put on a pair of boots and a long winter coat over her nightgown. It bothered her that the outdoor patio light was not working; only the underwater lights would turn on, and she was surprised to see that the water in the pool had finally frozen. That was the reason for the raft's arrested position. It was trapped as rigidly as a statue, like a ship seized in an ice floe. Being careful to hold tight to the pool curb, she kicked tentatively at the ice with the heel of her boot, but when she tugged the raft, it would not come free. If I walk out there, I'll fall right through, she thought.

That was when Homer came home. She heard the van in the driveway and she called to him.

"What do you want done with it?" Homer asked Olive about the raft.

"Just get it out," Olive said to him.

"And then what?" he asked.

"Throw it away," she said. "Meanwhile, I'll make you some hot chocolate."

Homer struggled with the raft. The ice, which would not support all his weight, was hard enough to have a firm grip on the raft. Very cleverly, he eased himself onto the raft, hoping it still had enough air in it so that it wouldn't sink once he broke the bond with the ice. He rocked back and forth on his knees on the raft until he could feel the ice breaking. Then he rocked his way through more of the ice and climbed up on the pool curb and pulled the raft out of the pool after him. Ice still clung to it; it was so heavy, he had to drag it. When he got to the trash barrels, he needed to deflate the raft in order to stuff it in a barrel. The nozzle was rusted shut, and even by jumping with both feet, he couldn't break the tough canvas hide.

He went into the garden shed and found a pair of hedge shears; with the thinner blade, he stabbed a gash in the raft and snipped upward—the stale, rubbery air blasting into his face. It was moist and fetid, and when he tore the hole wider, the smell washed over him—strangely warm in the cold night air, and strangely foul. It was not only the smell of someone's old sneakers left out in the rain; there was also something putrid about it and he couldn't help viewing the slashed object as he might have viewed a ripped intestine. He stuffed the raft into a trash barrel, but when he went into the house for his hot-chocolate reward, the smell remained on his hands even after he had washed them. He stuck his nose into the hollow in the palm of his hand; the smell was still there. Then he recognized the smell: it was what was left on his hands after he removed the rubber gloves.

"How's Candy?" Olive asked.

"Fine," said Homer Wells.

They sipped their hot chocolate—like mother and son, both of them were thinking; and, at the same time, *not* like mother and son, they both thought.

"And how are *you*?" Olive asked him, after a while.

"Just fine," said Homer Wells, but what he thought was: I'm going to wait and see.

/ / /

Wilbur Larch, inhaling and seeing the stars race across the ceiling of the dispensary, knew what a luxury it was: to be able to wait and see. Even if I last, he thought, I might get caught; an abortionist believes in odds. He had been in the business too long. What are the odds that someone will blow the whistle before I'm through? the old man wondered.

Only yesterday he had made a new enemy—a woman in her eighth month who said it was only her fourth. He had to refuse her. When the women were hysterical, he usually could wait them out; if they required firmness, he gave them Nurse Angela; Nurse Edna was better at hand-holding. In time, they calmed down. If, in his opinion, a woman was simply too late—if he felt he had to refuse to perform the abortion—he usually could convince the woman she would be safe at St. Cloud's; that he would deliver the baby and find it a home, and that this was preferable to the risk involved in a late abortion.

But not this woman. There had been no hysterics. The peacefulness of a long-standing hatred made the woman almost serene.

"So that's it—you won't do it," she said.

"I'm sorry," Dr. Larch said.

"How much do you want?" the woman asked him. "I can get it."

"Whatever you can afford to donate to the orphanage would be appreciated," Larch said. "If you can't afford anything, then everything is free. An abortion is free, delivery is free. A donation is appreciated. If you have nowhere to go, you're welcome to stay here. You don't have long to wait."

"Just tell me what I have to do," the woman said. "Do I fuck you? Okay, I'll fuck you."

"I want you to have this baby and let me find it a home," Wilbur Larch said. "That's all I want you to do."

But the woman had stared right through him. She struggled out of the overstuffed chair in Nurse Angela's office. She regarded the paperweight on Larch's desk; it was a weighted vaginal speculum, but it held down a lot of paper and most of the would-be foster families didn't know what it was. The woman who wanted the late abortion clearly knew what it was; she stared at it as if the sight of it gave her cramps. Then she looked out the window, where (Dr. Larch imagined) she intended to hurl the paperweight.

She picked up the weighted speculum and pointed the jaw of the thing at Larch, as if it were a gun.

"You'll be sorry," the woman said.

In his ether haze, Wilbur Larch saw the woman point the speculum at him again. How will I be sorry? he wondered.

"I'm sorry," he said aloud. Nurse Edna, passing in the hall—ever passing—thought, You're forgiven; I forgive you.

/ / /

It was Sunday, and overcast—as usual. The same Fred Astaire movie that was entertaining the residents of Bath was playing in Orono, and the students at the University of Maine in 194— were not yet so cynical that they failed to enjoy it. Wally went to the movie with some of his friends. During the afternoon matinee, they didn't interrupt the show with the news that interrupted the rest of the world. They allowed Fred Astaire to dance on, and on, and the moviegoers heard the news after the show, when they stepped out of the comforting dark of the theater into the late-afternoon daylight of downtown Orono.

Candy was returning to Camden with her father. Raymond Kendall was especially proud of the radio reception he had engineered for his Chevrolet; it was much clearer reception than was possible, at the time, in a standard car radio, and Ray had made the whiplash antenna himself. Candy and her father heard the news as soon as anyone in Maine heard it, and they heard it loud and clear.

Olive always had the radio on, and so she was one of those people who needed to hear things several times before she really heard them at all. She was baking an apple pie, and simmering applesauce, and only the unusual urgency in the announcer's voice caused her to pay attention to the radio at all.

Homer Wells was in Wally's room, reading *David Copperfield* and thinking about Heaven—" . . . that sky above me, where, in the mystery to come, I might yet love her with a love unknown on earth, and tell her what the strife had been within me when I loved her here." I think I would prefer to love Candy *here,* "on earth," Homer Wells was thinking—when Olive interrupted him.

"Homer!" Olive called upstairs. "Where is Pearl Harbor?"

He was the wrong person to ask; Homer Wells had seen the whole world only once, and briefly—and flat against the blackboard. He'd had difficulty locating South Carolina; not only did he not know where Pearl Harbor was, he also didn't know *what* it was.

"I don't know!" he called downstairs.

"Well, the Japanese have just bombed it!" Olive called to him.

"You mean, with planes?" asked Homer Wells. "From the sky?"

"Of course from the sky!" Olive shouted. "You better come listen to this."

"Where is Pearl Harbor?" Candy asked her father.

"Ssshhh!" said Raymond Kendall. "If we just listen, maybe they'll say."

"How could they get away with an attack?" Candy asked.

"Because someone wasn't doing his job," Ray said.

The first reports were garbled. There was mention of California falling under attack, or even being invaded. Many listeners were confused from the beginning; they thought Pearl Harbor was in California.

"Where is Hawaii?" Mrs. Grogan asked. They were having tea and cookies and listening to the radio, for music, when they'd heard the news.

"Hawaii is in the Pacific," said Wilbur Larch.

"Oh, that's very far away," Nurse Edna said.

"Not far enough away," Dr. Larch said.

"There's going to be another war, isn't there?" Nurse Angela asked.

"I guess it's already started," said Wilbur Larch, while Wally—to whom this war would mean the most—watched Fred Astaire; Fred just kept dancing and dancing, and Wally thought he could go on watching such a display of grace for hours.

Melony and Lorna were listening to the radio in the parlor of the boardinghouse where Lorna lived. It was a women-only boardinghouse; the women were either quite old or, like Lorna, only recently separated from their husbands. On this Sunday afternoon, most of the women listening to the radio were old.

"We should just bomb Japan," Melony said. "No messing around—just blow up the whole country."

"You know how come Japs got squinty eyes?" Lorna asked. Melony, and all the old women, listened intently. "Because they masturbate all the time—both the men and the women. They just do it all the time."

There was either a polite or a stunned silence, or both. In Melony's case, her silence was polite.

"Is this a joke?" she asked her friend respectfully.

"Of course it's a joke!" Lorna cried.

"I don't get it, I guess," Melony admitted.

"How come Japs got squinty eyes?" Lorna asked. "Because they masturbate all the time." She paused.

"That's what I thought you said," Melony said.

"Because they shut their eyes every time they come!" Lorna said. "Their eyes get tired from all that opening and closing. That's why they can't open their eyes all the way! Get it?" Lorna asked triumphantly.

Still self-conscious about her teeth, Melony managed a tight-lipped smile. Anyone seeing the old women in the boarding-house parlor would not have known exactly what filled them with fear and trembling: the news of the attack on Pearl Harbor, or Lorna and Melony.

And young Wally Worthington, who was so itchy to be a hero, danced out on the streets of Orono, where he heard the news. President Roosevelt would call it a "day of infamy," but that day meant more than infamy to Wally, whose noble and adventurous heart longed to fly a B-24 Liberator: a heavy bomber, four engines, used for bombing bridges, oil refineries, fuel depots, railroad tracks and so forth. Somewhere, on that "day of infamy," there was a B-24 Liberator bomber waiting for young Wally Worthington to learn how to fly it.

People in Heart's Haven and in Heart's Rock always said that Wally had everything: money, looks, goodness, charm, the girl of his dreams—but he had courage, too, and he had in abundance youth's most dangerous qualities: optimism and restlessness. He would risk everything he had to fly the plane that could carry the bomb within him.

/ / /

Wally enlisted in the Army Air Corps before Christmas, but they allowed him to spend Christmas at home. It would take the Army Air Corps more than a year to teach Wally the grim arts of aerial warfare.

"By that time," he told Olive and Candy in the kitchen at Ocean View, "all the fighting will probably be over. That would be just my luck."

"That *would* be lucky," Olive said. Candy nodded her head.

"Right!" said Homer Wells, from the other room. He was still thinking about being excused from his physical; Dr. Larch's account of Homer's heart history had sufficed. Physical examinations were given only to people who were Class I. Homer Wells was Class IV. According to his family physician, Homer had congenital pulmonic stenosis; Homer's "family physician" was Dr. Larch, whose letter to the local medical advisory board had been accepted as evidence enough for Homer's deferment—Larch was also a member of the local board.

"I asked her to marry me, but she wouldn't," Wally told Homer in their shared bedroom. "She said she'd wait for me, but she wouldn't marry me. She said she'd be my wife, but not my widow."

"Is that what you call waiting and seeing?" Homer asked Candy the next day.

"Yes," Candy said. "For years I've expected to be married to Wally. You came along second. I have to wait and see about you. And now comes the war. I have to wait and see about the war, too."

"But you made him a promise," said Homer Wells.

"Yes," Candy said. "Isn't a promise like waiting and seeing? Did you ever make a promise, and mean it—*and* break it?" Homer Wells's reaction was an involuntary cringe, as sudden and uncontrollable as if Candy had called him "Sunshine."

During Christmas dinner, Raymond Kendall, trying to relieve the silence, said, "I would have chosen submarines."

"You'd end up feeding lobsters," Wally said.

"That's okay," said Ray. "They been feeding me."

"You got a better chance in a plane," Wally said.

"Yes, a *chance,*" Candy said scornfully. "Why would you want to be anywhere where all you get is a *chance*?"

"Good question," Olive said crossly. She let the silver serving fork fall to the meat platter with such force that the goose appeared to flinch.

"A chance is enough," said Homer Wells, who did not immediately recognize the tone in his own voice. "A chance is all we get, right? In the air, or underwater, or right here, from the minute we're born." Or from the minute we're not born, he thought; now he recognized his tone of voice—it was Dr. Larch's.

"That's a rather grim philosophy," Olive said.

"I thought you were studying anatomy," Wally said to Homer, who looked at Candy, who looked away.

They sent Wally to Fort Meade, Maryland, for the month of January. He was a faithful but terrible letter writer; he wrote his mother, he wrote to Homer and to Candy, and even to Ray, but he never explained anything; if there was a plan to what they were teaching him, Wally either didn't know it or couldn't describe it. He simply wrote in tedious detail about the last thing that had occupied his mind before beginning the letter; this included the pouch he had devised to hang from his bunk bed to separate his shoe polish from his toothpaste and the best-name-for-a-plane competition that dominated the imaginative life of Company A. He was also delighted that a cook sergeant had taught him more limericks than Senior, in his last years, had been able to remember. Every letter Wally wrote, to anyone, included a limerick; Ray liked them, and Homer liked them, but they made Candy angry and Olive was appalled. Candy and Homer showed each other the limericks Wally sent them, until Homer realized that this made Candy even angrier: the limericks Wally chose to send Candy were very mild-mannered compared to the ones Wally sent to Homer. For example, he sent this to Candy:

> There was a young lady of Exeter,
> So pretty that men craned their necks at her.
> One was even so brave
> As to take out and wave
> The distinguishing mark of his sex at her.

He sent this to Homer Wells:

> There was a young lady named Brent
> With a cunt of enormous extent
> And so deep and so wide,
> The acoustics inside
> Were so good you could hear when you spent.

Wally sent Ray limericks of a similar kind:

> There's an unbroken babe from Toronto
> Exceedingly hard to get onto
> But when you get there
> And have parted the hair,
> You can fuck her as much as you want to.

God knows what limericks Wally sent to Olive—where does

Wally find ones that are decent enough? wondered Homer, who, in the evenings after Wally had gone and Candy had gone back to school, lay listening to his heart. It would help, he thought, if he knew what to listen for.

Wally was sent to St. Louis—the Jefferson Barracks, Flight 17, 28th School Squadron. It struck Homer Wells that the Army Air Corps might have modeled itself on *Gray's Anatomy*—manifesting a steadfast belief in categories and in everything having a name. It was reassuring to Homer Wells; in his mind, this endless categorizing made Wally safer, but Homer couldn't convince Candy of this.

"He's safe one minute, and in another minute he's not safe," she said, shrugging.

"Look after Homer, look after his heart," Wally had written her.

"And who's looking after *my* heart? Yes, I'm still angry," she wrote him, although he hadn't asked.

But if she was angry with Wally, she was also loyal; she was keeping her promise, about the waiting and seeing. She kissed Homer when she saw him, and when they said good-bye, but she wouldn't encourage him.

"We're just good pals," she told her father; Ray hadn't asked.

"I can see that," Ray said.

The work in the orchards was light that winter; pruning was the main job. The men took turns teaching Homer how to prune. "You make your big cuts in the subfreezing weather," Meany Hyde told him.

"A tree don't bleed so much when it's cold," was how Vernon Lynch put it, hacking away.

"There's less chance of an infection when it's cold," said Herb Fowler, who was not so free with the prophylactics in the winter months, perhaps because he would have needed to take his gloves off to get at them; but Homer felt sure that Herb was being wary ever since Homer had asked him about the holes.

"Are there holes?" Herb had replied. "Manufacturer's defect, I suppose."

But later he'd come up to Homer and whispered to him, "Not all of them's got holes."

"You have a system?" Homer asked. "Which ones have holes and which don't?"

"It's not my system," Herb Fowler said. "Some got holes, some don't. Manufacturer's defect."

"Right," said Homer Wells, but rubbers were rarely flung his way now.

Meany Hyde's wife, Florence, was pregnant again, and all winter Big Dot Taft and Irene Titcomb made jokes about Meany's potency.

"You keep away from me, Meany," Big Dot would say. "I'm not even lettin' you sip my coffee. I think all you gotta do is breathe on somebody and they're pregnant."

"Well, that's all he did to me!" Florence would say, and Big Dot Taft would roar.

"Don'tcha go givin' the men any breathin' lessons, Meany," Irene Titcomb said.

"Meany can knock you up just by kissin' your ears," Florence Hyde said proudly, glorying in her pregnancy.

"Gimme some earmuffs," said Squeeze Louise Tobey. "Gimme one of them ski hats."

"Gimme a dozen of Herb's rubbers!" said Irene Titcomb.

No, don't take any, thought Homer Wells. That's probably how she got that way. Homer was staring at Florence Hyde. It was riveting to him to see someone enjoying her pregnancy.

"Honestly, Homer," said Big Dot Taft, "ain't you ever seen anyone about to have a baby before?"

"Yes," said Homer Wells, who looked away. Grace Lynch was staring at him, and he looked away from her, too.

"If I was your age," Vernon Lynch told Homer, when they were pruning in an orchard called Cock Hill, "I'd enlist. I'd do what Wally's doing."

"I can't," said Homer Wells.

"They don't take orphans?" Vernon asked.

"No," Homer said. "I have a heart defect. Something I was born with."

Vernon Lynch was not a gossip, but that was all that Homer needed to say—the workers at Ocean View not only forgave Homer for not enlisting, they even began to take care of him. They treated him the way Dr. Larch would have liked to see him treated.

"You know, I didn't mean anything," Herb Fowler told Homer. "About the manufacturer's defect. I wouldn't have said that if I'd known about your heart."

"That's okay," Homer said.

And in the early spring, when it was time to mend the boxes for the beehives, Ira Titcomb rushed to assist Homer, who was struggling with a particularly heavy pallet.

"Don't strain yourself, Jesus!" Ira said.

"I can manage, Ira. I'm stronger than you are," Homer said, not understanding—at first—Ira's concern.

"I heard your heart's not as strong as the rest of you," Ira said.

On Mother's Day, Vernon Lynch taught him how to operate the sprayers by himself. He insisted on giving Homer another lecture on the use of the respirator. "You of all people," Vernon told him, "better keep this thing on, and keep it clean."

"Me of all people," said Homer Wells.

Even Debra Pettigrew forgave him for his seemingly undefined friendship with Candy. As the weather warmed up, they went parking again, and one night they managed some lingering kisses in the Pettigrews' unoccupied summer house on Drinkwater Lake; the shut-up, cold smell of the house reminded Homer of his first days in the cider house. When his kisses seemed too calm, Debra grew restless; when his kisses seemed too passionate, Debra said, "Careful! Don't get too excited." He was a young man with unusual kindness, or else he might have suggested to Debra that nothing she allowed him to do would ever endanger his heart.

It was spring. Wally was sent to Kelly Field—San Antonio, Texas—for Air Corps cadet training (Squadron 2, Flight C), and Melony thought that the time was right for her to hit the road again.

"You're crazy," Lorna told her. "The more of a war there is, the more good jobs there are for us. The country needs to build stuff—it don't need to eat more apples."

"Fuck what the country needs," Melony said. "I'm lookin' for Homer Wells, and I'm gonna find him."

"So will I see you next winter?" Lorna asked her friend.

"If I don't find Ocean View or Homer Wells," Melony said.

"So I'll see you next winter," Lorna said. "You're lettin' a man make an asshole out of you."

"That's just what I'm not lettin' him do," Melony said.

Mrs. Grogan's coat had seen better days, but the bundle of belongings contained within the grasp of Charley's belt had grown substantially. Melony had made money in the shipyards, and she'd treated herself to a few sturdy articles of a working-man's clothing, including a good pair of boots. Lorna gave her a present as she was leaving.

"I used to knit," Lorna explained. It was a child's woolen mitten—just the left-hand mitten—and too small for Melony, but the colors were very pretty. "It was gonna be for a baby I never had, 'cause I didn't stay married long enough. I never got the right hand finished." Melony stared at the mitten, which she held in her hand—the mitten was very heavy; it was full of ball bearings that Lorna had swiped from the shipyards. "It's a super weapon," Lorna explained, "in case you meet anyone who's a bigger asshole than you are!"

The gift brought tears to Melony's eyes, and the women hugged each other good-bye. Melony left Bath without saying good-bye to young Mary Agnes Cork, who would have done anything to please her, who asked all her school friends—and everyone who appeared at Ted and Patty Callahan's to browse the antiques—if any of them had ever heard of an apple orchard called Ocean View. If this knowledge might make Melony her friend, Mary Agnes Cork would never stop inquiring. After Melony left Bath, Lorna realized how much she missed her friend; Lorna discovered that she was asking about Ocean View all the time—as if this inquiry was as necessary and loyal a part of her friendship with Melony as the gift of that woolen weapon.

This meant that now there were three of them, all looking for Homer Wells.

/ / /

That summer they moved Wally from San Antonio to Coleman, Texas. "I wish someone would declare war on Texas," he wrote Homer. "That might be some justification for being here." He claimed he was flying in his undershorts and socks—that was all any of them could stand to wear in such unrelenting heat.

"Where does he think he's going?" Candy complained to Homer. "Does he expect a perfect climate? He's going to a *war*!" Homer sat opposite her on Ray Kendall's dock, the snail population forever influenced by their conversation.

In the cool cement-floor classroom at Cape Kenneth High, Homer would unroll the map of the world; there would rarely be anyone present besides the janitor, who was no better informed about geography than Homer Wells. Homer used the summer solitude to study the places of the world where he thought it would be likely that Wally would go.

Once Mr. Hood surprised him in his studies. Perhaps Mr. Hood was visiting his old classroom out of nostalgia, or perhaps it was time to place an order for the next year's rabbits.

"I suppose you'll be enlisting," Mr. Hood said to Homer.

"No, sir," Homer said. "I've got a bad heart—*pulmonary valve stenosis.*"

Mr. Hood stared at Homer's chest; Homer knew that the man had eyes for rabbits only—and not very sharp eyes, at that. "You had a heart murmur, from birth?" Mr. Hood asked.

"Yes, sir," Homer said.

"And do you still have a murmur?" Mr. Hood asked.

"Not much of one, not anymore," Homer said.

"That's not such a bad heart, then," Mr. Hood said encouragingly.

But why would Homer Wells feel that Mr. Hood was an authority? He couldn't keep his *uteri* straight; he didn't know rabbits from sheep.

Even the migrants were different that harvest—they were both older and younger; the men in their prime had enlisted, except for Mr. Rose.

"Slim pickin's for pickers this year," he told Olive. "There's too many fools think the war's more interestin' than pickin' apples."

"Yes, I know," Olive said. "You don't have to tell me about it."

That harvest there was a woman Mr. Rose called Mama, although she wasn't old enough to be any of their mothers. Her allegiance seemed quite exclusively assigned to Mr. Rose; Homer knew this because the woman did what she wanted to do—she picked a little, when she felt like it or when Mr. Rose suggested it; she cooked a little, but she was not the cook every night, and she was not everyone's cook. Some nights she even sat on the roof, but only when Mr. Rose sat there with her. She was a tall, heavy young woman with a deliberate slowness that made her movements seem copied from Mr. Rose, and she wore a nearly constant smile that was not quite relaxed and not quite smirking—also copied from Mr. Rose.

It surprised Homer that no special sleeping arrangements were made regarding the woman; she had her own bed, next to Mr. Rose, but no attempt was made to curtain-off their beds or otherwise construct a little privacy. There was only this: every once in a while, when Homer would drive by the cider house, he would note that everyone except Mr. Rose and his woman was either standing outside the house or sitting on the roof. That must have been their time together, and Mr. Rose must have orchestrated those meetings as deliberately as he appeared to direct everything else.

There was a ban on shore lights by the end of that summer; there was no Ferris wheel to watch at night, no magic lights to call by other names, but these blackout conditions didn't keep the pickers off the roof. They would sit in the dark, looking at the dark, and Mr. Rose would say, "It used to be over there—it was much higher than this roof, and brighter than all the stars if you hitched the stars all together. It went 'round and 'round," Mr. Rose would say, the tall, heavy woman leaning against him, the dark heads above the roofline nodding. "Now there's stuff out there, under the ocean—stuff with bombs, underwater guns. That stuff knows when there's a light on, and the bombs get drawn to the lights—like metal to them magnets. It happens automatically."

"There's no people, holding no triggers?" someone asked.

"There's no triggers," said Mr. Rose. "Everythin's automatic. But there's people. They just there to look the stuff over, make sure it work right."

"There's people out there, under the ocean?" someone asked.

"Sure," said Mr. Rose. "Lots of people. They real smart. They got this stuff so they can see you."

"On land?"

"Sure," said Mr. Rose. "They can see you anywhere."

A kind of communal sighing made the sitters on the roof resemble a chorus resting between numbers. In Wally's bedroom Homer marveled how the world was simultaneously being invented and destroyed.

Nothing marvelous about that, Dr. Larch would have assured him. At St. Cloud's, except for the irritation about sugar stamps and other aspects of the rationing, very little was changed by the war. (Or by what other people once singled out as the Depression, thought Wilbur Larch.)

We are an orphanage; we provide these services; we stay the same—if we're allowed to stay the same, he thought. When he would almost despair, when the ether was too overpowering, when his own age seemed like the last obstacle and the vulnerability of his illegal enterprise was as apparent to him as the silhouettes of the fir trees against the sharp night skies of autumn, Wilbur Larch would save himself with this one thought: I love Homer Wells, and I have saved him from the war.

Homer Wells did not feel saved. Did anyone who was in love and was unsatisfied with how he was loved in return ever feel *saved*? On the contrary, Homer Wells felt that he'd been singled out for special persecution. What young man—even an orphan—is patient enough to wait and see about love? And if Wilbur Larch had saved Homer Wells from the war, even Dr. Larch was powerless to interfere with Melony.

During the harvest that year, Wally moved again—to Perrin Field in Sherman, Texas (basic training, Company D)—but Melony moved five times. She had enough money; she didn't need to work. She took a job in one orchard after another, leaving as soon as she discovered that no one working there had ever heard of an Ocean View. She worked in an orchard in Harpswell, and in another in Arrowsic; she worked as far north as Rockport, and as far inland as Appleton and Lisbon. She took a side trip to Wiscasset because someone told her there was an Ocean View there; there was, but it was a rooming house. An ice-cream vendor told her he'd seen an Ocean View in Friendship; it turned out to be the name of a resident sailboat. Melony got in a fistfight with a head waiter in a seafood restaurant in South Thomaston because she insisted on asking each of the patrons about Ocean View; she won the fight, but she was fined for creating a disturbance; she was a little low on money when she passed through Boothbay Harbor in early November. The sea was slate gray and whitecapped, the pretty boats of summer were in dry dock, the wind had plenty of the coming winter in it; Melony's own pores, as well as the earth's, were closing as tightly as her disappointed heart.

She did not recognize the sallow-faced, sulky juvenile who served the ice-cream sodas to the candy-counter customers in Rinfret's Pharmacy, but young Roy Rinfret—the former (and deeply disappointed) Curly Day—recognized Melony in an instant.

"I used to be Curly Day! Remember me?" Curly asked Melony excitedly. He thrust a lot of free candy and chewing gum at her and insisted on treating her to an ice-cream soda. "A double scooper, on me," Curly said; his adoptive parents would have disapproved.

"Boy, you didn't turn out so good," Melony told him. She meant nothing insulting by this remark; it was a reference to his color, which was pasty, and to his size—he hadn't grown very much. She meant nothing more, but the remark triggered everything that was morose and waiting to be fired in Curly Day.

"You're not kidding, I didn't turn out so good," he said angrily. "I got ditched. Homer Wells stole the people I was meant for."

Melony's teeth were too weak for chewing gum, but she pocketed it, anyway; it would make a nice gift for Lorna. Melony's cavities howled when she sucked hard candy, but she liked it occasionally in spite of this pain—or perhaps because of it—and she had never had an ice-cream soda before.

To demonstrate his loathing for his environment, Curly Day squirted a runny glob of strawberry syrup on the floor—checking, first, to be sure that only Melony could see. He did this as if he were exercising the nozzle before he squirted the stuff on Melony's soda. "It draws ants," he explained; Melony doubted there were many ants left in November. "That's what they're always telling me," Curly said. " 'Don't spill, it draws ants.' " He squirted the floor a few more times. "I'm tryin' to get the ants to carry this place away."

"You still pissed at Homer Wells?" Melony asked him slyly.

She explained that Curly should simply inquire—of every customer—about Ocean View. Curly had never thought concretely about what he would do or say to Homer Wells if he ever encountered him again; he was resentful, but he was not a vengeful boy and he had a sudden, clear memory of Melony's violence. He became suspicious.

"What do you want to find Homer for?" Curly asked.

"What *for*?" Melony asked sweetly; it wasn't clear if she had considered it. "Well, what would *you* like to find him for, Curly?" she asked.

"Well," Curly said, struggling. "I guess I'd just like to see him, and tell him that I was really fucked up by his going off and leaving me there—when I thought I was the one who should be going, instead of him." When Curly thought about it, he realized he'd just like to see Homer Wells—maybe be his friend, maybe do stuff together. He'd always admired Homer. If he felt a little deserted by him, that was all he felt. He started to cry. Melony used the paper napkin that went with her ice-cream soda to wipe Curly's tears for him.

"Hey, I know what you mean," she said nicely. "I know how you feel. I got left, too, you know. Really, I just miss the guy. I just want to see him."

Curly's weeping attracted the attention of one of his adoptive parents, Mr. Rinfret, the pharmacist, who was stationed in that end of the store where the serious drugs were dispensed.

"I'm from Saint Cloud's," Melony explained to Mr. Rinfret. "We were all so close there—whenever we run into each other, it takes a little gettin' used to." She hugged Curly in a motherly, if somewhat burly, way, and Mr. Rinfret allowed them their privacy.

"Try to remember, Curly," Melony whispered, rocking the boy in her arms as if she were telling him a bedtime story. "Ocean View, just keep asking about Ocean View." When she calmed him down, she gave him Lorna's address in Bath.

On her way back to Bath, Melony hoped that the shipyards would hire her back and that the so-called war effort would keep the stuff on the assembly line changing—that she might look forward to a task somewhat different from the insertion of those ball bearings into that hamlike sprocket. With that thought she removed Lorna's gift mitten from the pocket of Mrs. Grogan's overcoat; she had not yet needed it as a weapon but many nights its presence had comforted her. And it's not been a thoroughly wasted year, Melony reflected warmly, socking the heavy mitten with a painful smack into the palm of her big hand. Now there are four of us looking for you, Sunshine.

/ / /

They kept Wally in Texas, yet they moved him once more—to Lubbock Flying School (Barracks 12, D3). He would spend November and most of December there, but the Army Air Corps had promised to send him home for Christmas.

"Soon to be in the bosom of my family!" he wrote to Candy, and Homer, and Olive—and even to Ray, who had contributed to the war effort by joining the force of mechanics at the Navy Yard in Kittery; Ray was building torpedoes. He had hired some local boys who were still in school to help him keep his lobster business from sinking, and he worked on the vehicles at Ocean View on the weekends. He enthusiastically demonstrated the gyroscope on Olive's kitchen table to Olive and Homer Wells.

"Before a fella can fathom the torpedo," Ray liked to say, "he has to understand the gyroscope." Homer was interested, Olive was polite—and what's more, thoroughly dependent on Ray; if he didn't fix all the machinery at Ocean View, Olive was convinced that the apples would stop growing.

Candy was cross much of the time—everyone's war effort seemed to depress her, although she had volunteered to pitch in herself and had worked some very long hours at the Cape Kenneth Hospital as a nurse's aide. She agreed it would be "indulgent" to go to college, and she'd had no trouble convincing Homer that he should pitch in, too—with his background, he could be a more useful nurse's aide than most.

"Right," Homer had said.

But if Homer had returned to a semi-hospital life against his will, he soon found he felt comfortable there; however, it was at times difficult to withhold his expert opinion on certain subjects and to play the beginner in a role he was disquietingly born to. Even the nurses were condescending to the nurse's aides, and Homer was irritated to see that the doctors were condescending to everyone—most of all, to their patients.

Candy and Homer were not allowed to give shots or medication, but they had more to do than make beds, empty bedpans, give back rubs and baths, and run those errands of friendliness that gave the modern hospital such a constant scuff of feet. They were given delivery-room duties, for example; Homer was unimpressed with the obstetrical procedure he witnessed. It could not hold a candle to Dr. Larch's work, and in some cases it could not hold a candle to his own. If Dr. Larch had often criticized Homer for his heavy touch with ether, Homer could not imagine how the old man would react to the heavy-handedness that was applied to that inhalation at Cape Kenneth Hospital. In St. Cloud's, Homer had seen many patients who were so lightly etherized that they could converse throughout their own operations; in Cape Kenneth's recovery rooms, the patients struggling to emerge from their ether doses looked bludgeoned—they snored gap-mouthed, with their hands hanging deadweight and the muscles in their cheeks so slack that at times their eyes were pulled half open.

It especially angered Homer to see how they dosed the children—as if the doctors or the anesthesiologists were so uninformed that they didn't pause to consider the patient's body weight.

One day he sat with Candy on either side of a five-year-old boy who was recovering from a tonsillectomy. That was nurse's aide work: you sat with the patients coming out of ether, especially the children, especially the tonsillectomies—they were often frightened and in pain and nauseous when they woke. Homer claimed they wouldn't be nearly so nauseous if they'd been given a little less ether.

One of the nurses was in the recovery room with them; it was the one they liked—a young, homely girl about their age. Her name was Caroline, and she was nice to the patients and tough to the doctors.

"You know a lot about ether, Homer," Nurse Caroline said.

"It seems overused to me, in certain cases," Homer mumbled.

"Hospitals aren't perfect, they're just expected to be," Nurse Caroline said. "And doctors aren't perfect, either; they just think they are."

"Right," said Homer Wells.

The five-year-old's throat was very sore when he finally woke up, and he went on retching for quite some time before any ice cream would slide down his throat, and stay down. One of the things the nurse's aides did was to be sure that the children, in such condition, didn't choke on their own vomit. Homer explained to Candy that it was very important that the child, in a semi-etherized state, not *aspirate,* or inhale, any fluid such as vomit into the lungs.

"Aspirate," Nurse Caroline said. "Was your father a doctor, Homer?"

"Not exactly," said Homer Wells.

It was Nurse Caroline who introduced Homer to young Dr. Harlow, who was in the throes of growing out his bangs; a cowlick persisted in making his forehead look meager; a floppy shelf of straw-colored hair gave Dr. Harlow's eyes the constant anxiousness of someone peering from under the brim of a hat.

"Oh yes, Wells—our ether expert," Dr. Harlow said snidely.

"I grew up in an orphanage," said Homer Wells. "I did a lot of helping out around the hospital."

"But surely you never administered any ether?" said Dr. Harlow.

"Surely not," lied Homer Wells. As Dr. Larch had discovered with the board of trustees, it was especially gratifying to lie to unlikable people.

"Don't show off," Candy told Homer when they were driving back to Heart's Haven together. "It doesn't become you, and it could get your Doctor Larch in trouble."

"When did I show off?" Homer asked.

"You really haven't, yet," Candy said. "Just don't, okay?" Homer sulked.

"And don't sulk," Candy told him. "That doesn't become you, either."

"I'm just waiting and seeing," said Homer Wells. "You know how that is." He let her out at the lobster pound; he usually came in with her and chatted with Ray. But Homer was mistaken to confuse Candy's irritability either with coldness toward him or with anything but the profoundest confusion of her own.

She slammed the door and walked around to his side of the van before he could drive away. She indicated he should roll down his window. Then she leaned inside and kissed him on the mouth, she yanked his hair, hard—with both hands, tilting his head back—and then she bit him, quite sharply, in the throat. She banged her head on the window frame when she pulled herself back from him; her eyes were watery, but no tears spilled to her face.

"Do you think I'm having a good time?" she asked him. "Do you think I'm teasing you? Do you think I *know* whether I want you or Wally?"

He drove back to Cape Kenneth Hospital; he needed work more substantial than mousing. It was the Goddamn mousing season again—how he hated handling the poison!

He arrived simultaneously with a sailor slashed up in a knife fight; it had happened where Ray worked—in Kittery Navy Yard—and the sailor's buddies had driven him around in a makeshift tourniquet, running out of gas coupons and getting lost on the way to several hospitals much nearer to the scene of the fight than the one in Cape Kenneth. The gash, into the fleshy web between the sailor's thumb and forefinger, extended nearly to the sailor's wrist. Homer helped Nurse Caroline wash the wound with ordinary white soap and sterile water. Homer could not help himself—he was accustomed to speaking to Nurse Angela and to Nurse Edna in the voice of an authority.

"Take his blood pressure, opposite arm," he said to Nurse Caroline, "and put the blood-pressure cuff on over a bandage—to protect the skin," he added, because Nurse Caroline was staring at him curiously. "The cuff might have to be on there for a half hour or more," said Homer Wells.

"I think *I* can give instructions to Nurse Caroline, if you don't mind," Dr. Harlow said to Homer; both the doctor and his nurse stared at Homer Wells as if they had witnessed an ordinary animal touched with divine powers—as if they half expected Homer to pass his hand over the profusely bleeding sailor and stop the flow of blood as quickly as the tourniquet stopped it.

"Very neat job, Wells," Dr. Harlow said. Homer observed the injection of the 0.5 percent Procaine into the wound and the subsequent probing of Dr. Harlow. The knife had entered on the palmar side of the hand, observed Homer Wells. He remembered his *Gray's,* and he remembered the movie he had seen with Debra Pettigrew: the cavalry officer with the arrow in his hand, the arrow that fortunately missed the branch of the median nerve that goes to the muscles of the thumb. He watched the sailor move his thumb.

Dr. Harlow was looking. "There's a rather important branch of the median nerve," Dr. Harlow said slowly, to the cut-up sailor. "You're lucky if that's not cut."

"The knife missed it," said Homer Wells.

"Yes, it did," said Dr. Harlow, looking up from the wound. "How do *you* know?" he asked Homer Wells, who held up the thumb of his right hand and wiggled it.

"Not only an ether expert, I see," said Dr. Harlow, still snidely. "Knows all about muscles, too!"

"Just about that one," said Homer Wells. "I used to read *Gray's Anatomy*—for fun," he added.

"For *fun*?" said Dr. Harlow. "I suppose you know all about blood vessels, then. Why not tell me where all this blood is coming from."

Homer Wells felt Nurse Caroline brush his hand with her hip; it was surely sympathetic contact—Nurse Caroline didn't care for Dr. Harlow, either. Despite Candy's certain disapproval, Homer couldn't help himself. "The blood vessel is a branch of the palmar arch," he said.

"Very good," said Dr. Harlow, disappointed. "And what would you recommend I do about it?"

"Tie it," said Homer Wells. "Three-o chromic."

"Precisely," said Dr. Harlow. "You didn't get that from *Gray's*." He pointed out to Homer Wells that the knife had also cut the tendons of the *flexor digitorum profundus* and the *flexor digitorum sublimis*. "And where might they go?" he asked Homer Wells.

"To the index finger," Homer said.

"Is it necessary to repair both tendons?" asked Dr. Harlow.

"I don't know," said Homer Wells. "I don't know a lot about tendons," he added.

"How surprising!" said Dr. Harlow. "It is only necessary to repair the *profundus*," he explained. "I'm going to use two-o silk. I'll need something finer to bring the edges of the tendon together."

"Four-o silk," recommended Homer Wells.

"Very good," said Dr. Harlow. "And something to close the palmar *fascia*?"

"Three-o chromic," said Homer Wells.

"This boy knows his stitches!" Dr. Harlow said to Nurse Caroline, who was staring intently at Homer Wells.

"Close the skin with four-o silk," Homer said. "And then I'd recommend a pressure dressing on the palm—you'll want to curve the fingers a little bit around the dressing."

"That's called 'the position of function,' " Dr. Harlow said.

"I don't know what it's called," Homer said.

"Were you ever in medical school, Wells?" Dr. Harlow asked him.

"Not exactly," said Homer Wells.

"Do you plan to go?" Dr. Harlow asked.

"It's not likely," Homer said. He tried to leave the operating room then, but Dr. Harlow called after him.

"Why aren't you in the service?" he called.

"I've got a heart problem," Homer said.

"I don't suppose you know what it's called," said Dr. Harlow.

"Right," said Homer Wells.

He might have found out about his pulmonary valve stenosis on the spot, if he had only asked; he might have had an X ray, and an expert reading—he could have learned the truth. But who seeks the truth from unlikable sources?

He went and read some stories to the tonsillectomy patients. They were all dumb stories—children's books didn't impress Homer Wells. But the tonsillectomy patients were not likely to be around long enough to hear *David Copperfield* or *Great Expectations*.

Nurse Caroline asked him if he would give a bath and a back rub to the large man recovering from the prostate operation.

"Don't ever underestimate the pleasure of pissing," the big man told Homer Wells.

"No, sir," Homer said, rubbing the mountain of flesh until the big man shone a healthy pink.

Olive was not home when Homer returned to Ocean View; it was her time for plane spotting. They used what was called the yacht-watching tower at the Haven Club, but Homer didn't think any planes had been spotted. All the men spotters—most of them Senior's former drinking companions—had the silhouettes of the enemy planes tacked on their lockers; the women brought the silhouettes home and stuck them on places like the refrigerator door. Olive was a plane spotter for two hours every day.

Homer studied the silhouettes that Olive had on the refrigerator.

I could learn all those, he was thinking. And I can learn everything there is to know about apple farming. But what he already knew, he knew, was near-perfect obstetrical procedure and the far easier procedure—the one that was against the rules.

He thought about rules. That sailor with the slashed hand had not been in a knife fight that was according to anyone's rules. In a fight with Mr. Rose, there would be Mr. Rose's own rules, whatever they were. A knife fight with Mr. Rose would be like being pecked to death by a small bird, thought Homer Wells. Mr. Rose was an artist—he would take just the tip of a nose, just a button or a nipple. The *real* cider house rules were Mr. Rose's.

And what were the rules at St. Cloud's? What were Larch's rules? Which rules did Dr. Larch observe, which ones did he break, or replace—and with what confidence? Clearly Candy was observing some rules, but whose? And did Wally know what the rules were? And Melony—did Melony obey *any* rules? wondered Homer Wells.

/ / /

"Look," said Lorna. "There's a war, have you noticed?"

"So what?" said Melony.

"Because he's probably in it, that's so what!" Lorna said. "Because he either enlisted or he's gonna get drafted."

Melony shook her head. "I can't see him in a war, not him. He just doesn't belong there."

"For Christ's sake," Lorna said. "You think everyone in a war *belongs* there?"

"If he goes, then he'll come back," Melony said. The ice on the Kennebec in December was not secure; it was a tidal river, it was brackish, and there was open water, gray and choppy, in the middle. But not even Melony could throw a beer bottle as far as the middle of that river in Bath. Her bottle, bouncing off the creaky ice, made a hollow sound and rolled toward the open water it couldn't reach. It disturbed a gull, who got up and walked a short way along the ice, like an old woman holding up a number of cumbersome petticoats above a puddle.

"Not everyone's comin' back from this war—that's all I'm sayin'," Lorna replied.

/ / /

Wally had trouble coming back from Texas. There were a series of delays, and bad weather; the landing field was closed—when Homer and Candy picked him up in Boston, the first thing he told them was that he had only forty-eight hours. He was still happy, however—"He was still Wally," Candy would say later—and especially pleased that he'd received his commission.

"Second Lieutenant Worthington!" Wally announced to Olive. Everyone cried, even Ray.

With the gas rationing, they couldn't manage the usual driving around and around. Homer wondered when Wally would want to be alone with Candy and how they would manage it. Surely *he* wants to manage it, Homer thought. Does *she* want to, too? he wondered.

For Christmas Eve everyone was together. And Christmas Day there was nowhere to go; Olive was home, and Ray wasn't building torpedoes or pulling lobster traps. And the day after Christmas, Candy and Homer would have to take Wally back to Boston.

Oh, Candy and Wally did plenty of hugging and kissing—everyone could see that. On Christmas night, in Wally's bedroom, Homer realized that he'd been so glad to see Wally that he'd forgotten to notice very much about his second Christmas away from St. Cloud's. He also realized he'd forgotten to send Dr. Larch anything—not even a Christmas card.

"I've got more flying school to get through," Wally was saying, "but I think it's going to be India for me."

"India," said Homer Wells.

"The Burma run," said Wally. "To go from India to China, you got to go over Burma. The Japs are in Burma."

Homer Wells had studied the maps at Cape Kenneth High. He knew that Burma was mountains, that Burma was jungles. When they shot your plane down, there would be quite a wide range of possible things to land on.

"How are things with Candy?" Homer asked.

"Great!" Wally said. "Well, I'll see tomorrow," he added.

Ray went early to build the torpedoes, and Homer observed that Wally left Ocean View at about the same time Ray would be leaving for Kittery. Homer spent the early morning being of little comfort to Olive. "Forty-eight hours is not what I'd call coming home," she said. "He hasn't been here for a year—does he call this a proper visit? Does the Army call it a proper visit?"

Candy and Wally came to pick up Homer before noon. Homer imagined that they had "managed it." But how does one know such things, short of asking?

"Do you want me to drive?" Homer asked; he had the window seat, and Candy sat between them.

"Why?" Wally asked.

"Maybe you want to hold hands," Homer said; Candy looked at him.

"We've already held hands," Wally said, laughing. "But thank you, anyway!"

Candy did not look amused, Homer thought.

"So you've done it, you mean?" Homer Wells asked them both.

Candy stared straight ahead, and Wally didn't laugh this time.

"What's that, old boy?" he asked.

"I said, 'So you've done it?'—had sex, I mean," said Homer Wells.

"Jesus, Homer," said Wally. "That's a fine thing to ask."

"Yes, we've done it—had sex," Candy said, still looking straight ahead.

"I hope you were careful," Homer said, to both of them. "I hope you took some precautions."

"Jesus, Homer!" Wally said.

"Yes, we were careful," Candy said. Now she stared at him, her look as neutral as possible.

"Well, I'm glad you were careful," Homer said, speaking

directly to Candy. "You should be careful—having sex with someone who's about to fly over Burma."

"Burma?" Candy turned to Wally. "You didn't say where you were going," she said. "Is it Burma?"

"I don't know where I'm going," Wally said irritably. "Jesus, Homer, what's the matter with you?"

"I love you both," said Homer Wells. "If I love you, I've got a right to ask anything I want—I've got a right to know anything I want to know."

It was, as they say in Maine, a real conversation stopper. They rode almost all the way to Boston in silence, except that Wally said—trying to be funny—"I don't know about you, Homer. You're becoming very philosophical."

It was a rough good-bye. "I love you both, too—you know," Wally said, in parting.

"I know you do," Homer said.

On the way home, Candy said to Homer Wells: "I wouldn't say 'philosophical'; I would say *eccentric.* You're becoming very eccentric, in my opinion. And you *don't* have a right to know everything about me, whether you love me or not."

"All you've got to know is, do you really love him?" Homer said. "Do you love Wally?"

"I've grown up loving Wally," Candy said. "I have always loved Wally, and I always will."

"Fine," Homer said. "That's all there is to it, then."

"But I don't even know Wally, anymore," Candy said. "I know you better, and I love you, too."

Homer Wells sighed. So we're in for more waiting and seeing, he thought. His feelings were hurt: Wally hadn't once asked him about his heart. What would he have answered, anyway?

Wilbur Larch, who knew that there was absolutely nothing wrong with Homer's heart, wondered *where* Homer's heart was. Not in St. Cloud's, he feared.

And Wally went to Victorville, California—advanced flying school. U.S. ARMY AIR FORCES—that is what his stationery said. Wally spent several months in Victorville—all the pruning months, as Homer Wells would remember them. Shortly after apple blossom time, when Ira Titcomb's bees had spread their marvelous life energies through the orchards of Ocean View, Wally was sent to India.

The Japanese held Mandalay. Wally dropped his first bombs

on the railroad bridge in Myitnge. Tracks and the embankment of the south approach were badly smashed, and the south span of the bridge was destroyed. All aircraft and crews returned safely. Wally also dropped his bombs on the industrial area of Myingyan, but heavy clouds prevented adequate observation of the destruction. In that summer, when Homer Wells was painting the cider house white again, Wally bombed the jetty at Akyab and the Shweli bridge in northern Burma; later he hit the railroad yards at Prome. He contributed to the ten tons of bombs that were dropped on the railroad yards at Shwebo, and to the fires that were left burning in the warehouses at Kawlin and Thanbyuzayat. The most spectacular hits he would remember were in the oil fields in Yenangyat—the sight of those oil derricks ablaze would stay with Wally on his return flight, across the jungles, across the mountains. All aircraft and crews returned safely.

They made him a captain and gave him what he called "easy work."

"Always be suspicious of easy work," Dr. Wilbur Larch once said to Homer Wells.

Wally had won the best-name-for-a-plane competition at Fort Meade; now he finally got to use it; he got to name his own plane. *Opportunity Knocks,* he called it. The painted fist under the inscription looked very authoritative. It would later puzzle Candy and Homer Wells that the name was not *Knocks Once* (or *Twice*), but just *Knocks.*

He flew the India–China route, over the Himalayas—over Burma. He carried gasoline and bombs and artillery and rifles and ammunition and clothing and aircraft engines and spare parts and food to China; he brought military personnel back to India. It was a seven-hour, round-trip flight—about five hundred miles. For six of the hours he wore an oxygen mask—they had to fly so high. Over the mountains they flew high because of the mountains; over the jungles they flew high because of the Japanese. The Himalayas have the most vicious air currents in the world.

When he left Assam, the temperature was a hundred and ten degrees, Fahrenheit. It was like Texas, Wally would think. They wore just their shorts and socks.

The heavily loaded transports needed to climb to fifteen thousand feet in thirty-five minutes; that was when they reached the first mountain pass.

At nine thousand feet, Wally put on his pants. At fourteen thousand, he put on the fleece-lined suit. It was twenty degrees below zero up there. In the monsoon weather, they flew mostly on instrument.

They called that aerial route "the lifeline"; they called it flying "over the hump."

Here were the headlines on the Fourth of July:

YANKS WRECK RAIL BRIDGE IN BURMA
CHINESE ROUT JAPS IN HUPEH PROVINCE

Here is what Wally wrote to Candy, and to Homer. Wally was getting lazy; he sent the same limerick to both:

> There was a young man of Bombay
> Who fashioned a cunt out of clay,
> But the heat of his prick
> Turned it into a brick,
> And chafed all his foreskin away.

That summer of 194__ the public interest in keeping use of the shore lights to a minimum forced the temporary closing of the Cape Kenneth Drive-In Theater, which Homer Wells did not feel as a tragic loss. Since he would have had no choice but to attend the movies with Candy *and* Debra Pettigrew, he was grateful to the war effort for sparing him that awkwardness.

Mr. Rose informed Olive that he would be unable to provide a worthwhile picking crew for the harvest. "Considering the men who are gone," he wrote. "And the travel. I mean the gas rationing."

"Then we've spruced up the cider house for nothing," Homer said to Olive.

"Nothing is ever improved for nothing, Homer," she said. The Yankee justification for hard work in the summer months is both desperate and undone by the rare pleasure of that fleeting season.

Homer Wells—nurse's aide and orchardman—was mowing in the rows between the trees when the news came to him. On a sweltering June day, he was driving the International Harvester and he had his eye on the sickle bar; he didn't want to snag a stump or a fallen branch; for that reason he didn't see the green van, which was trying to head him off. He almost ran into it. Because the tractor was running—and the mower blades, too—he didn't hear what Candy was yelling when she jumped out of the van and ran to him. Olive was driving, her face a stone.

"Shot down!" Candy was screaming, when Homer finally shut off the ignition. "He was shot down—over Burma!"

"Over Burma," said Homer Wells. He dismounted from the tractor and held the sobbing girl in his arms. The tractor was shut off but the engine still knocked, and then shuddered, and then throbbed; its heat made the air shimmer. Maybe, thought Homer Wells, the air is always shimmering over Burma.

9/ Over Burma

Two weeks after Wally's plane was shot down, Captain Worthington and the crew of *Opportunity Knocks* were still listed as missing.

A plane making the same run had noted that approximately one square mile of the Burmese jungle, roughly halfway between India and China, had been consumed by fire—presumably caused by the exploding plane; the cargo was identified as jeep engines, spare parts and gasoline. There was no evidence of the crew; the jungle was dense in that area and believed to be unpopulated.

A spokesman for the U.S. Army Air Forces paid a personal visit to Olive and told her that there was some reason to be optimistic. That the plane obviously had not exploded in the air meant that the crew might have had time to bail out. What would have happened afterward was anyone's guess.

That would have been a better name for the plane, thought Homer Wells: *"Anyone's Guess."* But Homer was supportive of Olive and Candy's view that Wally was not dead, that he was "just missing." Privately, Homer and Ray Kendall agreed that there wasn't much hope for Wally.

"Just suppose he didn't go down with the plane," Ray said to Homer, when they were pulling lobster pots. "So then he's in the middle of the jungle, and what does he do there? He can't let the Japs find him, and there's got to be Japs around—they shot down the plane, didn't they?"

"There could be natives," said Homer Wells. "Friendly Burmese villagers," he suggested.

"Or nobody at all," Ray Kendall said. "Some tigers, and lots of snakes," he added. "Aw, shit. He shoulda been in a submarine."

"If your friend survived all the rest," wrote Wilbur Larch to Homer Wells, "he's got all the diseases of Asia to worry about—lots of diseases."

It was horrible to imagine Wally suffering, and not even Homer's longing for Candy could allow him any comfort with the idea that Wally was already dead; in that case, Homer knew, Candy would always imagine that she loved Wally best. Reality, for orphans, is so often outdistanced by their ideals; if Homer wanted Candy, he wanted her *ideally*. In order for Candy to choose Homer, Wally had to be alive; and because Homer loved Wally, he also wanted Wally's blessing. Wouldn't any other way be compromising to them all?

Wilbur Larch was flattered that Homer asked his advice—and on a matter of romantic love, of all things! ("How should I behave with Candy?" Homer had asked.) The old man was used to being such an authority that he found it natural to assume an authoritative voice—"Even regarding a subject he knows nothing about!" Nurse Angela said to Nurse Edna indignantly. Larch was so proud of what he had written Homer that he showed his letter to his old nurses before sending it along.

"Have you forgotten what life is like at St. Cloud's?" Dr. Larch asked Homer. "Have you drifted so far away from us that you find a life of compromise to be unacceptable? And you, an orphan—of all people. Have you forgotten how to be of use? Don't think so badly of compromises; we don't always get to choose the ways we can be of use. You say you love her—then let her use you. It may not be the way you had in mind, but if you love her, you have to give her what she needs—and when she needs it, not necessarily when you think the time is right. And what can she give you of herself? Only what she has left—and if that's not everything you had in mind, whose fault is that? Are you not going to accept her because she hasn't got 100 percent of herself to give? Some of her is over Burma—are you going to reject the rest? Are you going to hold out for all or nothing? And do you call that being of use?"

"It's not very romantic," Nurse Angela said to Nurse Edna.

"When was Wilbur ever romantic?" Nurse Edna asked.

"Your advice is awfully utilitarian," Nurse Angela said to Dr. Larch.

"Well, I should hope so!" Dr. Larch said, sealing the letter.

Now Homer had a companion in sleeplessness. He and Candy preferred the night shift at Cape Kenneth Hospital. When there was a lull in their work, they were allowed to doze on the beds in the children's noncommunicable ward. Homer found that the music of the restless children soothed him—their troubles and pains familiar, their whimpers and outcries and night terrors transporting him beyond his own anxieties. And Candy felt that the drawn, black curtains in the nighttime hospital were suitable for mourning. The prevailing blackout conditions—which she and Homer had to observe in driving to and from the hospital, if it was after dark—were also to Candy's liking. They used Wally's Cadillac for these occasions—they were permitted to travel with only parking lights on, and the Cadillac's parking lights were the brightest. Even so, the dark coastal roads seemed barely lit; they drove at funeral speed. If the stationmaster at St. Cloud's (formerly, the stationmaster's assistant) had ever seen them passing, he would have thought again that they were driving a white hearse.

Meany Hyde, whose wife, Florence, was expecting, told Homer that he was sure his new baby would share something of Wally's soul (if Wally was truly dead)—and if Wally was alive, Meany said, the appearance of the new baby would signify Wally's escape from Burma. Everett Taft told Homer that his wife, Big Dot, had been plagued by dreams that could only mean that Wally was struggling to communicate with Ocean View. Even Ray Kendall, dividing his underwater attention between his lobsters and his torpedoes, said that he was "reading" his lobster pots, by which he meant that he found the content of the traps hauled from the deep to be worthy of interpretation. Untouched bait was a special sign; if the lobsters (which prefer food that's truly dead) wouldn't take the bait, it must mean that the bait was manifesting a living spirit.

"And you know I ain't religious," Ray said to Homer.

"Right," Homer said.

Because Homer Wells had spent many years wondering if his mother would ever return to claim him, if she even thought about him, if she was alive or dead, he was better at accepting Wally's undefined status than the rest of them were. An orphan understands what it means that someone important is "just missing." Olive and Candy, mistaking Homer's composure for indifference, were occasionally short-tempered with him.

"I'm only doing what we all have to do," he said—reserving special emphasis for Candy. "I'm just waiting and seeing."

There were few fireworks that Fourth of July; for one thing, they would have violated the blackout conditions, and for another, any simulation of bombs and gunfire would have been disrespectful to those among "our boys" who were facing the real music. In the nighttime hospital at Cape Kenneth, the nurse's aides conducted a quiet Independence Day celebration, which was interrupted by the hysterics of a woman who demanded an abortion from the young and imperious Dr. Harlow, who believed in obeying the law. "But there is a war!" the woman countered. Her husband was dead; he'd been killed in the Pacific; she had the wire from the War Department to prove it. She was nineteen, and not quite three months pregnant.

"I'll be glad to speak with her again, when she's behaving reasonably," Dr. Harlow told Nurse Caroline.

"Why should she behave reasonably?" Nurse Caroline asked him.

Homer Wells had to trust his instincts regarding Nurse Caroline; besides, she had told him and Candy that she was a socialist. "And I'm not pretty," she added truthfully. "Therefore, I'm not interested in marriage. In my case, I'd be expected to appear grateful—or, at least, to consider myself lucky."

The hysterical woman would not be calmed, perhaps because Nurse Caroline's heart wasn't in it. "I'm not asking for anything *secret*!" the woman shouted. "Why should I have to have this baby?"

Homer Wells found a piece of paper with columns for laboratory analysis. He wrote the following across the columns:

YOU GO TO ST. CLOUD'S, YOU ASK FOR THE ORPHANAGE.

He gave the piece of paper to Candy, who gave it to Nurse Caroline—who looked at it before she gave it to the woman, who instantly stopped protesting.

When the woman had gone, Nurse Caroline made Homer and Candy accompany her to the dispensary.

"I'll tell you what I usually do," Nurse Caroline said, as if she were furious with them. "I perform a perfectly safe dilatation without the curettage. I just dilate the cervix. I do this in my kitchen, and I'm very careful. They have to come to the hospital for a completion, of course. Someone might think they tried to do it to themselves, but there's no infection and nothing's damaged; they've just miscarried. They've had the D without the C. All they need is a good scraping. And the bastards have to be accommodating—there's all the bleeding, and it's clear the woman's already lost it." She paused, and glared at Homer Wells. "You're an expert about this, too, aren't you?"

"Right," Homer said.

"And you know a better way than my way?" she asked.

"Not that much better," he said. "It's a complete D and C, and the doctor is a gentleman."

"A gentleman," Nurse Caroline said doubtfully. "What's the gentleman cost?"

"He's free," Homer said.

"I'm free, too," Nurse Caroline said.

"He asks you to make a donation to the orphanage, if you can afford it," said Homer Wells.

"Why hasn't he been caught?" Nurse Caroline asked.

"I don't know," Homer said. "Maybe people are grateful."

"People are people," Nurse Caroline said, in her socialist voice. "You took a stupid chance, telling me. And a more stupid chance telling that woman—you don't even know her."

"Yes," Homer agreed.

"Your doctor isn't going to last if you keep that up," Nurse Caroline said.

"Right," Homer said.

Dr. Harlow found them all in the dispensary; only Candy looked guilty, and therefore he stared at her.

"What are these two experts telling you?" Dr. Harlow asked. He spent a lot of time looking at Candy when he thought no one saw him, but Homer Wells saw him and Nurse Caroline was very sensitive to the longings other women inspired. Candy was tongue-tied, which made her seem more guilty, and Dr. Harlow turned to Nurse Caroline. "You got rid of the hysteric?" he asked her.

"No problem," Nurse Caroline said.

"I know that you disapprove," Dr. Harlow told her, "but rules exist for reasons."

"Rules exist for reasons," said Homer Wells, uncontrollably;

it was such a stupid thing to say, he felt compelled to repeat it. Dr. Harlow stared at him.

"No doubt you're an abortion expert, too, Wells," Dr. Harlow said.

"It's not very hard to be an abortion expert," Homer Wells said. "It's a pretty easy thing to do."

"You think so?" Dr. Harlow asked aggressively.

"Well, what do I know?" Homer Wells said, shrugging.

"Yes, what do you know?" Dr. Harlow said.

"Not much," Nurse Caroline said gruffly; even Dr. Harlow appreciated this. Even Candy smiled. Homer Wells smiled sheepishly, too. *You see? I'm getting smarter!* That is what he smiled to Nurse Caroline, who viewed him with an expression of condescension that was proper for nurses to exhibit only to nurse's aides. Dr. Harlow seemed to feel that the pecking order he revered was being treated with the reverence that was mandatory from them all. A kind of glaze appeared to coat his face, a texture composed of righteousness and adrenaline. Homer Wells gave himself a brief sensation of pleasure by imagining something that could wake up Dr. Harlow, and humble him. Mr. Rose's knife work might have that effect on Dr. Harlow—Homer imagined Mr. Rose undressing Dr. Harlow with his knife; every article of clothing would be gathered around the doctor's ankles, in strips and tatters, yet on the doctor's naked body there wouldn't be a scratch.

/ / /

A month after Wally's plane was shot down, they heard from the crew of *Opportunity Knocks.*

"We were halfway to China," the co-pilot wrote, "when the Nips took some potshots. Captain Worthington ordered the crew to bail out."

The crew chief and the radioman jumped close together; the co-pilot jumped third. The roof of the jungle was so dense that when the first man crashed through it, he could not see the other parachutes. The jungle itself was so thick that the crew chief had to search for the others—it took him seven hours to find the radioman. The rain was so heavy—it made such a din against the broad palm leaves—none of the men heard the plane explode. The atmosphere was so rich with its own scents that the smell of the burning gasoline and the smoke from the fire never reached them. They wondered if the plane had not miraculously recovered itself and flown on. When they looked up, they could not see through the treetops (which everywhere glittered with bright green pigeons).

In seven hours, the crew chief contacted thirteen leeches of various sizes—which the radioman thoughtfully removed; the crew chief plucked fifteen leeches off the radioman. They found that the best way to remove the leeches was to touch the lighted end of a cigarette to their posterior ends; that way, they would release their contact with the flesh. If you just pulled them, they kept breaking; their strong sucking mouths would remain attached.

The radioman and the crew chief ate nothing for five days. When it rained—which it did, most of the time—they drank the rainwater that gathered in puddles in the big palm leaves. They were afraid to drink the other water they encountered. In some of the water they thought they saw crocodiles. Because the radioman was afraid of snakes, the crew chief did not point out the snakes he saw; the crew chief was afraid of tigers, and he thought he saw one, once, but the radioman maintained that they only heard a tiger, or several tigers—or the same tiger several times. The crew chief said that the same tiger followed them for five days.

The leeches tired them out, they said. Although the roof of the jungle made the pelting rain louder, it did keep the rain from falling directly on the two men; yet the jungle was so saturated that the rain almost constantly dripped on them—and when, for brief intervals, the rain stopped, the roof of the jungle allowed no sunlight to penetrate to the jungle floor, and the raucous birds, silent in the rain, were louder than the rain when they had their opportunities to protest the monsoon.

The radioman and the crew chief had no idea where Wally and the co-pilot were. On the fifth day they met up with the co-pilot, who had reached a native village only a day ahead of them. He was quite badly drained by the leeches—since he'd been traveling alone, he'd had no one to burn off the leeches he couldn't reach. In the middle of his back, there had been quite a gathering of them, which the natives were skillful at removing. They used a lighted stalk of bamboo, like a cigar. The natives were Burmese, and friendly; although they spoke no English, they made it clear that they had no fondness for the Japanese invasion, and also that they knew the way to China.

But where was Wally? The co-pilot had landed in a grove of

ironwood; and the canes of bamboo that he had to hack his way through were as stout as a man's thigh. The edge of his machete was as dull and round as the back of the blade.

The Burmese let them know they were not safe to stay and wait for Wally where they were; some of the villagers would lead the co-pilot, the crew chief and the radioman into China. For that trip, they darkened their skin with mashed peepul berries and tied orchids in their hair; they didn't want to look like white men.

The trip took twenty days, walking. They traveled two hundred twenty-five miles. They cooked no food; at the end of the journey, their rice was moldy—there was so much rain. The crew chief claimed he was terminally constipated; the co-pilot claimed he was dying of diarrhea. The radioman shat rabbit pellets and carried a low-grade fever for fifteen of the twenty days; he grew a helmet of ringworm. Each man lost about forty pounds.

When they reached their base in China, they were hospitalized for a week. Then they were flown back to India, where the co-pilot was retained in the hospital for diagnosis and treatment of an amoeba—no one could say what amoeba it was. The crew chief had a colon problem; he was also retained. The radioman (and his ringworm) went back to work. "They took all our gear when they put us in the hospital in China," he wrote to Olive. "When they gave it back to us, it was all lumped together. There was four compasses. There was just three of us, but there was four compasses. One of us jumped out of the plane with Captain Worthington's compass." In the radioman's opinion, it was better to have crashed with the plane than to have landed in that part of Burma without a compass.

In August of 194__, Burma officially declared war against Great Britain and the United States. Candy told Homer that she needed a new place to sit, to be left alone. The dock made her want to jump off; she'd sat too many times on that dock with Wally. It didn't help that Homer would sit there with her now.

"I know a place," Homer told her.

Maybe Olive was right, he thought; maybe they hadn't cleaned the cider house for nothing. When it rained, Candy sat inside and listened to the drops on the tin roof. She wondered if the jungle sounded as loud as that, or louder, and if the sweet rot smell of the cider apples was anything like the stifling decay-in-progress smell of the jungle floor. When the weather was clear, Candy sat on the roof. Some nights she allowed Homer Wells to tell her stories there. Perhaps it was the absence of the Ferris wheel and of Mr. Rose's interpretations of the darkness that prompted Homer Wells to tell Candy everything.

/ / /

That summer, Wilbur Larch wrote to the Roosevelts again. He had written to them both so many times under the constellations of ether that he was unsure whether he had actually written to them or had only imagined doing it. He never wrote to one without writing to the other.

He usually began "Dear Mr. President," and "Dear Mrs. Roosevelt," but occasionally he felt more informal and began "Dear Franklin Delano Roosevelt"; once he even began "Dear Eleanor."

That summer he addressed the President quite plainly. "Mr. Roosevelt," he wrote, dispensing with the endearment, "I know that you must be terribly busy with the war, yet I feel such confidence in your humanitarianism—and in your commitment to the poor, to the forgotten, and especially to children ..." To Mrs. Roosevelt, he wrote: "I know your husband must be very busy, but perhaps you could point out to him a matter of the utmost urgency—for it concerns the rights of women and the plight of the unwanted child ..."

The confusing configurations of light that dazzled the dispensary ceiling contributed to the strident and incomprehensible manner of the letter.

"These same people who tell us we must defend the lives of the unborn—they are the same people who seem not so interested in defending anyone but themselves after the accident of birth is complete! These same people who profess their love of the unborn's soul—they don't care to make much of a contribution to the poor, they don't care to offer much assistance to the unwanted or the oppressed! How do they justify such a concern for the fetus and such a lack of concern for unwanted and abused children? They condemn others for the accident of conception; they condemn the poor—as if the poor can help being poor. One way the poor could help themselves would be to be in control of the size of their families. I thought that freedom of choice was obviously democratic—was obviously American!

"You Roosevelts are national heroes! You are my heroes, anyway. How can you tolerate this country's anti-American, anti-democratic abortion laws?"

By now Dr. Larch had stopped writing and was ranting in the dispensary. Nurse Edna went to the dispensary door and rattled the frosted-glass panels.

"Is it a democratic society that condemns people to the accident of conception?" roared Wilbur Larch. "What are we—monkeys? If you expect people to be responsible for their children, you have to give them the right to choose whether or not to have children. What are you people thinking of? You're not only crazy! You're ogres!" Wilbur Larch was yelling so loudly that Nurse Edna went into the dispensary and shook him.

"Wilbur, the children can hear you," she told him. "And the mothers. Everyone can hear you."

"No one hears me," said Dr. Larch. Nurse Edna recognized the involuntary twitching in Wilbur Larch's cheeks and the slackness in his lower lip; the doctor was just emerging from ether. "The President doesn't answer my letters," Larch complained to Nurse Edna.

"He's very busy," Nurse Edna said. "He may not even get to read your letters."

"What about Eleanor?" Wilbur Larch asked.

"What about Eleanor?" Nurse Edna asked.

"Doesn't she get to read her letters?" Wilbur Larch's tone of voice was whiny, like a child's, and Nurse Edna patted the back of his hand, which was spotted with brown freckles.

"Missus Roosevelt is very busy, too," Nurse Edna said. "But I'm sure she'll get around to answering you."

"It's been years," Dr. Larch said quietly, turning his face to the wall. Nurse Edna let him doze in that position for a while. She restrained herself from touching him; she was inclined to brush his hair back from his forehead, in the manner that she often soothed any number of the little ones. Were they all becoming children again? And were they, as Nurse Angela claimed, all becoming the same, all resembling each other, even physically? Anyone visiting St. Cloud's for the first time might suspect that they were all members of the same family.

Suddenly Nurse Angela surprised her in the dispensary.

"Well, are we out of it?" she asked Nurse Edna. "What's the trouble? I was sure I ordered a whole case."

"A case of what?" Nurse Edna asked.

"Merthiolate—red," Nurse Angela said crossly. "I asked you to get me some red Merthiolate—there's not a drop left in the delivery room."

"Oh, I forgot!" said Nurse Edna, bursting into tears.

Wilbur Larch woke up.

"I know how busy you both are," he said to the Roosevelts, although he gradually recognized Nurse Edna and Nurse Angela—their tired arms held out to him. "My faithful friends," he said, as if he were addressing a vast audience of well-wishers. "My fellow laborers," said Wilbur Larch, as if he were running for reelection—a little tiredly, but no less earnestly seeking the support of his companions who also honored the Lord's work.

/ / /

Olive Worthington sat in Wally's room with the lights off; that way, if Homer looked into the house from the outside, he wouldn't see her sitting there. She knew that Homer and Candy were at the cider house, and she tried to tell herself that she did not resent the apparent comfort Homer could give to Candy. (He was powerless to comfort Olive in the slightest; in truth, Homer's presence—given Wally's absence—irritated Olive, and it was testimony to her strength of character that she was able to criticize herself for this irritation; only rarely did she allow her irritation to show.) And she would never have considered Candy unfaithful—not even if Candy had announced to everyone that she was giving Wally up and marrying Homer Wells. It was only that Olive knew Candy: Olive realized that Candy could not give Wally up without giving him up for dead, and Olive would have resented that. He doesn't *feel* dead! Olive thought. And it isn't Homer's fault that he is here and Wally is there, she reminded herself.

A mosquito was in the room, and its needlelike whine so disturbed Olive that she forgot why she was keeping Wally's room in darkness; she turned on the lights to hunt for the mosquito. Wouldn't there be terrible mosquitoes where Wally was? The Burmese mosquitoes were speckled (and much larger than the Maine variety).

Ray Kendall was also alone, but he was only mildly bothered by the mosquitoes. It was a still night, and Ray watched the silent heat lightning violate the blackout conditions along the coast. He was worried about Candy. Raymond Kendall knew how someone else's death could arrest your own life, and he regretted (in advance) how the forward motion of Candy's life might be halted by her losing Wally. "If it was me," Ray said aloud, "I'd take the other fella."

"The other fella," Ray knew, was more like Ray; it wasn't that Ray preferred Homer Wells to Wally—it was that Ray understood Homer better. Yet Ray did not disrupt a single snail while he sat on his dock; he knew that it took a snail too long to get where it was going.

"Every time you throw a snail off the dock," Ray teased Homer Wells, "you're making someone start his whole life over."

"Maybe I'm doing him a favor," said Homer Wells, the orphan. Ray had to admit that he liked that boy.

The heat lightning was less spectacular from the cider house roof—the sea was not visible even in the brightest flashes. Yet the lightning was more disquieting there; both its distance and its silence reminded Candy and Homer Wells of a war they could not feel or hear. For them, it was a war of far-off flashes.

"I think he's alive," Candy said to Homer. When they sat together on the roof, they held hands.

"I think he's dead," said Homer Wells. That was when they both saw the lights go on in Wally's room.

That night in August, the trees were full, the boughs bent and heavy, and the apples—all but the bright, waxy-green Gravensteins—were a pale green-going-to-pink. The grass in the rows between the trees was knee-high; there would be one more mowing before the harvest. That night there was an owl hooting from the orchard called Cock Hill; Candy and Homer also heard a fox bark from the orchard called Frying Pan.

"Foxes can climb trees," said Homer Wells.

"No, they can't," Candy said.

"Apple trees, anyway," Homer said. "Wally told me."

"He's alive," Candy whispered.

In the flash of heat lightning that illuminated her face, Homer saw her tears sparkle; her face was wet and salty when he kissed her. It was a trembling, awkward proposition—kissing on the cider house roof.

"I love you," said Homer Wells.

"I love you, too," Candy said. "But he's alive."

"He isn't," Homer said.

"I love him," Candy said.

"I know you do," said Homer Wells. "*I* love him, too."

Candy lowered her shoulder and put her head against Homer's chest so that he couldn't kiss her; he held her with one arm while his other hand strayed to her breast, where it stayed.

"This is so hard," she whispered, but she let his hand stay where it was. There were those distant flashes of light, out to sea, and a warm breeze so faint it barely stirred the apple leaves or Candy's hair.

Olive, in Wally's room, followed the mosquito from a lampshade (against which she was unable to strike it) to a spot on the white wall above Homer's bed. When she mashed the mosquito with the heel of her hand, the dime-sized spot of blood left on the wall surprised her—the filthy little creature had been gorging itself. Olive wet her index finger and dabbed at the blood spot, which only made the mess worse. Angry at herself, she got up from Homer's bed, unnecessarily smoothing his untouched pillow; she smoothed Wally's untouched pillow, too; then she turned off the night-table lamp. She paused in the doorway of the empty room to look things over, and turned off the overhead light.

Homer Wells held Candy around her hips—to help her off the roof. They must have known it was precarious to kiss on top of the cider house; it was more dangerous for them on the ground. They were standing together, arms loosely around each other's waists—his chin touching her forehead (she was shaking her head, No, No, but just a little)—when they both became aware that the lights from Wally's room were out. They leaned against each other as they walked to the cider house, the tall grass clutching at their legs.

They were careful not to let the screen door bang. Who could have heard it? They preferred the darkness; because they did not reach for the light switch in the kitchen, they never came in contact with the cider house rules that were tacked next to it. Only the palest flashes of the heat lightning showed them the way to the sleeping quarters, where the twin rows of iron beds stood with their harsh springs exposed—the old mattresses rolled in Army barracks fashion at the foot of each bed. They unrolled one.

It was a bed that had held many transients. The history of the dreams encountered upon that bed was rich. The small moan that caught in the back of Candy's throat was soft and difficult to hear above the iron screeching of the bed's rusted springs; the moan was as delicate in that fermented air as the fluttery touch of Candy's hands, lighting like butterflies upon Homer's shoulders, before he felt her hands grip him hard—her fingers sinking in as she held him tight. The moan that escaped her then was sharper than the grinding bed springs and nearly as loud as Homer's own sound. Oh, this boy whose crying had once been a legend upriver in Three Mile Falls—oh, how he could sound!

Olive Worthington, rigid in her bed, listened to what she thought was an owl on Cock Hill. What is it hooting about? she thought. She thought of anything that would distract her from her vision of the mosquitoes in the jungles of Burma.

Mrs. Grogan lay wide awake, momentarily frightened for her soul; the good woman had absolutely nothing to fear. It *was* an owl she heard—it made such a mournful sound.

Wilbur Larch, who seemed always to be wide awake, passed his skillful, careful fingers across the keyboard of the typewriter in Nurse Angela's office. "Oh please, Mr. President," he wrote.

Young Steerforth, who suffered allergies to dust and to mold, found the night oppressive; it seemed to him that he couldn't breathe. He was lazy about getting out of bed, and therefore blew his nose on his pillowcase. Nurse Edna rushed to him at the sound of such thick and troubled trumpeting. Although Steerforth's allergies were not severe, the last orphan who was allergic to dust and mold was Fuzzy Stone.

"You have done so much good, already," Wilbur Larch wrote to Franklin D. Roosevelt. "And your voice on the radio gives me hope. As a member of the medical profession, I am aware of the insidiousness of the disease you have personally triumphed over. After you, anyone who holds your office will be ashamed if he fails to serve the poor and the neglected—or *should* be ashamed . . ."

Ray Kendall, stretched out upon his dock as if the sea had cast him up there, could not make himself get up, go inside and go to bed. It was rare for the coastal air to be so torpid; the air was simply air-as-usual at St. Cloud's.

"I saw a picture of you and your wife—you were attending a church service. I think it was Episcopal," wrote Wilbur Larch to the President. "I don't know what they tell you in that church about abortion, but here is something you should know. Thirty-five to forty-five percent of our country's population growth can be attributed to unplanned, unwanted births. Couples who are well-to-do usually want their babies; only seventeen percent of the babies born to well-to-do parents are unwanted. BUT WHAT ABOUT THE POOR? Forty-two percent of the babies born to parents living in poverty are unwanted. Mr. President, that is almost half. And these are not the times of Ben Franklin, who (as you probably know) was so keen to increase the population. It has been the goal of your administration to find enough things for the present population to do, and to better provide for the present population. Those who plead for the lives of the unborn should consider the lives of the living. Mr. Roosevelt—you, of all people!—you should know that the unborn are not as wretched or as in need of our assistance as the *born*! Please take pity on the born!"

Olive Worthington tossed and turned. Oh, take pity on my son! she prayed and prayed.

Medium high in an apple tree in the orchard called Frying Pan—crouched warily in the crotch between the tree's largest branches—a red fox, its ears and nose alert, its tail poised as lightly as a feather, surveyed the orchard with a predatory eye. To the fox, the ground below twitched with rodents, although the fox had not climbed the tree for the view—it had run up the tree to eat a bird, a feather of which was thrust through the fox's whiskers and into the rust-colored goatee on the fierce little animal's pointed chin.

Candy Kendall clung to Homer Wells—oh, how she clung! —as the breath left them both and stirred the otherwise unmoving air. And the trembling mice beneath the floor of the cider house stopped in their tracks between the cider house walls to listen to the lovers. The mice knew there was the owl to worry about, and the fox. But what animal was this whose sound was petrifying them? The owl does not hoot when it hunts, and the fox does not bark when it pounces. But what is this new animal? wondered the cider house mice—what new beast has charged and disturbed the air?

And is it safe?

/ / /

In Wilbur Larch's opinion, love was certainly not safe—not ever. For his own advancing frailty since Homer Wells had departed St. Cloud's, he would have said love was to blame; how tentative he had become concerning some things and how suddenly irritable concerning others. Nurse Angela might have suggested to him that his more recent bouts of gloom and anger were as much the result of his fifty-year-old addiction to ether and of his advanced age as they were the result of his anxious love for Homer Wells. Mrs. Grogan, had she been asked, would have told him that he suffered more from what she called St. Cloud's syndrome than from love; Nurse Edna would never have held love to blame for anything.

But Wilbur Larch viewed love as a disease even more insidious than the polio that President Roosevelt had stood up to so courageously. And could anyone blame Larch if he occasionally referred to the so-called products of conception as the "results of love"?—although his dear nurses were upset with him when he spoke like this. Did he not have a right to judge love harshly? After all, there was much evidence—in both the products of conception, and their attendant pain, and in the injured lives of many of Dr. Larch's orphans—to justify his view that there was no more safety to be found in love than there was to be found in a virus.

Had he felt the force of the collision between Candy Kendall and Homer Wells—had he tasted their sweat and touched the tension in the muscles of their shining backs; had he heard the agony and the release from agony that could be detected in their voices—Wilbur Larch would not have changed his mind. A passing glimpse of such passion would have confirmed his opinion of the danger of love; he would have been as petrified as the mice.

In Dr. Larch's opinion, even when he could prevail on his patients to practice some method of birth control, love was never safe.

"Consider the so-called rhythm method," wrote Wilbur Larch. "Here in St. Cloud's we see many results of the rhythm method."

He had a pamphlet printed, in the plainest block letters:

COMMON MISUSES OF THE PROPHYLACTIC

He wrote as if he were writing for children; in some cases, he was.

1. SOME MEN PUT THE PROPHYLACTIC ON JUST THE TIP OF THE PENIS: THIS IS A MISTAKE, BECAUSE THE PROPHYLACTIC WILL COME OFF. IT MUST BE PUT OVER

THE WHOLE PENIS, AND IT MUST BE PUT
ON WHEN THE PENIS IS ERECT.

2. SOME MEN TRY TO USE THE PROPHYLAC-
TIC A SECOND TIME: THIS IS ALSO A
MISTAKE. ONCE YOU REMOVE A PROPHY-
LACTIC, THROW IT AWAY! AND WASH YOUR
GENITAL AREA THOROUGHLY BEFORE AL-
LOWING YOURSELF FURTHER CONTACT
WITH YOUR PARTNER—SPERM ARE LIVING
THINGS (AT LEAST, FOR A SHORT TIME),
AND THEY CAN SWIM!

3. SOME MEN TAKE THE PROPHYLACTIC OUT
OF ITS WRAPPER: THEY EXPOSE THE RUB-
BER TO LIGHT AND AIR FOR TOO LONG A
TIME BEFORE USING IT; CONSEQUENTLY,
THE RUBBER DRIES OUT AND IT DEVEL-
OPS CRACKS AND HOLES. THIS IS A MIS-
TAKE! SPERM ARE VERY TINY—THEY CAN
SWIM THROUGH CRACKS AND HOLES!

4. SOME MEN STAY INSIDE THEIR PARTNERS
FOR A LONG TIME AFTER THEY HAVE
EJACULATED; WHAT A MISTAKE THIS IS!
THE PENIS SHRINKS! WHEN THE PENIS IS
NO LONGER ERECT, AND WHEN THE MAN
FINALLY PULLS HIS PENIS OUT OF HIS
PARTNER, THE PROPHYLACTIC CAN SLIDE
COMPLETELY OFF. MOST MEN CAN'T EVEN
FEEL THIS HAPPENING, BUT WHAT A MESS!
INSIDE THE WOMAN YOU HAVE JUST DE-
POSITED A WHOLE PROPHYLACTIC, AND
ALL THOSE SPERM!

And some men, Homer Wells could have added—thinking
of Herb Fowler—distribute prophylactics with holes in them to
their fellow man.

In the cider house at Ocean View, huddled with the huddled
mice, Homer Wells and Candy Kendall could not move from
their embrace. For one thing, the mattress was so narrow—it
was only possible to share that mattress if they remained joined
together—and for another, they had waited so long; they had
anticipated so much. And, to both of them, so much was

meant by having allowed themselves to come together. They shared both a love and a grief, for neither of them would have permitted each other this moment if there were not at least parts of each of them that had accepted Wally's death. And, after lovemaking, those parts of them that felt Wally's loss were forced to acknowledge the moment with reverence and with solemnity; therefore, their expressions were not so full of rapture and not so void of worry as the expressions of most lovers after lovemaking.

Homer Wells, with his face pressed into Candy's hair, lay dreaming that he was only now arriving at the white Cadillac's original destination; he felt as if Wally were still driving him and Candy away from St. Cloud's—as if Wally were still in charge; surely Wally was a true benefactor to have driven him safely to this resting place. The pulse in Candy's temple, which lightly touched his own pulse, was as soothing to Homer as the tire hum when the great white Cadillac had rescued him from the prison into which he was born. There was a tear on Homer's face; he would have thanked Wally, if he could.

And if, in the darkness, he could have seen Candy's face, he would have known that a part of her was still over Burma.

They lay still for so long—the first mouse bold enough to run across their bare legs surprised them. Homer Wells jerked up to a kneeling position; a moment passed before he realized that he had left *a whole prophylactic, and all those sperm* inside Candy. It was number 4 on Wilbur Larch's list of the COMMON MISUSES OF THE PROPHYLACTIC.

"Oh-oh," said Homer Wells, whose fingers were quick, and sensitive, and trained; he needed only the index and middle fingers of his right hand to retrieve the lost rubber; although he was very fast, he doubted he'd been fast enough.

Despite the careful detail of Homer's instructions to Candy, she cut him off. "I think I know how to douche myself, Homer," she said.

And so their first night of passion, which had been so slowly building between them, ended in the haste typical of the measures taken to avoid an unwanted pregnancy—the possible cause of which was fairly typical, too.

"I love you," Homer repeated, kissing her good night. There were both fervor and anger in Candy's good-night kiss, both ferocity and resignation in the way she clutched his hands. Homer stood for a while in the parking lot behind the lobster pound; the only sound was the aeration device that circulated fresh oxygen through the water tank that kept the lobsters alive. The quality of the air in the parking lot was divided between brine and motor oil. The night's heat was gone. A cool, damp fog rolled in from the sea; there was no more heat lightning to illuminate, however slightly, the view across the Atlantic.

It seemed to Homer Wells that there had been so much waiting and seeing to his life, and now there was something else to wait and see about.

/ / /

Wilbur Larch, who was seventy-something and the grand master of Maine in the field of waiting and seeing, gazed once again upon the starry ceiling of the dispensary. One of ether's pleasures was its occasional transportation of the inhaler to a position that afforded him a bird's-eye view of himself; Wilbur Larch was thus permitted to smile from afar upon a vision of himself. It was the night that he blessed the adoption of young Copperfield, the lisper.

"Let us be happy for young Copperfield," Dr. Larch had said. "Young Copperfield has found a family. Good night, Copperfield!"

Only this time, in ether's memory, it was a joyous occasion. There was even unison in the responses, as if Larch conducted a choir of angels—all singing Copperfield merrily on his way. It hadn't been like that. Copperfield had been especially popular with the littlest orphans; he was what Nurse Angela called a "binder"—in his good-natured, lisping presence, the spirits of the other orphans rose and held together. That night no one had joined Larch in wishing Copperfield good night and good-bye. But Copperfield's departure had been especially hard for Dr. Larch, because with Copperfield's passing there went from St. Cloud's not only the last orphan to be named by Homer Wells but also the last orphan to have known Homer. With Copperfield's leaving, a little more of Homer Wells left, too. Little Steerforth—second-born and second-named—had been adopted first.

But good for ether! How it allowed Dr. Larch to revise his history. Perhaps it had been the ether, all along, that had provided Dr. Larch with the impulse to be a revisionist with Fuzzy Stone. And in Larch's ether dreams he had many times rescued Wally Worthington—the exploding plane had reassembled itself and returned to the sky; the parachute had opened, and the gentle currents of the Burmese air had borne Wally all the way to China. Safely above the Japanese, above the tigers and the snakes, and above the dread diseases of Asia—how peacefully Wilbur Larch had seen Wally fly. And how the Chinese had been impressed with Wally's noble good looks—with those patrician bones in that handsome face. In time, the Chinese would help Wally to find his base, and he would come home to his girlfriend—this was what Wilbur Larch wanted most: he wanted Wally back with Candy, for only then would there be any hope of Homer Wells returning to St. Cloud's.

/ / /

Nearly three months after Wally's plane was shot down, the harvest at Ocean View began and Candy Kendall knew she was pregnant. After all, she was familiar with the symptoms; so was Homer Wells.

A ragtag crew of pickers mauled the orchards that year; there were housewives and war brides falling out of trees, and students dismissed from the local schools so that they might contribute to the harvest. Even the apple harvest in 194__ was considered a part of the war effort. Olive made Homer a crew boss of the high school kids, whose methods of bruising the fruit were so various that Homer was kept very busy.

Candy worked in the mart; she told Olive that her frequent bouts of nausea were probably caused by the smell of diesel fuel and exhaust that was constant around the farm vehicles. Olive remarked that she thought the daughter of a mechanic and lobsterman would be less sensitive to strong odors, and when she suggested that Candy might be more comfortable working in the fields, Candy admitted that climbing trees also made her feel queasy.

"I never knew you were so delicate," Olive said. Olive had never been more active in a harvest, or more grateful for there being one. But the harvest that year reminded Homer Wells of learning to tread water; both Candy and Olive had taught him how. ("Swimming in place," Olive had called it.)

"I'm just swimming in place," Homer told Candy. "We can't leave Olive during the harvest."

"If I work as hard as I can," Candy told him, "it's possible that I'll miscarry."

It was not very possible, Homer Wells knew.

"What if I don't want you to miscarry?" Homer asked her.

"What if?" Candy asked.

"What if I want you to marry me, and to have the baby?" Homer asked.

They stood at one end of the conveyor belt in the packing-house; Candy was at the head of the line of women who sized and sorted the apples—who either packaged them or banished them to cider. Candy was retching, even though she had chosen the head of the line because that put her nearest the open door.

"We have to wait and see," Candy said between retches.

"We don't have long to wait," said Homer Wells. "We don't have long to see."

"I shouldn't marry you for a year, or more," Candy said. "I really *want* to marry you, but what about Olive? We have to wait."

"The baby won't wait," Homer said.

"We both know where to go—to not have the baby," Candy said.

"Or to have it," said Homer Wells. "It's my baby, too."

"How do I have a baby without anyone knowing I've had it?" Candy asked; she retched again, and Big Dot Taft came up the packing line to see what was the matter.

"Homer, ain't you got no better manners than to watch a young lady puke?" Big Dot asked him. She put her huge arm around Candy's shoulder. "You get away from the door, darlin'," Big Dot Taft said to Candy. "You come on and work down the line—there's only apples to smell down there. The tractor exhaust comes in the door."

"I'll see you soon," Homer mumbled, to both Candy and Big Dot.

"No one likes to be sick around the opposite sex, Homer," Big Dot informed him.

"Right," said Homer Wells, orphan and would-be father.

In Maine, it is considered wiser just to know something than to talk about it; that no one said Candy Kendall was pregnant didn't necessarily mean that they didn't know she was. In Maine, it is a given that any boy can get any girl in trouble. What they do about it is their business; if they want advice, they should ask.

"If *you* were an orphan, what would *you* have?" Wilbur

Larch once wrote in *A Brief History of St. Cloud's.* "An orphan, or an abortion?"

"An abortion, definitely," Melony had said once, when Homer Wells had asked her. "How about you?"

"I'd have the orphan," Homer had said.

"You're just a dreamer, Sunshine," Melony had told him.

Now he supposed it was true; he was just a dreamer. He confused the high school kids with each other, and gave some of them credit for picking bushels that other kids had picked. He stopped two of the boys from throwing apples at each other, and felt that he had to make an example of them—in order to protect the fruit and establish his authority. But while he was driving the boys back to the apple mart, where he forced them to wait without getting in any trouble—and to miss a morning's picking—a full-scale apple fight broke out among the other high school kids, and when Homer returned to the field, he interrupted a war. The crates that were already loaded on the flatbed were splattered with apple seeds, and the hot parts of the tractor gave off a burned-apple stench (someone must have tried to use the tractor for "cover"). Perhaps Vernon Lynch would have made a better foreman for the high school kids, Homer thought. All Homer wanted to do was to make things right with Candy.

When they sat on Ray Kendall's dock now, they sat close together, and they didn't sit for long—it was getting cold. They sat huddled against one of the posts at the dock's end, where Ray had seen Candy sit with Wally—so many times—and in somewhat the same position (although, Ray noted, Wally had always sat up straighter, as if he were already fastened to the pilot's seat).

Ray Kendall understood why it was necessary for them to brood about the process of falling in love, but he felt sorry for them; he knew that falling in love was never meant to be such a morose moment. Yet Ray had every respect for Olive, and it was for Olive, he knew, that Homer and Candy were forced to be mourners at their own love story. "You should just go away," Ray said out the window to Homer and Candy; he spoke very softly and the window was closed.

Homer was afraid that if he insisted to Candy that she marry him—insisted that she have their baby—that he would force her to reject him completely. He also knew that Candy was afraid of Olive; it was not that Candy was so eager to have a second abortion—Homer knew that Candy would marry him, and have their baby on the same day, if she thought she could avoid telling Olive the truth. Candy was not ashamed of Homer; she was not ashamed of being pregnant, either. Candy was ashamed that Olive would judge her harshly for her insufficient feelings for Wally—Candy's faith (in Wally being alive) had not been as strong as Olive's. It is not unusual for the mother of an only son and the young woman who is the son's lover to envision themselves as competitors.

More shocking (to Homer's mind) was what he could gather of his own feelings. He already knew that he loved Candy, and wanted her; now he discovered that—more than wanting her—he wanted her child.

They were just another trapped couple, more comfortable with their illusions than they were with the reality of their situation.

"After the harvest," Homer said to Candy, "we'll go to Saint Cloud's. I'll say that they need me there. It's probably true, anyway. And because of the war, no one else is paying attention to them. You could tell your dad that it's just another kind of war effort. We could both tell Olive that we feel an obligation—to be where we're really needed; to be of more use."

"You want me to have the baby?" Candy asked him.

"I want you to have *our* baby," said Homer Wells. "And after the baby's born, and you're both recovered, we'll come back here. We'll tell your dad, and Olive—or we'll write them—that we've fallen in love, and that we've gotten married."

"And that we conceived a child before we did any of that?" Candy asked.

Homer Wells, who saw the real stars above the blackened coast of Maine—bright and cold—envisioned the whole story very clearly. "We'll say the baby is adopted," he said. "We'll say we felt a further obligation—to the orphanage. I do feel that, in a way, anyway," he added.

"Our baby is adopted?" Candy asked. "So we have a baby who thinks it's an orphan?"

"No," Homer said. "We have our own baby, and it knows it's all ours. We just *say* it's adopted—just for Olive's sake, and just for a while."

"That's lying," Candy said.

"Right," said Homer Wells. "That's lying for a while."

"Maybe—when we came back, with the baby—maybe we

vouldn't have to say it was adopted. Maybe we could tell the ruth then," Candy said.

"Maybe," Homer said. Maybe everything is waiting and seeing, he thought. He put his mouth on the back of her neck; ne nuzzled into her hair.

"If we thought that Olive could accept it, if we thought that he could accept—about Wally," Candy added, "then we vouldn't have to lie about the baby being adopted, would ve?"

"Right," said Homer Wells. What is all this worrying about ying? he wondered, holding Candy tightly as she softly cried. Was it true that Wilbur Larch had no memory of Homer's nother? Was it true that Nurse Angela and Nurse Edna had 10 memory of his mother, either? Maybe it was true, but Homer Wells would never have blamed them if they had lied; hey would have lied only to protect him. And if they'd remembered his mother, and his mother was a monster, wasn't it better that they'd lied? To orphans, not every truth is wanted.

And if Homer had discovered that Wally had died in terrible pain or with prolonged suffering—if Wally had been tortured, or had burned to death, or had been eaten by an animal— Homer certainly would have lied about that. If Homer Wells had been an amateur historian, he would have been as much of a revisionist as Wilbur Larch—he would have tried to make everything come out all right in the end. Homer Wells, who always said to Wilbur Larch that *he* (Larch) was the doctor, was more of a doctor than he knew.

/ / /

The first night of cider making he shared the work of the press and grinder with Meany Hyde and Everett Taft; Big Dot and her kid sister, Debra Pettigrew, were the bottlers. Debra was sullen at the prospect of messy work; she complained about the slopping and the spilling, and her irritation was further enhanced by the presence of Homer Wells, to whom she had not been speaking—Debra's understanding that Candy and Homer had become partners in a certain grief was markedly colored by her suspicion that Candy and Homer had become partners in a certain pleasure, too. At least Debra had not reacted generously to Homer's suggestion that they just be friends. Homer was puzzled by Debra's hostility, and assumed that his years in the orphanage had deprived him of some perfectly sensible explanation for her behavior. It seemed to

Homer that Debra had always denied him access to anything more than her friendship. Why was she now incensed that he asked no more of her than that?

Meany Hyde announced to Homer and Everett Taft that this would be his first and last night press of the harvest because he wanted to stay home with Florence—"Now that her time is approachin'," Meany said.

When Mr. Rose pressed cider, there was a very different feeling in the fermented air. For one thing, everything went more quickly; the pressing was a kind of contest. For another, there was a tension that Mr. Rose's authority created—and the knowledge of those tired men asleep, or trying to sleep, in the next room, lent to the working of the grinder and the press a sense of hurry (and of perfection) that one feels only on the edge of exhaustion.

Debra Pettigrew's future heaviness grew more and more apparent the wetter she got; there was a matching slope in the sisters' shoulders, and even a slackness in the backs of Debra's arms that would one day yield the massive jiggles that shivered through Big Dot. In sisterly imitation, they wiped the sweat from their eyes with their biceps—not wanting to touch their faces with their cider-sweet and sticky hands.

After midnight, Olive brought them cold beer and hot coffee. When she had gone, Meany Hyde said, "That Missus Worthington is a thoughtful woman—here she is not only bringin' us somethin' but givin' us a choice."

"And her with Wally gone," said Everett Taft. "It's a wonder she even thought of us."

Whatever is brought to me, whatever is coming, Homer thought, I will not move out of its way. Life was finally about to happen to him—the journey he proposed making, back to St. Cloud's, was actually going to give him his freedom from St. Cloud's. He would have a baby (if not a wife, too); he would need a job.

Of course I'll take the baby trees, and plant them, he was thinking—as if apple trees would satisfy St. Cloud's, as if his planting them would satisfy what Wilbur Larch wanted from him.

By the end of the harvest, the light grew grayer and the orchards were darker in the daytime, although more light passed through the empty trees. The picking crew's inexperience was visible in the shriveled apples still clinging to the hard-to-reach limbs. The ground was already frozen in St. Cloud's. Homer would have to make a special trip for the baby trees. He would plant them in the spring; it would be a spring baby.

Homer and Candy worked only the night shifts at Cape Kenneth Hospital now. The days when Ray was building the torpedoes were the days Homer could spend with Candy, in her room above the lobster pound.

There was a freedom about their lovemaking, now that Candy was already pregnant. Although she could not tell him—not yet—Candy loved making love to Homer Wells; she enjoyed herself much more than she had been able to with Wally. But she could not bring herself to say aloud that anything was *better than with Wally;* although making love was better with Homer, she doubted that this was Wally's fault. She and Wally had never had the time to feel so free.

"The girl and I are coming," Homer wrote to Dr. Larch. "She's going to have my baby—neither an abortion nor an orphan."

"A *wanted* baby!" Nurse Angela said. "We're going to have a *wanted* baby!"

"If not a planned one," said Wilbur Larch, who stared out the window of Nurse Angela's office as if the hill that rose outside the window had personally risen against him. "And I suppose he's going to plant the damn trees," said Dr. Larch. "What does he want a baby for? How can he have a baby and go to college—or to medical school?"

"When was he ever going to go to medical school, Wilbur?" Nurse Edna asked.

"I knew he'd be back!" Nurse Angela shouted. "He belongs with us!"

"Yes, he does," said Wilbur Larch. Involuntarily, and somewhat stiffly, his back straightened, his knees braced, his arms reached out and the fingers of his hands partially opened—as if he were preparing to receive a heavy package. Nurse Edna shuddered to see him in such a pose, which reminded her of the fetus from Three Mile Falls, that dead baby whose posture of such extreme supplication had been arranged by Homer Wells.

/ / /

Homer said to Olive Worthington: "I hate to leave, especially with Christmas coming, and all those memories—but there is something, and someone, I've been neglecting. It's really all of them at Saint Cloud's—nothing changes there. They always need the same things, and now that there's a war, and everyone is making an effort for the war, I think Saint Cloud's is more forgotten than ever. And Doctor Larch isn't getting any younger. I should be of more use than I am here. With the harvest over, I don't feel I have enough to do. At Saint Cloud's, there's always too much to do."

"You're a fine young man," said Olive Worthington, but Homer hung his head. He remembered what Mr. Rochester said to Jane Eyre:

"Dread remorse when you are tempted to err, Miss Eyre: remorse is the poison of life."

It was an early November morning in the kitchen at Ocean View; Olive had not done her hair or put her makeup on. The gray in the light, and in her face and in her hair, made Mrs. Worthington look older to Homer. She was using the string of her tea bag to wring the last of the tea from the bag, and Homer could not raise his eyes from the ropy, knotted veins in the backs of her hands. She had always smoked too much, and in the morning she always coughed.

"Candy is coming with me," said Homer Wells.

"Candy is a fine young woman," Olive said. "It is most unselfish of you both—when you could be enjoying yourselves —to give comfort and companionship to unwanted children." The string across the belly of the tea bag was so taut that Homer thought it would slice through the bag. Olive's voice was so formal that she might have been speaking at an awards ceremony describing the heroism that was worthy of prizes. She was trying her hardest not to cough. When the string tore the tea bag, some of the wet leaves stuck to the yolk of her uneaten soft-boiled egg, which was perched in a china egg cup that Homer Wells had once mistaken for a candlestick holder.

"I could never thank you enough for everything you've done for me," Homer said. Olive Worthington just shook her head; her shoulders were squared, her chin was up, the straightness of her back was formidable. "I'm so sorry about Wally," said Homer Wells. There was the slightest movement in Olive's throat, but the muscles of her neck were rigid.

"He's just missing," Olive said.

"Right," said Homer Wells. He put his hand on Olive's shoulder. She gave no indication that the presence of his hand as either a burden or a comfort, but after they remained like that for a while, she turned her face enough to rest her cheek on top of his hand; there they remained for a while longer, as if posing for a painter of the old school—or for a photographer who was waiting for the unlikely: for the November sun to come out.

Olive insisted that he take the white Cadillac.

"Well," Ray said to Candy and to Homer, "I think it's good for you both that you stick together." Ray was disappointed that neither Homer nor Candy acknowledged his observation with any enthusiasm; as the Cadillac was leaving the lobster pound parking lot, Ray called out to them: "And try havin' some *fun* together!" Somehow, he doubted that they had heard him.

Who goes to St. Cloud's to have fun?

I have not really been adopted, thought Homer Wells. I am not really betraying Mrs. Worthington; she never said she was my mother. Even so, Homer and Candy did not talk a lot on the drive.

On their journey inland, the farther north they drove, the more the leaves had abandoned the trees; there was a little snow in Skowhegan, where the ground resembled an old man's face in need of a shave. There was more snow in Blanchard and in East Moxie and in Moxie Gore, and they had to wait an hour in Ten Thousand Acre Tract where a tree was down—across the road. The snow had drifted over the tree, the mashed shape of which resembled a toppled dinosaur. In Moose River and in Misery Gore, and in Tomhegan, too, the snow had come to stay. The drifts along the roadside were shorn so sharply by the plow—and they stood so high—that Candy and Homer could detect the presence of a house only by chimney smoke, or by the narrow paths chopped through the drifts that were here and there stained by the territorial pissing of dogs.

Olive and Ray and Meany Hyde had given them extra gas coupons. They had decided to take the car because they thought that it would be nice to have a means to get away from St. Cloud's—if only for short drives—but by the time they reached Black Rapids and Homer had put the chains on the rear tires, they realized that the winter roads (and this was only the beginning of the winter) would make most driving impossible.

If they had asked him, Dr. Larch would have saved them the

trouble of bringing the car. He would have said that no one
comes to St. Cloud's for the purpose of taking little trips away
from it; he would have suggested, for fun, that they could
always take the train to Three Mile Falls.

With the bad roads and the failing light and the snow that
began to fall after Ellenville, it was already dark when they
reached St. Cloud's. The headlights of the white Cadillac,
climbing the hill past the girls' division, illuminated two women
walking down the hill toward the railroad station—their faces
turning away from the light. Their footing looked unsure; one
of them didn't have a scarf; the other one didn't have a hat; the
snow winked in the headlights as if the women were throwing
diamonds in the air.

Homer Wells stopped the car and rolled down the window.
"May I give you a ride?" he asked the women.

"You're goin' the wrong way," one of them said.

"I could turn around!" he called to them. When they walked
on without answering him, he drove ahead to the hospital
entrance of the boys' division and turned out the headlights.
The snow falling in front of the light in the dispensary was the
same kind of snow that had been falling the night that he
arrived in St. Cloud's after his escape from the Drapers in
Waterville.

There had been something of a brouhaha between Larch and
his nurses about where Homer and Candy would sleep. Larch
assumed that Candy would sleep in the girls' division and that
Homer would sleep where he used to sleep, with the other boys,
but the women reacted strongly to this suggestion.

"They're lovers!" Nurse Edna pointed out. "Surely they
sleep together!"

"Well, surely they *have*," Larch said. "That doesn't mean
that they have to sleep together here."

"Homer said he was going to marry her," Nurse Edna
pointed out.

"Going to," grumbled Wilbur Larch.

"I think it would be nice to have someone sleeping with
someone else here," Nurse Angela said.

"It seems to me," said Wilbur Larch, "that we're in business
because there's entirely too much sleeping together."

"They're lovers!" Nurse Edna repeated indignantly.

And so the women decided it. Candy and Homer would
share a room with two beds on the ground floor of the girls'

ivision; how they arranged the beds was their own business.
Mrs. Grogan said that she liked the idea of having a man in the
girls' division; occasionally, the girls complained of a prowler
or a peeping tom; having a man around at night was a good
idea.

"Besides," Mrs. Grogan said, "I'm all alone over there—you
three have each other."

"We all *sleep* alone over here," Dr. Larch said.

"Well, Wilbur," Nurse Edna said, "don't be so proud of it."

/ / /

Olive Worthington, alone in Wally's room, regarded the two
beds, Homer's and Wally's—both beds were freshly made up,
both pillows were without a crease. On the night table between
their beds was a photograph of Candy teaching Homer how to
swim. Because there was no ashtray in the boys' room, Olive
held her free hand in a cupped position under the long, dangling ash of her cigarette.

Raymond Kendall, alone above the lobster pound, viewed
the triptych of photographs that stood like an altarpiece on his
night table, next to his socket wrench set. The middle photograph was of himself as a young man; he was seated in an
uncomfortable-looking chair, his wife was in his lap; she was
pregnant with Candy; the chair was in apparent danger. The
left-hand photograph was Candy's graduation picture, the right-
hand photograph was of Candy with Wally—their tennis rac-
quets pointed at each other, like guns. Ray had no picture of
Homer Wells; he needed only to look out the window at his
dock in order to imagine Homer clearly; Ray could not look at
his dock and think of Homer Wells without hearing the snails
rain upon the water.

Nurse Edna had tried to keep a little supper warm for
Homer and Candy; she had put the disappointing pot roast in
the instrument sterilizer, which she checked from time to time.
Mrs. Grogan, who was praying in the girls' division, did not
see the Cadillac come up the hill. Nurse Angela was in the
delivery room, shaving a woman who had already broken her
bag of waters.

Homer and Candy passed by the empty and brightly lit
dispensary; they peeked into Nurse Angela's empty office.
Homer knew better than to peek into the delivery room when
the light was on. From the dormitory, they could hear Dr.
Larch's reading voice. Although Candy held tightly to his

hand, Homer Wells was inclined to hurry—in order not to miss the bedtime story.

/ / /

Meany Hyde's wife, Florence, was delivered of a healthy baby boy—nine pounds, two ounces—shortly after Thanksgiving, which Olive Worthington and Raymond Kendall celebrated in a fairly formal and quiet fashion at Ocean View. Olive invited all her apple workers for an open house; she asked Ray to help her host the occasion. Meany Hyde insisted to Olive that his new baby was a definite sign that Wally was alive.

"Yes, I know he's alive," Olive told Meany calmly.

It was not too trying a day for her, but she did find Debra Pettigrew sitting on Homer's bed in Wally's room, staring at the photograph of Candy teaching Homer how to swim. And not long after ushering Debra from the room, Olive discovered Grace Lynch sitting in the same dent Debra had made on Homer's bed. Grace, however, was staring at the questionnaire from the board of trustees at St. Cloud's, the one that Homer had never filled out and had left tacked to the wall of Wally's room as if they were unwritten rules.

And Big Dot Taft broke down in the kitchen while telling Olive about one of her dreams. Everett had found her, in her sleep, dragging herself across the bedroom floor toward the bathroom. "I didn't have no legs," Big Dot told Olive. "It was the night Florence's boy was born, and I woke up without no legs—only I didn't really wake up, I was just dreamin' that there was nothin' left of me, below the waist."

"Except that you had to go to the bathroom," Everett Taft pointed out. "Otherwise, why was you crawlin' on the floor?"

"The important thing was that I was injured," Big Dot told her husband crossly.

"Oh," said Everett Taft.

"The point is," Meany Hyde said to Olive, "my baby was born just fine but Big Dot had a dream that she couldn't walk. Don'tcha see, Olive?" Meany asked. "I think God is tellin' us that Wally is okay—that he's alive—but that he's been hurt."

"He's injured, or somethin'," Big Dot said, bursting into tears.

"Of course," Olive said abruptly. "It's what I've always thought." Her words startled them all—even Ray Kendall. "If he weren't injured, we would have heard from him by now.

And if he weren't alive, I'd know it," Olive said. She handed her handkerchief to Big Dot Taft and lit a fresh cigarette from the butt end of the cigarette she had almost finished.

Thanksgiving at St. Cloud's was not nearly so mystical, and the food wasn't as good, but everyone had a good time. In lieu of balloons, Dr. Larch distributed prophylactics to Nurse Angela and Nurse Edna, who—despite their distaste for the job—inflated the rubbers and dipped them in bowls of green and red food coloring. When the coloring dried, Mrs. Grogan painted the orphans' names on the rubbers, and Homer and Candy hid the brightly colored prophylactics all over the orphanage.

"It's a rubber hunt," said Wilbur Larch. "We should have saved the idea for Easter. Eggs are expensive."

"We'll not give up eggs for Easter, Wilbur," Nurse Edna said indignantly.

"I suppose not," Dr. Larch said tiredly.

Olive Worthington had sent a case of champagne. Wilbur Larch had never drunk a drop of champagne before—he was not a drinker—but the way the bubbles tightened the roof of his mouth, opened his nasal passages and made his eyes feel dry but clear reminded him of that lightest of vapors, of that famous inhalation he was addicted to. He drank and drank. He even sang for the children—something he'd heard the French soldiers sing in World War I. That song was no more suitable for children than those prophylactics were, but—because of an ignorance of French and an innocence of sex—the French song (which was filthier than any limerick Wally Worthington would ever know) was mistaken for a pleasing ditty and the green and red rubbers were mistaken for balloons.

Even Nurse Edna got a little drunk; champagne was new to her, too, although she sometimes put sherry in hot soup. Nurse Angela didn't drink, but she became emotional—to the degree that she threw her arms around Homer's neck and kissed him nightly, all the while proclaiming that the spirit of St. Cloud's had been in a noticeable slump during Homer's absence and that Homer had been sent by a clearly sympathetic God to revive them.

"But Homer's not staying," Wilbur Larch said, hiccuping.

They had all been impressed with Candy, whom even Dr. Larch referred to as "our angelic volunteer," and over whom Mrs. Grogan daily fussed as if Candy were her daughter. Nurse

Edna busied herself around the young lovers the way a moth flaps around a light.

On Thanksgiving Day, Dr. Larch even flirted with Candy—a little. "I never saw such a pretty girl who was willing to give enemas," Larch said, patting Candy's knee.

"I'm not squeamish," Candy told him.

"There's no room for squeamishness here," Larch said, burping.

"There's still a little room for sensitivity, I hope," Nurse Angela complained. Larch had never praised her *or* Nurse Edna for their willingness to give enemas.

"Of course, I wanted him to go to medical school, to be a doctor, to come back and relieve me here," Wilbur Larch told Candy in a loud voice—as if Homer weren't sitting right across the table. Larch patted Candy's knee again. "But that's all right!" he said. "Who wouldn't rather get a girl like you pregnant—and grow apples!" He said something in French and drank another glass of champagne. "Of course," he whispered to Candy, "he doesn't need to go to medical school to be a doctor *here*. There's just a few more procedures he ought to be familiar with. Hell!" Larch said, indicating the orphans eating their turkey—each with a colored rubber, like a name tag, stationed in front of his or her plate, "this isn't a bad place to raise a family. And if Homer ever gets around to planting the damn hillside, then you'll get to grow apples here, too."

When Dr. Larch fell asleep at the table, Homer Wells carried him back to the dispensary. In his time away from St. Cloud's, Homer wondered, had Dr. Larch gone completely crazy? There was no one to ask. Mrs. Grogan, Nurse Edna and especially Nurse Angela might agree that Larch had traveled around the bend—that he had one oar out of the water, as Ray Kendall would say; that he had one wheel in the sand, as Wally used to say—but Mrs. Grogan and the nurses would most emphatically defend Dr. Larch. Their view, Homer could tell, was that Homer had left them for too long, that his judgment was rusty. Fortunately, Homer's obstetrical procedure had not suffered from his absence.

Pregnant women have no respect for holidays. The trains run at different times, but they run. It was after six in the evening when the woman arrived in St. Cloud's; although it was not his usual practice, the stationmaster escorted her to the hospital entrance because the woman was already engaged in

he second stage of labor—her membranes were ruptured, and
ier bearing-down pains were at regular intervals. Homer Wells
vas palpating the baby's head through the perineum when
Nurse Angela informed him that Dr. Larch was too drunk to
be aroused, and Nurse Edna had also fallen asleep. Homer
vas concerned that the perineum showed signs of bulging, and
he woman's response to a rather heavy ether sedation was
quite slow.

Homer was obliged to hold back the infant's head in order
o protect the perineum from tearing; the mediolateral incision,
vhich Homer elected to perform, was made at a point corre-
ponding to seven on the face of a clock. It was a safer episiotomy, in Homer's view, because the cut could, if necessary, be
carried back considerably farther than the midline type of
operation.

Immediately after the birth of the head, Homer slipped his
inger around the neck of the child to see if the umbilical cord
vas coiled there, but it was an easy birth, both shoulders
emerging spontaneously. He applied two ligatures to the umbilical and cut the cord between the two. He still had his
urgical gown on when he went to the dispensary to see how
Dr. Larch was recovering from his Thanksgiving Day champagne. If Larch was familiar with the transitions he encoun-
ered in moving from a world of ether to a world without
anesthesia, he was unfamiliar with the transition between drunkenness and hangover. Seeing Homer Wells in the bloody smock
of his business, Wilbur Larch imagined he was saved.

"Ah, Doctor Stone," he said, extending his hand to Homer
vith a self-congratulatory formality famous among colleagues
n the medical profession.

"Doctor Who?" said Homer Wells.

"Doctor Stone," said Wilbur Larch, withdrawing his hand,
his hangover settling on him—a dust so thick on the roof of his
mouth that he could only repeat himself. "Fuzzy Stone, Fuzzy
Stone, Fuzzy Stone."

"Homer?" Candy asked, when they lay together in one of
the twin beds given them in their room in the girls' division.
'Why would Doctor Larch say that you don't need to go to
medical school to be a doctor here?"

"Maybe he means that half the work here is illegal, anyway,"
said Homer Wells. "So what's the point of being a legitimate
doctor?"

"But no one would hire you if you weren't a legitimate doctor, would they?" Candy asked.

"Maybe Doctor Larch would," said Homer Wells. "I know some things."

"You don't *want* to be a doctor here, anyway—do you?" Candy asked.

"That's right, I don't want to," he said. What is all this about Fuzzy Stone? he was wondering as he fell asleep.

Homer was still asleep when Dr. Larch bent over the Thanksgiving woman and examined the episiotomy. Nurse Angela was telling him about it, stitch by stitch, but although Larch appreciated the description, it wasn't really necessary; the look and feel of the woman's healthy tissue told him everything he wanted to know. Homer Wells had not lost his confidence; he still had the correct touch.

He also possessed the self-righteousness of the young and wounded; Homer Wells had no doubts to soften his contempt for people who'd bungled their lives so badly that they didn't want the children they'd conceived. Wilbur Larch would have told him that he was simply an arrogant, young doctor who'd never been sick—that he was guilty of a young doctor's disease, manifesting a sick superiority toward *all* patients. But Homer was wielding an ideal of marriage and family like a club; he was more sure of the rightness of his goal than a couple celebrating their sixty-fifth wedding anniversary.

He must have imagined that the sacredness with which he viewed his union with Candy would hover like a halo above the young couple and shed a conspicuously forgiving light upon them and their child when they returned to Heart's Haven and Heart's Rock. He must have thought that the goodness of his and Candy's intentions would glow with such a powerful radiance that Olive and Ray and the rest of that all-knowing, say-nothing community would be blinded. Homer and Candy must have envisioned that their child—conceived in a moment of love that overshadowed Wally's being lost or dead or "just missing"—would be greeted as a descending angel.

And so they enjoyed the life of a young married couple that winter in St. Cloud's. Never had being of use been such good fun. There was no chore the lovely and growingly pregnant young woman thought herself to be above; her beauty and her physical energy were inspiring to the girls in the girls' division. Dr. Larch devoted himself to teaching Homer more about pediatrics—since he could find no fault with Homer's obstetrical procedure and since Homer was emphatic about his refusal to participate in the abortions. The rigidity of this latter position perplexed even Candy, who was fond of saying to Homer, "Just explain it to me again—how you're not disapproving of the procedure, but that you will not yourself be party to what you feel is wrong."

"Right," said Homer Wells; he had no doubts. "You've got it. There's nothing else to explain. I think an abortion should be available to anyone who wants one, but *I* never want to perform one. What's hard to understand about that?"

"Nothing," Candy said, but she would keep asking him about it. "You think it's wrong, yet you think it should be legal—right?"

"Right," said Homer Wells. "I think it's wrong, but I also think it should be everyone's personal choice. What could be more personal than deciding whether you want a child or not?"

"I don't know," Candy said, although it occurred to her that she and Homer Wells had "decided" that Wally was dead—which seemed especially personal to her.

In her fifth month, they began sleeping in separate beds, but they drew the beds together and attempted to make them up as if they were one big bed—a problem, since there were no double-bed sheets at St. Cloud's.

Mrs. Grogan wanted to make a present of double-bed sheets to Homer and Candy, but she had no money of her own to buy them and she wondered if purchasing them for the orphanage would seem strange. "Very strange," Larch said, vetoing the idea.

"In other parts of the world, they have double-bed sheets," wrote Wilbur Larch in *A Brief History of St. Cloud's*. "Here in St. Cloud's we do without—we just do without."

Yet it was the best Christmas ever in St. Cloud's. Olive sent so many presents, and Candy's example—as the first happily pregnant woman in any of their memories—was a present to them all. They had a turkey and a ham, and Dr. Larch and Homer Wells had a carving contest, which everyone said Homer won. He finished carving the turkey before Larch finished carving the ham.

"Well, turkeys are easier to cut than pigs," Larch said. Secretly, he was very pleased with Homer's knife work. That

Homer had learned his touch for cutting under circumstances different from Mr. Rose's was often on Homer's mind. Given certain advantages of education, Homer thought, Mr. Rose might have made an excellent surgeon.

"Might have made," Homer mumbled to himself. He had never been happier.

He was of use, he was in love—and was loved—and he was expecting a child. What more is there? he thought, making the daily rounds. Other people may look for a break from routine, but an orphan craves daily life.

/ / /

In midwinter, in a blizzard, when the women were having tea in the girls' division with Mrs. Grogan and Dr. Larch was at the railroad station, personally accusing the stationmaster of losing an expected delivery of sulfa, a woman arrived at the hospital entrance, bent double with cramps and bleeding. She'd had the D without the C, as Nurse Caroline would have observed; whoever had managed the dilatation appeared to have managed it safely. What was required now was a completion curettage, which Homer performed alone. One very small piece of the products of conception was recognizable in the scraping, which caused Homer Wells a single, small thought. About four months, was what he estimated—looking quickly at the piece, and quickly throwing it away.

At night, when he touched Candy without waking her up, he marveled at how peacefully she slept; and he observed how life in St. Cloud's seemed timeless, placeless and constant, how it seemed grim but caring, how it seemed somehow safer than life in Heart's Rock or in Heart's Haven—certainly safer than life over Burma. That was the night he got up and went to the boys' division; perhaps he was looking for his history in the big room where all the boys slept, but what he found instead was Dr. Larch kissing every boy a late good night. Homer imagined then that Dr. Larch had kissed him like that, when he'd been small; Homer could not have imagined how those kisses, even now, were still kisses meant for him. They were kisses seeking Homer Wells.

That was the same night that he saw the lynx on the barren, unplanted hillside—glazed with snow that had thawed and then refrozen into a thick crust. Homer had stepped outside for just a minute; after witnessing the kisses, he desired the bracing air. It was a Canada lynx—a dark, gunmetal gray against the lighter gray of the moonlit snow, its wildcat stench so strong Homer gagged to smell the thing. Its wildcat sense was keen enough to keep it treading within a single leap's distance of the safety of the woods. The lynx was crossing the brow of the hill when it began to slide; its claws couldn't grip the crust of the snow, and the hill had suddenly grown steeper. The cat moved from the dull moonlight into the sharper light from Nurse Angela's office window; it could not help its sideways descent. It traveled closer to the orphanage than it would ever have chosen to come, its ferocious death smell clashing with the freezing cold. The lynx's helplessness on the ice had rendered its expression both terrified and resigned; both madness and fatalism were caught in the cat's fierce, yellow eyes and in its involuntary, spitting cough as it slid on, actually bumping against the hospital before its claws could find a purchase on the crusted snow. It spit its rage at Homer Wells, as if Homer had caused its unwilling descent.

Its breath had frozen on its chin whiskers and its tufted ears were beaded with ice. The panicked animal tried to dash up the hill; it was less than halfway up when it began to slide down again, drawn toward the orphanage against its will. When it set out from the bottom of the hill a second time, the lynx was panting; it ran diagonally uphill, slipping but catching itself, and slipping again, finally escaping into the softer snow in the woods—nowhere near where it had meant to go; yet the lynx would accept *any* route of escape from the dark hospital.

Homer Wells, staring into the woods after the departed lynx, did not imagine that he would ever leave St. Cloud's more easily.

/ / /

There was a false spring very early that March; all over Maine the river ice buckled under the wet snow, the ponds split apart with gunshots sharp enough to put birds to wing, and the bigger, inland lakes groaned and sang and cracked like boxcars colliding in the station yards.

In the apartment she shared with Lorna in Bath, Melony was awakened by the Kennebec—its ice bending under a foot of slush and giving way with a deep, gonging alarm that caused one of the older women in the boardinghouse to sit up in her bed and howl. Melony was reminded of the nights in her bed in the girls' division in St. Cloud's when the March ice was grinding downriver from Three Mile Falls. She got out of bed and went into Lorna's room to talk, but Lorna was so sleepy that she wouldn't get up; Melony got in bed beside her friend. "It's just the ice," Lorna whispered. That was how she and Melony became lovers, listening to the false spring.

"There's just one thing," Lorna said to Melony. "If we're gonna be together, you gotta stop lookin' for this Homer character. Either you want me or you want him."

"I want you," Melony told Lorna. "Just don't ever leave me."

A permanent couple, an orphan's ideal; but Melony wondered where her rage would go. If she stopped looking for Homer Wells, would she stop thinking about him, too?

There was too much snow; the brief thaw never penetrated the frozen ground, and when the temperature dropped and it snowed again, the rivers hardened up fast. An old mill pond, behind the orphanage in St. Cloud's, became a trap for geese. Confused by the thaw, the geese landed on the slush that they mistook for open water; the slush refroze at night and the geese's paddle feet were caught in it. When Homer Wells found the geese, they were frozen statues of their former selves—dusted with the new snow, they were stony guardians of the pond. There was nothing to do but chip them out of the ice and scald them; they were easier to pluck because they were partially frozen. When Mrs. Grogan roasted them—pricking them constantly, to bleed their fat—she retained the sense that she was only warming them up before sending them on their dangerous way.

It was already April by the time the ice broke free in Three Mile Falls and the river overran its banks in St. Cloud's; water filled the basement of the former whore hotel and exerted such a force against the underbeams that the saloon bar with its brass footrail fell through the floor and floated out and away through a bulkhead. The stationmaster saw it go; as obsessed with omens as he was, he slept two nights in a row in his office for fear that the station house was in danger.

Candy was so huge she hardly slept at all. The morning that the hill was bare, Homer Wells tested the ground; he could work a spade almost a foot down before he hit frozen earth—he needed another six inches of thawing before he could plant apple trees, but he dared not wait any longer before making the trip to Heart's Rock to get the trees. He didn't want to be away when Candy delivered.

Olive was surprised to see him, and by his request to trade the Cadillac for one of the pickup trucks to transport the baby trees.

"I want to plant a standard forty-by-forty," Homer told Olive. "Half Macs, about ten percent Red Delicious, another ten or fifteen percent Cortlands and Baldwins."

Olive reminded him to throw in a few Northern Spies, and some Gravensteins—for apple pie. She asked him how Candy was and why she hadn't come with him; he told her Candy was too busy. (Everyone liked her, and the kids just hung on her.) It would be hard to leave, when the time came, Homer confided to Olive; they were of so much use—they were so needed. And the constancy of the demands—"Well, even a day off, like this, is hard to squeeze in," Homer said.

"You mean you won't spend the night?" Olive asked.

"Too busy," Homer said, "but we'll both be back in time to put out the bees."

"That'll be about Mother's Day," Olive observed.

"Right," said Homer Wells; he kissed Olive, whose skin was cool and smelled like ash.

Meany Hyde and Herb Fowler helped him load the pickup.

"You gonna plant a whole forty-by-forty by yourself?" Meany asked him. "You better hope the ground unfreezes."

"You better hope your back holds out," Herb Fowler said. "You better hope your pecker don't fall off."

"How's Candy?" Big Dot Taft asked Homer. Almost as big as you are, Homer thought.

"Just fine," he said. "But busy."

"I'll bet," said Debra Pettigrew.

In the furnace room, under the lobster tank, Ray Kendall was building his own torpedo.

"What for?" Homer asked.

"Just to see if I can do it," Ray said.

"But what will you fire it at?" Homer asked. "And what will you fire it from?"

"The hard part is the gyroscope," Ray said. "It ain't hard to fire it—what's hard is *guidin'* it."

"I don't understand," said Homer Wells.

"Well, look at you," Ray said. "You're plantin' an apple orchard at an orphanage. You been there five months, but my daughter's too busy to visit me for a day. I don't understand everythin', either."

"We'll be back about blossom time," Homer said guiltily.

"That's a nice time of year," said Ray.

On the drive back to St. Cloud's, Homer wondered if Ray's coolness, or evasiveness, was intentional. He decided that Ray's message was clear: if you keep things from me, I won't explain myself to you.

"A torpedo!" Candy said to Homer, when he arrived with the baby trees. "What for?"

"Wait and see," said Homer Wells.

Dr. Larch helped him unload the trees.

"They're kind of scrawny, aren't they?" Larch asked.

"They won't give much fruit for eight or ten years," Homer said.

"Then I doubt I'll get to eat any of it," said Wilbur Larch.

"Well," Homer said, "even before there are apples on the trees, think how the trees will look on the hill."

"They'll look scrawny," said Wilbur Larch.

Near the top of the hill the ground was still frozen; Homer couldn't work his spade down far enough. And at the bottom, the holes he dug filled with water—the runoff from the snow that was still melting in the woods. Because he would have to wait to plant the trees, he worried about the roots mildewing, or getting savaged by mice—but mainly he was peeved that he could not control, exactly, the calendar of his life. He'd wanted to plant the trees before Candy delivered. He wanted the hillside entirely planted when the baby was born.

"What did I do to you to make you so compulsively neat?" asked Wilbur Larch.

"Surgery is neat," said Homer Wells.

It was the middle of April before Homer could dig the holes and plant the forty-by-forty orchard—which he did in three days, his back so stiff at night that he slept as restlessly and uncomfortably as Candy, tossing and turning with her. It was the first warm night of the spring; they were much too hot under the winter-weight blanket; when Candy broke water, they both, for a second, confused the puddle with their sweat.

Homer helped her to the hospital entrance of the boys' division. Nurse Edna prepared Candy while Homer went to talk to Dr. Larch, who was waiting in Nurse Angela's office.

"*I* deliver this one," Larch said. "There are certain advantages to detachment. Fathers are a bother in the delivery room. If you want to be there, just mind your own business."

"Right," said Homer Wells. He was fidgeting, uncharacteristically, and Dr. Larch smiled at him.

Nurse Edna was with Candy, while Nurse Angela scrubbed for Dr. Larch. Homer had already put his mask on when he heard a commotion from the boys' sleeping room. He left the mask on when he went to investigate. One of the John Larches or the Wilbur Walshes had got up and gone outside to pee against a trash barrel—with considerable noise. This in turn had disturbed a large raccoon, busy at the trash, and the coon had startled the peeing orphan into wetting his pajamas. Homer tried to sort this out, calmly; he wanted to get back to the delivery room.

"Peeing indoors is better, at night," he observed to the room at large. "Candy's having her baby, now."

"What's she havin'?" one of the boys asked.

"Either a boy or a girl," said Homer Wells.

"What will you name it?" another one asked.

"Nurse Angela named me," Homer said.

"Me, too!" several of them said.

"If it's a girl, I'm naming her Angela," said Homer Wells.

"And if it's a boy?"

"If it's a boy, I'll name him Angel," Homer said. "That's really just Angela without the last A."

"Angel?" someone asked.

"Right," said Homer Wells, and kissed them all good night.

As he was leaving, someone asked him, "And will you leave it here?"

"No," mumbled Homer Wells, having pulled his mask back up.

"What?" the orphans shouted.

"No," Homer said more clearly, pulling down the mask.

It was hot in the delivery room. The warm weather had been unexpected; because no one had put the screens on, Larch refused to open any windows.

At the knowledge that the child, one way or another, would be named after her, Nurse Angela wept so hard that Larch insisted that she change her mask. Nurse Edna was too short to reach the sweat on Larch's forehead; she missed some of it. As the baby's head emerged, a drop of Larch's sweat baptized the child squarely on its temple—literally before it was entirely born—and Homer Wells could not help thinking that this was not unlike David Copperfield being born with a caul.

When the shoulders did not follow quickly enough to please Larch, he took the chin and occiput in both hands and drew the infant downward until, in a single, easy, upward motion, he delivered the posterior shoulder first. Homer Wells, biting his lip, nodded his approval as the anterior shoulder—and the rest of the child—followed.

"It's an Angel!" Nurse Edna announced to Candy, who was still smiling an ether smile. Nurse Angela, who had soaked through another mask, had to turn away.

Only after the placenta was born did Dr. Larch say, as he sometimes did, "Perfect!" Then, as he never before had done, he kissed Candy—albeit through his mask—squarely between her wide-open, out-of-ether eyes.

The next day it snowed, and snowed—an angry April snowstorm, desperate not to relinquish the winter—and Homer looked at his newly planted apple orchard with concern; the frail, snow-covered trees reminded him of the luckless geese who'd made an ill-timed landing in the mill pond.

"Stop worrying about the trees," said Wilbur Larch. "They're on their own now."

So was Angel Wells—eight pounds, seven ounces and neither an orphan nor an abortion.

/ / /

One week short of May, there was still too much snow in St. Cloud's for it to be mud season yet. Homer Wells had shaken the individual branches of each of his apple trees; and mouse tracks around one particularly vulnerable-looking Winter Banana had caused him to scatter poison oats and poison corn. Every tree had a metal sleeve around its slender trunk. Deer had already nibbled the row of Macs planted nearest the woods. Homer put out a salt lick for the deer, deeper into the woods, in hopes that the salt would keep them there.

Candy was nursing Angel, whose crusty remnant of an umbilical had fallen off cleanly and whose circumcision had healed. Homer had circumcised his son.

"You need the practice," Dr. Larch had told him.

"You want me to practice on my son?" Homer had asked.

"May it be the only pain you ever cause him," Wilbur Larch had replied.

There was still ice on the inside of the windowpanes in the morning. Homer would hold his finger to the pane until his finger was bright red, wet and cold, and then he'd touch Candy with the finger—which woke her up when she was slow to respond to his gentler touching of her stubble. Homer and Candy loved how they fit together in the bed again and how Angel could fit between them when Candy was nursing him, and how Candy's milk would sometimes wake them both up before Angel's crying would. They agreed: they had never been happier. So what if the sky, when it was almost May, was still the slate color of February, and still streaked with sleet? So what if the secret they kept in St. Cloud's could not be kept forever—and was already a secret that half of Heart's Haven and Heart's Rock had the sense to figure out for themselves? People from Maine don't crowd you; they let you come to your senses in your own, good time.

Every two days there was a ritual weighing of Angel Wells, which was always conducted in the dispensary—Nurse Angela keeping the record, Dr. Larch and Homer taking turns at poking Angel's belly, looking into Angel's eyes and feeling Angel's grip. "Admit it," Nurse Edna said to Candy and Homer at one such weighing-in ceremony. "You like it here."

That day, in St. Cloud's, it was thirty-three degrees; the wet snow, with which the morning had begun, had turned to freezing rain. That day, in Heart's Rock, Olive Worthington had her own secret. Perhaps if Homer and Candy had been more forthcoming to her, Olive would have shared her secret with them; she would have grabbed the phone and called them. But people from Maine don't like the telephone, a rude invention; especially in the case of important news, a telephone catches you too off-guard. A telegram provides you with a decent, respectful interval in which to gather your senses and respond. Olive sent them her secret in a telegram; that gave everyone a little more time.

Candy would see the telegram first. She was nursing Angel in the girls' division, to quite an appreciative audience of girl orphans, when Mrs. Grogan brought her the telegram, which one of the lackeys who slaved for the stationmaster had finally gotten around to delivering. The telegram was an obvious shock to Candy, who quite abruptly handed Angel to Mrs. Grogan, although Angel did not appear to be through nursing. It astonished Mrs. Grogan that Candy did not even pause to properly replace her breast in her bra—she just buttoned her blouse over herself and, in spite of the weather, ran outdoors and across to the hospital entrance of the boys' division.

At the time, Homer was asking Dr. Larch if he (Larch) thought that an X ray of his (Homer's) heart might prove instructive to Homer. Wilbur Larch was thinking very carefully about his answer when Candy burst upon them.

Olive Worthington was a Yankee who knew the price of a telegram, the cost of words, yet her enthusiasm for her subject had clearly carried her away; she went far beyond her usual, shorthand self.

WALLY FOUND ALIVE/STOP/
RECOVERING ENCEPHALITIS CEYLON/STOP/
LIBERATED FROM RANGOON BURMA/STOP/
TEMPERATURE NINETY-TWO DEGREES/STOP/
WEIGHT ONE HUNDRED FIVE POUNDS/STOP/
PARALYZED/STOP/
LOVE OLIVE

"A hundred and five pounds," said Homer Wells.

"*Alive,*" Candy whispered.

"Paralyzed," Nurse Angela said.

"Encephalitis," said Wilbur Larch.

"How *could* his temperature be ninety-two degrees, Wilbur?" Nurse Edna asked.

Dr. Larch didn't know; he wouldn't venture a guess. It was another one of those details—the clarification of which would take quite a long time. For Captain Worthington, who had abandoned his plane over Burma—about ten months ago—the clarification of many such details would take years.

It was raining so heavily when he jumped, it seemed to Wally that his parachute had to push against the rain to open. Yet the roar of the plane was so near, Wally was afraid he'd pulled the cord too soon. He was afraid of the bamboo—he'd heard stories of fliers being impaled by it—but he missed the bamboo and landed in a teak tree, a branch of which separated his shoulder. His head may have hit the trunk, or else the pain in his shoulder caused him to lose consciousness. It was dark when he woke up, and since he couldn't see how far below the ground was, he didn't dare to free himself from the chute cords until morning. Then he gave himself too much morphine—for his shoulder—and lost the syringe in the dark. In his haste to abandon the plane, he'd not had time to locate a machete; in the morning he spent quite a while cutting through the chute cords—using only the bayonet in his ankle sheath, and having the use of only one strong arm. He was lowering himself to the ground when his dog tags caught on a vine, and because of his bad shoulder he could neither support all his weight with one arm nor free the tags, and so he lost them; the chain cut his neck when the tags came off, and he landed on an old teakwood log that was hidden under the ferns and the dead palm fronds. The log rolled, and he sprained his ankle. When he realized that in the monsoon weather he would never know east from west, that was when he discovered that his compass was gone. He rubbed some sulfa powder on his cut neck.

Wally had no idea where China was; he picked his way by moving through whatever was the least dense. In this way, after three days, he had the impression that the jungle was either thinning out or that he was getting better at picking his way through it. China was east of Wally, but Wally went south; China was up—over the mountains—but Wally sought the valleys. Where Wally was, the valleys ran southwesterly. He was right about one thing: the jungle was thinning out. It was also getting warmer. Every night he climbed a tree and slept in its crotch. The large, twisted trunks of the peepul tree—as gnarled as giant, wooden cables—made the best crotches for sleeping, but Wally wasn't the first creature to figure this out. One night, at eye level, in the crotch of a peepul tree next to him, a leopard was examining itself for ticks. Wally followed the leopard's example, and discovered several. He gave up trying to remove the leeches.

One day he saw a python—a small one, about fifteen feet. It was lying on a rock, swallowing something the approximate size and shape of a beagle. Wally guessed it was a monkey, although he couldn't remember if he had seen any monkeys. He had seen monkeys, of course, but he'd forgotten them; he had a fever. He tried to take his temperature, but the thermometer in his first-aid kit was broken.

The day he saw a tiger swim across a river was the day he began to notice the mosquitoes; the climate was changing. The river with the tiger in it had produced a broader valley; the forest was changing, too. He caught a fish with his hands and ate its liver raw; he cooked frogs as big as cats, but their legs were fishier than the frog legs he remembered. Perhaps it was the lack of garlic.

He ate something that was the consistency of a mango and had no taste whatsoever; the fruit left a musty aftertaste, and for a whole day he vomited and had chills. Then the river where he'd seen the tiger turned into a bigger river; the monsoon water had a powerful current; Wally was encouraged to build a raft. He remembered the rafts he had engineered for travel on Drinkwater Lake, and he cried to think how much harder it was to build a raft with bamboo and vines than with pitch pine and ropes—and stray boards and nails. And how much heavier the green bamboo was, too. It didn't matter that the raft leaked; it barely floated; and if he needed to portage, he knew he couldn't carry it.

He noticed more mosquitoes, especially when the river broadened and the current slowed down, and he just drifted. He had no idea how many days he drifted, or when he first knew for certain that he had a fever; about the time he saw the rice paddies and the water buffaloes, he would say later. One day he would remember waving to the women in the rice paddies; they looked so surprised to see him.

When Wally saw the rice paddies, he must have known he'd gone the wrong way. He had gone into the heart of Burma, which is shaped like a kite with a long tail; he was much nearer to Mandalay than he was to China, and the Japanese held Mandalay. But Wally had a fever of one hundred four; he just drifted; sometimes, he couldn't tell the river from the rice paddies. It was strange how both the men and women wore long skirts, but only the men covered their hair; they wore what looked like baskets on their heads, and the baskets were wrapped with strips of brightly colored silk. The women's heads were bare, but many of them put flowers in their hair. Both the men and the women braided their hair. They seemed to be eating all the time, but they were just chewing betel nuts. Their teeth were stained; their lips made them appear as if they'd been drinking blood, but that was just the betel juice.

The shelters they took Wally to were all alike—one-story, thatched houses on bamboo stilts; the families ate outdoors on a porch. They gave him rice and tea and lots of things with curry. When his fever went down, Wally ate *panthay khowse* (noodles and chicken) and *nga sak kin* (curried fish balls). Those were the first words that his Burmese rescuers tried to teach him, but Wally misunderstood; he thought *nga sak kin* was the name of the man who had carried him off the raft and held Wally's head steady while the man's wife fed Wally with her fingers. She was wonderfully small and wore a sheer white blouse; her husband touched the blouse and called it by name, trying to teach Wally more of his language.

"Aingyis," the man said, and Wally thought that was the wife's name. She smelled like the inside of the thatched houses—she smelled like chintz and lemon rind.

They were such a nice couple, *Nga Sak Kin* and *Aingyis;* Wally repeated their names out loud and smiled. They smiled back at him, Mr. Curried Fish Balls and his wife, Mrs. Blouse. She smelled as sticky-sweet as frangipani; she smelled as citrus as bergamot.

With the fever had come the stiffness in his neck and back, but when the fever broke and he stopped vomiting—when the headaches were over and the shaking chills were gone, and he wasn't even nauseous anymore—that was when he noticed the paralysis. At that time, it was a stiff paralysis in both his lower and upper extremities. ("Spasticity," Wilbur Larch would have called it.) Wally's arms and legs stuck straight out and he couldn't move them; he was delirious for two or three weeks and when he tried to talk, his speech was thick and slow. He had trouble eating because of the tremors in his lips and tongue. He couldn't empty his bladder, and the natives had to catheterize him with a tiny, rough bamboo shoot—in order for him to urinate at all.

And they kept moving him. They always moved him over water. Once he saw elephants; they were dragging logs out of the forests. The surface of the water was forever interrupted with turtles and black snakes and water hyacinths, and betel juice—a darker red than the blood that traced Wally's urine.

"Nga Sak Kin?" Wally asked. *"Aingyis?"* he asked. Where had they gone? Although the faces of his rescuers kept changing, they seemed to understand him. Must come from a big family, Wally thought. "I'm paralyzed, aren't I?" he asked the small, pretty men and women, who always smiled. One of the women washed and combed his hair; her whole family watched Wally's hair drying in the sun—the blond light leaping into it as it dried: how that impressed them!

They gave him a long sheer white blouse to wear. *"Aingyis,"* they said. Oh, it's a present from her! he thought. Then they covered his blond hair with a dark wig—it was a waxy pigtail, and they piled it high on top of his head and studded it with flowers. The children giggled. They shaved his face so close his skin burned; they shaved his legs—below the knee, where his legs protruded from the long skirt they made him wear. The game was to make him a woman. The game was to make him safe, to make him blend in. Because his face was so pretty, it was easier for them to make him a woman than a man; the ideal Burmese woman has no breasts.

It is a shame that they weren't more careful when they catheterized him—they were so careful about everything else. The bamboo shoot wasn't always clean; the catheter's roughness hurt him and made him bleed, but it was the dirtiness that would give him the infection. The infection would make him sterile. The epididymis, Wilbur Larch could have informed him, is a single coiled tube in which the sperm mature after leaving the testicle. Epididymitis (an infection of that little tube) prevents sperm from reaching the sperm duct. In Wally's case, the infection would permanently seal his tube.

They were correct to catheterize him—it was only the how that was wrong. He suffered urinary retention, his bladder was distended—they had no choice but to relieve him. At times, Wally would wonder if there wasn't an easier way—or if the bamboo was clean—but what could he say to them? *"Aingyis,"* he would say. *"Nga Sak Kin?"* he would ask them.

Months later, he would hear bombing. "Irrawaddy," they would explain. They were bombing the oil fields along the Irrawaddy. Wally knew where he was. He used to bomb those fields, too. Before he heard the bombing (and, as always, disguised as a woman), he was taken to a doctor in Mandalay. His eyes were smarting because they'd rubbed a curry paste on his face to make him look brown. But, up close, with those blue eyes and that patrician nose, he couldn't have fooled anyone. He saw many Japanese in Mandalay. The doctor had trouble explaining to Wally what was wrong with him. He said the following in English: "Japanese B mosquito."

"I was bitten by a Japanese mosquito?" Wally said. But what's a B mosquito? he wondered. He no longer needed a catheter to pee, but the infection had done its damage.

By the time he heard the bombing of the Irrawaddy, the paralysis had left his upper extremities—he had the full use of his arms, again—and the spasticity had left his legs; although his legs were still paralyzed, it was a flaccid paralysis and not quite symmetrical (his left leg was more dead than his right).

His bladder was okay, and except for the effects of curry, his bowels were okay, too; what he could detect of his sexual function felt normal.

"There are no autonomic effects to encephalitis," Wilbur Larch would explain to Candy and to Homer Wells.

"What's that mean?" Candy asked.

"It means that Wally can have a normal sex life," said Homer Wells, who didn't know about Wally's epididymis. Wally would have a normal sex life, but he wouldn't have an adequate sperm count. He would still have orgasm and ejaculation—since so much of the ejaculate is made in the prostate, which is quite a way downstream. He just could never make his own baby.

At the time, none of them knew Wally had been sterilized; they knew only about the encephalitis.

Wally caught it from the mosquitoes. It was called Japanese B encephalitis, and it was quite common in Asia during the war. "It is an arthropod-borne virus," Wilbur Larch explained.

Residual flaccid paralysis of the lower extremities was not a common effect of the disease, but it was well enough known to be documented. There are numerous changes that occur in the tissue of the brain, but the changes in the spinal cord look very much like polio. The incubation period is about a week long and the acute disease process lasts only a week or ten days; the recovery is very slow, with muscular tremors lasting sometimes for months.

"Considering that it comes from birds, it's a big disease," Wilbur Larch said to Nurse Edna and Nurse Angela. The mosquito picks up the virus from birds and transmits it to men and other large animals.

Wally's face was so pretty, and he'd lost so much weight: that was why they disguised him as a woman. The Japanese were both attracted to and intimidated by the Burmese women—especially the Padaung women with their high brass collars wound in spirals to stretch their necks. That Wally was a woman *and* an invalid made him an untouchable. That they had made him look Eurasian also made him an outcast.

When the monsoon season ended, in October, they either traveled on the river at nights or they protected him from the sun with an umbrella—and with more curry paste. He got very tired of curried fish balls, but he kept asking for them—or so the Burmese thought; that was all they gave him. And when he was delirious, he said Candy's name. One of the boatmen asked him about it.

"Candy?" the boatman inquired politely. That day they were in a sampan; Wally lay under a roof of mats and watched the boatman sculling.

"*Aingyis,*" Wally said. He meant, like her—a good woman, a wife.

The boatman nodded. At the next port on the river—Wally didn't know where: it might have been Yandoon—they gave him another sheer white blouse.

"Candy!" the boatman said. Wally thought he meant, give it to Candy. He smiled; he just kept drifting. The sampan's sharp nose seemed to smell the way. It was a country of smells to Wally—it was a fragrant dream.

Wilbur Larch could imagine Wally's journey. It was an ether journey, of course. Elephants and oil fields, rice paddies and bombs falling, dressed up as a woman and paralyzed from the waist down—Larch had been there; he had been everywhere. He had no trouble imagining Rangoon and water buffaloes. Every ether dream has its equivalent of British underground agents smuggling American pilots across the Bay of Bengal. Wally's trip through Burma was a voyage Wilbur Larch had often undertaken. The black-currant odor of petunias was at war with the odor of dung, all the way.

They flew Wally across the Bay of Bengal in a small plane with a British pilot and a Sinhalese crew. Wilbur Larch had taken many such flights.

"Do you speak Sinhala?" the Englishman asked Wally, who sat in the co-pilot's seat. The pilot smelled of garlic and turmeric.

"I don't even know what Sinhala is," Wally said. When he shut his eyes, he could still see the white, waxy flowers of the wild lime bushes; he could still see the jungle.

"Principal language of Ceylon, my boy," the pilot said. The pilot also smelled like tea.

"We're going to Ceylon?" Wally asked.

"Can't keep a blond in Burma, lad," the Englishman said. "Don't you know Burma's full of Nips?" But Wally preferred to remember his native friends. They had taught him to salaam—a low bow with the right hand on the forehead (always the right hand, they'd explained); it was a bow of salutation. And when he was sick, someone had always stirred the punkah for him—a punkah is a large, screen-shaped fan that is moved by a rope (pulled by a servant).

"Punkah," Wally said to the English pilot.

"What's that, lad?" the pilot asked.

"It's so hot," said Wally, who felt drowsy; they were flying at a very low altitude, and the little plane was an oven. A brief scent of sandalwood came through the stronger garlic in the pilot's sweat.

"Ninety-two degrees, American, when we left Rangoon," the pilot said. The pilot got a kick out of saying "American" instead of "Fahrenheit," but Wally didn't notice.

"Ninety-two degrees!" Wally said. It felt like the first fact he could hang his hat on, as they say in Maine.

"What happened to the legs?" the Englishman asked casually.

"Japanese B mosquito," Wally explained. The British pilot looked very grave; he thought that Wally meant a plane—that the Japanese B mosquito was the name of the fighter plane that shot Wally's plane down.

"I don't know that one, lad," the pilot admitted to Wally. "Thought I'd seen them all, but you can't trust the Nips."

The Sinhalese crew had slathered themselves with coconut oil and were wearing sarongs and long, collarless shirts. Two of them were eating something and one of them was screeching into the radio; the pilot said something sharply to the radioman, who instantly lowered his voice.

"Sinhala is an awful language," the pilot confided to Wally. "Sounds like cats fucking."

When Wally didn't respond to his humor, the Englishman asked him if he'd ever been to Ceylon. When Wally didn't answer him—Wally seemed to be daydreaming—the Englishman said, "We not only planted the first rubber trees *and* developed their bloody rubber plantations—we taught them how to brew tea. They knew how to grow it, all right, but you couldn't get a decent cup of tea on the whole bloody island. And now they want to be independent," the Englishman said.

"Ninety-two degrees," Wally said, smiling.

"Yes, just try to relax, lad," the pilot said. When Wally

burped, he tasted cinnamon; when he shut his eyes, he saw African marigolds come out like stars.

Suddenly the three Sinhalese began to speak at once. First the radio would say something, then the three of them would speak in unison.

"Bloody Buddhists, all of them," the pilot explained. "They even pray on the bloody radio. That's Ceylon," the Englishman said. "Two thirds tea and one third rubber and prayer." He yelled something at the Sinhalese, who lowered their voices.

Somewhere over the Indian Ocean, shortly before sighting Ceylon, the pilot was worried about an aircraft in his vicinity. "Pray now, damn you," he said to the Sinhalese, who were all asleep. "That Japanese B mosquito," the Englishman said to Wally. "What does it look like?" he asked. "Or did it get you from behind?"

But all Wally would say was, "Ninety-two degrees."

After the war, Ceylon would become an independent nation; twenty-four years after that, the country would change its name to Sri Lanka. But all Wally would remember was how hot it had been. In a way, his parachute had never touched down; in a way, he had remained over Burma for ten months—just floating there. All Wally would remember of his own story would never make as much sense as an ether frolic. And how he would survive the war—sterile, paralyzed, both legs flaccid—had already been dreamed by Big Dot Taft.

/ / /

It was thirty-four degrees in St. Cloud's when Homer Wells went to the railroad station and dictated a telegram to Olive to the stationmaster. Homer could not have phoned her, and lied to her *that* directly. And hadn't Olive telegramed them? She must have had her reasons for not wanting to talk on the phone. It was with the almost certain feeling that Ray and Olive knew everything that Homer and Candy were doing that Homer dictated his telegram to Olive—respecting a polite formality as faint as a suspicion. It was a suspicion that could be proven only impolitely, and Homer Wells was polite.

GOD BLESS YOU AND WALLY/STOP
WHEN WILL WE SEE HIM/STOP
CANDY AND I HOME SOON/STOP

I HAVE ADOPTED A BABY BOY/STOP
LOVE HOMER

"You're kind of young to adopt somebody, ain't you?" the stationmaster asked.

"Right," said Homer Wells.

Candy telephoned her father.

"It's gonna be weeks, or maybe months before they can move him," Ray told her. "He's gotta gain some weight before he can travel so far, and there's probably tests they've gotta do—and there's still a war on, don't forget."

At her end of the phone, Candy just cried and cried.

"Tell me how you are, darlin'," Ray Kendall said. That was when she could have told him that she'd just had Homer's baby, but what she said was, "Homer's adopted one of the orphans."

After a pause, Raymond Kendall said, "Just one of them?"

"He's adopted a baby boy," Candy said. "Of course, I'll help, too. We've kind of adopted a baby together."

"You have?" Ray said.

"His name is Angel," Candy said.

"Bless his heart," Ray said. "Bless you both, too."

Candy cried some more.

"Adopted, huh?" Ray asked his daughter.

"Yes," said Candy Kendall. "One of the orphans."

She quit the breast-feeding, and Nurse Edna introduced her to the device for pumping her breasts. Angel disliked his conversion to formula milk, and for a few days he displayed a cranky temperament. Candy displayed a cranky temperament, too. When Homer observed that her pubic hair would be very nearly grown back by the time she returned to Heart's Haven, she snapped at him.

"For God's sake, who's going to see whether I have pubic hair or not—except you?" Candy asked.

Homer showed signs of strain, too.

He was impatient with Dr. Larch's suggestion that Homer's future lay in the medical profession. Larch insisted on giving Homer a brand-new copy of *Gray's Anatomy;* he also gave him the standard Greenhill's *Office Gynecology* and the British masterpiece *Diseases of Women.*

"Jesus Christ," said Homer Wells. "I'm a father, and I'm going to be an apple farmer."

"You have near-perfect obstetrical procedure," Larch told him. "You just need a little more of the gynecological—and the pediatric, of course."

"Maybe I'll end up a lobsterman," Homer said.

"And I'll send you a subscription to *The New England Journal of Medicine*," Dr. Larch said. "And *JAMA*, and *S, G and O . . .*"

"You're the doctor," said Homer Wells tiredly.

"How do you feel?" Candy asked Homer.

"Like an orphan," Homer said. They held each other tightly, but they did not make love. "How do *you* feel?" Homer asked.

"I won't know until I see him," Candy said honestly.

"What will you know then?" Homer asked.

"If I love him, or you, or both of you," she said. "Or else I won't know any more than I know now."

"It's always wait and see, isn't it?" Homer asked.

"You don't expect me to tell him anything when he's still over there, do you?" Candy asked.

"No, of course I don't expect that," he said softly. She held him tighter; she began to cry again.

"Oh, Homer," she said. "How can he weigh only a hundred and five pounds?"

"I'm sure he'll gain some weight," Homer said, but his entire body shivered suddenly; Wally's body had been so strong. Homer remembered the first time Wally had taken him to the ocean; the surf had been unusually rough, and Wally had warned him about the undertow. Wally had taken him by the hand and shown him how to duck under the waves, and how to ride them. They had walked along the beach for an hour, undistracted by Candy; she had been tanning.

"I don't understand all this stupid lying down in the sun," Wally had told Homer, who agreed. "You're either doing something in the sun and you pick up a little color, or you're doing something else—but you're doing something. That's the main thing."

They were picking up shells and stones—the beachcombers' search for specimens. Homer was immediately impressed with the smoothness of the stones and the broken pieces of shell—how the water and the sand had softened them.

"This is a very experienced piece," Wally had said, handing Homer an especially worn bit of shell; it had no edges.

"Experienced," Homer had said.

And after that, Wally had said, "And this is a worldly stone," exhibiting an old, smooth one.

Homer thought that his desire for Candy had changed everything, even the natural process of the grinding smooth of stones and shells. If he and Wally went back to the beach, would they still be beachcombers, or was it inevitable that the love of a woman would alter even their most commonplace experiences together? Was he my friend for five minutes? wondered Homer Wells—and my rival for the rest of my life?

Homer entrusted Nurse Edna with the care of the hillside orchard. He explained that the wire-mesh sleeves around the trees could not be wrapped so tightly that they didn't permit the trees to grow—but also not so loosely that the mice could girdle the trees. He showed her how to spot the tunnels of the pine mice who ate the roots.

Everyone kissed Candy good-bye, even Wilbur Larch—who, when he reached to shake Homer's hand, appeared embarrassed that Homer brushed past his hand and hugged him, and kissed him on his leathery neck. Nurse Edna sobbed the most freely. As soon as the pickup truck rolled past the girls' division, Wilbur Larch closed himself in the dispensary.

It was a Sunday, so Raymond Kendall was at work on his homemade torpedo when Homer brought Candy home. Candy told Homer that she could not face seeing Olive until the next morning, but she was gripped by an unforeseen panic when Homer drove off with Angel. Although her milk was gone, she knew she would still wake up to her baby's clock—even though it would be Homer, alone, who was hearing the actual cries. And how many nights had it been since she had slept alone?

She would tell Homer the next day: "We've got to find a way to share him. I mean, even before we tell Olive—not to mention, Wally—we have to *both* take care of him, we have to *both* be with him. I just miss him too much."

"I miss you," Homer Wells told her.

He was an orphan who'd had a family for less than a month of his life, and he was not prepared to not have a family again.

When he and Angel arrived at Ocean View, Olive greeted

Homer as if she were his mother; she threw her arms around him, and kissed him, and wept. "Show me that baby—oh, he's darling!" she cried. "Whatever possessed you? You're so young, and you're all alone."

"Well, the baby was all alone, too," Homer mumbled. "And Candy will help me with him."

"Of course," Olive said. "I'll help you, too." She carried Angel to Wally's room, where Homer was surprised to see a crib—and more baby things, for just one baby, than could have been collected in a thorough search of both the boys' and girls' divisions in St. Cloud's.

An army of bottles, for the formula, awaited Homer in the kitchen. Olive had even bought a special pot for sterilizing the nipples. In the linen closet, there were more diapers than there were pillowcases and sheets and towels. For the first time in his life, Homer felt that he'd been adopted. To his horror, he saw that Olive loved him.

"I think that you and Angel should have Wally's room," Olive said; she had obviously been busy, planning. "Wally won't be able to climb stairs, so I'm having the dining room made into a bedroom—we can always eat in the kitchen, and the dining room has that terrace for when the weather's nice. I'm having a ramp built from the terrace to the patio around the pool, for the wheelchair."

As Homer held her while she cried, a new guilt surrounded him, like the nightfall, that ever-old, ever-new remorse that Mr. Rochester had told Jane Eyre to dread, that "poison of life."

/ / /

In the second week of May, Ira Titcomb and Homer worked alongside each other, putting the bees out in the orchards. It was the start of blossom time, the night before Mother's Day, when they put out the hives. Everyone remembered Mother's Day that year; no one forgot Olive. The house was full of little presents and lots of apple blossoms, and some of the work crew even gave Homer a Mother's Day present—they thought it was so funny that he'd adopted a baby.

"Just imagine you with your very own baby!" was the way Big Dot Taft put it.

In the apple mart, where they were giving the display tables a fresh coat of paint, there were two babies on display—Angel Wells and Florence and Meany Hyde's boy, Pete. Pete Hyde looked like a potato compared to Angel Wells—which is to say that his disposition was entirely bland and he had no apparent bones in his face.

"Well, Homer, your Angel is an Angel," Florence Hyde would say, "and my Pete's a Pete."

The apple-mart women teased him endlessly; Homer just smiled. Debra Pettigrew was especially interested in handling Angel Wells; she would look intently into the baby's face for the longest time before announcing that she was sure the baby was going to look just like Homer. "Only more aristocratic," she guessed. Squeeze Louise said the baby was "too precious for words." When Homer was out in the field, either Olive or one of the apple-mart women looked after Angel, but most of the time Candy looked after her baby.

"We kind of adopted him together," she would explain. She said it so often that Olive said Candy was as much of a mother to that child as Homer was, and Olive therefore—as a kind of joke—gave Candy a Mother's Day present, too. All the while, the bees did their work, carrying pollen from the Frying Pan to Cock Hill, and the honey leaked between the clapboards that housed the hives.

One morning, on a corner of the newspaper, Homer Wells saw Olive's handwriting—a penciled remark above the day's headlines, any one of which might have prompted Olive to respond. But somehow Homer thought the remark was written to him.

INTOLERABLE DISHONESTY

Olive had written.

And one night Candy overheard Ray. Her bedroom light was out; in the pitch dark she heard her father say, "It's not wrong, but it's not right." At first she thought he was on the telephone. After she drifted back to sleep, the sound of her door opening and closing woke her up again, and she realized Ray had been sitting in her room with her—addressing her in her sleep, in the darkness.

And some of the nights in blossom time, Candy would say to Homer, "You're an overworked father."

"Isn't he?" Olive would say admiringly.

"I'm going to take this kid off your hands for the night," Candy would say, and Homer would smile through the tension of these exchanges. He would wake up alone in Wally's room in anticipation of Angel needing his bottle. He could imagine Raymond Kendall getting up to heat the formula and Candy being in her bed with the bottle of formula in as near an approximation of the correct angle of her breast as she could arrange it.

Ray's torpedo parts were stolen from Kittery Navy Yard; both Homer and Candy knew that's how he got them, but only Candy criticized Ray for it.

"I've caught more mistakes in the way they do things than they know things to do," Ray said. "Not likely they could catch me."

"But what's it for, anyway?" Candy asked her father. "I don't like there being a bomb here—especially when there's a baby in the house."

"Well, when I got the torpedo," Ray explained, "I didn't know about the baby."

"Well, you know now," Candy said. "Why don't you fire it at something—at something far away."

"When it's ready, I'll fire it," Ray said.

"What are you going to fire it at?" Homer asked Raymond Kendall.

"I don't know,". Ray said. "Maybe the Haven Club—the next time they tell me I spoil their view."

"I don't like not knowing what you're doing something *for,*" Candy told her father when they were alone.

"It's like this," Ray said slowly. "I'll tell you what it's like—a torpedo. It's like Wally, comin' home. You know he's comin', you can't calculate the damage."

Candy asked Homer for an interpretation of Ray's meaning.

"He's not telling you anything," Homer said. "He's fishing—he wants you to tell him."

"Suppose it all just goes on, the way it is?" Candy asked Homer, after they had made love in the cider house—which had not yet been cleaned for use in the harvest.

"The way it is," said Homer Wells..

"Yes," she said. "Just suppose that we wait, and we wait. How long could we wait?" she asked. "I mean, after a while, suppose it gets easier to wait than to tell?"

"We'll have to tell, sometime," said Homer Wells.

"When?" Candy asked.

"When Wally comes home," Homer said.

"When he comes home paralyzed and weighing less than I weigh," Candy said. "Is that when we spring it on him?" she asked.

Are there things you can't ease into? wondered Homer Wells. The scalpel, he remembered, has a certain heft; one does not need to press on it—it seems to cut on its own—but one does need to take charge of it in a certain way. When one takes it up, one has to move it. A scalpel does not require the authority of force, but it demands of the user the authority of motion.

"We have to know where we're going," said Homer Wells.

"But what if we don't know?" Candy asked. "What if we know only how we want to stay? What if we wait and wait?"

"Do you mean that you won't ever know if you love him or me?" Homer asked her.

"It may be all confused by how much he's going to need me," Candy said. Homer put his hand on her—where her pubic hair had grown back, almost exactly as it was.

"You don't think I'll need you, too?" he asked her. She rolled to her other hip, turning her back to him—but at the same time taking his hand from where he'd touched her and clamping his hand to her breast.

"We'll have to wait and see," she said.

"Past a certain point, I won't wait," said Homer Wells.

"What point is that?" Candy asked. Because his hand was on her breast, he could feel her holding her breath.

"When Angel is old enough to either know he's an orphan or know who his parents are," Homer said. "That's the point. I won't have Angel thinking he's adopted. I won't have him not knowing who his mother and father are."

"I'm not worried about Angel," Candy said. "Angel will get lots of love. I'm worried about you and me."

"And Wally," Homer said.

"We'll go crazy," Candy said.

"We won't go crazy," Homer said. "We've got to take care of Angel and make him feel loved."

"But what if *I* don't feel loved, or *you* don't—what then?" Candy asked him.

"We'll wait until then," said Homer Wells. "We'll just wait and see," he said, almost with a vengeance. A spring breeze blew over them, bearing with it the sickly-sweet stench of rotten apples. The smell had an almost-ammonia power that so overwhelmed Homer Wells that he released Candy's breast and covered his mouth and nose with his hand.

It was not until the summer when Candy first heard directly from Wally. She got an actual letter—her first communication from him since he'd been shot down a year ago.

Wally had spent six weeks in Mt. Lavinia Hospital in Ceylon. They had not wanted to move him from there until he'd gained fifteen pounds, until his muscle tremors had ceased and his speech had lost the daydreaming vacantness of malnutrition. He wrote the letter from another hospital, in New Delhi; after a month in India, he had gained an additional ten pounds. He said that he'd learned to put cinnamon in his tea, and that the slap of sandals was nearly constant in the hospital.

They were promising him that they would allow him to commence the long trip home when he weighed one hundred forty pounds and when he had mastered a few basic exercises that were essential to his rehabilitation. He couldn't describe the route of his proposed voyage home because of the censors. Wally hoped that the censors would understand—in the light of his paralysis—that it was necessary for him to say something about his "perfectly normal" sexual function. The censors had allowed this to pass. Wally still didn't know he was sterile; he knew he'd had a urinary tract infection, and that the infection was gone.

"And how is Homer? How I miss him!" Wally wrote.

But that was not the part of the letter that devastated Candy. Candy was so devastated by the beginning of the letter that the rest of the letter was simply a continuing devastation to her.

"I'm so afraid that you won't want to marry a cripple," Wally began.

In her single bed, tugged into sleep and into wakefulness by the tide, Candy stared at the picture of her mother on the night table. She would have liked a mother to talk to at the moment, and perhaps because she had no memory of her mother she remembered the first night she had arrived at the orphanage. Dr. Larch had been reading to the boys from *Great Expectations*. Candy would never forget the line that she and Homer had walked in on.

" 'I awoke without having parted in my sleep with the

erception of my wretchedness,'" Wilbur Larch had read
loud. Either Dr. Larch had predetermined that he would end
he evening's reading with that line, or else he had only then
.oticed Candy and Homer Wells in the open doorway—the
arsh hall light, a naked bulb, formed a kind of institutional
alo above their heads—and had lost his place in the book,
ausing him, spur-of-the-moment, to stop reading. For what-
ver reason, that perception of wretchedness had been Candy's
ntroduction to St. Cloud's, and the beginning and the end of
er bedtime story.

10/ Fifteen Years

For fifteen years they were a couple: Lorna and Melony. They were set in their ways. Once the young rebels of the women-only boardinghouse, they now occupied the choicest rooms—with the river view—and they served as superintendents to the building for a consideration regarding their rent. Melony was handy. She had learned plumbing and electricity at the shipyard where she was one of a staff of three electricians. (The other two were men, but they never messed with Melony; no one ever would.)

Lorna became more domestic. She lacked the concentration for advanced training at the shipyard, but she remained an employee—"Stay on for the pension plan," Melony had advised her. Lorna actually liked the assembly-line monotony, and she was smart about signing up for the overtime pay shifts—she was willing to work at odd hours if she could work less. Her being out late bothered Melony.

Lorna became increasingly feminine. She not only wore dresses (even to work) and used more makeup and perfume (and watched her weight); her voice, which had once been harsh, actually softened and she developed a smile (especially when she was being criticized). Melony found her increasingly passive.

As a couple, they rarely fought because Lorna would not fight back. In fifteen years, she had discovered that Melony relented if there wasn't a struggle; given any resistance, Melony would never quit.

"You don't fight fair," Melony would occasionally complain.

"You're much bigger than I am," Lorna would say coyly.

An understatement. By 195__, when Melony was forty-something (no one knew exactly how old she was), she weighed one hundred seventy-five pounds. She was five feet eight inches all; she was almost fifty inches around at her chest, which meant that she wore men's shirts (large; anything smaller than a seventeen-inch neck wouldn't fit her; because her arms were short, she always had to roll up the sleeves). She had a thirty-six-inch waist, but only a twenty-eight-inch inseam (which meant that she had to roll up the cuffs of her trousers or have Lorna shorten them). Melony's pants were always so tight across her thighs that they quickly lost their crease there, but they were very baggy in the seat—Melony was not fat-assed, and she had the nondescript hips of most men. She had small feet, which always hurt her.

In fifteen years she'd been arrested only once—for fighting. Actually, the charge was assault, but in the end she was stuck with nothing more damaging than a disturbance of the peace. She'd been in the ladies' room of a pizza bar in Bath when some college boy had tried to engage Lorna in conversation. When he saw Melony take her place beside Lorna at the bar, he whispered to Lorna, "I don't think I could find anyone for your friend." He was imagining a possible double-date situation.

"Speak up!" Melony said. "Whispering is impolite."

"I said, I don't think I could find a date for you," the boy said boldly.

Melony put her arm around Lorna and cupped her breast.

"I couldn't find a sheep dog that would hold still for you," Melony told the college boy.

"Fucking dyke," he said as he was leaving. He thought he'd spoken quietly enough—and strictly to impress the shipyard workers at the far end of the bar; he couldn't have known that the men were Melony's co-workers. They held the college boy while Melony broke his nose with a metal napkin container.

The way that Melony liked to fall asleep was with her big face on Lorna's tight bare belly; Lorna could always tell when Melony had fallen asleep because of the change in Melony's breathing, which Lorna could feel against her pubic hair. In fifteen years, there was only one night when Lorna had to ask her friend to move her heavy head before she had soundly fallen asleep.

"What is it? You got cramps?" Melony asked.

"No, I'm pregnant," Lorna said. Melony thought it was a joke until Lorna went into the bathroom to be sick.

When Lorna came back to bed, Melony said, "I want to try to understand this, calmly. We've been like a married couple for fifteen years, and now you're pregnant." Lorna curled herself into a ball around one of the pillows; she covered her head with the other pillow. Her face and her stomach and her private parts were protected, but still she trembled; she began to cry. "I guess what you're telling me," Melony went on, "is that when women are fucking each other, it takes a lot longer for one of them to get pregnant than when a woman is fucking some guy. Right?" Lorna didn't answer her; she just went on sniveling. "Like about fifteen years—like *that* long. It takes fifteen years for women to get pregnant when they're just fucking other women. Boy, that's some effort," Melony said.

She went to the window and looked at the view of the Kennebec; in the summer, the trees were so leafy that the river was hard to see. She let a summer breeze dry the sweat on her neck and chest before she started packing.

"Please don't go—don't leave me," Lorna said; she was still all balled up on the bed.

"I'm packing up *your* things," Melony said. "I'm not the one who's pregnant. I don't have to go nowhere."

"Don't throw me out," Lorna said miserably. "Beat me, but don't throw me out."

"You take the train to Saint Cloud's. When you get there, you ask for the orphanage," Melony told her friend.

"It was just a guy—just one guy, and it was just once!" Lorna cried.

"No, it wasn't," Melony said. "A guy gets you pregnant *fast*. With women, it takes fifteen years."

When she had packed up Lorna's things, Melony stood over the bed and shook her friend, who tried to hide under the bedcovers. "Fifteen years!" Melony cried. She shook Lorna, and shook her, but that was all she did to her. She even walked Lorna to the train. Lorna looked very disheveled, and it was only the early morning of what would be a wilting summer day.

"I ask for the orphanage?" Lorna asked numbly. In addition to her suitcase, Melony handed Lorna a large carton.

"And you give this to an old woman named Grogan—if she's still alive," Melony said. "Don't say nothing to her, just give it to her. And if she's dead, or not there anymore," Melony started to say; then she stopped. "Forget that," she said. "She's either there or she's dead, and if she's dead, bring the carton back. You can give it back to me when you pick up the rest of your stuff."

"The rest of my stuff?" Lorna said.

"I was faithful to you. I was loyal as a dog," Melony said, more loudly than she'd meant to speak, because a conductor looked at her strangely—as if she were a dog. "You see somethin' you want, shitface?" Melony asked the conductor.

"The train is about to leave," he mumbled.

"Please don't throw me out," Lorna whispered to Melony.

"I hope you have a real monster inside you," Melony told her friend. "I hope it tears you to pieces when they drag it out your door."

Lorna fell down in the aisle of the train, as if she'd been punched, and Melony left her in a heap. The conductor helped Lorna to her feet and into her seat; out the window of the moving train, he watched Melony walking away. That was when the conductor noticed that he was shaking almost as violently as Lorna.

Melony thought about Lorna arriving in St. Cloud's—that turd of a stationmaster (would he still be there?), that long walk uphill with her suitcase and the large carton for Mrs. Grogan (could Lorna make it?), and would the old man still be in the business? She'd not been angry for fifteen years, but now here was another betrayal and Melony pondered how readily her anger had returned; it made all her senses keener. She felt the itch to pick apples again.

She was surprised that it was not with vengeance that she thought of Homer Wells. She remembered how she'd first loved having Lorna as a pal—in part, because she could complain to Lorna about what Homer had done to her. Now Melony imagined she'd like to complain about Lorna to Homer Wells.

"That little bitch," she'd tell Homer. "If there was anybody with a bulge in his pants, she couldn't keep her eyes off it."

"Right," Homer would say, and together they would demolish a building—just shove it into time. When time passes, it's the people who knew you whom you want to see; they're the ones you can talk to. When enough time passes, what's it matter what they did to you?

Melony discovered that she could think like this for one minute; but in the next minute, when she thought of Homer Wells, she thought she'd like to kill him.

When Lorna came back from St. Cloud's and went to the boardinghouse to retrieve her things, she found that everything had been neatly packed and boxed and gathered in one corner of the room; Melony was at work, so Lorna took her things and left.

After that, they would see each other perhaps once a week at the shipyard, or at the pizza bar in Bath where everyone from the yard went; on these occasions, they were polite but silent. Only once did Melony speak to her.

"The old woman, Grogan—she was alive?" Melony asked.

"I didn't bring the box back, did I?" Lorna asked.

"So you gave it to her?" Melony asked. "And you didn't say nothing?"

"I just asked if she was alive, and one of the nurses said she was, so I gave the carton to one of the nurses—as I was leavin'," Lorna said.

"And the doctor?" Melony asked. "Old Larch—is he alive?"

"Barely," Lorna said.

"I'll be damned," said Melony. "Did it hurt?"

"Not much," Lorna said cautiously.

"Too bad," Melony said. "It shoulda hurt a lot."

In her boardinghouse, where she was now the sole superintendent, she took from a very old electrician's catalogue a yellowed article and photograph from the local newspaper. She went to the antiques shop that was run by her old, dim-witted devotee, Mary Agnes Cork, whose adoptive parents had treated her well; they'd even put her in charge of the family store. Melony asked Mary Agnes for a suitable frame for the newspaper article and the photograph, and Mary Agnes was delighted to come up with something perfect. It was a genuine Victorian frame taken from a ship that had been overhauled in the Bath yards. Mary Agnes sold Melony the frame for much less than it was worth, even though Melony was rich. Electricians are well paid, and Melony had been working full-time for the shipyard for fifteen years; because she was the superintendent of the boardinghouse, she lived almost rent-free. She didn't own a car and she bought all her clothes at Sam's Army-Navy Men's Store.

It was fitting that the frame was teak—the wood of the tree that had held Wally Worthington in the air over Burma for one whole night—because the newspaper article was about Captain Worthington, and the picture—which Melony had recognized, fifteen years ago—was also of Wally. The article was all about the miraculous rescue of the downed (and paralyzed) pilot, who had been awarded the Purple Heart. As far as Melony was oncerned, the whole story resembled the plot of a cheap and nlikely adventure movie, but she liked the picture—and the art of the article that said Wally was a local hero, a Worthington rom those Worthingtons who for years had owned and managed the Ocean View Orchards in Heart's Rock.

In her bedroom, in her boardinghouse in Bath, Melony hung he antique frame containing the article and photograph over er bed. In the darkness she liked knowing it was there—over er head, like history. She liked that as much as looking at the hotograph in the daylight hours. And in the darkness, she vould linger over the syllables of that hero's name.

"Worthington," she liked to say aloud. "Ocean View," she aid, at other times; she was more familiar with saying this. 'Heart's Rock," she would say, quickly spitting the short words ut.

In those predawn hours, which are the toughest for insomniacs, Melony would whisper, "Fifteen years." And just before she vould fall asleep, she would ask of the first, flat light that crept nto her bedroom, "Are you still there, Sunshine?" What is ardest to accept about the passage of time is that the people vho once mattered the most to us are wrapped up in parentheses.

/ / /

For fifteen years, Homer Wells had taken responsibility for he writing and the posting of the cider house rules. Every ear, it was the last thing he attached to the wall after the fresh oat of paint had dried. Some years he tried being jolly with he rules; other years he tried sounding nonchalant; perhaps it ad been Olive's tone and not the rules themselves that had aused some offense, and thereby made it a matter of pride vith the migrants that the rules should never be obeyed.

The rules themselves did not change much. The rotary screen ad to be cleaned out. A word of warning about the drinking nd the falling asleep in the cold-storage room was mandatory. And long after the Ferris wheel at Cape Kenneth was torn lown and there were so many lights on the coast that the view rom the cider house roof resembled a glimpse of some distant ity, the migrants still sat on the roof and drank too much and ell off, and Homer Wells would ask (or tell) them not to. Rules, he guessed, never *asked;* rules *told.*

But he tried to make the cider house rules seem friendly. He hrased the rules in a confiding voice. "There have been some ccidents on the roof, over the years—especially at night, and

especially in combination with having a great deal to drink
while sitting on the roof. We recommend that you do your
drinking with both feet on the ground," Homer would write.

But every year, the piece of paper itself would become worn
and tattered and used for other things—a kind of desperation
grocery list, for example, always by someone who couldn't
spell.

CORN MEEL
REGULAR FLOWER

was written across Homer's rules one year.

At times, the solitary sheet of paper gathered little insults
and mockeries of a semi-literate nature.

"No fucking on the roof!" or "Beat-off only in cold storage!"
Wally told Homer that only Mr. Rose knew how to write—
that the pranks, and insults, and shopping lists were all composed by Mr. Rose, but Homer could never be sure.

Every summer Mr. Rose would write to Wally and Wally
would tell Mr. Rose how many pickers he needed—and Mr.
Rose would say how many he was bringing and the day they
would arrive (give or take). No contract ever existed—just the
short, reliable assurances from Mr. Rose.

Some summers he came with a woman—large and soft and
quiet, with a baby girl riding her hip. By the time the little girl
could run around and get into trouble (she was about the age
of Angel Wells), Mr. Rose stopped bringing her or the woman.

For fifteen years the only migrant who was as constant as
Mr. Rose was Black Pan, the cook.

"How's your little girl?" Homer Wells would ask Mr. Rose—
every year that the woman and the daughter didn't show up
again.

"She growin', like your boy," Mr. Rose would say.

"And how's your lady?" Homer would ask.

"She lookin' after the little girl," Mr. Rose would say.

Only once in fifteen years did Homer Wells approach Mr.
Rose on the subject of the cider house rules. "I hope they don't
offend anyone," Homer began. "I'm responsible—I write them
every year—and if anyone takes offense, I hope you'll tell me."

"No offense," said Mr. Rose, smiling.

"They're just little rules," Homer said.

"Yes," said Mr. Rose. "They are."

"But it does concern me that no one seems to pay attention to them," Homer finally said.

Mr. Rose, whose bland face was unchanged by the years and whose body had remained thin and lithe, looked at Homer mildly. "We got our own rules, too, Homer," he said.

"Your own rules," said Homer Wells.

" 'Bout lots of things," said Mr. Rose. " 'Bout how much we can have to do with you, for one thing."

"With me?" Homer said.

"With white people," said Mr. Rose. "We got our rules 'bout that."

"I see," Homer said, but he didn't really see.

"And about fightin'," said Mr. Rose.

"Fighting," said Homer Wells.

"With each other," said Mr. Rose. "One rule is, we can't cut each other bad. Not bad enough for no hospital, not bad enough for no police. We can cut each other, but not bad."

"I see," Homer said.

"No, you don't," said Mr. Rose. "You *don't* see—that's the point. We can cut each other only so bad that you never see—you never know we was cut. You see?"

"Right," said Homer Wells.

"When you gonna say somethin' else?" Mr. Rose asked, smiling.

"Just be careful on the roof," Homer advised him.

"Nothin' too bad can happen up there," Mr. Rose told him. "Worse things can happen on the ground."

Homer Wells was on the verge of saying "Right," again, when he discovered that he couldn't talk; Mr. Rose had seized his tongue between his blunt, square-ended index finger and his thumb. A vague taste, like dust, was in Homer's mouth; Mr. Rose's hand had been so fast, Homer had never seen it—he never knew before that someone could actually catch hold of someone's tongue.

"Caught ya," said Mr. Rose, smiling; he let Homer's tongue go.

Homer managed to say, "You're very fast."

"Right," said Mr. Rose alertly. "Ain't no one faster."

Wally complained to Homer about the yearly wear and tear on the cider house roof. Every two or three years, they had to re-tin the roof, or fix the flashing, or put up new gutters.

"What's having his own rules got to do with not payin, attention to ours?" Wally asked Homer.

"I don't know," Homer said. "Write him a letter and asl him."

But no one wanted to offend Mr. Rose; he was a reliabl crew boss. He made the picking and the pressing go smoothl every harvest.

Candy, who managed the money at Ocean View, claimec that whatever costs they absorbed in repairs to the cider hous roof were more than compensated for by Mr. Rose's reliability

"There's something a little gangland style about the guy, Wally said—not exactly complaining. "I mean, I don't reall want to know how he gets all those pickers to behav themselves."

"But they *do* behave themselves," Homer said.

"He does a good job," Candy said. "Let him have his ow rules."

Homer Wells looked away; he knew that rules, for Candy were all private contracts.

Fifteen years ago, they had made their own rules—or, really Candy had made them (before Wally came home). They stooc in the cider house (after Angel was born, on a night wher Olive was looking after Angel). They had just made love, bu not happily; something was wrong. It would be wrong fo fifteen years, but that night Candy had said, "Let's agree tc something."

"Okay," Homer said.

"Whatever happens, we share Angel."

"Of course," Homer said.

"I mean, you get to be his father—you get all the father tim you want to have—and I get to have all the mother time need," Candy said.

"Always," said Homer Wells, but something was wrong.

"I mean, regardless of what happens—whether I'm with you or with Wally," Candy said.

Homer was quiet for a while. "So you're leaning towarc Wally?" he asked.

"I'm not *leaning* anywhere," Candy said. "I'm standing righ here, and we're agreeing to certain rules."

"I didn't know they were rules," said Homer Wells.

"We share Angel," Candy said. "We both get to live witl him. We get to be his family. Nobody ever moves out."

"Even if you're with Wally?" Homer said, after a while.

"Remember what you told me when you wanted me to have Angel?" Candy asked him.

Homer Wells was cautious, now. "Remind me," he said.

"You said that he was your baby, too—that he was *ours*. That I couldn't decide, all by myself, not to have him—that was the point," Candy said.

"Yes," Homer said. "I remember."

"Well, if he was ours then, he's ours now—whatever happens," Candy repeated.

"In the same house?" asked Homer Wells. "Even if you go with Wally?"

"Like a family," Candy said.

"Like a family," said Homer Wells. It was a word that took a strong grip of him. An orphan is a child, forever; an orphan detests change; an orphan hates to move; an orphan loves routine.

For fifteen years, Homer Wells knew that there were possibly as many cider house rules as there were people who had passed through the cider house. Even so, every year, he posted a fresh list.

/ / /

For fifteen years, the board of trustees had tried and failed to replace Dr. Larch; they couldn't find anyone who wanted the job. There were people dying to throw themselves into unrewarded service of their fellow man, but there were more exotic places than St. Cloud's where their services were needed—and where they could also suffer. The board of trustees couldn't manage to entice a new nurse into service there, either; they couldn't hire even an administrative assistant.

When Dr. Gingrich retired—not from the board; he would never retire from the board—he mused about accepting the position in St. Cloud's, but Mrs. Goodhall pointed out to him that he wasn't an obstetrician. His psychiatric practice had never flourished in Maine, yet Dr. Gingrich was surprised and a little hurt to learn that Mrs. Goodhall enjoyed pointing this out to him. Mrs. Goodhall had reached retirement age herself, but nothing could have been farther from that woman's zealous mind. Wilbur Larch was ninety-something, and Mrs. Goodhall was obsessed with retiring him before he died; she realized that to have Larch die, while still in service, would register as a kind of defeat for her.

Not long ago—perhaps in an effort to invigorate the board—Dr. Gingrich had proposed they hold a meeting in an off-season hotel in Ogunquit, simply to break the routine of meeting in their usual offices in Portland. "Make it a kind of outing," he proposed. "The ocean air and all."

But it rained. In the colder weather, the wood shrank; the sand got in the windows and doors and crunched underfoot; the drapes and the towels and the bedsheets were gritty. The wind was off the ocean; no one could sit on the veranda because the wind blew the rain under the roof. The hotel provided them with a long, dark, empty dining room; they held their meeting under a chandelier that no one could turn on—no one could find the right switch.

It was appropriate to their discussion of St. Cloud's that they attempted to conduct their business in a former ballroom that had seen better days, in a hotel so deeply in the off-season that anyone seeing them there would have suspected they'd been quarantined. In fact, when he got a glimpse of them, that is what Homer Wells thought; he and Candy were the hotel's only other off-season guests. They had taken a room for half the day; they were a long way from Ocean View, but they'd come this far to be sure that no one would recognize them.

It was time for them to leave. They stood outside on the veranda, Candy with her back against Homer's chest, his arms wrapped around her; they both faced out to sea. He appeared to like the way the wind whipped her hair back in his face, and neither of them seemed to mind the rain.

Inside the hotel, Mrs. Goodhall looked through the streaked window, frowning at the weather and at the young couple braving the elements. In her opinion, nothing could ever be normal enough. That was what was wrong with Larch; not everyone who is ninety-something is senile, she would grant you, but Larch wasn't normal. And even if they were a young married couple, public displays of affection were not acceptable to Mrs. Goodhall—and they were calling all the more attention to themselves by their defiance of the rain.

"What's more," she remarked to Dr. Gingrich, who was given no warning and had no map with which he could have followed her thoughts, "I'll bet they're not married."

The young couple, he thought, looked a little sad. Perhaps they needed a psychiatrist; perhaps it was the weather—they'd been planning to sail.

"I've figured out what he is," Mrs. Goodhall told Dr. Gingrich, who thought she was referring to the young man, Homer Wells. "He's a nonpracticing homosexual," Mrs. Goodhall announced. She meant Dr. Larch, who was on her mind night and day.

Dr. Gingrich was rather amazed at what struck him as Mrs. Goodhall's wild guess, but he looked at the young man with renewed interest. True, he was not actually fondling the young woman; he seemed a trifle distant.

"If we could catch him at it, we'd have him out in a minute," Mrs. Goodhall observed. "Of course we'd still have to find someone willing to replace him."

Dr. Gingrich was lost. He realized that Mrs. Goodhall couldn't be interested in replacing the young man on the veranda, and that therefore she was still thinking about Dr. Larch. But if Dr. Larch were a "nonpracticing homosexual," what could they ever catch him at?

"We would catch him at *being* a homosexual, just not practicing as such?" Dr. Gingrich asked cautiously; it was not hard to rile Mrs. Goodhall.

"He's obviously queer," she snapped.

Dr. Gingrich, in all his years of psychiatric service to Maine, had never been moved to apply the label of "nonpracticing homosexual" to anyone, although he had often heard of such a thing; usually, someone was complaining about someone else's peculiarity. In Mrs. Goodhall's case, she despised men who lived alone. It wasn't normal. And she despised young couples who displayed their affection, or weren't married, or both; too much of what was normal also enraged her. Although he shared with Mrs. Goodhall the desire to replace Dr. Larch and his staff at St. Cloud's, it occurred to Dr. Gingrich that he should have had Mrs. Goodhall as a patient—she might have kept him out of retirement for a few more years.

When the young couple came inside the hotel, Mrs. Goodhall gave them such a look that the young woman turned away.

"Did you see her turn away in shame?" Mrs. Goodhall would ask Dr. Gingrich, later.

But the young man stared her down. He looked right through her! Dr. Gingrich marveled. It was one of the best looks, in the tradition of "withering," that Dr. Gingrich had ever seen and he found himself smiling at the young couple.

"Did you see that couple?" Candy asked him later, in the long drive back to Ocean View.

"I don't think they were married," said Homer Wells. "Or if they're married, they hate each other."

"Maybe that's why I thought they were married," Candy said.

"He looked a little stupid, and she looked completely crazy," Homer said.

"I know they were married," Candy said.

In the sad, dingy dining room in Ogunquit, while the rain pelted down, Mrs. Goodhall said, "It's just not normal. Doctor Larch, those old nurses—the whole bit. If someone new, in some capacity, isn't hired soon, I say we send a janitor up there—just anyone who can look the place over and tell us how bad it is."

"Maybe it's not as bad as we think," Dr. Gingrich said tiredly. He had seen the young couple leave the hotel, and they had filled him with melancholy.

"Let somebody go there and see," Mrs. Goodhall said, the dark chandelier above her small gray head.

Then, in the nick of time—in everyone's opinion—a new nurse came to St. Cloud's. Remarkably, she appeared to have found out about the place all by herself. Nurse Caroline, they called her; she was constantly of use, and a great help when Melony's present for Mrs. Grogan arrived.

"What is it?" Mrs. Grogan asked. The carton was almost too heavy for her to lift; Nurse Edna and Nurse Angela had brought it over to the girls' division together. It was a sweltering summer afternoon; still, because it had been a perfectly windless day, Nurse Edna had sprayed the apple trees.

Dr. Larch came to the girls' division to see what was in the package.

"Well, go on, open it," he said to Mrs. Grogan. "I haven't got all day."

Mrs. Grogan was not sure how to attack the carton, which was sealed with wire and twine and tape—as if a savage had attempted to contain a wild animal. Nurse Caroline was called for her help.

What would they do without Nurse Caroline? Larch wondered. Before the package for Mrs. Grogan, Nurse Caroline had been the only large gift that anyone sent to St. Cloud's; Homer Wells had sent her from the hospital in Cape Kenneth.

Homer Wells knew that Nurse Caroline believed in the Lord's work, and he had persuaded her to go where her devotion would be welcome. But Nurse Caroline had trouble opening Melony's present.

"Who left it?" Mrs. Grogan asked.

"Someone named Lorna," Nurse Angela said. "I never saw her before."

"I never saw her before, either," said Wilbur Larch.

When the package was opened, there was still a mystery. Inside was a huge coat, much too large for Mrs. Grogan. An Army surplus coat, made for the Alaskan service, it had a hood and a fur collar and was so heavy that when Mrs. Grogan tried it on, it almost dragged her to the floor—she lost her balance a little and wobbled around like a top losing its spin. The coat had all sorts of secret pockets, which were probably for weapons or mess kits—"Or the severed arms and legs of enemies," said Dr. Larch.

Mrs. Grogan, lost in the coat and perspiring, said, "I don't get it." Then she felt the money in one of the pockets. She took out several loose bills and counted them, which was when she remembered that it was the exact amount of money that Melony had stolen from her when Melony had left St. Cloud's—and taken Mrs. Grogan's coat with her—more than fifteen years ago.

"Oh, my God!" Mrs. Grogan cried, fainting.

Nurse Caroline ran to the train station, but Lorna's train had already left. When Mrs. Grogan was revived, she cried and cried.

"Oh, that dear girl!" she cried, while everyone soothed her and no one spoke; Larch and Nurse Angela and Nurse Edna remembered Melony as anything but "dear." Larch tried on the coat, which was also too big and heavy for him; he staggered around in it for a while, frightening one of the smaller girls in the girls' division who'd come into the lobby to investigate Mrs. Grogan's cries.

Larch found something in another pocket: the snipped, twisted ends of some copper wire and a pair of rubber-handled, insulated wire-cutters.

On his way back to the boys' division, Larch whispered to Nurse Angela: "I'll bet she robbed some electrician."

"A *big* electrician," Nurse Angela said.

"You two," Nurse Edna scolded them. "It's a warm coat, anyway—at least it will keep her warm."

"It'll give her a heart attack, lugging it around," Dr. Larch said.

"I can wear it," Nurse Caroline commented. It was the first time that Larch and his old nurses realized that Nurse Caroline was not only young and energetic, she was also big and strong—and, in a much less crude and vulgar way, a little reminiscent of Melony (if Melony had been a Marxist, thought Wilbur Larch—and an angel).

Larch had trouble with the word "angel" since Homer Wells and Candy had taken their son away from St. Cloud's. Larch had trouble with the whole idea of how Homer was living. For fifteen years, Wilbur Larch had been amazed that the three of them—Homer and Candy and Wally—had managed it; he wasn't at all sure what they had managed, or at what cost. He knew, of course, that Angel was a wanted child, and well loved, and well looked after—or else Larch couldn't have remained silent. It was difficult for him to remain silent about the rest of it. How had they arranged it?

But who am I to advocate honesty in all relationships? he wondered. Me with my fictional histories, me with my fictional heart defects—me with my Fuzzy Stone.

And who was he to ask exactly what the sexual relationship was? Did he need to remind himself that he had slept with someone else's mother and dressed himself in the light of her daughter's cigar? That he had allowed to die a woman who had put a pony's penis in her mouth for money?

Larch looked out the window at the apple orchard on the hill. That summer of 195__, the trees were thriving; the apples were mostly pale green and pink, the leaves were a vibrant dark green. The trees were almost too tall for Nurse Edna to spray with the Indian pump. I should ask Nurse Caroline to take over the tending of them, Dr. Larch thought. He wrote a note to himself and left it in the typewriter. The heat made him drowsy. He went to the dispensary and stretched himself out on the bed. In the summer, with the windows open, he could risk a slightly heavier dose, he thought.

/ / /

The last summer that Mr. Rose was in charge of the picking crew at Ocean View was the summer of 195__, when Angel Wells was fifteen. All that summer, Angel had been looking forward to the next summer—when he would be sixteen, old enough to have his driver's license. By that time, he imagined, he would have saved enough money—from his summer jobs in the orchards and from his contribution to the harvests—to buy his first car.

His father, Homer Wells, didn't own a car. When Homer went shopping in town or when he volunteered at the hospital in Cape Kenneth, he used one of the farm vehicles. The old Cadillac, which had been equipped with a hand-operated brake and accelerator so Wally could drive it, was often available, and Candy had her own car—a lemon-yellow Jeep, in which she had taught Angel to drive and which was as reliable in the orchards as it was sturdy on the public roads.

"I taught your father how to swim," Candy always told Angel. "I guess I can teach you how to drive."

Of course Angel knew how to drive all the farm vehicles, too. He knew how to mow, and how to spray, and how to operate the forklift. The driver's license was simply necessary, official approval of something Angel already did very well on the farm.

And, for a fifteen-year-old, he looked much older. He could have driven all over Maine and no one would have questioned him. He would be taller than his boyish, round-faced father (they were dead-even as the summer began), and there was a defined angularity in the bones of his face that made him seem already grown up; even the trace of a beard was there. The shadows under his eyes were not unhealthy-looking; they served only to accent the vivid darkness of his eyes. It was a joke between father and son: that the shadows under Angel's eyes were "inherited." "You get your insomnia from me," Homer Wells would tell his son, who still thought he was adopted. "You've got no reason to *feel* adopted," his father had told him. "You've got three parents, really. The best that most people get is two."

Candy had been like a mother to him, and Wally was a second father—or the favorite, eccentric uncle. The only life Angel had known was a life with all of them. At fifteen, he'd never suffered so much as a change of rooms; everything had been the same since he could remember it.

He had what had been Wally's room, the one Wally had shared with Homer. Angel had been born into a real boy's room: he'd grown up surrounded by Wally's tennis and swimming trophies, and the pictures of Candy with Wally (when Wally's legs worked), and even the picture of Candy teaching Homer how to swim. Wally's Purple Heart (which Wally had given to Angel) was hung on the wall over the boy's bed; it concealed an oddly smeared fingerprint—Olive's fingerprint, from the night when she'd crushed a mosquito against that wall, which was the same night Angel Wells had been conceived in the cider house. After fifteen years, the wall needed a fresh coat of paint.

Homer's room down the hall had been the master bedroom; it had been Olive's room and the room where Senior had died. Olive herself had died in Cape Kenneth Hospital before the war was over, even before they'd sent Wally home. It was an inoperable cancer, which spread very quickly after they'd done the exploratory.

Homer and Candy and Ray had taken turns visiting her; one of them was always with Angel but Olive was never alone. Homer and Candy had said—privately, only to each other—that things might have worked out differently if Wally had made it back to the States before Olive died. Because of Wally's precariousness and the added difficulty of moving him in wartime, it was thought best not to tell Wally of Olive's cancer; that was how Olive had wanted it, too.

In the end, Olive thought Wally had come home. She was pumped so full of pain-killers that she mistook Homer for Wally in their last few meetings. Homer had been in the habit of reading to her—from *Jane Eyre,* from *David Copperfield* and from *Great Expectations*—but he gave that up when Olive's attention began to wander. The first few times Olive confused Homer with Wally, Homer couldn't be sure whom she thought she was addressing.

"You must forgive him," Olive said. Her speech was slurred. She took Homer's hand, which she did not really hold so much as contain in her lap.

"Forgive him?" said Homer Wells.

"Yes," Olive said. "He can't help how much he loves her, or how much he needs her."

To Candy, Olive was clearer. "He's going to be crippled. And he's going to lose me. If he loses you, too, who's going to look after him?"

"I'll always look after him," Candy said. "Homer and I will look after him."

But Olive was not so drugged that she failed to detect and dislike the ambiguity of Candy's answer. "It's not right to hurt or deceive someone who's already been hurt and deceived, Candy," she said. With the drugs she was taking, Olive felt a perfect freedom. It was not for her to tell them that she knew what she knew; it was for them to tell her what they were keeping from her. Until they told her, she could keep them guessing about what she knew.

To Homer, Olive said: "He's an orphan."

"Who is?" Homer asked.

"*He* is," she said. "Don't you forget how needy an orphan is. He'll take everything. He's come from having nothing—when he sees what he can have, he'll take everything he sees. My son," Olive said, "don't blame anyone. Blame will kill you."

"Yes," said Homer Wells, who held Olive's hand. When he bent over her, to hear how she was breathing, she kissed him as if he were Wally.

"Blame will kill you," he repeated to Candy, after Olive had died. "'Dread remorse,'" said Homer Wells, forever recalling Mr. Rochester's advice.

"Don't *quote* to me," Candy told him. "The thing is, he's coming home. And he doesn't even know his mother's dead. Not to mention," Candy said; then she stopped talking.

"Not to mention," said Homer Wells.

/ / /

Candy and Wally were married less than a month after Wally returned to Ocean View; Wally weighed one hundred forty-seven pounds, and Homer Wells pushed the wheelchair down the church aisle. Candy and Wally occupied the converted bedroom on the ground floor of the big house.

Homer Wells had written to Wilbur Larch, shortly after Wally had come home. Olive's death (Homer wrote to Larch) had "fixed" things for Candy and Wally more securely than Wally's paralysis, or than whatever sense of betrayal and guilt might have plagued Candy.

"Candy's right: don't worry about Angel," Wilbur Larch had written to Homer Wells. "Angel will get enough love. Why would he feel like an orphan if he never is one? If you're a good father to him, and Candy's a good mother to him—and if he's got Wally loving him, too—do you think he's going to start missing some *idea* of who his so-called *real* father is? The problem is not going to be Angel's problem. It's going to be yours. You're going to want him to know you're his real father, because of *you*—not because he's going to need to know. The problem is, you're going to need to tell. You and Candy. You're going to be proud. It will be for you, and not for Angel, that you're going to want to tell him he's no orphan."

And to himself, or as an entry in *A Brief History of St. Cloud's,* Wilbur Larch wrote: "Here in St. Cloud's we have just one problem. His name is Homer Wells. He's a problem, wherever he goes."

Aside from the darkness in his eyes and an ability to sustain a pensive, faraway look that was both alert and dreaming, Angel Wells resembled his father very little. He never thought of himself as an orphan; he knew he had been adopted, and he knew he came from where his father came from. And he knew he was loved; he had always felt it. What did it matter that he called Candy "Candy" and Homer "Dad"—and Wally "Wally"?

This was the second summer that Angel Wells had been strong enough to carry Wally—up some steps, or into the surf, or out of the shallow end of the pool and back into the wheelchair. Homer had taught Angel how to carry Wally into the surf, when they went to the beach. Wally was a better swimmer than any of them, but he needed to get into deep enough water so that he could either float over a wave or duck under one.

"You just can't let him get dragged around in the shallow water," Homer had explained to his son.

There were some rules regarding Wally (there were always rules, Angel had observed). As good a swimmer as he was, Wally was never allowed to swim alone, and for many summers now, Angel Wells had been Wally's lifeguard whenever Wally swam his laps or just floated in the pool. Almost half the physical contact between Wally and Angel occurred in the water, where they resembled otters or seals. They wrestled and dunked each other so ferociously that Candy couldn't help being anxious at times for both of them.

And Wally was not allowed to drive alone; even though the Cadillac had hand-operated controls, someone else had to collapse the wheelchair and put it in or take it out of the back of the car. The first collapsible wheelchairs were quite heavy. Although Wally would occasionally drag himself through the ground floor of the house using one of those metal walkers, his legs were mere props; in unfamiliar terrain, he needed his wheelchair—and in rough terrain, he needed a pusher.

So many times the pusher had been Angel; and so many times Angel had been the passenger in the Cadillac. Although Homer and Candy might have complained if they had known, Wally had long ago taught Angel to drive the Cadillac.

"The hand controls make it easy, kiddo," Wally would say. "Your legs don't have to be long enough to reach the pedals." That was not what Candy had told Angel about teaching him to drive in the Jeep. "Just as soon as your legs are long enough to reach the pedals," she had told him, kissing him (which she did whenever she had the excuse), "I'll teach you how to drive."

When the time came, it never occurred to Candy that Angel had been so easy to teach because he'd been driving the Cadillac for years.

"Some rules are good rules, kiddo," Wally would tell the boy, kissing him (which Wally did a lot, especially in the water). "But some rules are just rules. You just got to break them carefully."

"It's dumb that I have to be sixteen before I get a driver's license," Angel told his father.

"Right," said Homer Wells. "They should make an exception for kids who grow up on farms."

Sometimes Angel played tennis with Candy, but more often he hit balls back to Wally, who maintained his good strokes even sitting down. The club members had complained a little about the wheelchair tracks on the clay—but what would the Haven Club have been without tolerating one or another Worthington eccentricity? Wally would set the wheelchair in a fixed position and hit only forehands for fifteen or twenty minutes; Angel's responsibility was to get the ball exactly to him. Then Wally would move the chair and hit only backhands.

"It's actually better practice for you than for me, kiddo," Wally would tell Angel. "At least, I'm not getting any better." Angel got a lot better; he was so much better than Candy that it sometimes hurt his mother's feelings when she detected how boring it was for Angel to play with her.

Homer Wells didn't play tennis. He had never been a games man, he had resisted even the indoor football at St. Cloud's—although he occasionally dreamed of stickball, usually with Nurse Angela pitching; she was always the hardest to hit. And

Homer Wells had no hobbies—nothing beyond following Angel around, as if Homer were his son's pet, a dog waiting to be played with. Pillow fights in the dark; they'd been popular for a few years. Kissing each other good night, and then finding excuses to repeat the ritual—and finding novel ways to wake each other in the mornings. If Homer was bored, he was also busy. He had continued his volunteer work for Cape Kenneth Hospital; in a sense, he had never stopped his war effort, his service as a nurse's aide. And he was a veteran reader of medical literature. *The Journal of the American Medical Association* and *The New England Journal of Medicine* were very acceptably piled up on the tables and in the bookcases of the Ocean View house. Candy objected to the illustrations in *The American Journal of Obstetrics and Gynecology.*

"I need a little intellectual stimulation around here," Homer Wells would say whenever Candy complained about the graphic nature of this material.

"I just don't think that Angel has to see it," Candy said.

"He knows I have a little background in the subject," Homer said.

"I don't object to what he knows, I object to the pictures," Candy said.

"There's no reason to mystify the subject for the child," Wally said, taking Homer's side.

"There's no need to make the subject grotesque, either," Candy argued.

"*I* don't think it's either a mystery or grotesque," Angel said, that summer he was fifteen. "It's just interesting."

"You're not even going out with girls, yet," Candy said, laughing, and taking the opportunity to kiss him. But when she bent over him to kiss him, she saw in her son's lap the illustration that was featured in an article on vaginal operations. The illustration indicated the lines of incision for the removal of the vulva and a primary tumor in an extended radical vulvectomy.

"Homer!" Candy shouted. Homer was upstairs in his very spare bedroom. His life was so spare, he'd tacked only two things on his walls—and one of those was in his bathroom. By his bed he had a picture of Wally in his flier's scarf and sheepskin. Wally was posing with the crew of *Opportunity Knocks;* the shadow from the wing of the dark plane completely obscured the face of the radioman, and the glare of the

Indian sun completely whited out the face of the crew chief (who had eventually died of his colon complication); only Wally and the co-pilot were correctly illuminated, although Homer had seen better pictures of them both. The co-pilot sent Wally a picture of himself and his growing family every Christmas; he had five or six children and a plump wife; but every year the co-pilot looked thinner (the amoeba he'd contracted in Burma had never entirely left him).

And in the bathroom Homer had tacked up the blank questionnaire, the extra copy—the one he'd never sent to the board of trustees of St. Cloud's. The exposure to the steam from the shower had given to the paper of the questionnaire the texture of a parchment lampshade, but each question had remained readable and idiotic.

The master bed was higher than most (because, in his day, Senior Worthington had enjoyed looking out the window while lying down); it was a feature Homer also appreciated about the bed. He could oversee the pool from up there, and he could see the cider house roof; he liked to lie on that bed for hours, just looking out the window. "Homer!" Candy called to him. "Please come see what your son is reading!"

That was the way they all talked. Candy said "your son" to Homer, and that's how Wally spoke, too, and Angel always said "Dad" or "Pop" when he addressed his father. It had been an uninterrupted, fifteen-year relationship—Homer and Angel upstairs, Wally and Candy in the former dining room downstairs. The four of them ate their meals together.

Some nights—especially in winter, when the bare trees permitted more of a view of the lit dining room and kitchen windows of strangers' houses—Homer Wells liked to take a short car ride before dinner. He wondered about the families who were eating dinner together—what were their real lives like? St. Cloud's had been more predictable. What did anyone really know about all those families sitting down to have a meal?

"We *are* a family. Isn't that the main thing?" Candy asked Homer Wells, whenever Homer appeared to her to be taking longer and longer drives before dinner.

"Angel has a family, a really wonderful family. Yes, that's the main thing," Homer agreed.

And when Wally would tell her how happy he was, how he felt he was the luckiest man alive—how anyone would give up his legs to be as happy as Wally was—those were the nights that Candy couldn't sleep; those were the nights when she'd be aware of Homer Wells, who was wide awake, too. Some nights they would meet in the kitchen—they'd have some milk and apple pie. Some nights, when it was warm, they'd sit by the swimming pool not touching each other; to any observer, the space between them would have indicated a quarrel (although they rarely quarreled), or else indifference (but they were never indifferent to each other). The way they sat by the pool reminded them both of how they used to sit on Ray Kendall's dock, before they'd sat closer together. If ever they were too conscious of this memory—and of missing that dock, or of missing Ray (who'd died before Angel was old enough to have any memory of him)—this would spoil their evening by the swimming pool and they would be forced back to their separate bedrooms, where they would lie awake a little longer.

As he grew older (and almost as insomniac as his father), Angel Wells would often watch Homer and Candy sitting by the pool, which he could also see out the window of his room. If Angel ever thought anything about the two of them sitting out there, it was why such old friends sat so far apart.

Raymond Kendall had died shortly after Wally and Candy were married. He was killed when the lobster pound blew up; his whole dock was blown apart, and his lobster boat sank, and two old heaps of automobiles he was working on were jolted across his parking lot a good twenty-five yards down the coastal highway by the explosion—as if they'd been driven under their own power. Even the picture window at the Haven Club was collapsed by the blast, but it happened so late at night that the bar was closed and none of the Haven Club's regular drinkers was on hand to see their favorite eyesore obliterated from their view of Heart's Haven Harbor.

Ray had been tinkering with his homemade torpedo; for all of his legendary mechanical genius, he must have found out something about a torpedo that he didn't know. The misfortune of someone you love can bring out the guilt in you; Candy regretted that she'd not told her father about Homer and Angel Wells. It was no consolation to her that she imagined Ray already knew everything; she had been able to understand, by his silences, that he wanted to hear it from her. Yet not even the death of her father could prompt Candy Kendall to tell her story to anyone.

As far south along the coastal highway as Powell's Ice Cream Palace, there had been dead lobsters and lobster parts in the parking lot and in the road. This had prompted Herb Fowler (who was never caught without something funny to say) to ask old Mr. Powell if he was inventing a new ice cream flavor.

Herb had waited for the summer that Angel Wells was fifteen before he flicked Angel his first rubber. Angel's feelings were slightly hurt that Herb had not initiated him sooner. Angel's pal and co-worker, pudgy Pete Hyde, was only a few months older than Angel (and not nearly so grown up, in countless ways), and Angel knew that Herb Fowler had bounced a rubber off Pete Hyde's head when Pete was only thirteen. What Angel hadn't yet fathomed was that Pete Hyde was a part of Ocean View's working-class family, and Angel—although he worked with the workers—was from the boss's family.

The workers knew that Homer Wells ran Ocean View. He was the one most in charge. This would not have surprised Olive, and it was clear that Candy and Wally were grateful for Homer's authority. Perhaps because the workers knew that Homer had come from St. Cloud's, they felt that he was closer to them; he lived in what Big Dot Taft called "the fancy house," but he was like one of them. None of the workers resented that Homer was the boss, with the possible exception of Vernon Lynch, who resented any and every authority—all the more so since Grace Lynch had died.

Candy, who looked into the matters concerning the workers' wives, discovered that Grace had been pregnant; she'd died of acute peritonitis, following a misguided attempt to abort herself. Homer, who would often wonder why she had not chosen to make a second trip to St. Cloud's, liked to think that she had not died in vain. It had been her death (and Dr. Harlow's particularly unsympathetic response to it) that had prompted Nurse Caroline to resign from the Cape Kenneth Hospital staff, as Homer Wells had been encouraging her to do. Nurse Caroline finally took Homer's suggestion and offered her services to St. Cloud's.

"Homer Wells sent me," Nurse Caroline said, when she introduced herself to Wilbur Larch. The old man had not grown too careless.

"Sent you for what?" Larch asked.

"I'm a trained nurse," she said. "I'm here to help you."

"Help me do what?" asked Larch, who was not very convincing at portraying innocence.

"I believe in the Lord's work," Nurse Caroline said, exasperated.

"Well, why didn't you say so?" Wilbur Larch asked.

So he's given me something besides apple trees, the old man mused. So there's still hope for him.

Nurse Angela and Nurse Edna were so relieved to get Nurse Caroline that they weren't even jealous. Here was the new blood that might hold the board of trustees at bay a while longer.

"The new nurse is a definite improvement to the situation," Dr. Gingrich confided to the board. "I would say that she takes a lot of pressure off making any immediate decision." (As if they weren't trying to replace the old man every minute!)

"I'd prefer a young doctor to a young nurse," Mrs. Goodhall declared. "A young doctor *and* a young administrator. You know how I feel about the records; the records of that place are pure whimsy. But it's at least a temporary improvement; I'll buy that," she said.

If Wilbur Larch could have heard her, he would have said: "Just give me the time, lady, and you'll buy more than that."

But in 195—, Wilbur Larch was ninety-something. Sometimes his face would hold so still under the ether cone that the mask would stay in place after his hand had dropped to his side; only the force of his exhalations would make the cone fall. He had lost a lot of weight. In a mirror, or traveling with his beloved ether, he had the impression that he was becoming a bird. Only Nurse Caroline had the courage to criticize his drug habit. "You should know, of all people," Nurse Caroline told him roughly.

"Me of all people?" Larch asked innocently. Sometimes, he found it was fun to provoke her.

"You have a low opinion of religion," Nurse Caroline remarked to him.

"I suppose so," he said cautiously. She was a little too young and quick for him, he knew.

"Well, what do you suppose a drug dependency is—if not a kind of religion?" Nurse Caroline asked.

"I have no quarrel with anyone at prayer," Wilbur Larch said. "Prayer is personal—prayer is anyone's choice. Pray to whom or what you want! It's when you start making rules," said Wilbur Larch, but he felt lost. He knew she could talk circles around him. He admired socialism, but talking to a damn socialist was like talking to any true believer. He had heard her say, so many times, that a society that approved of making abortion illegal was a society that approved of violence against women; that making abortion illegal was simply a sanctimonious, self-righteous form of violence against women—it was just a way of legalizing violence against women, Nurse Caroline would say. He had heard her say, so many times, that abortions were not only a personal freedom of choice but also a responsibility of the state—to provide them.

"Once the state starts providing, it feels free to hand out the rules, too!" Larch blurted hastily. It was a Yankee thing to say—very Maine. But Nurse Caroline smiled. That led him into another of her arguments; she could always trap him. He was not a systems man, he was just a good one.

"In a better world . . ." she began patiently. Her patience with him could make Larch furious.

"No, *not* in a better world!" he cried. "In this one—in *this* world! I take this world as a given. Talk to me about *this* world!" But it all made him so tired. It made him want a little ether. The more he tried to keep up with Nurse Caroline, the more he needed ether; and the stronger he felt his need for it, the more that made her right.

"Oh, I can't always be right," Larch said tiredly.

"Yes, I know," Nurse Caroline said sympathetically. "It's because even a good man can't always be right that we need a society, that we need certain rules—call them priorities, if you prefer," she said.

"You can call them whatever you want," said Wilbur Larch testily. "I don't have time for philosophy, or for government, or for religion. I don't have enough time," said Wilbur Larch.

Always, in the background of his mind, there was a newborn baby crying; even when the orphanage was as silent as the few, remaining, abandoned buildings of St. Cloud's—even when it was ghostly quiet—Wilbur Larch heard babies crying. And they were not crying to be born, he knew; they were crying because they were born.

/ / /

That summer, Mr. Rose wrote that he "and the daughter" might be arriving a day or so ahead of the picking crew; he hoped the cider house would be ready.

"It's been a while since we've seen the daughter," Wally remarked, in the apple-mart office. Everett Taft was outside oiling Wally's wheelchair for him, so Wally sat on the desk—his withered legs swinging limply, his unused feet in a perfectly polished pair of loafers; the loafers were more than fifteen years old.

Candy was playing with the adding machine. "I think the daughter is about Angel's age," she said.

"Right," said Homer Wells, and Wally hit Homer with a very well-thrown jab—the only sort of punch he could really throw, sitting down. Because Homer had been leaning on the desk and Wally had been sitting up straight, the punch caught Homer completely by surprise, and very solidly, in the cheek. The punch surprised Candy so much that she pushed the adding machine off the far corner of the desk. The machine crashed to the office floor; when Homer hit the floor, he did not land quite as loudly or as deadweight as the adding machine, but he landed hard. He put his hand to his cheek, where he would soon have some swelling and the start of a slight shiner.

"Wally!" Candy said.

"I'm so *sick* of it!" Wally shouted. "It's time you learned a new word, Homer," Wally said.

"Jesus, Wally," Candy said.

"I'm okay," Homer said, but he remained sitting on the office floor.

"I'm sorry," Wally said. "It just gets on my nerves—you saying 'Right' all the time." And although he had not made this particular mistake for years, he lifted himself off the desk with his arms—it must have seemed to him that the appropriate thing to do would be to swing his legs to the floor and help Homer up to his feet; he'd forgotten that he couldn't walk. If Candy had not caught him under the arms, and hugged him—chest to chest—Wally would have fallen. Homer got to his feet and helped Candy put Wally back on the desk.

"I'm sorry, buddy," Wally said. He put his head on Homer's shoulder.

Homer did not say "Right." Candy went to get a piece of ice in a towel for Homer's face, and Homer said, "It's okay, Wally. Everything's okay." Wally slumped a little forward, and Homer leaned over him; their foreheads touched. They maintained that position until Candy returned with the ice.

Most days, for fifteen years, Candy and Homer thought that Wally knew everything, that he accepted everything, but that he resented not being told. At the same time, Homer and Candy imagined that it was a relief to Wally—that he didn't have to admit that he knew everything. What new, uncomfortable position would they put him in by telling him now? Wasn't the main thing that Angel not know?—not until Candy and Homer told him; the main thing was that Angel shouldn't hear it from anyone else. Whatever Wally knew, he would never tell Angel.

If Homer was surprised, he was surprised that Wally had never hit him before.

"What was that all about?" Candy asked Homer when they were alone that night by the swimming pool. Some kind of large, whirring insect was caught in the leaf skimmer; they heard its wings beating against the soggy leaves. Whatever it was, it grew weaker and weaker.

"I guess it is irritating how I say 'Right' all the time," Homer said.

"Wally knows," Candy said.

"That's what you've thought for fifteen years," said Homer Wells.

"You think he doesn't know?" Candy asked.

"I think he loves you, and you love him," Homer said. "I think he knows we love Angel. I think Wally loves Angel, too."

"But do you think he knows Angel is *ours*?" Candy asked.

"I don't know," Homer said. "I know that one day Angel has to know he's ours. I think that Wally knows I love you," he said.

"And that I love you?" Candy asked. "Does he know that?"

"You love me sometimes," Homer said. "Not very often."

"I wasn't talking about sex," Candy whispered.

"I was," said Homer Wells.

They had been careful, and—in their opinion—almost good. Since Wally had come home from the war, Homer and Candy had made love only two hundred seventy times—an average of only eighteen times a year, only one and a half times a month; they were simply as extremely careful as they knew how. It was another thing that Candy had insisted Homer agree to: that for Wally's sake and for Angel's—for the sake of what Candy called their family—they would never be caught; they would never cause anyone even the slightest embarrassment. If anyone ever saw them, they would stop, forever.

That was why they hadn't told Wally. Why wouldn't Wally accept that they'd thought he was dead—not just missing—and that they had needed each other, and that they'd wanted Angel, too? They knew Wally would have accepted that. Who couldn't accept what *had* happened? What was happening *now* was what they knew Wally wanted to know, and they couldn't tell him.

They had another thing to be careful about. Because Wally was sterile, Candy's becoming pregnant would seem too miraculous to be believed. Because Wally's sterility was not the result of encephalitis, it would take him several years to discover that he was sterile. He would remember the unclean instrumentation of his urethra, but he would remember it gradually—the way he remembered the rest of Burma. Once he learned that his epididymis was sealed, for life, the specificity of the various bamboo shoots came back to him; sometimes it seemed to him that he could recall, exactly, every catheter that had ever relieved him.

There is no difference in the feeling of orgasm; Wally was fond of emphasizing this particular point to Homer Wells. Wally called it "shooting"; Homer was the only person with whom Wally could joke about his condition. "I can still aim the gun, and the gun still goes off," Wally said, "and it still goes off with a bang—for me," he said. "It's just that no one ever finds the bullet."

Wally remembered, from time to time, that when one of the Burmese on the sampan would instrument him—for which he was always so grateful—there was never very much bleeding, even when the bamboo shoot was not exactly straight; his blood seemed pale and minimal by comparison to the bloodier stains of the betel juice that everyone spat on the deck.

If Homer Wells got Candy pregnant again, Candy made him promise that—this time—*he* would give her an abortion. She could not fool Wally about another trip to St. Cloud's; she *would* not fool him, she said. And so this added consideration—that Candy never get pregnant—contributed to the moderation of their coupling, which was almost always managed under conditions harsh enough to win the approval of New England's founding fathers. It still would not have won Wilbur Larch's approval.

They established no pattern of behavior that could make anyone suspicious. (As if everyone wasn't already suspicious, regardless of how they behaved!) There was no one place that they met, no one day, no one time of day. In the winter months, when Angel—after school—would take Wally for a swim in the indoor pool of a private boys' academy, Homer and Candy could manage an occasional late afternoon together. But Homer's bed, which had been Olive's bed, which also suffered from all the master-bedroom connotations, was full of conflicting emotions for them both—and the bed Candy shared with Wally had its own set of taboos. Rarely, they took trips. The cider house was fit to be used only in the late summer, after it had been made ready for the picking crew; but ever since Angel had learned to drive, he'd been given the run of the orchards—he was allowed to drive any of the farm vehicles, just so he kept off the public roads, and his pudgy pal, Pete Hyde, often drove around with him. Homer suspected that Pete and Angel used the cider house to drink beer in secret, whenever they could convince Herb Fowler to buy beer for them; or that they went there for the fifteen-year-old thrill of smoking cigarettes. And at night, trapped by their own insomnia, where could Candy and Homer have disappeared to—now that Angel was an insomniac, too?

Homer Wells knew that there was no reason ever to have an accident—no reason for Candy ever to get pregnant (certainly not, knowing what Homer knew)—and no reason for them ever to get caught, either. But by being so reasonable and so discreet, Homer regretted the loss of the passion with which he and Candy had at first collided. Although she insisted (and he agreed), he thought it was quite unnecessary for him to write to Dr. Larch to request (which he did) the proper equipment with which to treat the emergency that Candy feared.

For fifteen years Homer had told her: "You won't get pregnant. You can't."

"Do you have everything you need, if you need it?" she always asked him.

"Yes," he said.

He'd gotten better about not saying "Right," since Wally had hit him. And when the word would slip out, it was often attended by an equally involuntary wince—as if in anticipation of another punch, as if anyone he might say the word to would feel as strongly about it as Wally and might be as fast as Mr. Rose.

Wilbur Larch had misunderstood about the instruments Ho mer had requested. For fifteen years, he'd misunderstood Larch had sent everything promptly. There were both a me dium and a large vaginal speculum, and an Auvard's weighted speculum; there was a set of dilators with Douglass points— and one uterine sound, one uterine biopsy curette, two vulsellum forceps, a set of Sim's uterine curettes, and a Rheinstater's uterine flushing curette. Larch sent enough Dakin's solution and red Merthiolate (and enough sterile vulval pads) for Ho mer Wells to perform abortions into the next century.

"I'm NOT going into the business!" Homer wrote to Dr Larch, but Larch remained encouraged by the simple fact of Homer's possessing the necessary equipment.

Homer wrapped the instruments in a whole bale of cotton and gauze; he then put the bundle in a waterproof bag that had once contained Angel's diapers. He stored the instruments along with the Merthiolate, the Dakin's solution and all the vulval pads, in the very back of the upstairs linen closet Homer kept the ether in the shed with the lawn and garden tools. Ether was flammable; he didn't want it in the house.

However, in the one and a half times a month that he could be with Candy, it jolted him to realize that in their union there was (even after fifteen years) a frenzy with which they clung to each other that would not have appeared pale in comparison to their first such meeting in the cider house. But since Melony had first introduced Homer Wells to sex—and it had been only during that brief period of what seemed to him to be his "married life" with Candy in St. Cloud's that he had expe rienced anything of what sex ideally is—it was Homer's opin ion that sex had little to do with love; that love was much more focused and felt in moments of tenderness and of concern. It had been years (for example) since he had seen Candy asleep, or had been the one to waken her; years since he had watched her fall asleep, and had stayed awake to watch her.

This tenderness he reserved for Angel. When Angel had been smaller, Homer had occasionally encountered Candy in the darkness of Angel's room, and they had even shared a few evenings of that silent wondering parents engage in while watch ing their children sleep. But Homer had fallen asleep, many nights, in the empty twin bed beside Angel's bed, just listening to the breathing of his son; after all, Homer had spent his childhood trying to sleep in a room where an entire population lay breathing.

And was there a feeling more full of love, he wondered, than to wake up a child in the morning? Full of love and apology, both, Homer Wells concluded. It was with Angel that he felt love like that; if Candy had such moments, Homer imagined, she had to have them with Wally. An orphan's pleasures are compartmental. In St. Cloud's, it was best to be hungry in the morning; they didn't run out of pancakes. There was sex, which called for good weather (and, of course, Melony); there were acts of wandering and destruction (Melony again, in any weather); there were solitary acts and moments of reflection, which could occur only when it rained (and only without Melony). As much as he desired a family, Homer Wells was not trained to appreciate a family's flexible nature.

That July—it was one hot and lazy Saturday afternoon—Homer was floating in the pool; he had been in the orchards all morning, mulching the young trees. Angel had been working with him, and now Angel was out of the pool, but still dripping wet; he was tossing a baseball back and forth with Wally. Wally sat on the lawn, on a slight knoll above the pool, and Angel stood on the deck. They would throw the hardball back and forth, not talking but concentrating on their throws; Wally would fire the ball with considerable sting for someone in a sitting position but Angel had more zip on the ball. The ball popped pleasantly in their big gloves.

Candy came down to the pool from the apple-mart office. She was wearing her work clothes—jeans; a khaki field shirt, with oversized pockets and epaulettes; work boots; a Boston Red Sox baseball cap with the visor turned backward. (She cared more about protecting her hair from the sun than her face, because in the summer her blondness could turn whiter, which she knew showed more of the gray.)

"I know the men are out of the fields at noon on Saturday," she said, her hands on her hips, "but the women are working in the mart until three."

Homer stopped floating; he let his feet touch the bottom and he stood chest deep in the pool, looking at Candy. Wally looked over his shoulder at her, then fired the ball to Angel, who fired it back.

"Please hold the ball, while I'm trying to say something," Candy said.

Wally held the ball. "What are you trying to say?" he asked.

"I think that on Saturdays, as long as there are people

working at the mart, you should refrain from playing at the pool—everyone can hear you, and I think it kind of rubs it in.'

"Rubs what in?" Angel asked.

"That you get to play and live in the fancy house, as they call it, and they get to work," Candy said.

"Pete's not working," Angel said. "Pete got a ride to the beach."

"Pete Hyde is a kid," Candy said. "His mother is still working."

"Well, I'm a kid, aren't I?" Angel asked playfully.

"Well, I don't mean you, especially," Candy said. "What about you two?" she asked Homer and Wally.

"Well, I'm a kid, too," Wally said, throwing the ball back to Angel. "I just play all day long, anyway." Angel laughed and threw the ball back, but Homer Wells glowered at Candy from his chest-deep position in the pool.

"Do *you* see what I mean, Homer?" Candy asked him. Homer allowed himself to sink; he held his breath for a while and when he came up for air, Candy was going through the kitchen door. The screen door banged.

"Oh, come on!" Wally called after her. "Of course we see what you mean!"

And that was when Homer said it. Homer spat out some water and said to Angel, "Go tell your mother that if she changes her clothes, we'll take her to the beach."

Angel was halfway to the house before it registered with Homer what he'd said, and Wally said to Angel, "Tell her to change her mood, too."

When Angel went in the kitchen, Wally said, "I don't think he even noticed what you said, old boy."

"It's just that she *is* such a mother to him—I can't help thinking of her that way," Homer said.

"I'm sure it's hard," Wally said, "not to think of her any way that you want."

"What?" Homer asked.

"She certainly is manipulative, isn't she?" Wally asked him. Homer ducked his head underwater again—it was a cool place to think.

"Manipulative?" he said, when he surfaced.

"Well, someone has to know what to do," Wally said. "Someone's got to make the decisions."

Homer Wells, who felt the word "Right!" rising in him, like

an unstoppable bubble surfacing from the swimming pool, put
his hand over his mouth and looked at Wally, who was sitting
on the knoll on the lawn, his back very straight, the baseball
mitt in his lap, the baseball held in his hand (his throwing arm
cocked). Homer Wells knew that if the word had escaped him,
the ball would have been on its fast way to him as soon as the
word was in the air—and quite probably before Homer could
have ducked underwater again.

"She has a point," said Homer Wells.

"She always does," Wally said. "And she's aging well, don't
you think?"

"Very well," Homer said, climbing out of the pool. He
buried his wet face in a towel; with his eyes closed, he could
see the delicate latticework of wrinkles at the corners of Candy's eyes and the freckles on her chest, where, over the years,
she'd allowed herself too much sun. There were also the very
few but deeper wrinkles that ran across her otherwise taut
abdomen; they were stretch marks, Homer knew; he wondered
if Wally knew what they were from. And there were the veins
that had gained more prominence in the backs of Candy's long
hands, but she was still a beautiful woman.

When Angel and Candy came out of the house—they were
ready to go to the beach—Homer watched his son closely, to
see if Angel had noticed that Homer had referred to Candy as
"your mother," but Angel was the way he always was, and
Homer couldn't tell if Angel had caught the slip. Homer
wondered if he should tell Candy that Wally had caught it.

They took Candy's lemon-yellow Jeep. Candy drove; Wally
sat up front, in the comfortable seat, and Homer and Angel
shared the back. All the way to the beach, Wally just looked
out the window intently, as if he were seeing the road between
Heart's Rock and Heart's Haven for the first time. As if,
thought Homer Wells, Wally had just abandoned the plane—
over Burma—and his chute had just opened, and he was
searching for a spot to land.

That was the first time that Homer knew for certain that
Candy was right.

He knows, Homer thought. Wally knows.

/ / /

The apple mart never changed. It was also a family. Only
Debra Pettigrew was gone; Big Dot Taft's kid sister had married a man from New Hampshire, and she came back to

Heart's Rock only at Christmas. Every Christmas, Homer Wells took Angel to St. Cloud's. They had an early Christmas breakfast with Candy and Wally, and a lot of opening presents; then they took a lot more presents to St. Cloud's. They would arrive late in the day, or in the early evening, and have Christmas dinner with everyone. How Nurse Angela cried! Nurse Edna cried when they left. Dr. Larch was friendly but reserved.

The apple mart was nearly as constant as St. Cloud's—in some ways, the apple mart was more constant, because the people didn't change, and at St. Cloud's the orphans were always changing.

Herb Fowler still went out with Louise Tobey, who was still called Squeeze Louise; she was almost fifty, now; she'd never married Herb (she'd never been asked), yet she had acquired a wife's matronly charms and postures. Herb Fowler was still a very coarse, very worn-out joke (about the rubbers); he was one of those thin, gray men in his sixties, with an outrageous pot belly (for such a skinny fellow); he carried his paunch like something stolen and badly hidden beneath his shirt. And Meany Hyde was uniformly fat and bald, and as nice as ever; his wife, Florence, and Big Dot Taft still ruled the roost in the apple mart. Only momentarily sobered by Grace Lynch's death, these two women (with their thigh-sized upper arms) still kept Irene Titcomb giggling (and she still turned the side of her face with the burn scar away). Everett Taft, who was the mellowest foreman, seemed relieved that Homer did the hiring, now, and that the burden of hiring the extra help at harvest had been lifted off him. And Vernon Lynch's resentment was so monumental that it didn't confine itself to mere particulars—either to Homer's being in charge, or to Grace's death. It was just anger that possessed him—seething and constant and unrestrained by the ravages of Vernon's sixty-something years.

Homer Wells said that Vernon Lynch had a constant brain tumor; it never grew, it always exerted the same pressure and the same interference. "It's just there, like the weather, huh?" Ira Titcomb, the beekeeper, kidded with Homer. Ira was sixty-five, but he had another number marked on the trailer he used to carry his hives: the number of times he'd been stung by his bees.

"Only two hundred and forty-one times," Ira said. "I been keepin' bees since I was nineteen," he said, "so that amounts to only five point two stings a year. Pretty good, huh?" Ira asked Homer.

"Right," mumbled Homer Wells, ducking the expected punch, cringing in anticipation of the baseball whistling toward his face at the speed of Mr. Rose's knife work.

Homer kept his own accounts, of course. The number of times he'd made love with Candy since Wally came home from the war was written in pencil (and then erased, and then rewritten) on the back of the photograph of Wally with the crew of *Opportunity Knocks*. Two hundred seventy—only a few more times than Ira Titcomb had been stung by bees. What Homer didn't know was that Candy also kept a record—also written in pencil, she wrote "270" on the back of another print of the photograph of her teaching Homer how to swim. She kept the photograph, almost casually, in the bathroom she shared with Wally, where the photograph was always partially concealed by a box of tissues, or a bottle of shampoo. It was a cluttered bathroom, which Olive had outfitted properly before she died, and before Wally came home; it had the convenient handrails Wally needed to help himself on and off the toilet and in and out of the tub.

"It's your standard cripple's bathroom," Wally would say. "An ape would have a good time in there. There's all that stuff to swing from."

And once, that summer, returning from the beach, they had stopped the car at the playground of the elementary school in Heart's Haven. Wally and Angel wanted to play on the jungle gym. Angel was very agile on the thing, and Wally's arms were so developed that he could move through it with an alarmingly apelike strength and grace—the two of them hooting like monkeys at Homer and Candy, who waited in the car.

"Our two children," Homer had said to the love of his life.

"Yes, our family," Candy had said, smiling—watching Wally and Angel climb and swing, climb and swing.

"It's better for them than watching television," said Homer Wells, who would always think of Wally and Angel as children. Homer and Candy shared the opinion that Wally watched too much television, which was a bad influence on Angel, who liked to watch it with him.

Wally was so fond of television that he had even given a TV to Homer to take to St. Cloud's. Of course the reception was very poor up there, which had perhaps improved the McCarthy hearings, which had been Wilbur Larch's first, sustained experience with television.

"Thank God it didn't come in clearly," he wrote to Homer.

Nurse Caroline had been in a bad mood all that year. If the U.S. Army really was "coddling Communists," as Senator McCarthy claimed, Nurse Caroline said that she'd consider joining up.

Wilbur Larch, straining to see Senator McCarthy through the television's snow and zigzagging lines, said, "He looks like a drunk to me. I'll bet he dies young."

"Not young enough to suit me," Nurse Caroline said.

Finally, they gave the television away. Nurse Edna and Mrs. Grogan were becoming addicted to it, and Larch considered that it was worse for the orphans than organized religion. "It's better for anyone than ether, Wilbur," Nurse Edna complained, but Larch was firm. He gave the thing to the stationmaster, who (in Larch's opinion) was the perfect sort of moron for the invention; it was just the right thing to occupy the mind of someone who waited all day for trains. It was Wilbur Larch who was the first man in Maine to call a television what it was: "an idiot box." Maine, of course—and St. Cloud's, especially—seemed to get everything more slowly than the rest of the country.

But Wally loved to watch it, and Angel watched it with him whenever Candy and Homer didn't object. Wally argued, for example, that such televised events as the McCarthy hearings were educational for Angel. "He ought to know," Wally said, "that the country is always in danger from right-wing nut cases."

Although Senator McCarthy lost the support of millions of people as a result of the hearings—and although the Senate condemned him for his "contemptuous" conduct toward a subcommittee that had investigated his finances and for his abuse of a committee that recommended he be censured, the board of trustees of St. Cloud's had been favorably impressed by Senator McCarthy. Mrs. Goodhall and Dr. Gingrich, especially, were encouraged to complain about Nurse Caroline's socialist views and involvements, which they considered tinged the orphanage a shade of pink.

Nurse Caroline's arrival had stolen a bit of the board's fire. If Mrs. Goodhall was at first relieved to learn that someone "new" had invaded St. Cloud's, she was later irritated to discover that Nurse Caroline approved of Dr. Larch. This led Mrs. Goodhall to investigate Nurse Caroline, whose nursing redentials were perfect but whose political activities gave Mrs. Goodhall a glow of hope.

Many times had Mrs. Goodhall advanced her thesis to the board that Dr. Larch was not only ninety-something, he was also a nonpracticing homosexual. Now she warned the board that Dr. Larch had hired a young Red.

"They're all so old, they'll be easily brainwashed," Mrs. Goodhall said.

Dr. Gingrich, who was increasingly fascinated with the leaps of Mrs. Goodhall's mind, was still marveling over the confusing image of a nonpracticing homosexual; it struck him as a brilliant accusation to make of anyone who was slightly (or hugely) different. It was the best rumor to start about anyone because it could never be proved or disproved. Dr. Gingrich wished he'd considered the accusation—just as a means of provocation—when he'd still been practicing psychiatry.

And now, not only was Dr. Larch old and homosexual and nonpracticing—he was also in danger of being brainwashed by a young Red.

Dr. Gingrich was dying to find out what Dr. Larch's responses might be to the accusation that he was a nonpracticing homosexual, because Dr. Larch was so outspoken on the issue of Nurse Caroline's politics.

"She's a socialist, not a Communist!" Dr. Larch protested to the board.

"Same difference," as they say in Maine—about so many things.

"The next thing you know," Larch complained to his nurses, "they'll be asking us to denounce things."

"What would we denounce?" Nurse Edna asked worriedly.

"Let's make a list," Larch said.

"The abortion laws," Nurse Angela said.

"At the top of the list!" Larch agreed.

"Oh my!" Nurse Edna said.

"Republicans," said Wilbur Larch. "And the board of trustees," he added.

"Oh dear," Nurse Edna said.

"Capitalism," Nurse Caroline said.

"There's never been any capital around here," Dr. Larch said.

"Insects and scab!" Nurse Edna said. They all stared at her. "And maggots," Nurse Edna added. "They're what I have to spray the apple trees for. Insects and scab and maggots."

As a result, Wilbur Larch dug out of a closet the old black leather bag he'd had at the Boston Lying-In; he took the bag to a cobbler in Three Mile Falls who also repaired ladies' hand bags and put gold initials on saddles, and he had the cobbler engrave on his old black bag the gold initials F.S.—for Fuzzy Stone.

That August of 195__, just a few days before the picking crew was expected at Ocean View, Wilbur Larch sent the doctor's bag to Homer Wells. It was the time of year, every year, when Melony took her vacation.

Most of the shipyard workers, even the electricians, took a couple of weeks in the summer and a couple of weeks around Christmas, but Melony took a whole month during harvest time; it made her feel good—or, maybe, young again—to pick apples. This year, she had decided, she'd try working at Ocean View.

She still hitchhiked whenever and wherever she traveled, and because she wore only men's work clothes, she still looked like a tramp; no one would ever know that she was a shipyard's skilled electrician, with enough money in a savings account to buy a nice house and a couple of cars.

When Melony arrived at the apple mart, Big Dot Taft was the first to see her. Big Dot and Florence Hyde were arranging some of the display tables, although the only new apples they had available were the Gravensteins. They had mostly jellies and jams and honey. Irene Titcomb was working the pie ovens. Wally was in the office; he was on the telephone and didn't see Melony—and she didn't see him.

Candy was in the kitchen of the fancy house, talking real estate to Olive's vulgar brother, Bucky Bean. Bucky had bought what was left of the point of land Ray Kendall had owned on Heart's Haven Harbor. Bucky had put a very cheap and shabby seafood restaurant there—one of Maine's first carhop restaurants, one of those places where young girls dressed like cheerleaders bring you mostly fried and mostly tepid food, which you consume in your car. The food attaches itself to the cars by means of wobbly little trays that cling to the doors of the cars when the windows are rolled down. Homer always wanted to take Wilbur Larch to such a place—only to hear what the old man would say. Larch's response, Homer was sure, would be related to his response to television and to Senator Joe McCarthy.

Bucky Bean's new idea was to buy the part of the orchard

called Cock Hill and sell it in one-acre lots as "summer property" with a view of the ocean.

Candy was in the process of rejecting the offer when Melony arrived at the apple mart. Candy's opinion was that one-acre lots were too small and that the unsuspecting new owners would be unprepared for the chemical spray used on the apples that would regularly float over and descend upon their property every summer. Also, the families who bought property and built houses would doubtlessly believe it was their right to climb the fences and pick all the apples they wanted.

"You're just like Olive," Bucky Bean complained. "You've got no imagination concerning the future."

That was when Melony approached Big Dot Taft, not only because Big Dot appeared to be in charge but also because Melony felt comfortable with big, fat women. Big Dot smiled to see how hefty Melony was; the two women appeared predisposed to like each other when Melony spoke—her voice reverberating through the near-empty stalls and surprising Meany Hyde and Vernon Lynch, who were putting water in the John Deere's radiator. When Melony tried to speak normally, her voice was peculiarly deep; when she tried to raise the pitch of her voice, most people thought she was shouting.

"Does a guy named Homer Wells work here?" Melony asked Big Dot.

"He sure does," Big Dot said cheerfully. "Are you a pal of Homer's?"

"I used to be," Melony said. "I haven't seen him in a while," she added coyly—at least coyly for Melony, whose love affair with Lorna had made her occasionally self-conscious and shy with other women; her self-confidence around men was as steadfast as ever.

"Where's Homer?" Florence Hyde asked Meany. He was staring at Melony.

"He's puttin' out crates in the Frying Pan," said Meany Hyde. Something made him shiver.

"You just come to say hello?" Big Dot asked Melony, whose fingers—Dot noticed—were instinctively opening and closing, making fists and then relaxing.

"I actually come for work," Melony said. "I done a lot of pickin'."

"Homer hires the pickers," Big Dot said. "I guess you're in luck—you bein' old friends."

"It's too early for hirin' pickers," Vernon Lynch said. Something about the way Melony looked at him made him not insist on that point.

"Just go tell Homer there's someone to see him," Big Dot told Vernon. "Homer's the boss."

"The boss?" Melony said.

Irene Titcomb giggled, and turned her burn scar away. "It's actually a kind of secret—who's boss around here," Irene said.

Vernon Lynch gunned the tractor so hard that an oily, black smoke barked out of the exhaust pipe and washed over the women in the mart.

"If you're gonna work here," Big Dot told Melony, "you might as well know it: that guy drivin' the tractor is the number one asshole."

Melony shrugged. "There's just one?" she asked, and Big Dot laughed.

"Oh, my pies!" said Irene Titcomb, who went running off. Florence Hyde sized Melony up, in a friendly way, and Big Dot put her meaty paw on Melony's shoulder as if they were lifelong pals. Irene Titcomb ran back to them and announced that the pies were saved.

"So tell us how you know Homer Wells," Florence Hyde said to Melony.

"From where and since when?" asked Big Dot Taft.

"From Saint Cloud's, since forever," Melony told them. "He was my guy," she told the women, her lips parting, showing the damage done to her teeth.

"You don't say?" said Big Dot Taft.

/ / /

Homer Wells and his son, Angel, were talking about masturbation—or, rather, Homer was talking. They were taking their lunch break under one of the old trees in the Frying Pan; they'd been putting crates out in the orchards all morning—taking turns driving the tractor and unloading the crates. They'd finished their sandwiches, and Angel had shaken up his soda and squirted his father with it, and Homer had tried to find a casual way to bring up the subject of masturbation. Candy had mentioned to Homer that the evidence on Angel's bedsheets suggested that this might be the time for a father-and-son conversation regarding Angel's obviously emerging sexuality.

"Boy, when I was your age—in Saint Cloud's—it was really tough to beat off with any privacy," Homer had begun (he thought, casually).

They'd been lying on their backs in the tall grass, under the fullest tree in the Frying Pan—the sun couldn't filter through the lush, bent branches and all the heavy apples.

"Really," Angel said indifferently, after a while.

"Yup," Homer said. "You know, I was the oldest—about your age—and I was supposed to be in charge of all the other kids, more or less. I knew they weren't even old enough to have pubic hair, or they didn't even know what to make of their little hard-ons."

Angel laughed. Homer laughed, too.

"So how'd you manage it?" Angel asked his father, after a while.

"I waited until I thought they were all asleep, and then I tried to keep the bed quiet," Homer said. "But you've got no idea how long it can take twelve or fifteen boys to fall asleep!"

They both laughed some more.

"There was one other kid who was old enough to know about it," Homer confided. "I think he was just beginning to experiment with playing with himself—I think the first time that he actually did it, he didn't have any idea what would happen. And when he actually squirted—when he ejaculated, you know—he thought he'd hurt himself. In the dark, he probably thought he was bleeding!"

This story was a complete fiction, but Angel Wells loved it; he laughed in a very worldly way, which encouraged his father to go on.

"Well, he was so worried—he kept asking me to turn on the light, he said something had broken inside him," Homer said.

"Broken?" Angel said, and they both howled.

"Yes!" Homer said. "And when I turned on the light and he got a look at himself, he said, 'Oh, God, it went off!'—as if he were talking about a gun, and he'd just shot himself with it!"

Father and son laughed over that for a while.

Then Homer said, more seriously, "Of course I tried to explain it all to him. It was hard to make him understand that he hadn't done anything wrong—because it's natural; it's perfectly healthy and normal, but these things have a way of getting distorted."

Angel was quiet now; perhaps he saw the reason for the story.

"But just imagine me trying to explain to this kid—he was quite a bit younger than you are—that it was only natural that he would have feelings about girls, and about sex, long before he would have the opportunity to have anything to do with girls. Or to actually have sex," Homer added. He had truly labored the point into submission, and he paused to see how his son was taking it in; Angel, who had a long stalk of grass in his mouth, lay on his back staring at the sprawling trunk of the huge tree.

They were quiet for a while, and then Homer said: "Is there anything you'd like to ask me—about anything?"

Angel gave a short laugh; then he paused. "Yes," Angel said to his father. "I wonder why you don't have a girlfriend—why you don't even seem interested."

This was not the question Homer had expected, following his birds-and-bees invitation, but after a few seconds he realized that the question should have been anticipated and that some reasonable answer was doubtlessly pressing more on Angel's mind than any truths regarding masturbation.

"I had a girlfriend, in Saint Cloud's," Homer said. "She was kind of rough on me. She was something of a bully. Older than me, and at the time, she was stronger than me!" he said, laughing.

"No kidding," Angel said; he wasn't laughing; he had rolled over on his elbows and was watching his father intently.

"Well, we weren't very much alike," Homer said. "It was one of those cases of the sex happening before there was a friendship, or there really being no friendship—and, after a short while, there wasn't any more sex, either. After that, I'm not sure what the relationship was."

"It was a sort of bad way to start, you mean?" Angel asked.

"Right," his father said.

"So what happened after that?" Angel asked.

"I met Wally and Candy," Homer said carefully. "I guess I would have married Candy—if she hadn't married Wally. She was almost my girlfriend, for about five minutes. That was when Wally was in the war, when we wondered if he was still alive," Homer said quickly. "I've always been so close to Wally and Candy, and then—once I had you—I started to feel that I already had everything I wanted."

Angel Wells rolled over on his back, gazing up the trunk of the tree. "So you still kind of like Candy?" he asked. "You're not interested in anybody else?"

"Kind of," said Homer Wells. "Have you met anybody you're interested in?" he asked, hoping to change the subject.

"Nobody who'd be interested in me," his son said. "I mean, the girls I think about are all too old to even look at me."

"That will change," Homer said, poking Angel in the ribs; the boy doubled up his knees and rolled on his side, poking back at his father. "Pretty soon," Homer said, "the girls are going to stand in line to look at you." He grabbed Angel in a headlock and they started wrestling. Wrestling with Angel was one way Homer could keep in close physical contact with the boy—long after Angel had grown self-conscious about being hugged and kissed, in public. A fifteen-year-old boy doesn't want his father draped all over him, but wrestling was perfectly respectable; that was still allowed. They were wrestling so hard, and laughing—and breathing so heavily—that they did not hear Vernon Lynch approach them.

"Hey, Homer!" Vernon said sharply, kicking at them as they rolled on the ground under the big tree—the way he might, tentatively, attempt to break up a dogfight. When they saw him standing over them, they froze in an awkward embrace—as if they'd been caught doing something they shouldn't. "If you quit dickin' around," Vernon said, "I got a message for you."

"For me?" said Homer Wells.

"There's a fat woman who says she knows you. She's at the mart," Vernon said. Homer smiled. He knew several fat women at the mart; he assumed that Vernon meant Big Dot Taft or Florence Hyde. Even Squeeze Louise had been putting on weight in recent years.

"I mean a *new* fat woman," Vernon said. He started walking back to his tractor. "She says she wants to be a picker, and she asked for you. She knows you."

Homer got slowly to his feet; he'd rolled over a root of the big tree, and the root had hurt him in the ribs. Also, Angel had stuffed grass down the back of his shirt. Angel said to his father, "Oh, a fat woman, huh? I guess you didn't tell me about the fat woman." As Homer unbuttoned his shirt to shake out the grass, Angel poked his father's bare stomach. That was when Angel noticed that his father had aged. He was still a trim man, and strong from all the orchard work he'd done, but just a bit of belly rolled over the belt of his jeans, and his hair, tousled from the wrestling, was more flecked with gray than it was with grass. There was something grim around the corners of Homer's eyes that Angel had also never noticed before.

"Pop?" Angel asked him softly. "Who's the woman?" But his father was looking at him in a panic; he started buttoning his shirt askew, and Angel had to help him with it. "It can't be the bully, can it?" Angel was trying to joke with his father—their manner together was often full of joking; but Homer wouldn't speak, he wouldn't even smile. Half a trailer of apple crates still needed to be unloaded, but Homer drove too fast, dumping an occasional crate. They had an empty trailer in no time, and on the way back to the apple mart, Homer took the public road instead of winding through the back orchards. The public road was faster, although Homer had told all the drivers to keep off it whenever they could—to avoid any possible accidents with the beach traffic along that road in the summers.

Children are most impressed with the importance of a moment when they witness a parent breaking the parent's own rule.

"Do you think it's her?" Angel shouted to his father. He stood over his father's shoulders, his hands on the tractor seat, his feet braced against the trailer hitch. "You've got to admit, it's a little exciting," the boy added, but Homer looked grim.

Homer parked the tractor and trailer by the storage barns, next to the mart. "You can start putting on another load," he told Angel, but he was not going to get rid of Angel so easily. The boy dogged his footsteps to the apple mart, where Big Dot and Florence and Irene were surrounding the implacable and massive Melony.

"It *is* her, isn't it?" Angel whispered to his father.

"Hello, Melony," said Homer Wells. There was not a sound in the still, summer air.

"How you doin', Sunshine?" Melony asked him.

"Sunshine!" said Big Dot Taft.

Even Angel had to say it out loud. Imagine: his father a "Sunshine"!

But although she had waited years to see him, Melony's gaze was riveted not on Homer Wells but on Angel. Melony could not take her eyes off the boy. Homer Wells, a pleasant-looking man in his forties, did not very precisely remind Melony of the Homer Wells she had known; rather, it was Angel who struck Melony with a force quite unexpected by her. She had not anticipated being swept off her feet by the near-spitting image of the boy she had known. Poor Angel felt a little wilted by the

ruffian eye Melony cast over him, but he was a young gentleman and he smiled appealingly at the stranger.

"There's no doubt about who *you* are," Melony said to the
boy. "You look more like your father than your father." Big
Dot and the apple-mart ladies were hanging on her every word.

"It's nice that you see a resemblance," said Homer Wells,
"but my son is adopted."

Hadn't Homer Wells learned anything? Through those years
of hard knocks, those years of muscle and fat and betrayal and
growing decidedly older, could he still not see in Melony's
fierce, sad eyes that she possessed a quality that could never be
bullshitted?

"Adopted?" Melony said, her yellow-gray eyes never once
leaving Angel. She was disappointed in her oldest friend: that
he should, after all these years, still try to deceive her.

That was when Candy—who had finally gotten rid of Bucky
Bean—strolled into the apple mart, removed a Gravenstein
from a basket on the first display table, took a sharp bite,
noticed that no one seemed to be working and walked over to
the small crowd.

Since the most natural space for Candy to enter this gathering was between Homer and Angel, she stepped between them;
and since her mouth was quite full of the new apple, she was a
little embarrassed to speak to the stranger.

"Hi!" she managed to say to Melony, who recognized
instantly—in Candy's face—those few parts of Angel she had
failed to locate in her memory of Homer Wells.

"This is Melony," Homer said to Candy, who had difficulty
swallowing—long ago, on the cider house roof, she had heard
all about Melony. "This is Missus Worthington," Homer mumbled to Melony.

"How do you do?" Candy managed to say.

"Missus Worthington?" Melony said, her lynxlike eyes now
darting from Angel to Candy, and from Angel to Homer Wells.

That was when Wally wheeled himself out of the office and
into the mart.

"Isn't anybody working today?" he asked, in his friendly
way. When he saw there was a stranger, he was polite. "Oh,
hello!" he said.

"Hi," said Melony.

"This is my husband," Candy said, through lots of apple.

"Your husband?" Melony said.

"This is Mister Worthington," mumbled Homer Wells.

"Everybody calls me Wally," Wally said.

"Melony and I were in the orphanage together," Homer explained.

"Really?" Wally said enthusiastically. "That's great," he said. "Get them to show you around. Show her the house, too," Wally told Homer. "Maybe you'd like to take a swim?" he asked Melony, who, for once in her life, did not know what to say. "Dot?" Wally said to Big Dot Taft. "Get me a count of the number of bushels of Gravs we have in storage. I got a phone order waiting." He turned the wheelchair very smoothly and started to roll back to the office.

"Meany knows how many we got," Florence Hyde said. "He was just in there."

"Then someone get Meany to tell me," Wally said. "It's nice to meet you!" he called to Melony. "Please stay for supper."

Candy almost choked, but she managed a hard swallow.

"Thank you!" Melony called after Wally.

He didn't need any help going in and out of the office, because Everett Taft had (years ago) taken the threshold off and arranged for the screen door to swing both ways—like a saloon door. Wally could come and go without assistance.

He's the only hero here, Melony thought, watching the door swing closed behind the wheelchair; she could not control her hands. She wanted to touch Angel, to hug him—she'd wanted to get her hands on Homer Wells for years, but now she didn't know what she wanted to do to him. If she'd suddenly dropped to all fours, or had crouched into a stance more suitable for a fight, she knew that Homer Wells would be prepared; she noticed he had no control of his hands, either—his fingers were playing pitty-pat against his thighs. Hardest for Melony was to recognize that there was no love for her in his eyes; he looked like a trapped animal—there was no enthusiasm or curiosity about seeing her in any part of him. She thought that if she'd opened her mouth, beginning with the boy—how he was clearly no orphan!—Homer Wells would be at her throat before she could spit out the story.

No one seemed to remember that Melony had come—among other reasons—for a job. Angel said, "Would you like to see the pool first?"

"Well, I don't swim," Melony said, "but it would be nice to see it." She smiled at Homer with such an uncharacteristic warmth—which revealed everything about her bad teeth—that Homer shivered. The apple, from which only one, uncomfortable bite had been taken, hung like a lead weight at the end of Candy's limp arm.

"I'll show you the house," Candy said. "After Angel's shown you the pool." She dropped the uneaten apple, then laughed at herself.

"I'll show you the orchards," Homer mumbled.

"You don't have to show me no orchards, Sunshine," Melony said. "I seen lots of orchards, before."

"Oh," he said.

"Sunshine," Candy said blankly.

Angel poked his father in the back as they were walking toward the house and pool; Angel still thought that this surprise was great and unexpected fun. Homer turned briefly and frowned at his son, which Angel found all the more amusing. While the boy was showing Melony the swimming pool—and making special note of the ramp for Wally's wheelchair—Candy and Homer awaited her arrival in the kitchen.

"She knows," Homer said to Candy.

"What?" Candy said. "What does she know?"

"Melony knows everything," said Homer Wells, in a trance of almost ether intensity.

"How could she?" Candy asked him. "Did you tell her?"

"Don't be ridiculous," Homer said. "She just knows—she always knows."

"Don't *you* be ridiculous," Candy said crossly.

"Wally's a great swimmer," Angel explained to Melony. "In the ocean, he just needs to get carried out past the breakers. I can carry him."

"You're a good-lookin' guy," Melony said to Angel. "You're better-lookin' than your dad ever was."

Angel was embarrassed; he took the temperature of the pool. "It's warm," he said. "Too bad you don't swim. You could stay in the shallow end, or I could teach you how to float. Candy taught my dad how to swim."

"Incredible," Melony said. She walked out on the diving board and jounced a little; she needed to jounce very little to make the board dip close to the water. "If I fell in, I'll bet you could save me," she said to Angel, who couldn't tell if the big woman was being flirtatious or threatening—or if she was idly fooling around. That was what was exciting about her, Angel thought: she gave him the impression that—from one minute to the next—she might do anything.

"I could probably save you, if you were drowning," Angel offered cautiously. But Melony retreated from the end of the diving board, which lent to her step the sense of springing power that one detects in the larger members of the cat family.

"Incredible," she repeated, her eyes trying to take in everything.

"Want to see the house now?" Angel asked her. She was making him nervous.

"Gee, it's some place you got," Melony told Candy, who showed her the downstairs; Homer showed her the upstairs. In the hallway between Homer's and Angel's rooms, Melony whispered to him, "Boy, you really done all right for yourself. How'd you manage it, Sunshine?" How she feasted on him with her tawny eyes! "You even got a great view!" she pointed out, sitting on the master bed and looking out the window.

When she asked if she could use the bathroom, Homer went downstairs to have a word with Candy, but Angel was still hanging around—still very much enjoying himself, and still curious. The impact that the thuglike nature of his father's first girlfriend had made on the boy was considerable; if Angel had been troubled in trying to imagine why his father chose such a solitary life, the violent apparition that had presented herself today had done much to reassure him. If this menacing woman had been his father's first experience, it was more understandable (to Angel) why Homer had been reluctant to repeat the relationship.

Melony seemed to spend a long time in the bathroom, and Homer Wells was grateful for the time; he needed it—to convince Candy and Angel to go back to work, to leave him alone with Melony. "She wants a *job*," he told them forcefully. "I need to have a little time with her, alone."

"A job," Candy said—a new horror coming into her face; the thought of it made her squint her pretty eyes.

Mirrors had never been Melony's friends, but the mirror in Homer's bathroom was especially harsh to her. She went through the medicine cabinet quickly; for no reason, she dumped some of the pills down the toilet. She began ejecting razor blades from a crude, metal dispenser; she emptied the dispenser before she could make herself stop. She cut her finger trying to pick up one of the blades from the floor. She had her finger stuck in her mouth when she first looked at herself in the mirror. She held the razor blade in her other hand while she reviewed the forty-something years she saw in her face. Oh, she had never been attractive, she had never been nice, but once she had been an efficient weapon, she thought; now she wasn't so sure. She held the razor blade against the pouch under one eye; she shut that eye, as if the eye itself couldn't watch what she was going to do. Then she did nothing. After a while, she put the blade down on the edge of the sink and cried.

Later, she found a cigarette lighter; Candy must have left it in the bathroom; Homer didn't smoke; Wally couldn't climb stairs. She used the lighter to melt the handle of Homer's toothbrush; she sunk the razor blade in the softest part and waited for the handle to harden. When she clutched the brush end in her hand, she had quite a nice little weapon, she thought.

Then she saw the fifteen-year-old questionnaire from the St. Cloud's board of trustees; the paper was so old, she had to be careful not to tear it. How those questions spun her mind around! She threw the toothbrush with the razor blade in the sink, then she picked it up again, then she put it in the medicine cabinet, then she took it out. She was sick once and flushed the toilet twice.

Melony stayed upstairs in the bathroom a long time. When she came downstairs, she found Homer waiting for her in the kitchen; she'd had enough time alone for her disposition to change and rechange—for her to grasp hold of her real feelings about finding Homer in these surroundings, and in what she presumed was a sleazy situation. She might have enjoyed a few minutes of the discomfort she had caused him, but by the time she came downstairs she was no longer enjoying herself and her disappointment in Homer Wells was even deeper than her steadfast anger—it was nearly level with grief.

"I somehow thought you'd end up doin' somethin' better than ballin' a poor cripple's wife and pretendin' your own child ain't your own," Melony said to Homer Wells. "You of all people—you, an orphan," she reminded him.

"It's not quite like that," he started to tell her, but she shook her huge head and looked away from him.

"I got eyes," Melony said. "I can see what it's like—it's like *shit*. It's ordinary, middle-class shit—bein' unfaithful and lyin' to the kids. You of all people!" Melony said. She had her hands thrust in her pockets; she took them out and clasped them behind her back; then she jammed them back in her pockets again. Every time she moved her hands, Homer flinched.

Homer Wells had expected to be attacked by her; Melony was an attacker; but this was not the attack he had expected. He had imagined that he would, one day—when he saw her again—be a match for her, but now he knew that he would never be a match for Melony.

"Do you think I get my rocks off embarrassin' you?" Melony asked him. "Do you think I was always lookin' for you—only to give you a bad time?"

"I didn't know you were looking for me," said Homer Wells.

"I had you figured all wrong," said Melony. Looking at her, Homer Wells realized that he'd had Melony figured all wrong, too. "I always thought you'd end up like the old man."

"Like Larch?" Homer said.

"Of course, like Larch!" Melony snapped at him. "I figured you for that—you know, the missionary. The do-gooder with his nose in the air."

"I don't see Larch quite that way," Homer said.

"Don't be snotty to me!" Melony cried, her raw face streaked with tears. "You've got your nose in the air—I got that part right. But you ain't exactly no missionary. You're a creep! You knocked up somebody you shouldn't 'a' been fuckin' in the first place, and you couldn't even come clean about it to your own kid. Some missionary! Ain't that *brave*? In my book, Sunshine, that's a creep," Melony told him.

Then she left; she never asked him about the job; he never got to ask her how her life had been.

He went upstairs to the bathroom and threw up; he filled the sink with cold water and soaked his head, but the throbbing had no end. One hundred seventy-five pounds of truth had struck him in the face and neck and chest—had constricted his breathing and made him ache. A vomit taste was in his mouth; he tried to brush his teeth but he cut himself in the hand before he saw the blade. He felt nearly as paralyzed above the waist as he knew Wally must feel below. When he reached for the towel by the shower door, he saw what else was wrong, he saw what was missing from the bathroom: the blank questionnaire, the one he'd never returned to the board of trustees of St. Cloud's was gone. It didn't take Homer Wells long to imagine how Melony might answer some of the questions.

This new panic momentarily elevated him above his own self-pity. He called the orphanage immediately, and got Nurse Edna on the phone.

"Oh, Homer!" she cried, so glad to hear his voice.

"This is important," he told her. "I saw Melony."

"Oh, Melony!" Nurse Edna cried happily. "Missus Grogan will be thrilled!"

"Melony has a copy of the questionnaire," Homer said. "Please tell Doctor Larch—I don't think this is good news. That old questionnaire from the board of trustees."

"Oh, dear," Nurse Edna said.

"Of course she might never fill it out," Homer said, "but she has it—it says where to send it, right on the thing. And I don't know where she's gone; I don't know where she came from."

"Was she married?" Nurse Edna asked. "Was she happy?"

Jesus Christ, thought Homer Wells. Nurse Edna always shouted into the telephone; she was so old that she remembered only the days of bad connections.

"Just tell Doctor Larch that Melony has the questionnaire. I thought he should know," said Homer Wells.

"Yes, yes!" Nurse Edna shouted. "But was she happy?"

"I don't think so," Homer said.

"Oh, dear."

/ / /

"I thought she was going to stay for supper," Wally said, serving the swordfish.

"I thought she wanted a job," Angel said.

"What's she been doing with herself?" Wally asked.

"If she wanted to pick apples," Candy said, "she can't be doing too much with herself."

"I don't think she needed the job," Homer said.

"She just wanted to look you over, Pop," Angel said, and Wally laughed. Angel had told Wally that Melony had been Homer's girlfriend, which Wally had thought was very funny.

"I'll bet your dad never told you about Debra Pettigrew, kiddo," Wally said to Angel.

"Oh, come on, Wally," Candy said. "That wasn't serious."

"You left something out," Angel said to his father; Angel pointed his finger at Homer.

"Yes," Homer admitted. "But Debra Pettigrew wasn't any-one special."

"We used to double-date," Wally told Angel. "Your old man usually got the backseat."

"Come on, Wally!" Candy said. She'd given Homer and Angel too many asparagus; she had to take some back, or there wouldn't be any for Wally or herself.

"You should have seen your old man at his first drive-in," Wally said to Angel. "He didn't know what drive-ins were for!"

"Maybe Angel doesn't know what they're for!" Candy said sharply to her husband.

"Of course I know!" Angel said, laughing.

"Of course he knows!" Wally said, also laughing.

"Only Bedouins don't know," said Homer Wells, trying to go along with the fun.

After supper, he helped Candy with the dishes while Angel drove around the orchards with Pete Hyde; after supper, al-most every night, the boys had a game—they tried to drive through all the orchards before it was dark. Homer wouldn't let them drive in the orchards after dark—not after the apple crates had been put out for the pickers.

Wally liked the twilight by the swimming pool. From the kitchen window, Homer and Candy could see him sitting in the wheelchair; he had tipped his head back, as if he were staring at the sky, but he was watching the spiral drifting of a hawk over the orchard called Cock Hill—some smaller birds were pestering the hawk, flying dangerously close to it, trying to drive it away.

"It's time to tell," Homer said to Candy.

"No, please," Candy said; she reached around him, where he was working at the sink, and dropped the broiler rack that the swordfish had been cooked on into the soapy water. The rack was greasy and stuck all over with charred bits of fish, but Homer Wells immediately pulled it out of the water—without letting it soak—and started scrubbing it.

"It's time to tell everyone everything," said Homer Wells. "No more waiting and seeing."

She stood behind him and put her arms around his hips; she pressed her face between his shoulder blades, but he did not return her embrace—or even turn to face her. He just kept scrubbing the broiler rack.

"I'll work it out with you, any way you want to do it," Homer said. "Whether you want to be with me, when I tell Angel—whether you want me with you, when you tell Wally. Any way you want it, it'll be okay," he said.

She hugged him as hard as she could but he just kept scrubbing. She buried her face between his shoulder blades and bit him in the back. He had to turn toward her then; he had to push her away.

"You're going to make Angel hate me!" Candy cried.

"Angel will never hate you," Homer said to her. "To Angel, you've always been just what you are—a good mother."

She held the serving tongs for the asparagus, and Homer thought that she might attack him, but she just kept wrenching the tongs, open and closed, in her hands.

"Wally will hate me!" she cried miserably.

"You're always telling me that Wally knows," said Homer Wells. "Wally loves you."

"And you *don't* love me, anymore, do you?" Candy said; she started to blubber; then she threw the serving tongs at Homer, then she clenched her fists against her thighs. She bit down so hard on her lower lip that it bled; when Homer tried to dab at her lip with a clean dish towel, she pushed him away.

"I love you, but we're becoming bad people," he said.

She stamped her foot. "We're *not* bad people!" she cried. "We're trying to do the right thing, we're trying not to hurt anybody!"

"We're doing the wrong thing," said Homer Wells. "It's time to do everything right."

In a panic, Candy looked out the window; Wally was gone from his position at the far corner of the deep end of the pool. "We'll talk later," she whispered to Homer. She grabbed an ice cube out of someone's drinking glass; she held the cube to her lower lip. "I'll see you by the pool."

"We can't talk about this around the pool," he told her.

"I'll meet you at the cider house," she said; she was looking everywhere for Wally, wondering what door he'd come in—any second.

"That's not a good idea, to meet there," said Homer Wells.

"Just take a walk!" she snapped at him. "You walk there your way, I'll walk there my way—I'll meet you, Goddamn it," she said. She made it into the bathroom before Homer heard Wally at the terrace door.

Candy was grateful for the special bathroom equipment—especially the sink at wheelchair level, like a sink for children in a kindergarten, like the sinks at St. Cloud's (she remembered). She knelt on the bathroom floor and hung her head in the sink; she turned her face under a faucet; the cold water was continuous against her lip.

"How are the dishes coming?" Wally asked Homer, who was still laboring over the broiler rack.

"Kind of messy tonight," Homer said.

"I'm sorry," Wally said genuinely. "Where's Candy?" he asked.

"I think she's in the bathroom."

"Oh," said Wally. He wheeled himself over to the corner of the kitchen where the serving tongs and a few broken bits of asparagus were on the floor. He leaned down and picked up the tongs, which he delivered to Homer at the sink. "Want to see the last couple of innings of the ball game?" he asked Homer. "Let Candy do the fucking dishes." Wally wheeled himself out of the kitchen; he waited in the driveway for Homer Wells to bring the car around.

They took Candy's Jeep, keeping the top down. It wasn't necessary to take the wheelchair; it was just a Little League game, and Homer could drive the Jeep right up to the foul line and they could watch the game from the car seats. The town was thrilled to have a lighted field, although it was stupid to play Little League games after dark; it kept the little kids up later than was necessary, and the field wasn't that well lit—home runs and long foul balls were always lost. The tiny infielders seemed to lose the high pop-ups. But Wally loved watching the kids play; when Angel had played, Wally had never missed a game. Angel was too old for Little League now, and he found watching the games the depths of boredom.

The game was nearly over when they arrived, which relieved Homer Wells (who hated baseball). A worried fat boy was pitching; he took the longest time between pitches, as if he were waiting for it to grow so dark (or for the lights to fail so completely) that the batter could no longer see the ball at all.

"You know what I miss?" Wally asked Homer Wells.

"What's that?" said Homer, who dreaded the answer. Maybe walking, Homer thought—or maybe he's going to say, "Loving my wife; that's what I miss."

But Wally said, "Flying. I really miss flying. I miss being up there." Wally was not watching the ball game but looking above the tall field lights at some point high in the darkness. "Above everything," he said. "That's how it was."

"I never did it," said Homer Wells.

"My God, that's true!" Wally said, genuinely shocked. "That's right, you've never flown! My God, you'd love it. We've got to arrange that, somehow. And Angel would really find it exciting," Wally added. "It's the thing I miss most."

When the game was over and they were driving home, Wally reached across to the gearshift and popped the Jeep into neutral. "Cut the engine just a second," he said to Homer. "Let's just coast." Homer turned off the key and the Jeep ambled silently along. "Cut the headlights, too," Wally said. "Just for a second." And Homer Wells cut the lights. They could see the lights from the Ocean View house ahead of them, and both of them knew the road so well that they felt fairly secure just freewheeling in the darkness, but then the trees rose up and cut their view of the lighted house, and there was an unfamiliar dip in the road. For just a moment they seemed to be completely lost, possibly plunging off the road into the dark trees, and Homer Wells turned the headlights back on.

"That was flying," Wally said, when they pulled into the driveway—ahead of them, gleaming in the headlights, the wheelchair was parked in waiting. When Homer carried Wally from the Jeep to the wheelchair, Wally let both his arms lock around Homer's neck. "Don't ever think I'm not grateful to you, for all you've done, old boy," Wally told Homer, who put him very gently in the chair.

"Come on," Homer said.

"No, I mean it. I know how much you've done for me, and I don't usually get the opportunity to say how grateful I really am," Wally said. He kissed Homer smack between the eyes, then, and Homer straightened up, clearly embarrassed.

"You've certainly done everything for me, Wally," Homer said, but Wally dismissed this with a wave; he was already wheeling himself toward the house.

"It's not the same, old boy," Wally said, and Homer went to park the Jeep.

That night when Homer put Angel to bed, Angel said, "You know, you really don't have to put me to bed anymore."

"I don't do it because I have to," Homer said. "I like to."

"You know what I think?" Angel said.

"What's that?" asked Homer, who dreaded the answer.

"I think you ought to try having a girlfriend," Angel said cautiously. Homer laughed.

"Maybe when you try having one, I'll try one, too," Homer said.

"Sure, we can double-date!" Angel said.

"I get the backseat," Homer said.

"Sure, I'd rather get to drive, anyway," Angel said.

"Not for long, you won't rather drive," his father told him.

"Sure!" Angel said, laughing. Then he asked his father: "Was Debra Pettigrew big like Melony?"

"No!" Homer said. "Well, she was on her way to being big, but she wasn't that big—not when I knew her."

"There's no way Big Dot Taft's sister could have been small," Angel said.

"Well, I never said she was small," Homer said, and they both laughed. It was a lighthearted enough moment for Homer to lean over Angel and kiss the boy—smack between the eyes, where Wally had just kissed Homer. It was a good place to kiss Angel, in Homer's opinion, because he liked to smell his son's hair.

"Good night, I love you," Homer said.

"I love you. Good night, Pop," Angel said, but when Homer was almost out the door, Angel asked him, "What's the thing you love best?"

"You," Homer told his son. "I love you best."

"Next to me," said Angel Wells.

"Candy and Wally," Homer said, making them as close to one word as his tongue could manage.

"Next to them," Angel said.

"Well, Doctor Larch—and all of them, in Saint Cloud's, I guess," said Homer Wells.

"And what's the best thing you ever did?" Angel asked his father.

"I got you," Homer said softly.

"Next best," Angel said.

"Well, I guess it was meeting Candy and Wally," Homer said.

"You mean, *when* you met them?" Angel asked.

"I guess so," said Homer Wells.

"*Next* best," Angel insisted.

"I saved a woman's life, once," Homer said. "Doctor Larch was away. The woman had convulsions."

"You told me," Angel said. Angel had never been especially interested that his father had become a highly qualified assistant to Dr. Larch; Homer had never told him about the abortions. "What else?" Angel asked his father.

Tell him now, thought Homer Wells, tell him all of it. But what he said to his son was, "Nothing else, really. I'm no hero. I haven't done any best things, or even any one best thing."

"That's okay, Pop," Angel said cheerfully. "Good night."

"Good night," said Homer Wells.

Downstairs, he couldn't tell if Wally and Candy had gone to bed, or if Wally was in bed alone; the bedroom door was closed, and there was no light coming from the crack under the door. But someone had left a light on in the kitchen, and the outdoor light on the post at the head of the driveway was still on. He went to the apple-mart office to read the mail; with the light on in the office, Candy would know where he was. And if she'd already gone to the cider house, he could walk there from the office; it would be smart, in that case, to leave the office light on and not turn it out until he came back from the cider house. That way, if Wally woke up and saw the light, he'd figure that Homer or Candy was still working in the office.

The package from St. Cloud's, arriving so exactly on the day of Melony's visit, startled Homer. He almost didn't want to open it. *The old man has probably sent me enema bags!* Homer Wells thought. He was shocked to see the black leather doctor's bag; the leather was scuffed and soft, and the brass clasp was so tarnished that its luster was as dull as the cinch buckle of an old saddle, but everything that was worn and used about the bag's appearance only made the gold initials that much brighter.

F.S.

Homer Wells opened the bag and sniffed deeply inside it; he was anticipating the hearty and manly smell of old leather, but mixed with the leather smell were the feminine traces of ether's tangy perfume. That was when—in one whiff—Homer Wells detected something of the identity that Dr. Larch had fashioned for Fuzzy Stone.

"Doctor Stone," Homer said aloud, remembering when Larch had addressed him as if he were Fuzzy.

He didn't want to walk back to the house to put the doctor's bag away, but he didn't want to leave the bag in the office, either; when he came back to the office to turn out the light, he thought he might forget the bag. And the thing about a good doctor's bag is that it's comfortable to carry. That was why he took it with him to the cider house. The bag was empty, of course—which didn't feel quite right to Homer—so he picked some Gravensteins and a couple of early Macs on his way to the cider house and put the apples in the bag. Naturally, the apples rolled back and forth; that didn't feel quite authentic. "Doctor Stone," he mumbled once, his head nodding as he took high steps through the tall grass.

Candy had been waiting for him for a while, long enough so her nerves were shot. He thought that if it had happened the other way around—if she'd been the one to break things off—he would have been as upset as she was.

It was heartbreaking for him to see that she had made up one of the beds. The clean linen and the blankets had already been put in the cider house in anticipation of the picking crew's arrival, the mattresses rolled and waiting at the opposite ends of the beds. Candy had made up the bed the farthest from the kitchen doorway. She'd brought a candle from the house, and had lit it—it gave the harsh barracks a softer light, although candles were against the rules. Recently, Homer had found it necessary to emphasize candles on the list; one of the pickers had started a small fire with one some years ago.

PLEASE DON'T SMOKE IN BED—AND
NO CANDLES, PLEASE!

was the way he'd written that rule.

The candlelight was faint; it couldn't be seen from the fancy house.

Candy had not undressed herself, but she was sitting on the bed—and she had brushed her hair out. Her hairbrush was on the apple crate that served as a night table, and this commonplace article of such familiarity and domesticity gave Homer Wells (with the black doctor's bag in his hand) a shiver of such magnitude that he envisioned himself as a helpless physician paying a house call to someone with not long to live.

"I'm sorry," he said softly to her. "We've tried it—we've

certainly tried—but it just doesn't work. Only the truth will work." His voice was croaking at his own pomposity.

Candy sat with her knees together and her hands in her lap; she was shivering. "Do you really think Angel's old enough to know all this?" she whispered, as if the flickering room were full of sleeping apple pickers.

"He's old enough to beat off, he's old enough to know what drive-ins are for—I think he's old enough," said Homer Wells.

"Don't be coarse," Candy said.

"I'm sorry," he said again.

"There's always so much to do during harvest," Candy said; she picked at her white, summery dress as if there were lint on it (but it was spotlessly clean), and Homer Wells remembered that Senior Worthington had this habit—that in Senior's case it was a symptom of his Alzheimer's disease and that Dr. Larch had even known the name for the symptom. What did the neurologists call it? Homer tried to remember.

"We'll wait and tell them after the harvest, then," Homer said. "We've waited fifteen years. I guess we can wait another six weeks."

She stretched out on her back on the thin bed, as if she were a little girl waiting to be tucked in and kissed good night in a foreign country. He went to the bed and sat uncomfortably on the edge of it, at her waist, and she put her hand on his knee. He covered her hand with his hand.

"Oh, Homer," she said, but he wouldn't turn to look at her. She took his hand and pulled it under her dress and made him touch her; she wasn't wearing anything under the dress. He didn't pull his hand away, but he wouldn't allow his hand to be more than a deadweight presence against her. "What do you imagine will happen?" she asked him coolly—after she realized that his hand was dead.

"I can't imagine anything," he said.

"Wally will throw me out," Candy said, blandly and without self-pity.

"He won't," Homer said. "And if he did, *I* wouldn't—then you'd be with me. That's why he won't."

"What will Angel do?" Candy asked.

"What he wants," Homer said. "I imagine he'll be with you when he wants, and with me when he wants." This part was hard to say—and harder to imagine.

"He'll hate me," Candy said.

"He won't," said Homer Wells.

She pushed his hand away from her and he returned the dead thing to his own lap; in another moment, her hand found his knee again, and he held her hand lightly there—at the wrist, almost as if he were taking her pulse. At his feet, the shabby doctor's bag, heavy with apples, crouched like a cat drawn in upon itself and waiting; in the flickering room, the doctor's bag looked like the only natural object—that bag would look at home wherever anyone took it; it was a bag that belonged wherever it was.

"Where will you go?" Candy asked him after a while.

"Will I have to go anywhere?" he asked her.

"I imagine so," Candy said.

Homer Wells was trying to imagine it all when he heard the car. Candy must have heard it in the same instant because she sat up and blew out the candle. They sat holding each other on the bed, listening to the car approach them.

It was an old car, or else it was not very well cared for; the valves were tapping and something like the tailpipe was loose and rattled. The car was heavy and low; they heard it scrape on the high crown of the dirt road through the orchard, and the driver had to be familiar with the way through the orchard because the headlights were off—that's how the car had gotten so close without their knowing it was coming.

Candy hurried to unmake the bed; in the darkness, she probably wasn't refolding the blankets and the linen very neatly, and Homer had to help her roll up the mattress.

"It's Wally!" Candy whispered, and indeed the car sounded like the Cadillac, which (since Raymond Kendall's death) had lost its pinpoint timing. In fact, Homer remembered, the Cadillac's muffler was loose, and it had a rebuilt engine, which already needed a valve job. And it was too heavy and low-built a car for proper use on the ragged dirt roads that wound through the orchards.

But how could Wally have managed it? wondered Homer Wells. Wally would have had to crawl to the Cadillac (Homer himself had parked it behind one of the storage barns, where the road was much too rocky and broken up for the wheelchair).

"Maybe it's some local kid," Homer whispered to Candy; the cider house was not unknown to a few locals; the orchard roads had been lovers' lanes for more than one couple.

The heavy car pulled right up to the cider house wall. Candy and Homer felt the front bumper nudge against the building.

"It's Wally!" Candy whispered; why would some local kid bother to park so close? The motor knocked for a while after the key was turned off. And then there was that ping of engine heat from the heavy car as it settled into place.

Homer let go of Candy; he tripped on the doctor's bag as he started for the door, and Candy caught hold of him, pulling him back against her.

"I'm not going to make him *crawl* in here," Homer said to her, but Candy could not make herself move out of the darkest corner of the cider house.

Homer picked up the doctor's bag and felt his way into the dark kitchen; his hand groped for the light switch, his hand brushing over his new list of rules. He had not heard the car door open, but he suddenly heard low voices; he paused, with his hand on the light switch. Oh Wally, this isn't fair! he thought; if there were voices Homer knew that Wally had brought Angel with him. That would have made it easier for Wally to get to the Cadillac—Angel could have brought the car around for him. But regardless of the torment that burdened Wally, Homer was angry at his friend for involving Angel. But wasn't Angel involved in it, anyway? Homer wondered. (Now they turned the headlights on—to light their way to the door?)

It was not the way Homer had imagined telling them both, but what did the way matter? Homer Wells turned on the light, which momentarily blinded him. He thought that he must be as lit up as a Christmas tree in the cider house door. And, he thought, wasn't it fitting that it had been the Cadillac that had rescued him from St. Cloud's, and now here was the Cadillac—in a way, come to rescue him again? For here he was, with the well-worn doctor's bag in hand, at last prepared to tell the truth—ready, at last, to take his medicine.

In the bright light, he nervously picked the imaginary lint off his clothes. He remembered what the neurologists call it: carphologia.

He tightened his grip on Dr. Larch's bag and peered into the darkness. Suddenly, it was clear to him—where he was going. He was only what he always was: an orphan who'd never been adopted. He had managed to steal some time away from the orphanage, but St. Cloud's had the only legitimate claim to him. In his forties, a man should know where he belongs.

/ / /

Dr. Larch began another letter to Harry Truman, before he remembered that Eisenhower had been President for a few years. He had written several letters to Roosevelt after Roosevelt had died, and he'd written many more to Eleanor, but the Roosevelts had never written back. Harry Truman had never written back, either, and Larch couldn't remember if he'd written to Mrs. Truman, too, or to Truman's daughter—whichever one it was hadn't answered, either.

He tried not to get depressed at the thought of writing to Eisenhower; he tried to recall how he'd begun the last one. He'd begun "Dear General," but after that he couldn't remember; he'd said something about how he'd been a doctor to the "troops" in World War I—he'd tried to sneak up on his real subject, a kind of flanking maneuver. Maybe it was time to try Mrs. Eisenhower. But when Larch wrote "Dear Mamie," he felt ridiculous.

Oh, what's the use? thought Wilbur Larch. You have to be crazy to write to Eisenhower about abortion. He tore the letter out of the typewriter; out of the blue, he decided that the President's head resembled that of a baby.

Then he remembered that Melony had the questionnaire. There was no time to fool around. He told Nurse Angela that there would be a meeting after supper, after the children had been put to bed.

Nurse Angela could not recall that there had ever been a meeting at St. Cloud's, except that most uncomfortable meeting with the board of trustees; she assumed that if there was going to be another meeting, the board was probably involved.

"Oh dear, a meeting," Nurse Edna said; she fretted all day. Mrs. Grogan was worried, too. She was concerned about where the meeting would take place—as if it would be possible to miss it or not find it.

"I think we can narrow down the possibilities," Nurse Caroline assured her.

All day Wilbur Larch worked in Nurse Angela's office. No babies were born that day; and the one woman who wanted an abortion was welcomed, and made comfortable, and told that she could have her abortion tomorrow. Wilbur Larch would not leave Nurse Angela's office, not even for lunch, not even for tea and not even for the Lord's work.

He was reviewing and putting the finishing touches to the

history of Fuzzy Stone, that good doctor; Larch was also writing the obituary of Homer Wells. Poor Homer's heart: the rigors of an agricultural life and a high-cholesterol diet—"An orphan is a meat eater, an orphan is always hungry," wrote Wilbur Larch.

Dr. Stone, on the other hand, was not a typical orphan. Larch characterized Fuzzy Stone as "lean and mean." After all, who among the orphans had ever dared to challenge Dr. Larch? And here was Fuzzy Stone threatening to turn his old mentor in! Not only did he dare to attack Dr. Larch's beliefs regarding the abortions, but also Fuzzy had such strong views on the subject that he repeatedly threatened to expose Dr. Larch to the board. And now Fuzzy's zeal was fired with the self-righteousness of a true missionary, for Larch knew that the safest place for Dr. Stone to be practicing medicine was where the board could never trace him. Fuzzy was fighting diarrhea amid the dying children of Asia. Larch had just read an article in *The Lancet* about diarrhea being the number one killer of kids in that part of the world. (Homer Wells, who did not know that his heart had given out, had read the same article.) The other little details about Burma and India—which lent such a missionary authenticity to Fuzzy's angry letters to Wilbur Larch—were things that Larch remembered hearing about Wally's excruciating travels there.

It had been an exhausting day for Larch, who had also written—in other voices—to the board of trustees. He would have preferred ether to supper, although supper, he knew, would make him more stable for the meeting that his bullied staff was dreading. Larch read such a short passage from *Jane Eyre* that every girl in the girls' division was still awake when he left them, and he read such a short section of *David Copperfield* that two of the boys complained.

"I'm sorry, that's all that happened to David Copperfield today," Dr. Larch told them. "David didn't have a very big day."

Wilbur Larch had had a big day, and Mrs. Grogan and his nurses knew it. He made them all meet in Nurse Angela's office, as if he took comfort from the litter of paper and the gloomy, surrounding presence of his massive *A Brief History of St. Cloud's,* which was gathered around him. He leaned on his overworked typewriter as if the machine were a podium.

"Now!" he said, because the women were chatting. "Now!"

he repeated, using the word like a gavel to call the meeting to order. "Now we're going to head them off at the pass."

Nurse Edna wondered if he'd been sneaking down to the train station to watch the Westerns on the TV with the station master; Nurse Edna did this quite often. She liked Roy Rogers better than Hopalong Cassidy; she wished Roy wouldn't sing; she preferred Tom Mix to them all. Although she loathed the Lone Ranger, she had a soft spot in her heart for Tonto—for all the world's sidekicks.

"*Whom* are we heading off?" Nurse Caroline asked aggressively.

"And *you*!" Dr. Larch said to Nurse Caroline, pointing his finger at her. "You're my top gun. You're the one who's going to pull the trigger. You get to fire the first shot."

Mrs. Grogan, who feared for her own sanity, feared that Dr. Larch had finally lost his. Nurse Angela suspected Larch had been slipping for a long time. Nurse Edna loved him so much that she couldn't judge him. Nurse Caroline just wanted the facts.

"Okay," Nurse Caroline said. "Let's begin at the beginning. *Whom* do I shoot?"

"You're going to turn me in," Larch told her. "You're going to blow the whistle on me—on all of us here."

"I'll do no such thing!" Nurse Caroline said.

Very patiently, he explained it to them. It was so simple—to *him* it was simple because he'd been thinking of it for years. It was not simple to the rest of them, and he had to take them very slowly through the steps toward their salvation.

They must assume that Melony would respond to the questionnaire. They must believe that her response would be negative—not because Melony was necessarily negative, as Larch pointed out to Mrs. Grogan (who was ready to defend her), but because Melony was angry. "She was born angry, she will always be angry, and even if she means us no harm, one day she will be angry enough—about something, about *anything*—so that she will respond to the questionnaire. And she'll say what she knows," Larch added, "because, whatever else Melony is, she's no liar."

Therefore, he argued, he wanted the board to hear that he was an abortionist from someone else first. It was the only way they might be saved. Nurse Caroline was the logical betrayer, she was young, she was relatively new, she had struggled with her conscience for an acceptably short period of time, and she had decided that she could remain silent no longer. Mrs. Grogan and the older nurses had been bullied into accepting a doctor's authority as absolute; Nurse Caroline would maintain that they were not to blame. Nurse Caroline, however, had a challenging attitude toward the authority figures of this (or of any) society. She would present her protest as a matter of women's rights—that even nurses should never allow doctors to tyrannize them; that when a doctor was breaking the law, even if it was not a nurse's role to challenge him, it was her right and her moral obligation to expose him. Larch was sure that Mrs. Goodhall would like that bit about "moral obligation" —Mrs. Goodhall doubtlessly labored under the illusion that her own moral obligations were the guiding lights of her life, and Dr. Larch felt that it was the overwhelming burden of these obligations that had made her a sour, joyless woman.

Nurse Edna and Nurse Angela listened to Larch as if they were baby birds awaiting a parent's return to the nest; their heads were sunk into their shoulders, their faces were tilted up, their mouths silently forming the words they heard Larch speak—in anticipation of swallowing worms.

Mrs. Grogan wished that she'd brought her knitting; if this was what a meeting was, she never wanted to attend another. But Nurse Caroline began to see; she had a basically brave and a fundamentally political conscience; and once she grasped the portrait of the board as her enemy, she was most attentive to her commander who had so arduously plotted the board's defeat. It was a kind of revolt, and Nurse Caroline was all for revolution.

"Also," Larch pointed out to her, "you need to win a few points with the right-wingers on the board; they've colored you pink. Now you color yourself Christian. They're not only going to end up forgiving you, they're also going to want to promote you. They're going to want you in charge.

"And *you*," Larch said, pointing to Nurse Angela.

"Me?" said Nurse Angela; she looked frightened, but Larch knew that she would be the perfect one to recommend Fuzzy Stone. Hadn't she named him? And hadn't she almost dared, all those times, to join Fuzzy in his righteous debate with Dr. Larch? Because Fuzzy knew them all, and loved them all; he knew what they needed, and his beliefs (regarding the abortions) were so much more in sympathy with Nurse Angela's own beliefs.

"They *are*?" Nurse Angela said. "But I believe in abortion!"

"Of course you do!" Larch said. "And if you want Saint Cloud's to continue to offer abortions, you better pretend that you're on the other side. You'd better *all* pretend."

"What do *I* pretend, Wilbur?" Nurse Edna asked.

"That it's a great load off your conscience—that I have been caught," Larch told her. Perhaps, if Fuzzy Stone came back, Nurse Edna's conscience would let her sleep. And Mrs. Grogan could lighten up on the praying; perhaps she would not be so driven to pray, if they had that wonderfully decent Dr. Stone around.

Not that we don't all *adore* Dr. Larch! Nurse Angela would tell the board. And not that the poor old man didn't believe in himself, and in what he was doing—and for whom he was doing it. He was always devoted to the orphans. It was just that this social problem got the best of him and of his judgment. And how this issue has upset us all! How it has taken its toll!

How, indeed, Nurse Edna thought, her mouth still open, her head lolling between her shoulders—she was more in love with him than ever. He really *was* devoted to his orphans; he really would do anything for them.

"But what will happen to you, Wilbur—if we expose you?" Nurse Edna asked, a slim tear making its difficult way down her wrinkled cheek.

"I'm almost a hundred years old, Edna," he said softly. "I suppose, I'll retire."

"You won't go away, will you?" Mrs. Grogan asked him.

"I wouldn't get very far, if I tried," he said.

He had been so convincing about Fuzzy Stone—he had presented them with such marvelous details—that Nurse Caroline was the only one to spot the problem.

"What if Homer Wells won't come here and pretend to be Fuzzy Stone?" she asked Dr. Larch.

"Homer belongs here," Nurse Angela said, by rote; that Homer Wells belonged to St. Cloud's was (to Nurse Angela) as obvious a fact as the weather—even if this fact (to Homer) had been his life's crucible.

"But he doesn't believe in performing abortions," Nurse Caroline reminded all the old people. "When did you last talk to him about it?" she asked Larch. "*I've* talked to him pretty recently, and he believes in *your* right to perform them—he even sent me here, to help you. And he believes it should be legal—to have one. But he also says that he could never, personally, do it—to him, it's killing someone. That's how he sees it. That's what he says."

"He has near-perfect procedure," Wilbur Larch said tiredly. When Nurse Caroline looked at all of them, she saw them as if they were dinosaurs—not just prehistoric but also almost willfully too large for the world. How could the planet ever provide enough for them? It was not a very socialist thought, but this was the conviction with which her heart sank as she looked at them.

"Homer Wells thinks it's killing someone," Nurse Caroline repeated.

As she spoke, she felt she was personally responsible for starving the dinosaurs; the old people looked gaunt and feeble to her—despite their size.

"Is the alternative just waiting and seeing?" Nurse Angela asked.

No one answered her.

" 'O Lord, support us all the day long, until the shadows lengthen and the evening comes,' " Mrs. Grogan began softly, but Dr. Larch wouldn't hear her out.

"Whatever the alternative is—if there is one—it isn't *prayer*," he said.

"It's always been an alternative for me," Mrs. Grogan said defiantly.

"Then say it to yourself," he said.

Dr. Larch moved slowly in the small room. He handed Nurse Angela the letter to the board he had written for her. He handed Nurse Caroline her letter, too.

"Just sign them," he said. "Read them over, if you want."

"You don't *know* that Melony will expose you," Mrs. Grogan said to him.

"Does it really matter?" Larch asked. "Just look at me. Do I have a lot of time?" They looked away. "I don't want to leave it up to Melony. Or to old age," he added. "Or to ether," he admitted, which caused Nurse Edna to cover her face with her hands. "I prefer to take my chances with Homer Wells."

Nurse Angela and Nurse Caroline signed the letters. Several examples of the correspondence between Wilbur Larch and Fuzzy Stone were also submitted to the board of trustees;

Nurse Angela would include these in the envelope with her letter. The board would understand that all the nurses, and Mrs. Grogan, had discussed the matter together. Wilbur Larch would not need ether to help him sleep—not that night.

Mrs. Grogan, who usually slept like a stone, would be awake all night; she was praying. Nurse Edna took a long walk through the apple orchard on the hill. Even when they all pitched in for the harvest, it was hard to keep up with the apples Homer had provided. Nurse Caroline, who (everyone agreed) was the most alert, was assigned the task of familiarizing herself with the details of the life and training of the zealous missionary Dr. Stone; if the board asked questions— and surely they would—someone had to be ready with the right answers. Despite her youth and her energy, Nurse Caroline was forced to take Fuzzy's history with her to her bed, where sleep overcame her before she got to the part about the children's diarrhea.

Nurse Angela was on duty. She gave the woman who was expecting an abortion another sedative; she gave a woman who was expecting a baby a glass of water; she tucked one of the smaller boys back into his bed—he must have had a dream; he was completely on top of his covers and his feet were on his pillow. Dr. Larch had been so tired that he had gone to bed without kissing any of the boys, so Nurse Angela decided to do this for him—and, perhaps, for herself. When she'd kissed the last boy, her back was hurting her and she sat down on one of the unoccupied beds. She listened to the boys' breathing; she tried to remember Homer Wells as a boy, to recall the particular sound of his breathing; she tried to get a picture of the postures of his style of sleep. It calmed her to think of him. Given old age, given ether, given Melony, she, too, would prefer to take her chances with Homer Wells.

"Please come home, Homer," Nurse Angela whispered. "Please come home."

It was one of the few times that Nurse Angela fell asleep when she was on duty, and the first time, ever, that she fell asleep in the boys' sleeping room. The boys were astonished to discover her with them in the morning; she woke up with the boys climbing on her, and she needed to busy herself to assure the younger ones that no great change in the order of their lives was being heralded by her being found asleep among them. She hoped she was telling the truth. A particularly small and superstitious boy did not believe her; he believed in things he referred to as "woods creatures," which he refused to describe, and he remained convinced that one of these demons had turned Nurse Angela into an orphan overnight.

"When you fall asleep, the bark grows over your eyes," he explained to her.

"Heavens, no!" she said.

"Yes," he said. "And then only the trees will adopt you."

"Nonsense," Nurse Angela told him. "The trees are just trees. And bark can't hurt you."

"Some of the trees used to be people," the little boy told her. "They used to be orphans."

"No, no, dear. No, they didn't," Nurse Angela said. She made him sit on her lap.

Although it was early in the morning, she could hear the typewriter; Dr. Larch had more to say. The little boy in her lap was trembling; he was listening to the typewriter, too.

"Do you hear that?" he whispered to Nurse Angela.

"The typewriter?" she asked him.

"The what?" he said.

"That's a typewriter," she said, but he shook his head.

"No, it's the bark," he said. "It gets in at night, and in the morning."

Although her back still hurt her, Nurse Angela carried the boy all the way to her office; she showed him the noise he'd heard—Dr. Larch at the typewriter—but she wondered if Larch, in the state he was in when he was writing, was not even more terrifying to the little boy than his imagined tree people.

"You see?" Nurse Angela asked the boy. "It's a typewriter, and that's Doctor Larch." Larch scowled at them; irritated by the interruption, he grumbled something they couldn't hear. "You know Doctor Larch, don't you?" Nurse Angela asked the little boy.

But the child had no doubt. He threw his arms around Nurse Angela's neck; then, tentatively, he let go with one hand, with which he pointed at the typewriter and at Dr. Larch. "Woods creature," he whispered.

/ / /

This time the letter was written in Larch's most didactic voice; he wrote to Homer Wells; he told Homer everything. He didn't beg. He did not characterize Fuzzy Stone as having an altogether more important job than Homer had; he did not

point out that both Homer Wells and Fuzzy Stone were impos-
ters. Larch said that he was sure Angel would accept his
father's sacrifice—"He'll value your need to be of use," was
how Wilbur Larch put it.

"Young people find risk-taking admirable. They find it he-
roic," Larch argued. "If abortions were legal, you could
refuse—in fact, given your beliefs, you *should* refuse. But as
long as they're against the law, how can you refuse? How can
you allow yourself a choice in the matter when there are so
many women who haven't the freedom to make the choice
themselves? The women have no choice. I know you know
that's not right, but how can you—you of all people, knowing
what you know—HOW CAN YOU FEEL FREE TO CHOOSE
NOT TO HELP PEOPLE WHO ARE NOT FREE TO GET
OTHER HELP? You have to help them because you know
how. Think about who's going to help them if you refuse."
Wilbur Larch was so tired that if he had allowed himself to go
to sleep, the bark would have grown over his eyes.

"Here is the trap you are in," Dr. Larch wrote to Homer.
"And it's not my trap—I haven't trapped you. Because abortions are illegal, women who need and want them have no
choice in the matter, and you—because you know how to
perform them—have no choice, either. What has been violated
here is your freedom of choice, and every woman's freedom of
choice, too. If abortion was legal, a woman would have a
choice—and so would you. You could feel free not to do it
because someone else would. But the way it is, you're trapped.
Women are trapped. Women are victims, and so are you.

"You are my work of art," Wilbur Larch told Homer Wells.
"Everything else has just been a job. I don't know if you've got
a work of art in you," Larch concluded in his letter to Homer,
"but I know what your job is, and you know what it is, too.
You're the doctor."

It went out in the same mail with the letters and the "evidence" to the board of trustees; Nurse Caroline not only
carried the letters to the railroad station, she also watched the
mail being put on the train. When the train left, she observed a
particularly lost-looking young woman who'd gotten off the
train on the wrong side of the tracks; the stationmaster, who
was watching television, was not available to give directions.
Nurse Caroline asked the woozy young woman if she was
looking for the orphanage, which she was. Unable to speak, or

else choosing not to, she simply nodded and accompanied Nurse Caroline up the hill.

Dr. Larch was just finishing with the abortion patient who'd arrived the day before and had spent the night. "I'm sorry you had to wait. I hope you were comfortable," he told her.

"Yes, everyone's been very nice," she said. "Even the children seem nice—what I saw of them." Dr. Larch was puzzled by the "even"; why *wouldn't* the children seem nice? Then he wondered if he had any idea how everything at St. Cloud's might appear to others.

He was on his way to the dispensary to rest for a while when Nurse Caroline introduced him to the next patient. The young woman still wouldn't speak, which made it hard for Larch to trust her.

"You're sure you're pregnant?" he asked her. She nodded. "Second month?" Larch guessed. The woman shook her head; she held up three fingers. "Third month," Larch said, but the woman shrugged; she held up four fingers. "Maybe four?" Larch asked. She held up five fingers. "You're five months pregnant?" Larch asked. Now she held up six fingers. "Maybe six?" Larch asked. The woman shrugged.

"Are you sure you're pregnant?" Larch began again. Yes, she nodded. "You have no idea how long you've been pregnant?" Larch asked her, while Nurse Caroline helped the woman undress; she was so undernourished, both Larch and Nurse Caroline saw instantly that she was more pregnant than they first supposed. After Larch examined the woman, who was extremely jumpy to his touch, and feverish, he said, "You might be seven months. You might be too late," Larch pointed out to her. The woman shook her head.

Larch wanted to look more closely, but Nurse Caroline was having difficulty getting the woman to assume the proper position. And while Nurse Caroline took the woman's temperature, all Larch could do was press his hand against the woman's abdomen, which was extremely tense—whenever Larch barely touched her, she would hold her breath.

"Have you tried to do something to yourself?" he asked the woman gently. "Have you hurt yourself?" The woman froze. "Why won't you talk?" Larch asked; the woman shook her head. "Are you mute?" She shook her head. "Have you been injured?" Larch asked. The woman shrugged.

Finally, Nurse Caroline made the woman comfortable in the

stirrups. "I'm going to look inside you, now," Larch explained "This is a speculum," he said, holding up the instrument. "I may feel cold, but it doesn't hurt." The woman shook he head. "No, really, I'm not going to hurt you—I'm just going to look."

"Her temperature is a hundred and four," Nurse Caroline whispered to Dr. Larch.

"This will be more comfortable for you if you can relax," Larch said; he could feel the woman's resistance to the speculum. As he bent to look, the young woman spoke to him.

"It wasn't me," she said. "I would never have put all that inside of me."

"All that?" Larch said. "All what?" Suddenly, he didn't want to look before he knew.

"It wasn't me," she repeated. "I would never do such a thing."

Dr. Larch bent so close to the speculum, he had to hold his breath. The smell of sepsis and putrefaction was strong enough to gag him if he breathed or swallowed, and the familiar, fiery colors of her infection (even clouded by her discharge) were dazzling enough to blind the intrepid or the untrained. But Wilbur Larch started to breathe again, slowly and regularly; it was the only way to keep a steady hand. He just kept looking and marveling at the young woman's inflamed tissue; it looked hot enough to burn the world. Now do you see, Homer? Larch asked himself. Through the speculum, he felt her heat against his eye.

11/ Breaking the Rules

Melony, who had hitchhiked from Bath to Ocean View, hitchhiked back on the same day; she'd lost her zeal for apple picking. She retreated, to plan another vacation—or to plead to return to work. Melony went to the pizza bar where everyone went, and she was looking so woebegone that Lorna left the lout she was with at the bar and sat down in the booth opposite her.

"I guess you found him," Lorna said.

"He's changed," Melony said; she told Lorna the story. "It wasn't for *me* that I felt so bad," Melony said. "I mean, I didn't really expect him to run away with me, or anythin' like that. It was just him—he was really better than that, I thought. He was someone I thought was gonna be a hero. I guess that's dumb, but that's what he looked like—like he had hero stuff in him. He seemed so much better than everybody else, but he was just a fake."

"You don't know everythin' that's happened to him," Lorna said philosophically; she didn't know Homer Wells, but she had sympathy for sexual entanglements.

Her present sexual entanglement grew impatient at the bar, where he'd been waiting for her; he was a bum named Bob, and he came over to Melony's booth where the two women were holding hands.

"I guess what's the matter with Homer is that he's a man," Melony observed. "I only ever met one who didn't let his dong run his life"—she meant Dr. Larch—"and he was an ether addict."

"Are you with me, or have you gone back to her?" Bob asked Lorna, but he stared at Melony.

"We was just talkin', she was just bein' an old friend," Melony said.

"I thought you was on vacation," Bob said to Melony. "Why don'tcha go somewhere where there's cannibals?"

"Go beat off in a bucket," Melony told him. "Go try to fill a pail, go drip in a teaspoon," she told him, and Bob twisted her arm too sharply—he broke it. Then Bob broke her nose against the Formica tabletop before some of the shipyard workers pulled him off her.

Lorna took her friend to the hospital, and when they'd put the cast on her arm and had set her nose—they set it almost straight—Lorna took Melony back to the women-only boardinghouse, where they both agreed they belonged: together. Lorna moved her things back in while Melony was convalescing. The swelling in her face went down after a few days, and her eyes turned from black to a purplish-green to yellow in about a week.

"The thing is," Melony said, with her sore face against Lorna's tummy, with Lorna's hand stroking her hair, "when he was a boy, he had that kind of bravery that's really special—no one could make him just go along with what was goin' on. And now look at him: bangin' a cripple's wife, lyin' to his own son."

"It's disgusting," Lorna agreed. "Why not forget it?" When Melony didn't answer her, Lorna asked, "How come you're not gonna press charges against Bob?"

"Suppose it works?" Melony asked.

"Pardon me?" Lorna said.

"Suppose they really put Bob in jail, or send him off somewheres?" Melony asked. "Then when I'm all better, I won't be able to find him."

"Oh," Lorna said.

/ / /

Homer Wells did not recognize the voice that spoke to him from the headlights' glare.

"What you got in the bag, Homer?" asked Mr. Rose. It had been a long drive from the Carolinas, and Mr. Rose's old car creaked and popped with heat and with apparent pain. "It's nice of you workin' all night to make my house nice for me, Homer," he said. When he stepped in front of his headlights, his black face was still hard to see, but Homer recognized the way he moved—so slowly, but with a felt potential for moving so fast.

"Mister Rose!" Homer said.

"Mistuh Wells," said Mr. Rose, smiling. They shook hands, while Homer's heart calmed down. Candy was still hiding in the cider house, and Mr. Rose sensed that Homer wasn't alone. He was peering through the lit kitchen, looking into the shadowy bunkroom, when Candy walked, guiltily, into the light.

"Missus Worthington!" said Mr. Rose.

"Mister Rose," Candy said, smiling, shaking his hand. "We're just in time," she said to Homer, poking him. "We just this minute got all the bed linen ready," she told Mr. Rose, but Mr. Rose observed that there was no car or truck—that they had walked to the cider house. Had they carried all the blankets and sheets?

"Just this minute, we got it all folded up, I mean," Candy said.

Homer Wells thought that Mr. Rose might have seen the light in the apple-mart office when he drove by. "We were working late in the office," Homer said, "and we remembered the linen was down here—all in a heap."

Mr. Rose nodded and smiled. Then the baby cried. Candy jumped.

"I wrote to Wally 'bout bringin' the daughter," Mr. Rose explained, as a young woman, about Angel's age, walked into the light with a baby in her arms.

"I haven't seen you since you were a little girl," Homer Wells told the young woman, who looked at him blankly; it must have been an exhausting trip with a small child.

"My daughter," Mr. Rose said in introduction. "And *her* daughter," he added. "Missus Worthington," said Mr. Rose, introducing her, "and Homer Wells."

"Candy," Candy said, shaking the young woman's hand.

"Homer," Homer said. He couldn't remember the daughter's name, and so he asked her. She looked a little startled, and looked at her father—as if for clarification, or advice.

"Rose," Mr. Rose said.

Everyone laughed—the daughter, too. The baby stopped crying and looked with wonder at the laughter. "No, I mean your first name!" said Homer Wells.

"Rose is her first name," said Mr. Rose. "You already heard it."

"Rose Rose?" Candy asked. The daughter smiled; she didn't look very sure.

"Rose Rose," said Mr. Rose proudly.

Everyone laughed again; the baby was cheering up, and Candy played with the little girl's fingers. "And what's *her* name?" Candy asked Rose Rose. This time, the young woman answered for herself.

"She don't have a name, yet," Rose Rose replied.

"We're still thinking it out," said Mr. Rose.

"What a good idea," said Homer Wells, who knew that too many names were given frivolously, or just temporarily—or, in the cases of John Wilbur and Wilbur Walsh, that they were repeated without imagination.

"The cider house isn't really set up for a baby," Candy said to Rose Rose. "If you'd like to come up to the house, I may have some baby things you could use—there's even a playpen in the attic, isn't there, Homer?"

"We don't need nothin'," Mr. Rose said pleasantly. "Maybe she'll look another day."

"I could sleep a whole day, I think," said Rose Rose prettily.

"If you'd like," Candy told her, "I could look after the baby for you—so you could sleep."

"We don't need nothin'," Mr. Rose repeated. "Not today, anyway," he said, smiling.

"Want a hand unpacking?" Homer asked him.

"Not today, anyway," Mr. Rose said. "What's in the bag, Homer?" he asked when they'd all said good night and Homer and Candy were leaving.

"Apples," Homer admitted.

"That would be strange," said Mr. Rose. Homer unzipped the bag and showed him the apples.

"You the apple doctor?" Mr. Rose asked him.

Homer almost said "Right."

"He knows," Homer said to Candy, as they were walking back to the office.

"Of course he knows," Candy said. "But what's it matter if we're stopping?"

"I guess it doesn't matter," Homer said.

"Since you were prepared to tell Wally and Angel," she said, "I guess it won't be that hard to really do it."

"After the harvest," he said; he took her hand, but when they came near the apple mart and the office light, they dropped hands and walked their separate ways.

"What's the bag for?" Candy asked him, before she kissed him good night.

"It's for me," said Homer Wells. "I think it's for me."

He fell asleep, marveling at what seemed to him to be the extreme control Mr. Rose had of his world—he even controlled the speed at which his daughter's daughter would be named (not to mention, probably, the name itself)! Homer woke up near dawn and took a fountain pen from his night table and used it to write, with a heavy finality, over the penciled number on the back of the photograph of the crew of *Opportunity Knocks*. With the dark ink he followed the outline of the pencil; this permanency was reassuring—as if ink, as on a contract, was more binding than pencil. He couldn't have known that Candy was also awake; her stomach was upset, and she was looking for some medicine in her and Wally's bathroom. She also found it necessary to address the subject of the two hundred seventy times she and Homer had made love together since Wally had come home from the war, but Candy honored the finality of this number with less significance than Homer honored it. Instead of writing over the number in ink, Candy used her eraser to remove the evidence from the back of the photograph of her teaching Homer how to swim. Then her stomach calmed and she was able to sleep. It astonished her: how completely relaxed she was at the prospect that after the harvest, her life (as she'd grown used to it) would be over.

Homer Wells didn't try to go back to sleep; he knew his history on the subject of sleep; he knew there was no fighting history. He read an article in *The New England Journal of Medicine* about antibiotic therapy; he'd followed, for many years, the uses of penicillin and streptomycin. He was less familiar with Aureomycin and Terramycin, but he thought that antibiotics were easy to figure out. He read about the limited usage of neomycin; he made note of the fact that Achromycin and tetracycline were the same. He wrote erythromycin in the margin of the article, several times, until he was sure he knew how to spell it; Dr. Larch had taught him that method of familiarizing himself with something new.

"E-R-Y-T-H-R-O-M-Y-C-I-N," wrote Homer Wells—the apple doctor, as Mr. Rose had called him. He wrote that in the margin, too. "The apple doctor." And just before he got out of bed, he wrote, "A Bedouin Again."

In the morning, Candy sent Angel to the cider house to

inquire if Rose Rose needed anything for the baby, and that was when Angel fell in love. He was shy with girls his own age; boys his own age, and a little older, always teased him about his name. He thought he was the only Angel in Maine. He was even shy in advance of meeting girls, anticipating when he would have to tell them his name. In Heart's Rock and Heart's Haven, the prettier, more confident girls in his class ignored him; they were interested in the older boys. The girls who appeared to like him were plain, sullen gossips who most enjoyed talking to other girls like themselves, about themselves—or about which boys had said what to whom. Every time Angel spoke to a girl, he knew his remarks were relayed that evening over the telephone to every other neglected girl in his class. The following morning, they would all smirk at him—as if he'd said the same, foolish thing to each of them. And so he learned to keep quiet. He watched the older girls in school; he approved of the ones who did the least amount of talking to their girlfriends. They struck him as more mature, by which he meant that they were actually doing things they would not want their girlfriends to know.

In 195__, girls Angel's age looked forward to dating; boys Angel's age—as in other times—looked forward to doing things.

Mr. Rose's daughter was not only the most exotic young woman Angel had ever seen; if she had a daughter, she must also have done things.

It was cold and damp in the cider house in the mornings; when Angel arrived there, Rose Rose was outside, in the sun, washing Baby Rose in a bucket. The baby was splashing, and Rose Rose was talking to her daughter; she didn't hear Angel walking up to her. Perhaps—since Angel had been brought up more by his father than by his mother—Angel was predisposed to be attracted to a Madonna scene. Rose Rose was only a few years older than Angel—she was so young that her maternity was startling. When she was with her baby, her gestures and her expressions were womanly, and she had a full, womanly figure. She was a little taller than Angel. She had a round, boyish face.

"Good morning," Angel said, startling Baby Rose in the bucket. Rose Rose wrapped her daughter in a towel and stood up.

"You must be Angel," she said shyly. She had a fine scar that sliced across the flange of one nostril and her upper lip; it made a nick in her gum, which Angel could see when she parted her lips. Later, he would see that the knife had stopped at the eyetooth and removed it, which accounted for her only partial smile. She would explain to him that the wound had killed the root of the tooth and that the tooth had fallen out later. He was so smitten when he first met her that even the scar was beautiful to him; it was her only apparent flaw.

"I wondered if I could help you get anything for the baby," Angel said.

"She seem to be teethin'," Rose Rose reported on her daughter. "She kind of cranky today."

Mr. Rose came out of the cider house; when he saw Angel, he waved and smiled, and then he walked over and put his arm around the boy. "How you doin'?" he asked. "You still growin', I think. I used to carry him on top of my head," he told Rose Rose. "He used to grab them apples I couldn't reach," Mr. Rose explained, punching Angel affectionately on the arm.

"I'm counting on growing a little more," Angel said—for Rose Rose's benefit. He wouldn't want her to think he had stopped growing; he wanted her to know that he would be taller than she, one day.

He wished he'd worn a shirt; it was not that he wasn't muscular, it was somehow more grown-up to wear a shirt. Then he imagined that she might approve of his summer tan, and so he relaxed about not having a shirt; he put his hands in the hip pockets of his jeans, and he wished he'd worn his baseball cap. It was a Boston Red Sox cap, and he had to get hold of it first thing in the morning if he was going to wear it—otherwise, Candy would wear it. They had been meaning to buy another baseball cap for two summers now; Candy owed him one because she'd admitted to tearing one of the sweat holes in the cap by poking a pencil through it.

Candy worked as a checker during the harvest, and she needed her pencil. This would be the second harvest that Angel would be a checker, and the second summer that he got to drive one of the tractors that hauled the apples out of the orchards.

When Angel told his father that Rose Rose's baby was teething, Homer knew what to do. He sent Angel (with Wally) to town to buy some pacifiers, and then he sent Angel back to the cider house with a package of pacifiers and a fifth of bourbon; Wally drank a very little bourbon from time to time, and the bottle was three-quarters full. Homer showed Angel how to dab whiskey on Baby Rose's gums.

"It numbs the gums," Angel explained to Rose Rose. He dipped his pinky finger in the whiskey, then he stuck his finger in Baby Rose's tiny mouth. At first, he was afraid he'd gag the baby girl, whose eyes instantly grew large and watery at the bourbon fumes; but then Baby Rose went to work on Angel's finger so ferociously that when he removed his finger to apply more bourbon, the baby cried to have the finger back.

"You gonna make her drunk," Rose Rose warned.

"No, I won't," Angel assured her. "I'm just putting her gums to sleep."

Rose Rose examined the pacifiers. They were rubber nipples, like the nipple on a baby's bottle, but without the hole and attached to a baby-blue plastic ring that was too big to swallow. The problem with using a regular bottle nipple, Angel Wells explained, was that the baby would keep sucking in air through the hole, and the air would give the baby burping fits or a gassy stomach.

"How come you know so much?" Rose Rose asked Angel, smiling. "How old are you?"

"I'm almost sixteen," Angel said. "How old are you?"

" 'Bout your age," she told him.

In the afternoon, when Angel came back to the cider house to see how the teething was going, Baby Rose was not the only Rose with a pacifier stuck in her mouth. Mr. Rose was sitting on the cider house roof, and Angel could see—from a considerable distance, because of the unreal, baby-blue hue of the plastic ring—that he had a pacifier in his mouth.

"Are you teething, too?" Angel called up to him. Mr. Rose removed the pacifier from his mouth slowly—the way he did everything.

"I'm cuttin' out smokin'," said Mr. Rose. "You got a nipple in your mouth all day, who needs a cigarette?" He stuck the pacifier back in his mouth and grinned at Angel broadly.

In the cider house, Baby Rose had fallen asleep with a pacifier in her mouth and Angel surprised Rose Rose as she was washing her hair. She was bent over the kitchen sink with her back to him; he couldn't see her breasts, although she was bare from the waist up.

"Is that you?" she asked ambiguously, keeping her back turned to him—but not jumping to cover herself.

"Sorry," Angel said, stepping back outside. "I should have knocked." Then she jumped and covered herself, her hair still soapy; she must have thought it was her father.

"I was checking on how the teething was going," Angel explained.

"It goin' fine," Rose Rose said. "You a good doctor. You my hero, for today." She was smiling her partial smile.

A stream of bright suds from the shampoo ran around her neck and down her chest, over her arms, which she'd folded, with a towel, across her unseen breasts. Angel Wells, smiling, backed so far away from the cider house door that he bumped into the old car, which was parked close enough against the cider house to appear to be helping hold the building up. He heard a tiny pebble come rolling down the cider house roof, but when it hit him on the head—even though he'd had time to steal the baseball cap away from Candy and now wore it at a casual angle, with the visor shading his forehead—the pebble hurt. He looked up at Mr. Rose, who had rolled the pebble in his direction—a perfect shot.

"Gotcha!" Mr. Rose said, smiling.

But it was Rose Rose who'd really gotten him; Angel staggered back to the apple mart and into the fancy house as if he'd been struck by a boulder.

Who was the baby's father? Angel Wells wondered. And where was he? And where was Mrs. Rose? Were Mr. Rose and his daughter all alone?

Angel went to his room and began to compose a list of names—girls' names. He took some names he liked out of the dictionary, and then he added other names that the dictionary had overlooked. How else do you impress a girl who hasn't been able to think of a name for her baby?

Angel would have been a blessing to St. Cloud's, where the practice of naming the babies was a little worn out. Although Nurse Caroline had contributed her youthful energy to the nearly constant occasion, her rather political choices had been met with some resistance. She was fond of Karl (for Marx), and Eugene (for Debs), but everyone balked at Friedrich (for Engels), and so she had been reduced to Fred (which she didn't like). Nurse Angela also complained about Norman (for Thomas)—to her it was a name like Wilbur. But it was difficult to know if Angel Wells could have kept his passion for names intact when the task was almost a daily business. Finding a name for Rose Rose's daughter was a devotion quite unexpected—yet it was typical of a boy's first love.

Abby? thought Angel Wells. Alberta? Alexandra? Amanda? Amelia? Antoinette? Audrey? Aurora? "Aurora Rose," Angel said aloud. "God, no," he said, plunging into the alphabet. The scar on the face of the young woman he loved was so extremely thin, so very fine—Angel imagined that if he could kiss that scar, he could make it disappear; and he began working his way through the B's.

Bathsheba? Beatrice? Bernice? Bianca? Blanche? Bridget?

/ / /

Dr. Larch was facing a different problem. The dead patient had come to St. Cloud's without a scrap of identification—she'd brought only her burning infection, her overpowering discharge, her dead but unexpelled fetus (and several of the instruments she—or someone else—had put into herself in order to expel the fetus), her punctured uterus, her unstoppable fever, her acute peritonitis. She reached Dr. Larch too late for him to save her, yet Larch blamed himself.

"She was alive when she got here," Larch told Nurse Caroline. "I'm supposed to be a doctor."

"Then *be* one," Nurse Caroline said, "and stop being maudlin."

"I'm too old," Larch said. "Someone younger, someone quicker, might have saved her."

"If that's what you think, maybe you *are* too old," Nurse Caroline told him. "You're not seeing things as they are."

"As they are," said Wilbur Larch, who closed himself off in the dispensary. He'd never been good about losing patients, but this one, Nurse Caroline knew, was quite lost when she'd arrived.

"If he can hold himself responsible for a case like that," Nurse Caroline told Nurse Angela, "then I think he ought to be replaced—he *is* too old."

Nurse Angela agreed. "It's not that he's incompetent, but once he starts thinking he's incompetent, he's had it."

Nurse Edna would not contribute to this conversation. She went and stood outside the dispensary door, where she repeated, and repeated, "You're *not* too old, you're *not* incompetent, you're *not* too old," but Wilbur Larch could not hear her; he was under ether, and he was traveling. He was far away, in Burma—which he saw almost as clearly as Wally ever saw it, although Larch (even with ether's assistance) could never have imagined such heat. The shade that he saw under the peepul trees was deceiving; it was not really cool there—not at that time of the day that the Burmese refer to as "when feet are silent." Larch was observing the missionary Dr. Stone making his rounds. Even the noonday heat would not keep Fuzzy Stone from saving the diarrhetic children.

Wally could have informed Larch's dream with some better detail. How slippery the bamboo leaves were when one was trying to walk uphill—for example. How the sleeping mats were always damp with sweat; how it seemed (to Wally) to be a country of submagistrates, corrupted by the British—either into being like the British, or into being consumed by their hatred of the British. Wally had once been carried across a plateau shot through with sprouting weeds and befouled with pigshit; on it was a former tennis court, built by someone British. The net was now a magistrate's hammock. The court itself, because of the high fence that enclosed it, was a good place to keep the pigs; the fence, which had once kept tennis balls from being lost in the jungle, now made it more difficult for the leopards to kill the pigs. At that way station, Wally would remember, the magistrate himself had instrumented his urinary tract for him; a kindly, round-faced man with patient, steady hands, he had used a long, silver swizzle stick—something else the British had left behind. Although the magistrate's English was poor, Wally had made him understand what the swizzle stick was for.

"British ees crazy," the Burmese gentleman had said to Wally. "Yes?"

"Yes, I think so," Wally had agreed. He hadn't known many British, but some of them seemed crazy to him, and so it seemed a small thing to agree to—and Wally thought it was wise to agree with whoever it was who held the catheter.

The silver swizzle stick was too inflexible for a proper catheter, and the top of the thing was adorned with a kind of heraldic shield, Queen Victoria's stern face presiding (in this one case, she was observing a use of the instrument she adorned that might have shocked her).

"Only British ees crazy enough to make something to stir a drink," the magistrate said, chuckling. He lubricated the catheter with his own saliva.

Through his tears, Wally tried to laugh.

And in the rounds that Dr. Stone was making, wouldn't many of the diarrhetic children suffer urinary retention, wouldn't Dr. Stone have to relieve their little, distended bladders, and wouldn't his catheter be proper and his method of instrumentation sound? In Wilbur Larch's eyes, which were over Burma, Dr. Stone would be perfect—Fuzzy Stone wouldn't lose a single patient.

Nurse Caroline, understanding that the coincidence of the woman dying without a name would not sit well alongside the recent "evidence" submitted to the board of trustees, knew it was time for her to write to Homer Wells. While Dr. Larch rested in the dispensary, Nurse Caroline worked with a vengeance over the typewriter in Nurse Angela's office.

"Don't be a hypocrite," she began. "I hope you recall how vehemently you were always telling me to leave Cape Kenneth, that my services were more needed here—and you were right. And do you think your services aren't needed here, or that they aren't needed right now? Do you think the apples can't grow without you? Just who do you think the board's going to replace him with if you don't step forward? One of the usual cowards who does what he's told, one of your typically careful, mousy, medical men—a little law-abiding citizen who will be of absolutely NO USE!"

She mailed that letter at the same time she alerted the stationmaster that there was a body at the orphanage; various authorities would have to be sent for. It had been a long time since the stationmaster had seen bodies at the orphanage, but he would never forget the bodies he had seen—not his predecessor, after the sternum shears had opened him up, and certainly never the fetal autopsy from Three Mile Falls.

"A body?" the stationmaster asked. He gripped the sides of the small table where the constant television revealed to him its blurry, fade-in and fade-out images—any one of which the stationmaster found preferable to the more vivid picture of those long-ago bodies.

"Someone who didn't want to have a baby," Nurse Caroline told him. "She butchered herself, trying to get the baby out. She got to us too late for us to be able to do anything about it."

Unanswering, and never taking his eyes from the snowy, zigzagging figures on the TV screen, the stationmaster clung to the table as if it were an altar and the television was his god—at least, he knew, he would never see on that television anything resembling what Nurse Caroline described, and so the stationmaster continued to watch the TV instead of looking into Nurse Caroline's eyes.

/ / /

Carmen? Cecelia? Charity? Claudia? Constance? Cookie? Cordelia? Angel Wells cocked the Red Sox cap at the correct angle; although it was cool in the early morning, he elected not to wear a shirt. Dagmar? he thought. Daisy? Dolores? Dotty?

"Where are you going in my hat?" Candy asked him; she was picking up the breakfast dishes.

"It's *my* hat," Angel said, going out the door.

"Love is blind," Wally said, pushing his wheelchair away from the table.

Does he mean me or Angel? Candy wondered. Homer and Wally were worried about Angel's puppylike infatuation with Rose Rose, but that is all it seemed to Candy: puppylike. Candy knew that Rose Rose had too much experience to allow Angel to get carried away. That wasn't the point, Homer had said. Candy imagined that Rose Rose had more experience in her little finger than . . . but that wasn't the point, either, Wally had said.

"Well, I hope the point isn't that she's *colored*," Candy had said.

"The point is Mister Rose," Wally had said. The word "Right!" had been almost visible on Homer's lips. Men want to control everything, Candy thought.

Homer Wells was in the apple-mart office. In the mail there was a letter for him from Dr. Larch, but Homer didn't look through the mail. That was Wally's job; besides, the picking crew had arrived. The harvest would be starting as soon as Homer could get it organized. He looked out the office window and saw his son not wearing any shirt and talking to Big Dot Taft. He opened the screen door and hollered at Angel. "Hey, it's cold this morning—put on a shirt!" Angel was already walking toward the barns beyond the apple mart.

"I got to warm up the tractor!" he told his father.

"Warm yourself up first!" Homer told him, but the boy was already very warm this morning.

Edith? Angel asked himself. Ernestine? Esmeralda? Eve! he thought.

He bumped into Vernon Lynch, who was glowering over a cup of hot coffee.

"Watch where yer goin'," Vernon told Angel.

"Faith!" Angel said to him. "Felicia! Francesca! Frederica!"

"Asshole," said Vernon Lynch.

"No, that's you," Big Dot Taft told him. "You're the asshole, Vernon."

"God, I love the harvest!" Wally said, cruising around the kitchen table, while Candy washed the dishes. "It's my favorite time."

"Mine, too," Candy said, smiling. What she thought was: I have six more weeks to live.

Black Pan, the cook, was back; Candy had to hurry—she had to take Black Pan shopping. A man named Peaches had picked for them before, but not for several years; he was called Peaches because his beard never grew. Also, a man named Muddy was back; no one had seen Muddy for years. He'd been badly knifed at the cider house one night, and Homer had driven him to the hospital in Cape Kenneth. Muddy had taken one hundred twenty-three stitches; Homer Wells thought he'd looked like a kind of experimental sausage.

The man who'd cut him was long gone. That was one of Mr. Rose's rules; Homer guessed it might have been the dominant rule of the cider house. No hurting each other. You cut people to scare them, to show them who's boss, but you don't send people to the hospital. Then the law comes, and everyone at the cider house feels small. The man who'd cut Muddy hadn't been thinking about the community.

"He was really tryin' to cut my ass off, man," Muddy had said, as if he were surprised.

"He was an amateur," Mr. Rose had said. "He long gone now, anyway."

The rest of the crew, except for Mr. Rose's daughter, hadn't been to Ocean View before. Mr. Rose arranged, with Angel, how Rose Rose and her daughter would spend the day.

"She gonna ride around with you and help you out," Mr. Rose told Angel. "She can sit on the fender, or stand behind the seat. She can ride on the trailer, before it full."

"Sure!" Angel said.

"If she need to take the baby back to the cider house, she can walk," Mr. Rose said. "She don't need no special favors."

"No," Angel said; it surprised him that Mr. Rose would speak this way about his daughter when she was standing beside him, looking a little embarrassed. Baby Rose—pacifier in place—rode her hip.

"Sometimes Black Pan can look after the baby," Mr. Rose said, and Rose Rose nodded.

"Candy said she'd look after her, too," Angel offered.

"No need botherin' Missus Worthington," said Mr. Rose, and Rose Rose shook her head.

When Angel drove the tractor, he always stood up; if he sat down without a cushion on the seat (and he thought a cushion was for an old man with piles), he couldn't quite see the radiator cap. He was afraid that, if he sat down, the engine might overheat and the radiator would boil over without his noticing it. But most of all, it looked better to drive a tractor standing up.

He was glad he was driving the International Harvester; years ago, Raymond Kendall had built a swivel for the seat. He could let Rose Rose sit down—with or without Baby Rose in her lap—and he could stand a little to one side of the swivel seat and operate the tractor without awkwardness. There was a foot clutch, a foot brake and a hand throttle. The emergency hand brake was next to Rose Rose's hip; the gearshift was by her knee.

"Why you wear that old baseball cap?" she asked him. "You got nice eyes, but nobody see 'em. You got nice hair, but nobody see it. And you got one pale forehead 'cause the sun can't find your face. If you didn't wear that dumb cap, your face would be as brown as your body."

This implied to Angel, of course, that Rose Rose liked his body being brown, didn't care for his forehead being pale and had managed—despite the hat—to notice his eyes and hair (and to like them, too).

After filling the trailer with his first load of apples, Angel took a long drink from a water jug in the orchard, twisting the baseball cap backward on his head as he drank. Then he wore it that way, the way a catcher wears a baseball cap—or the way Candy wore it, with the visor tipped over her hair and the back of her neck. Somehow it looked better that way on Candy. When Rose Rose saw Angel wearing the cap that way, she said, "Now you look real stupid, like you got a ball for a head."

The next day, Angel let Candy wear the cap.

Baby Rose was sucking the pacifier, like a three-horsepower pump, and Rose Rose smiled at Angel. "Where's that nice hat?" she asked him.

"I lost it," he lied.

"Too bad," she said. "It was nice."

"I thought you didn't like that hat," he said.

"I didn't like that hat on *you,*" said Rose Rose.

The next day he brought the hat and put it on her head as soon as she was settled into the tractor seat. Rose Rose looked awfully pleased; she wore the hat the same way Angel had worn it—low, over her eyes. Baby Rose looked cross-eyed at the visor.

"You lost it and then you found it, huh?" Rose Rose asked Angel.

"Right," Angel said.

"You better be careful," she told him. "You don't wanna get involved with me."

But Angel was flattered and encouraged that she'd even noticed his interest—especially since he was unsure how to express his interest.

"How old *are* you?" he asked her casually, later that day.

" 'Bout your age, Angel," was all she said. Baby Rose slumped against her breast; a floppy-brimmed white sailor's hat protected the baby from the sun, but under the brim of the hat, the little girl looked glassy-eyed and exhausted from chomping on the pacifier all day. "I don't believe you can still be teethin'," Rose Rose said to her daughter. She took hold of the baby-blue plastic ring and pulled the pacifier out of the little girl's mouth; it made a *pop* like a wine cork, which startled Baby Rose. "You becomin' an addict," Rose Rose said, but when Baby Rose started to cry, her mother put the nipple back.

"How do you like the name Gabriella?" Angel asked Rose Rose.

"I never heard it before," she said.

"How about Ginger?" Angel asked.

"That somethin' you eat," Rose Rose said.

"Gloria?" Angel asked.

"That nice," said Rose Rose. "Who it for?"

"Your baby!" Angel said. "I've been thinking of names for your baby." Rose Rose raised the visor of the Boston Red Sox cap and looked into Angel's eyes.

"Why you thinkin' of that?" she asked him.

"Just to be of help," he said awkwardly. "Just to help you decide."

"Decide?" Rose Rose asked.

"To help you make up your mind," said Angel Wells.

The picker named Peaches was almost as fast as Mr. Rose. He was emptying his canvas bag into a bushel crate, and he interrupted Rose Rose and Angel.

"You countin' me, Angel?" Peaches asked.

"I got you," Angel said. Sometimes Angel examined the fruit if he didn't know the picker very well—to make sure they weren't bruising it; if they were bruising it, or if there were other signs that they were picking too fast, Angel wouldn't give them the top price for a bushel. But Angel knew Peaches was a good picker, so he just put a number on the list without getting off the tractor to look at the apples.

"Ain't you a checker?" Peaches asked Angel, then.

"Sure, I got you!" Angel said to him.

"Don't you wanna check me, then? Better make sure I ain't pickin' pears, or somethin'," Peaches said, grinning. Angel went to look over the apples, and that was when Peaches said to him: "You don't wanna go into the knife business with Mistuh Rose." Then he walked away, with his bag and his ladder, before Angel could say anything about his apples—which were, of course, perfect.

Back on the tractor, Angel got up his nerve. "Are you still married to the baby's father?" he asked Rose Rose.

"Wasn't ever married," she said.

"Are you still together, you and the father?" Angel asked.

"Baby got no father," Rose Rose said. "I wasn't ever *together*."

"I like Hazel and Heather," Angel said, after a while. "They're both names of plants, so they sort of go with Rose."

"I don't have no plant, I got a little girl," Rose Rose said, smiling.

"I also like the name Hope," Angel said.

"Hope ain't no name," Rose Rose said.

"Iris is nice," Angel said. "But it's sort of cute, because it's another flower. Then there's Isadora."

"Whew!" said Rose Rose. "No name is better than some."

"Well, how about plain old Jane?" asked Angel Wells, who was getting frustrated. "Jennifer? Jessica? Jewel? Jill? Joyce? Julia? Justine?"

She touched him. She just put her hand on his hip, which nearly caused him to jackknife the trailer and spill the load. "Don't never stop," she told him. "I never knew there was so many names. Go on," she said, her hand urging him—it was just a little shove, before she returned her hand to her lap, where Baby Rose sat mesmerized by the tractor's motion and the tractor's sound.

"Katherine? Kathleen? Kirsten? Kitty?" Angel Wells began.

"Go on," Rose Rose said, her hand grazing his hip again.

"Laura? Laurie? Laverne? Lavinia? Leah? That means 'weary,' " he told her. "Leslie? Libby? Loretta? Lucy? Mabel? That means 'lovable,' " he told her. "Malvina? That means 'smooth snow,' " he explained.

"I never livin' where they got snow," Rose Rose said.

"Maria?" Angel said. "Marigold? That's another flower. Mavis? That means a 'thrush,' it's a kind of bird," he said.

"Don't tell me what they mean," Rose Rose instructed him.

"Melissa? Mercedes?" Angel said.

"Ain't that a car?" Rose Rose asked him.

"It's a good car," Angel said. "A German car. Very expensive."

"I seen one, I think," Rose Rose said. "They got a funny bull's-eye on the hood."

"Their insignia," said Angel Wells.

"Their what?" she asked.

"It's a kind of bull's-eye, you're right," Angel said.

"Say it again," Rose Rose said.

"Mercedes," he said.

"It for rich people, ain't it?" Rose Rose asked.

"The car?" he asked.

"The name or the car," she said.

"Well," Angel said, "it's an expensive car, but the name means 'Our Lady of Mercies.' "

"Well, fuck it, then," Rose Rose said. "Didn't I tell you not to tell me what the names mean?"

"Sorry," he said.

"How come you never wear a shirt?" she asked him. "Ain't you never cold?"

Angel shrugged.

"You can go on with them names, any time," she told him.

After the first four or five days of the harvest, the wind shifted; there was a strong sea breeze off the Atlantic, and the early mornings were especially cold. Angel wore a T-shirt and a sweat shirt over that. One morning, when it was so cold that Rose Rose had left Baby Rose with Candy, Angel saw that she was shivering and he gave her his sweat shirt. She wore it all day. She was still wearing it when Angel went to help with the cider press that night, and for a while they sat on the cider house roof together. Black Pan sat up there with them, and he told them about the time when there'd been an Army installation on the coast, which they could see at night.

"It was a secret weapon," he told them. "And your father," Black Pan told Angel, "he made up a name for it—he had us all shittin' our pants, we was so scared. It was a kind of wheel, he told us—it sent people to the moon, or somethin'."

"It was a Ferris wheel," said Mr. Rose in the darkness. "It was just a Ferris wheel."

"Yeah, that what it was!" Black Pan said. "I seen one, once."

"But it was somethin' else that used to be out there," Mr. Rose said dreamily. "It got used in the war."

"Yeah," Black Pan said. "They shot it at somebody."

Watching the lights on the coast, Rose Rose announced: "I'm movin' to the city."

"Maybe, when you old enough," said Mr. Rose.

"Maybe Atlanta," she said. "I been in Atlanta," she told Angel—"at night, too."

"That was Charleston," Mr. Rose said. "Unless you was in Atlanta some other time."

"You said it was Atlanta," she told him.

"Maybe I *said* it was Atlanta," said Mr. Rose, "but it was Charleston." Black Pan laughed.

Rose Rose forgot to give the sweat shirt back, but in the morning, when it was still cold, she was wearing one of Mr. Rose's old sweaters and she handed the sweat shirt back to Angel.

"Got my own clothes, sort of, this mornin'," she told Angel, the baseball cap pulled lower than usual over her eyes. Black Pan was watching after Baby Rose, and it took Angel a while to see that Rose Rose had a black eye—a white person doesn't spot a black eye on a black person right away, but she had a good one.

"He say it okay if I wear your hat, but for you to wear your own shirt," Rose Rose told Angel. "I told you," she said. "You don't wanna get involved with me."

After the picking that day, Angel went to the cider house to have a word with Mr. Rose. Angel told Mr. Rose that he meant nothing improper by letting Rose Rose wear his sweat shirt; Angel added that he really liked Mr. Rose's daughter, and so forth. Angel got pretty worked up about it, although Mr. Rose remained a calm, calm man. Of course, Angel (and all the rest of them) had seen Mr. Rose peel and core an apple in about three or four seconds—it was widely presumed that Mr. Rose could bleed a man in half a minute. He could have made the whole mess of a human being look like a series of slight shaving injuries.

"Who told you I beat my daughter, Angel?" Mr. Rose asked gently. Rose Rose had told Angel, of course, but now Angel saw the trap; he was only making trouble for her. Mr. Rose would never allow himself to have any trouble with Angel. Mr. Rose knew the rules: they were the *real* cider house rules, they were the pickers' rules.

"I just thought you had hit her," Angel said, backing off.

"Not me," said Mr. Rose.

Before he put the tractor away, Angel spoke with Rose Rose. He told her that if she was frightened about staying in the cider house, she could always stay with him—that he had an extra bed in his room, or that he could vacate his room and make it into a guest room for her and her baby.

"A guest room?" Rose Rose said; she laughed. She told him he was the nicest man she ever knew. She had such a languid manner, like someone who was used to sleeping while standing up—her heavy limbs as relaxed as if she were underwater. She had a lazy body, yet in her presence Angel felt the same potential for lightning-quick movement that surrounded her father as intimately as someone's scent. Rose Rose gave Angel the shivers.

At supper, his father asked him, "How are you getting along with Mister Rose?"

"I'm more curious how you're getting along with Rose Rose," Candy said.

"How he's getting along with the girl is his own business," Wally said.

"Right," said Homer Wells, and Wally let it pass.

"How you're getting along with Mister Rose is our business, Angel," Wally said.

"Because we love you," Homer said.

"Mister Rose won't hurt me," Angel told them.

"Of course he won't!" Candy said.

"Mister Rose does what he wants," Wally said.

"He's got his own rules," said Homer Wells.

"He beats his daughter," Angel told them. "He hit her once, anyway."

"Don't make that your business, Angel," Wally told the boy.

"That's right," Homer said.

"I'll make it *my* business!" Candy told them. "If he's beating that girl, he'll hear about it from me."

"No, he won't," Wally said.

"Better not," Homer told her.

"Don't tell me what to do," she told them, and they were quiet; they both knew better than to try to tell Candy what to do.

"Are you sure it's true, Angel?" Candy asked.

"Almost sure," the boy said. "Ninety-nine percent."

"Make it a hundred percent, Angel, before you say it's true," his father told him.

"Right," Angel said as he got up from the table and cleared his dishes.

"Good thing we got all that straightened out," Wally said when Angel was in the kitchen. "Good thing we're all such experts at the truth," he said as Candy got up from the table to clear her dishes. Homer Wells kept sitting where he was.

The next morning Angel learned that Rose Rose had never been in the ocean—that she'd picked citrus in Florida and peaches in Georgia, and she'd driven up the East Coast all the way to Maine, but she'd never stuck so much as her toe in the Atlantic. She'd never even felt the sand.

"That's crazy!" said Angel Wells. "We'll go to the beach some Sunday."

"What for?" she said. "You think I gonna look better with a tan? What would I go to a beach for?"

"To swim!" Angel said. "The ocean! The salt water!"

"I don't know how to swim," Rose Rose informed him.

"Oh," he said. "Well, you don't have to swim to enjoy the ocean. You don't have to go in over your head."

"I don't have no bathin' suit," she said.

"Oh," Angel said. "Well, I can get you one. I'll bet one of Candy's would fit you." Rose Rose looked only mildly surprised. Any bathing suit of Candy's would be a tight fit.

For their lunch break, after Rose Rose had seen how Baby Rose was getting along with Black Pan, Angel drove her to the baby-tree orchard near Cock Hill; they were not picking the baby trees, so there was no one there. You could barely see the ocean. You could see the unnatural end of the horizon, how the sky inexplicably flattened out—and by standing on the tractor, they could distinguish the different tones of blue and gray where the sky bled into the sea. Rose Rose remained unimpressed.

"Come on," Angel said to her. "You got to let me take you to see it!" He tugged her by one arm—just fooling around, just an affectionate gesture—but she suddenly cried out; his hand grazed the small of her back as she turned away from him, and when he looked at his hand, he saw her blood.

"It's my period," she lied. Even a fifteen-year-old boy knows that the blood from anyone's period isn't usually found on the *back*.

After they kissed for a while, she showed him some of the wounds—not the ones on the backs of her legs, and not the ones on her rump; he had to take her word for those. She showed him only the cuts on her back—they were fine, thread-thin, razorlike cuts; they were extremely deliberate, very careful cuts that would heal completely in a day or two. They were slightly deeper than scratches; they were not intended to leave scars.

"I told you," she said to Angel, but she still kissed him hard. "You shouldn't have no business with me. I ain't really available."

Angel agreed not to bring up the matter of the cuts with Mr. Rose; that would only make things worse—Rose Rose convinced him of that. And if Angel wanted to take her to the beach—somehow, some Sunday, they should both be as nice to Mr. Rose as they could manage.

The man named Muddy, who'd been reassembled with one hundred twenty-three stitches, had said it the best. What he said once was, "If old Rose had cut me, I wouldn't of needed *one* stitch. I would of bled a pint an hour, or even slower, and when it was finally all over it would have looked like someone hadn't used anythin' on me except a stiff toothbrush."

When Angel was putting the tractor away on Saturday, it was Muddy instead of Peaches who spoke to him. "You don't wanna get involved with Rose Rose, you know. The knife business ain't your business, Angel," Muddy said, putting his arm around the boy and giving him a squeeze. Muddy liked Angel; he remembered, fondly, how Angel's father had gotten him to Cape Kenneth Hospital in time.

When there was another night pressing, Angel sat with Rose Rose on the cider house roof and told her all about the ocean:

the strange tiredness one feels at the edge of the sea, the weight in the air, the haze in the middle of a summer day, the way the surf softens sharp things. He told her the whole, familiar story. How we love to love things for other people; how we love to have other people love things through our eyes.

But Angel could not keep secret what he imagined was the enormity of Mr. Rose's wrongdoing. He told the whole story to his father, and to Candy and Wally.

"He cut her? He deliberately cut her?" Wally asked Angel.

"No doubt about it," Angel said. "I'm a hundred percent sure."

"I can't imagine how he could do that to his own daughter," said Homer Wells.

"I can't believe how we're always saying how wonderful it is: that Mister Rose is so *in charge* of everything," Candy said, shivering. "We have to do something about this."

"We do?" Wally asked.

"Well, we can't do nothing!" Candy told him.

"People do," Wally said.

"If you speak to him, he'll hurt her more," Angel told them. "And she'll know I told you. I want your advice, I don't want you to *do* anything."

"I wasn't thinking of speaking to *him,*" Candy said angrily. "I was thinking of speaking to the police. You can't carve up your own children!"

"But will it help her—if he gets in trouble?" Homer asked.

"Precisely," Wally said. "We're not helping her by going to the police."

"Or by speaking to him," Angel said.

"There's always waiting and seeing," said Homer Wells. For fifteen years, Candy had learned to ignore this.

"I could ask her to stay with us," Angel suggested. "That would get her away from him. I mean, she could just stay here, even after the harvest."

"But what would she do?" Candy asked.

"There aren't any jobs around," said Homer Wells. "Not after the harvest."

"It's one thing having them pick," Wally said carefully. "I mean, everyone accepts them, but they're only migrants—they're transients. They're supposed to move on. I don't think that a colored woman with an illegitimate child is going to be made to feel all that welcome in Maine. Not if she's *staying.*"

Candy was cross. She said, "Wally, in all the years I've bee
here, I've never heard anyone call them niggers, or say anythin
bad about them. This isn't the South," she added proudly.

"Come on," Wally said. "It only isn't the South because the
don't live here. Let one of them actually try to live here and se
what they call her."

"I don't believe that," Candy said.

"Then you're dumb," Wally said. "Isn't she, old boy?
Wally asked Homer.

But Homer Wells was watching Angel. "Are you in love wit
Rose Rose, Angel?" Homer asked his son.

"Yes," Angel said. "And I think she likes me—at least
little." He cleared his own dishes and went upstairs to h
room.

"He's in love with the girl," Homer said to Candy an
Wally.

"As plain as the nose on your face, old boy," Wally sai
"Where have you been?" He wheeled himself out on th
terrace and took a few turns around the swimming pool.

"What do you think of that?" Homer asked Candy. "Angel'
in love!"

"I hope it makes him more sympathetic to us," Candy tol
him. "That's what I think about it."

But Homer Wells was thinking about Mr. Rose. How fa
would he go? What were his rules?

When Wally wheeled himself back into the house, he tol
Homer that there was some mail for him in the apple-ma
office. "I keep meaning to bring it up to the house," Wall
told him, "but I keep forgetting it."

"Just keep forgetting it," Homer advised him. "It's th
harvest. Since I don't have time to answer any mail, I might a
well not read it."

Nurse Caroline's letter had also arrived; it was waiting fo
him with Dr. Larch's letter, and with a letter from Melony.

Melony had returned the questionnaire to Homer. She hadn
filled it out; she'd just been curious, and she'd wanted to loo
it over more closely. After she'd read it a few times, she coul
tell—by the nature of the questions—that the board of trustee
were, in her opinion, a collection of the usual assholes. "Th
guys in suits," she called them. "Don't you hate men in suits?
she'd asked Lorna.

"Come on," Lorna had told her. "You just hate men, a
men."

"Men in suits, especially," Melony had said.

Across the questionnaire, which would never be filled out, Melony had written a brief message to Homer Wells.

> DEAR SUNSHINE,
> I THOUGHT YOU WAS GOING TO BE
> A HERO. MY MISTAKE. SORRY
> FOR HARD TIME.
>
> LOVE, MELONY

Homer Wells would read that, much later that same night, when he couldn't sleep, as usual, and he decided to get up and read his mail. He would read Dr. Larch's letter, and Nurse Caroline's, too, and any doubts that were remaining about the doctor's bag with the initials F.S. engraved in gold had disappeared with the darkness just before dawn.

Homer saw no reason to add irony to their predicament; he decided not to send Melony's response to the questionnaire to Larch or to Nurse Caroline—how would it help them to know that they had turned themselves in when they might have gone on for another few years? He sent a single, short note, addressed to them both. The note was simple and mathematical.

1. I AM NOT A DOCTOR.

2. I BELIEVE THE FETUS HAS A SOUL.

3. I'M SORRY.

"Sorry?" said Wilbur Larch, when Nurse Caroline read him the note. "He says he's *sorry?*"

"Of course, he isn't a doctor," Nurse Angela admitted. "There'd always be something he'd think he didn't know; he'd always be thinking he was going to make an amateur mistake."

"That's why he'd be a good doctor," said Dr. Larch. "Doctors who think they know everything are the ones who make the most amateur mistakes. That's how a good doctor should be thinking: that there's always something he doesn't know, that he can always kill someone."

"We're in for it, now," Nurse Edna said.

"He believes the fetus has a soul, does he?" Larch asked. "Fine. He believes that a creature that lives like a fish has a soul—and what sort of soul does he believe those of us walking around have? He should believe in what he can see! If he's going to play God and tell us who's got a soul, he should take care of the souls who can talk back to him!" He was ranting.

Then Nurse Angela said, "So. We wait and see."

"Not me," said Wilbur Larch. "Homer can wait and see," he said, "but not me."

He sat at the typewriter in Nurse Angela's office; he wrote this simple, mathematical note to Homer Wells.

1. YOU KNOW EVERYTHING I KNOW, PLUS WHAT YOU'VE TAUGHT YOURSELF. YOU'RE A BETTER DOCTOR THAN I AM—AND YOU KNOW IT.

2. YOU THINK WHAT I DO IS PLAYING GOD, BUT YOU PRESUME YOU KNOW WHAT GOD WANTS. DO YOU THINK THAT'S NOT PLAY-ING GOD?

3. I AM NOT SORRY—NOT FOR ANYTHING I'VE DONE (ONE ABORTION I DID NOT PER-FORM IS THE ONLY ONE I'M SORRY FOR). I'M NOT EVEN SORRY THAT I LOVE YOU.

Then Dr. Larch walked to the railroad station and waited for the train; he wanted to see the note sent on its way. Later, the stationmaster whom Larch rarely acknowledged admitted he was surprised that Larch spoke to him; but because Larch spoke after the train had gone, the stationmaster thought that Larch might have been addressing the departed train.

"Good-bye," Dr. Larch said. He walked back up the hill to the orphanage. Mrs. Grogan asked him if he wanted some tea, but Dr. Larch told her that he felt too tired for tea; he wanted to lie down.

Nurse Caroline and Nurse Edna were picking apples, and Larch went a little way up the hill to speak to them. "You're too old to pick apples, Edna," Larch told her. "Let Caroline and the children do it." He then walked a short distance with Nurse Caroline, back toward the orphanage. "If I had to be anything," he told her, "I'd probably be a socialist, but I don't want to be anything."

Then he went into the dispensary and closed the door. Despite the harvest weather, it was still warm enough to have he window open during the day; he closed the window, too. It was a new, full can of ether; perhaps he jabbed the safety pin too roughly into the can, or else he wiggled it around too impatiently. The ether dripped onto the face mask more freely than usual; his hand kept slipping off the cone before he could get enough to satisfy himself. He turned a little toward the wall; that way, the edge of the windowsill maintained contact with the mask over his mouth and nose after his fingers relaxed their grip. There was just enough pressure from the windowsill to hold the cone in place.

This time he traveled to Paris; how lively it was there, at the end of World War I. The young doctor was constantly embraced by the natives. He remembered sitting with an American soldier—an amputee—in a café; all the patrons bought them Cognac. The soldier put out his cigar in a snifter of Cognac that he couldn't finish—not if he intended to stand on his crutches, with his one leg—and Wilbur Larch breathed deeply of that aroma. That was how Paris smelled—like Cognac and ash.

That, and like perfume. Larch had walked the soldier home— he'd been a good doctor, even there, even then. He was a third crutch to the drunken man, he was the man's missing leg. That was when the woman had accosted them. She was a whore, quite clearly, and she was quite young, and quite pregnant; Larch, who didn't understand French very well, assumed that she wanted an abortion. He was trying to tell her that she was too late, that she'd have to go through with having this baby, when he suddenly understood that she was asking only what a whore is usually asking.

"*Plaisir d'amour?*" she asked them. The amputated soldier was passing out in Larch's arms; it was to Larch alone that the woman was offering the "pleasure of love."

"*Non, merci,*" Wilbur Larch mumbled. But the soldier collapsed; Larch needed the pregnant prostitute to help carry him. When they delivered the soldier to his room, the woman renewed her offer to Wilbur Larch. He had to hold her at arm's length to keep her away from him—and still she would slip through his grasp and push her firm belly into him.

"*Plaisir d'amour!*" she said.

"*Non, non!*" he told her; he had to wave his arms to keep her away. One hand, swinging back and forth beside the bed, knocked over the ether can with the loose pin. Slowly, the puddle developed on the linoleum floor; it spread under the bed, and all around him. The strength of the fumes overpowered him—the woman in Paris had smelled very strongly, too. Her perfume was strong, and stronger still was the effluvia of her trade. By the time Larch moved his face away from the windowsill and the cone fell, he was already gagging.

"Princes of Maine!" He tried to call for them, but he didn't make a sound. "Kings of New England!" He thought he was summoning them, but no one could hear him, and the French woman lay down beside him and snuggled her heavy belly against him. She hugged him so tightly that he couldn't breathe, and her flavorful, tangy aroma made the tears run down his cheeks. He thought he was vomiting; he was.

"Plaisir d'amour," she whispered.

"Oui, merci," he said, giving in to her. *"Oui, merci."*

The cause of death would be respiratory failure, due to aspiration of vomit, which would lead to cardiac arrest. The board of trustees—in light of the evidence submitted against him—would privately call it a suicide; the man was about to be disgraced, they told themselves. But those who knew him and understood his ether habit would say that it was the kind of accident a tired man would have. Certainly, Mrs. Grogan knew—and Nurse Angela, and Nurse Edna, and Nurse Caroline knew, too—that he was *not* a man "about to be disgraced"; rather, he was a man about to be no longer of use. And a man *of use,* Wilbur Larch had thought, was all that he was born to be.

Nurse Edna, who for some time would remain almost speechless, found his body. The dispensary door was not a perfect seal, and she thought that the odor was especially strong and that Dr. Larch had been in there longer than usual.

Mrs. Grogan, who hoped he'd gone to a better world, read, in the voice of a troubled thrush, a quavering passage of *Jane Eyre* to the girls' division.

An orphan loves and needs routine, the women reminded each other.

Nurse Caroline, who was tough as nails and found Dickens a sentimental bore, had a firm grasp of the language; she read aloud an almost hearty passage of *David Copperfield* to the boys' division. But she found herself broken by the prospect of the expected benediction.

It was Nurse Angela who said it all, according to the rules.

"Let us be happy for Doctor Larch," she said to the attentive children. "Doctor Larch has found a family. Good night, Doctor Larch," Nurse Angela said.

"Good night, Doctor Larch!" the children called.

"Good night, Wilbur!" Nurse Edna managed to say, while Nurse Angela summoned her strength for the usual refrain, and Nurse Caroline, who hoped the evening wind would dry her tears, marched down the hill to the railroad station—once again to inform the frightened stationmaster that there was a body in St. Cloud's.

/ / /

That Sunday at Ocean View was an Indian summer day, and Homer Wells was fishing. Not real fishing: Homer was trying to find out more about the relationship between Mr. Rose and his daughter. The two men sat on the cider house roof—for the most part, they weren't talking. Not talking too much, Homer assumed, was the only way to go fishing with Mr. Rose.

Below them, Angel was trying to teach Rose Rose how to ride a bicycle. Homer had offered to drive Rose Rose and Angel to the beach (and to drive back and pick them up at some designated hour), but it mattered to Angel that he and Rose Rose were independent—to be driven to the beach only emphasized that he was still waiting to be old enough to get his driver's license. The beach was too far to walk to, and Homer wouldn't allow Angel to hitchhike; but it was only a four- or five-mile ride on a bike, and the road was mostly flat.

Mr. Rose observed the lesson placidly, but Homer grew anxious for Rose Rose to succeed on the bicycle; he knew how much preparation had gone into the proposed trip—how Angel had fussed over both his own and Candy's bicycles, and how Angel had discussed (with Candy) which of Candy's bathing suits would be the most suitable for Rose Rose. Together, they had chosen an emerald-green one—it had one pink, spiraled, barber-pole stripe, and Candy was sure the suit would fit Rose Rose better than it fit her; it had always been too loose in the bust and in the hips for Candy.

"It's the kind of thing you're supposed to learn when you're a little kid, I guess," Homer Wells observed of the bicycle lesson. Angel would run alongside the wobbly bicycle, which Rose Rose struggled to ride. After the bike was moving at a comfortable speed, Angel would release his hold on it. Rose Rose would either not pedal—hugging the bike until it simply ran out of speed and toppled—or else she would pedal furiously, but without guidance. She seemed unable to balance the bicycle and pedal it at the same time. And her hands appeared frozen on the handlebars; for her to balance, and pedal, *and* steer simultaneously looked, increasingly, like a distant miracle.

"Can you ride one?" Mr. Rose asked Homer.

"I never tried," said Homer Wells. "I'd probably have a little trouble," he admitted; it looked easy enough to him. There were no bicycles at the orphanage; the children might have used them to ride away. The only bicycle in St. Cloud's was the stationmaster's, and he rarely rode it.

"I never tried, either," said Mr. Rose. He watched his daughter careen over a slight hill; she shrieked, the bike jackknifed, she fell—and Angel Wells ran to her, to help her up.

A line of men sat with their backs against the cider house wall; some were drinking coffee, some were drinking beer, but all of them watched the bicycle lesson. Some were encouraging—and as vocal as local fans, rooting at a sporting event—and others watched the procedure as placidly as Mr. Rose.

It had been going on for a while, and the applause—what there'd been of it—grew spottier and more random.

"Don't give up," Angel said to Rose Rose.

"I *not* givin' up," Rose Rose said. "Did I say I was givin' up?"

"You remember what you said to me, once, about the rules?" Homer asked Mr. Rose.

"What rules?" Mr. Rose asked.

"You know, those rules I put up every year in the cider house," Homer said. "And you mentioned that you had other rules—your own rules for living here."

"Yeah, those rules," said Mr. Rose.

"I thought you meant that your rules were about not hurting each other—I thought they were about being careful," Homer said. "Sort of like my rules, too, I guess."

"Say what you mean, Homer," said Mr. Rose.

"Is someone getting hurt?" Homer asked. "I mean, this year—is there some kind of trouble?"

Rose Rose was up on the bicycle; her look was grim; both she and Angel were sweating. It appeared to Homer that Rose Rose was jouncing on the seat too hard, almost intentionally hurting herself; or else she was treating herself so roughly in order to give herself the intensity she needed to master the machine. She wobbled off a knoll, out of sight behind some apple trees, and Angel sprinted after her.

"Why don't they just walk?" the picker named Peaches asked. "They coulda been there by now."

"Why don't someone take 'em in some car?" another man asked.

"They wanna do it they own way," Muddy said. There was a little laughter about that.

"Show some respect," said Mr. Rose. Homer thought Mr. Rose was speaking to him, but he was speaking to the men, who stopped laughing. "Pretty soon, that bicycle gonna break," Mr. Rose said to Homer.

Rose Rose was wearing a pair of blue jeans, some heavy work shoes and a white T-shirt; because she was sweating, the outline and the colors of the emerald-green and pink bathing suit were visible through her shirt.

"Imagine her learnin' to swim," said Mr. Rose.

Homer Wells felt bad for Angel, but another subject weighed more heavily on his mind.

"About someone being hurt," Homer said. "About the rules."

Mr. Rose reached into his pocket, slowly, and Homer half expected to see the knife, but it was not the knife that Mr. Rose removed from his pocket and very gently placed in Homer's hand—it was the burned-down nub of a candle. It was what was left of the candle Candy had lit for their lovemaking in the cider house. In her panic—when she thought it was Wally who had caught them there—she had forgotten it.

Homer closed his fingers around the candle, and Mr. Rose patted his hand.

"That 'gainst the rules, ain't it?" Mr. Rose asked Homer.

Black Pan was baking corn bread and the smell rose from the cider house and hung deliciously over the roof, which was warming in the late-morning sun; pretty soon, it would be uncomfortably hot on the roof.

"Ain't that bread ready to eat yet?" Peaches hollered into the kitchen.

"No it ain't," Black Pan said from inside the cider house. "And pipe down, or you wake the baby."

"Shit," Peaches said. Black Pan came outside and kicked Peaches—not terribly hard—where he was leaning against the cider house wall.

"When that bread ready, you won't call it 'shit,' will you?" Black Pan asked him.

"I wasn't callin' nothin' 'shit,' man—I was just sayin' it," Peaches said.

"Just pipe down," Black Pan said. He observed the bicycle lesson. "How it comin' with that?" he asked.

"They tryin' hard," Muddy said.

"They inventin' a new sport," Peaches said, and everyone laughed.

"Show some respect," said Mr. Rose, and everyone piped down. Black Pan went back inside the cider house.

"What you bet he burns the bread?" Peaches asked quietly.

"If he burns it, it 'cause he took the time to kick your ass," Muddy told him.

The bicycle was broken; either the rear wheel wouldn't turn or else the chain was jammed in the wheel.

"There's another bicycle," Angel told Rose Rose. "You try that one, while I fix this one." But while he fixed Candy's bicycle, Rose Rose had to suffer with a boy's bicycle, so that in addition to her troubles, she slipped and hurt her crotch against the crossbar. Homer was actually worried about how hard a fall she had, and he asked her if she was all right.

"It just like a cramp," she called to him, but she remained bent over until Angel managed to get Candy's bicycle running again.

"It looks hopeless," Homer confided to Mr. Rose.

"What about them rules?" Mr. Rose asked him. Homer put the candle in his pocket. He and Mr. Rose regarded each other—it was almost a contest, the way they looked at each other.

"I'm worried about your daughter," said Homer Wells, after a while. Together they watched Rose Rose fall off the bicycle again.

"Don't worry about her," said Mr. Rose.

"She looks unhappy, sometimes," Homer said.

"She ain't unhappy," Mr. Rose said.

"Are you worried about her?" Homer asked him.

"Once you start worryin', you can worry 'bout anybody, can't you?" said Mr. Rose.

It appeared to Homer Wells that her fall against the crossbar was still giving Rose Rose some pain because she stood for a while with her hands on her knees and her head down (as if her stomach hurt her) each time she fell off the bicycle.

Homer and Mr. Rose missed the moment when she gave up. They just noticed that she was running off, in the direction of the orchard called Frying Pan, and that Angel was running after her; both bicycles were left behind.

"That's too bad," Homer said. "They would have had a good time at the beach. Maybe I can convince them to let me drive them there."

"Leave 'em alone," said Mr. Rose; the way Homer heard it, it was more of a command than a suggestion. "They don't have to go to no beach," Mr. Rose said, more mildly. "They just young, they not sure how to have a good time," he said. "Just think what might happen at the beach. They might get drowned. Or some people might not like seein' a white boy with a colored girl—and they both in bathin' suits. It better they don't go nowhere," Mr. Rose concluded. That was the end of that subject, because then Mr. Rose asked, "Are you happy, Homer?"

"Am I happy?" said Homer Wells.

"Why you repeat every single thing?" Mr. Rose asked him.

"I don't know," Homer said. "I'm happy, sometimes," he said cautiously.

"That good," said Mr. Rose. "And Mistuh and Missus Worthington—are they happy?"

"I think they're pretty happy, most of the time," Homer told him.

"That good," said Mr. Rose.

Peaches, who'd had a few beers, approached Angel's bicycle warily, as if the machine were dangerous even when it was lying on the ground.

"Careful it don't bite you," Muddy warned him. Peaches mounted the bike and grinned at the men.

"How do it start?" he asked them, and they all laughed.

Muddy got up from against the wall and went over to Candy's bicycle.

"I have you a race," he said to Peaches.

"Yeah," said Black Pan, in the cider house door. "We see which one of you falls down first."

"Mine ain't got no middle," Muddy observed of Candy's bike.

"That make it go faster," Peaches said. He tried to move Angel's bike forward, as if his feet were paddles.

"You ain't ridin' that thing, you fuckin' it," one of the men said, and everyone laughed. Black Pan ran up behind Peaches and started pushing him faster.

"Cut that shit out!" Peaches cried, but Black Pan got the bike rolling so fast that he couldn't keep up with it.

"I can't be in no race if someone don't push me, too," Muddy said, and two of the men got him rolling faster than Peaches, who had disappeared over a hill into the next field (from which the men could hear him screaming).

"Holy shit!" said Muddy, when he was under way. He pedaled so hard that the front wheel rose off the ground, and then the bicycle rode right out from under him. The men were howling now, and Black Pan picked up Muddy's fallen bicycle; he was the next to try it.

"You gonna try it, too?" Mr. Rose asked Homer.

As long as Angel and Candy weren't around to watch him, Homer thought he would. "Sure," Homer said. "I'm next!" he yelled at Black Pan, who was balancing the bicycle in place, his feet slipping off the pedals; he fell over on his side before he could get moving.

"That was no *real* turn!" Black Pan said. "I get another try."

"Are you going to try it?" Homer asked Mr. Rose.

"Not me," said Mr. Rose.

"The baby's cryin'," someone said.

"Go pick her up," said someone else.

"I'll take care of that," said Mr. Rose to all of them. "I'll watch the baby—you all play."

Peaches appeared over the hill; he was walking the bicycle beside him, and he was limping.

"It hit a tree," he explained. "It went right at the tree like the tree was its enemy."

"You supposed to steer it," Muddy told him.

"It steer itself," Peaches said. "It don't listen to me."

Homer supported Black Pan while the cook mounted Candy's bike a second time. "Here we go," Black Pan said with determination, but he kept one arm wrapped around Homer's neck; he had only one hand on the handlebars, and he wasn't pedaling.

"You've got to pedal it, to make it go," Homer told him.

"You got to push me first," Black Pan said.

"Somethin' burnin'!" someone shouted.

"Oh shit, my corn bread!" Black Pan said. He lunged to one side, his arm still around Homer's neck so that Homer fell over with him—on top of the bicycle.

"I told you he was gonna burn that bread," Peaches told Muddy.

"Give me that bike," Muddy said, taking Angel's bike away from Peaches.

Two of the men were giving Homer a push.

"I got it, I got it," Homer told them, so they let go. But he didn't have it. He veered sharply in one direction, then he veered back toward the men, who had to run out of his way; then he jackknifed the bike and went tumbling one way—the bike went another.

Everyone was laughing now. Peaches looked at Homer Wells lying on the ground.

"Sometimes, it don't help if you white!" Peaches told Homer, and everyone howled.

"It help, if you white, most of the time," said Mr. Rose. He stood in the cider house door, the smoke from the burning corn bread billowing behind him, his daughter's daughter in his arms—the pacifier a seemingly permanent fixture in her mouth. And after Mr. Rose had spoken, he stuck a pacifier in his mouth, too.

/ / /

In the heart of the valley that was at the bottom of Frying Pan, where the ocean might be a hundred miles away and no breath from the sea ever reached, Rose Rose was stretched out in the dark grass under a Northern Spy that no one had picked yet; Angel Wells was stretched out beside her. She let her arm loll on his waist; he ran his finger very lightly over her face, following the line of her scar down her nose to her lip. When he got to her lip, she held his hand still and kissed his finger.

She had taken off the work shoes and the blue jeans, but she kept Candy's bathing suit and the T-shirt on.

"Wouldn't of had no fun at no beach, anyway," she said.

"We'll go another day," Angel said.

"We won't go nowhere," she said. They kissed each other for a while. Then Rose Rose said, "Tell me 'bout it again." Angel Wells began to describe the ocean, but she interrupted him. "No, not that part," she said. "I don't care 'bout no ocean. Tell me 'bout the other part—where we all livin' together in the same house. You and me and my baby and your father and Mistuh and Missus Worthington," Rose Rose said. "That the part that get to me," she said, smiling.

And he began again: about how it was possible. He was sure that his father and Wally and Candy wouldn't object.

"You all crazy," she told Angel. "But go on," she said.

There was plenty of room, Angel assured her.

"Ain't nobody gonna mind 'bout the baby?" she asked him; she shut her eyes; with her eyes shut, she could see what Angel was describing a little better.

That was when Angel Wells became a fiction writer, whether he knew it or not. That's when he learned how to make the make-believe matter to him more than real life mattered to him; that's when he learned how to paint a picture that was not real and never would be real, but in order to be believed at all—even on a sunny Indian summer day—it had to be better made and seem more real than real; it had to sound at least possible. Angel talked all day; he just went on and on and on; he would be a novelist before nightfall. In his story, Rose Rose and everyone else got along famously. No one objected to anything anyone else did. All of it, as they say in Maine, worked out.

Sometimes, Rose Rose cried a little; more often, they just kissed. Only a few times did she interrupt him, usually because she wanted him to repeat something that had seemed especially unlikely to her. "Hold on a minute," she'd say to Angel. "Better go over that again, 'cause I must be slow."

In the late afternoon, the mosquitoes began to bother them, and it crossed Angel's mind how, some evening, Rose Rose could ask Wally to tell her what the rice paddy mosquitoes were like.

"An Ocean View mosquito isn't anything compared to a Japanese B mosquito," Wally would have told her, but Angel didn't get to tell Rose Rose this part of the fantasy. She was starting to stand up when an apparent cramp, or the pain from her fall against the bicycle's crossbar, dropped her to her knees as if she'd been kicked, and Angel caught her around her shoulders.

"You hurt yourself on the bicycle, didn't you?" he asked her.

"I was tryin' to," she said then.

"What?" he asked her.

"I was *tryin'* to hurt myself," Rose Rose told him, "but I don't think I hurt myself enough."

"Enough for what?" he asked.

"To lose the baby," she told him.

"You're pregnant?" Angel asked her.

"Again," she said. "Again and again, I guess," she said. "Somebody must want me to keep havin' babies."

"Who?" Angel asked her.

"Never mind," she told him.

"Someone who's not here?" he asked.

"Oh, he here," Rose Rose said. "But never mind."

"The father is here?" Angel asked.

"The father of *this* one—yeah, he here," she said, patting her flat stomach.

"Who is he?" Angel asked.

"Never mind who he is," she told Angel. "Tell me that part again—only better make it *two* babies. Now they me and you, and everybody else, and *two* babies," she said. "Won't we all have fun?"

Angel looked as if she'd slapped him; Rose Rose kissed him and hugged him—and she changed her tone of voice.

"You see?" she whispered to him, holding him tight. "We wouldn't of had no fun at no beach, Angel."

"Do you want the baby?" he asked her.

"I want the one I got," she told him. "I don't want this other one!" She struck herself as hard as she could when she said "other"; she bent herself over again, she'd knocked the wind out of herself. She lay in the grass in what Angel could not help observing was a fetal position.

"You wanna love me or help me?" she asked him.

"Both," he said miserably.

"Ain't no such thing as *both*," she said. "If you smart, you just stick with helpin' me, that easier."

"You can stay with me," Angel began—again.

"Don't tell me no more 'bout that!" Rose Rose said angrily. "Don't tell me no more names for my baby, either. Just plain help me," she said.

"How?" Angel asked. "Anything," he told her.

"Just get me an abortion," Rose Rose said. "I don't live 'round here, I don't know nobody to ask, and I got no money."

/ / /

Angel thought that the money he'd been saving to buy his first car would probably be enough money for an abortion—he had saved about five hundred dollars—but the problem was that the money was in a savings account, the trustees of which were his father and Candy; Angel couldn't take any money out without their signatures. And when Angel called Herb Fowler at home, the news regarding the abortionist was typically vague.

"There's some old fart named Hood who does 'em," Herb

told Angel. "He's a retired doctor from Cape Kenneth. But he does the business in his summer house over on Drinkwater. Lucky for you it's still almost summer. I heard he does 'em in the summer house even if it's the middle of the winter."

"Do you know what it costs?" Angel asked Herb.

"A lot," Herb said. "But it don't cost as much as a baby."

"Thanks, Herb," Angel said.

"Congratulations," Herb Fowler told the boy. "I didn't know your pecker was long enough."

"It's long enough," Angel said bravely.

But when Angel looked in the phone book, there was no Dr. Hood among the many Hoods in that part of Maine, and Herb Fowler didn't know the man's first name. Angel knew he couldn't call everyone named Hood and ask, each time, if this was the abortionist. Angel also knew he'd have to speak to Candy and his father in order to get the money, and so he didn't delay in telling them the whole story.

"God, what a good boy Angel is!" Wally would say later. "He never tries to keep anything from anybody. He just comes right out with it—no matter what it is."

"She wouldn't tell you who the father is?" Homer Wells asked Angel.

"No, she wouldn't," Angel said.

"Maybe Muddy," Wally said.

"Probably Peaches," Candy said.

"What's it matter if she doesn't want to say who the father is? The main thing is she doesn't want the baby," said Homer Wells. "The main thing is to get her an abortion." Wally and Candy were quiet; they wouldn't question Homer's authority on this subject.

"The problem is, how do we know which Hood to call, when the phone book doesn't say which one is the doctor?" Angel asked.

"I know which one it is," Homer said, "and he's not a doctor."

"Herb said he was a retired doctor," Angel said.

"He's a retired biology teacher," said Homer Wells, who knew exactly which Mr. Hood it was. Homer also remembered that Mr. Hood had once confused a rabbit's uteri with a sheep's. He wondered how many uteri Mr. Hood imagined women had? And would he be more careful if he knew a woman had only one?

"A biology teacher?" Angel asked.

"Not a very good one, either," Homer said.

"Herb Fowler has never known shit about anything," Wally said.

The thought of what Mr. Hood might not know gave Homer Wells the shivers.

"She's not going anywhere near Mister Hood," Homer said. "You'll have to take her to Saint Cloud's," he told Angel.

"But I don't think she wants to have the baby," Angel said. "And if she had it, I don't think she'd want to leave it in the orphanage."

"Angel," Homer said, "she doesn't have to have a baby in Saint Cloud's. She can have an abortion there."

Wally moved the wheelchair back and forth.

Candy said: "*I* had an abortion there, once, Angel."

"You did?" Angel said.

"At the time," Wally told the boy, "we thought we'd always be able to have another baby."

"It was before Wally was hurt—before the war," Candy began.

"Doctor Larch does it?" Angel asked his father.

"Right," said Homer Wells. He was thinking that he should put Angel and Rose Rose on a train to St. Cloud's as soon as possible; with all the "evidence" that had been submitted to the board of trustees, Homer didn't know how much more time Dr. Larch would have to practice.

"I'll call Doctor Larch right now," Homer said. "We'll put you and Rose Rose on the next train."

"Or I could drive them in the Cadillac," Wally said.

"It's too far for you to drive, Wally," Homer told him.

"Baby Rose can stay here, with me," Candy said.

They decided that it would be best if Candy went to the cider house and brought Rose Rose and her baby back to the house. Mr. Rose might give Rose Rose an argument if Angel showed up at night, wanting Rose Rose and the baby to go off with him.

"He won't argue with me," Candy said. "I'll just say I've found a lot of old baby clothes, and that Rose Rose and I are going to dress up the baby in everything that fits her."

"At night?" Wally said. "For Christ's sake, Mister Rose isn't a fool."

"I don't care if he believes me," Candy said. "I just want to get the girl and her baby out of there."

"Is there that much of a rush?" Wally asked.

"Yes, I'm afraid there is," said Homer Wells. He had not told Candy or Wally about Dr. Larch's desire to replace himself, or what revelations and fictions had been delivered to the board. An orphan learns to keep things to himself; an orphan holds things in. What comes out of orphans comes out of them slowly.

When Homer called St. Cloud's, he got Nurse Caroline; in their shock, in their grief, in their mourning for Dr. Larch, they had determined that Nurse Caroline had the sturdiest voice over the phone. And they had all been trying to familiarize themselves with Dr. Larch's plans, for everything, and with his massive *A Brief History of St. Cloud's* as well. Every time the phone rang, they assumed it was someone from the board of trustees.

"Caroline?" said Homer Wells. "It's Homer. Let me speak with the old man."

Nurse Angela and Nurse Edna, and even Mrs. Grogan, would love Homer Wells forever—in spite of his note of denial—but Nurse Caroline was younger than any of them; she did not feel the abiding sweetness for Homer Wells that comes from knowing someone when he's a baby. She felt he had betrayed Larch. And, of course, it was a bad time for him to ask for "the old man." When Larch had died, Nurse Angela and Nurse Edna and Mrs. Grogan had said they were not up to calling Homer; Nurse Caroline hadn't wanted to call him.

"What do you want?" Nurse Caroline asked him coldly. "Or have you changed your mind?"

"There's a friend of my son's," said Homer Wells. "She's one of the migrants here. She's already got a baby who's got no father, and now she's going to have another."

"Then she'll have two," Nurse Caroline informed him.

"Caroline!" said Homer Wells. "Cut the shit. I want to talk to the old man."

"I'd like to talk to him, too," Nurse Caroline told him, her voice rising. "Larch is dead, Homer," she said more quietly.

"Cut the shit," said Homer Wells; he felt his heart dancing.

"Too much ether," she said. "There's no more Lord's work in Saint Cloud's. If you know someone who needs it, you'll have to do it yourself."

Then she hung up on him—she really slammed the phone down. His ear rang; he heard the sound of the logs bashing together in the water that swept the Winkles away. His eyes had not stung so sharply since that night in the Drapers' furnace room, in Waterville, when he had dressed himself for his getaway. His throat had not ached so deeply—the pain pushing down, into his lungs—since that night he had yelled across the river, trying to make the Maine woods repeat the name of Fuzzy Stone.

Snowy Meadows had found happiness with the furniture Marshes; good for Snowy, thought Homer Wells. He imagined that the other orphans would have difficulty finding happiness in the furniture business. At times, he admitted, he had been very happy in the apple business. He knew what Larch would have told him: that his happiness was not the point, or that it wasn't as important as his usefulness.

Homer shut his eyes and watched the women getting off the train. They always looked a little lost. He remembered them in the gaslit sleigh—their faces were especially vivid to him when the sled runners would cut through the snow and strike sparks against the ground; how the women had winced at that grating sound. And, briefly, when the town had cared enough to provide a bus service, how isolated the women had seemed in the sealed buses, their faces cloudy behind the fogged glass; through the windows they had appeared to Homer Wells the way the world appeared to them, just before the ether transported them.

And now they walked from the station. Homer saw them marching uphill; there were more of them than he'd remembered. They were an army, advancing on the orphanage hospital, bearing with them a single wound.

Nurse Caroline was tough; but where would Nurse Edna and Nurse Angela go, and what would happen to Mrs. Grogan? worried Homer Wells. He remembered the hatred and contempt in Melony's eyes. If Melony were pregnant, I would help her, he thought. And with that thought he realized that he was willing to play God, a little.

Wilbur Larch would have told him there was no such thing as playing a *little* God; when you were willing to play God—at all—you played a lot.

Homer Wells was thinking hard when he reached into his pocket and found the burned-down nub of the candle Mr. Rose had returned to him—"That 'gainst the rules, ain't it?" Mr. Rose had asked him.

On his bedside table, between the reading lamp and the telephone, was his battered copy of *David Copperfield*. Homer didn't have to open the book to know how the story began. " 'Whether I shall turn out to be the hero of my own life, or whether that station will be held by anybody else, these pages must show,' " he recited from memory.

His memory was exceedingly keen. He could recall the different sizes of the ether cones that Larch insisted upon making himself. The apparatus was rudimentary: Larch shaped a cone out of an ordinary huckaback towel; between the layers of the towel were layers of stiff paper to keep the cone from collapsing. At the open tip of the cone was a wad of cotton—to absorb the ether. Crude, but Larch could make one in three minutes; they were different sizes for different faces.

Homer had preferred the ready-made Yankauer mask—a wire-mesh mask, shaped like a soup ladle, wrapped with ten or twelve layers of gauze. It was into the old Yankauer mask on his bedside table that Homer deposited the remains of the cider house candle. He kept change in the mask, and sometimes his watch. Now he peered into it; the mask contained a piece of chewing gum in a faded green wrapper and the tortoiseshell button from his tweed jacket. The gauze in the mask was yellow and dusty, but all the mask needed was fresh gauze. Homer Wells made up his mind; he would be a hero.

He went downstairs to the kitchen where Angel was pushing Wally around in the wheelchair—it was a game they played when they were both restless. Angel stood on the back of the wheelchair and pushed it, the way you push a scooter; he got the chair going faster and faster—much faster than Wally could make it move by himself. Wally just steered—he kept turning and turning. Wally kept trying to miss the furniture, but despite his skill as a pilot and the good size of the kitchen floor, eventually Angel would get the chair going too fast to control and they'd crash into something. Candy got angry at them for it, but they did it, anyway (especially when she was out of the house). Wally called it "flying"; most of all, it was something they did when they were bored. Candy had gone to the cider house to get Rose Rose and her baby. Angel and Wally were freewheeling.

When they saw how Homer looked, they stopped.

"What's the matter, old boy?" Wally asked his friend.

Homer knelt by Wally's wheelchair and put his head in Wally's lap.

"Doctor Larch is dead," he told Wally, who held Homer while he cried. He cried a very short time; in Homer's memory, Curly Day had been the only orphan who ever cried for a long time. When Homer stopped crying, he said to Angel, "I've got a little story for you—and I'm going to need your help."

They went outside to the shed where the garden things were kept, and Homer opened one of the quarter-pound ether cans with a safety pin. The fumes made his eyes tear a little; he'd never understood how Larch could like the stuff.

"He got addicted to it," Homer told his son. "But he used to have the lightest touch. I've seen patients talking back to him while they were under, and still they didn't feel a thing."

They took the ether upstairs and Homer told Angel to make up the extra bed in his room—first with the rubber sheet they'd used when Angel had still been in diapers; then the usual sheets (but clean ones) over that.

"For Baby Rose?" Angel asked his father.

"No, not for Baby Rose," Homer said. When he unpacked the instruments, Angel sat down on the other bed and watched him.

"The water's boiling!" Wally called upstairs.

"You remember how I used to tell you that I was Doctor Larch's *helper*?" Homer asked Angel.

"Right," said Angel Wells.

"Well, I got very good—at helping him," Homer said. "Very good. I'm not an amateur," he told his son. "That's really it—that's the little story," Homer said, when he'd arranged everything he needed where he could see it; everything looked timeless, everything looked perfect.

"Go on," Angel Wells told his father. "Go on with the story."

Downstairs, in the quiet house, they heard Wally in his wheelchair, rolling from room to room; he was still flying.

Upstairs, Homer Wells was talking to his son while he changed the gauze on the Yankauer mask. He began with that old business about the Lord's work and the Devil's—how, to Wilbur Larch, it was all the work of the Lord.

/ / /

It startled Candy: how the headlights from her Jeep caught all the men in the starkest silhouettes against the sky; how they were perched in a row, like huge birds, along the cider house roof. She thought that everyone must be up there—but not everyone was. Mr. Rose and his daughter were inside the cider house, and the men were waiting where they'd been told to wait.

When Candy got out of the Jeep, no one spoke to her. There were no lights on in the cider house; if her headlights hadn't exposed the men on the roof, Candy would have thought that everyone had gone to bed.

"Hello!" Candy called up to the roof. "One day, that whole roof is going to cave in." It suddenly frightened her: how they wouldn't speak to her. But the men were more frightened than Candy was; the men didn't know what to say—they knew only that what Mr. Rose was doing to his daughter was wrong, and that they were too afraid to do anything about it.

"Muddy?" Candy asked in the darkness.

"Yes, Missus Worthington!" Muddy called down to her. She went over to the corner of the cider house where the roof dipped closest to the ground; it was where everyone climbed up; an old picking ladder was leaned up against the roof there, but no one on the roof moved to hold the ladder steady for her.

"Peaches?" Candy said.

"Yes, ma'am," Peaches said.

"Please, someone hold the ladder," she said. Muddy and Peaches held the ladder, and Black Pan held her hand when she climbed up on the roof. The men made room for her, and she sat down with them.

She could not see very clearly, but she would have known if Rose Rose was there; and if Mr. Rose had been there, Candy knew he would have spoken to her.

The first time she heard the sound from the cider house—it came from directly under her—Candy thought it was the baby, just babbling or maybe beginning to cry.

"When your Wally was a boy, it was different—out there," Black Pan said to her. "It look like another country then." His gaze was fixed upon the twinkling coast.

The noise under the cider house roof grew more distinct, and Peaches said, "Ain't it a pretty night, ma'am?" It was decidedly not a pretty night; it was a darker night than usual, and the sound from the cider house was now comprehensible to her. For a second, she thought she was going to be sick.

"Careful when you stand up, Missus Worthington," Muddy

said to her, but Candy stamped her feet on the roof; then she knelt down and began to beat on the tin with both her hands.

"It's so old a roof, Missus Worthington," Black Pan said to her. "You best be careful you don't fall through it."

"Get me down, get me off," Candy said to them. Muddy and Peaches took her arms and Black Pan preceded them to the ladder. Even walking down the roof, Candy tried to keep stamping her feet.

Going down the ladder, she called, "Rose!" She could not say the ridiculous name of "Rose Rose," and she couldn't make herself say "Mister Rose," either. "Rose!" she called ambiguously. She wasn't even sure which one she was summoning, but it was Mr. Rose who met her at the cider house door. He was still getting dressed—he was tucking his shirt in and buttoning his trousers. He looked thinner and older to her than he'd looked before, and although he smiled at her, he didn't look into her eyes with his usual confidence—with his usual, polite indifference.

"Don't you speak to me," Candy told him, but what would he have said? "Your daughter and her baby are coming with me." Candy walked by him into the cider house; she felt the tattered rules with her fingers as she found the light.

Rose Rose was sitting up on the bed. She had pulled her blue jeans on, but she hadn't closed them, and she had pulled the T-shirt on, but she held Candy's bathing suit in her lap—she was unfamiliar with wearing it, and she'd not been able to put it on in a hurry. She had found only one of her work shoes, which she held in one hand. The other one was under the bed. Candy found it and put it on the correct foot—Rose Rose wore no socks. Then Candy tied the laces for her, too. Rose Rose just sat on the bed while Candy put on and tied her other shoe.

"You're coming with me. Your baby, too," Candy told the girl.

"Yes, ma'am," Rose Rose said.

Candy took the bathing suit from her and used the suit to wipe the tears from Rose Rose's face.

"You're fine, you're just fine," Candy said to the girl. "And you're going to feel better. No one's going to hurt you."

Baby Rose was sound asleep, and Candy was careful not to wake her when she picked her up and handed her to her mother. Rose Rose moved uncertainly and Candy put her arm around her when they walked out of the cider house together.

"You're going to be just fine," Candy said to Rose Rose; she kissed the young woman on her neck, and Rose Rose, who was sweating, leaned against her.

Mr. Rose was standing in the darkness between the Jeep and the cider house, but the rest of the men still sat on the roof.

"You comin' back," Mr. Rose said—nothing was raised at the end of his voice; it was not a question.

"I told you not to speak to me," Candy told him. She helped Rose Rose and her baby into the Jeep.

"I was speakin' to my daughter," Mr. Rose said with dignity.

But Rose Rose would not answer her father. She sat like a statue of a woman with a baby in her arms while Candy turned the Jeep around and drove away. Before they went into the fancy house together, Rose Rose slumped against Candy and said to her, "I never could do nothin' about it."

"Of course you couldn't," Candy told her.

"He hated the father of the other one," Rose Rose said. "He been after me ever since."

"You're going to be all right now," Candy told the girl before they went inside; through the windows, they could watch Wally flying back and forth in the house.

"I know my father, Missus Worthington," Rose Rose whispered. "He gonna want me back."

"He can't have you," Candy told her. "He can't make you go back to him."

"He make his own rules," said Rose Rose.

"And the father of your beautiful daughter?" Candy asked, holding the door open for Rose Rose and her baby girl. "Where is he?"

"My father cut him up. He long gone," Rose Rose said. "He don't wanna be involved with me no more."

"And your mother?" Candy asked, as they went in the house.

"She dead," Rose Rose said.

That was when Wally told Candy that Dr. Larch was dead, too. She would not have known it to look at Homer, who was all business; an orphan learns how to hold back, how to keep things in.

"Are you all right?" Candy asked Homer, while Wally wheeled Baby Rose around the downstairs of the house and Angel took Rose Rose to his room, which was prepared for her.

"I'm a little nervous," Homer admitted to Candy. "It's

certainly not a matter of technique, and I've got everything I need—I know I can do it. It's just that, to me, it is a living human being. I can't describe to you what it feels like—just to hold the curette, for example. When living tissue is touched, it responds—somehow," Homer said, but Candy cut him off.

"It may help you to know who the father is," she said. "It's Mister Rose. Her father is the father—if that makes it any easier."

The crisply made-up bed in Angel's childhood room and the gleaming instruments—which were displayed so neatly on the adjacent bed—made Rose Rose both talkative and rigid.

"This don't look like no fun," the girl said, holding her fists in her lap. "They took the other one out through the top—not the way she was supposed to come out," Rose Rose explained. She'd had a Caesarean, Homer Wells could see, perhaps because of her age and her size at the time. But Homer could not quite convince her that this time everything would be much easier. He wouldn't need to take anything "out through the top."

"Go stay with Wally, Angel," Candy told the boy. "Go give Baby Rose a ride in the wheelchair. Knock over all the furniture, if you want," she told him, kissing her son.

"Yeah, you go away," Rose Rose told Angel.

"Don't be afraid," Candy told Rose Rose. "Homer knows what he's doing. You're in very safe hands." She swabbed Rose Rose with the red Merthiolate, while Homer began to show Rose Rose the instruments.

"This is a speculum," he said to her. "It may feel cold, but it doesn't hurt. You won't feel any of this," he assured her. "These are dilators," Homer said, but Rose Rose shut her eyes.

"You done this before, ain't you?" Rose Rose asked him. He had the ether ready.

"Just breathe normally," he told her. At the first whiff, she opened her eyes and turned her face away from the mask, but Candy put her hands at Rose Rose's temples and very gently moved her head into the right position. "The first smell is the sharpest," said Homer Wells.

"Please, have you done this before?" Rose Rose asked him. Her voice was muffled under the mask.

"I'm a good doctor—I really am," Homer Wells told her. "Just relax, and breathe normally."

"Don't be afraid," Rose Rose heard Candy tell her just before the ether began to take her out of her body.

"I can ride it," she said. Rose Rose meant a bicycle. Homer watched her wiggle her toes. Rose Rose was getting her first feel of the sand; the beach was warm. The tide was coming in; she felt the water around her ankles. "No big deal," she murmured. Rose Rose meant the ocean.

Homer Wells, adjusting the speculum until he had a perfect view of the cervix, introduced the first dilator until the os opened like an eye looking back at him. The cervix looked softened and slightly enlarged, and it was bathed in a healthy, clear mucus—it was the most breathtaking pink color that Homer had ever seen. Downstairs, he heard the wheelchair careening through the house—there was a wild and nonstop giggling from Baby Rose.

"Tell them not to get that baby overexcited," Homer said to Candy, as if she were his nurse of long-standing and he was used to giving her directions and she was used to following them, exactly. He did not let the ruckus (or Candy trying to quiet them down) distract him; he watched the cervix open until it opened wide enough. He chose the curette of the correct size. After the first one, thought Homer Wells, this might get easier. Because he knew now that he couldn't play God in the worst sense; if he could operate on Rose Rose, how could he refuse to help a stranger? How could he refuse anyone? Only a god makes that kind of decision. I'll just give them what they want, he thought. An orphan or an abortion.

Homer Wells breathed slowly and regularly; the steadiness of his hand surprised him. He did not even blink when he felt the curette make contact; he did not divert his eye from witnessing the miracle.

/ / /

For that night, Candy slept in the extra bed in Angel's room—she wanted to be close by if Rose Rose needed anything, but Rose Rose slept like a rock. The gap left by her missing tooth made a small whistling noise when her lips were parted; it was not at all disturbing, and Candy slept quite soundly, too.

Angel slept downstairs, sharing the big bed with Wally. They stayed awake quite late, talking. Wally told Angel about the time he first fell in love with Candy; although Angel had heard the story before, he listened to it more attentively—now that he thought he had fallen in love with Rose Rose. Wally also told Angel that he must never underestimate the darker necessities of the world where his father had grown up.

"It's the old story," Wally said to Angel. "You can get Homer out of Saint Cloud's, but you can't get Saint Cloud's out of Homer. And the thing about being in love," Wally said to Angel, "is that you can't force anyone. It's natural to want someone you love to do what you want, or what you think would be good for them, but you have to let everything happen to them. You can't interfere with people you love any more than you're supposed to interfere with people you don't even know. And that's hard," he added, "because you often feel like interfering—you want to be the one who makes the plans."

"It's hard to want to protect someone else, and not be able to," Angel pointed out.

"You can't protect people, kiddo," Wally said. "All you can do is love them."

When he fell asleep, Wally felt the movement of the raft on the Irrawaddy. One of his friendly Burmese rescuers was offering to catheterize him. First he dipped the bamboo shoot in the brown river, then he wiped it dry on one of the strips of silk that bound up his head basket, then he spat on it. "You want to *pees* now?" the Burmese asked Wally.

"No, thank you," Wally said in his sleep. "No piss now," he said aloud, which made Angel smile before he fell asleep, too.

Upstairs, in the master bedroom, Homer Wells was wide awake. He'd volunteered to have Baby Rose for the night. "Because I'll be up all night, anyway," he said. He'd forgotten how much he enjoyed having a baby to look after. Babies reminded Homer of himself; they were always wanting something in the middle of the night. But after he'd given Baby Rose her bottle, the child went back to sleep and left Homer Wells alone again; it was nonetheless a pleasure having the little girl to look at. Her black face in the bed beside him was no bigger than his hand, and occasionally her hands would reach up and her fingers would open and close, grasping at something she saw in her sleep. The presence of another breather in the room reminded Homer Wells of the sleeping quarters in St. Cloud's, where he had some difficulty imagining the necessary announcement.

"Let us be happy for Doctor Larch," Homer said softly. "Doctor Larch has found a family. Good night, Doctor Larch."

He tried to imagine which one of them would have said it. He imagined it would have been Nurse Angela, and so it was to her that he sent the letter.

Now that Dr. Larch had died, Mrs. Goodhall's pleasure at the thought of replacing the old, nonpracticing homosexual was less intense; it did stimulate her, however, to imagine replacing him with that young missionary who had antagonized him so. Dr. Gingrich saw some faint justice appear on the horizon at the thought of replacing Larch with someone who'd clearly driven the old man crazy, but Dr. Gingrich was not so interested in the outcome of the situation in St. Cloud's as he was fascinated with his secretive study of Mrs. Goodhall's mind, in which he found such a complex broth of righteous delusion and inspired hatred.

Of course, Dr. Gingrich and the other board members were eager to meet young Dr. Stone, but Dr. Gingrich was particularly eager to observe Mrs. Goodhall at such a meeting. Mrs. Goodhall had developed a tic—whenever someone provided her with unusual pleasure or displeasure, the right side of her face suffered an involuntary muscular contraction. Dr. Gingrich imagined that, upon meeting the missionary doctor, Mrs. Goodhall would enter a phase of nearly constant spasm, and he could not wait to observe this.

"You must stall the board," Homer wrote to Nurse Angela. "Tell them that your efforts to reach Dr. Stone are hampered by the doctor being in transit between two of the mission's hospitals in India. Say Assam is one, say New Delhi is the other. Say you don't expect to be able to communicate with him for a week or more, and that—if he was willing to consider the position at St. Cloud's—he couldn't possibly be available before November."

Homer Wells hoped that this would allow him the time to tell Angel everything, and to be finished with the harvest.

"You'll have to convince the board that you are competent midwives, in addition to being good nurses, and that you'll be able to recognize the patients who should be referred to a physician," Homer wrote to Nurse Angela. "You must forgive me for needing all this time, but perhaps I will seem more believable to the board of trustees if everyone has to wait for me. It takes time to leave Asia."

He also requested that they send him the available history of Fuzzy Stone, and tell him anything that Larch might have omitted—although Homer could not imagine that St. Larch had left out anything. It was with the shortest possible sentence that Homer told Nurse Angela that he had loved Larch "like a father," and that they had "nothing to fear from Melony."

Poor Bob, who had broken her nose and her arm, had plenty to fear from Melony, however, but Bob wasn't smart enough to be afraid of her. When the cast would come off her arm, and when her nose looked more or less normal again, Melony and Lorna would cruise the old, familiar spots—the pizza bar in Bath, among them—and Bob would have the charmless instinct to annoy them again. Melony would disarm him with her shy smile—the one that humbly revealed her bad teeth to him—and while Bob turned his oafish attention to Lorna, Melony snipped off the top half of his ear with her wire-cutters (the electrician's common and trusty tool). Then Melony broke several of Bob's ribs and his nose and beat him unconscious with a chair. She had her heart in the right place, regarding St. Cloud's, but Melony was an eye-for-an-eye and a tit-for-tat girl.

"My hero," Lorna called her. It was a touchy word to use around Melony, who had long thought that Homer Wells was made of hero stuff.

Homer was a hero in Rose Rose's eyes; she spent all of Monday in the bed in Angel's room, with Candy bringing her baby to her from time to time, and Angel visiting with her every chance he could get.

"You're going to love this room," Angel told her.

"You plain crazy," Rose Rose told him. "But I already love it."

It was a day that hurt the harvest; Mr. Rose wouldn't pick and half the men were sore from falling off the bicycles. Homer Wells, who never would master the terrible machine, had a puffy knee and a bruise between his shoulder blades the size of a melon. Peaches refused to go up a ladder; he would load the trailers and pick drops all day. Muddy groaned and complained; he was the only one among them who had actually learned to ride. Black Pan announced that it was a good day for a fast.

Mr. Rose, it appeared, was fasting. He sat outside the cider house in the weak sun, wrapped in a blanket from his bed; he sat Indian-style, not talking to anyone.

"He say he on a pickin' strike," Peaches whispered to Muddy, who told Homer that he thought Mr. Rose was on a hunger strike, too—"and every other kind of strike they is."

"We'll just have to get along without him," Homer told the men, but everyone pussyfooted their way past Mr. Rose, who appeared to have enthroned himself in front of the cider house.

"Or else he planted hisself, like a tree," Peaches said.

Black Pan brought him a cup of coffee and some fresh corn bread, but Mr. Rose wouldn't touch any of it. Sometimes, he appeared to be gnawing on one of the pacifiers. It was a cool day, and when the faint sun would drift behind the clouds, Mr. Rose would draw the blanket over his head; then he sat cloaked and robed and closed off completely from any of them.

"He like an Indian," Peaches said. "He don't make no treaty."

"He want to see his daughter," Muddy informed Homer at the end of the day. "That what he say to me—it all he say. Just *see* her. He say he won't touch her."

"Tell him he can come to the house and see her there," Homer Wells told Muddy.

But at suppertime, Muddy came to the kitchen door alone. Candy asked him in, and asked him to eat with them—Rose Rose was sitting with them, at the table—but Muddy was too nervous to stay. "He say he won't come here," Muddy told Homer. "He say for her to come to the cider house. He say to tell you they got they own rules. He say you breakin' the rules, Homer."

Rose Rose sat so still at the table that she was not even chewing; she wanted to be sure to hear everything Muddy was saying. Angel tried to take her hand, which was cold, but she pulled it away from him and kept both her hands wound up in her napkin, in her lap.

"Muddy," Wally said, "you tell him that Rose Rose is staying in my house, and that in my house we follow *my* rules. You tell him he's welcome to come here anytime."

"He won't do it," Muddy said.

"I have to go see him," Rose Rose said.

"No, you don't," Candy told her. "You tell him he sees her here, or nowhere, Muddy," Candy said.

"Yes, ma'am. I brung the bicycles back," Muddy said to Angel. "They a little banged up." Angel went outside to look at the bicycles, and that's when Muddy handed him the knife.

"You don't need this, Angel," Muddy told the boy, "but

you give it to Rose Rose. You say I want her to have it. Just so she have one."

Angel looked at Muddy's knife; it was a bone-handled jack-knife, and part of the bone was chipped. It was one of those jackknives where the blade locks in place when you open it so it can't close on your fingers. The blade was almost six inches long, which would make it prominent in anyone's pocket, and over the years it had seen a lot of whetstone; the blade was ground down very thin and the edge was very sharp.

"Don't you need it, Muddy?" Angel asked him.

"I never knew what to do with it," Muddy confessed. "I just get in trouble with it."

"I'll give it to her," Angel said.

"You tell her her father say he love her, and he just wanna see her," Muddy said. "Just *see*," he repeated.

Angel considered this message; then he said, "I love Rose Rose, you know, Muddy."

"Sure I know," Muddy said. "I love her, too. We all love her. Everybody love Rose Rose—that part of her problem."

"If Mister Rose just wants to see her," Angel said, "how come you're giving her your knife?"

"Just so she have one," Muddy repeated.

Angel gave her the knife when they were sitting in his room after supper.

"It's from Muddy," he told her.

"I know who it from," Rose Rose said. "I know what knife everyone got—I know what they all look like." Although it was not a switchblade, it made Angel jump to see how quickly she opened the knife using only one hand. "Look what Muddy do," she said, laughing. "He been sharpenin' it to death—he wore it half away." She closed the knife against her hip; her long fingers moved the knife around so quickly that Angel didn't notice where she put it.

"You know a lot about knives?" Angel asked her.

"From my father," she said. "He show me everythin'."

Angel moved and sat on the bed next to her, but Rose Rose regarded him neutrally. "I told you," she began patiently. "You don't wanna have no business with me—I could never tell you nothin' about me. You don't wanna know 'bout me, believe me."

"But I love you," Angel pleaded with her.

After she kissed him—and she allowed him to touch her

breasts—she said, "Angel. Lovin' someone don't always make
no difference."

Then Baby Rose woke up, and Rose Rose had to attend to
her daughter. "You know what I namin' her?" she asked
Angel. "Candy," Rose Rose said. "That who she is—she is
Candy."

In the morning, on the downhill side of the harvest, everyone got up early, but no one got up earlier than Rose Rose.
Angel, who had more or less been imagining that he was
guarding the house all night, noticed that Rose Rose and her
daughter had gone. Angel and Homer got in the Jeep and
drove out to the cider house before breakfast—but there was
nowhere they could go that morning that Rose Rose hadn't
been to ahead of them. The men were up and looking restless,
and Mr. Rose was already maintaining his stoical sitting position in the grass in front of the cider house—the blanket
completely covering him, except for his face.

"You too late," Mr. Rose said to them. "She long gone."

Angel ran and looked in the cider house, but there was no
sign of Rose Rose or her daughter.

"She gone with her thumb, she say," Mr. Rose told Homer
and Angel. He made the hitchhiking sign—his bare hand emerging from the blanket only for a second before it went back into
hiding.

"I didn't hurt her," Mr. Rose went on. "I didn't touch her,
Homer," he said. "I just love her, was all. I just wanna see
her—one more time."

"I'm sorry for your troubles," Homer Wells told the man,
but Angel ran off to find Muddy.

"She say to tell you you was the nicest," Muddy told the
boy. "She say to tell your dad he a hero, and that you was the
nicest."

"She didn't say where she was going?"

"She don't know where she goin', Angel," Muddy told him.
"She just know she gotta go."

"But she could have stayed with us!" Angel said. "With
me," he added.

"I know she thought about it," Muddy said. "You better
think about it, too."

"I *have* thought about it—I think about it all the time,"
Angel said angrily.

"I don't think you old enough to think about it, Angel," Muddy said gently.

"I loved her!" the boy said.

"She know," Muddy said. "She know who she is, too, but he also know you don't know who you is, yet."

Looking for her and thinking about her would help Angel to know that. He and Candy would drive south along the coast for an hour; then they would drive north, for two. They knew that even Rose Rose would know enough about Maine not to go inland. And they knew that a young black woman with a baby in her arms would be quite exotic among the hitchhikers of Maine; she certainly would have less trouble than Melony getting a ride—and Melony always got rides.

Mr. Rose would maintain his almost Buddhist position; he made it through lunch without moving, but in the afternoon he asked Black Pan to bring him some water, and when the men were through picking that day, he called Muddy over to him. Muddy was very frightened, but he approached Mr. Rose and stood at a distance of about six feet from him.

"Where your knife, Muddy?" Mr. Rose asked him. "You lose it?"

"I didn't lose it," Muddy told him. "But I can't find it," he added.

"It around, you mean?" Mr. Rose asked him. "It around somewhere, but you don't know where."

"I don't know where it is," Muddy admitted.

"Never do you no good, anyway—do it?" Mr. Rose asked him.

"I never could use it," Muddy admitted. It was a cold and sunless late afternoon, but Muddy was sweating; he held his hands at his sides as if his hands were dead fish.

"Where she get the knife, Muddy?" Mr. Rose asked.

"What knife?" Muddy asked him.

"It look like your knife—what I seen of it," said Mr. Rose.

"I gave it to her," Muddy admitted.

"Thank you for doin' that, Muddy," Mr. Rose said. "If she gone with her thumb, I glad she got a knife with her."

"Peaches!" Muddy screamed. "Go get Homer!" Peaches came out of the cider house and stared at Mr. Rose, who didn't move a muscle; Mr. Rose didn't look at Peaches at all. "Black Pan!" Muddy screamed, as Peaches went running off to get Homer Wells. Black Pan came out of the cider house and he and Muddy got down on their knees and peered at Mr. Rose together.

"You all stay calm," Mr. Rose advised them. "You too late," he told them. "No one gonna catch her now. She had all day to get away," Mr. Rose said proudly.

"Where she get you?" Muddy asked Mr. Rose, but neither he nor Black Pan dared to poke around under the blanket. They just watched Mr. Rose's eyes and his dry lips.

"She good with that knife—she better with it than *you* ever be!" Mr. Rose said to Muddy.

"I know she good," Muddy said.

"She almost the best," said Mr. Rose. "And who taught her?" he asked them.

"You did," they told him.

"That right," said Mr. Rose. "That why she almost as good as me." Very slowly, without exposing any of himself—keeping himself completely under the blanket, except for his face—Mr. Rose rolled over on his side and tucked his knees up to his chest. "I real tired of sittin' up," he told Muddy and Black Pan. "I gettin' sleepy."

"Where she get you?" Muddy asked him again.

"I didn't think it would take this long," said Mr. Rose. "I taken all day, but it felt like it was gonna go pretty fast."

All the men were standing around him when Homer Wells and Peaches arrived in the Jeep. Mr. Rose had very little left to say when Homer got to him.

"You breakin' them rules, too, Homer," Mr. Rose whispered to him. "Say you know how I feel."

"I know how you feel," said Homer Wells.

"Right," said Mr. Rose—grinning.

The knife had entered in the upper right quadrant, close to the rib margin. Homer knew that a knife moving in an upward direction would give a substantial liver laceration, which would continue to bleed—at a moderate rate—for many hours. Mr. Rose might have stopped bleeding several times, and started again. In most cases, a liver stab wound hemorrhages very slowly.

Mr. Rose died in Homer's arms before Candy and Angel arrived at the cider house, but long after his daughter had made good her escape. Mr. Rose had managed to soak the blade of his own knife in his wound, and the last thing he told Homer was that it should be clear to the authorities that he had stabbed himself. If he hadn't meant to kill himself, why would he have let himself bleed to death from what wasn't necessarily a mortal wound?

"My daughter run away," Mr. Rose told all of them. "And I so sorry that I stuck myself. You better say that what happen. Let me hear you say it!" He raised his voice to them.

"That what happen," Muddy said.

"You kill yourself," Peaches told him.

"That what happen," Black Pan said.

"You hearin' this right, Homer?" Mr. Rose asked him.

That was how Homer reported it, and that was how the death of Mr. Rose was received—the way he wanted it, according to the cider house rules. Rose Rose had broken the rules, of course, but everyone at Ocean View knew the rules Mr. Rose had broken with her.

At the end of the harvest, on a gray morning with a wild wind blowing in from the ocean, the overhead bulb that hung in the cider house kitchen blinked twice and burned out; the spatter of apple mash on the far wall, near the press and grinder, was cast so somberly in shadows that the dark clots of pomace looked like black leaves that had blown indoors and stuck against the wall in a storm.

The men were picking up their few things. Homer Wells was there—with the bonus checks—and Angel had come with him to say good-bye to Muddy and Peaches and Black Pan and the rest of them. Wally had made some arrangements with Black Pan to be crew boss the following year. Wally had been right about Mr. Rose being the only one of them who could read well and write at all. Muddy told Angel that he'd always thought the list of rules tacked to the kitchen wall was something to do with the building's electricity.

" 'Cause it was always near the light switch," Muddy explained. "I thought they was instructions 'bout the lights."

The other men, since they couldn't read at all, never noticed that the list was there.

"Muddy, if you should happen to see her," Angel said, when he was saying good-bye.

"I won't see her, Angel," Muddy told the boy. "She long gone."

Then they were all long gone. Angel would never see Muddy again, either—or Peaches, or any of the rest of them except Black Pan. It wouldn't work out, having Black Pan as a crew boss, as Wally would discover; the man was a cook, not a picker, and a boss had to be in the field with the men. Although Black Pan would gather a fair picking crew together, he was never quite in charge of them—in future years, of course, no one would ever be as in charge of a picking crew at Ocean View as Mr. Rose had been. For a while, Wally would try hiring French Canadians; they were, after all, closer to Maine than the Carolinas. But the French Canadian crews were often ill-tempered and alcoholic, and Wally would always be trying to get the French Canadians out of jail.

One year Wally would hire a commune, but that crew arrived with too many small children. The pregnant women on the ladders made everyone nervous. They left something cooking all day, and started a small fire in the kitchen. And when the men ran the press, they allowed their children to splash about in the vat.

Wally would finally settle on Jamaicans. They were friendly, nonviolent and good workers. They brought with them an interesting music and a straightforward but contained passion for beer (and for a little marijuana). They knew how to handle the fruit and they never hurt each other.

But after Mr. Rose's last summer at Ocean View, the pickers—whoever they were—would never sit on the cider house roof. It just never occurred to them. And no one would ever put up a list of rules again.

In future years, the only person who ever sat on the cider house roof was Angel Wells, who would do it because he liked that particular view of the ocean, and because he wanted to remember that November day in 195__, after Muddy and the rest of them had left, and his father turned to him (they were alone at the cider house) and said, "How about sitting on the roof for a while with me? It's time you knew the whole story."

"Another little story?" Angel asked.

"I said the whole story," said Homer Wells.

And although it was a cold day, that November, and the wind off the sea was briny and raw, father and son sat on that roof a long time. It was, after all, a long story, and Angel would ask a lot of questions.

Candy, who drove by the cider house and saw them sitting up there, was worried about how cold they must be. But she didn't interrupt them; she just kept driving. She hoped the truth would keep them warm. She drove to the barn nearest the apple mart and got Everett Taft to help her put the canvas canopy on the Jeep. Then she went and got Wally out of the office.

"Where are we going?" Wally asked her. She bundled him up in a blanket, as if she were taking him to the Arctic Circle. "We must be going north," he said, when she didn't answer him.

"My father's dock," she told him. Wally knew that Ray Kendall's dock, and everything else belonging to Ray, had been blown over land and sea; he kept quiet. The ugly little carhop restaurant that Bucky Bean had manufactured was closed for the season; they were alone. Candy drove the Jeep through the empty parking lot and out to a rocky embankment that served as a seawall against the waves in Heart's Haven Harbor. She stopped as near to the ocean's edge as she dared to, near the old pilings of what had been her father's dock—where she and Wally had spent so many evenings, so long ago.

Then, since this wasn't wheelchair terrain, she carried Wally about ten yards, over the rocks and the sand, and sat him down on a relatively smooth and flat shelf of the jagged coastline. She wrapped Wally's legs in the blanket and then she sat down behind him and straddled him with her legs—as a way of keeping them both warm. They sat facing Europe in this position, like riders on a sled about to plunge downhill.

"This is fun," Wally said. She stuck her chin over his shoulder; their cheeks were touching; she hugged him around his arms and his chest, and she squeezed his withered hips with her legs.

"I love you, Wally," Candy said, beginning her story.

/ / /

In late November, in the mousing season, the board of trustees at St. Cloud's approved the appointment of Dr. F. Stone as obstetrician-in-residence and the new director of the orphanage—having met the zealous missionary in the board's chambers in Portland, the birthplace of the late Wilbur Larch. Dr. Stone, who appeared a little tired from his Asian journeying and from what he described as "a touch of something dysenteric," made the correct impression on the board. His manner was somber, his hair was graying and cropped in an almost military fashion ("Hindu barbers," he apologized, showing a mild sense of humor; actually, Candy had cut his hair). Homer Wells was carelessly shaven, clean but tousled in his dress—both at ease and impatient with strangers, in the manner (the board thought) of a man with urgent business who was not in the least vain about his appearance; he hadn't the time. The board also approved of Dr. Stone's medical and religious credentials—the latter, in the estimation of the devout Mrs. Goodhall, would give to Dr. Stone's authority in St. Cloud's a "balance" that she noted had been missing in Dr. Larch.

Dr. Gingrich was excited to note the contortions registered on Mrs. Goodhall's face during the entire meeting with young Dr. Stone, who did not recognize Gingrich and Goodhall from his brief glimpse of them in the off-season, Ogunquit hotel. Dr. Gingrich found a comforting familiarity in the young man's face, although he would never associate the glow of a missionary with the sorrowful longing he had seen on the face of the lover. Perhaps Mrs. Goodhall's tic affected her vision—she did not recognize the young man from the hotel, either—or else her mind would never grasp the possibility that a man devoted to children could also be a man with a practicing sexual life.

To Homer Wells, Mrs. Goodhall and Dr. Gingrich were not special enough to remember; the peevish miseries compounded in their expressions were not unique. And the way that Homer looked when he was with Candy was not the way he looked most of the time.

On the matter of abortions, Dr. Stone surprised the board by the adamant conviction he held: that they *should* be legalized, and that he intended to work through the proper channels toward that end. However, Dr. Stone assured them, as long as abortions were illegal, he would rigorously uphold the law. He believed in rules, and in obeying them, he told the board. They liked the hardship and self-sacrifice that they imagined they could witness in the wrinkles around his dark eyes—and how the fierce Asian sun had blistered his nose and cheeks while he had toiled to save the diarrhetic children. (Actually, he had deliberately sat for too long in front of Candy's sunlamp.) And—on the religious grounds more comfortable to the board, and to Mrs. Goodhall especially—Dr. Stone said that he himself never would perform abortions, even if they were legalized. "I just couldn't do it," he lied calmly. If it ever was legal, of course, he would simply refer the unfortunate woman "to one of those doctors who could, and would." It was clear that Dr. Stone found "those doctors" not to his liking—that, despite his loyalty to Dr. Larch, Dr. Stone found that particular practice of Larch's to be an act decidedly against nature.

It was in large measure indicative of Dr. Stone's "Christian tolerance" that despite his long-standing disagreement with Dr. Larch on this delicate subject, the young missionary was forgiving of Larch—far more forgiving than the board, by no small portion. "I always prayed for him," Dr. Stone said of Dr. Larch, his eyes shining. "I still pray for him." It was an emotional moment, perhaps influenced by the aforementioned "touch of something dysenteric"—and the board was predictably moved by it. Mrs. Goodhall's tic went wild.

On the matter of Nurse Caroline's socialist views, Dr. Stone assured the board that the young woman's fervor to do the right thing had simply been—in her youth—misguided. He would tell her a few things about the Communist guerrilla activity in Burma that would open her eyes. And Dr. Stone convinced the board that the older nurses, and Mrs. Grogan, had a few more years of good service in them. "It's all a matter of guidance," Dr. Stone told the board. Now there was a word that pleased Dr. Gingrich!

Dr. Stone opened his hands; they were rather roughly calloused for the hands of a doctor, Mrs. Goodhall would observe—thinking it charming how this healer of children must have helped with building the huts or planting the gardens or whatever other rough work there'd been to do over there. When he said "guidance," Homer Wells opened his hands the way a minister received a congregation, thought the board; or the way a good doctor received the precious head of a newborn child, they thought.

And it was thrilling, after they had interviewed him, how he blessed them as he was leaving them. And how he salaamed to them!

"Nga sak kin," said the missionary doctor.

Oh, what had he said? they all wanted to know. Wally, of course, had taught Homer the correct pronunciation—it being one of the few Burmese things that Wally had ever heard correctly, although he'd never learned what it meant.

Homer Wells translated the phrase for them—Wally had always thought it was someone's name. "It means," Homer told the enraptured board: "May God watch over your soul, which no man may abuse."

There were loud murmurs of approval. Mrs. Goodhall said, "All that in such a short phrase!"

"It's a remarkable language," Dr. Stone told them dreamily. *"Nga sak kin,"* he told them again. He got them all to repeat it after him. He was pleased to imagine them, later, giving this meaningless blessing to each other. It would have pleased him more if he'd ever known what the phrase actually meant. It was the perfect thing for a board of trustees to go around saying to each other: "Curried fish balls."

"I think I got away with it," Homer told Wally and Candy and Angel when they were eating a late supper in the house at Ocean View.

"It doesn't surprise me," Wally told his friend. "I have every reason to believe that you can get away with anything."

Upstairs, after supper, Angel watched his father pack the old black doctor's bag—and some other bags, as well.

"Don't worry, Pop," Angel told his father. "You're going to do just fine."

"You're going to do just fine, too," Homer told his son. "I'm not worried about that." Downstairs they heard Candy pushing Wally around in the wheelchair. They were playing the game that Wally and Angel often played—the game Wally called "flying."

"Come on," Wally was saying. "Angel can make it go faster."

Candy was laughing. "I'm going as fast as I can," Candy said.

"Please stop thinking about the furniture," Wally told her.

"Please look after Wally," Homer said to Angel. "And mind your mother," he told his son.

"Right," said Angel Wells.

/ / /

In the constantly changing weather of Maine, especially on cloudy days, the presence of St. Cloud's could be felt in Heart's Rock; with a heavy certainty, the air of St. Cloud's could be distinguished in the trapped stillness that hovered above the water of Drinkwater Lake (like those water bugs, those water walkers, that were nearly constant there). And even in the fog that rolled over those bright, coastal lawns of Heart's Haven's well-to-do, there was sometimes in the storm-coming air that leaden, heart-sinking feeling that was the essence of the air of St. Cloud's.

Candy and Wally and Angel would go to St. Cloud's for

hristmas, and for the longer of Angel's school vacations, too;
nd after Angel had his driver's license, he was free to visit his
ather as often as he liked, which was often.

But when Homer Wells went to St. Cloud's—even though
Wally had offered him a car—Homer took the train. Homer
new he wouldn't need a car there, and he wanted to arrive the
ay most of his patients did; he wanted to get the feel of it.

In late November, there was already snow as the train moved
orth and inland, and by the time the train reached St. Cloud's,
e blue-cold snow was deeply on the ground and heavily bent
e trees. The stationmaster, who hated to leave the television,
as shoveling snow off the platform when the train pulled in.
he stationmaster thought he recognized Homer Wells, but the
tern, black doctor's bag and the new beard fooled him. Ho-
er had started the beard because it had hurt to shave (after
e'd burned his face with the sunlamp), and once the beard
ad grown for a while, he thought the change would be suit-
ble. Didn't a beard go with his new name?

"Doctor Stone," Homer said to the stationmaster, introduc-
g himself. "Fuzzy Stone," he said. "I used to be an orphan
ere. Now I'm the new doctor."

"Oh, I thought you was familiar!" the stationmaster said,
owing as he shook Homer's hand.

Only one other passenger had gotten off the train in St.
loud's, and Homer Wells had no difficulty imagining what
he wanted. She was a thin young woman in a long muskrat
oat with a scarf, and a ski hat pulled almost over her eyes, and
he hung back on the platform, waiting for Homer to move
way from the stationmaster. It was the doctor's bag that had
aught her attention, and after Homer had arranged for the
sual louts to tote his heavier luggage, he started up the hill to
he orphanage carrying just the doctor's bag; the young woman
ollowed him.

They walked uphill in this fashion, with the woman lagging
urposefully behind, until they almost reached the girls' divi-
ion. Then Homer stopped walking and waited for her.

"Is this the way to the orphanage?" the young woman asked
im.

"Right," said Homer Wells. Since he had grown the beard,
e tended to oversmile at people; he imagined that the beard
ade it hard for people to tell whether he was smiling.

"Are you the doctor?" the young woman asked him, staring

at the snow on both their boots—and, warily, at the doctor
bag.

"Yes, I'm Doctor Stone," he said, taking the woman's arm
and leading her toward the hospital entrance of the boy
division. "May I help you?" he asked her.

And so he arrived, as Nurse Edna would say, bringing th
Lord's work with him. Nurse Angela threw her arms aroun
his neck and whispered in his ear. "Oh, Homer!" she whis
pered. "I knew you'd be back!"

"Call me 'Fuzzy,'" he whispered to her, because he kne
that Homer Wells (like Rose Rose) was long gone.

For several days, Nurse Caroline would be shy with him, bu
he wouldn't need more than a few operations and a few
deliveries to convince her that he was the real thing. Dr. Stone
even as a name, would be a fitting successor to Dr. Larch. Fc
wasn't Stone a good, hard, feet-on-the-ground, reliable-soundin
sort of name for a physician?

And Mrs. Grogan would remark that she had not enjoye
being read aloud to so much since those hard-to-remembe
days of Homer Wells. And it was to everyone's relief tha
Fuzzy Stone would exhibit as few symptoms of his forme
respiratory difficulties as Homer Wells had exhibited signs of
weak and damaged heart.

Candy and Wally Worthington would throw themselves fu
tilt into apple farming. Wally would serve two terms as pres
dent of the Maine Horticultural Society; Candy would serve
term as director of the New York–New England Apple Inst
tute. And Angel Wells, whom Rose Rose had introduced t
love and to imagination, would one day be a novelist.

"The kid's got fiction in his blood," Wally would tell Home
Wells.

To Candy, a novelist was also what Homer Wells ha
become—for a novelist, in Candy's opinion, was also a kind c
imposter doctor, but a good doctor nonetheless.

Homer never minded giving up his name—it wasn't hi
actual name, to begin with—and it was as easy to be a Fuzzy a
it was to be a Homer—as easy (or as hard) to be a Stone as
was to be anything else.

When he was tired or plagued with insomnia (or both), h
would miss Angel, or he would think of Candy. Sometimes h
longed to carry Wally into the surf, or to fly with him. Som
nights Homer imagined he would be caught, or he worrie

about what he would do when Nurse Angela and Nurse Edna were too old for the Lord's work, and for all the other work in St. Cloud's. And how would he ever replace Mrs. Grogan? Sometimes, when he was especially tired, he dreamed that abortions were legal—that they were safe and available, and therefore he could stop performing them (because someone else would do them)—but he was rarely that tired.

And, after a while, he would write to Candy and say that he had become a socialist; or, at least, that he'd become sympathetic to socialist views. Candy understood by this confession that Homer was sleeping with Nurse Caroline, which she also understood would be good for them—that is, this new development was good for Homer and for Nurse Caroline, and it was good for Candy, too.

Homer Wells saw no end to the insights he perceived nightly, in his continuous reading from *Jane Eyre,* and from *David Copperfield* and *Great Expectations.* He would smile to remember how he had once thought Dickens was "better than" Brontë. When they both gave such huge entertainment and instruction, what did it matter? he thought—and from where comes this childish business of "better"? If not entertainment, he took continued instruction from *Gray's Anatomy.*

For a while, he lacked one thing—and he was about to order it when one came unordered to him. "As if from God," Mrs. Grogan would say.

The stationmaster sent him the message: there was a body at the railroad station, addressed to Dr. Stone. It was from the hospital in Bath—which had been Dr. Larch's long-standing source for bodies, in the days when he'd ordered them. It was some mistake, Homer Wells was sure, but he went to the railroad station to view the body anyway—and to spare the stationmaster any unnecessary agitation.

Homer stood staring at the cadaver (which had been correctly prepared) for such a long time that the stationmaster grew even more anxious. "I'd just as soon you either take it up the hill, or send it back," the stationmaster said, but Homer Wells waved the fool off; he wanted peace to look at Melony.

She had requested this use of her body, Lorna had told the pathologist at the Bath hospital. Melony had seen a photograph in the Bath paper, together with an article revealing Dr. Stone's appointment in St. Cloud's. In the event of her death (which was caused by an electrical accident), Melony had instructed

Lorna to send her body to Dr. Stone in St. Cloud's. "I might be of some use to him, finally," she had told her friend. Of course Homer remembered how Melony had been jealous of Clara.

He would write to Lorna; they would correspond for a while. Lorna would inform him that Melony was "a relatively happy woman at the time of her accident"; in Lorna's opinion, something to do with how relaxed Melony had become was responsible for her electrocuting herself. "She was a daydreamer," Lorna would write. Homer knew that all orphans were daydreamers. "You was her hero, finally," Lorna would tell him.

When he viewed her body, he knew he could never use it for a refresher course; he would send to Bath for another cadaver. Melony had been used enough.

"Should I send it back, Doctor?" the stationmaster whispered.

"No, she belongs here," Homer Wells told him, and so he had Melony brought uphill. It would be essential to keep the sight of her in her present form a secret from Mrs. Grogan. What Homer told them all was that Melony had requested she be buried in St. Cloud's, and so she was—on the hill, under the apple trees, where it was torturously hard to dig a correct hole (the root systems of the trees were everywhere). Finally, a large and deep enough hole was managed, although it was backbreaking labor, and Nurse Caroline said, "I don't know who she is, but she sure is *difficult*."

"She was always that," said Homer Wells.

("Here in St. Cloud's," Wilbur Larch had written, "we learn to love the difficult.")

Mrs. Grogan said her Cardinal Newman over Melony's grave, and Homer said his own prayer (to himself) about her. He had always expected much from Melony, but she had provided him with more than he'd ever expected—she had truly educated him, she had shown him the light. She was more Sunshine than he ever was, he thought. ("Let us be happy for Melony," he said to himself. "Melony has found a family.")

But chiefly, for his education, he would peruse (and linger over every word of) *A Brief History of St. Cloud's*. In this pursuit, he would have Nurse Angela's and Nurse Edna's and Mrs. Grogan's and Nurse Caroline's tireless company, for by this pursuit they would keep Wilbur Larch alive.

Not that everything was clear to Homer: the later entries in *A Brief History of St. Cloud's* were marred by shorthand inspirations and the whimsy conveyed to Larch through ether. For example, what did Larch mean by "rhymes with screams!"? And it seemed uncharacteristically harsh of Larch to have written: "*I* put the pony's penis in her mouth! *I* contributed to that!" How could he have thought that? Homer wondered, because Homer never knew how well Dr. Larch had known Mrs. Eames's daughter.

And as he grew older, Homer Wells (alias Fuzzy Stone) would take special comfort in an unexplained revelation he found in the writings of Wilbur Larch.

"Tell Dr. Stone," Dr. Larch wrote—and this was his very last entry; these were Wilbur Larch's last words: "There is absolutely nothing wrong with Homer's heart." Except for the ether, Homer Wells knew there had been very little that was wrong with the heart of Wilbur Larch.

To Nurse Edna, who was in love, and to Nurse Angela, who wasn't (but who had in her wisdom named both Homer Wells and Fuzzy Stone), there was no fault to be found in the hearts of either Dr. Stone or Dr. Larch, who were—if there ever were—Princes of Maine, Kings of New England.

Author's Notes

(*pp. 36–37*)   Anthony Trollope, who visited Portland, Maine, in 1861, and wrote about it in his *North America,* was mistaken—in the manner of Wilbur Larch's father—about the intended future of the *Great Eastern.*

(*p. 40*)   I am indebted to my grandfather Dr. Frederick C. Irving for this information regarding Dr. Ernst, the curve-ball pitcher—and for the particularly medical language in this chapter. My grandfather's books include *The Expectant Mother's Handbook, A Textbook of Obstetrics,* and *Safe Deliverance.* Dr. Ernst's studies of bacterial infections drew the attention of a Dr. Richardson of the Boston Lying-In Hospital, the maternity hospital where Wilbur Larch served an internship and later joined the staff. Dr. Richardson's article "The Use of Antiseptics in Obstetric Practice" would surely have caught the attention of that eager student of bacteriology, clap-sufferer Wilbur Larch.

    The interest in antiseptics among obstetricians was due to their effect in preventing the most deadly puerperal infection of that day, childbed fever. In 188__, in some maternity hospitals, the death rate among the mothers was about one in eight. In 189__, when Wilbur Larch was still at the Boston Lying-In, a mother's odds were better; the doctors and their patients were washed with a solution of bichloride of mercury. Before Larch would leave the Boston Lying-In, he would see the antiseptic technique advance to the aseptic—the latter meaning "free from bacteria," which meant that everything was sterilized (the sheets, the towels, the gowns, the gauze sponges); the instruments were boiled.

(pp. 41–42) On the use of ether: most historians of anesthesia agree with Dr. Sherwin B. Nuland that surgical anesthesia began at Massachusetts General Hospital on October 16, 1846, when William Morton demonstrated the effectiveness of ether. Dr. Nuland writes: "Everything that led up to it was prologue, everything that was tangential to it was byplay, and everything that followed it was amplification."

According to Dr. Nuland, ether in proper hands remains one of the safest inhalation agents known. At a concentration of only 1 to 2 percent it is a light, tasty vapor; in light concentration, even thirty years ago, hundreds of cases of cardiac surgery were done with light ether and partially awake (even talking) patients.

Some of Dr. Larch's colleagues, at the time, would have preferred nitrous oxide or chloroform, but Larch developed his preference for ether through self-administration. Someone would be crazy to self-administer chloroform. It is twenty-five times more toxic to heart muscle than is ether and has an extremely narrow margin of safety; a minimal overdose can result in cardiac irregularity and death.

Nitrous oxide requires a very high (at least 80 percent) concentration to do the job and is always accompanied by a degree of what is called hypoxia—insufficient oxygen. It requires careful monitoring and cumbersome apparatus, and the patient runs the risk of bizarre fantasies or giggling fits. Induction is very fast.

Ether is a perfect drug addiction for a conservative.

(pp. 42–43) The source of this story is, again, my grandfather, who graduated from Harvard Medical School in 1910. He became chief of staff of the Boston Lying-In Hospital and was William Lambert Richardson Professor of Obstetrics at Harvard for a number of years. I remember him as a good storyteller and an occasional bully—of the other members of his family. As a young doctor, he had many experiences delivering babies to Boston's poorer immigrant families, and to read him is to understand that he had as many opinions and prejudices as he had experiences and talents.

(p. 44) Ether was first synthesized in 1540 by a twenty-five-year-old Prussian botanist. People have been having ether frolics—and later, laughing-gas parties—ever since. In 1819, John Dalton published his study of the compound's physical and chemical properties. Coleridge was a laughing-gas man—a party sniffer, and a frequenter of the experiments with nitrous oxide conducted by Humphrey Davy. The poet was certainly familiar with ether; it was a pity—for him—that he apparently preferred opium.

(p. 45) A Caesarean section is, today, a relatively calm operation: the abdominal incision is small because the uterus is opened inside the abdominal cavity. But in Dr. Larch's days at the Boston Lying-In, in 188__ and 189__, the incision made in the abdominal wall was nearly a foot long; the uterus was lifted through the incision and placed upon the patient's abdomen. "The slashing of this great, plum-colored organ produced a dramatic gush of liquid and blood," my grandfather wrote. The uterus was then sutured with silk and returned to the abdominal cavity; the abdomen was closed in the same way. Considerably more discomfort followed such an operation than follows a Caesarean section now. The operation, in Larch's time—and without complications—would require nearly an hour.

(p. 48) This death by scurvy is based on an actual case: "The Strange Case of Ellen Bean," as told by my grandfather. "A spinster of thirty-five years and of New England stock," Grandfather wrote of Ms. Bean, whose condition (and cause of death) was the same fate I awarded to the unfortunate Mrs. Eames. As my grandfather wrote: "The pregnant state does not engender in all women the rapturous joy traditionally associated with this condition; indeed, there are some who view their future with a sour visage and a jaundiced eye. This much may be assumed from the case of Ellen Bean."

(p. 48) In Wilbur Larch's own state, in dear old Maine, performing an abortion was punishable by a year in jail or a one-thousand-dollar fine, or both—and, if you were a doctor, you might lose your license to practice. The Eastman-Everett Act of 1840 described the attempted abortion of any woman with child as an offense, "whether such child be quick or not"—and regardless of the method.

(p. 49) Instead of red merthiolate Dr. Larch might have used Dakin's solution, although it's likely he would have learned more about its uses during his short visit to France in World War I. That is where my grandfather learned of the many uses of Dakin's solution and where he learned how to *débride*—that is, to cut away all the devitalized tissue surrounding a wound; the French were good teachers of this, he said.

(pp. 52–58) In order for Dr. Larch to find the music in the 189__ abortion palace "remindful of Mahler's *Kindertotenlieder*," he would have to be gifted with a little precognition; Mahler's song cycle was written in 1902. That is implied in the line, "Of course they could not have been singing Mahler's *Songs on the Death of Children*, but those were the songs Wilbur Larch had heard.

(p. 59) This is my grandfather's description of the condition of an actual patient, an extremely small woman named Edith Fletcher—upon whom a Caesarean section was performed (Boston Lying-In Hospital; July 13, 1894). A pelvis this small is rare.

(pp. 59–60) Mrs. W. H. Maxwell's *A Female Physician to the Ladies of the United States: Being a Familiar and Practical Treatise of Matters of Utmost Importance Peculiar to Women* ("Adapted to Every Woman's Own Private Use") was published in New York in 1860. Mrs. Maxwell treated "all diseases peculiar to women, or which they may have unfortunately incurred through the dissipations or wanton unfaithfulness of husbands, or otherwise." (In short, she treated venereal diseases.) Mrs. Maxwell also wrote that she gave her attention, as well, "to women . . . who are forced by the malfunction of their genital organs, or other cause, to resort to premature delivery." (In short, she performed abortions.)

(p. 96) The New England Home for Little Wanderers was originally The Baldwin Place Home for Little Wanderers; the charter was granted by the Commonwealth of Massachusetts in 1865. The name was changed to The New England Home for Little Wanderers, its present name, in 1889—more than a decade before Wilbur Larch founded the orphanage in St. Cloud's.

(p. 106) In a 1928 gynecology textbook (Howard Kelly—the standard at that time), the term D and C is used. I think it's safe to assume that the term was in common use in 192__.

(p. 106) My grandfather said that he needed to use his *Gray's Anatomy* in France in World War I as a "navigational chart."

(pp. 114–115) This is the exact description of a D and C as viewed by Dr. Richard Selzer (Yale School of Medicine), a general surgeon and author (*Mortal Lessons: Notes on the Art of Surgery* and *Rituals of Surgery* are among his books). I'm grateful for his reading of the manuscript of this novel and his generous advice—especially his introducing me to Dr. Nuland, who was the overseer of all the medical aspects of this novel.

(p. 123) The source of my information concerning the physical and mental manifestations of Alzheimer's disease is *The Journal of the History of Medicine and Allied Sciences,* Volume XXXIV, Number 3, July 1979: the article by Dr. Sherwin B. Nuland, "The Enigma of Semmelweis—An Interpretation." Dr. Nuland first presented his material in a lecture at the Yale School of Medicine (the annual History of Surgery Series). His thesis is that Ignac Semmelweis, the tortured discoverer of the sources of puerperal fever, suffered from Alzheimer's disease and not from neurosyphilis; furthermore, Dr. Nuland believes that Semmelweis died of injuries received in a mental institution—i.e., he was beaten to death by his keepers. The records of Bedlam and of other institutions for the insane show that this was common as late as the early part of this century, and occasional reports still appear.

(pp. 127– 129) The source of the description of Homer Wells's first eclampsia patient is my grandfather's book *Safe Deliverance*—the chapter on puerperal convulsions. Grandfather examines the case of a Lucy Nickerson, who died in 1880 of an eclamptic condition that was further aggravated by a forced delivery—the only method known to physicians of the unfortunate Mrs. Nickerson's day.

(pp. 129– 130) The source of this treatment is again my grandfather, Dr. Frederick C. Irving (he was called Fritz). Grandfather describes this as the correct and lifesaving treatment given to one Mrs. Mary O'Toole in 1937.

(p. 134) As of 1942, these are my grandfather's findings. Syphilis—although a great source of agitation to the public-health officials of the day—afflicted only 2 percent of the pregnant women of Boston. The incidence of eclamptic convulsions was much higher. The disease developed in 8 percent of the country's childbearing women.

(p. 152) Spring would be considered too early to bother waxing the press boards; the first press wouldn't be until September, when you'd be pressing the early McIntoshes and the Gravensteins. The press boards, or racks, are wooden slats, over which the cider cloths (or press cloths) are folded. The press boards—they are stacked seven-high—take quite a beating, and the wax protects them. The mash, which is also called the pomace, is squeezed between these boards under a pressure of two thousand pounds. It takes eight hours to squeeze a thousand gallons of cider out of the press—about three gallons per bushel of apples.

The reason you wax the press boards before the first press is that you don't want to take the time to do it once the harvest has begun. And you're running the cider mill during the harvest maybe as much as every other night, and every day that it rains—when you can't pick apples. In the 1940s and the 1950s, the last good press would have come in January.

I'm indebted to my old friends Ben and Peter Wagner and to their mother, Jean, for this and other apple-farming information. The Wagners run the Applecrest Farm Orchards in Hampton Falls, New Hampshire, where I worked when I was a boy; Jean and her late husband, Bill, gave me my first job.

(*p. 153*) All orchards have names; it is common practice, too, for farmers to name their buildings. This is necessary for the shorthand language of simple directions, as in: "The Deere has a flat and needs fixing in the Frying Pan"; or, "I left the Dodge in Number Two because Wally is spraying in the Sanborn and he'll need a ride back." In the orchard where I worked, there was a building called Number Two—although there was no Number Three and I don't remember a Number One. Many of the orchards were named after the families who'd been the original homesteaders on that particular piece of land (Brown, Eaton, Coburn, and Curtis are some local names I remember). There was an orchard called Twenty Acres and another one called Nineteen, and there were the plainer names—an orchard called the Field, one called the Fountain, one called the Spring, and one called Old-New (because it was half old trees and half newly planted). The Frying Pan is also called Frying Pan—without the article.

(*p. 161*) Anyone who grew up near the ocean, as I did, could detect a sea breeze in Iowa (if one was blowing).

(*p. 219*) The prayer that Mrs. Grogan recites is credited to John Henry (Cardinal) Newman, the English theologian and author (1801–90); I'm told that the prayer was originally part of one of Cardinal Newman's sermons. It was also what served my family as a family prayer and was spoken at the graveside of my maternal grandmother—it was her favorite. Her name was Helen Bates Winslow, and she died just a month short of her hundredth birthday; the festivities the family had planned for that event would doubtlessly have killed my grandmother, had she lived until then. Cardinal Newman's prayer must be a very good one, or at least it worked very well— and for a very long time—for my grandmother, who was devoted to it. I was devoted to her.

(p. 237) Alzheimer described the disease he called presenile dementia in 1907. "Deterioration in cognition" occurs relatively early in the disease and is marked by a disturbance of recent memory and a loss of the ability to learn new things. Dr. Nuland of Yale also states that some patients are more likely to begin with personality changes and some with intellectual changes. The advance of the disease, in either case, is marked by a lowering threshold of frustration. Dr. Nuland notes that the sequence in which certain small jobs need to be done would be difficult to follow and that complex ideas are hard to comprehend and impossible to explain to others. It is a rapid deterioration that advances in Alzheimer victims: the average lifespan, from the time of diagnosis, is approximately seven years; there are patients who live much longer, and many who die within a few months. In recent years, it has been recognized that Alzheimer's is not only an uncommon disease that affects people in midlife, but also a relatively frequent cause of mental and physical degeneration in the elderly— many of whom were previously thought to have simple hardening of the arteries (arteriosclerosis).

(pp. 287– The famous Paris edition of 1957 (which was pri-
288) vately printed) collected seventeen hundred examples of the limerick. This limerick, which is categorized as an "organ limerick," originated in print in 1939; it may have been in spoken circulation earlier. In 194__, when Senior and Wally are saying it to each other, it would have been only a few years old.

(pp. 304– Benjamin Arthur Bensley's *Practical Anatomy of the*
305) *Rabbit* is a real book, published by the University of Toronto Press in 1918. Bensley is a clear, no-nonsense writer; his book, which he calls "an elementary laboratory textbook in mammalian anatomy," employs

the anatomy of the rabbit as an introduction to an understanding of human anatomy. Bensley's is not *Gray's*, but *Practical Anatomy of the Rabbit* is a good book of its kind. As a very "elementary" student of anatomy, I learned a lot from Bensley—his book made reading *Gray's* much easier for me.

(*p. 315*) The McIntosh apple was developed in Ontario, where the climate is similar to New England and New York's Hudson and Champlain valleys (where the apple has flourished).

(*p. 334*) In *Practical Anatomy of the Rabbit,* Bensley describes the ovary and oviducts of the rabbit and compares his findings to the same equipment in other animals.

(*p. 364*) The Exeter limerick is dated 1927–41; the town of Exeter appears in many limericks because it rhymes with "sex at her"—as in, "It was then that Jones pointed his sex at her!" (A famous last line.) I always heard a lot of Exeter limericks because I was born and grew up in Exeter, New Hampshire.

The Brent limerick is dated 1941. It is a classic "organ limerick," so called because there is a special category of limericks devoted to the peculiarities of the male and female organs. As in,

There was a young fellow named Cribbs
Whose cock was so big it had ribs.
                                   (1944–51)

And in the famous 1938 limerick that was voted Best Limerick by one of the graduating classes of Princeton:

There once was a Queen of Bulgaria
Whose bush had grown hairier and hairier,
Till a Prince from Peru
Who came up for a screw
Had to hunt for her cunt with a terrier.

The Toronto limerick is circa 1941.

(*p. 384*) The Bombay limerick is dated 1879—an old one.

(*pp. 399–400*) Dr. Larch would have been surprised to learn that his condemning statistics of unwanted children were still accurate in 1965. Dr. Charles F. Westoff of Princeton's Office of Population Research, and the co-director of the 1965 National Fertility Study, concluded that 750,000 to a million children—born to married couples between 1960 and 1965—were unwanted. This estimate is low. Even in a poll, many parents are unwilling to admit that any child of theirs was unwanted. Furthermore, unwed or abandoned mothers were not included in the survey; their opinions regarding how many of their children were unwanted were never counted. For more information on this subject, see James Trager's *The Bellybook* (1972).

Ben Franklin was the fifteenth of seventeen children; his faith in rapid population growth was declared in his *Observations Concerning the Increase of Mankind* (1755).

(*p. 419*) My source for this delivery is Chapter XV, "Conduct of Normal Labor," *Williams Obstetrics,* Henricus J. Stander—circa 1936. I base the described procedure on such a dated source—it is performed in my story in 1943—because I wish to emphasize that Homer's procedure, which has been learned from Dr. Larch, is somewhat old-fashioned but nonetheless correct.

(*p. 427*) "I was born with a caul, which was advertised for sale, in the newspapers, at the low price of fifteen guineas." From *David Copperfield,* Chapter 1 ("I Am Born"). The caul is the membrane that is usually ruptured and expelled at the onset of bearing-down pains but that in rare cases does not rupture—the child coming into the world surrounded by membrane. In the time of Dickens, this protective shroud was taken as a sign that the child would be lucky in life—and, more specifically, never be drowned. In the story of *David Copperfield,* this is an early indication that our hero will find his way and not meet with the form of poor Steerforth's undoing (Steerforth drowns).

Homer Wells, very familiar with *David Copperfield,* is interpreting the drop of sweat that prematurely baptizes his birthing child as having similar protective powers. Homer's child will be lucky in life; Angel will not drown.

(*p. 439*) The first edition of Greenhill's *Office Gynecology* was published in 1939; the eighth edition of *Diseases of Women* (Roquist, Clayton and Lewis) was published in 1949.

The medical journals that Larch would always have had on hand—in addition to *The New England Journal of Medicine*—are *The Journal of the American Medical Association* (in doctors' shorthand this is always called *JAMA*), *The American Journal of Obstetrics and Gynecology* (it has the most vivid illustrations), *The Lancet* (a British journal), and *Surgery, Gynecology and Obstetrics* (in doctors' shorthand this is always called *S, G and O;* in 194__, lots of surgeons did gynecology, too).

JOHN IRVING

A Novel

Every major character in *Until I Find You* has been marked for life—not only William Burns, a church organist who is addicted to being tattooed, but also William's son, Jack, an actor who, as a child, is shaped by his relationships with older women. And Jack's mother, Alice—a Toronto tattoo artist—has been permanently damaged by William's rejection of her. This is a novel about the loss of innocence, on many levels.

 BALLANTINE BOOKS | www.ballantinebooks.com